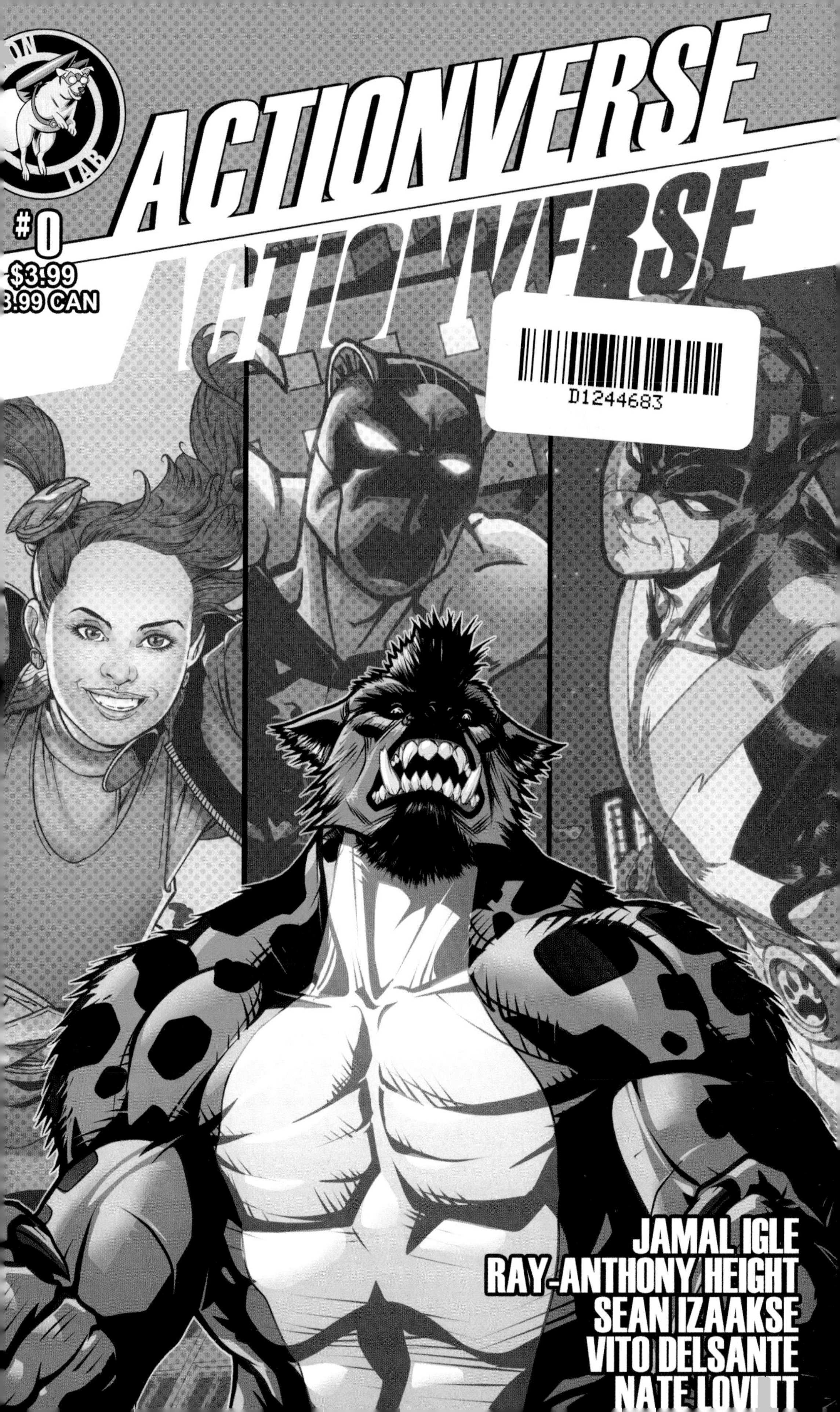
ACTIONVERSE
#0
$3.99
3.99 CAN
JAMAL IGLE
RAY-ANTHONY HEIGHT
SEAN IZAAKSE
VITO DELSANTE
NATE LOVI TT

ACTIONVERSE

THE SAVAGE MAXIM

Written by
Vito Delsante/Jamal Igle

Art by
Ray-Anthony Height/Sean Izaakse

Color by Nate Lovett, w/Ben Hunzeker/Tom Chu

Lettered by Full Court Press

Cover by Height/Igle/Izaakse

BRYAN SEATON - PUBLISHER
KEVIN FREEMAN - PRESIDENT
SHAWN GABBORIN - EDITOR IN CHIEF
DAVE DWONCH - CREATIVE DIRECTOR
JASON MARTIN - EDITOR
COLLEEN BOYD - ASSOCIATE EDITOR
JAMAL IGLE - DIRECTOR OF MARKETING
VITO DELSANTE - ASSOCIATE DIRECTOR OF MARKETING
JIM DIETZ - SOCIAL MEDIA DIRECTOR
CHAD CICCONI - WAS ONCE A FRIEND AND NOW... A VILLAIN!

ACTIONLABCOMICS.COM

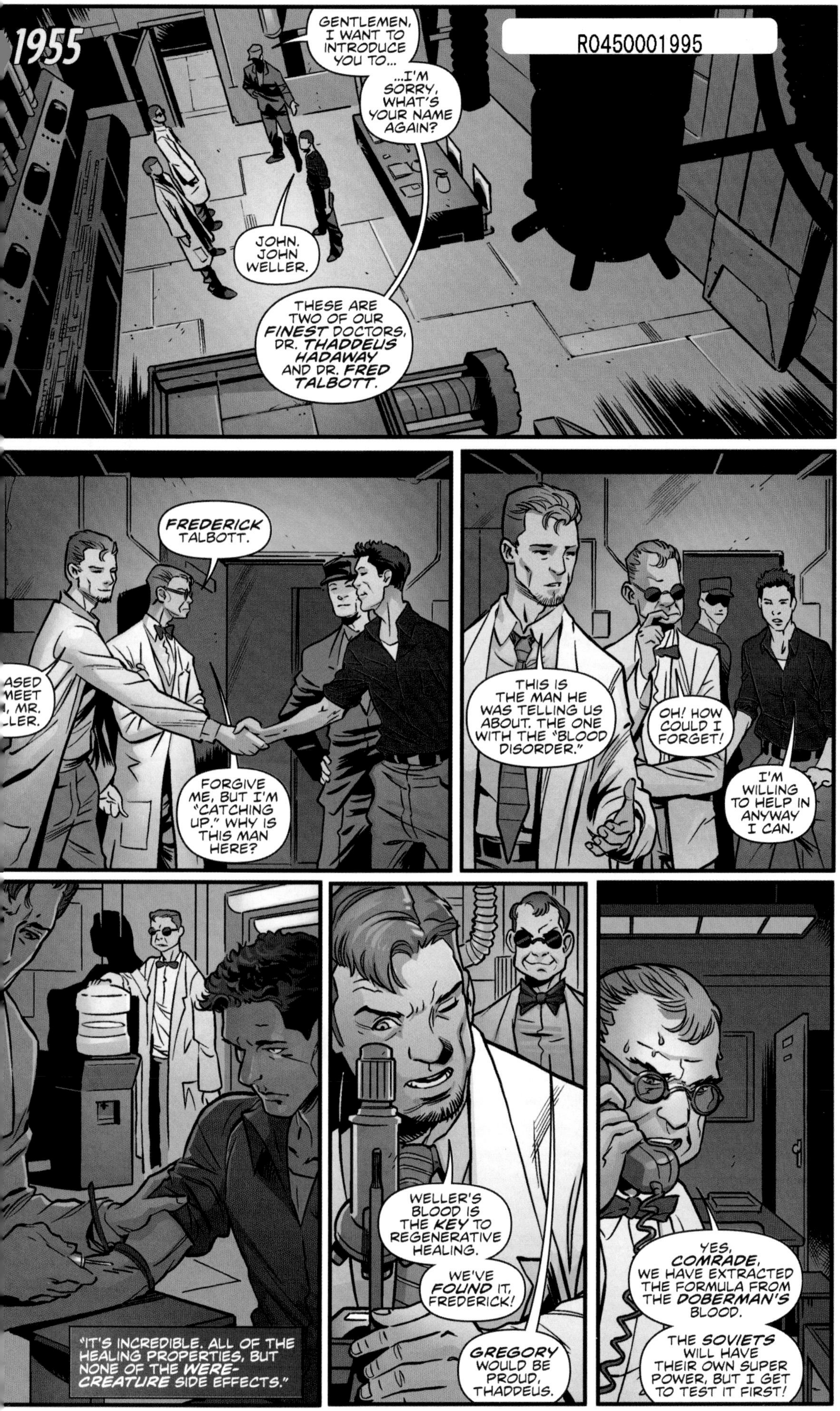
1955
GENTLEMEN, I WANT TO INTRODUCE YOU TO...
...I'M SORRY, WHAT'S YOUR NAME AGAIN?
JOHN. JOHN WELLER.
THESE ARE TWO OF OUR *FINEST* DOCTORS, DR. ***THADDEUS HADAWAY*** AND DR. ***FRED TALBOTT***.
FREDERICK TALBOTT.
FORGIVE ME, BUT I'M "CATCHING UP." WHY IS THIS MAN HERE?
THIS IS THE MAN HE WAS TELLING US ABOUT. THE ONE WITH THE "BLOOD DISORDER."
OH! HOW COULD I FORGET!
I'M WILLING TO HELP IN ANYWAY I CAN.
"IT'S INCREDIBLE. ALL OF THE HEALING PROPERTIES, BUT NONE OF THE ***WERE-CREATURE*** SIDE EFFECTS."
WELLER'S BLOOD IS THE ***KEY*** TO REGENERATIVE HEALING.
WE'VE ***FOUND*** IT, FREDERICK!
GREGORY WOULD BE PROUD, THADDEUS.
YES, ***COMRADE***, WE HAVE EXTRACTED THE FORMULA FROM THE ***DOBERMAN'S*** BLOOD.
THE ***SOVIETS*** WILL HAVE THEIR OWN SUPER POWER, BUT I GET TO TEST IT FIRST!

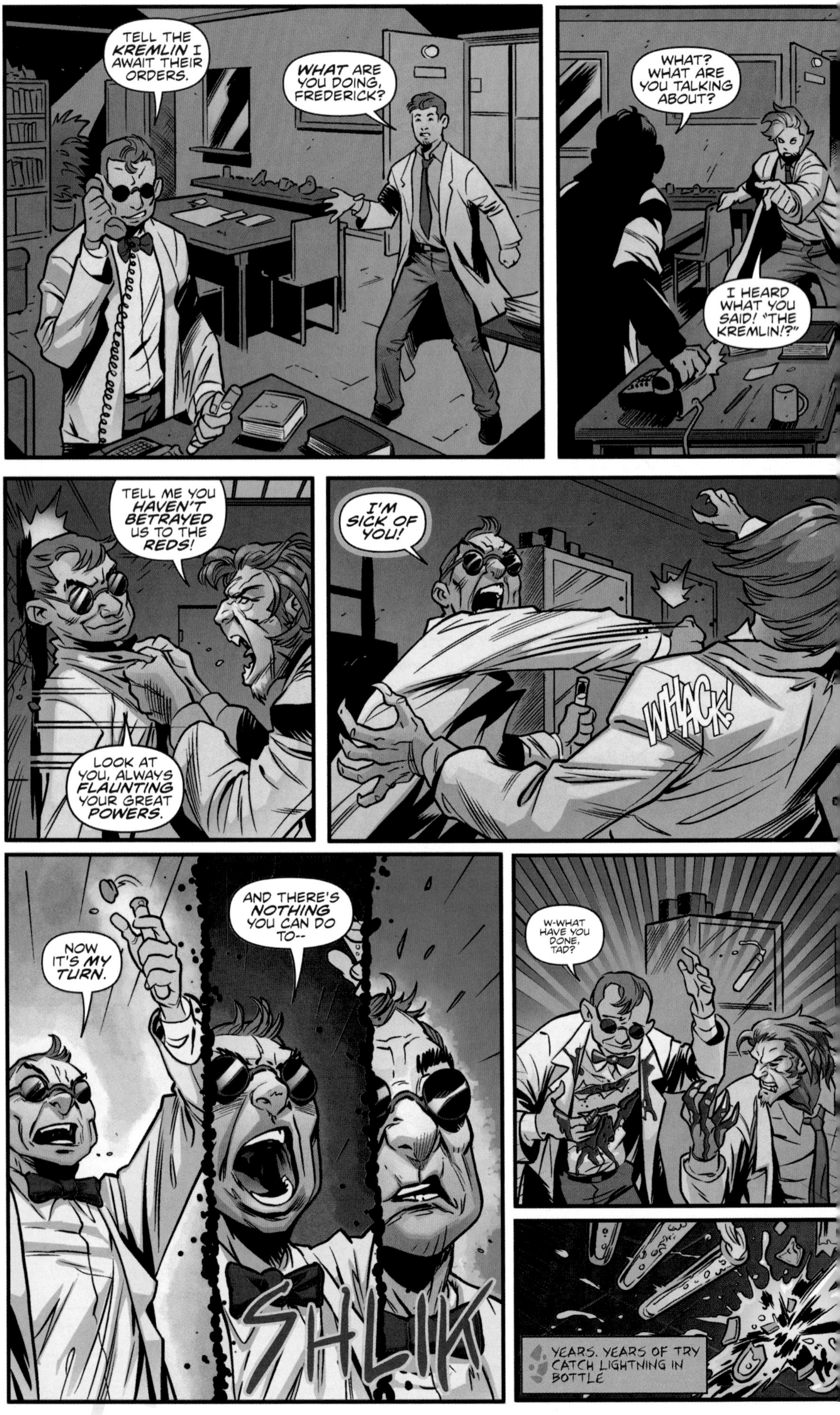

TELL THE KREMLIN I AWAIT THEIR ORDERS.
WHAT ARE YOU DOING, FREDERICK?
WHAT? WHAT ARE YOU TALKING ABOUT?
I HEARD WHAT YOU SAID! "THE KREMLIN!?"
TELL ME YOU HAVEN'T BETRAYED US TO THE REDS!
LOOK AT YOU, ALWAYS FLAUNTING YOUR GREAT POWERS.
I'M SICK OF YOU!
WHACK!
NOW IT'S MY TURN.
AND THERE'S NOTHING YOU CAN DO TO--
SHLIK
W-WHAT HAVE YOU DONE, TAD?
YEARS. YEARS OF TRY CATCH LIGHTNING IN BOTTLE

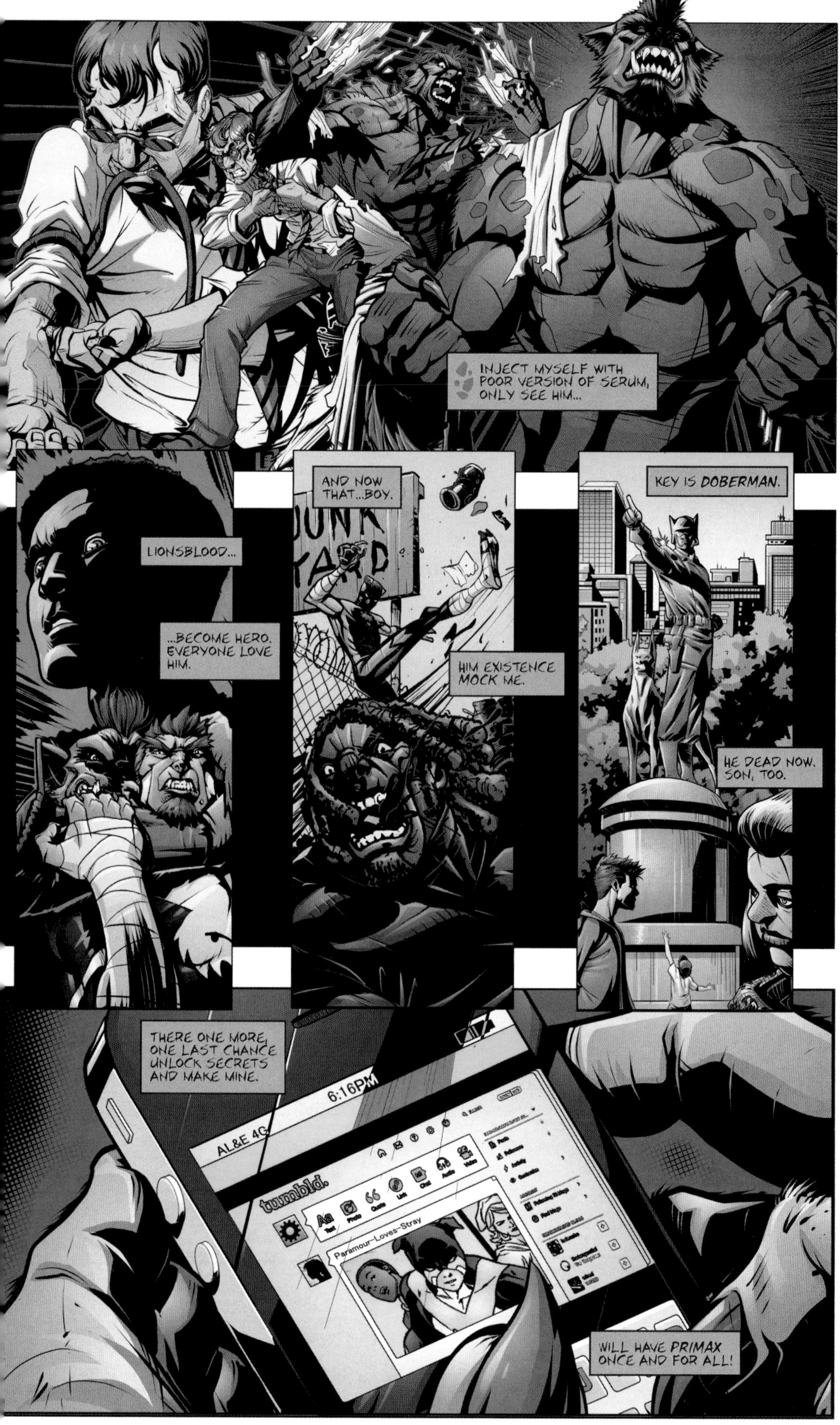
INJECT MYSELF WITH POOR VERSION OF SERUM, ONLY SEE HIM...
LIONSBLOOD...
...BECOME HERO. EVERYONE LOVE HIM.
AND NOW THAT...BOY.
JUNK YARD
HIM EXISTENCE MOCK ME.
KEY IS DOBERMAN.
HE DEAD NOW. SON, TOO.
THERE ONE MORE, ONE LAST CHANCE UNLOCK SECRETS AND MAKE MINE.
6:16PM
AL&E 4G
tumbld.
Paramour-Loves-Stray
WILL HAVE PRIMAX ONCE AND FOR ALL!

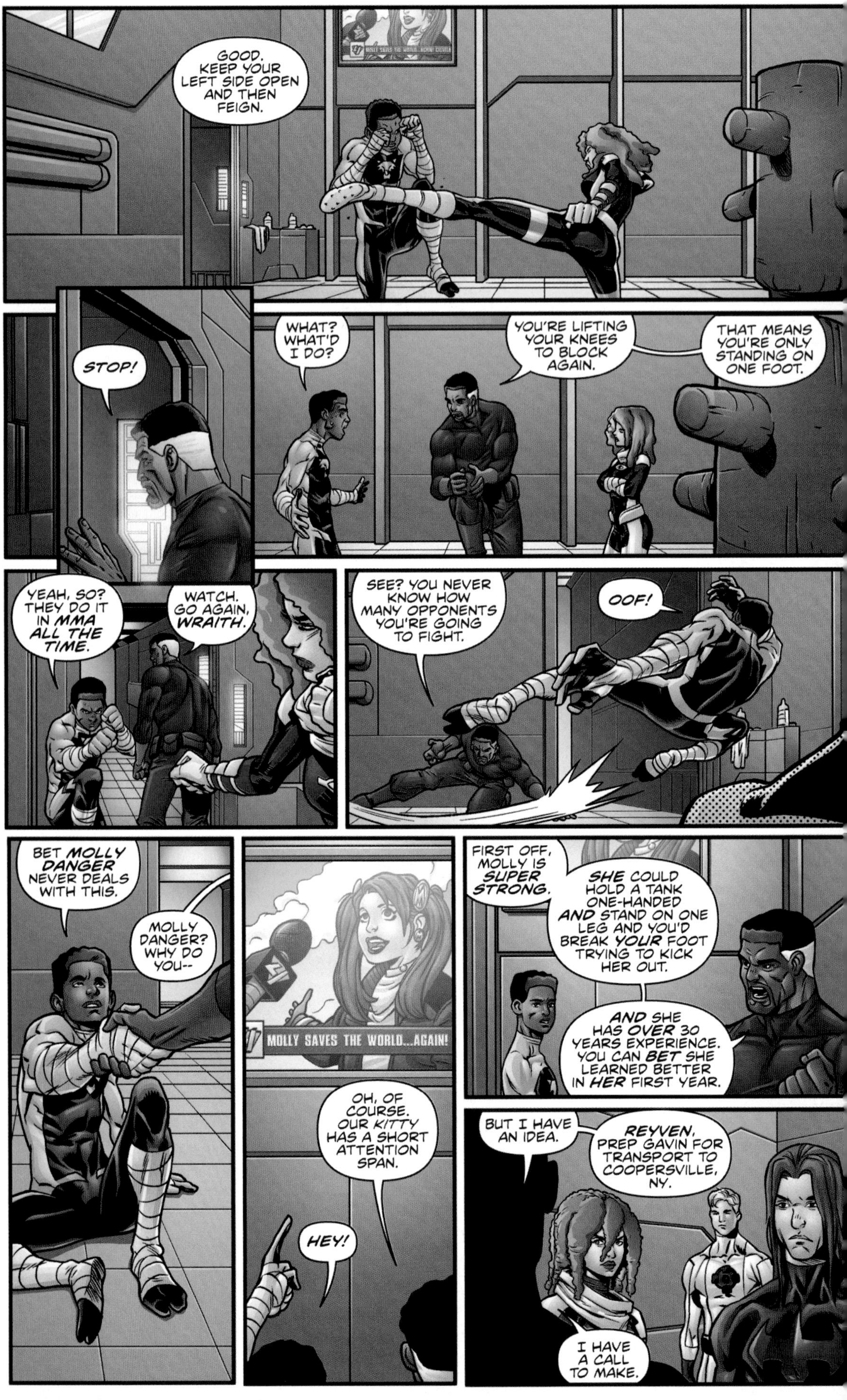

GOOD. KEEP YOUR LEFT SIDE OPEN AND THEN FEIGN.
STOP!
WHAT? WHAT'D I DO?
YOU'RE LIFTING YOUR KNEES TO BLOCK AGAIN.
THAT MEANS YOU'RE ONLY STANDING ON ONE FOOT.
YEAH, SO? THEY DO IT IN *MMA ALL THE TIME*.
WATCH. GO AGAIN, *WRAITH*.
SEE? YOU NEVER KNOW HOW MANY OPPONENTS YOU'RE GOING TO FIGHT.
OOF!
BET *MOLLY DANGER* NEVER DEALS WITH THIS.
MOLLY DANGER? WHY DO YOU--
MOLLY SAVES THE WORLD...AGAIN!
OH, OF COURSE. OUR *KITTY* HAS A SHORT ATTENTION SPAN.
HEY!
FIRST OFF, MOLLY IS *SUPER STRONG*.
SHE COULD HOLD A TANK ONE-HANDED *AND* STAND ON ONE LEG AND YOU'D BREAK *YOUR* FOOT TRYING TO KICK HER OUT.
AND SHE HAS *OVER* 30 YEARS EXPERIENCE. YOU CAN *BET* SHE LEARNED BETTER IN *HER* FIRST YEAR.
BUT I HAVE AN IDEA.
REYVEN, PREP GAVIN FOR TRANSPORT TO COOPERSVILLE, NY.
I HAVE A CALL TO MAKE.

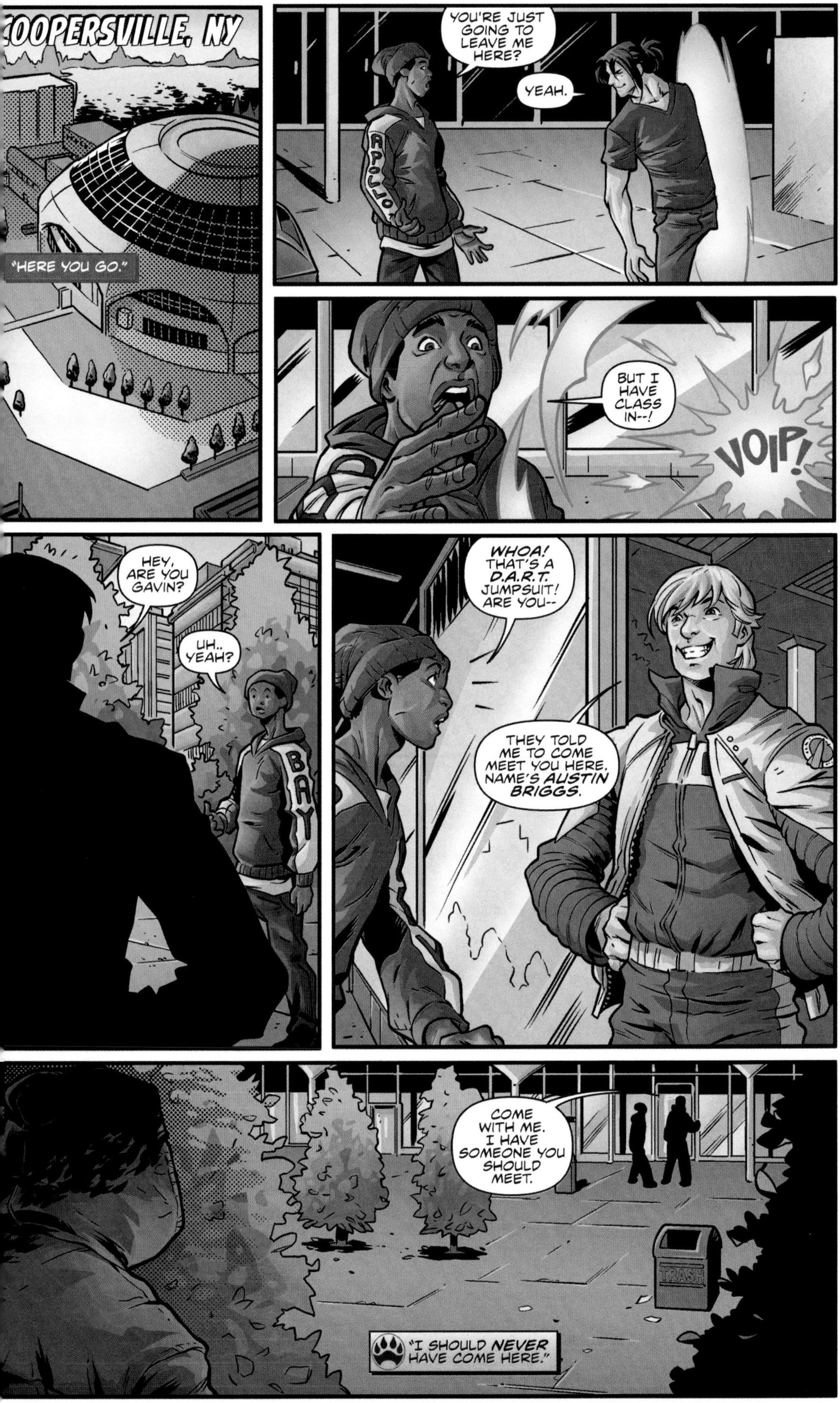
COOPERSVILLE, NY
"HERE YOU GO."
YOU'RE JUST GOING TO LEAVE ME HERE?
YEAH.
APOLLO
BUT I HAVE CLASS IN--!
VOIP!
HEY, ARE YOU GAVIN?
UH.. YEAH?
BAY
WHOA! THAT'S A D.A.R.T. JUMPSUIT! ARE YOU--
THEY TOLD ME TO COME MEET YOU HERE. NAME'S AUSTIN BRIGGS.
COME WITH ME. I HAVE SOMEONE YOU SHOULD MEET.
TRASH
"I SHOULD NEVER HAVE COME HERE."

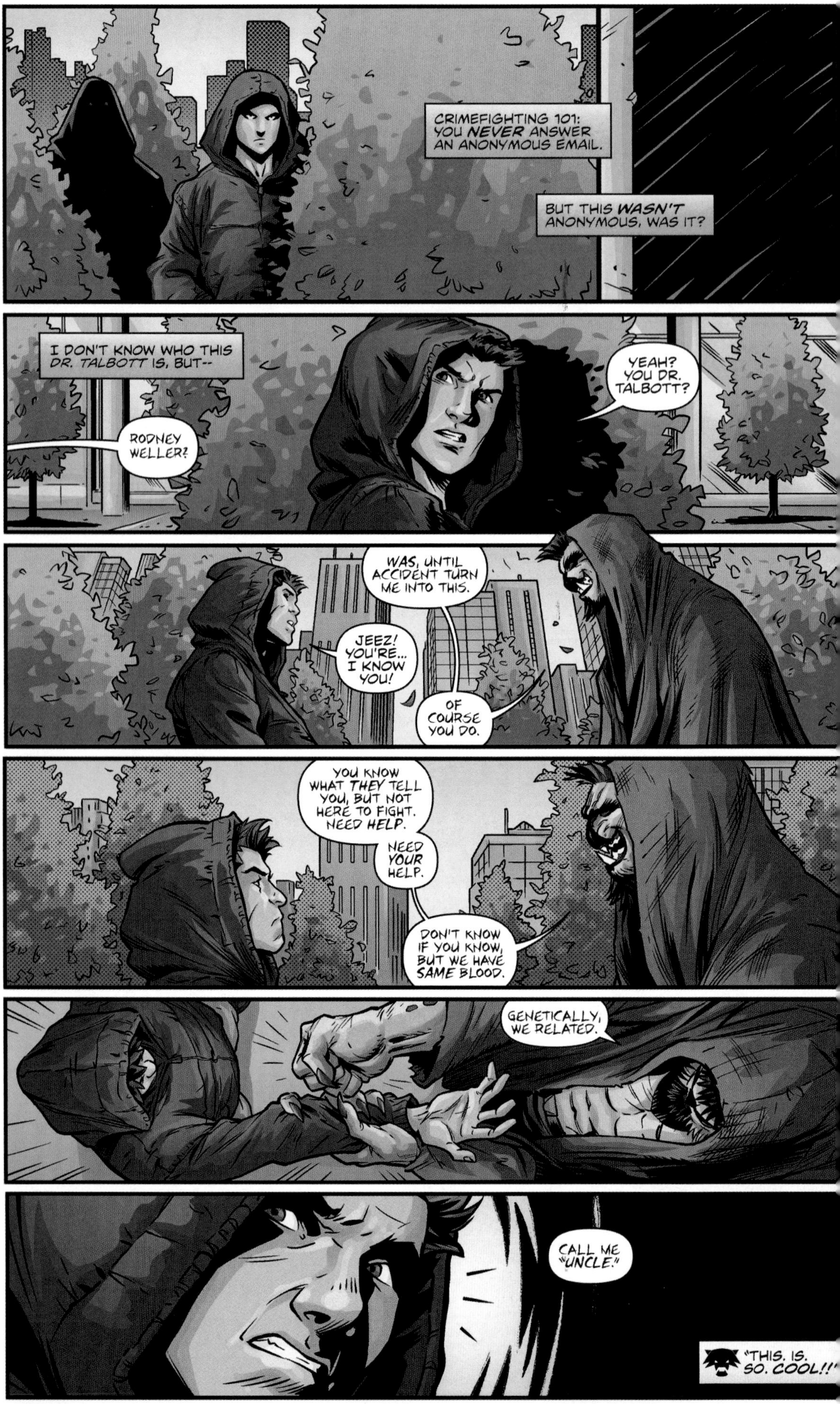

CRIMEFIGHTING 101: YOU NEVER ANSWER AN ANONYMOUS EMAIL.
BUT THIS WASN'T ANONYMOUS, WAS IT?
I DON'T KNOW WHO THIS DR. TALBOTT IS, BUT--
RODNEY WELLER?
YEAH? YOU DR. TALBOTT?
WAS, UNTIL ACCIDENT TURN ME INTO THIS.
JEEZ! YOU'RE... I KNOW YOU!
OF COURSE YOU DO.
YOU KNOW WHAT THEY TELL YOU, BUT NOT HERE TO FIGHT. NEED HELP.
NEED YOUR HELP.
DON'T KNOW IF YOU KNOW, BUT WE HAVE SAME BLOOD.
GENETICALLY, WE RELATED.
CALL ME "UNCLE."
"THIS. IS. SO. COOL!!"

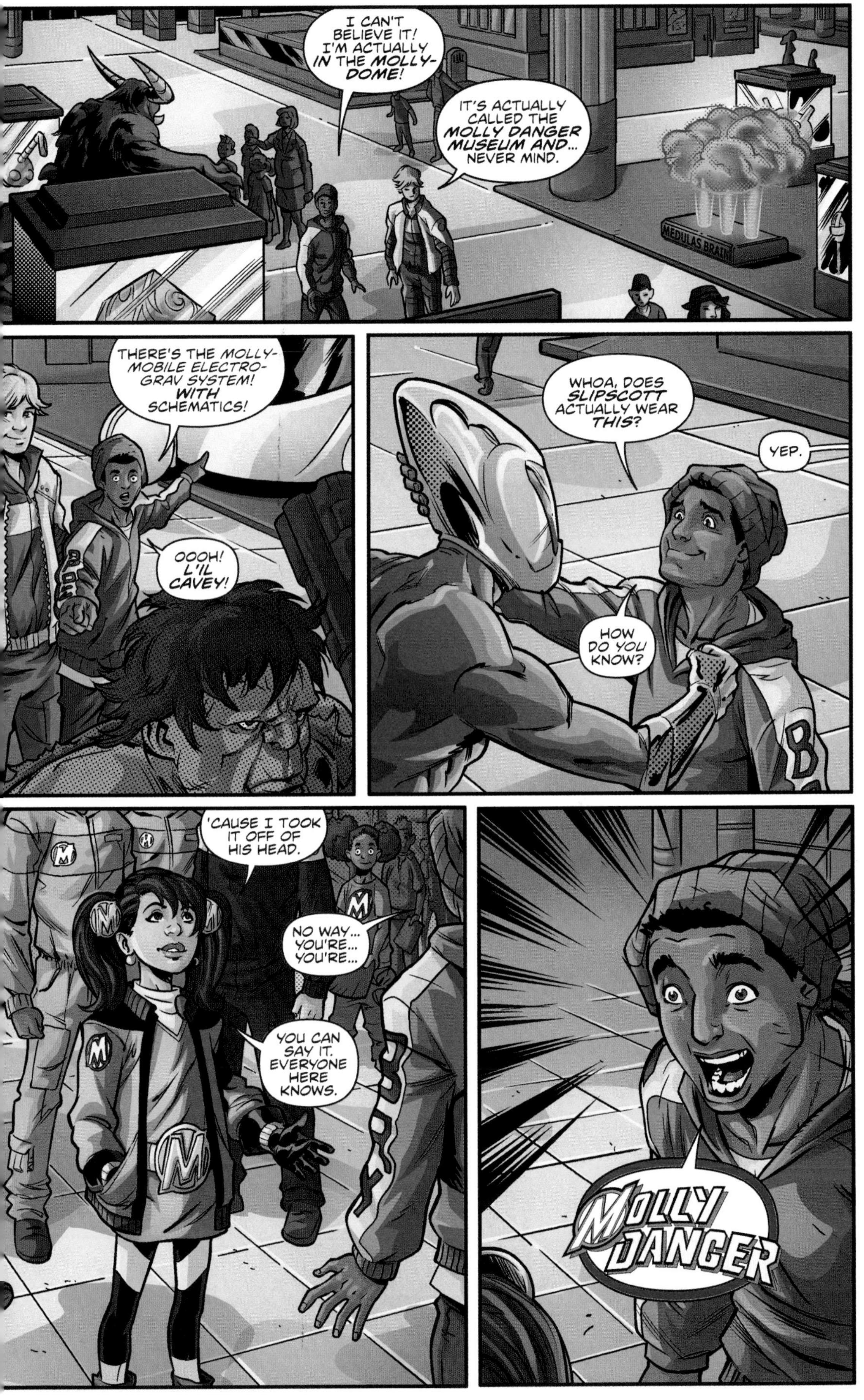
I CAN'T BELIEVE IT! I'M ACTUALLY IN THE MOLLY-DOME!
IT'S ACTUALLY CALLED THE MOLLY DANGER MUSEUM AND... NEVER MIND.
MEDULAS BRAIN
THERE'S THE MOLLY-MOBILE ELECTRO-GRAV SYSTEM! WITH SCHEMATICS!
OOOH! L'IL CAVEY!
WHOA, DOES SLIPSCOTT ACTUALLY WEAR THIS?
YEP.
HOW DO YOU KNOW?
'CAUSE I TOOK IT OFF OF HIS HEAD.
NO WAY... YOU'RE... YOU'RE...
YOU CAN SAY IT. EVERYONE HERE KNOWS.
MOLLY DANGER

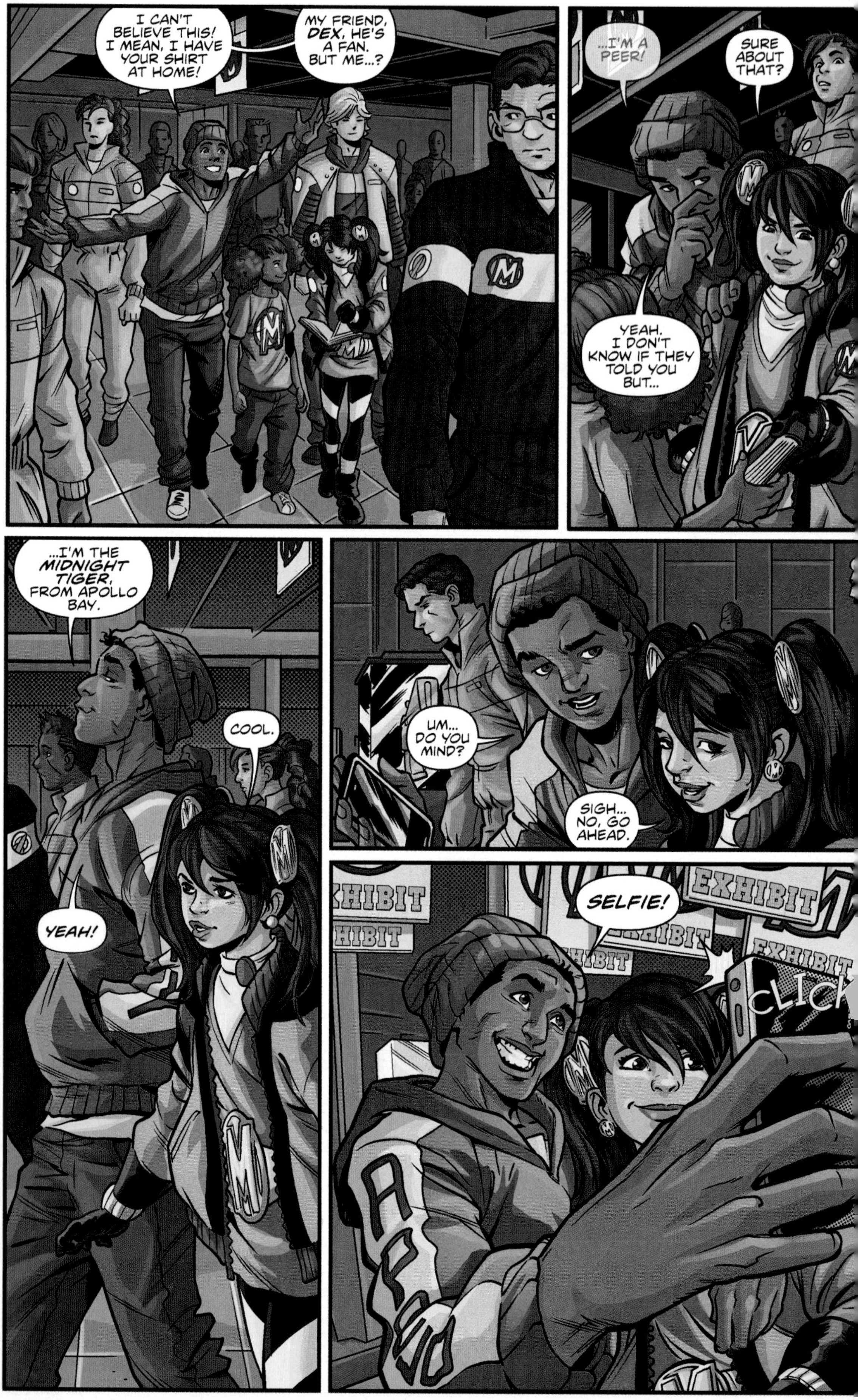
I CAN'T BELIEVE THIS! I MEAN, I HAVE YOUR SHIRT AT HOME!
MY FRIEND, DEX, HE'S A FAN. BUT ME...?
...I'M A PEER!
SURE ABOUT THAT?
YEAH. I DON'T KNOW IF THEY TOLD YOU BUT...
...I'M THE MIDNIGHT TIGER, FROM APOLLO BAY.
COOL.
YEAH!
UM... DO YOU MIND?
SIGH... NO, GO AHEAD.
EXHIBIT
SELFIE!
CLICK

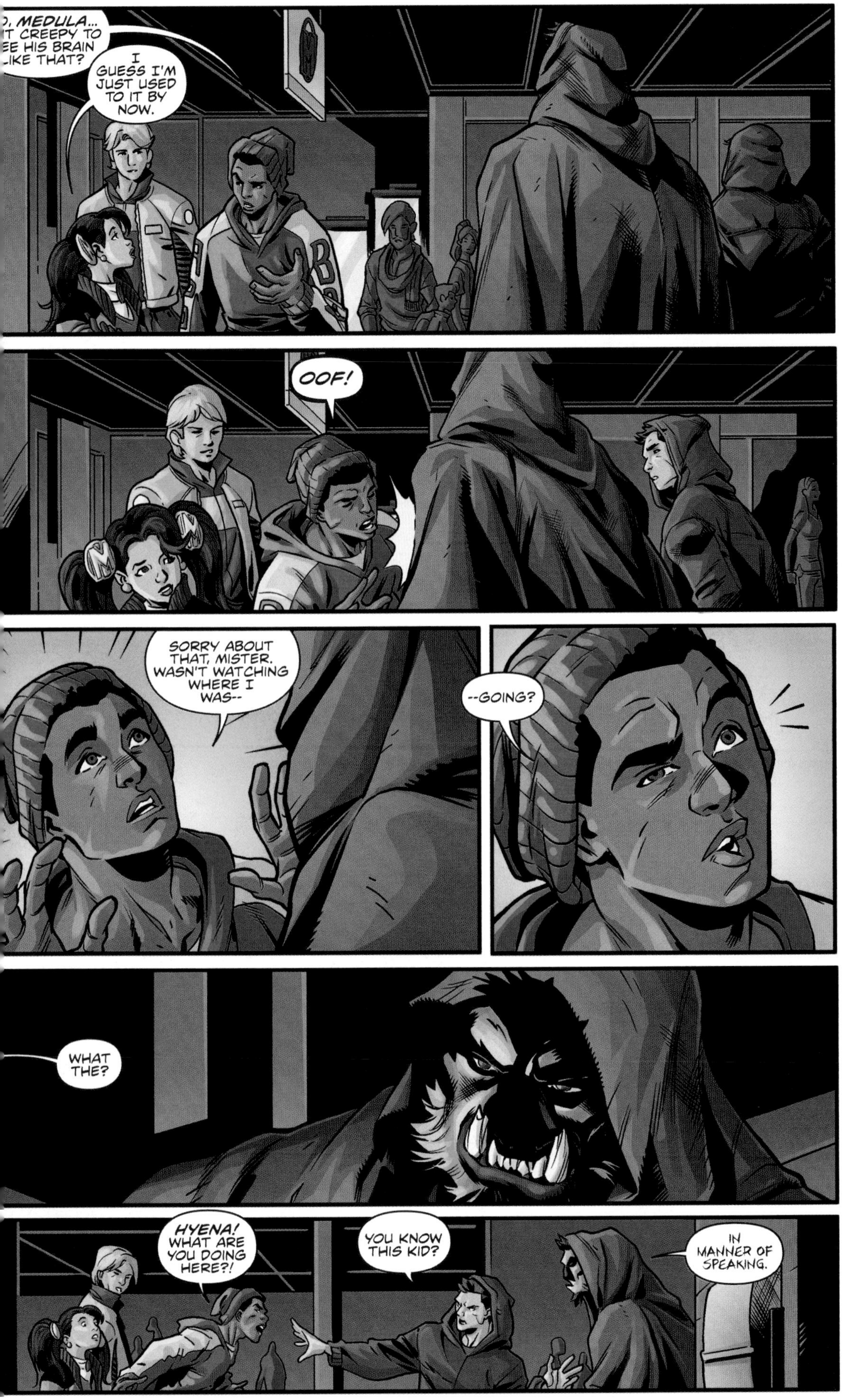

..., MEDULA...
...T CREEPY TO
...EE HIS BRAIN
...IKE THAT?
I GUESS I'M JUST USED TO IT BY NOW.
OOF!
SORRY ABOUT THAT, MISTER. WASN'T WATCHING WHERE I WAS--
--GOING?
WHAT THE?
HYENA! WHAT ARE YOU DOING HERE?!
YOU KNOW THIS KID?
IN MANNER OF SPEAKING.

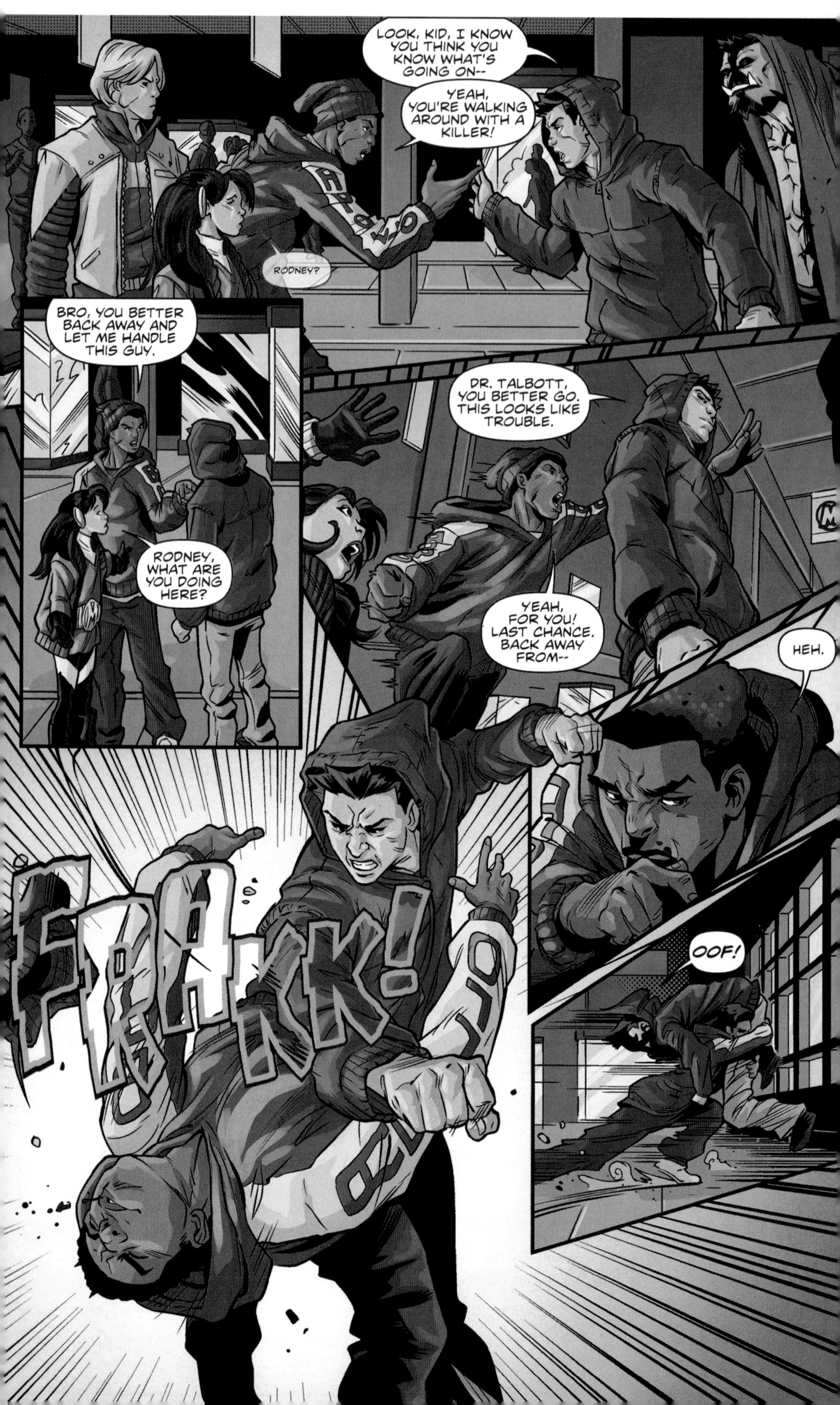
LOOK, KID, I KNOW YOU THINK YOU KNOW WHAT'S GOING ON--
YEAH, YOU'RE WALKING AROUND WITH A KILLER!
RODNEY?
BRO, YOU BETTER BACK AWAY AND LET ME HANDLE THIS GUY.
RODNEY, WHAT ARE YOU DOING HERE?
DR. TALBOTT, YOU BETTER GO. THIS LOOKS LIKE TROUBLE.
YEAH, FOR YOU! LAST CHANCE. BACK AWAY FROM--
HEH.
FRAKK!
OOF!

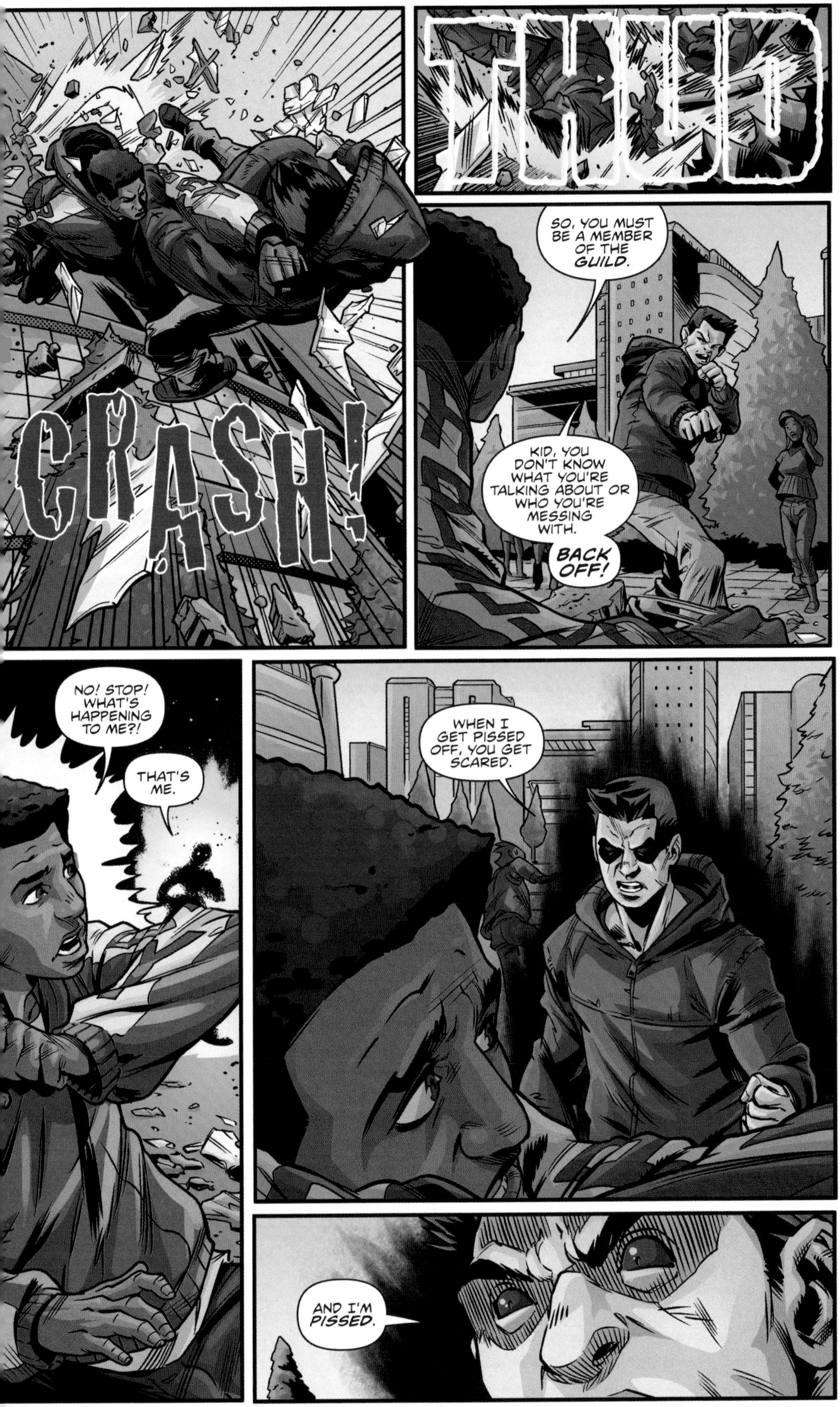
CRASH!
THUD
SO, YOU MUST BE A MEMBER OF THE GUILD.
KID, YOU DON'T KNOW WHAT YOU'RE TALKING ABOUT OR WHO YOU'RE MESSING WITH.
BACK OFF!
NO! STOP! WHAT'S HAPPENING TO ME?!
THAT'S ME.
WHEN I GET PISSED OFF, YOU GET SCARED.
AND I'M PISSED.

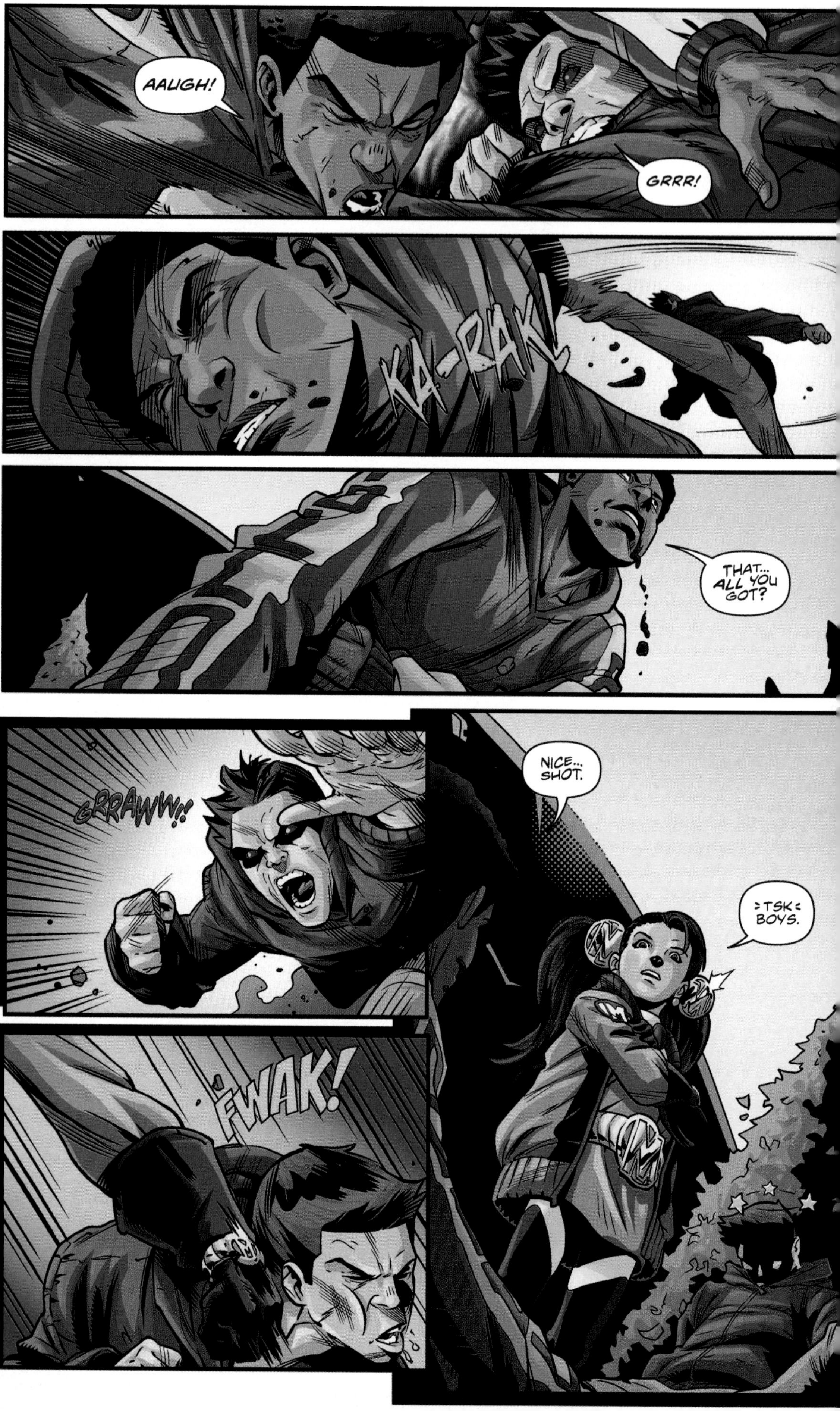
AAUGH!
GRRR!
KA-RAK!
THAT... ALL YOU GOT?
GRRAWW!!
NICE... SHOT.
FWAK!
=TSK= BOYS.

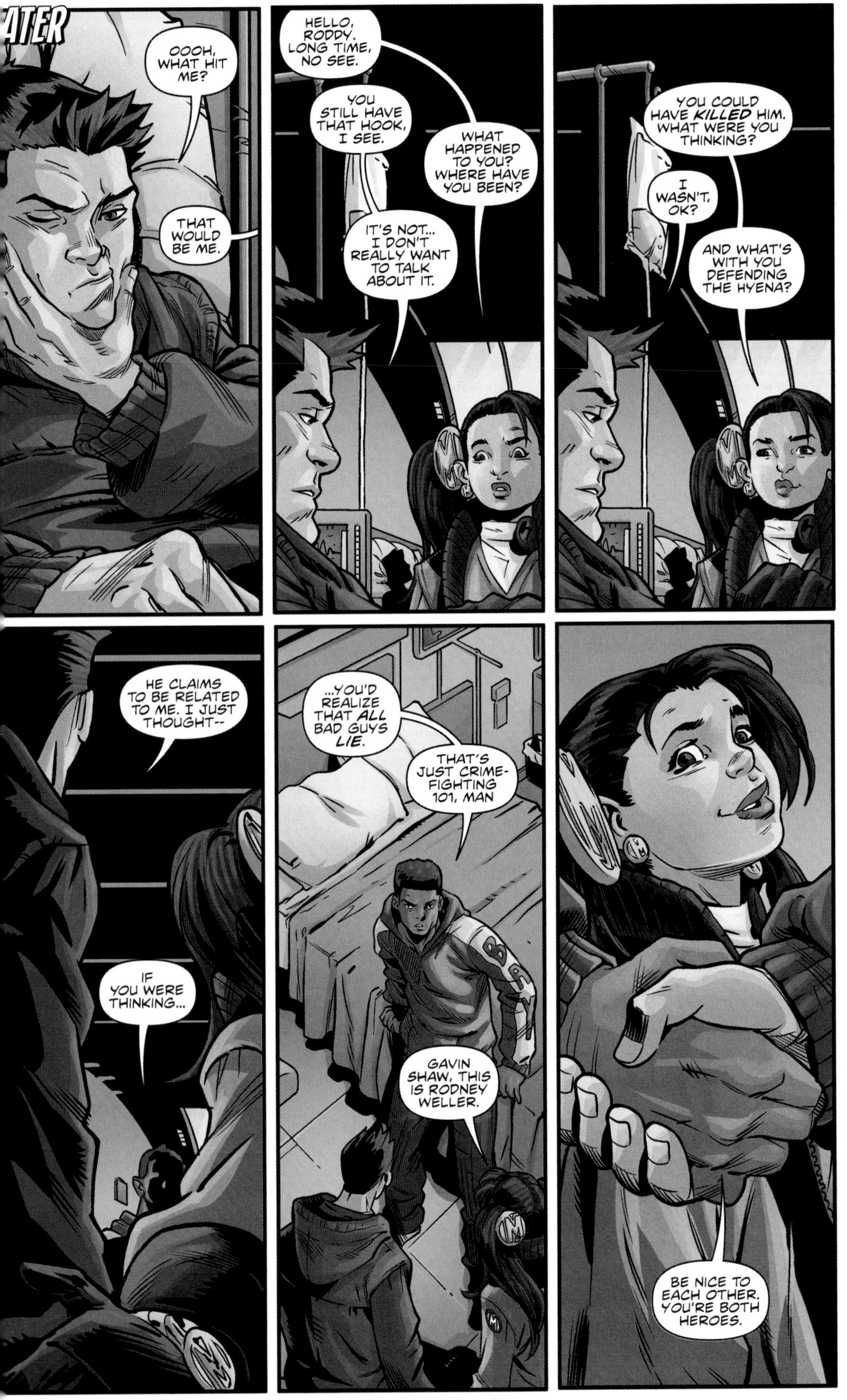
ATER
OOOH, WHAT HIT ME?
THAT WOULD BE ME.
HELLO, RODDY. LONG TIME, NO SEE.
YOU STILL HAVE THAT HOOK, I SEE.
WHAT HAPPENED TO YOU? WHERE HAVE YOU BEEN?
IT'S NOT... I DON'T REALLY WANT TO TALK ABOUT IT.
YOU COULD HAVE KILLED HIM. WHAT WERE YOU THINKING?
I WASN'T, OK?
AND WHAT'S WITH YOU DEFENDING THE HYENA?
HE CLAIMS TO BE RELATED TO ME. I JUST THOUGHT--
IF YOU WERE THINKING...
...YOU'D REALIZE THAT ALL BAD GUYS LIE.
THAT'S JUST CRIME-FIGHTING 101, MAN
GAVIN SHAW, THIS IS RODNEY WELLER.
BE NICE TO EACH OTHER. YOU'RE BOTH HEROES.

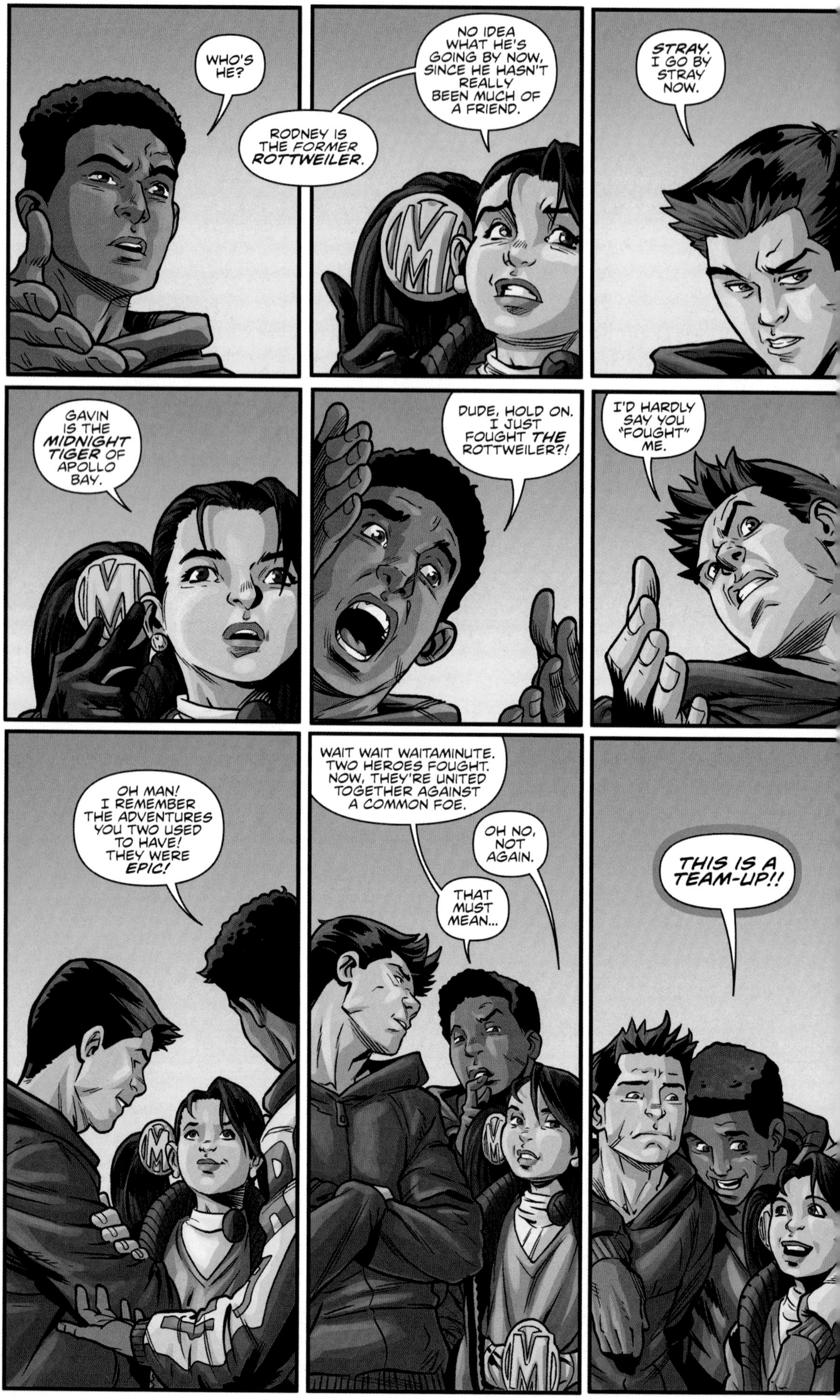
WHO'S HE?
RODNEY IS THE FORMER ROTTWEILER.
NO IDEA WHAT HE'S GOING BY NOW, SINCE HE HASN'T REALLY BEEN MUCH OF A FRIEND.
STRAY. I GO BY STRAY NOW.
GAVIN IS THE MIDNIGHT TIGER OF APOLLO BAY.
DUDE, HOLD ON. I JUST FOUGHT THE ROTTWEILER?!
I'D HARDLY SAY YOU "FOUGHT" ME.
OH MAN! I REMEMBER THE ADVENTURES YOU TWO USED TO HAVE! THEY WERE EPIC!
WAIT WAIT WAITAMINUTE. TWO HEROES FOUGHT. NOW, THEY'RE UNITED TOGETHER AGAINST A COMMON FOE.
OH NO, NOT AGAIN.
THAT MUST MEAN...
THIS IS A TEAM-UP!!

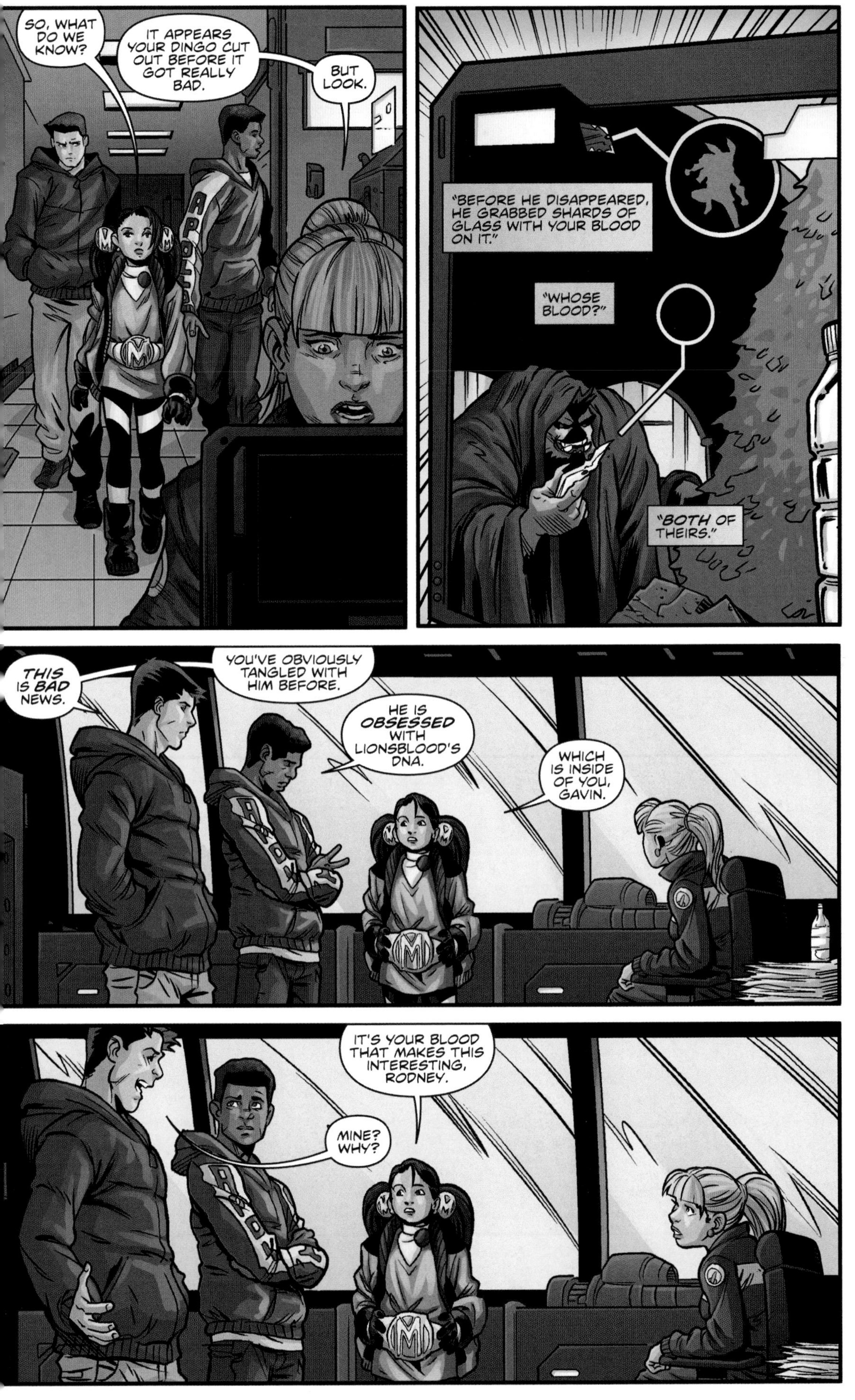
SO, WHAT DO WE KNOW?
IT APPEARS YOUR DINGO CUT OUT BEFORE IT GOT REALLY BAD.
BUT LOOK.
"BEFORE HE DISAPPEARED, HE GRABBED SHARDS OF GLASS WITH YOUR BLOOD ON IT."
"WHOSE BLOOD?"
"BOTH OF THEIRS."
THIS IS BAD NEWS.
YOU'VE OBVIOUSLY TANGLED WITH HIM BEFORE.
HE IS OBSESSED WITH LIONSBLOOD'S DNA.
WHICH IS INSIDE OF YOU, GAVIN.
IT'S YOUR BLOOD THAT MAKES THIS INTERESTING, RODNEY.
MINE? WHY?

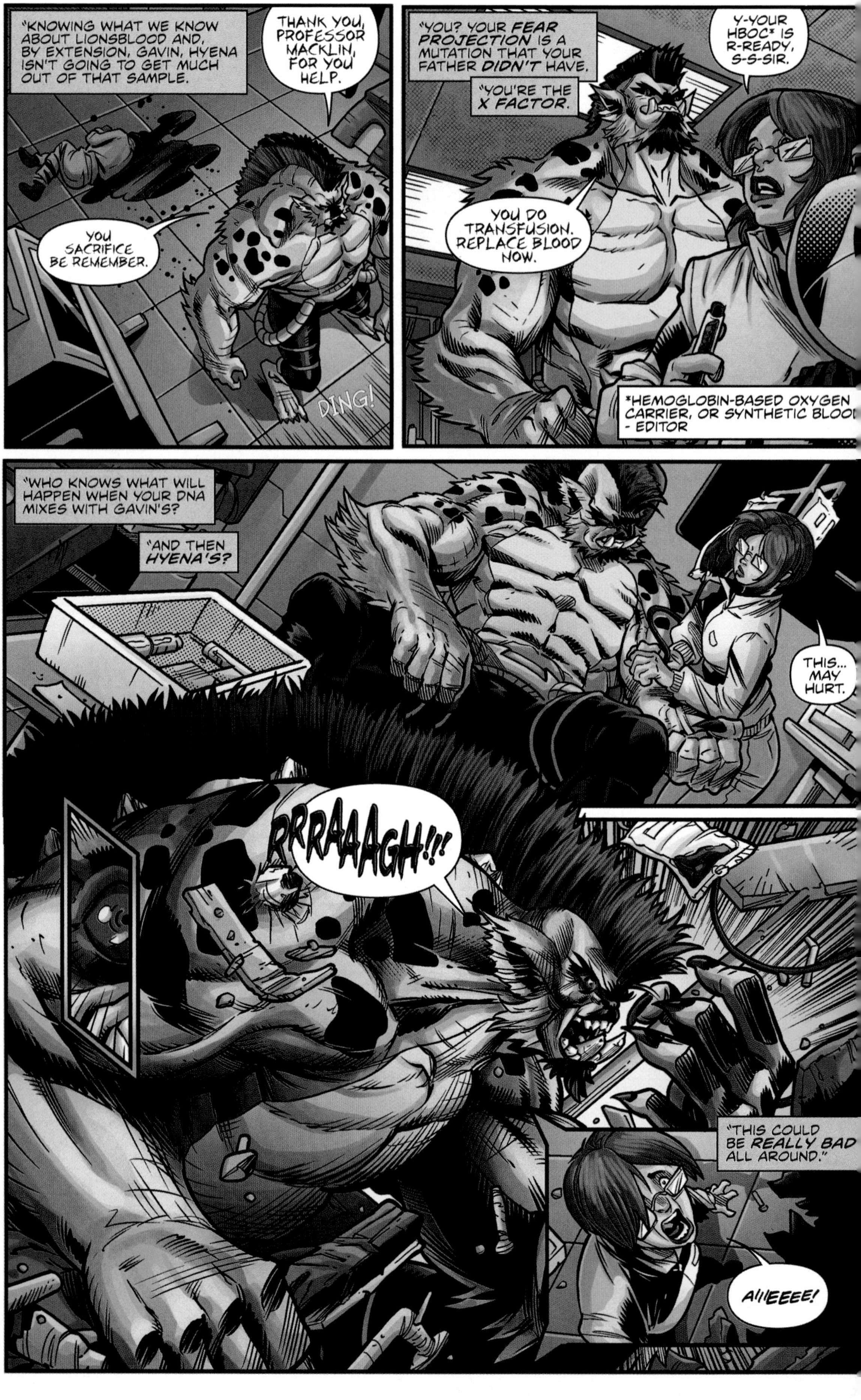

"KNOWING WHAT WE KNOW ABOUT LIONSBLOOD AND, BY EXTENSION, GAVIN, HYENA ISN'T GOING TO GET MUCH OUT OF THAT SAMPLE.
THANK YOU, PROFESSOR MACKLIN, FOR YOU HELP.
YOU SACRIFICE BE REMEMBER.
DING!
"YOU? YOUR FEAR PROJECTION IS A MUTATION THAT YOUR FATHER DIDN'T HAVE.
"YOU'RE THE X FACTOR.
Y-YOUR HBOC* IS R-READY, S-S-SIR.
YOU DO TRANSFUSION. REPLACE BLOOD NOW.
*HEMOGLOBIN-BASED OXYGEN CARRIER, OR SYNTHETIC BLOOD - EDITOR
"WHO KNOWS WHAT WILL HAPPEN WHEN YOUR DNA MIXES WITH GAVIN'S?
"AND THEN HYENA'S?
THIS... MAY HURT.
RRRAAAGH!!!
"THIS COULD BE REALLY BAD ALL AROUND."
AIIEEEE!

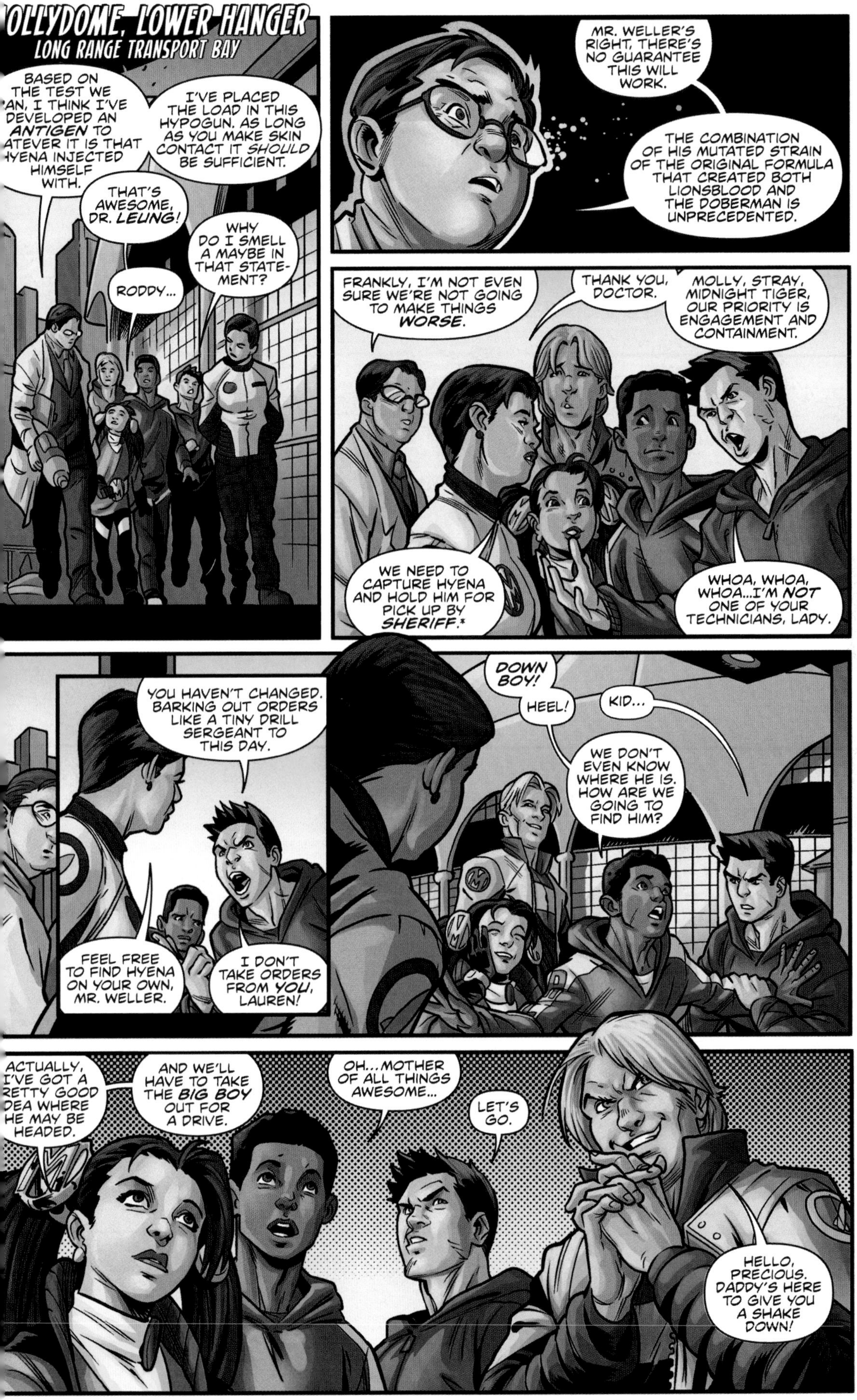

OLLYDOME, LOWER HANGER
LONG RANGE TRANSPORT BAY
BASED ON THE TEST WE AN, I THINK I'VE DEVELOPED AN ANTIGEN TO ATEVER IT IS THAT YENA INJECTED HIMSELF WITH.
I'VE PLACED THE LOAD IN THIS HYPOGUN. AS LONG AS YOU MAKE SKIN CONTACT IT SHOULD BE SUFFICIENT.
THAT'S AWESOME, DR. LEUNG!
WHY DO I SMELL A MAYBE IN THAT STATEMENT?
RODDY...
MR. WELLER'S RIGHT, THERE'S NO GUARANTEE THIS WILL WORK.
THE COMBINATION OF HIS MUTATED STRAIN OF THE ORIGINAL FORMULA THAT CREATED BOTH LIONSBLOOD AND THE DOBERMAN IS UNPRECEDENTED.
FRANKLY, I'M NOT EVEN SURE WE'RE NOT GOING TO MAKE THINGS WORSE.
THANK YOU, DOCTOR.
MOLLY, STRAY, MIDNIGHT TIGER, OUR PRIORITY IS ENGAGEMENT AND CONTAINMENT.
WE NEED TO CAPTURE HYENA AND HOLD HIM FOR PICK UP BY SHERIFF.*
WHOA, WHOA, WHOA...I'M NOT ONE OF YOUR TECHNICIANS, LADY.
YOU HAVEN'T CHANGED. BARKING OUT ORDERS LIKE A TINY DRILL SERGEANT TO THIS DAY.
FEEL FREE TO FIND HYENA ON YOUR OWN, MR. WELLER.
I DON'T TAKE ORDERS FROM YOU, LAUREN!
DOWN BOY!
HEEL!
KID...
WE DON'T EVEN KNOW WHERE HE IS. HOW ARE WE GOING TO FIND HIM?
ACTUALLY, I'VE GOT A RETTY GOOD DEA WHERE HE MAY BE HEADED.
AND WE'LL HAVE TO TAKE THE BIG BOY OUT FOR A DRIVE.
OH...MOTHER OF ALL THINGS AWESOME...
LET'S GO.
HELLO, PRECIOUS. DADDY'S HERE TO GIVE YOU A SHAKE DOWN!

*SUPER HUMAN ENFORCEMENT RECONNAISSANCE, AND INCARCERATION OF FUGITIVES FORCE

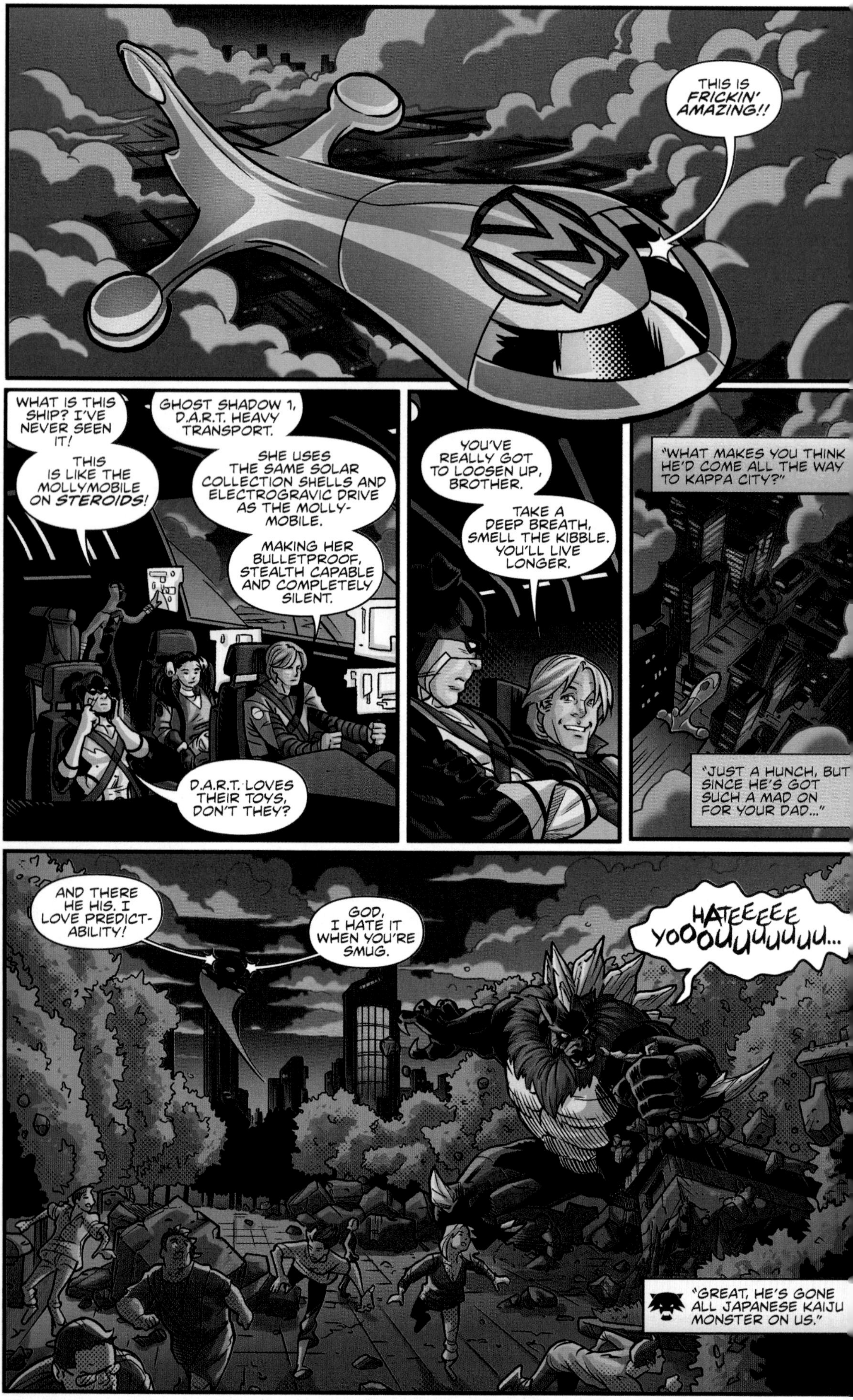
THIS IS FRICKIN' AMAZING!!
WHAT IS THIS SHIP? I'VE NEVER SEEN IT!
THIS IS LIKE THE MOLLYMOBILE ON STEROIDS!
GHOST SHADOW 1, D.A.R.T. HEAVY TRANSPORT.
SHE USES THE SAME SOLAR COLLECTION SHELLS AND ELECTROGRAVIC DRIVE AS THE MOLLY-MOBILE.
MAKING HER BULLETPROOF, STEALTH CAPABLE AND COMPLETELY SILENT.
D.A.R.T. LOVES THEIR TOYS, DON'T THEY?
YOU'VE REALLY GOT TO LOOSEN UP, BROTHER.
TAKE A DEEP BREATH, SMELL THE KIBBLE. YOU'LL LIVE LONGER.
"WHAT MAKES YOU THINK HE'D COME ALL THE WAY TO KAPPA CITY?"
"JUST A HUNCH, BUT SINCE HE'S GOT SUCH A MAD ON FOR YOUR DAD..."
AND THERE HE HIS. I LOVE PREDICT-ABILITY!
GOD, I HATE IT WHEN YOU'RE SMUG.
HATEEEEE YOOOUUUUUUU...
"GREAT, HE'S GONE ALL JAPANESE KAIJU MONSTER ON US."

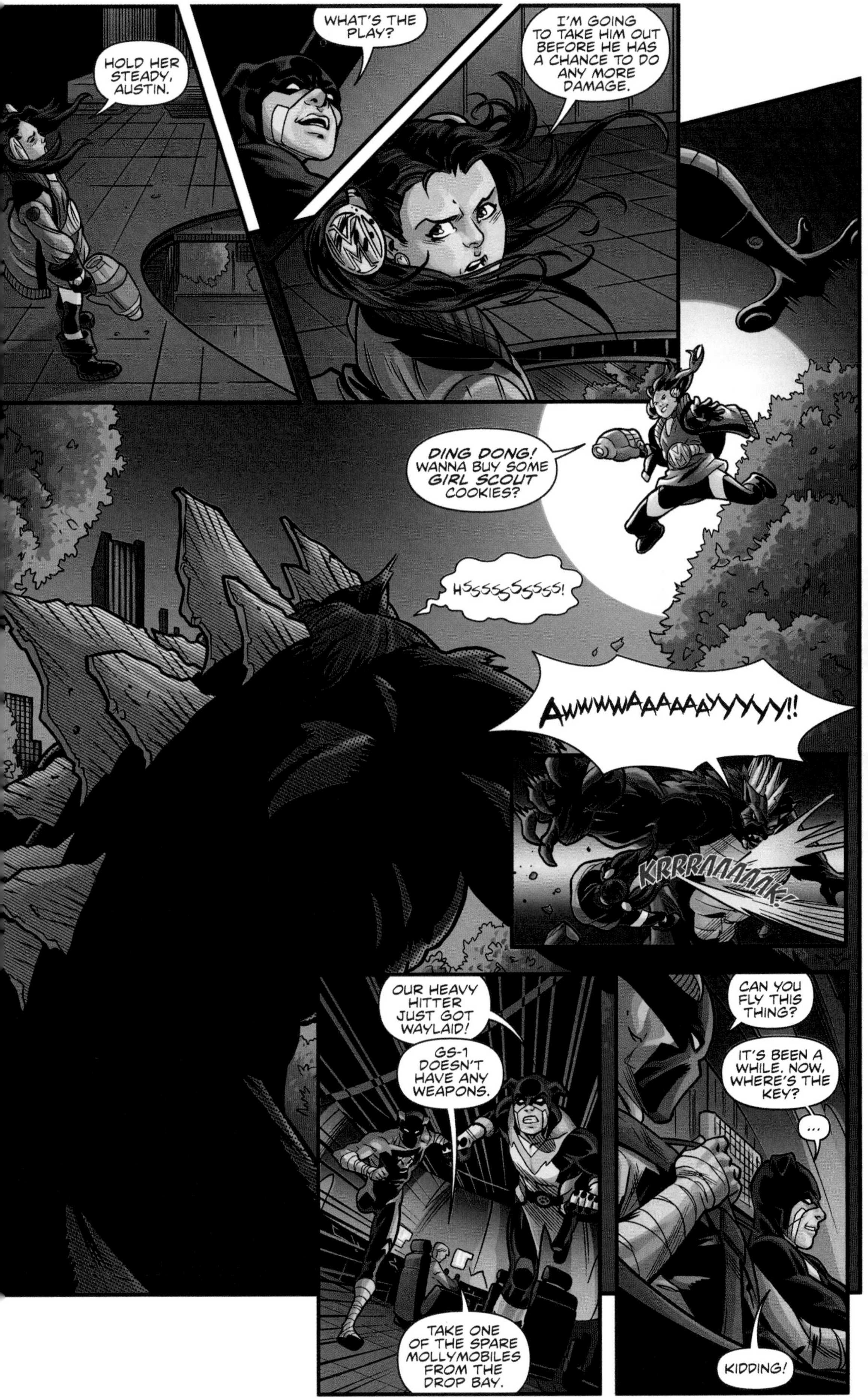
HOLD HER STEADY, AUSTIN.
WHAT'S THE PLAY?
I'M GOING TO TAKE HIM OUT BEFORE HE HAS A CHANCE TO DO ANY MORE DAMAGE.
DING DONG! WANNA BUY SOME GIRL SCOUT COOKIES?
HSSSSSSSSSS!
AWWWWAAAAAYYYYY!!
KRRRAAAAAAK!
OUR HEAVY HITTER JUST GOT WAYLAID!
GS-1 DOESN'T HAVE ANY WEAPONS.
TAKE ONE OF THE SPARE MOLLYMOBILES FROM THE DROP BAY.
CAN YOU FLY THIS THING?
IT'S BEEN A WHILE. NOW, WHERE'S THE KEY?
...
KIDDING!

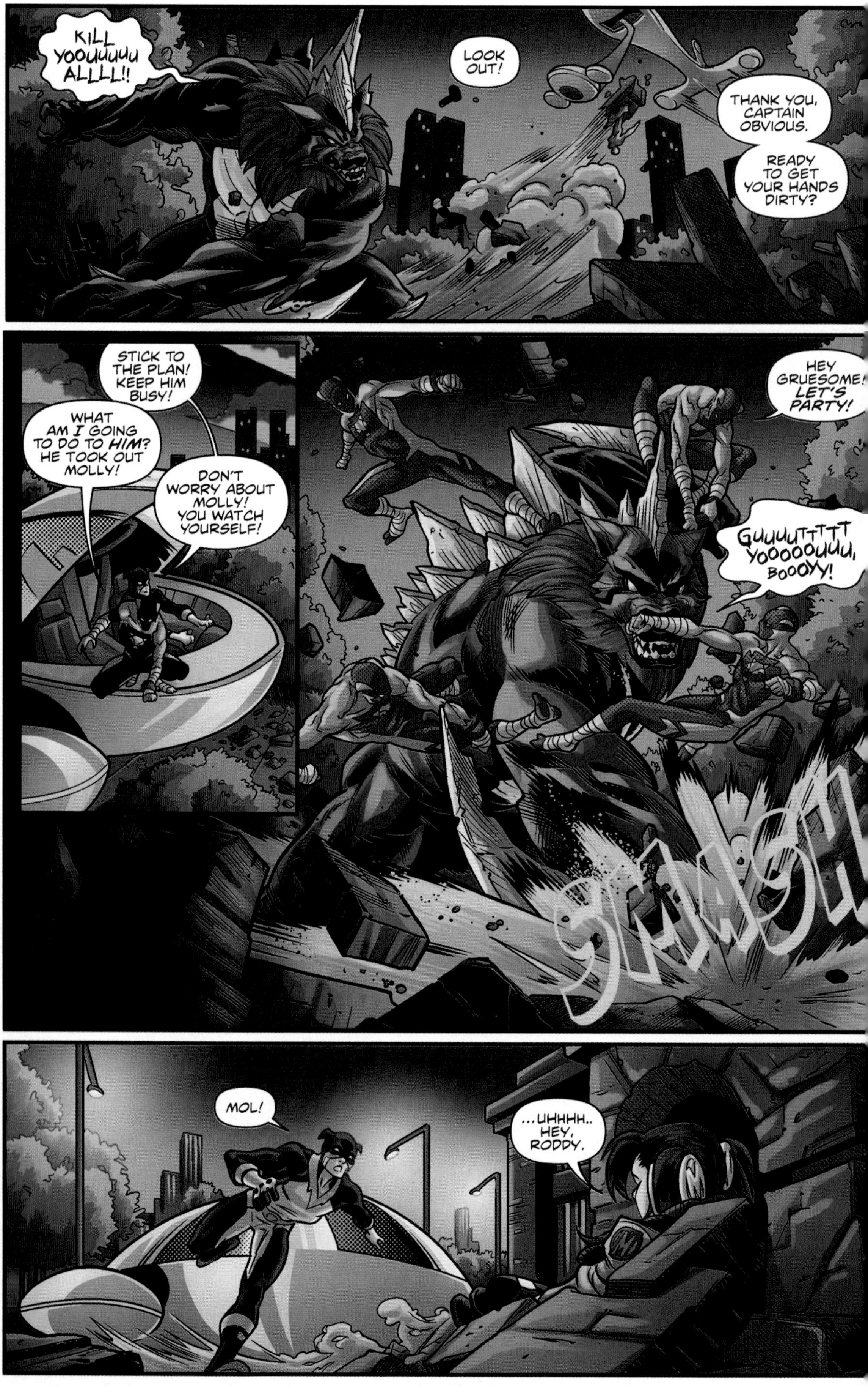
KILL YOOUUUUU ALLLL!!
LOOK OUT!
THANK YOU, CAPTAIN OBVIOUS.
READY TO GET YOUR HANDS DIRTY?
STICK TO THE PLAN! KEEP HIM BUSY!
WHAT AM *I* GOING TO DO TO *HIM*? HE TOOK OUT MOLLY!
DON'T WORRY ABOUT MOLLY! YOU WATCH YOURSELF!
HEY GRUESOME! *LET'S PARTY!*
GUUUUTTTTT YOOOOUUU, BOOOYY!
SMASH
MOL!
...UHHHH.. HEY, RODDY.

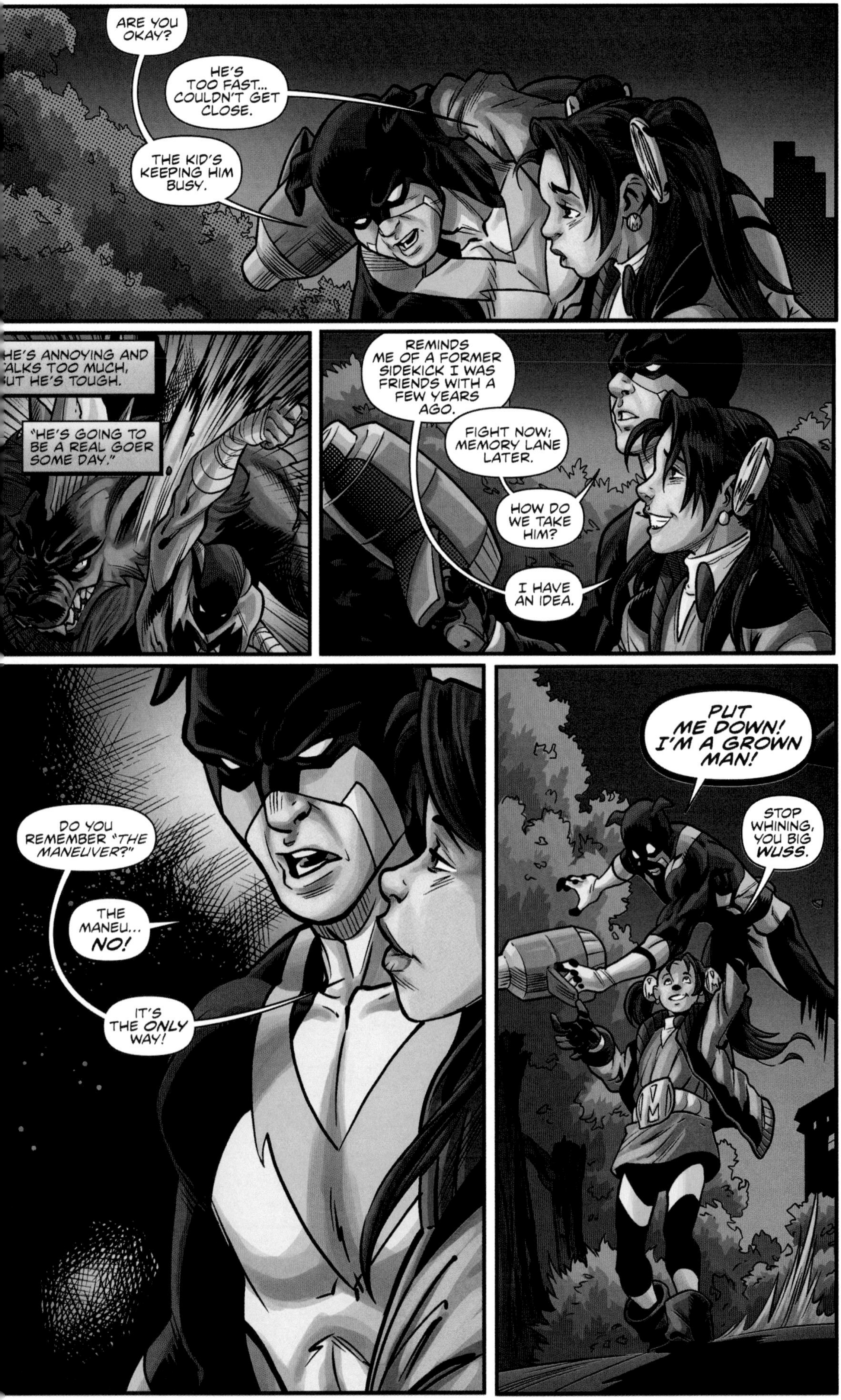
ARE YOU OKAY?
HE'S TOO FAST... COULDN'T GET CLOSE.
THE KID'S KEEPING HIM BUSY.
HE'S ANNOYING AND TALKS TOO MUCH, BUT HE'S TOUGH.
"HE'S GOING TO BE A REAL GOER SOME DAY."
REMINDS ME OF A FORMER SIDEKICK I WAS FRIENDS WITH A FEW YEARS AGO.
FIGHT NOW; MEMORY LANE LATER.
HOW DO WE TAKE HIM?
I HAVE AN IDEA.
DO YOU REMEMBER "THE MANEUVER?"
THE MANEU... NO!
IT'S THE ONLY WAY!
PUT ME DOWN! I'M A GROWN MAN!
STOP WHINING, YOU BIG WUSS.

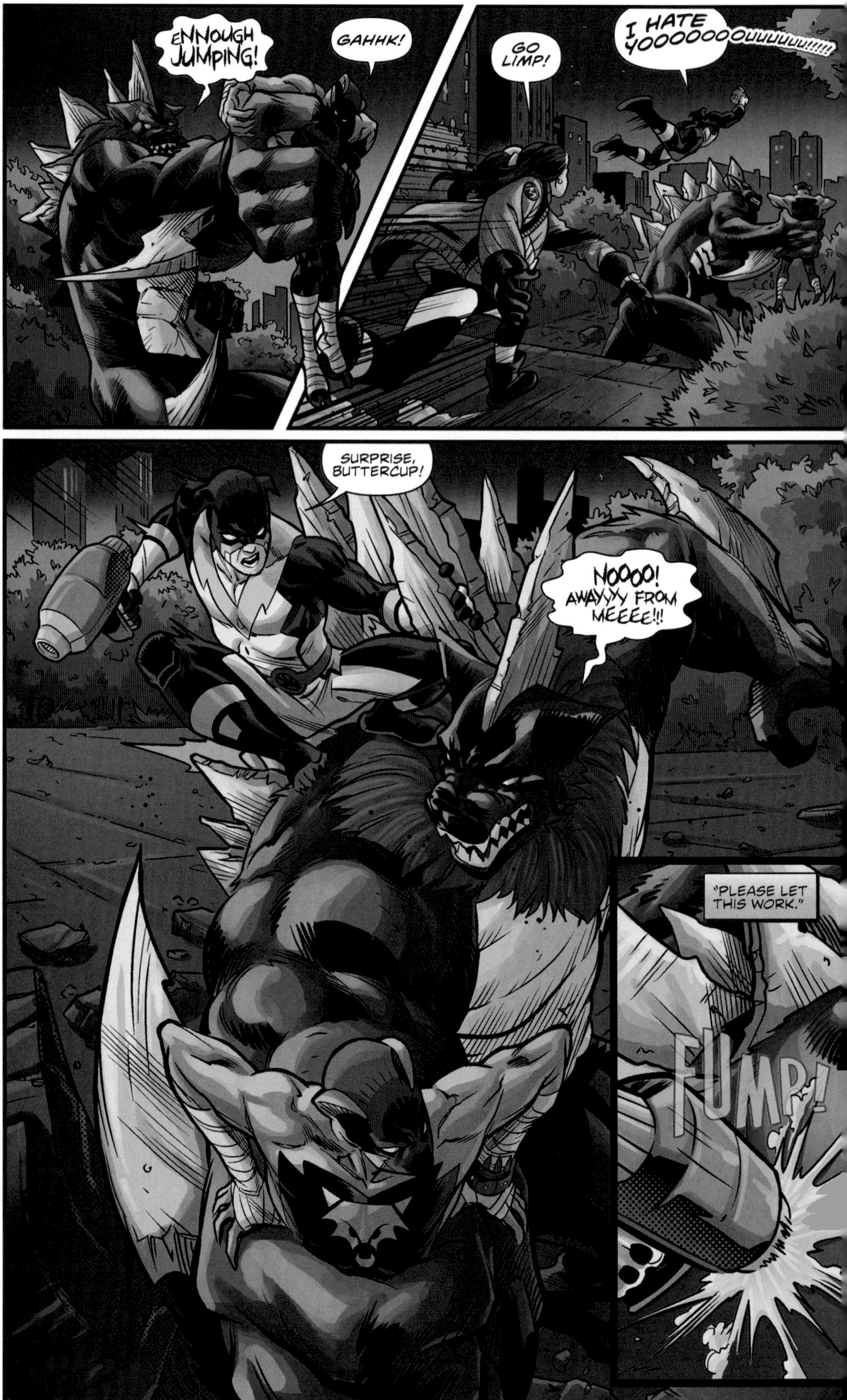
ENNOUGH JUMPING!
GAHHK!
GO LIMP!
I HATE YOOOOOOOuuuuuuu!!!!!
SURPRISE, BUTTERCUP!
NOOOO! AWAYYYY FROM MEEEE!!!
"PLEASE LET THIS WORK."
FUMP!

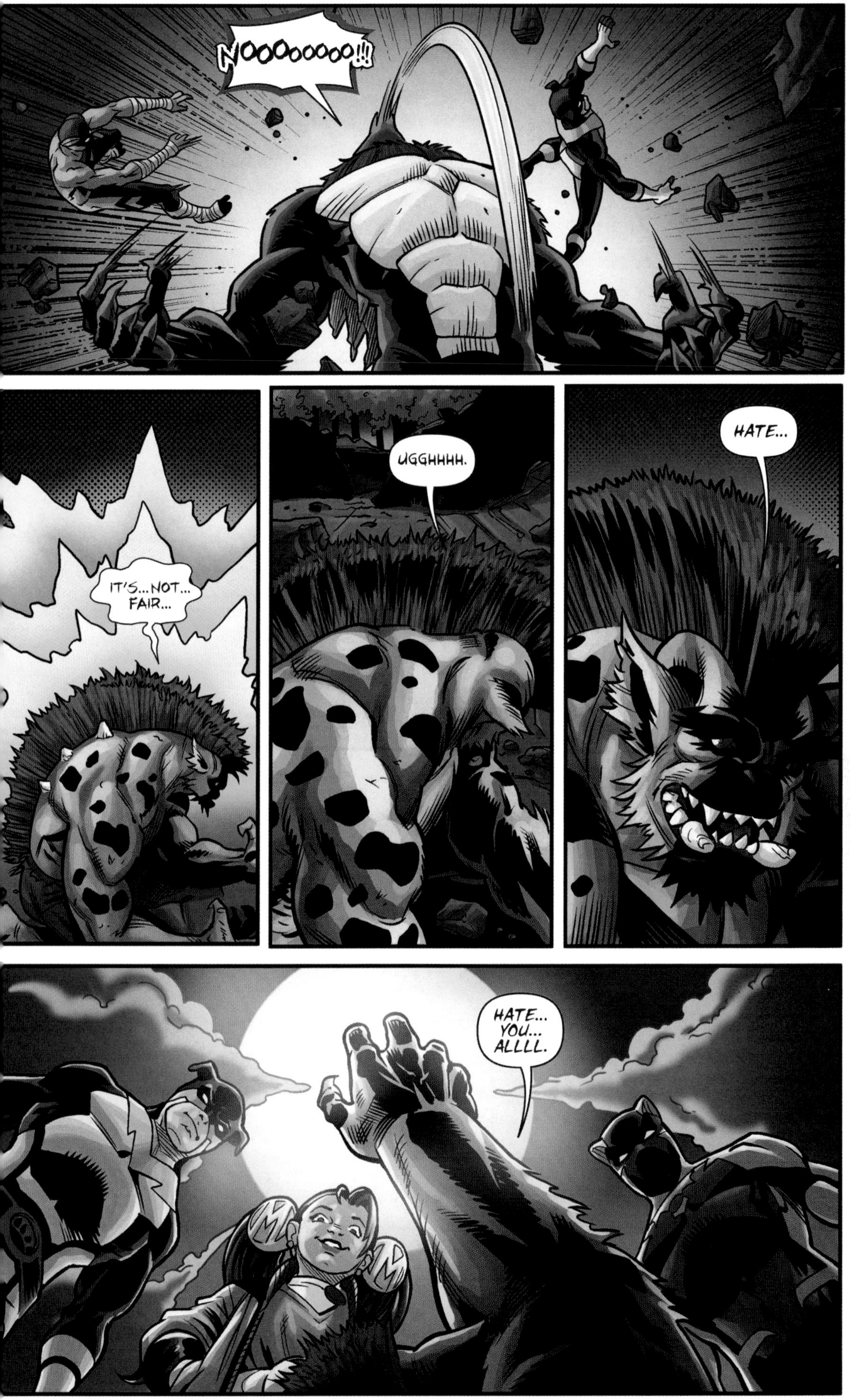
NOOOoooooo!!!
IT'S...NOT...
FAIR...
UGGHHHH.
HATE...
HATE...
YOU...
ALLLL.

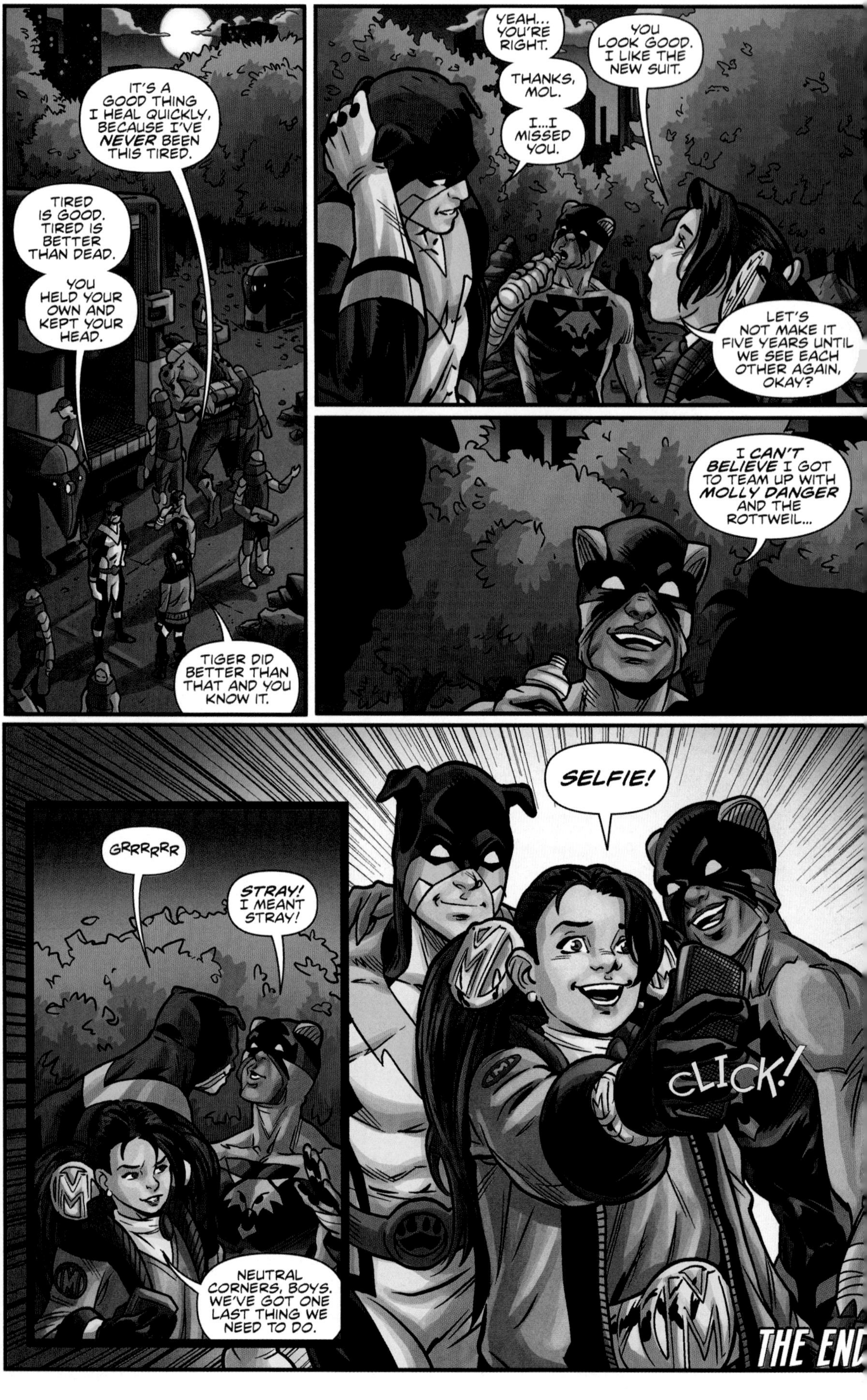
IT'S A GOOD THING I HEAL QUICKLY, BECAUSE I'VE NEVER BEEN THIS TIRED.
TIRED IS GOOD. TIRED IS BETTER THAN DEAD.
YOU HELD YOUR OWN AND KEPT YOUR HEAD.
TIGER DID BETTER THAN THAT AND YOU KNOW IT.
YEAH... YOU'RE RIGHT.
THANKS, MOL.
I...I MISSED YOU.
YOU LOOK GOOD. I LIKE THE NEW SUIT.
LET'S NOT MAKE IT FIVE YEARS UNTIL WE SEE EACH OTHER AGAIN, OKAY?
I CAN'T BELIEVE I GOT TO TEAM UP WITH MOLLY DANGER AND THE ROTTWEIL...
GRRRRRR
STRAY! I MEANT STRAY!
NEUTRAL CORNERS, BOYS. WE'VE GOT ONE LAST THING WE NEED TO DO.
SELFIE!
CLICK!
THE END

After the tragic events of last issue, Cyrus Perkins has gone from aimless Taxi Cab Driver to amateur Detective. Teaming with Michael, the ghost boy trapped in his car, Cyrus speeds into mystery, danger, and a conspiracy too twisted for words!

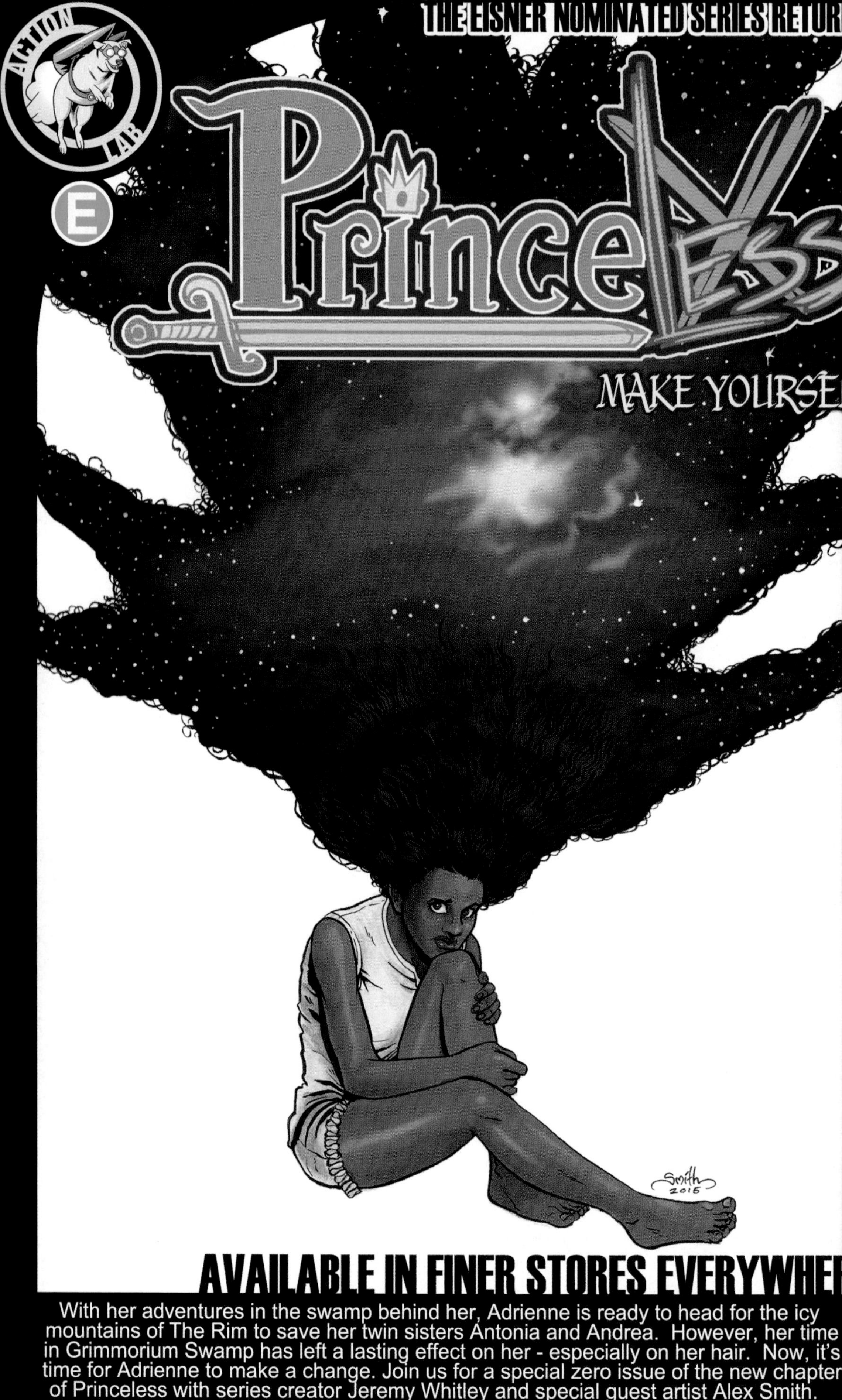

THE EISNER NOMINATED SERIES RETUR
ACTION LAB
E
Princeless
MAKE YOURSE
Smith 2015
AVAILABLE IN FINER STORES EVERYWHE
With her adventures in the swamp behind her, Adrienne is ready to head for the icy mountains of The Rim to save her twin sisters Antonia and Andrea. However, her time in Grimmorium Swamp has left a lasting effect on her - especially on her hair. Now, it's time for Adrienne to make a change. Join us for a special zero issue of the new chapter of Princeless with series creator Jeremy Whitley and special guest artist Alex Smith.

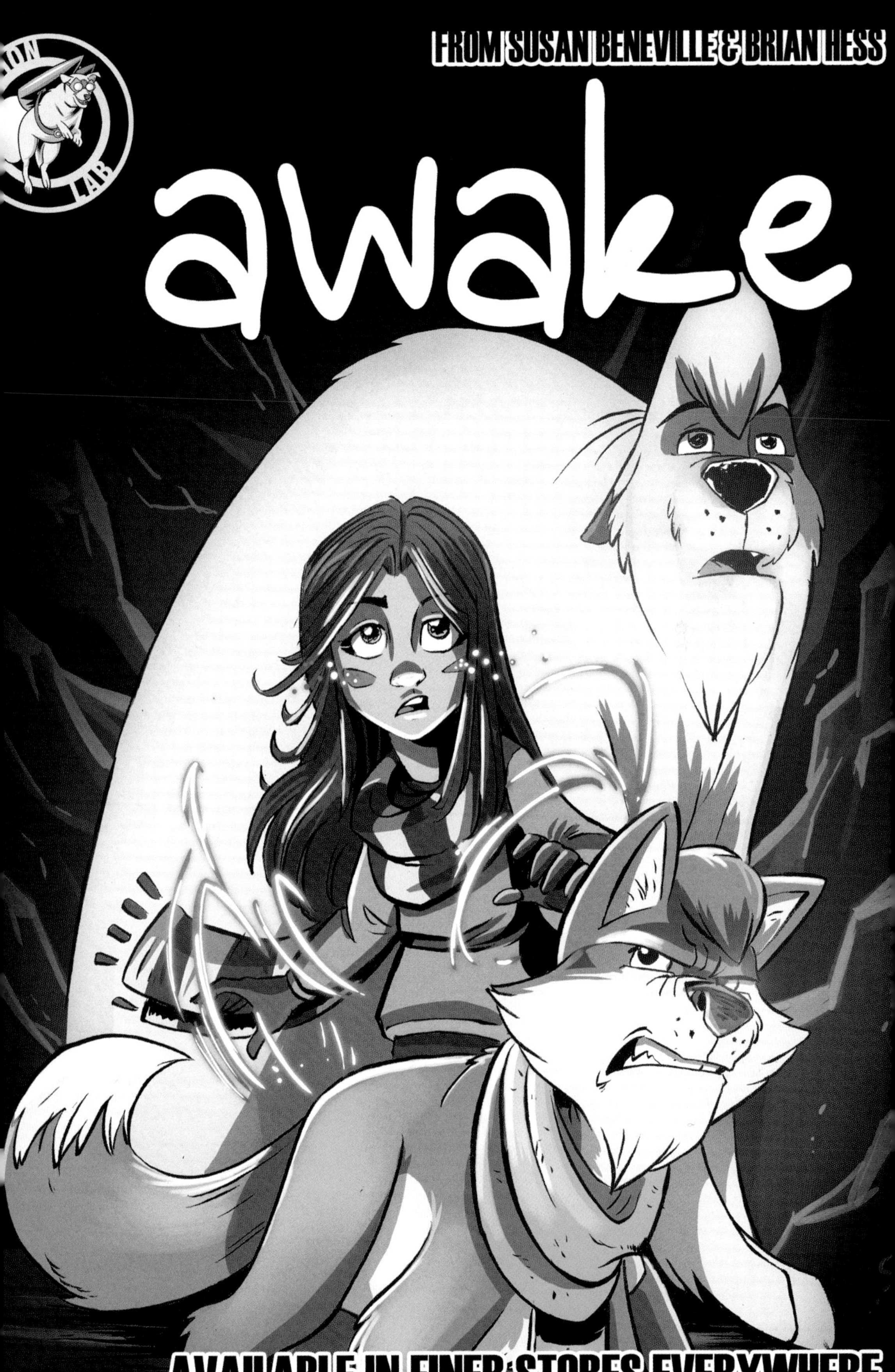
FROM SUSAN BENEVILLE & BRIAN HESS
awake
AVAILABLE IN FINER STORES EVERYWHERE

Twelve year-old Regn has the power to wake and heal planets. But, on her first mission, she lands on Gremon where she discovers an angry planet tearing itself apart, an irresponsible big brother, and a greedy baron who stokes the chaos for his own benefit. Her power may not be enough when she comes face-to-face with the planet's consciousness.

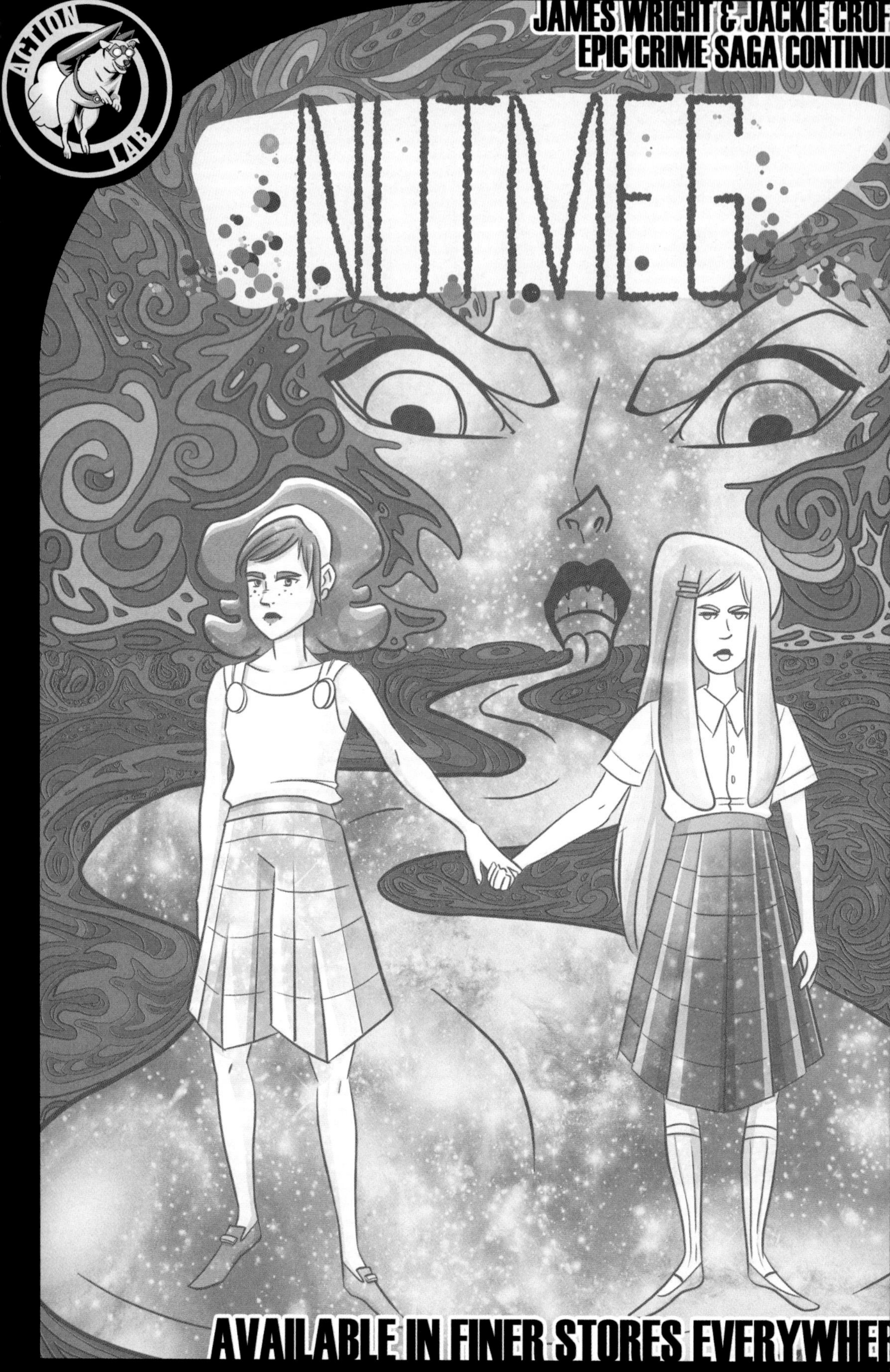
ACTION LAB
JAMES WRIGHT & JACKIE CROF
EPIC CRIME SAGA CONTINU
NUTMEG
AVAILABLE IN FINER STORES EVERYWHE

Fall, Part 5: “Pantry Raids” Poppy and Cassia, the teen masterminds behind the addictive Patty Cake brownies, hoping to better understand their product, violate one of the 10 Crime Commandments: they try their own supply.

FROM ALL-AGES TO MATURE READERS
ACTION LAB HAS YOU COVERED.

 Appropriate
for everyone.

 Appropriate for age 9 and up.
Absent of profanity or adult content.

 Suggested for 12 and Up. Comics
with this rating are comparable to a
PG-13 movie rating. Recommended
for our teen and young adult readers.

 Appropriate for older teens. Similar
to Teen, but featuring more mature
themes and/or more graphic imagery.

 Contains extreme viloence and some
nudity. Basically the Rated-R of
comics.

 FIND YOUR NEW FAVORITE COMICS.

ACTION LAB

READ MORE NOW

Actionverse - Action Lab
www.actionlabcomics.com
00011
7 02382 69113 4

ACTIONLABCOMICS.COM

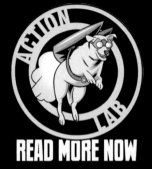

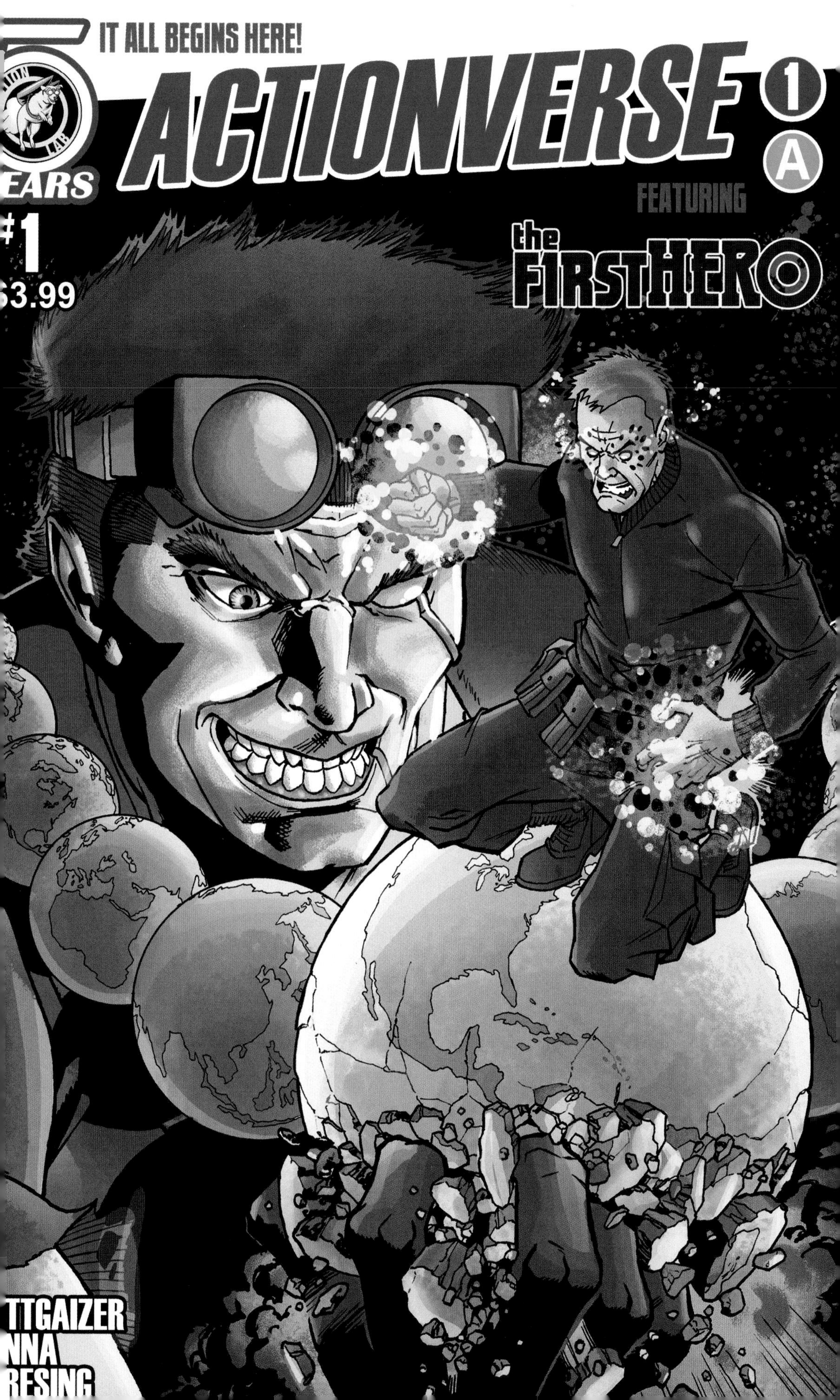

IT ALL BEGINS HERE!
5 YEARS
ACTIONVERSE
1
A
FEATURING
the FIRST HERO
#1
$3.99
TTGAIZER
NNA
RESING

ACTIONVERSE

FEATURING

the FIRST HERO

Written by Anthony Ruttgaizer

Art by Marco Renna

Color and Letters by Fred C. Stresing

Cover by Lee Moder and Fred C. Stresing

Variant Connecting Cover by Ron Frenz, Marc Deering
Ross Campbell and David Bednarski

Edited by Vito Delsante

THE FIRST HERO and all related characters
created by Anthony Ruttgaizer

PREVIOUSLY

On a world, just like ours, a man named Kyle Scordato tried to take on the villainous persona of Malice
only to be foiled by the hero, Virtue.
Meanwhile, on a parallel Earth, Jake Roth is the only superbeing to not go insane after manifesting super powers.
On his world, he is the first, and only, hero.

BRYAN SEATON - PUBLISHER
DAVE DWONCH - PRESIDENT
SHAWN GABBORIN - EDITOR IN CHIEF
JASON MARTIN - PUBLISHER, DANGER ZONE
JAMAL IGLE - VICE-PRESIDENT OF MARKETING
JIM DIETZ - SOCIAL MEDIA DIRECTOR
NICOLE D'ANDRIA - EDITOR
CHAD CICCONI - MULTIVERSAL MENSCH
COLLEEN BOYD - SUBMISSIONS EDITOR

ACTIONLABCOMICS.COM

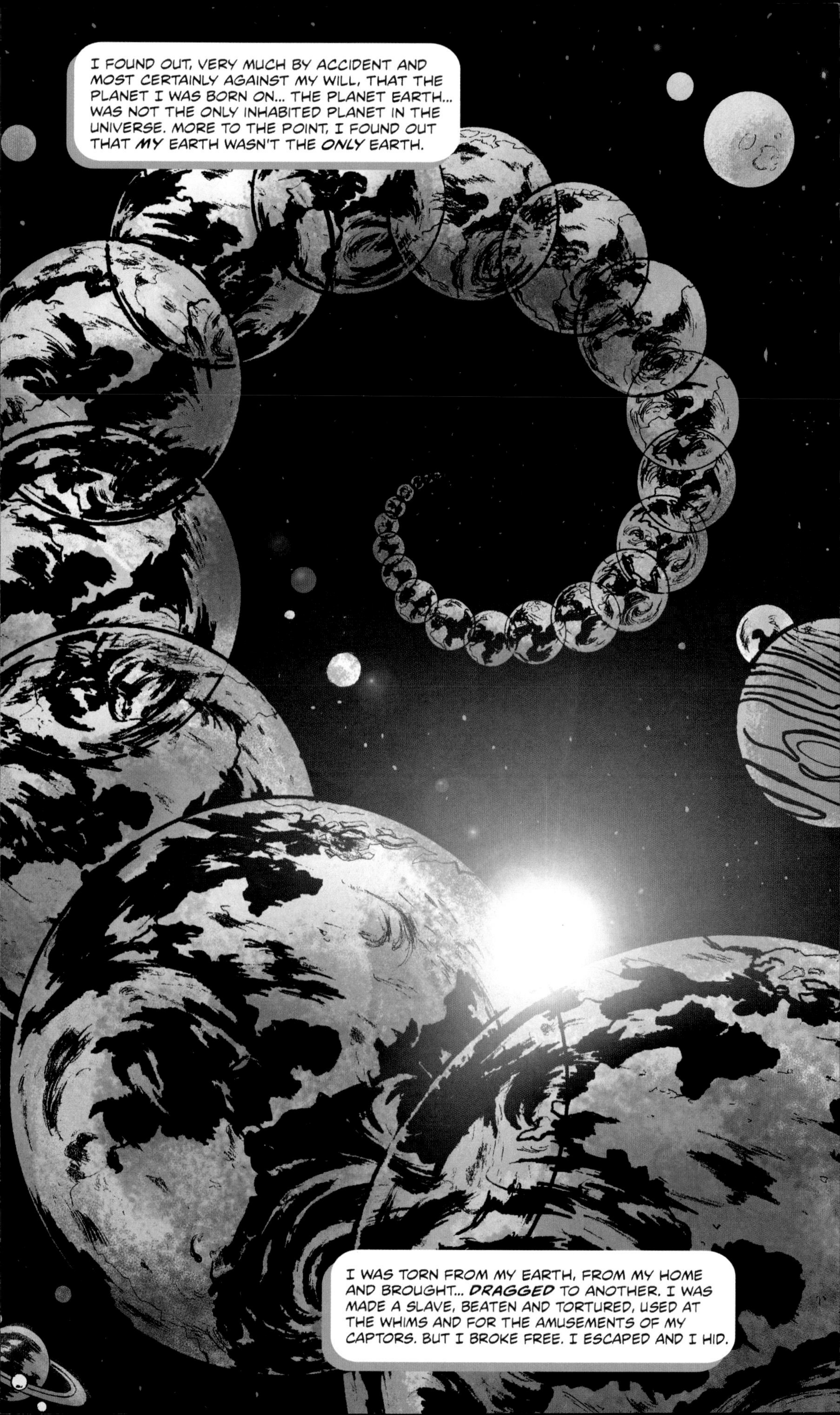
I FOUND OUT, VERY MUCH BY ACCIDENT AND MOST CERTAINLY AGAINST MY WILL, THAT THE PLANET I WAS BORN ON... THE PLANET EARTH... WAS NOT THE ONLY INHABITED PLANET IN THE UNIVERSE. MORE TO THE POINT, I FOUND OUT THAT *MY* EARTH WASN'T THE *ONLY* EARTH.
I WAS TORN FROM MY EARTH, FROM MY HOME AND BROUGHT... ***DRAGGED*** TO ANOTHER. I WAS MADE A SLAVE, BEATEN AND TORTURED, USED AT THE WHIMS AND FOR THE AMUSEMENTS OF MY CAPTORS. BUT I BROKE FREE. I ESCAPED AND I HID.

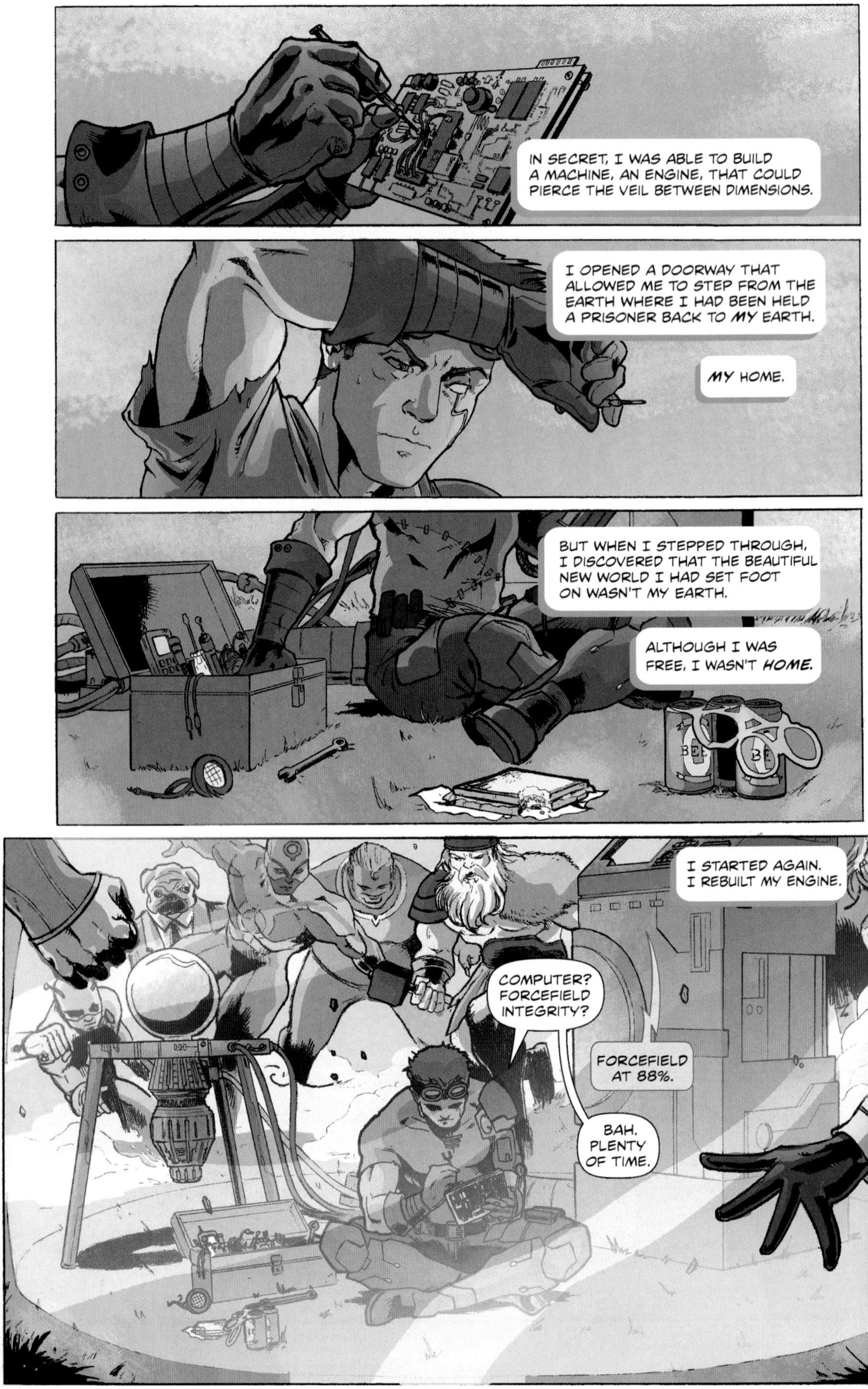
IN SECRET, I WAS ABLE TO BUILD A MACHINE, AN ENGINE, THAT COULD PIERCE THE VEIL BETWEEN DIMENSIONS.
I OPENED A DOORWAY THAT ALLOWED ME TO STEP FROM THE EARTH WHERE I HAD BEEN HELD A PRISONER BACK TO *MY* EARTH.
MY HOME.
BUT WHEN I STEPPED THROUGH, I DISCOVERED THAT THE BEAUTIFUL NEW WORLD I HAD SET FOOT ON WASN'T MY EARTH.
ALTHOUGH I WAS FREE, I WASN'T *HOME*.
I STARTED AGAIN. I REBUILT MY ENGINE.
COMPUTER? FORCEFIELD INTEGRITY?
FORCEFIELD AT 88%.
BAH. PLENTY OF TIME.

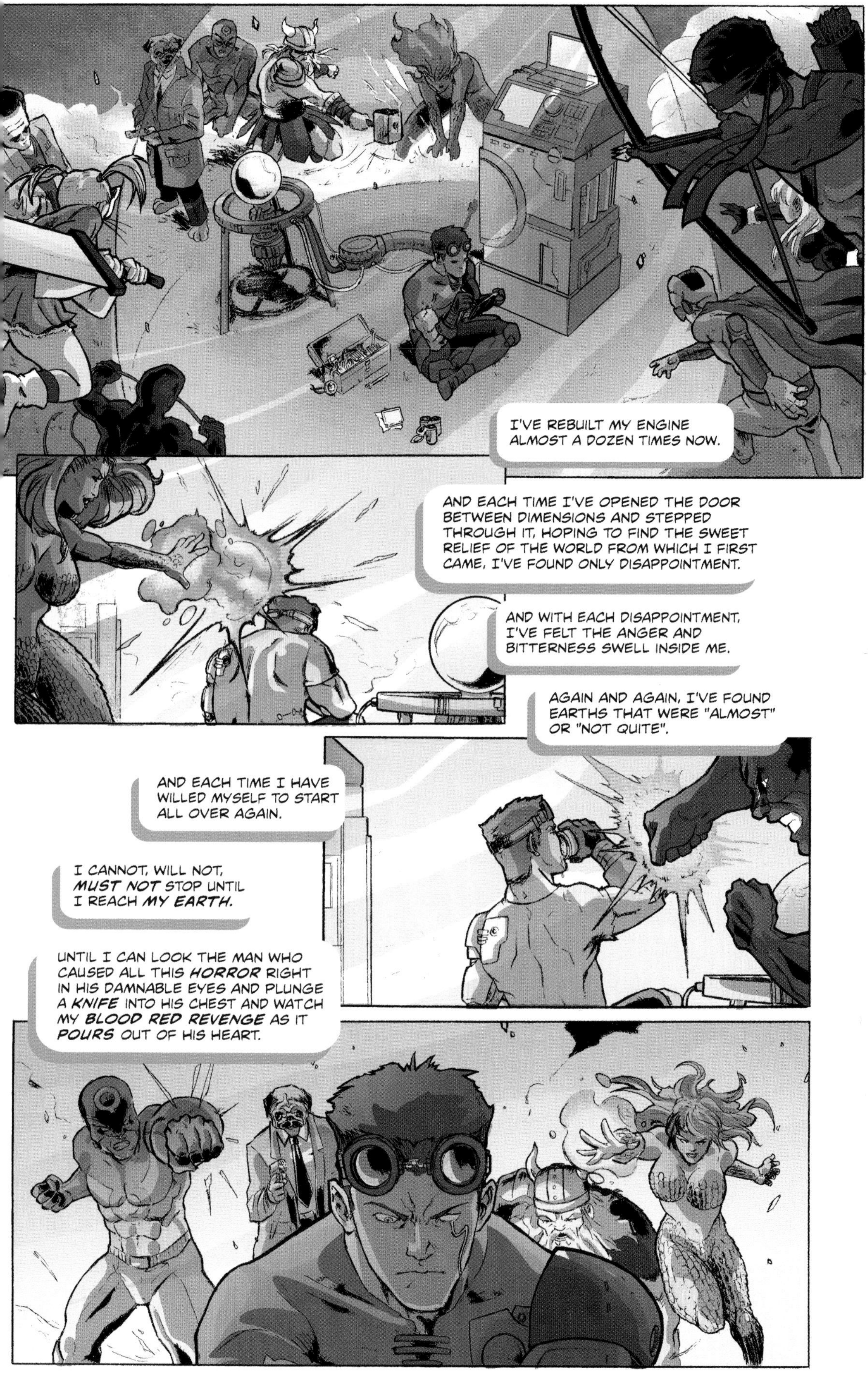
I'VE REBUILT MY ENGINE ALMOST A DOZEN TIMES NOW.
AND EACH TIME I'VE OPENED THE DOOR BETWEEN DIMENSIONS AND STEPPED THROUGH IT, HOPING TO FIND THE SWEET RELIEF OF THE WORLD FROM WHICH I FIRST CAME, I'VE FOUND ONLY DISAPPOINTMENT.
AND WITH EACH DISAPPOINTMENT, I'VE FELT THE ANGER AND BITTERNESS SWELL INSIDE ME.
AGAIN AND AGAIN, I'VE FOUND EARTHS THAT WERE "ALMOST" OR "NOT QUITE".
AND EACH TIME I HAVE WILLED MYSELF TO START ALL OVER AGAIN.
I CANNOT, WILL NOT, MUST NOT STOP UNTIL I REACH MY EARTH.
UNTIL I CAN LOOK THE MAN WHO CAUSED ALL THIS HORROR RIGHT IN HIS DAMNABLE EYES AND PLUNGE A KNIFE INTO HIS CHEST AND WATCH MY BLOOD RED REVENGE AS IT POURS OUT OF HIS HEART.

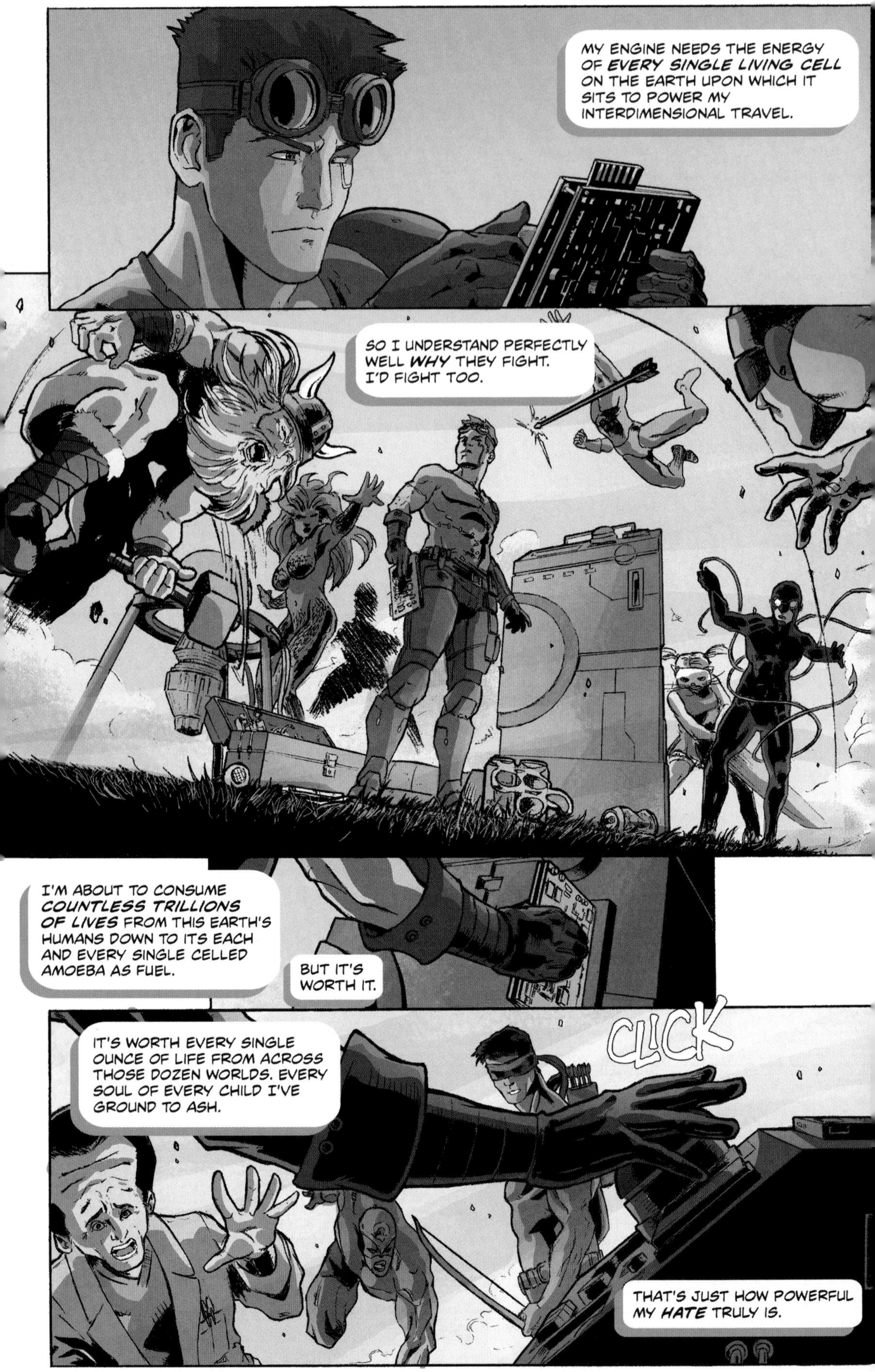

MY ENGINE NEEDS THE ENERGY OF *EVERY SINGLE LIVING CELL* ON THE EARTH UPON WHICH IT SITS TO POWER MY INTERDIMENSIONAL TRAVEL.
SO I UNDERSTAND PERFECTLY WELL *WHY* THEY FIGHT. I'D FIGHT TOO.
I'M ABOUT TO CONSUME *COUNTLESS TRILLIONS OF LIVES* FROM THIS EARTH'S HUMANS DOWN TO ITS EACH AND EVERY SINGLE CELLED AMOEBA AS FUEL.
BUT IT'S WORTH IT.
CLICK
IT'S WORTH EVERY SINGLE OUNCE OF LIFE FROM ACROSS THOSE DOZEN WORLDS. EVERY SOUL OF EVERY CHILD I'VE GROUND TO ASH.
THAT'S JUST HOW POWERFUL MY *HATE* TRULY IS.

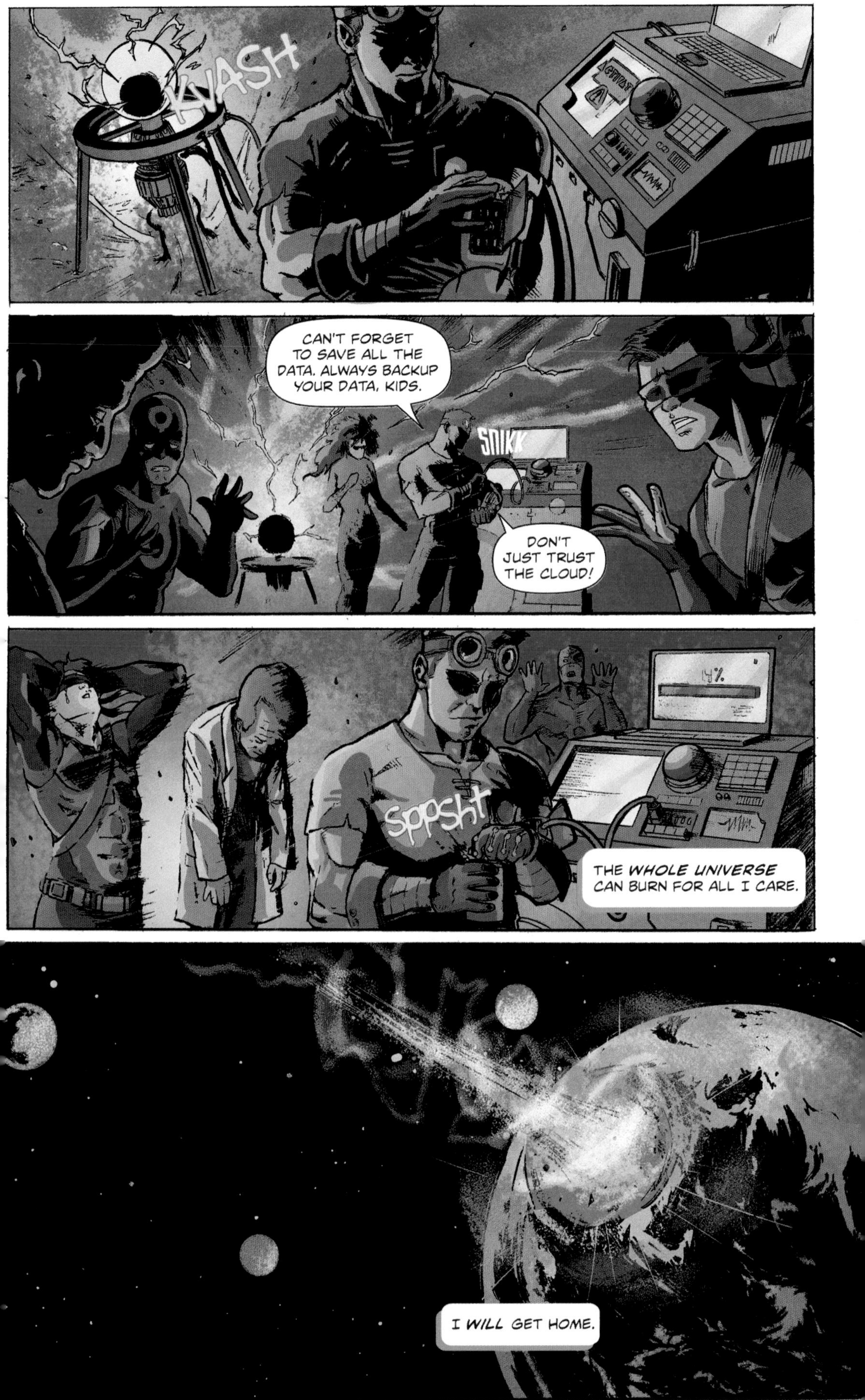
KVASH
CAN'T FORGET TO SAVE ALL THE DATA. ALWAYS BACKUP YOUR DATA, KIDS.
SNIKK
DON'T JUST TRUST THE CLOUD!
SPPSHT
THE *WHOLE UNIVERSE* CAN BURN FOR ALL I CARE.
I *WILL* GET HOME.

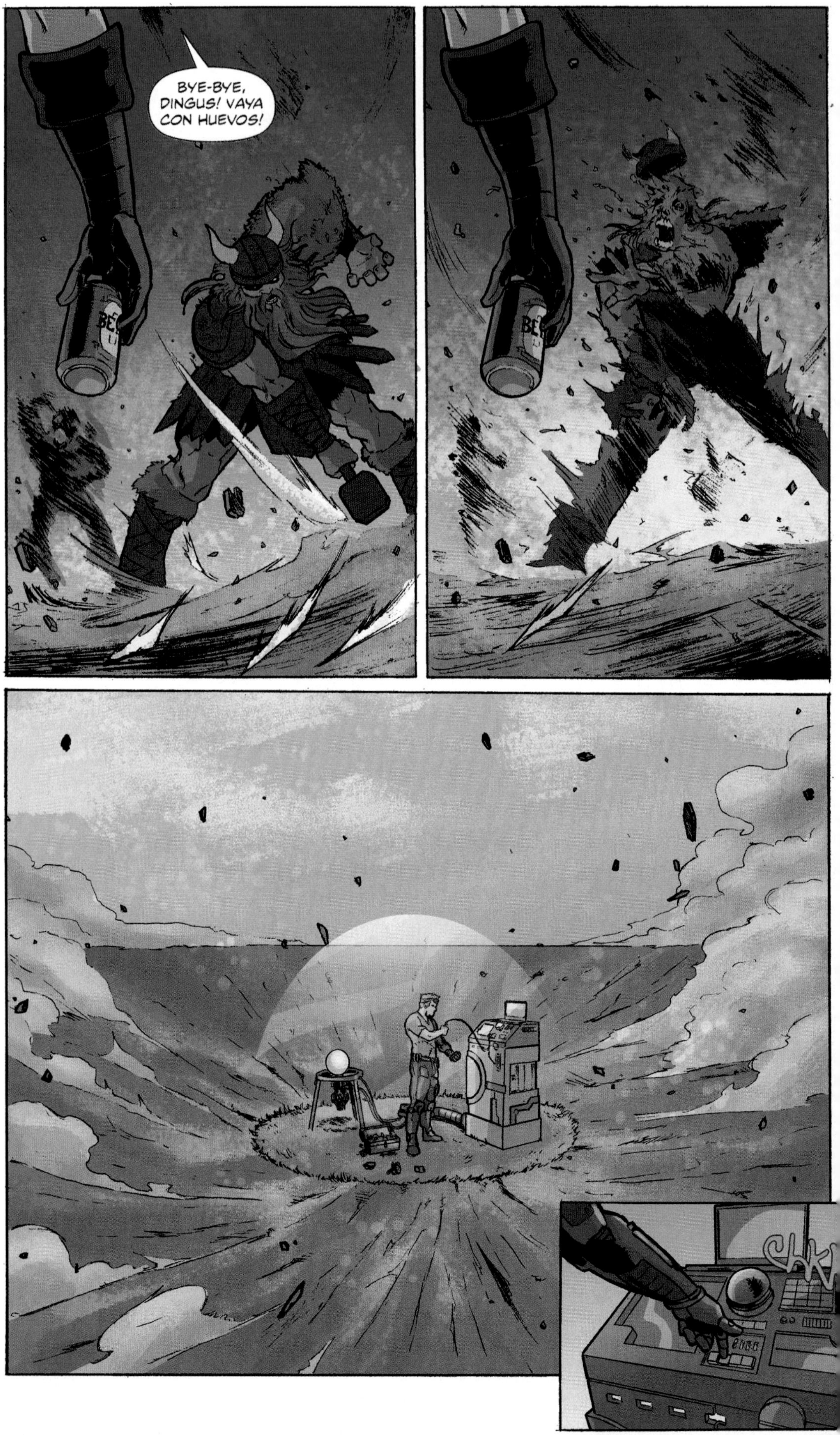
BYE-BYE, DINGUS! VAYA CON HUEVOS!
CHK

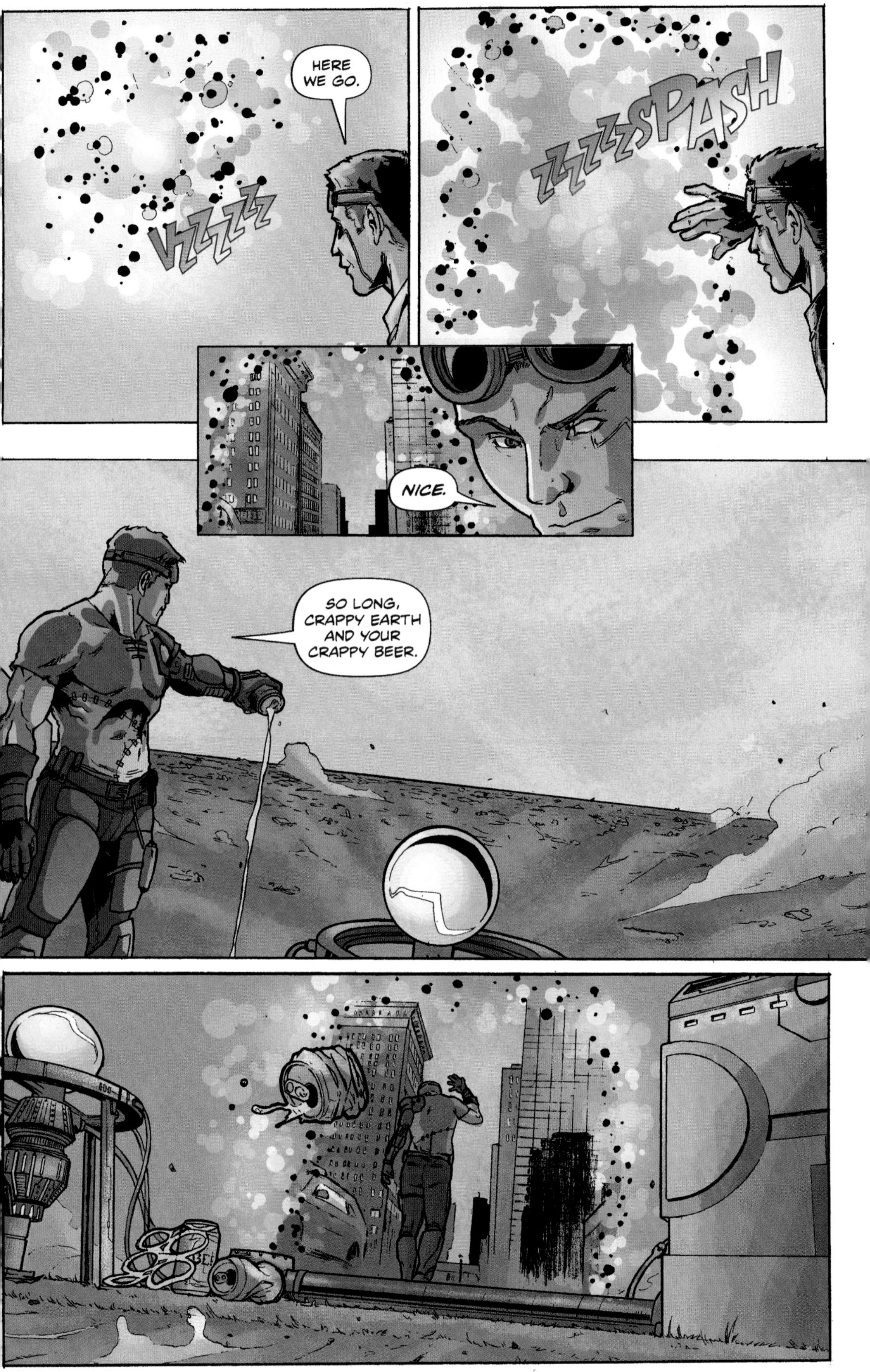
HERE WE GO.
VZZZZZZ
ZZZZZZSPASH
NICE.
SO LONG, CRAPPY EARTH AND YOUR CRAPPY BEER.

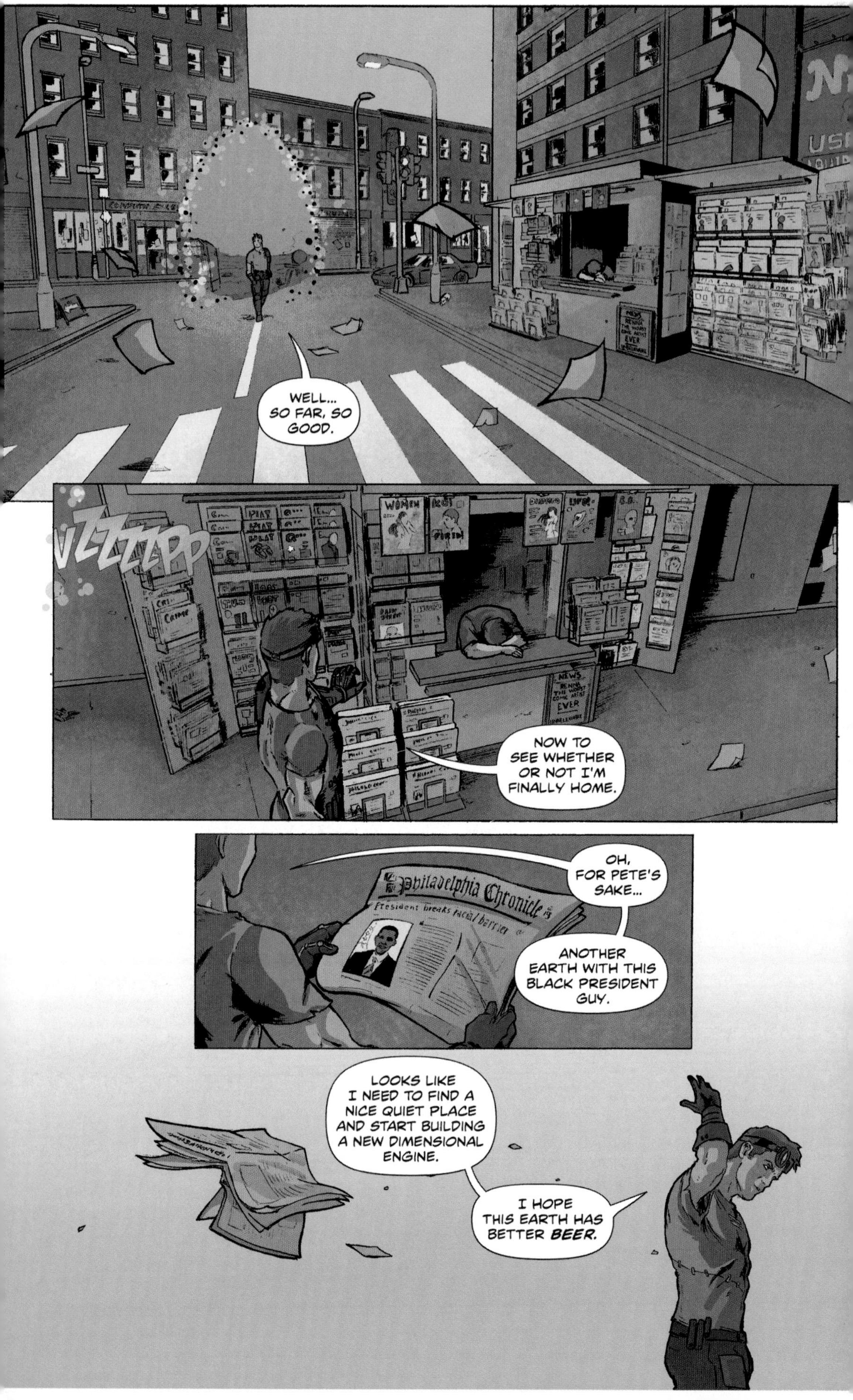
WELL... SO FAR, SO GOOD.
VZZZZPP
NOW TO SEE WHETHER OR NOT I'M FINALLY HOME.
Philadelphia Chronicle
President breaks racial barrier
OH, FOR PETE'S SAKE...
ANOTHER EARTH WITH THIS BLACK PRESIDENT GUY.
LOOKS LIKE I NEED TO FIND A NICE QUIET PLACE AND START BUILDING A NEW DIMENSIONAL ENGINE.
I HOPE THIS EARTH HAS BETTER *BEER*.

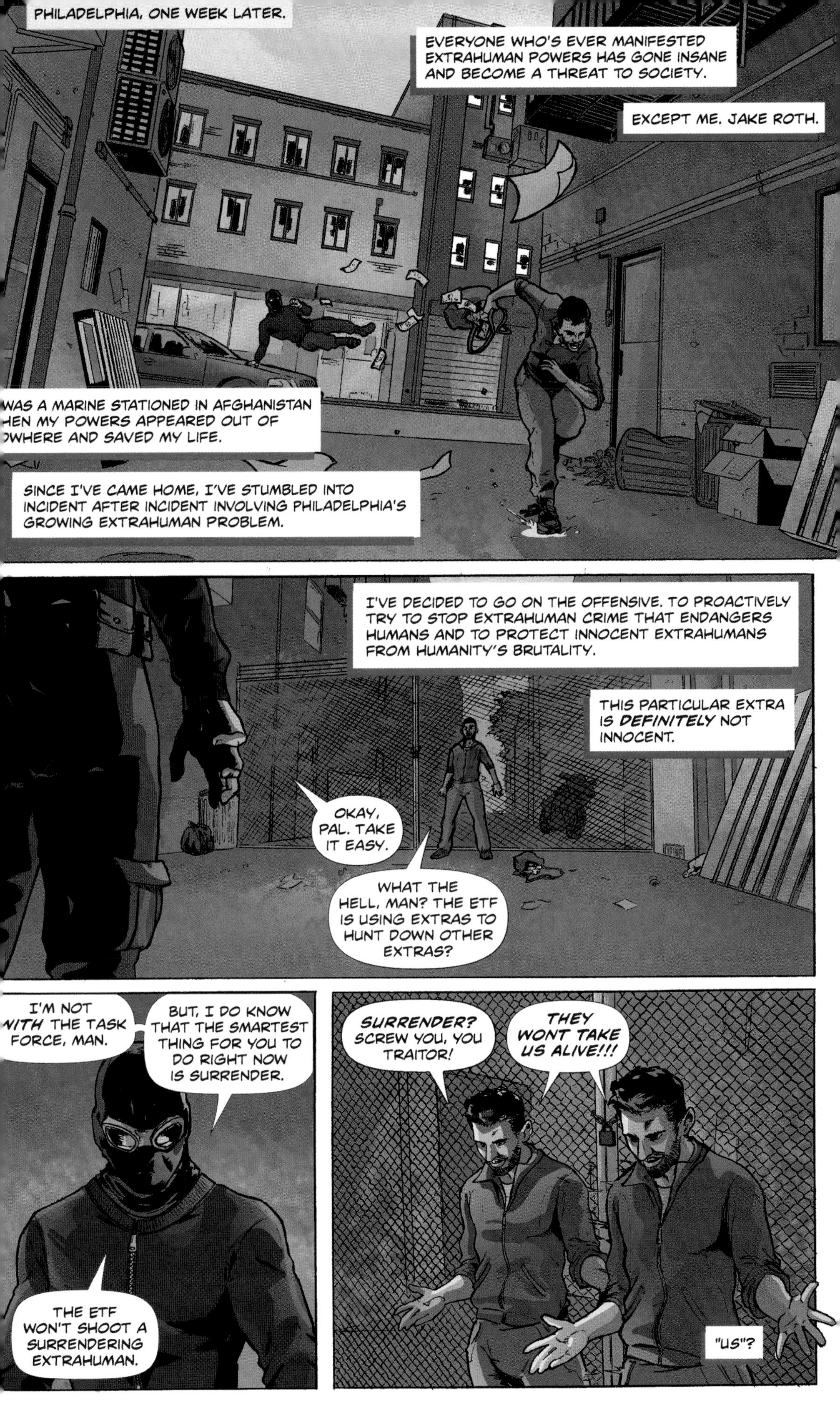

PHILADELPHIA, ONE WEEK LATER.
EVERYONE WHO'S EVER MANIFESTED EXTRAHUMAN POWERS HAS GONE INSANE AND BECOME A THREAT TO SOCIETY.
EXCEPT ME. JAKE ROTH.
WAS A MARINE STATIONED IN AFGHANISTAN HEN MY POWERS APPEARED OUT OF OWHERE AND SAVED MY LIFE.
SINCE I'VE CAME HOME, I'VE STUMBLED INTO INCIDENT AFTER INCIDENT INVOLVING PHILADELPHIA'S GROWING EXTRAHUMAN PROBLEM.
I'VE DECIDED TO GO ON THE OFFENSIVE. TO PROACTIVELY TRY TO STOP EXTRAHUMAN CRIME THAT ENDANGERS HUMANS AND TO PROTECT INNOCENT EXTRAHUMANS FROM HUMANITY'S BRUTALITY.
THIS PARTICULAR EXTRA IS *DEFINITELY* NOT INNOCENT.
OKAY, PAL. TAKE IT EASY.
WHAT THE HELL, MAN? THE ETF IS USING EXTRAS TO HUNT DOWN OTHER EXTRAS?
I'M NOT *WITH* THE TASK FORCE, MAN.
BUT, I DO KNOW THAT THE SMARTEST THING FOR YOU TO DO RIGHT NOW IS SURRENDER.
THE ETF WON'T SHOOT A SURRENDERING EXTRAHUMAN.
SURRENDER? SCREW YOU, YOU TRAITOR!
THEY WONT TAKE US ALIVE!!!
"US"?

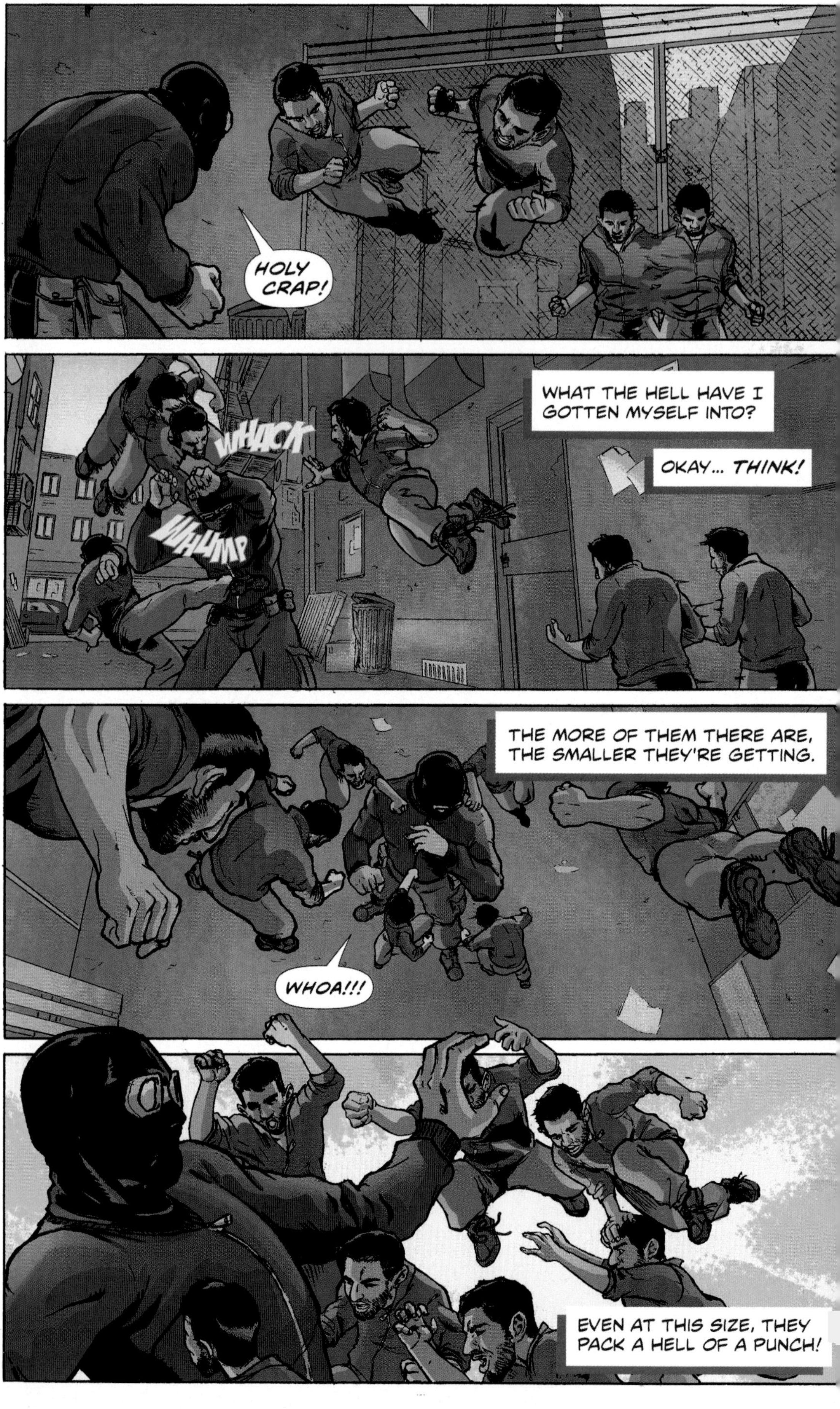
HOLY CRAP!
WHAT THE HELL HAVE I GOTTEN MYSELF INTO?
OKAY... THINK!
WHACK
WHUMP
THE MORE OF THEM THERE ARE, THE SMALLER THEY'RE GETTING.
WHOA!!!
EVEN AT THIS SIZE, THEY PACK A HELL OF A PUNCH!

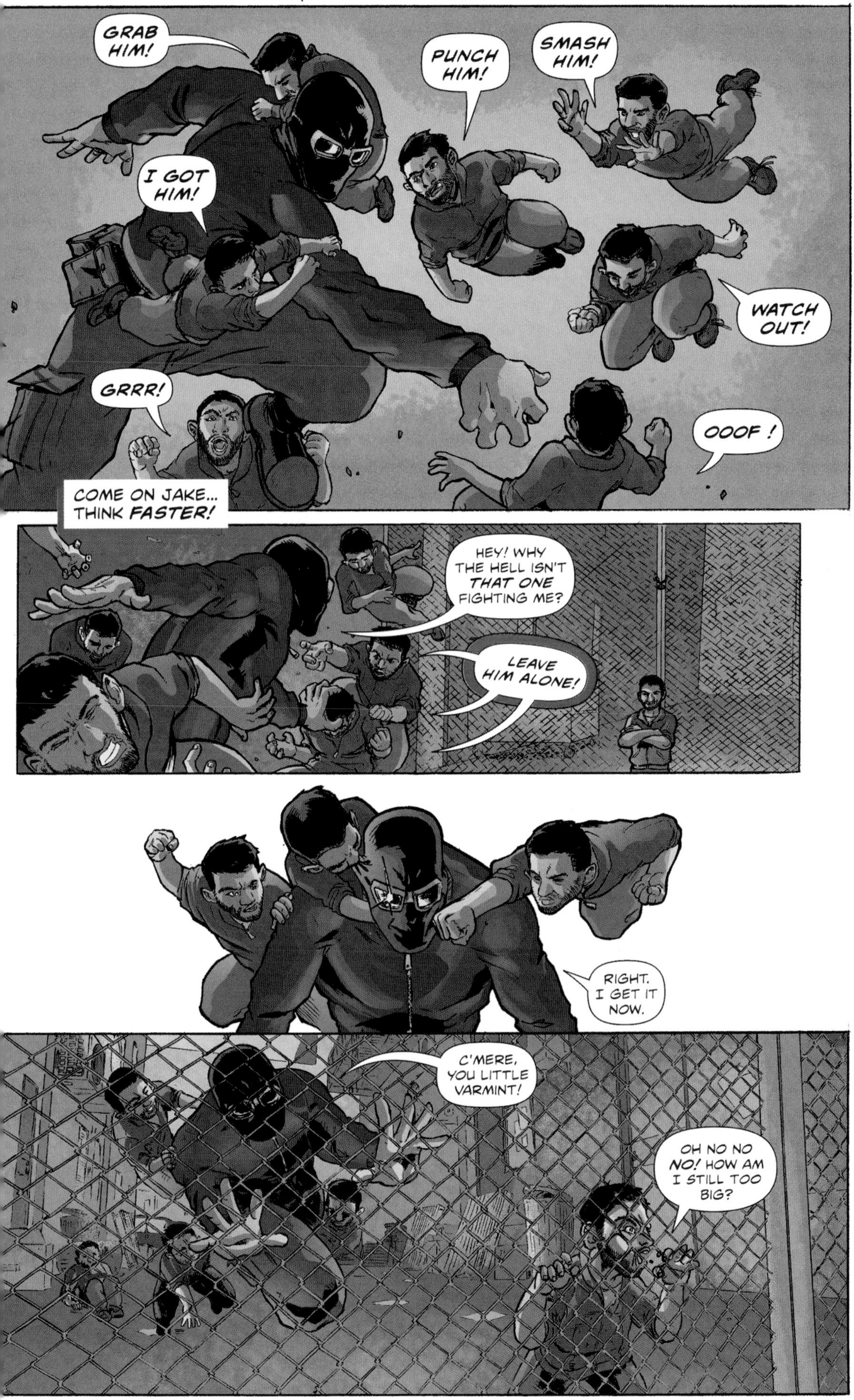
GRAB HIM!
PUNCH HIM!
SMASH HIM!
I GOT HIM!
WATCH OUT!
GRRR!
OOOF !
COME ON JAKE... THINK FASTER!
HEY! WHY THE HELL ISN'T THAT ONE FIGHTING ME?
LEAVE HIM ALONE!
RIGHT. I GET IT NOW.
C'MERE, YOU LITTLE VARMINT!
OH NO NO NO! HOW AM I STILL TOO BIG?

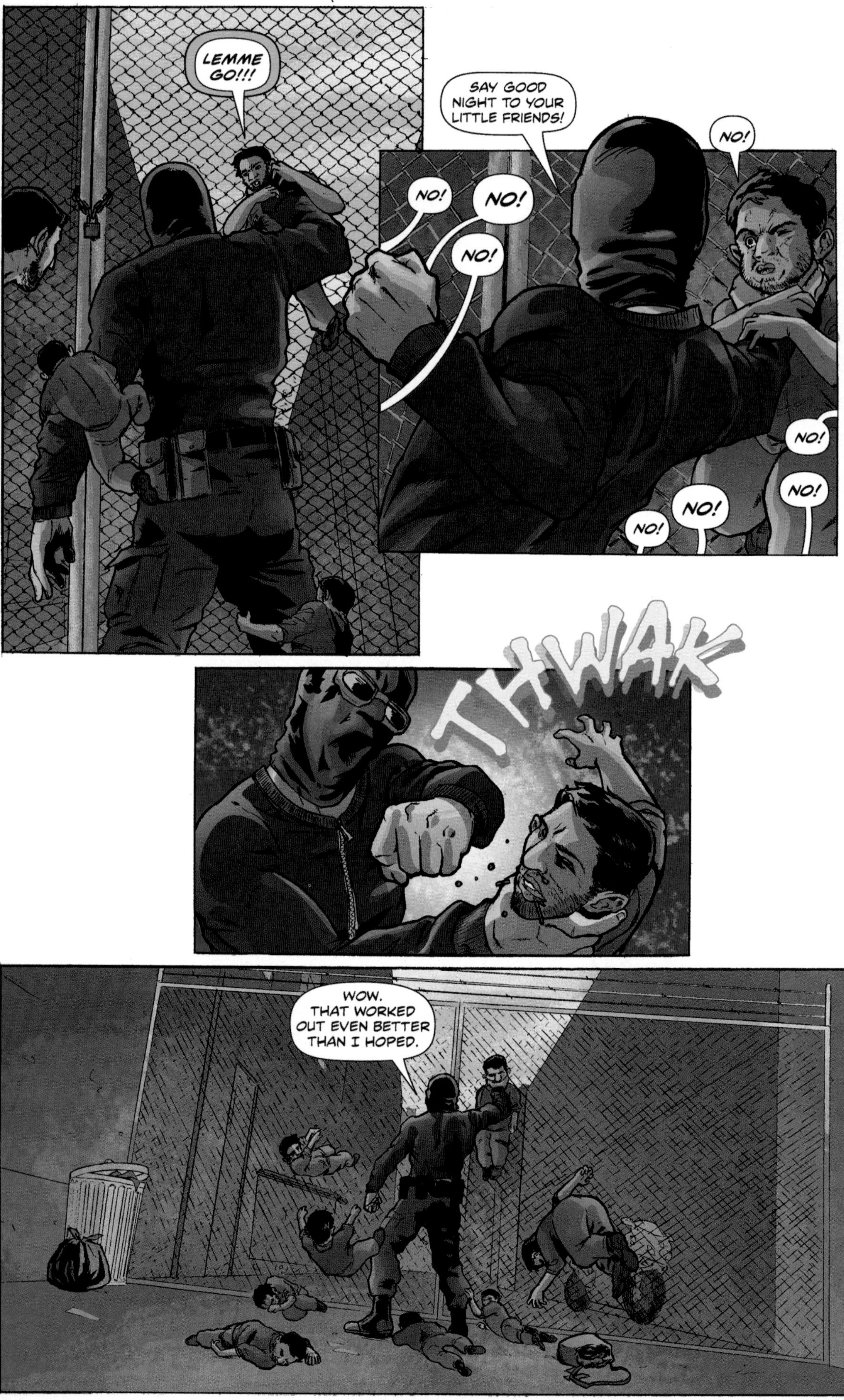

LEMME GO!!!
SAY GOOD NIGHT TO YOUR LITTLE FRIENDS!
NO!
NO!
NO!
NO!
NO!
NO!
NO!
NO!
THWAK
WOW. THAT WORKED OUT EVEN BETTER THAN I HOPED.

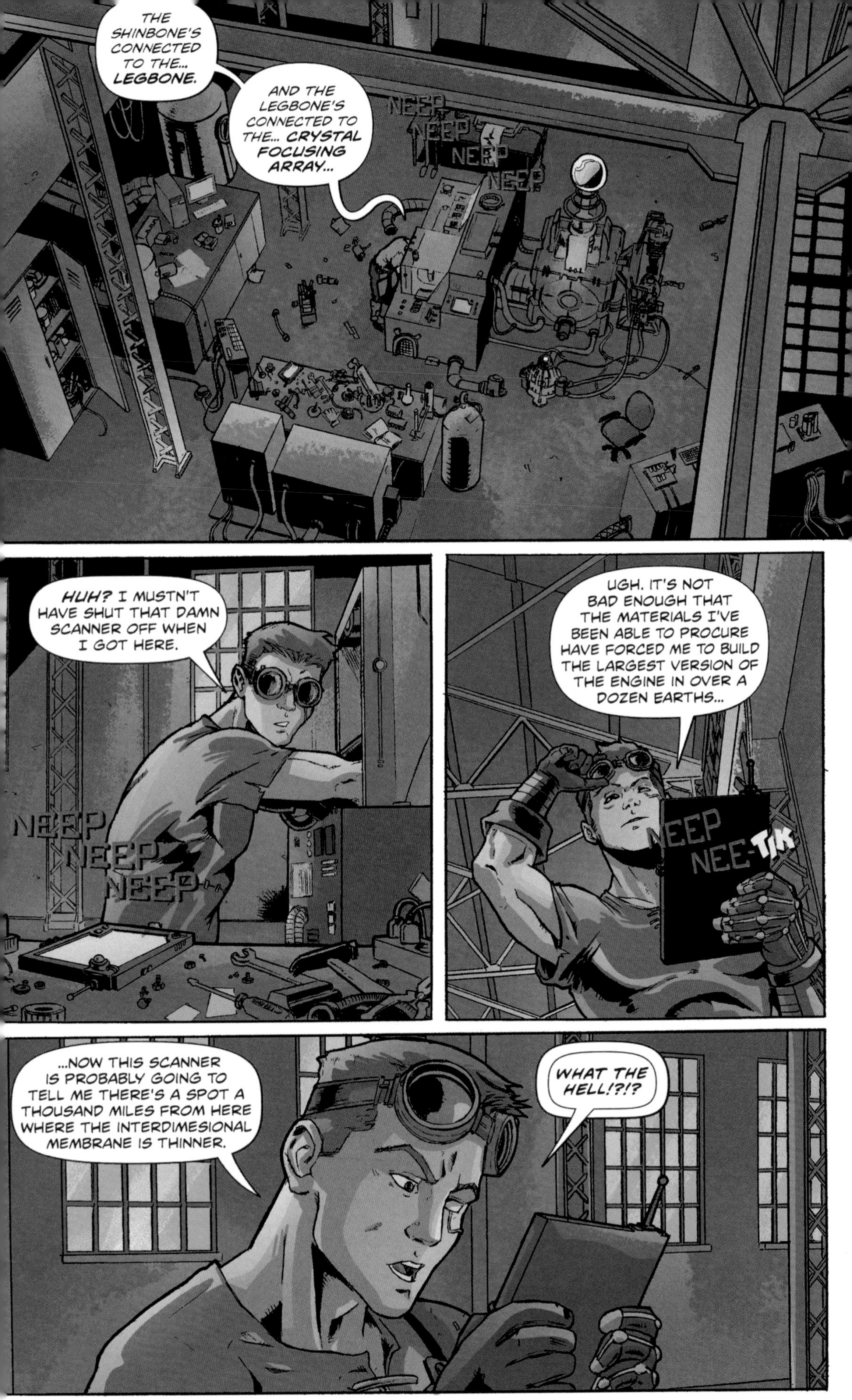
THE SHINBONE'S CONNECTED TO THE... LEGBONE.
AND THE LEGBONE'S CONNECTED TO THE... CRYSTAL FOCUSING ARRAY...
NEEP NEEP NEEP NEEP
HUH? I MUSTN'T HAVE SHUT THAT DAMN SCANNER OFF WHEN I GOT HERE.
NEEP NEEP NEEP
UGH. IT'S NOT BAD ENOUGH THAT THE MATERIALS I'VE BEEN ABLE TO PROCURE HAVE FORCED ME TO BUILD THE LARGEST VERSION OF THE ENGINE IN OVER A DOZEN EARTHS...
NEEP NEE-TIK
...NOW THIS SCANNER IS PROBABLY GOING TO TELL ME THERE'S A SPOT A THOUSAND MILES FROM HERE WHERE THE INTERDIMESIONAL MEMBRANE IS THINNER.
WHAT THE HELL!?!?

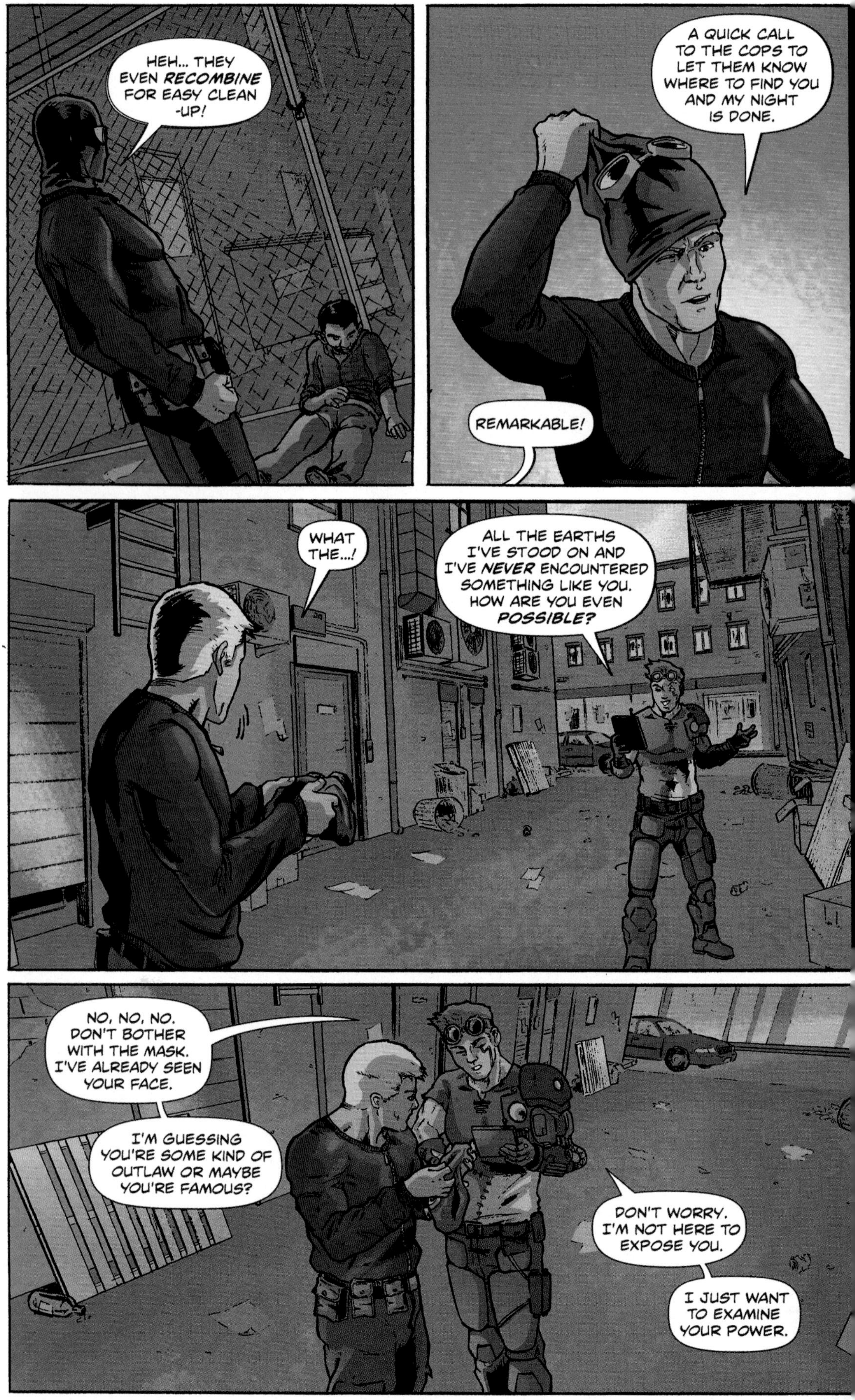
HEH... THEY EVEN *RECOMBINE* FOR EASY CLEAN -UP!
A QUICK CALL TO THE COPS TO LET THEM KNOW WHERE TO FIND YOU AND MY NIGHT IS DONE.
REMARKABLE!
WHAT THE...!
ALL THE EARTHS I'VE STOOD ON AND I'VE *NEVER* ENCOUNTERED SOMETHING LIKE YOU. HOW ARE YOU EVEN *POSSIBLE?*
NO, NO, NO. DON'T BOTHER WITH THE MASK. I'VE ALREADY SEEN YOUR FACE.
I'M GUESSING YOU'RE SOME KIND OF OUTLAW OR MAYBE YOU'RE FAMOUS?
DON'T WORRY. I'M NOT HERE TO EXPOSE YOU.
I JUST WANT TO EXAMINE YOUR POWER.

OKAY, I'M TRYING MY BEST NOT TO COMPLETELY FREAK OUT HERE BUT WHAT THE HELL IS GOING ON?

FINE. YOU'RE NOT GOING TO UNDERSTAND A *WORD* I'M SAYING BUT I'LL TELL YOU ANYWAYS.

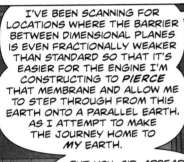

I'VE BEEN SCANNING FOR LOCATIONS WHERE THE BARRIER BETWEEN DIMENSIONAL PLANES IS EVEN FRACTIONALLY WEAKER THAN STANDARD SO THAT IT'S EASIER FOR THE ENGINE I'M CONSTRUCTING TO *PIERCE* THAT MEMBRANE AND ALLOW ME TO STEP THROUGH FROM THIS EARTH ONTO A PARALLEL EARTH, AS I ATTEMPT TO MAKE THE JOURNEY HOME TO *MY* EARTH.

BUT YOU, SIR, APPEAR TO BE SATURATED WITH THE ENERGY THAT SEPARATES THE DIMENSIONS. YOU ARE A *WALKING PINHOLE* IN THAT MEMBRANE.

IF I'M RIGHT, I MAY BE ABLE TO TURN THAT *PINHOLE* INTO A *DOORWAY.*

SNKT

NOW THIS NEXT PART MIGHT STING A LITTLE...

CHKKT

SO TRY NOT TO FLINCH.

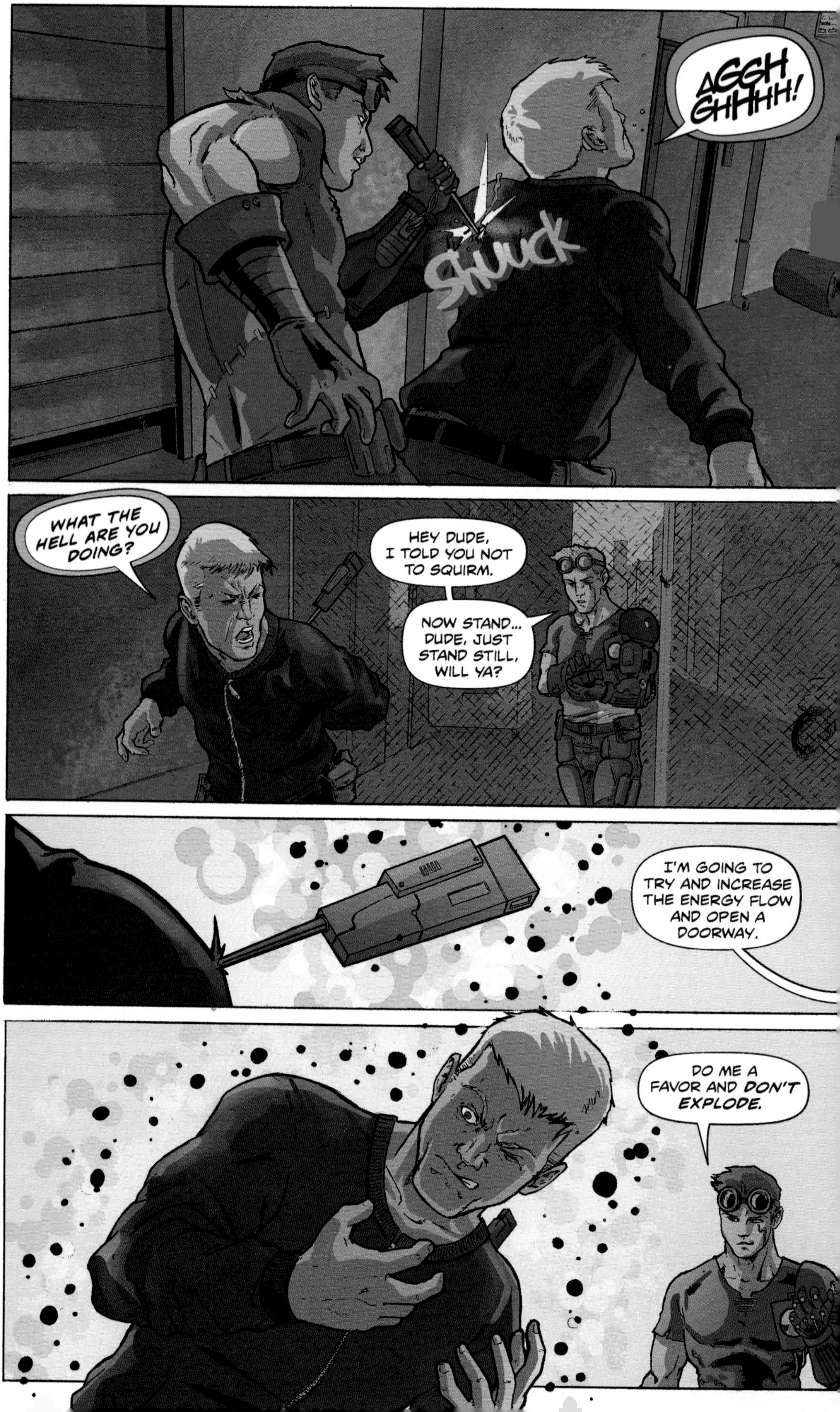

AGGH GHHHH!
SHUUCK
WHAT THE HELL ARE YOU DOING?
HEY DUDE, I TOLD YOU NOT TO SQUIRM.
NOW STAND... DUDE, JUST STAND STILL, WILL YA?
I'M GOING TO TRY AND INCREASE THE ENERGY FLOW AND OPEN A DOORWAY.
DO ME A FAVOR AND DON'T EXPLODE.

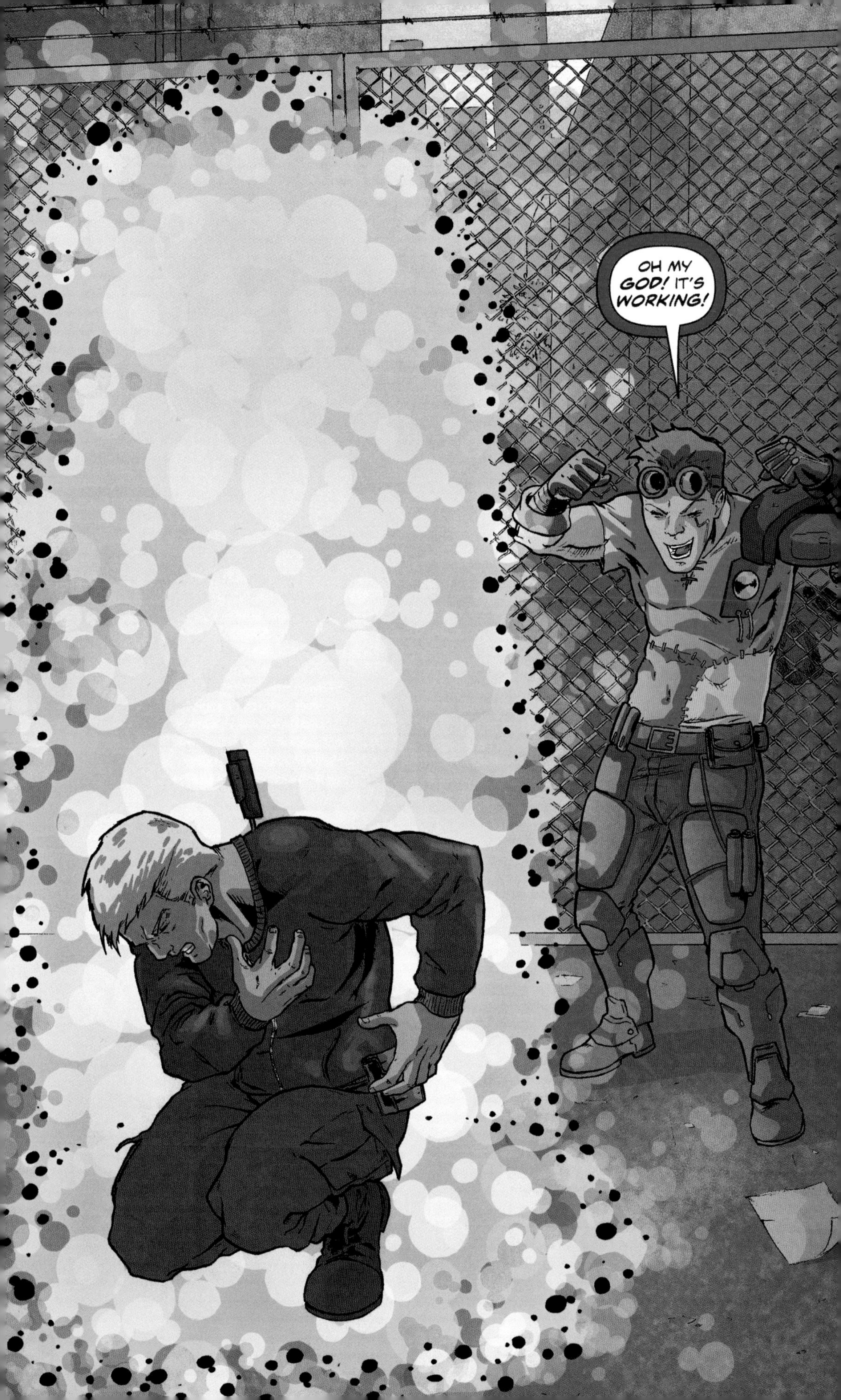
OH MY GOD! IT'S WORKING!

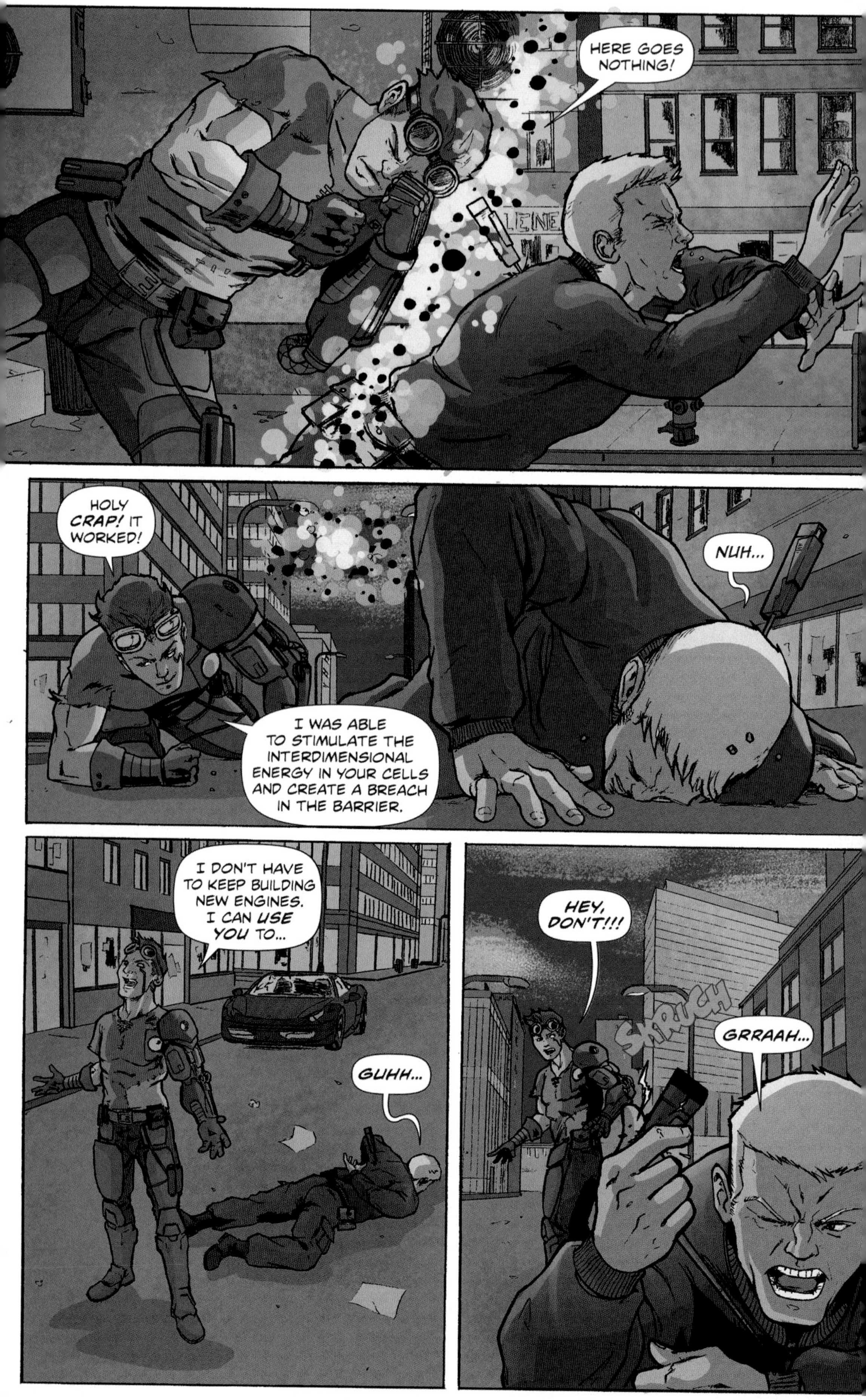
HERE GOES NOTHING!
LENE
HOLY CRAP! IT WORKED!
NUH...
I WAS ABLE TO STIMULATE THE INTERDIMENSIONAL ENERGY IN YOUR CELLS AND CREATE A BREACH IN THE BARRIER.
I DON'T HAVE TO KEEP BUILDING NEW ENGINES. I CAN USE YOU TO...
GUHH...
HEY, DON'T!!!
SKRUCH
GRRAAH...

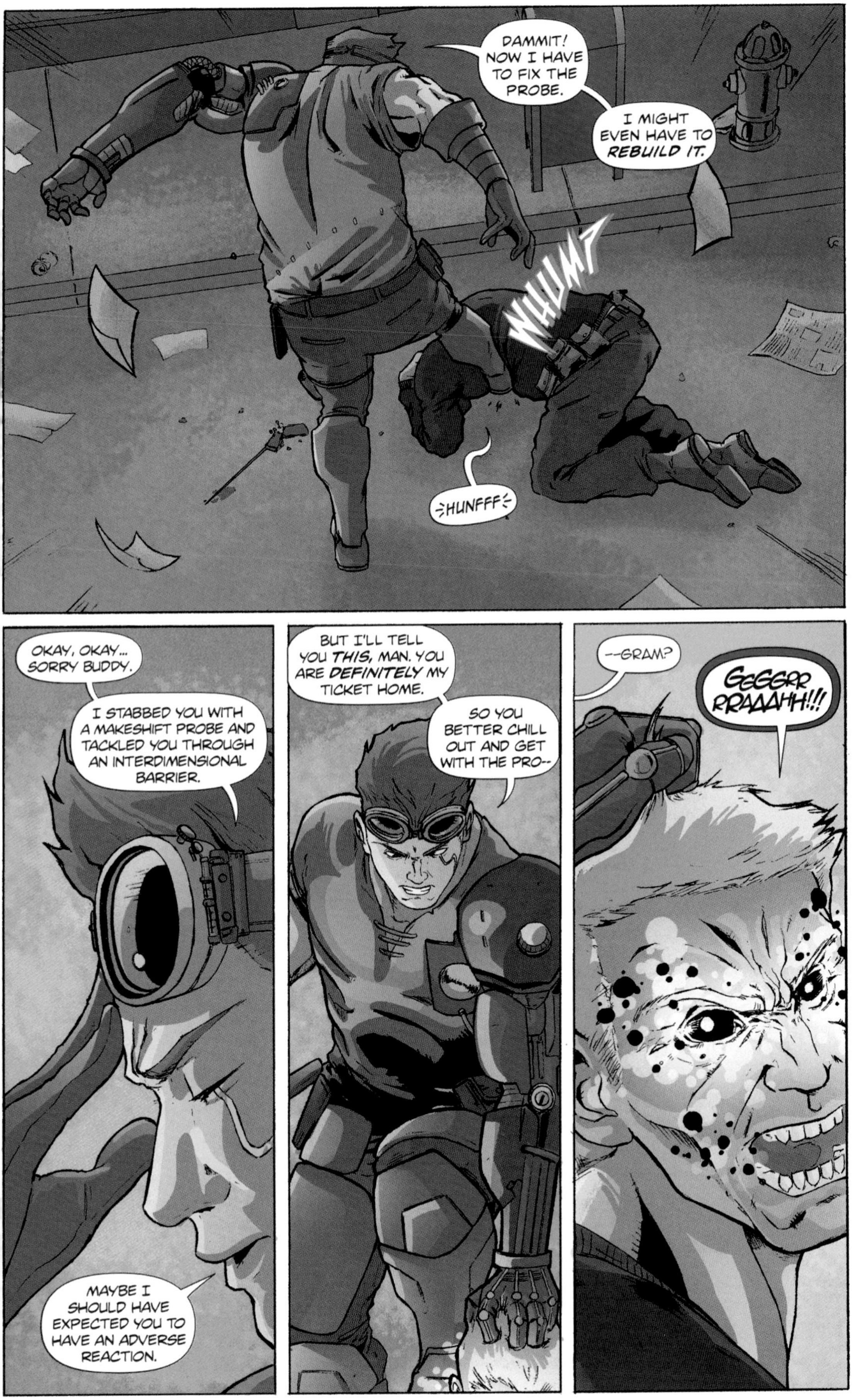
DAMMIT! NOW I HAVE TO FIX THE PROBE.
I MIGHT EVEN HAVE TO *REBUILD IT.*
WHUMP
HUNFFF
OKAY, OKAY... SORRY BUDDY.
I STABBED YOU WITH A MAKESHIFT PROBE AND TACKLED YOU THROUGH AN INTERDIMENSIONAL BARRIER.
MAYBE I SHOULD HAVE EXPECTED YOU TO HAVE AN ADVERSE REACTION.
BUT I'LL TELL YOU *THIS,* MAN. YOU ARE *DEFINITELY* MY TICKET HOME.
SO YOU BETTER CHILL OUT AND GET WITH THE PRO--
--GRAM?
GGGGRR RRAAAHH!!!

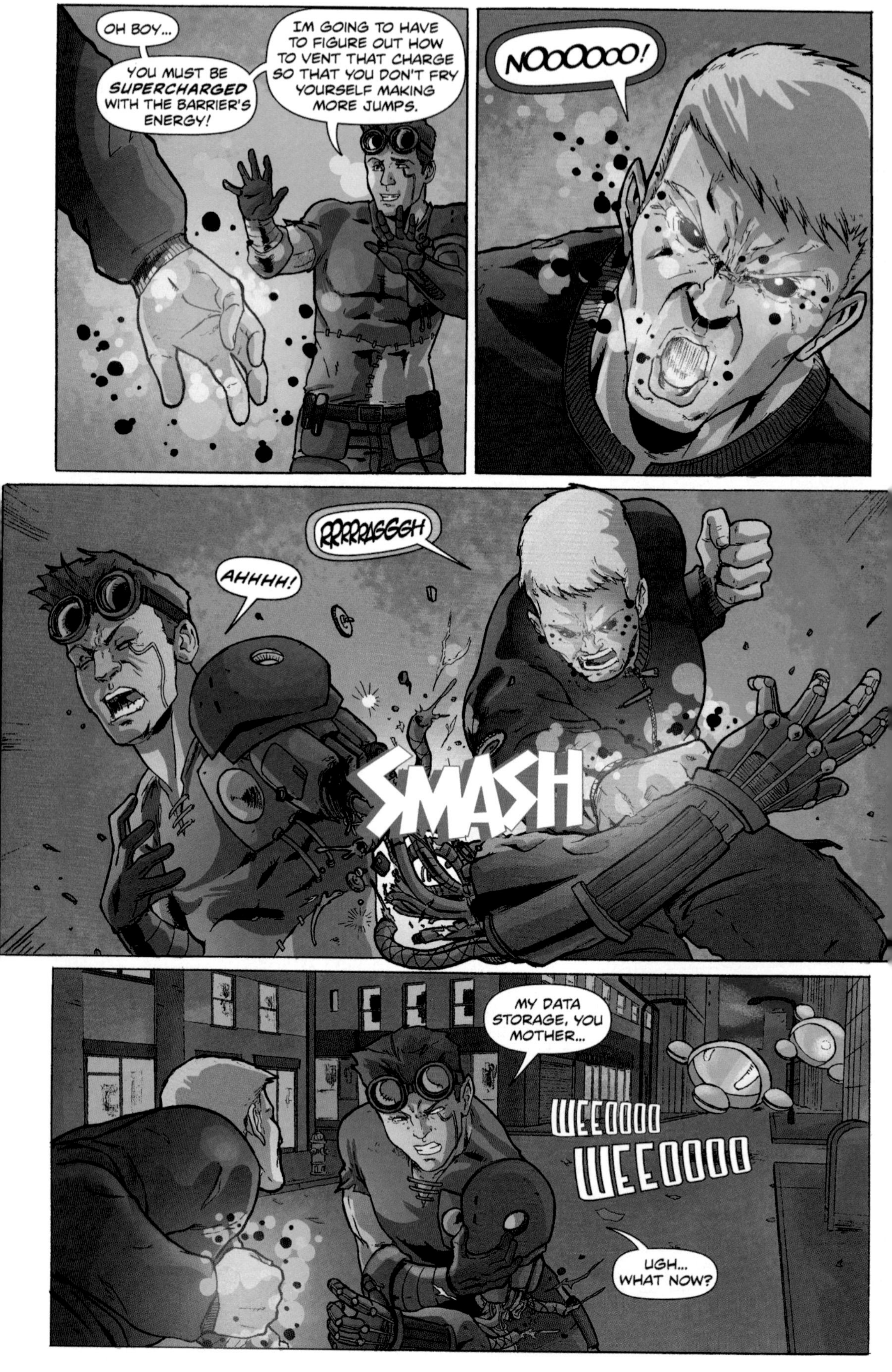
OH BOY...
YOU MUST BE SUPERCHARGED WITH THE BARRIER'S ENERGY!
IM GOING TO HAVE TO FIGURE OUT HOW TO VENT THAT CHARGE SO THAT YOU DON'T FRY YOURSELF MAKING MORE JUMPS.
NOOOOOO!
RRRRRAGGGH
AHHHH!
SMASH
MY DATA STORAGE, YOU MOTHER...
WEEOOOO
WEEOOOO
UGH... WHAT NOW?

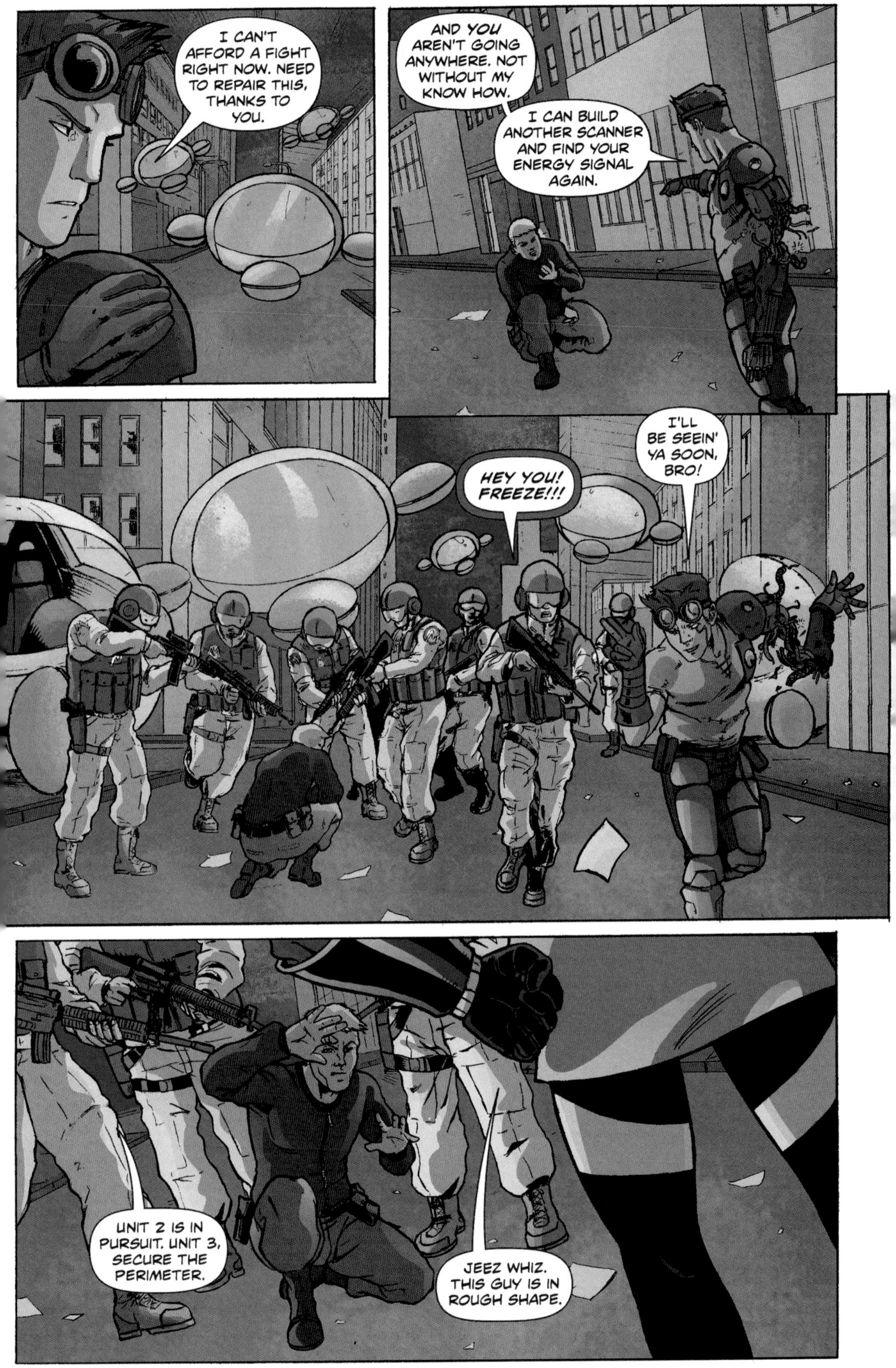
I CAN'T AFFORD A FIGHT RIGHT NOW. NEED TO REPAIR THIS, THANKS TO YOU.
AND YOU AREN'T GOING ANYWHERE. NOT WITHOUT MY KNOW HOW.
I CAN BUILD ANOTHER SCANNER AND FIND YOUR ENERGY SIGNAL AGAIN.
HEY YOU! FREEZE!!!
I'LL BE SEEIN' YA SOON, BRO!
UNIT 2 IS IN PURSUIT. UNIT 3, SECURE THE PERIMETER.
JEEZ WHIZ. THIS GUY IS IN ROUGH SHAPE.

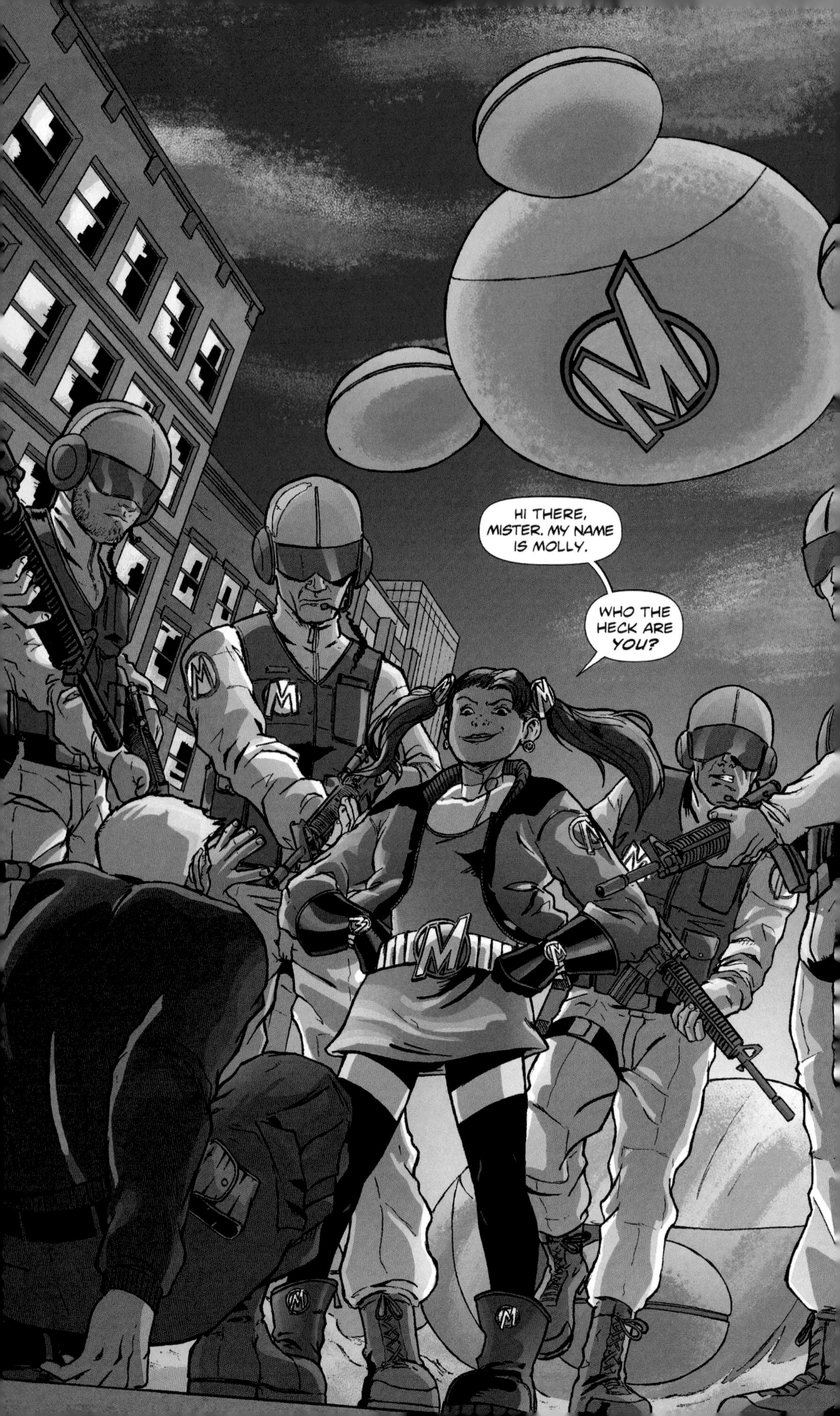
HI THERE, MISTER. MY NAME IS MOLLY.
WHO THE HECK ARE YOU?

ACTIONVERSE

...mother passed away two weeks ago.

...ay, maybe that's not exactly how you'd expect the editorial ...ge in the funnybook you just finished reading to start, but ...ar with me because that just happens to be where I am in ...y life right now.

...ctually tried to write this editorial the night she died. I had ...d Vito (Delsante) I would have something for him that ...ekend so that he could finish the typesetting on this issue. ...t I just couldn't. After writing a sentence very similar to the ...e that started this essay, I had no words left in me. The ...ful thing that I had been dreading for years and expecting ... weeks, if not months, had happened. Knowing that an ...ful thing is imminent doesn't make it's arrival any easier to ...e.

...at down with my older brother that night and cracked open a ...ttle of Crown Royal. I used to be a drinker. I'm not anymore. ...ave up the demon bottle as a sort of New Year's resolution ...the first day of 2009. But on this night, Saturday January ...h 2016, I came out of drinking retirement to put on an ...dre The Giant-level performance, polishing off one entire ...ttle of Crown on my own and cracking open a second.

...ot through a few phone calls with some of my friends before ...mbing into bed and succumbing to the liquor and exhaustion ...d, frankly, sadness. I woke up Sunday morning and got back ...the business at hand of settling her affairs and arranging ...r cremation and memorial service. (My brother, by the way, ...ked out a really terrific urn. I mention this purely as an ...cuse to tell my brother, here in print, that I love him and, if ...no other reason than that urn, I'm glad he was with me ...t day.)

...been difficult. I loved my mother. We had a pretty ...mbative relationship for a lot of years. But when she got ill a ...v years ago, I told her it was time to come home where I ...ld take charge of her care. The last four years have been ...tty stressful. My mother was a nurse for 4 decades. Nurses ...e the WORST patients. My mother was a headstrong woman ...o had an incredibly hard time accepting that there were now ...its to what she could and couldn't do.

...n essence, became her parent for those final years, trying to ...ep her safe and make her life a happy one. But, life, no ...tter how happy, has an inevitable conclusion. And we ...ched that inevitability two weeks ago.

...ish I could tell you that I wrote this with some grand notion ...delivering untold wisdom to you about the nature of life, ...ath, the universe and everything... but really, I just needed ...cleanse my soul a little. I'm no different then the millions of ...ople who go through this every day. You'll get your turn, ...fortunately. I hope when that turn comes around, you'll ...ve as many good people (friends, relatives and health care ...fessionals) around to help you and your family as my ...ther and I did.

...ve you, Mom.

So... ACTIONVERSE. It's here and, as Vito Delsante is so fond of saying, "It's All Connected." I should probably have written that as a hashtag. We've been working on this damn thing for almost 18 months. It was already underway when I was invited onboard. I'm grateful, not just to have received that invite, but also for the willingness of the assembled creative teams to make wholesale changes to the plot in order to accommodate the reality I've created for Jake Roth. Simply put, if Jake is the ONLY sane superpower on his Earth, then he simply cannot be sharing an Earth with characters like Molly Danger or Midnight Tiger.

And after a lot of writing and rewriting and editing and fine-tuning, we had a six-issue story that we could be proud of. Again, I have to express my gratitude to the other creators, as Jake's unique nature lead to THE F1RST HERO being the lead off issue of the series. As the old saying goes, where the head leads, the body must follow. By allowing me to write the first issue, the teams were allowing me to set the tone for the series.

So, you'll pardon me if I take a bow because I really love what I wrote and I love the story that follows it. And you're going to enjoy this story, kids. A whole bunch of really talented folks put their all into ACTIONVERSE and it's a 132-page thrill ride.

I want to say a big THANK YOU to Marco Renna, Fred C Stresing and Lee Moder.

Marco came onboard for this issue and for the upcoming third volume of THE F1RST HERO. Like Phillip Sevy and Danny Zabbal before him, Marco is a fantastic but previously undiscovered talent. His art gets stronger with each page he sends me and you are going to love THE F1RST HERO: WEDNESDAY'S CHILD when it debuts in a few weeks.

As for Fred...What can I say about Fred? He is one of the most talented, most adaptable colourists I've ever seen and I'm lucky man to have found such a talented man to help bring my books to life.

And Lee Moder is, simply put, one of the best friends I've ever had and one of the most criminally under-appreciated artists in the industry.

Thank you to Vito Delsante, who quarterbacked this whole thing and to Jamal Igle, Shawn Gabborin, Chad Cicconi, Ray-Anthony Height, Sean Izaakse and Steve Walker for the scripts and art for the other five issues of the series. Thank you to the incomparable Ron Frenz for the variant covers for the series. Thank you to Ross Hughes, Full Court Press, Meredith Moriarty, Nate Lovett, Wilson Ramos Jr., Marc Deering, Ross Campbell and David Bednarski for the colouring and lettering for those issues and the variant covers. And thank you to Bryan Seaton, Kevin Freeman and Dave Dwonch for giving us the sandbox to play in in the first place.

And thank you to you, the reader for recognizing the fact that "the Big Two" aren't the only players in the superhero game and for giving this series a chance.

Anthony Ruttgaizer
Toronto, 31 January 2016

the F1RST HERO

PERSONAL DATA

Alter Ego: Cpl. Jacob Joshua ("Jake") Roth, USMC
Occupation: Junior Executive, Roth Corporation (current); United States Marine (former, Corporal)
Marital Status: Single
Known Relatives: Bernard Roth (father), Philippa Roth (mother), Petra Roth-Michaels (sister)
Group Affiliation: None
Base of Operations: Philadelphia, PA
First Appearance: THE F1RST HERO (Vol 1) #1
Height: 5' 11" **Weight**: 202 lbs
Eyes: Blue **Hair**: Blonde (Sandy)

HISTORY

Everyone who develops superpowers goes criminally or clinically insane. These so-called "extrahumans" have been globally stripped of all their rights and are hunted down because of the threat they pose to society...until Jake Roth. As a United States Marine nearing the end of active duty in Afghanistan, Jake's platoon came under sniper fire. Charging headfirst into danger to stop the sniper and save his men, Jake instead found himself staring point blank down the barrel of the gunman's weapon. At the very moment the sniper pulled the trigger, Jake's own extrahuman power--an energy pulse that gives him immense strength and protects him from harm--manifested itself. Jake was able to defeat the enemy combatants and escape capture... all while maintaining his sanity.

With his new powers still a secret, Jake returned home to Philadelphia but fear that he might still lose his sanity made it difficult for him to settle into his normal life as a junior executive in his family's growing media empire. But when the police attempted a violent takedown on an extrahuman teenager who had just accidentally destroyed part of a South Philly sports arena with uncontrolled optic blasts, bystander Jake felt compelled to step in and help the boy. Donning a mask to hide his identity, Jake successfully fought off the local cops but was then set upon by a squad from the United States Extra-human Task Force, led by its National Director, Col. Paul Kirkson. When it seemed that Jake and the young boy had lost all hope of escaping, a rogue gang of extra-human thugs arrived on the scene. Attacking the ETF Troops, they turned the corner of Swanson and Ritner into a full-blown battlefield.

The extrahuman gang, following the orders "Fat Alvin" Crosby, rescued Jake and the boy and escaped by blowing up a section of the I-95 overpass, creating a barrier between themselves and Kirkson's ETF. Jake soon learned that his rescue would not come without a price as Fat Alvin expected both Jake and young Scotty Winters to join his growing stable of extrahuman soldiers. Jake refused and the ensuing brawl between him and Alvin's crew pushed Scotty over the edge. Scotty suffered a catastrophic loss of control of his powers, resulting in a massive explosion that decimated Fat Alvin's hideout and a portion of the surrounding industrial park. Jake (and unbeknownst to him, Fat Alvin) escaped the destruction but not without making himself a target for both sides of the growing human/extrahuman conflict. Jake vowed to use his powers to prevent what he saw as the impending all-out war coming to the streets of Philadelphia.

POWERS & WEAPONS

Jake is able to channel an energy pulse, currently of unknown origin, which create a visible discharge from his eyes and around his hands. The energy reinforces Jake's body's structural integrity and grants him immense, although as yet unmeasured, strength. Jake has also been able to energy pulse around his hands as a form of shield, deflecting bullets shot at him at point blank range. Prior to manifesting his extrahuman abilities, Jake was an active duty United States Marine. He is incredibly skilled in several hand-to-hand combat disciplines and is a highly proficient marksman. Jake is fully fluent in both English and Spanish and speaks a small amount of conversational Hebrew, Arabic and Pashto.

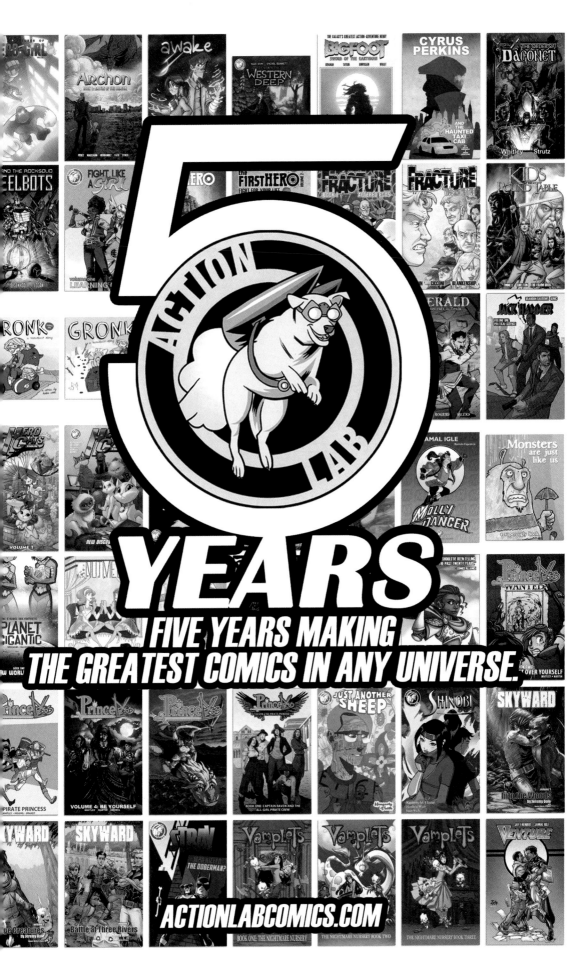

5 YEARS

FIVE YEARS MAKING THE GREATEST COMICS IN ANY UNIVERSE.

ACTIONLABCOMICS.COM

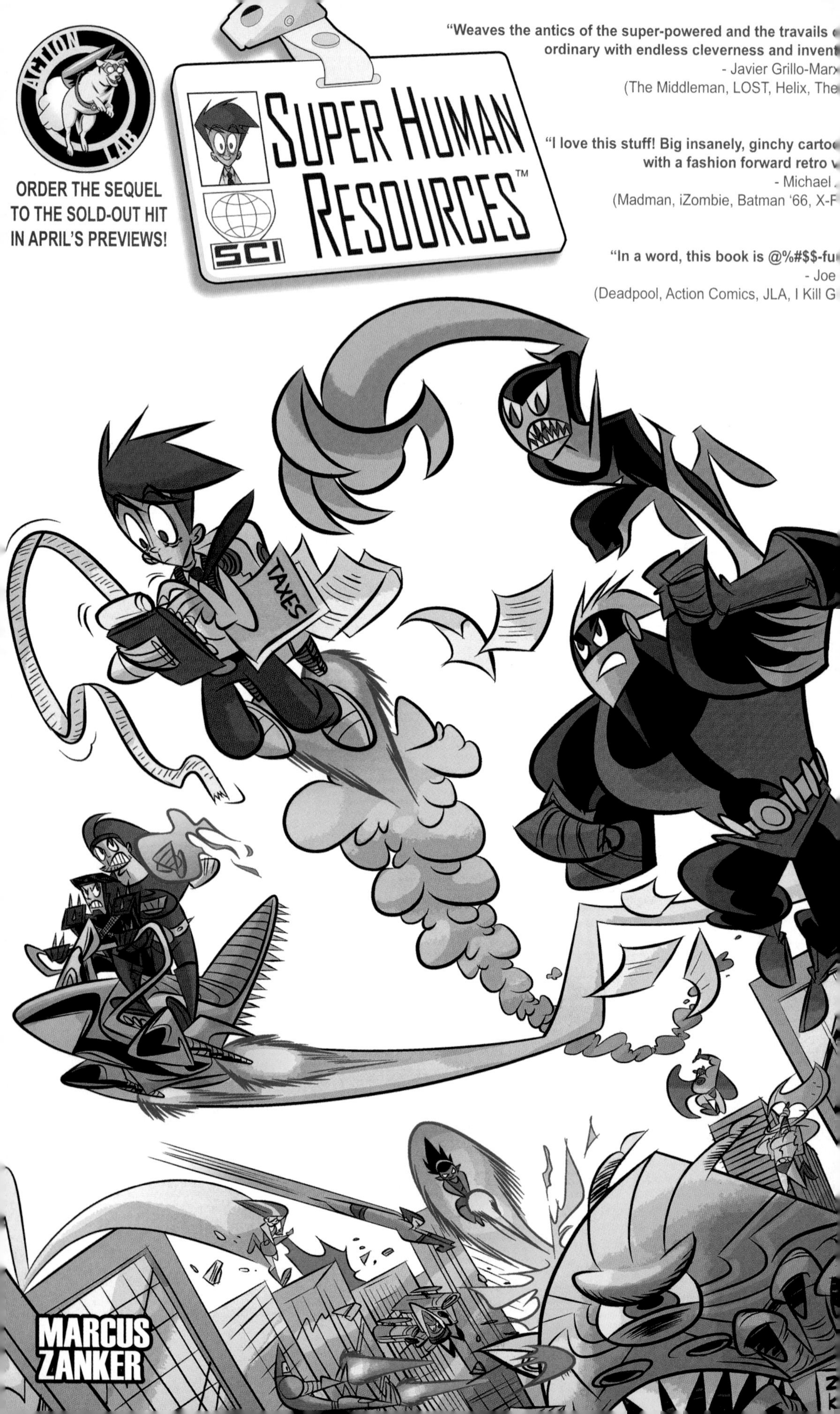
"Weaves the antics of the super-powered and the travails o
ordinary with endless cleverness and invent
- Javier Grillo-Marx
(The Middleman, LOST, Helix, The
"I love this stuff! Big insanely, ginchy carto
with a fashion forward retro v
- Michael
(Madman, iZombie, Batman '66, X-F
"In a word, this book is @%#$$-fu
- Joe
(Deadpool, Action Comics, JLA, I Kill G
ACTION LAB
ORDER THE SEQUEL
TO THE SOLD-OUT HIT
IN APRIL'S PREVIEWS!
SCI
SUPER HUMAN RESOURCES™
TAXES
MARCUS
ZANKER

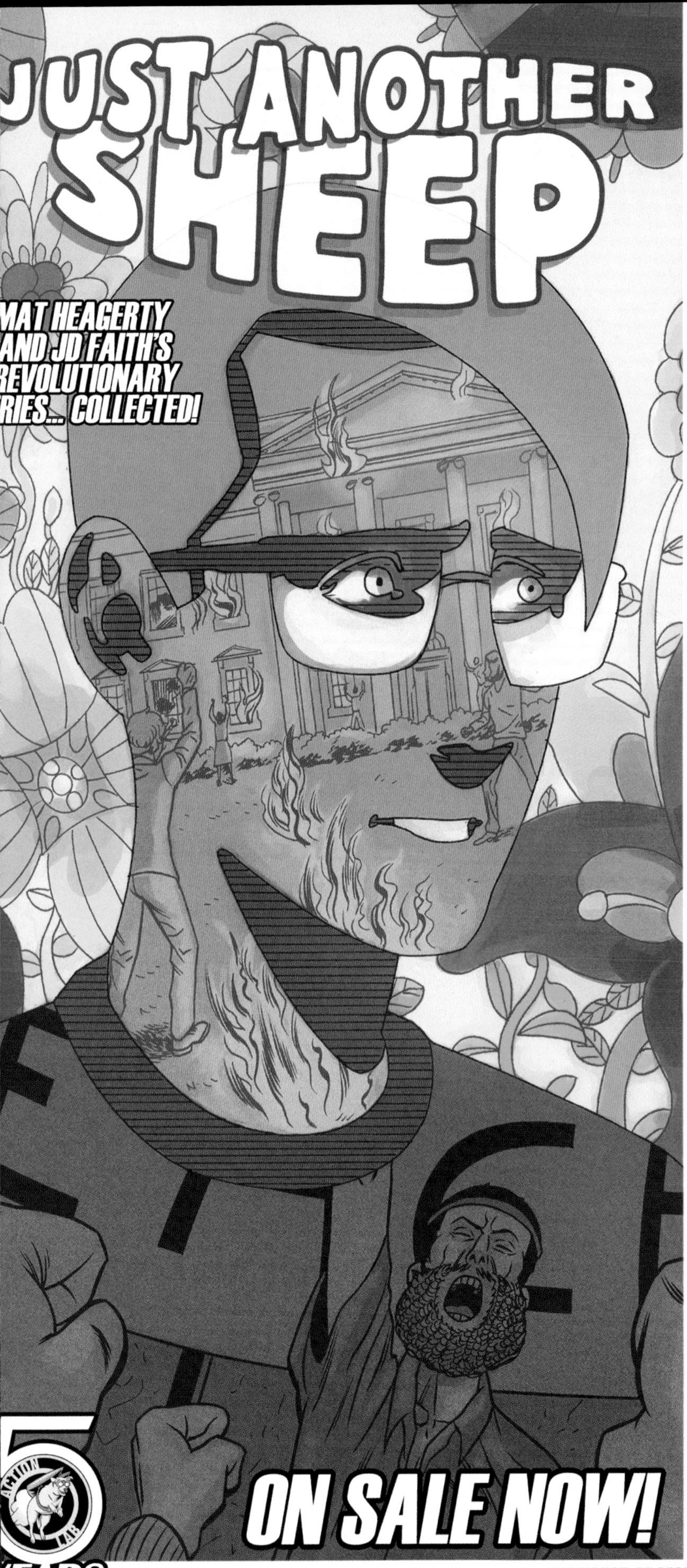

JUST ANOTHER SHEEP
MAT HEAGERTY AND JD FAITH'S REVOLUTIONARY RIES... COLLECTED!
5 YEARS
ACTION LAB
ON SALE NOW!

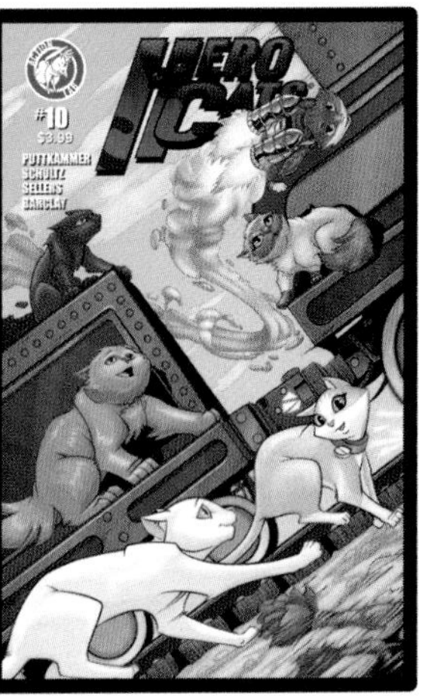

HERO CATS
#10
$3.99
PUTTKAMMER
SCHULTZ
SELLERS
BARCLAY

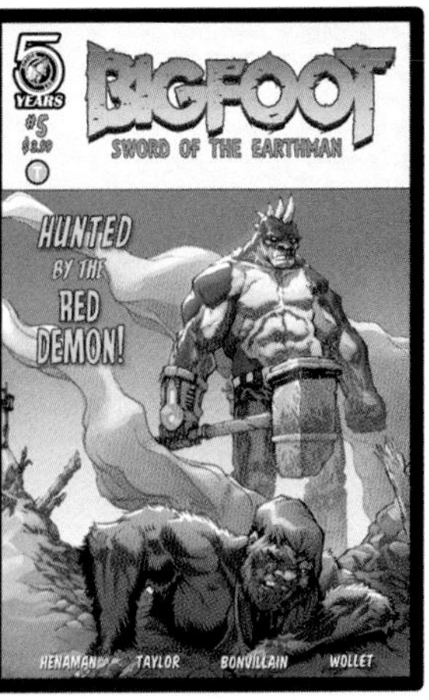

5 YEARS
BIGFOOT
#5
SWORD OF THE EARTHMAN
HUNTED BY THE RED DEMON!
HENAMAN TAYLOR BONVILLAIN WOLLET

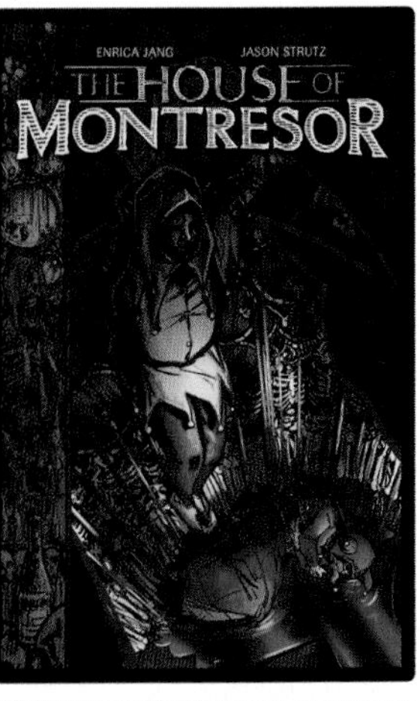

ENRICA JANG
JASON STRUTZ
THE HOUSE OF MONTRESOR

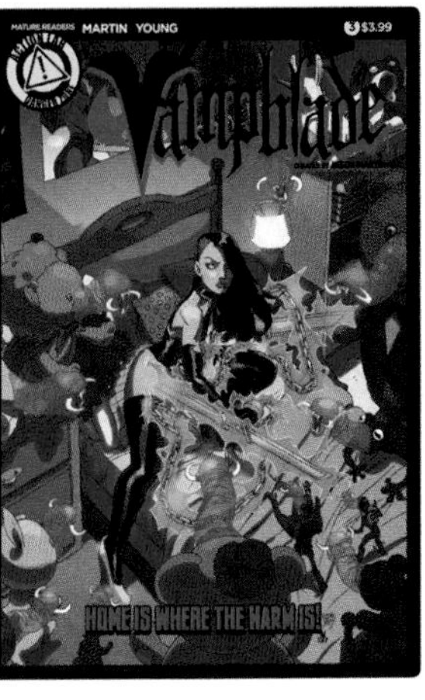

MATURE READERS
MARTIN YOUNG
$3.99
Vampblade
HOME IS WHERE THE HARM IS!

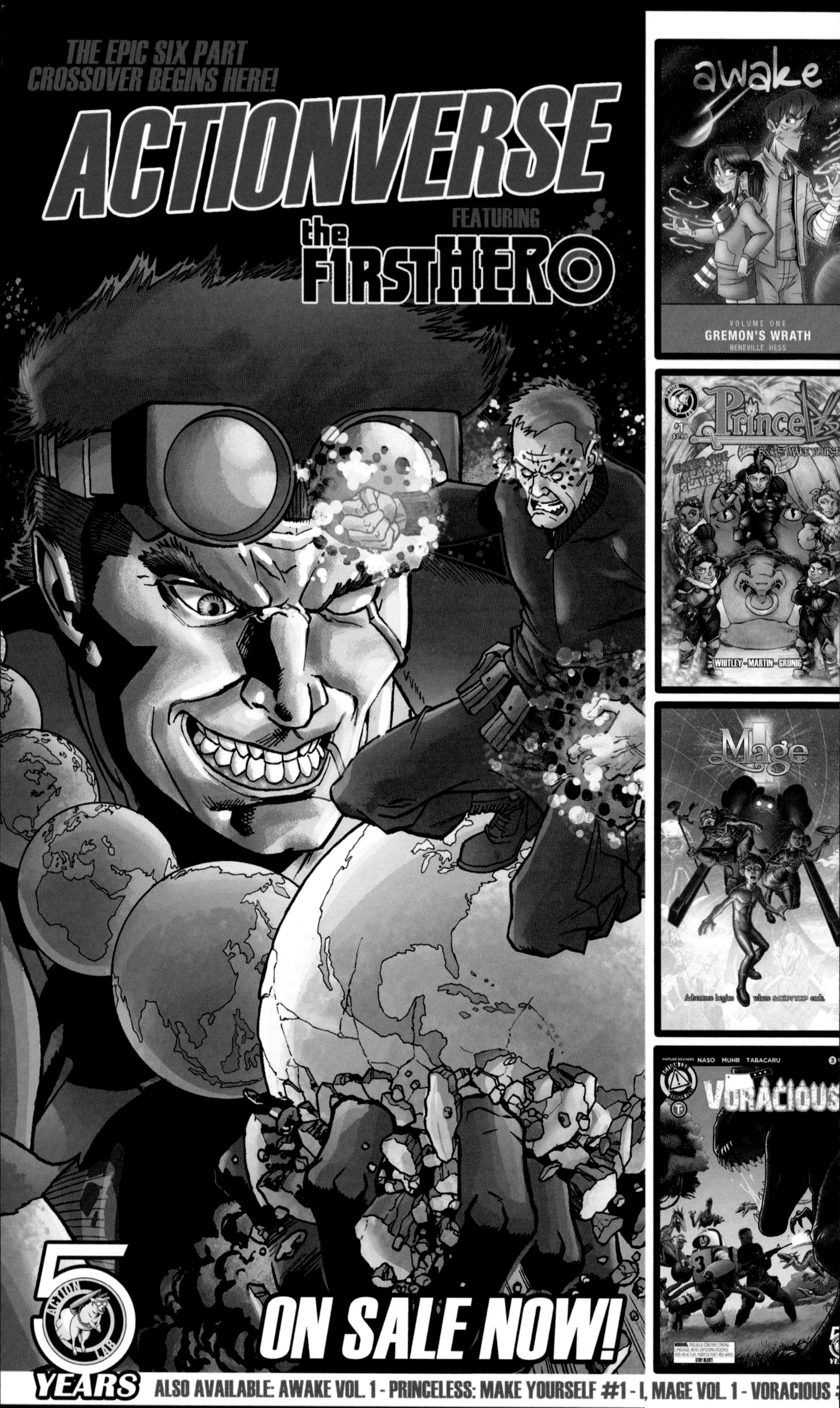

THE EPIC SIX PART
CROSSOVER BEGINS HERE!
ACTIONVERSE
FEATURING
the FIRSTHERO
awake
VOLUME ONE
GREMON'S WRATH
BENEVILLE HESS
Princeless
#1
$3.99
ENTER THE DRAGON SLAYERS!
WHITLEY - MARTIN - GRUNIG
Mage
Adventure begins where science ends.
MATURE READERS NASO MUHR TABACARU
VORACIOUS
ON SALE NOW!
5 YEARS
ALSO AVAILABLE: AWAKE VOL. 1 - PRINCELESS: MAKE YOURSELF #1 - I, MAGE VOL. 1 - VORACIOUS

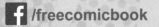

READ MORE NOW

ACTIONLABCOMICS.COM

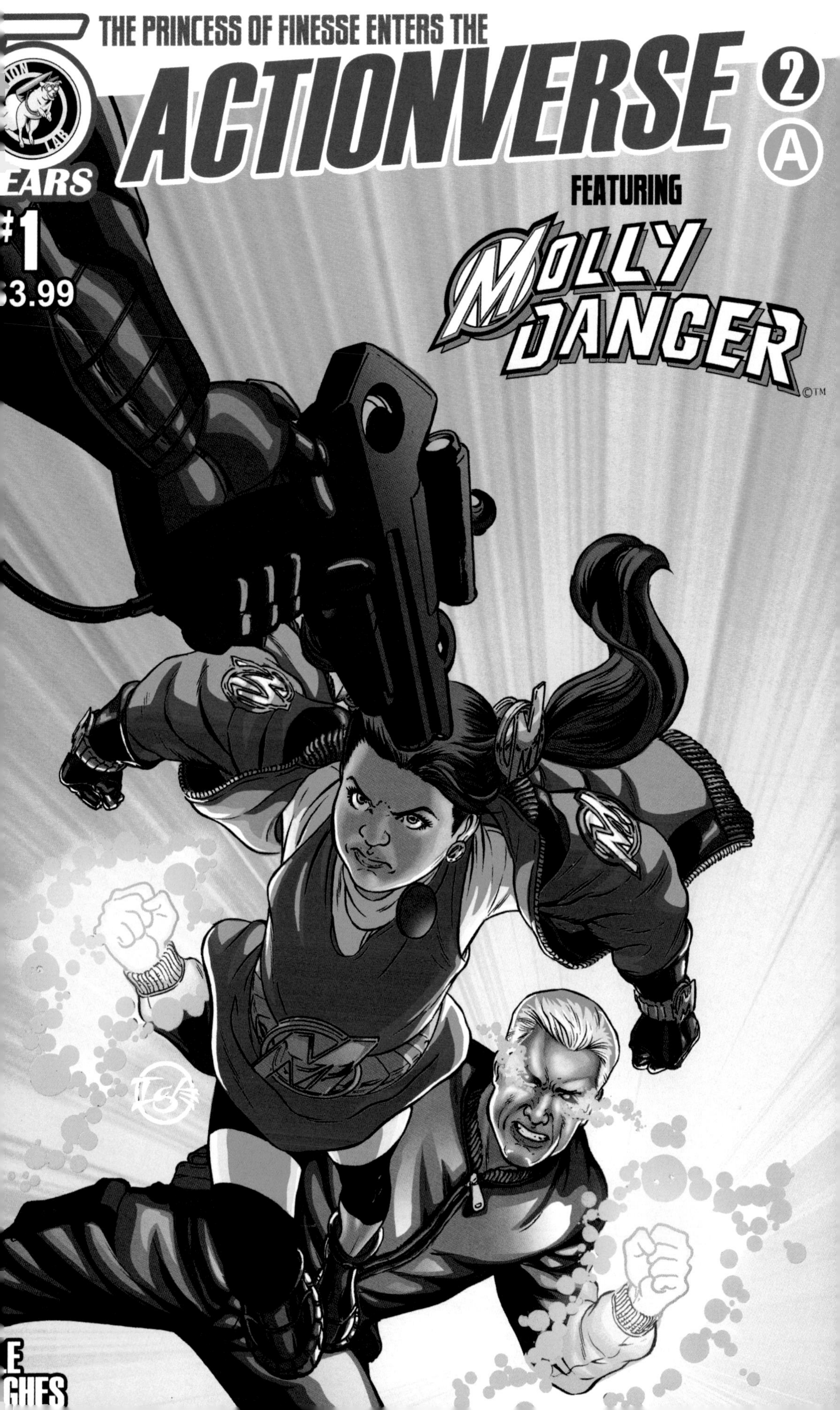

THE PRINCESS OF FINESSE ENTERS THE
ACTIONVERSE
2
A
FEATURING
MOLLY DANGER
©TM
EARS
#1
$3.99

ACTIONVERSE

FEATURING

MOLLY DANGER

Written and Drawn by Jamal Igle

Colors by Ross Hughes

Letters by Full Court Press

Cover by Jamal Igle

Variant Connecting Cover by Ron Frenz, Marc Deering
Ross Campbell and David Bednarski

Edited by Vito Delsante

MOLLY DANGER and all related characters created by Jamal Igle

PREVIOUSLY

Kyle Scordato, a dimension-hopping supervillan, has been searching for a way home. Destroying entire wor
in his wake to power his machine, Kyle has stumbled upon Jake Roth. Roth is the only sane super-powered
being on a world where superpowers cause criminal insanity. Kyle thinks Jake is the answer to his prayer.
but things don't go as planned.

BRYAN SEATON - PUBLISHER
KEVIN FREEMAN - PRESIDENT
SHAWN GABBORIN - EDITOR IN CHIEF
DAVE DWONCH - CREATIVE DIRECTOR
JASON MARTIN - EDITOR
COLLEEN BOYD - ASSOCIATE EDITOR
JAMAL IGLE - DIRECTOR OF MARKETING
VITO DELSANTE - ASSOCIATE DIRECTOR OF MARKETING
JIM DIETZ - SOCIAL MEDIA DIRECTOR
CHAD CICCONI - D.A.R.T. BOARD

ACTIONLABCOMICS.COM

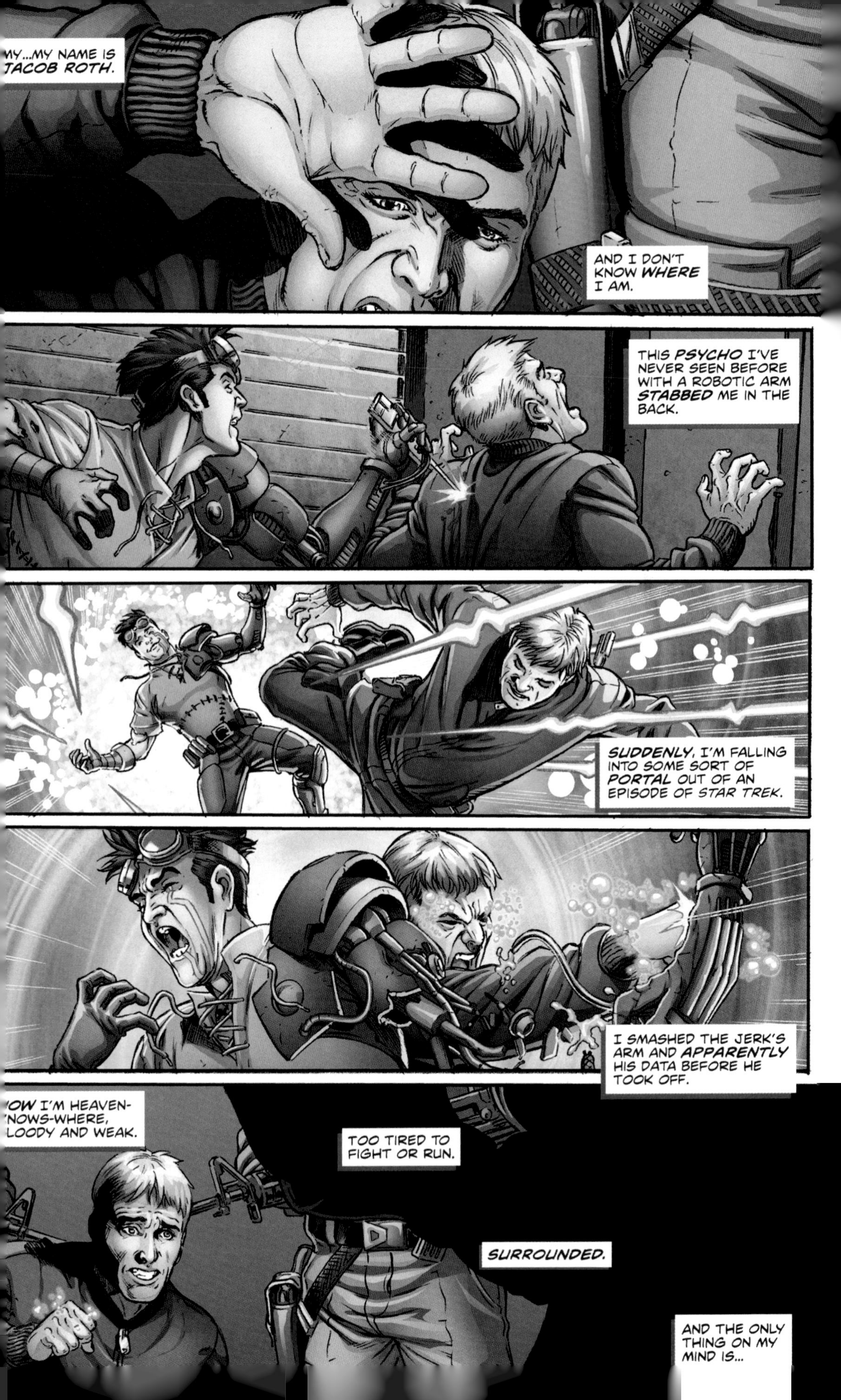

MY...MY NAME IS
JACOB ROTH.
AND I DON'T KNOW WHERE I AM.
THIS PSYCHO I'VE NEVER SEEN BEFORE WITH A ROBOTIC ARM STABBED ME IN THE BACK.
SUDDENLY, I'M FALLING INTO SOME SORT OF PORTAL OUT OF AN EPISODE OF STAR TREK.
I SMASHED THE JERK'S ARM AND APPARENTLY HIS DATA BEFORE HE TOOK OFF.
OW I'M HEAVEN-NOWS-WHERE, LOODY AND WEAK.
TOO TIRED TO FIGHT OR RUN.
SURROUNDED.
AND THE ONLY THING ON MY MIND IS...

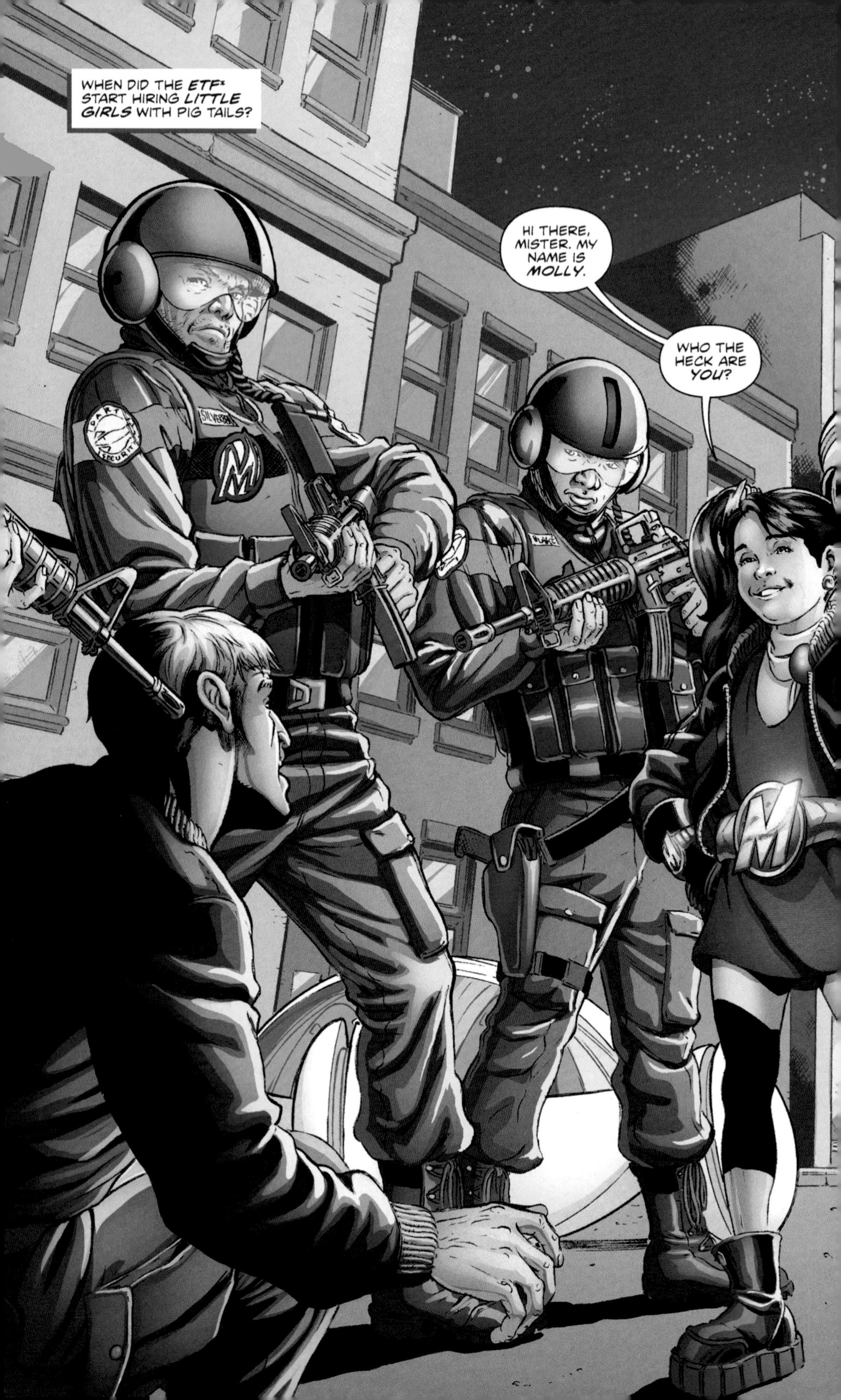
WHEN DID THE ETF* START HIRING LITTLE GIRLS WITH PIG TAILS?
HI THERE, MISTER. MY NAME IS MOLLY.
WHO THE HECK ARE YOU?

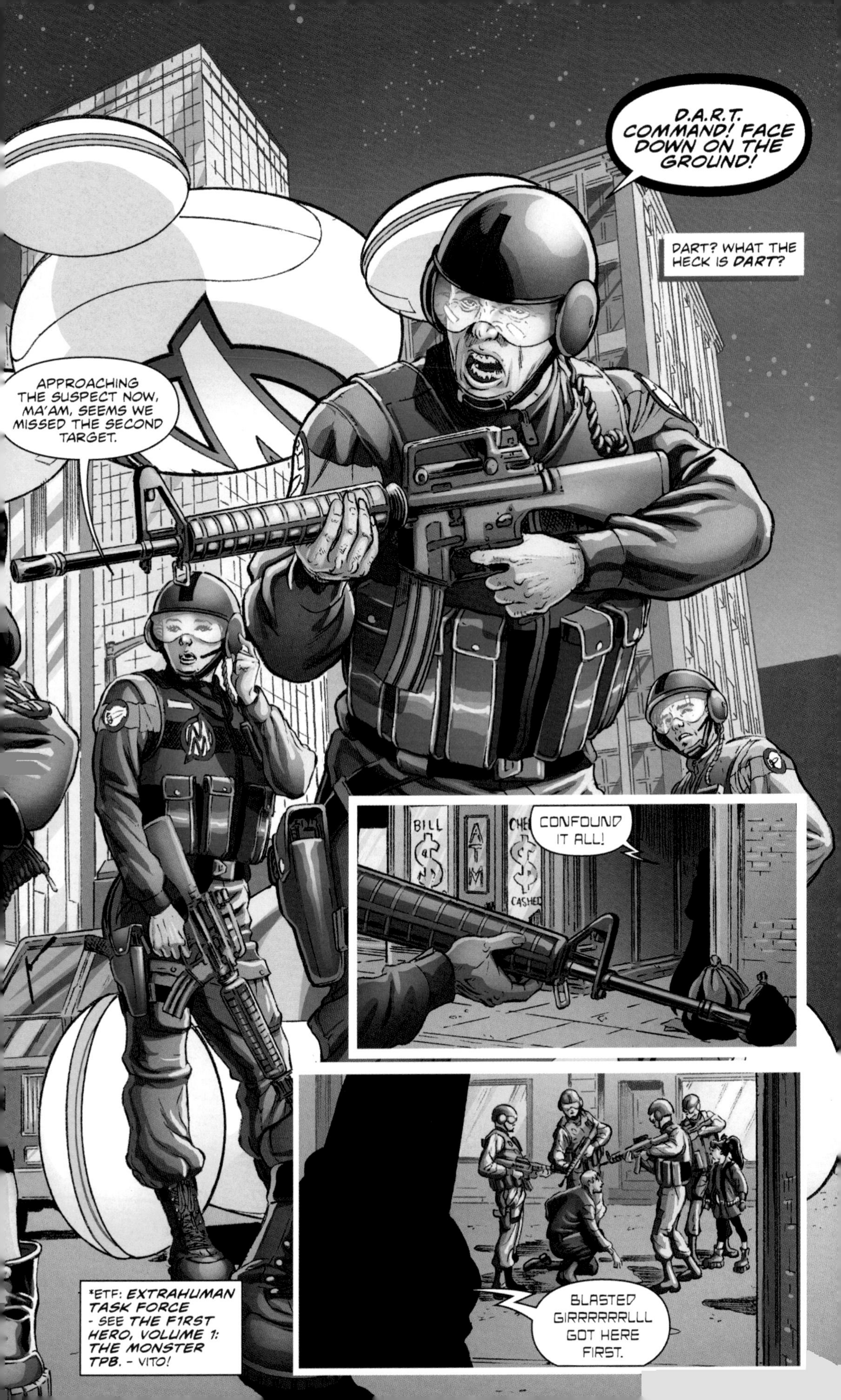
D.A.R.T. COMMAND! FACE DOWN ON THE GROUND!
DART? WHAT THE HECK IS DART?
APPROACHING THE SUSPECT NOW, MA'AM, SEEMS WE MISSED THE SECOND TARGET.
BILL
ATM
CHE
CASHED
CONFOUND IT ALL!
BLASTED GIRRRRRRLLL GOT HERE FIRST.
*ETF: EXTRAHUMAN TASK FORCE - SEE THE F1RST HERO, VOLUME 1: THE MONSTER TPB. - VITO!

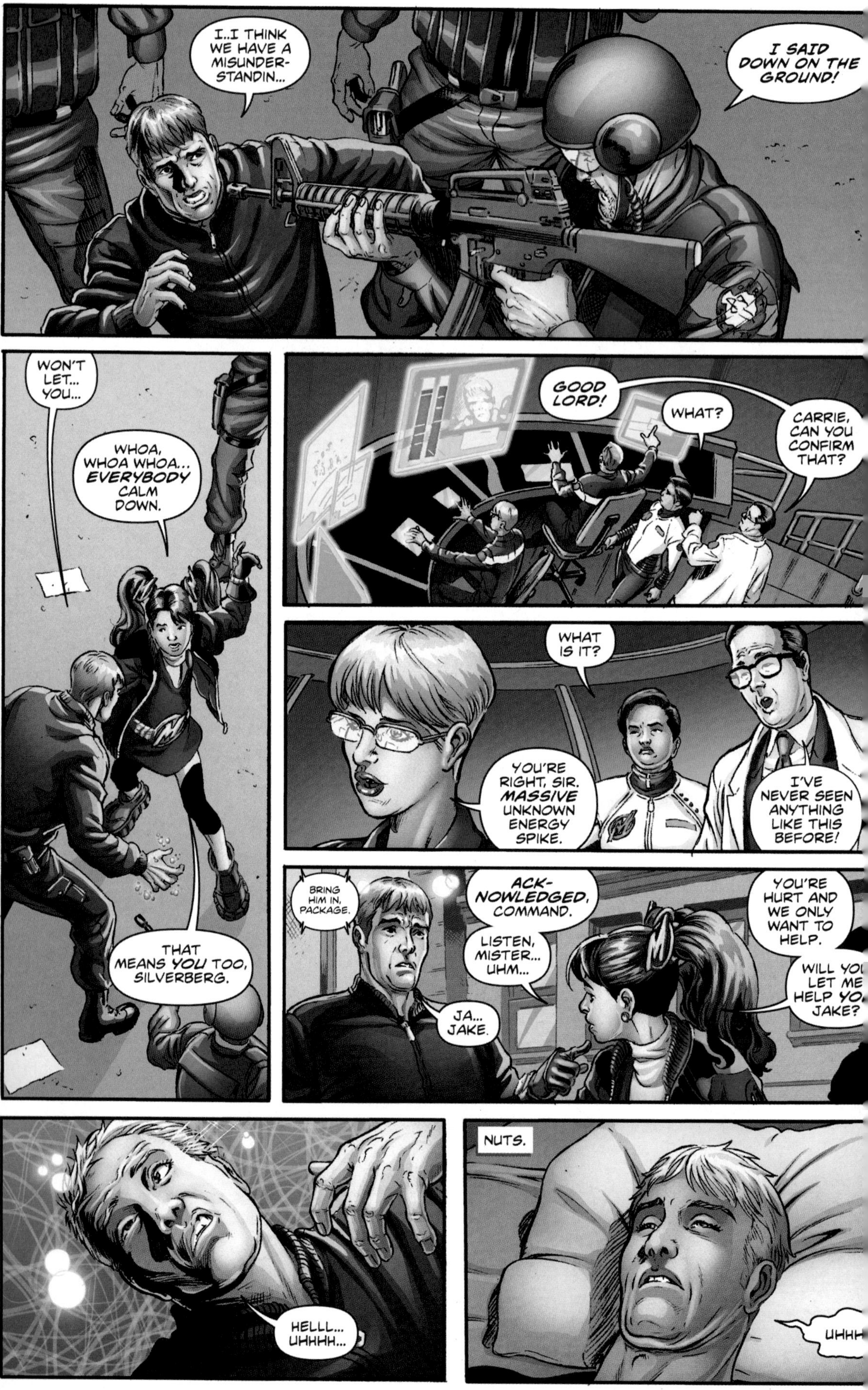

I..I THINK WE HAVE A MISUNDER-STANDIN...
I SAID DOWN ON THE GROUND!
WON'T LET... YOU...
WHOA, WHOA WHOA... EVERYBODY CALM DOWN.
THAT MEANS YOU TOO, SILVERBERG.
GOOD LORD!
WHAT?
CARRIE, CAN YOU CONFIRM THAT?
WHAT IS IT?
YOU'RE RIGHT, SIR. MASSIVE UNKNOWN ENERGY SPIKE.
I'VE NEVER SEEN ANYTHING LIKE THIS BEFORE!
BRING HIM IN, PACKAGE.
ACK-NOWLEDGED, COMMAND.
LISTEN, MISTER... UHM...
JA... JAKE.
YOU'RE HURT AND WE ONLY WANT TO HELP.
WILL YOU LET ME HELP YOU, JAKE?
HELLL... UHHHH...
NUTS.
UHHH

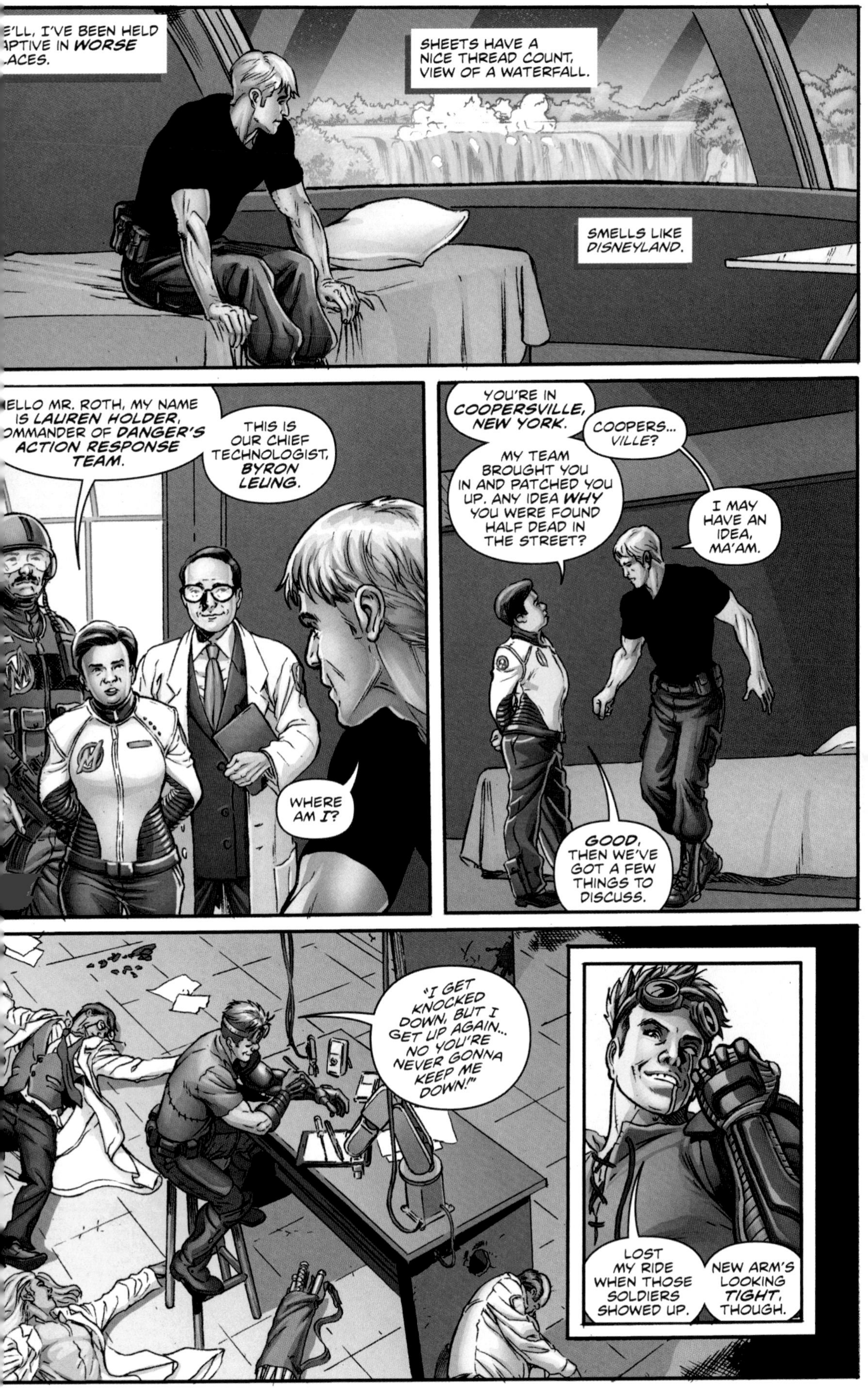

E'LL, I'VE BEEN HELD
APTIVE IN *WORSE*
ACES.
SHEETS HAVE A NICE THREAD COUNT, VIEW OF A WATERFALL.
SMELLS LIKE *DISNEYLAND*.
ELLO MR. ROTH, MY NAME IS *LAUREN HOLDER*, OMMANDER OF *DANGER'S ACTION RESPONSE TEAM*.
THIS IS OUR CHIEF TECHNOLOGIST, *BYRON LEUNG*.
WHERE AM *I*?
YOU'RE IN *COOPERSVILLE, NEW YORK*.
COOPERS... *VILLE*?
MY TEAM BROUGHT YOU IN AND PATCHED YOU UP. ANY IDEA *WHY* YOU WERE FOUND HALF DEAD IN THE STREET?
I MAY HAVE AN IDEA, MA'AM.
GOOD, THEN WE'VE GOT A FEW THINGS TO DISCUSS.
"I GET KNOCKED DOWN, BUT I GET UP AGAIN... NO YOU'RE NEVER GONNA KEEP ME DOWN!"
LOST MY RIDE WHEN THOSE SOLDIERS SHOWED UP.
NEW ARM'S LOOKING *TIGHT*, THOUGH.

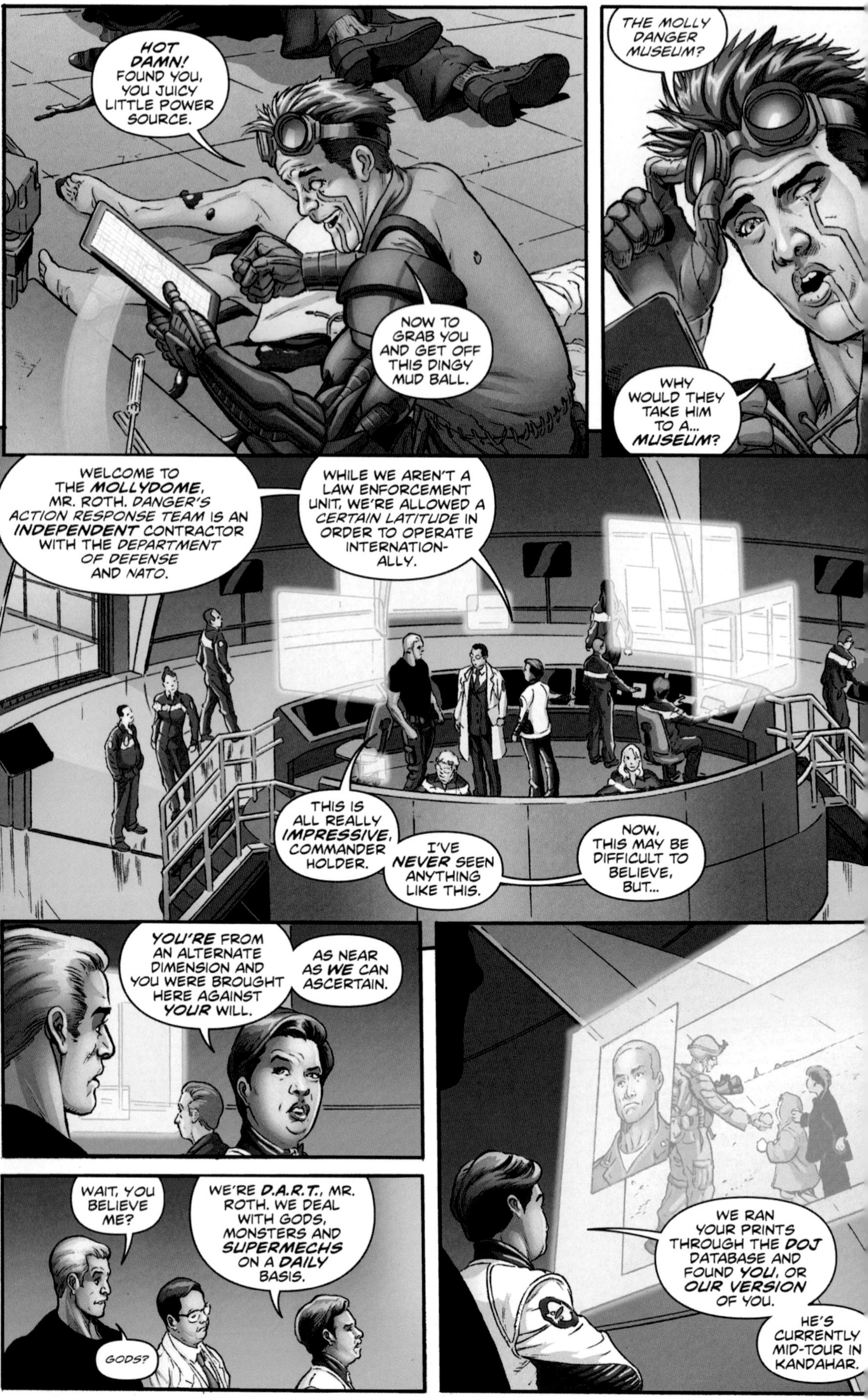
HOT DAMN! FOUND YOU, YOU JUICY LITTLE POWER SOURCE.
NOW TO GRAB YOU AND GET OFF THIS DINGY MUD BALL.
THE MOLLY DANGER MUSEUM?
WHY WOULD THEY TAKE HIM TO A... MUSEUM?
WELCOME TO THE MOLLYDOME, MR. ROTH. DANGER'S ACTION RESPONSE TEAM IS AN INDEPENDENT CONTRACTOR WITH THE DEPARTMENT OF DEFENSE AND NATO.
WHILE WE AREN'T A LAW ENFORCEMENT UNIT, WE'RE ALLOWED A CERTAIN LATITUDE IN ORDER TO OPERATE INTERNATION-ALLY.
THIS IS ALL REALLY IMPRESSIVE, COMMANDER HOLDER.
I'VE NEVER SEEN ANYTHING LIKE THIS.
NOW, THIS MAY BE DIFFICULT TO BELIEVE, BUT...
YOU'RE FROM AN ALTERNATE DIMENSION AND YOU WERE BROUGHT HERE AGAINST YOUR WILL.
AS NEAR AS WE CAN ASCERTAIN.
WAIT, YOU BELIEVE ME?
WE'RE D.A.R.T., MR. ROTH. WE DEAL WITH GODS, MONSTERS AND SUPERMECHS ON A DAILY BASIS.
GODS?
WE RAN YOUR PRINTS THROUGH THE DOJ DATABASE AND FOUND YOU, OR OUR VERSION OF YOU.
HE'S CURRENTLY MID-TOUR IN KANDAHAR.

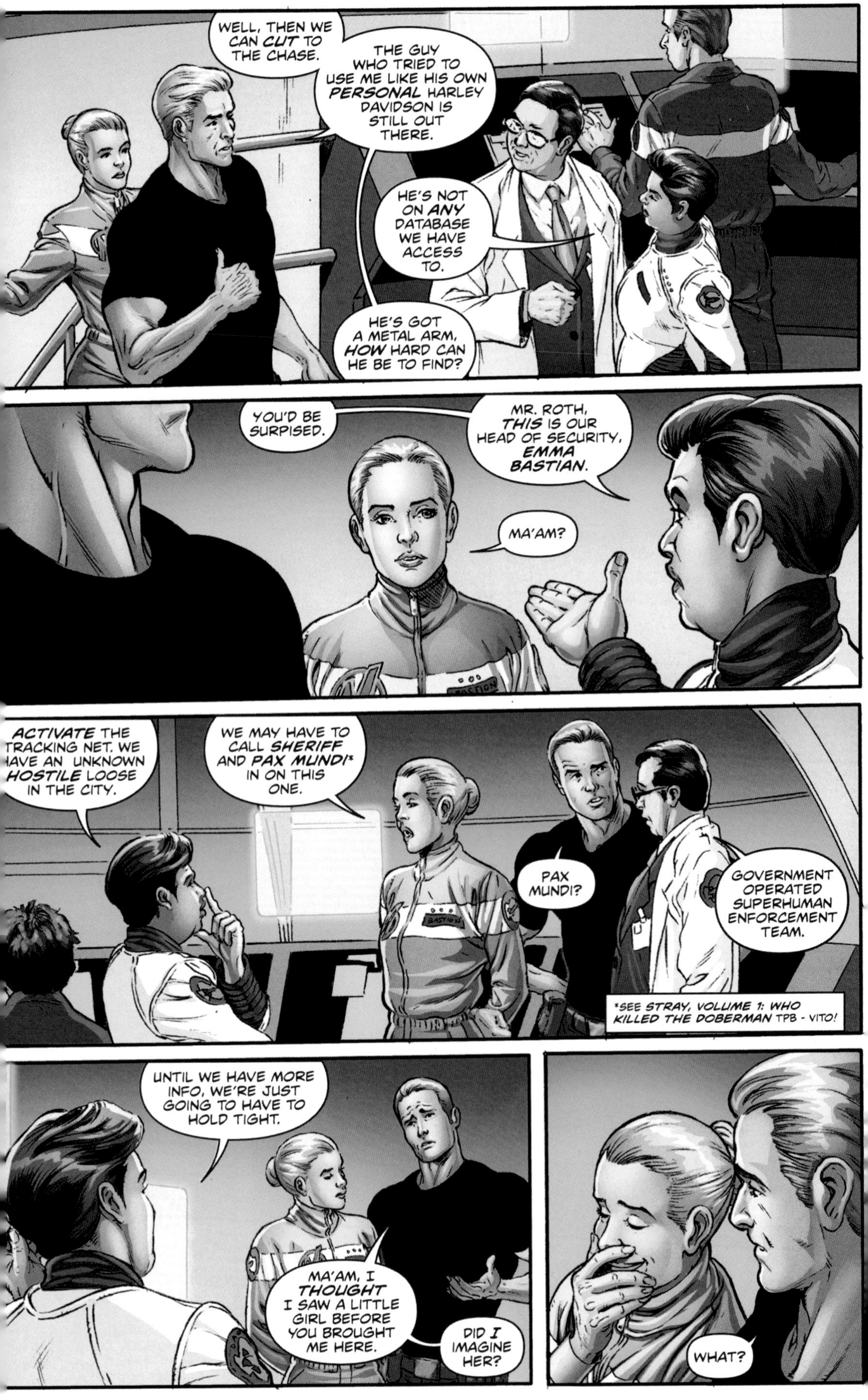
WELL, THEN WE CAN CUT TO THE CHASE.
THE GUY WHO TRIED TO USE ME LIKE HIS OWN PERSONAL HARLEY DAVIDSON IS STILL OUT THERE.
HE'S NOT ON ANY DATABASE WE HAVE ACCESS TO.
HE'S GOT A METAL ARM, HOW HARD CAN HE BE TO FIND?
YOU'D BE SURPISED.
MR. ROTH, THIS IS OUR HEAD OF SECURITY, EMMA BASTIAN.
MA'AM?
ACTIVATE THE TRACKING NET. WE HAVE AN UNKNOWN HOSTILE LOOSE IN THE CITY.
WE MAY HAVE TO CALL SHERIFF AND PAX MUNDI* IN ON THIS ONE.
PAX MUNDI?
GOVERNMENT OPERATED SUPERHUMAN ENFORCEMENT TEAM.
*SEE STRAY, VOLUME 1: WHO KILLED THE DOBERMAN TPB - VITO!
UNTIL WE HAVE MORE INFO, WE'RE JUST GOING TO HAVE TO HOLD TIGHT.
MA'AM, I THOUGHT I SAW A LITTLE GIRL BEFORE YOU BROUGHT ME HERE.
DID I IMAGINE HER?
WHAT?

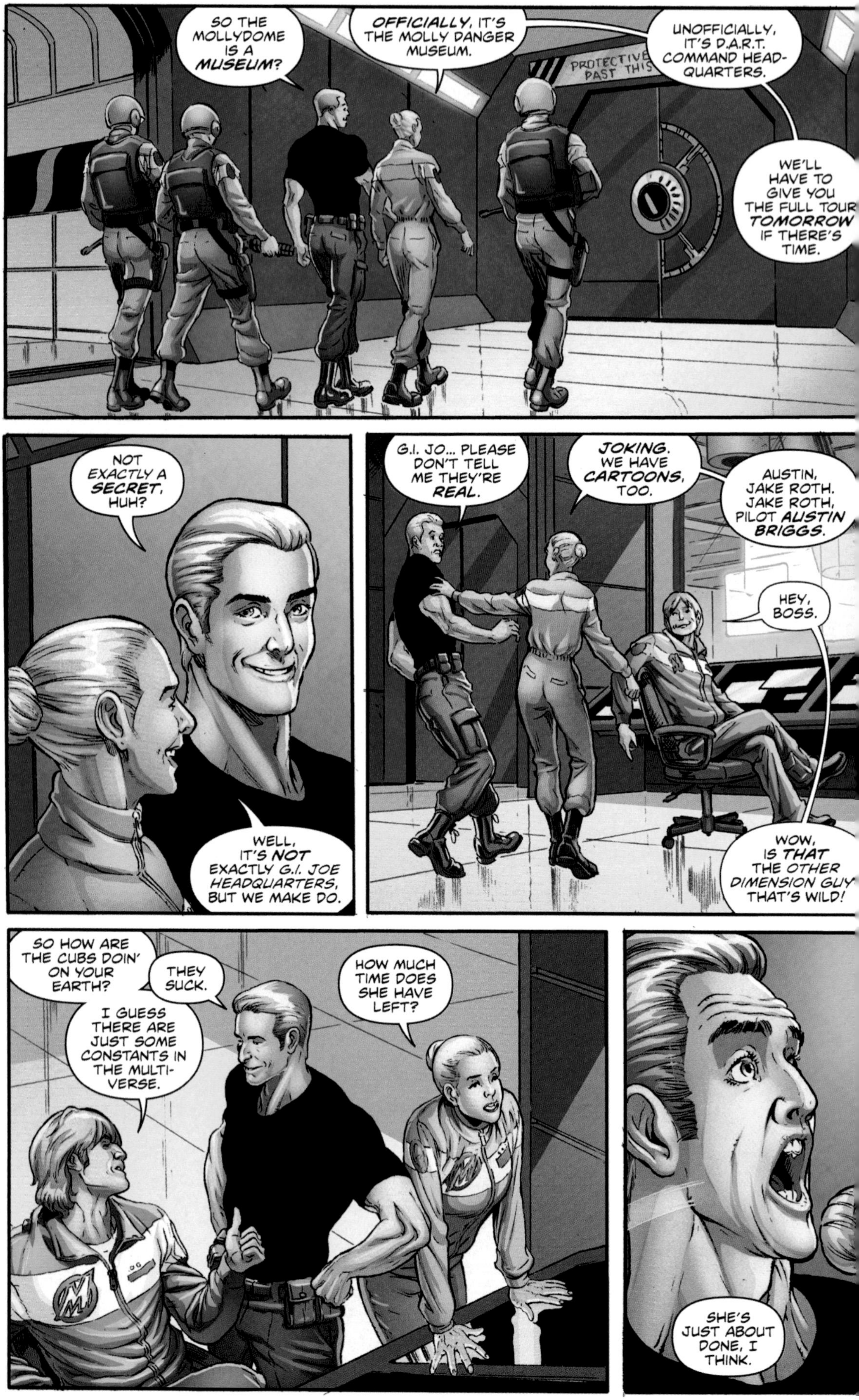

SO THE MOLLYDOME IS A MUSEUM?
OFFICIALLY, IT'S THE MOLLY DANGER MUSEUM.
UNOFFICIALLY, IT'S D.A.R.T. COMMAND HEAD-QUARTERS.
PROTECTIVE PAST THIS
WE'LL HAVE TO GIVE YOU THE FULL TOUR TOMORROW IF THERE'S TIME.
NOT EXACTLY A SECRET, HUH?
WELL, IT'S NOT EXACTLY G.I. JOE HEADQUARTERS, BUT WE MAKE DO.
G.I. JO... PLEASE DON'T TELL ME THEY'RE REAL.
JOKING. WE HAVE CARTOONS, TOO.
AUSTIN, JAKE ROTH. JAKE ROTH, PILOT AUSTIN BRIGGS.
HEY, BOSS.
WOW, IS THAT THE OTHER DIMENSION GUY THAT'S WILD!
SO HOW ARE THE CUBS DOIN' ON YOUR EARTH?
THEY SUCK.
I GUESS THERE ARE JUST SOME CONSTANTS IN THE MULTI-VERSE.
HOW MUCH TIME DOES SHE HAVE LEFT?
SHE'S JUST ABOUT DONE, I THINK.

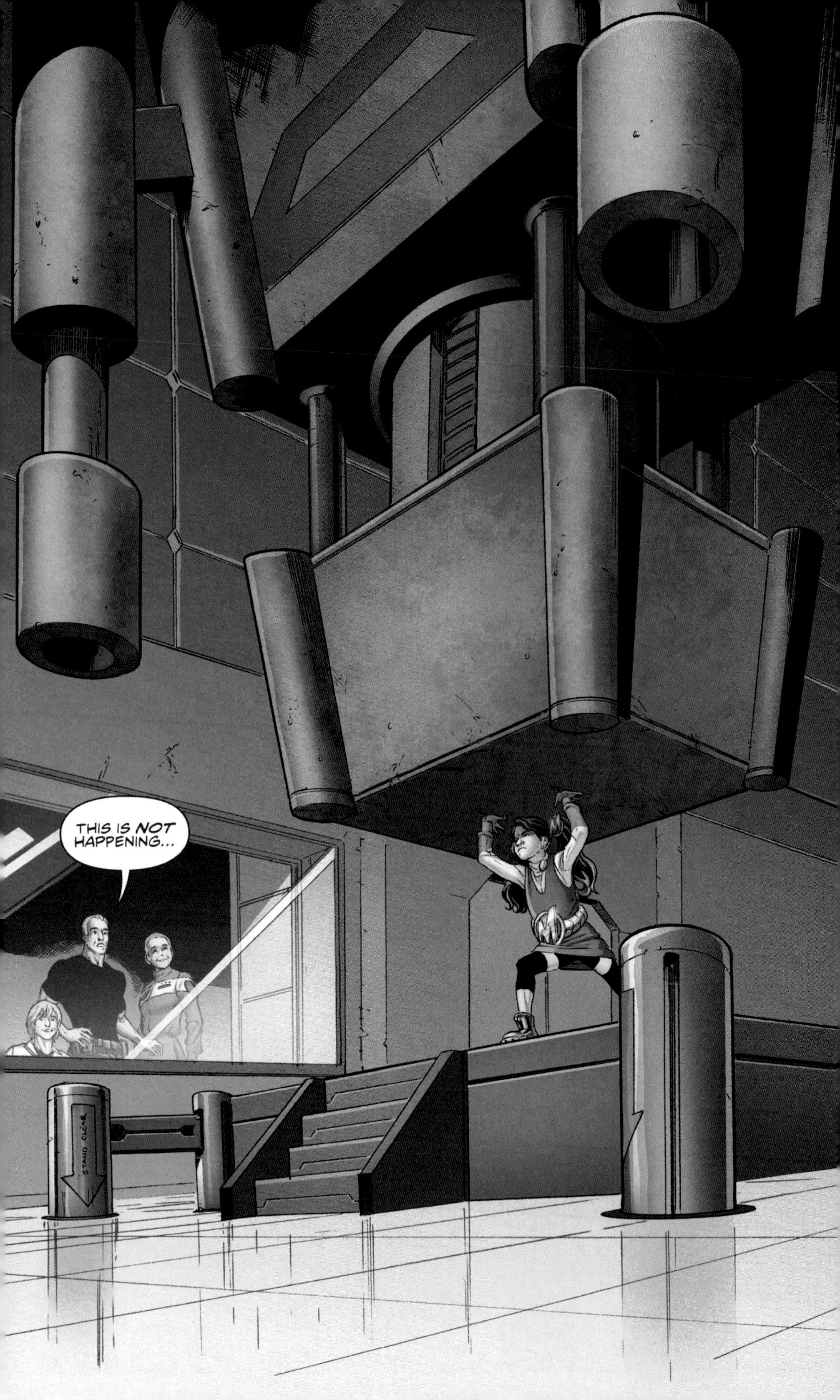
THIS IS NOT HAPPENING...
STAND CLEAR

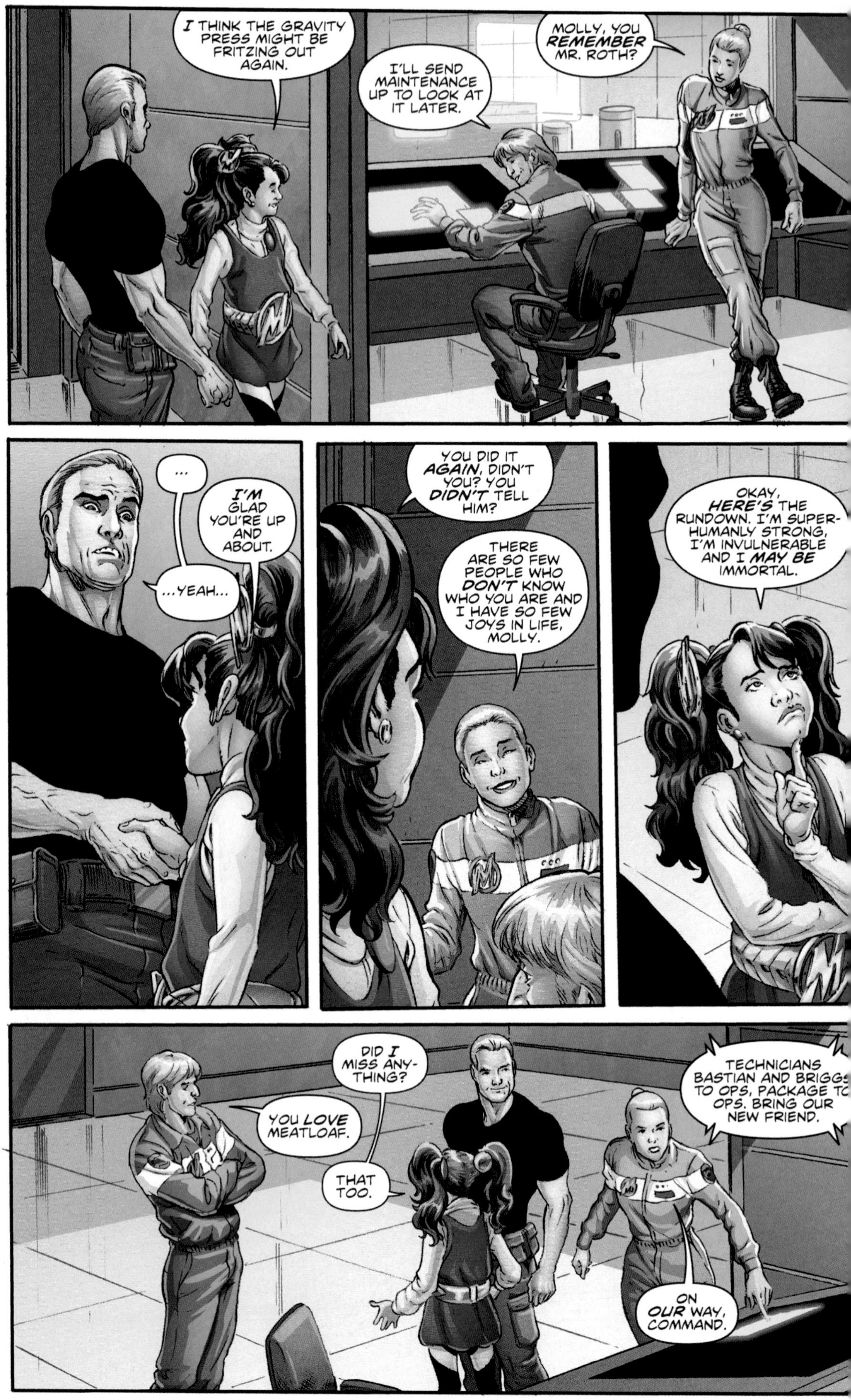
I THINK THE GRAVITY PRESS MIGHT BE FRITZING OUT AGAIN.
I'LL SEND MAINTENANCE UP TO LOOK AT IT LATER.
MOLLY, YOU REMEMBER MR. ROTH?
...
...YEAH...
I'M GLAD YOU'RE UP AND ABOUT.
YOU DID IT AGAIN, DIDN'T YOU? YOU DIDN'T TELL HIM?
THERE ARE SO FEW PEOPLE WHO DON'T KNOW WHO YOU ARE AND I HAVE SO FEW JOYS IN LIFE, MOLLY.
OKAY, HERE'S THE RUNDOWN. I'M SUPER-HUMANLY STRONG, I'M INVULNERABLE AND I MAY BE IMMORTAL.
DID I MISS ANY-THING?
YOU LOVE MEATLOAF.
THAT TOO.
TECHNICIANS BASTIAN AND BRIGGS TO OPS, PACKAGE TO OPS. BRING OUR NEW FRIEND.
ON OUR WAY, COMMAND.

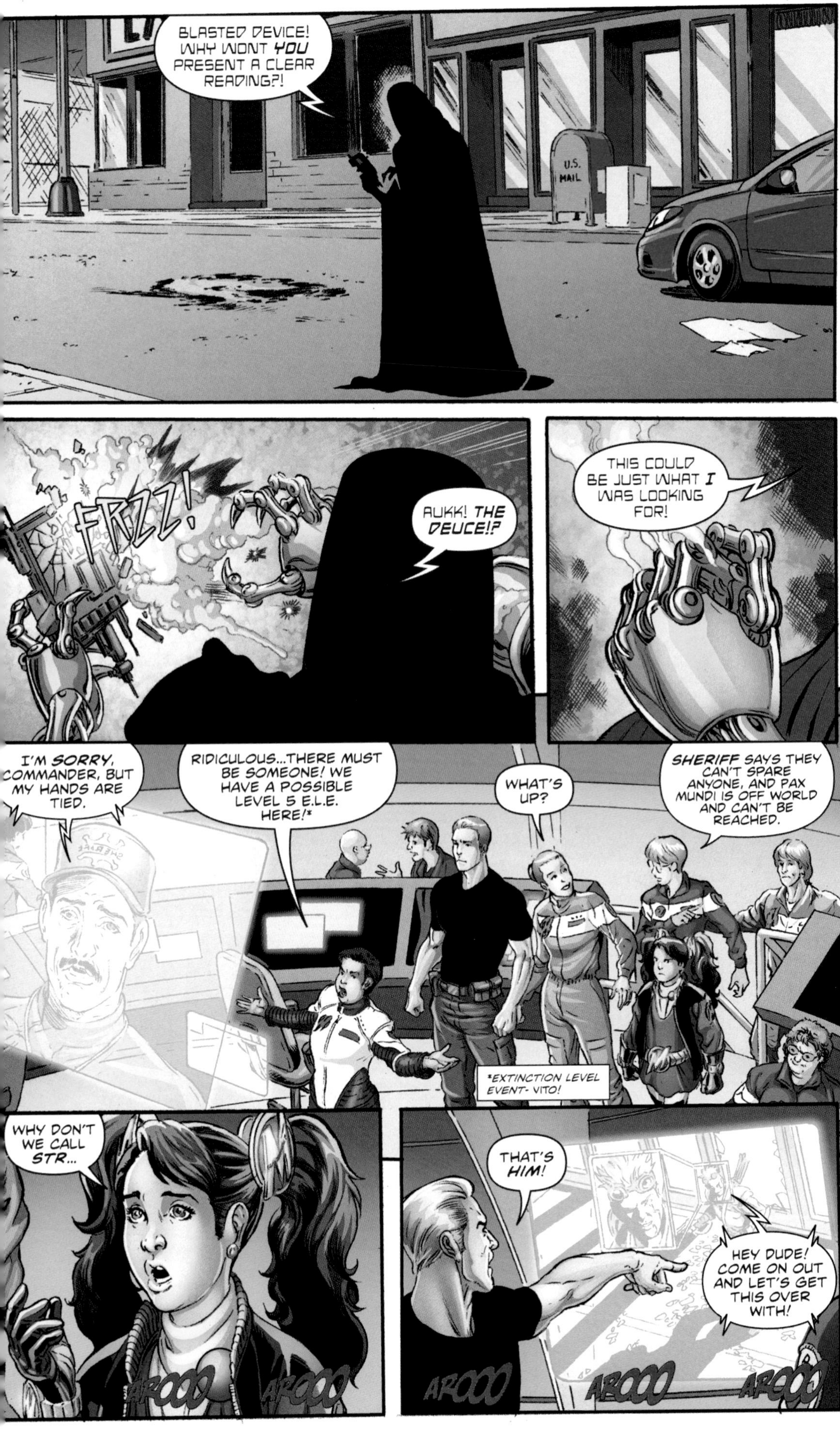
BLASTED DEVICE! WHY WONT *YOU* PRESENT A CLEAR READING?!
U.S. MAIL
FRZZ!
AUKK! *THE DEUCE!?*
THIS COULD BE JUST WHAT *I* WAS LOOKING FOR!
I'M *SORRY*, COMMANDER, BUT MY HANDS ARE TIED.
RIDICULOUS...THERE MUST BE SOMEONE! WE HAVE A POSSIBLE LEVEL 5 E.L.E. HERE!*
WHAT'S UP?
SHERIFF SAYS THEY CAN'T SPARE ANYONE, AND PAX MUNDI IS OFF WORLD AND CAN'T BE REACHED.
*EXTINCTION LEVEL EVENT- VITO!
WHY DON'T WE CALL *STR...*
THAT'S *HIM!*
HEY DUDE! COME ON OUT AND LET'S GET THIS OVER WITH!
AROOO AROOO AROOO AROOO AROOO

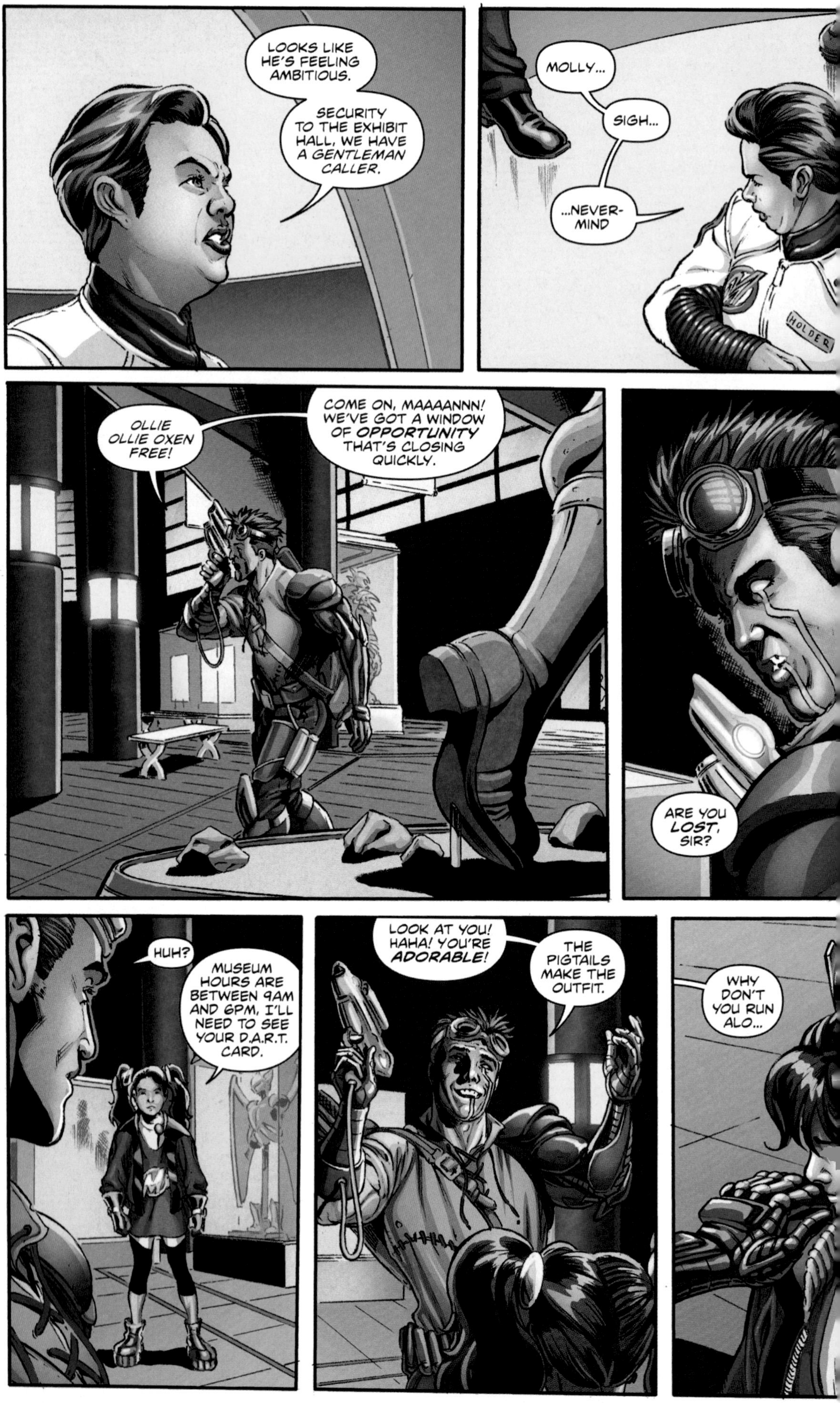
LOOKS LIKE HE'S FEELING AMBITIOUS.
SECURITY TO THE EXHIBIT HALL, WE HAVE A GENTLEMAN CALLER.
MOLLY...
SIGH...
...NEVER-MIND
HOLDER
OLLIE OLLIE OXEN FREE!
COME ON, MAAAANNN! WE'VE GOT A WINDOW OF OPPORTUNITY THAT'S CLOSING QUICKLY.
ARE YOU LOST, SIR?
HUH?
MUSEUM HOURS ARE BETWEEN 9AM AND 6PM, I'LL NEED TO SEE YOUR D.A.R.T. CARD.
LOOK AT YOU! HAHA! YOU'RE ADORABLE!
THE PIGTAILS MAKE THE OUTFIT.
WHY DON'T YOU RUN ALO...

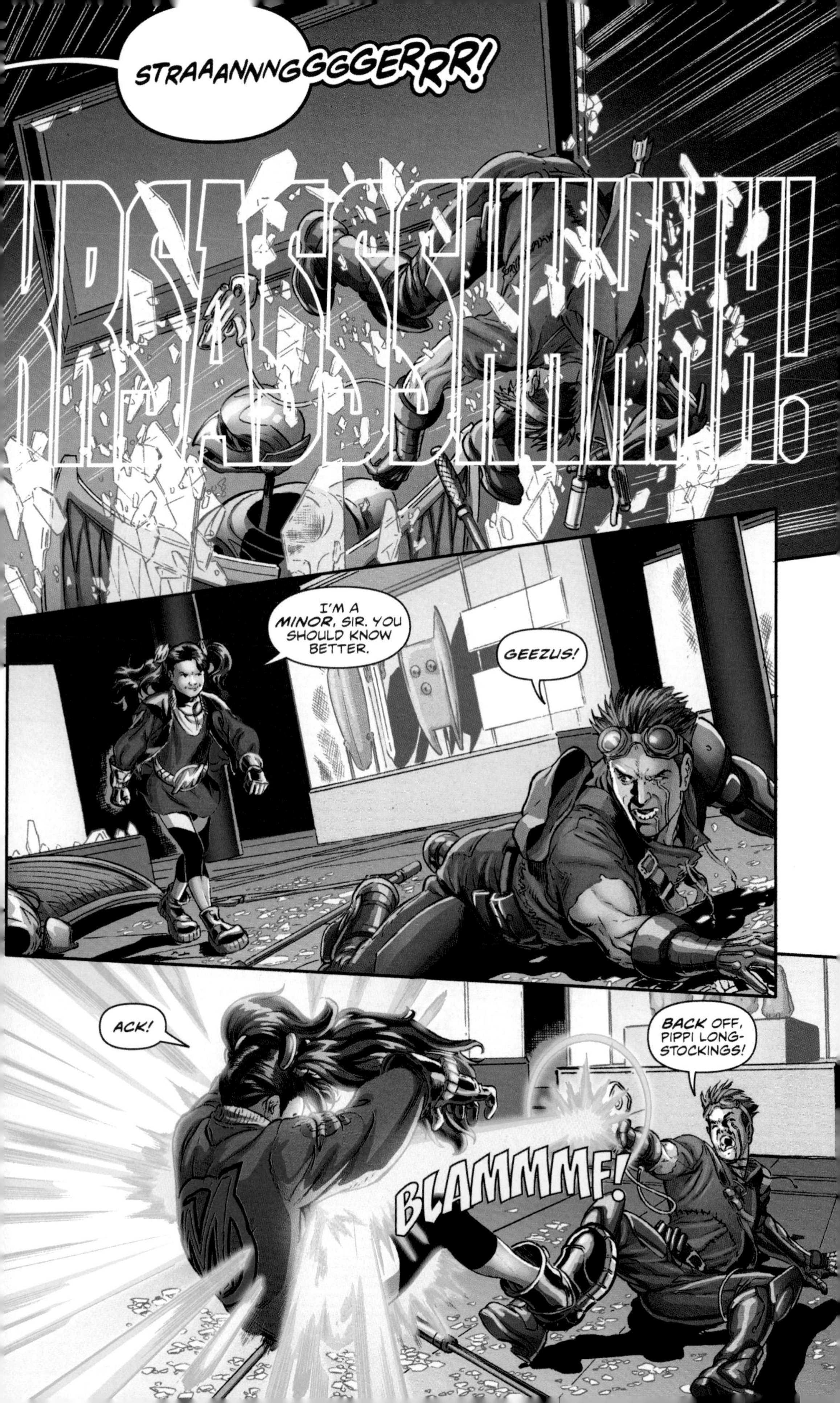
STRAAANNNGGGGERRR!
I'M A MINOR, SIR. YOU SHOULD KNOW BETTER.
GEEZUS!
ACK!
BACK OFF, PIPPI LONG-STOCKINGS!
BLAMMMMF!

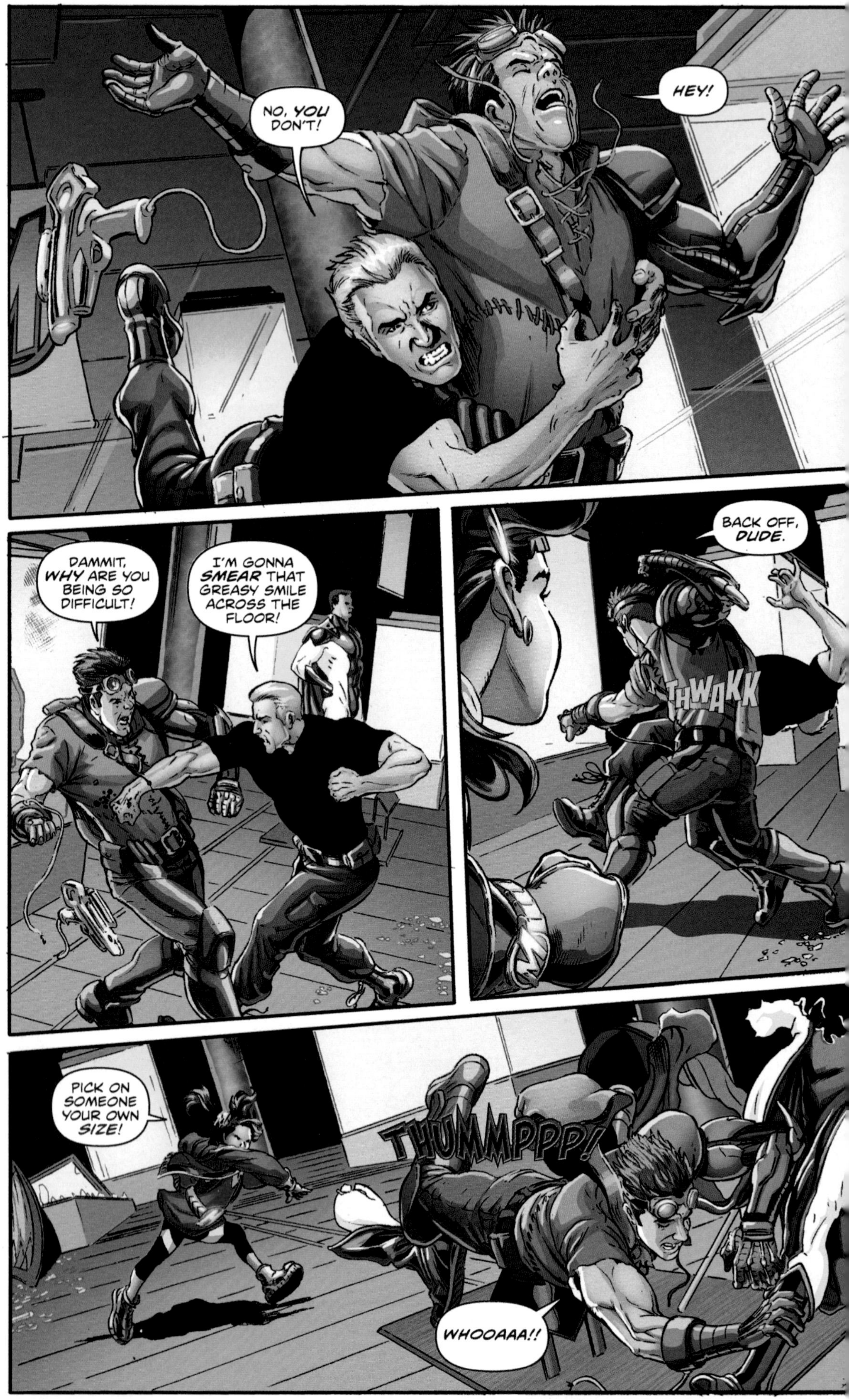
NO, YOU DON'T!
HEY!
DAMMIT, WHY ARE YOU BEING SO DIFFICULT!
I'M GONNA SMEAR THAT GREASY SMILE ACROSS THE FLOOR!
BACK OFF, DUDE.
THWAKK
PICK ON SOMEONE YOUR OWN SIZE!
THUMMPPP!
WHOOAAA!!

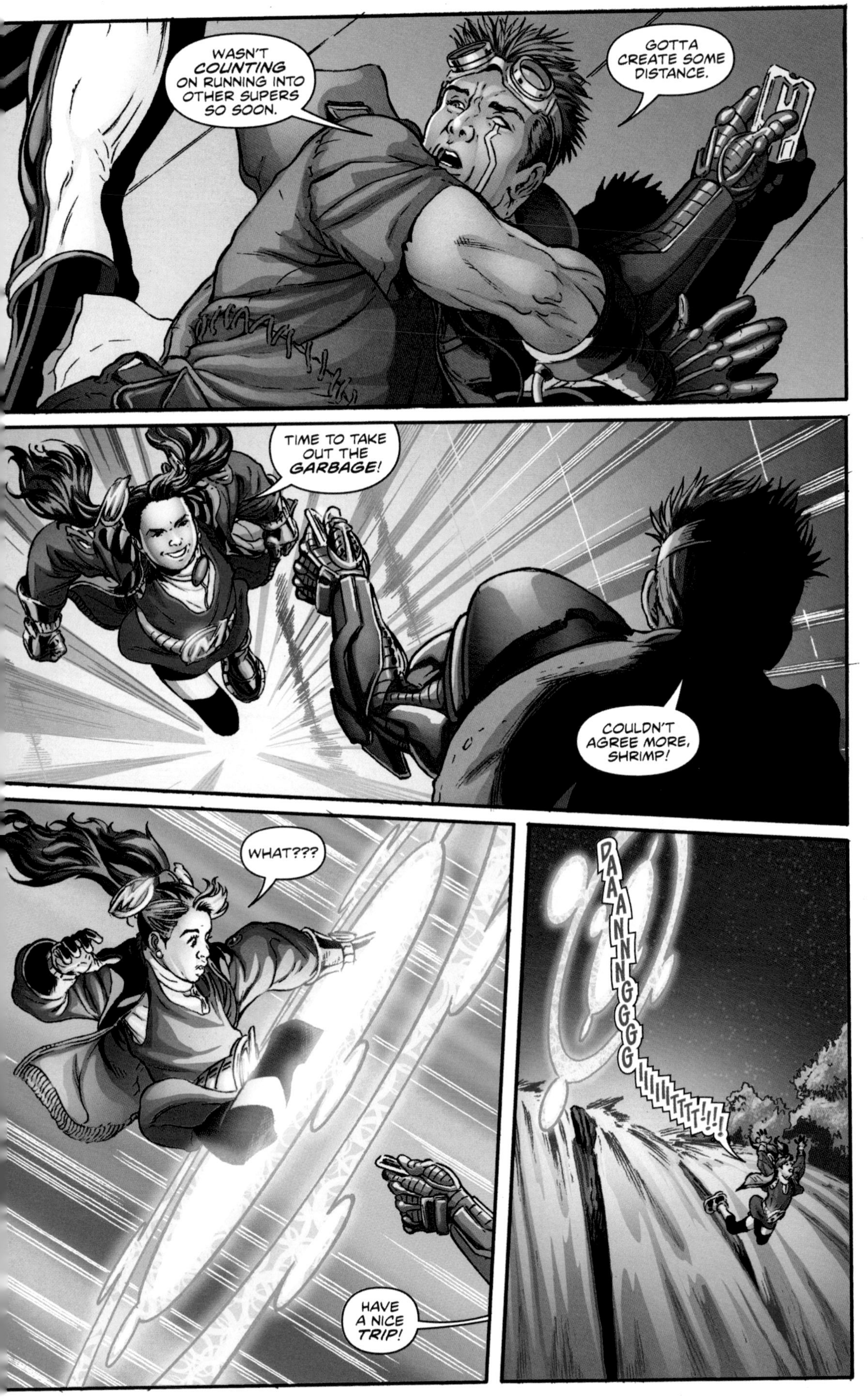
WASN'T COUNTING ON RUNNING INTO OTHER SUPERS SO SOON.
GOTTA CREATE SOME DISTANCE.
TIME TO TAKE OUT THE GARBAGE!
COULDN'T AGREE MORE, SHRIMP!
WHAT???
HAVE A NICE TRIP!
DAAANNNGGGIIIIITTTT!!!

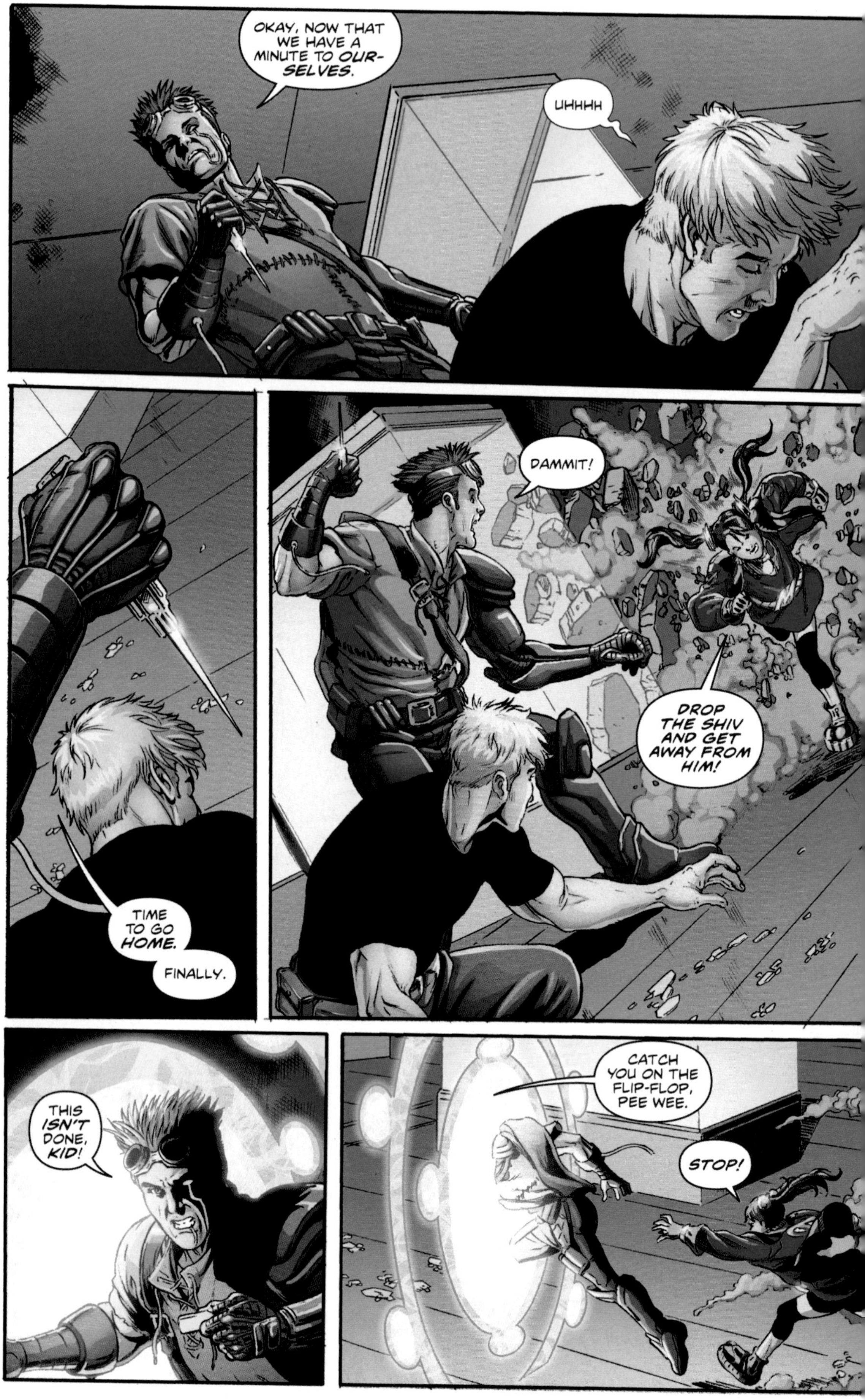
OKAY, NOW THAT WE HAVE A MINUTE TO OUR-SELVES.
UHHHH
TIME TO GO HOME.
FINALLY.
DAMMIT!
DROP THE SHIV AND GET AWAY FROM HIM!
THIS ISN'T DONE, KID!
CATCH YOU ON THE FLIP-FLOP, PEE WEE.
STOP!

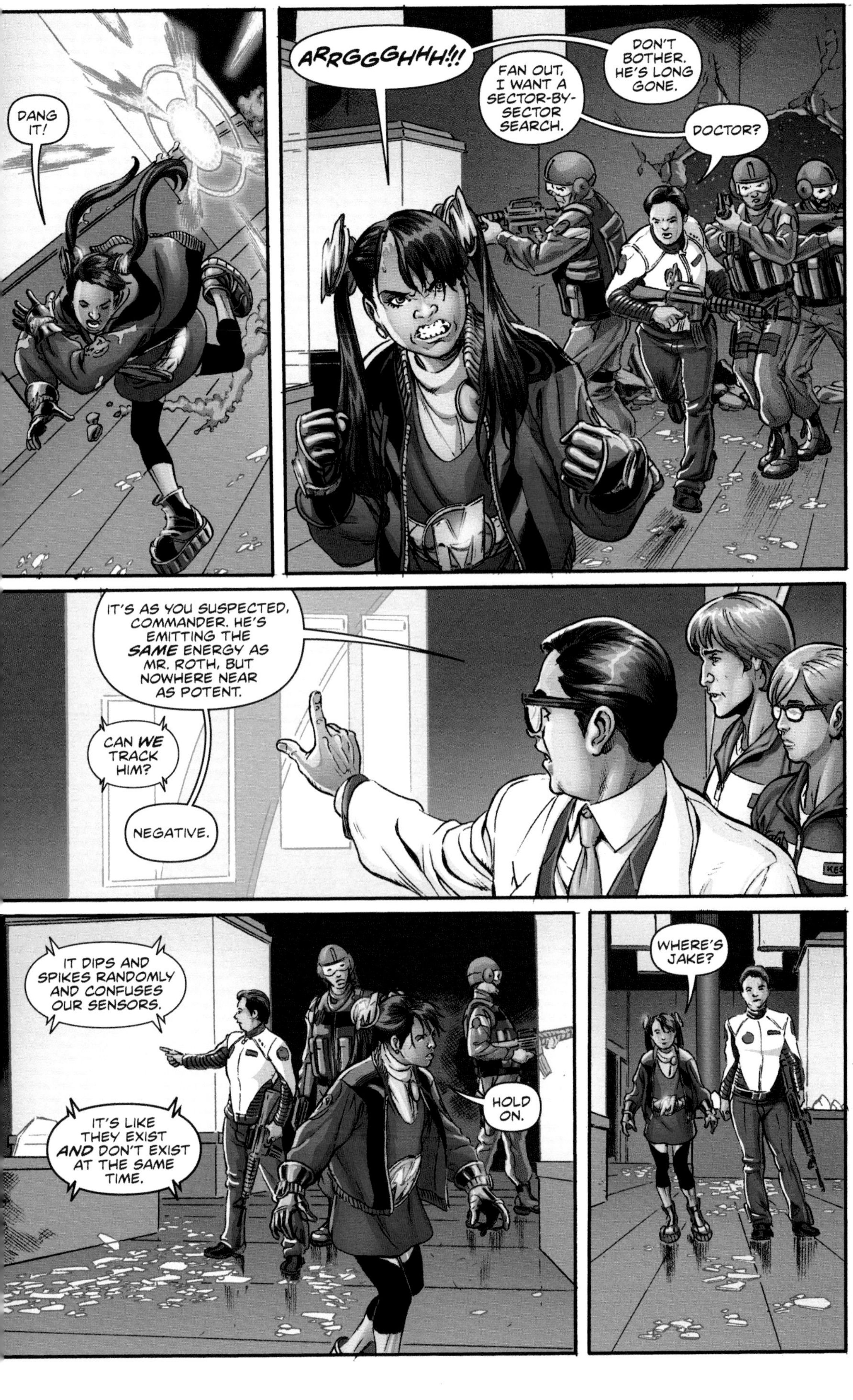

DANG IT!
ARRGGGHHH!!!
FAN OUT, I WANT A SECTOR-BY-SECTOR SEARCH.
DON'T BOTHER. HE'S LONG GONE.
DOCTOR?
IT'S AS YOU SUSPECTED, COMMANDER. HE'S EMITTING THE SAME ENERGY AS MR. ROTH, BUT NOWHERE NEAR AS POTENT.
CAN WE TRACK HIM?
NEGATIVE.
IT DIPS AND SPIKES RANDOMLY AND CONFUSES OUR SENSORS.
IT'S LIKE THEY EXIST AND DON'T EXIST AT THE SAME TIME.
HOLD ON.
WHERE'S JAKE?

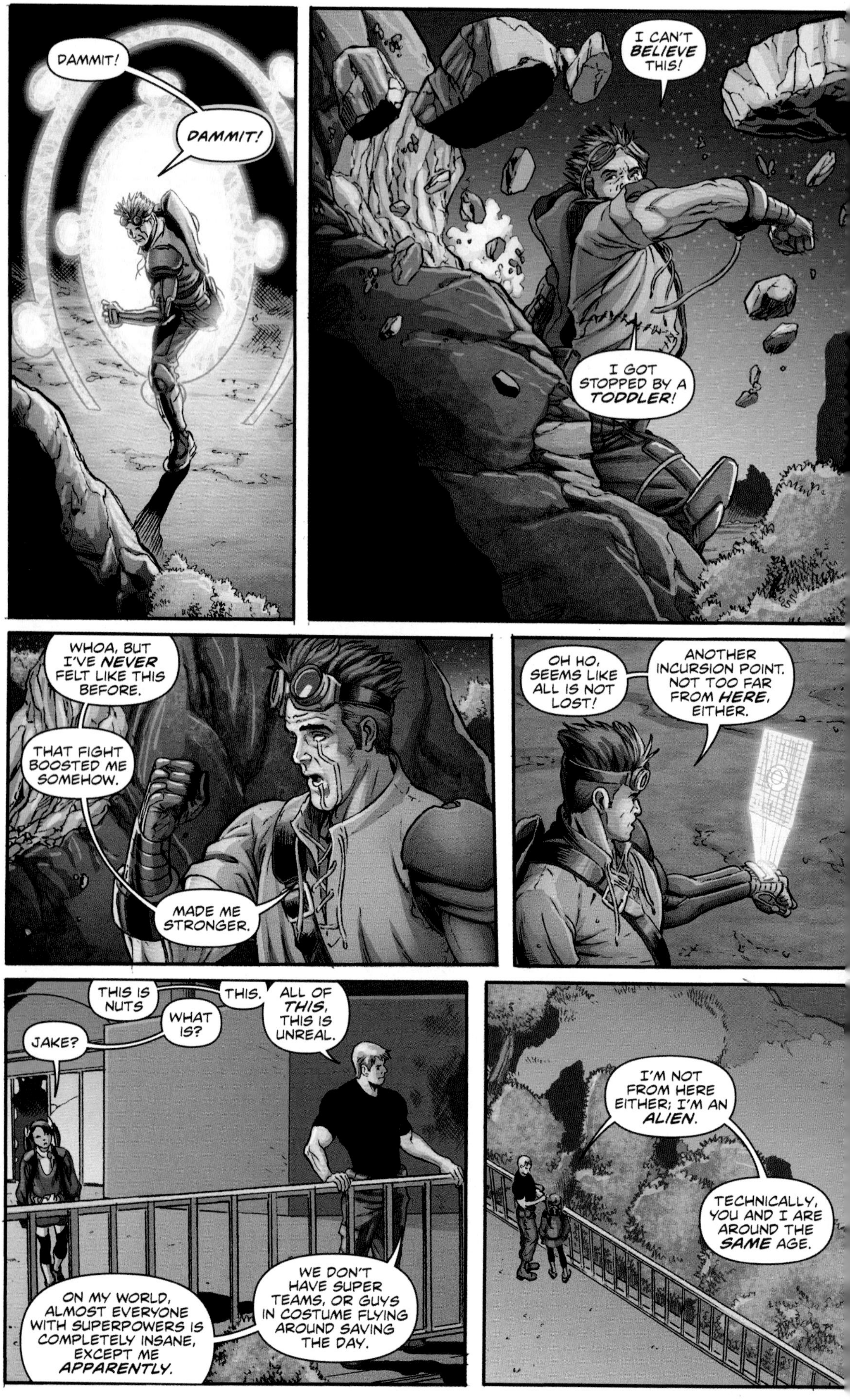
DAMMIT!
DAMMIT!
I CAN'T BELIEVE THIS!
I GOT STOPPED BY A TODDLER!
WHOA, BUT I'VE NEVER FELT LIKE THIS BEFORE.
THAT FIGHT BOOSTED ME SOMEHOW.
MADE ME STRONGER.
OH HO, SEEMS LIKE ALL IS NOT LOST!
ANOTHER INCURSION POINT. NOT TOO FAR FROM HERE, EITHER.
JAKE?
THIS IS NUTS
WHAT IS?
THIS.
ALL OF THIS, THIS IS UNREAL.
WE DON'T HAVE SUPER TEAMS, OR GUYS IN COSTUME FLYING AROUND SAVING THE DAY.
ON MY WORLD, ALMOST EVERYONE WITH SUPERPOWERS IS COMPLETELY INSANE, EXCEPT ME APPARENTLY.
I'M NOT FROM HERE EITHER; I'M AN ALIEN.
TECHNICALLY, YOU AND I ARE AROUND THE SAME AGE.

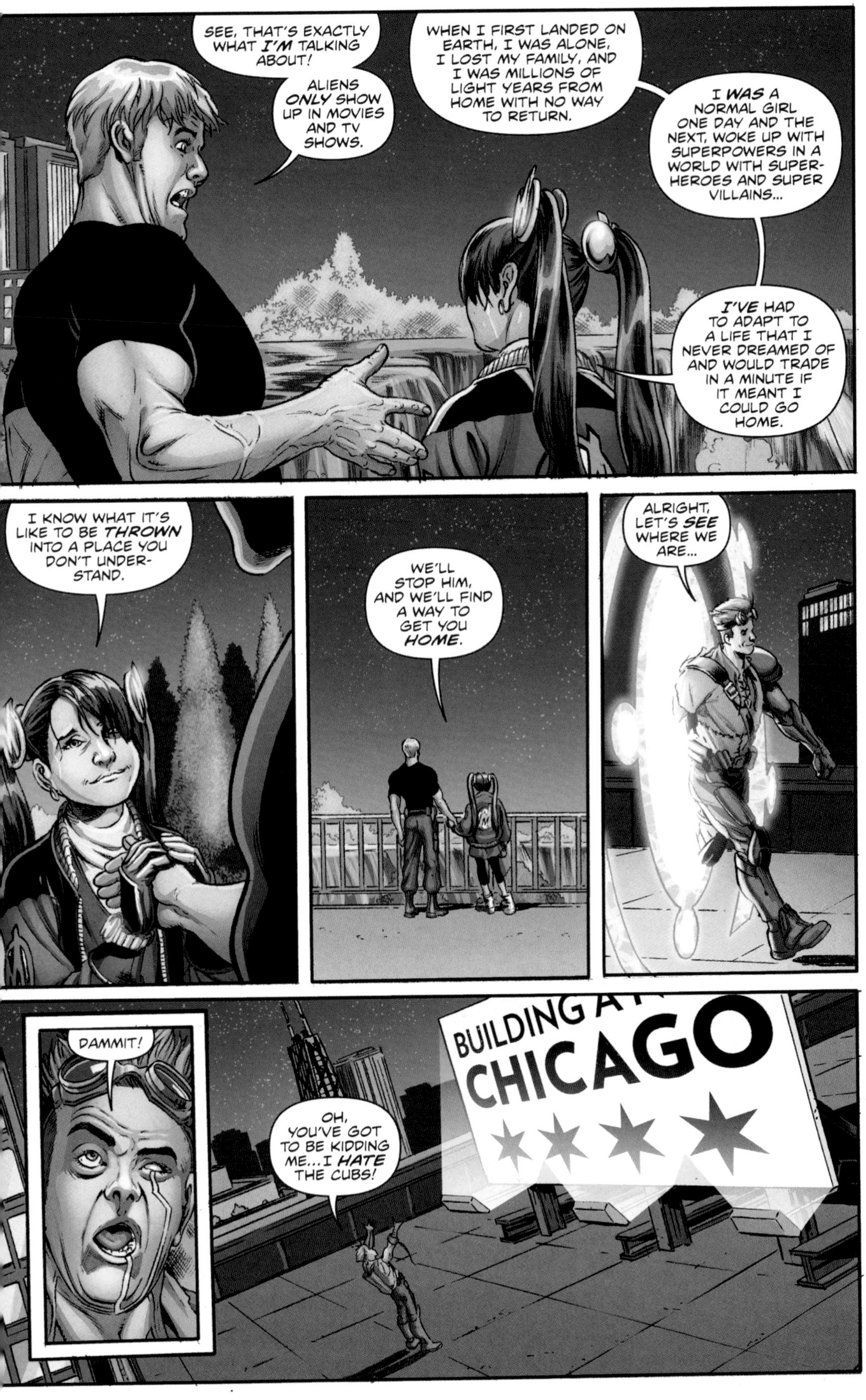

SEE, THAT'S EXACTLY WHAT *I'M* TALKING ABOUT!
ALIENS *ONLY* SHOW UP IN MOVIES AND TV SHOWS.
WHEN I FIRST LANDED ON EARTH, I WAS ALONE, I LOST MY FAMILY, AND I WAS MILLIONS OF LIGHT YEARS FROM HOME WITH NO WAY TO RETURN.
I *WAS* A NORMAL GIRL ONE DAY AND THE NEXT, WOKE UP WITH SUPERPOWERS IN A WORLD WITH SUPER-HEROES AND SUPER VILLAINS...
I'VE HAD TO ADAPT TO A LIFE THAT I NEVER DREAMED OF AND WOULD TRADE IN A MINUTE IF IT MEANT I COULD GO HOME.
I KNOW WHAT IT'S LIKE TO BE *THROWN* INTO A PLACE YOU DON'T UNDER-STAND.
WE'LL STOP HIM, AND WE'LL FIND A WAY TO GET YOU *HOME*.
ALRIGHT, LET'S *SEE* WHERE WE ARE...
DAMMIT!
OH, YOU'VE GOT TO BE KIDDING ME...I *HATE* THE CUBS!
CHICAGO

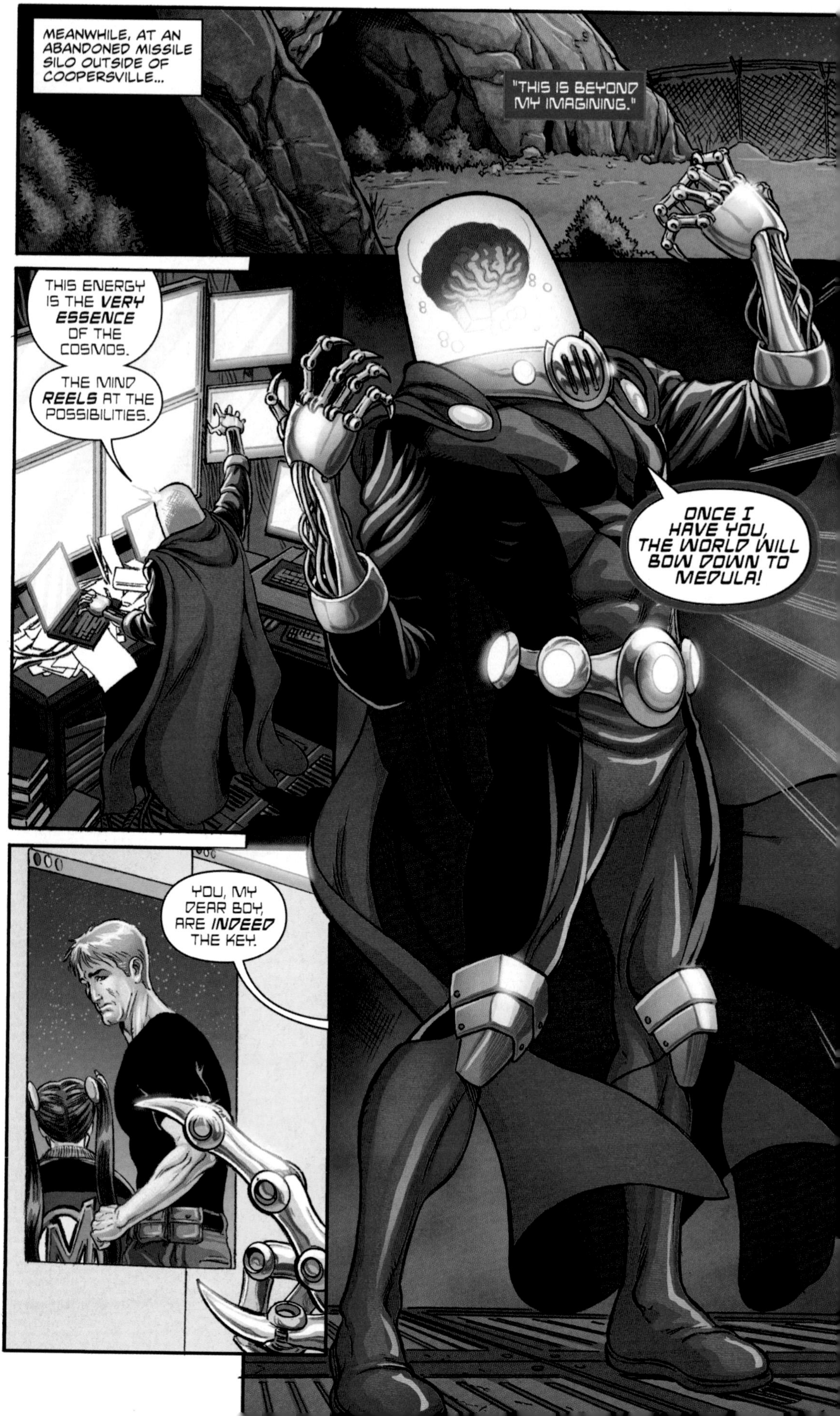

MEANWHILE, AT AN ABANDONED MISSILE SILO OUTSIDE OF COOPERSVILLE...
"THIS IS BEYOND MY IMAGINING."
THIS ENERGY IS THE VERY ESSENCE OF THE COSMOS.
THE MIND REELS AT THE POSSIBILITIES.
ONCE I HAVE YOU, THE WORLD WILL BOW DOWN TO MEDULA!
YOU, MY DEAR BOY, ARE INDEED THE KEY.

APOLLO BAY, CA

KRAKATHOBOOMMM!!

THIS CITY IS FILTHY. YOU CAN SMELL THE FOUL STENCH OF CORRUPTION EVEN FROM HERE.

INNOCENTS ARE THREATENED, AND WHERE ARE THE POLICE?

CRIME *CANNOT* BE ALLOWED TO STAND.

CRIMINALS *ONLY* UNDERSTAND *FEAR.*

BUT *FEAR OF PUNISHMENT ISN'T* ENOUGH.

OH, THANK YOU.

THANK Y...

SNAP!

AHHHHH... AHHHHH...

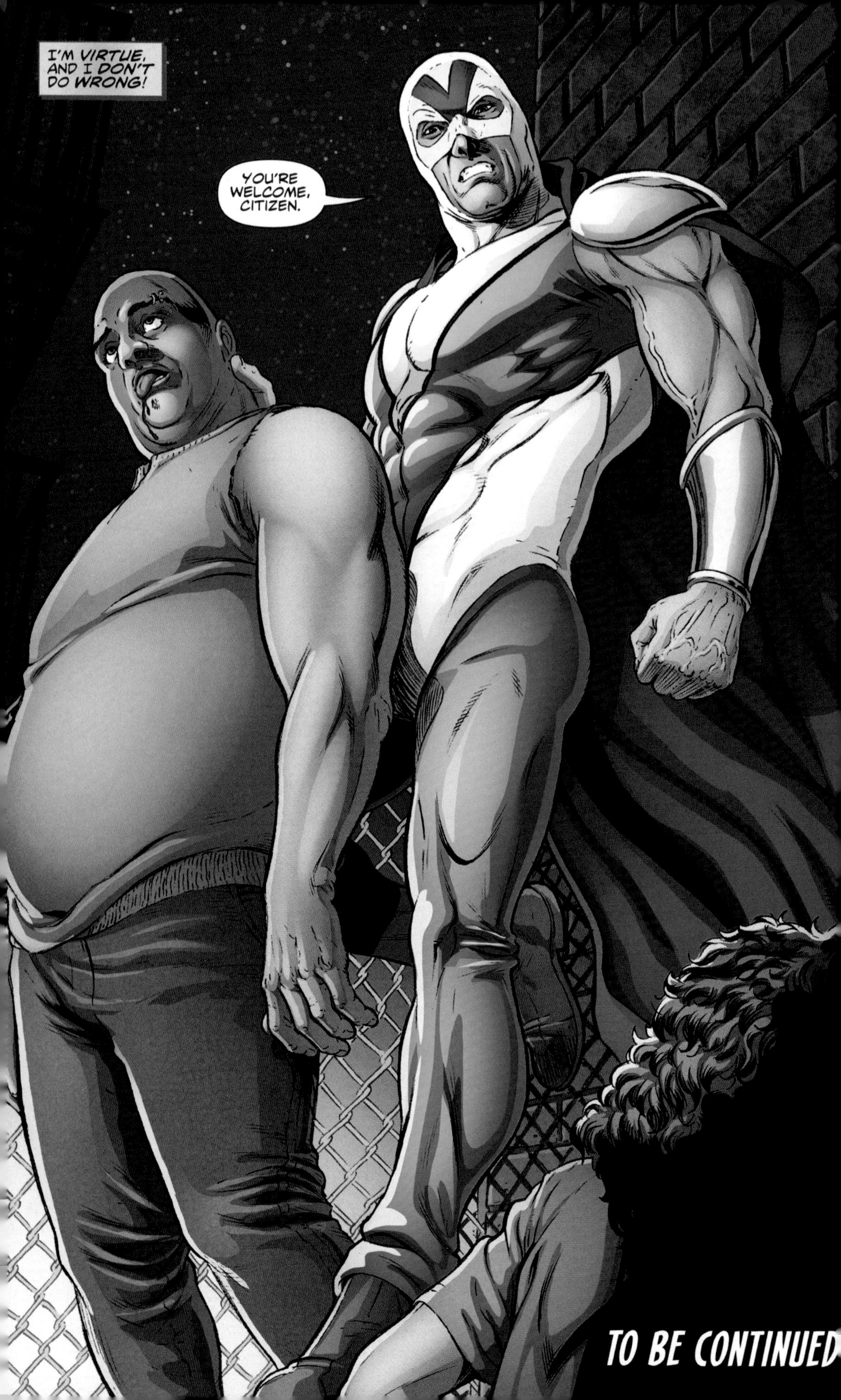

I'M VIRTUE, AND I DON'T DO WRONG!
YOU'RE WELCOME, CITIZEN.
TO BE CONTINUED

Sometimes all it takes is a little time.

When I first came up with the idea for Molly Danger, I had no idea what it would turn into. I started this idea with a name..nothing else. No firm concept other than she was a young female hero named Molly Danger. She was a nebulous concept for a very long time and, other than her physical powers, which were much more varied originally, I hadn't found a way to tackle her. I knew that I didn't want to create a typical hero, because a hero without emotional weight would be useless to me. I frankly didn't have the maturity at the time (being all of 30 years old, unmarried, without children of my own) to explore the topics I was looking to delve into.

So I sat on the concept, occasionally revisiting in sketches and notes in the margins of books. I would see something that would influence the story. Articles about bionics, or artificial intelligence, both pro and con. I read pieces on how certain gasses affect how materials, or the applications of carbon. I also became both a husband and a father. I began to think about what it may be like to be a child, because we forget what it's like as maturity sets its claws into our souls. Then I began to contemplate what it would be like for that same child to see the world transform around her, but not age, not grow, unchanging. How would that affect her? Then separate her from a public that loves her and not tell her why. What would she say, what would she do?

That became the story of Molly Danger. Molly is an eternal child, trapped in a world she can't change, trying to make the best of it as she can. I wanted to surround Molly with characters who weren't cardboard cutouts. I also want to make Molly as relatable as a superhumanly strong child can be. I know it will be an uphill climb, but I have one of the best sources of inspiration sleeping on a bunk bed in the bedroom next to mine.

I hope you enjoy this sampling of "The Princess of Finesse." I want you, the reader, to revel in her triumphs and care about her struggles. If I can make you laugh and cry, then I've done my job.

I always like to say that "I believe in Molly," and it's true. Molly in many ways is as real to me as my own daughter. So, like any parent, I anxiously send her out into the world and watch to see how she grows.

Believe in Molly.

- Jamal Igle
Brooklyn, NY
March 2016

MOLLY DANGER ©™

RETURNS THIS FALL!

PERSONAL DATA

Alter Ego: None (publicly known)
Occupation: Adventurer
Marital Status: Single
Known Relatives: Unnamed father (Deceased), unnamed mother (Deceased), unnamed brother (Deceased)
Group Affiliation: D.A.R.T. Command (Danger's Action Reponse Team)
Base of Operations: Coopersville, New York
First Appearance: MOLLY DANGER: Book One
Height: 4' 8" **Weight**: 80 lbs (normal); 2,000 lbs (fully powered)
Eyes: Green **Hair**: Brown

HISTORY

Very little is known about the life of the girl who would become known as Molly Danger. Most of what we know has been pieced together by various biographies written over the years.

Molly is an alien from a planet known as Gama Seven, part of the Gama sector of "The Great Galactic Rim," a system of inhabited worlds on the far side of the our galaxy. Twenty-two years ago, Molly's family was part of an expeditionary mission, seeking uninhabited worlds for colonization. Sometime during the mission, there was an accident that sent their ship out of control, forcing them to seek the closest inhabited planet for help.

Molly was found in the woods outside of Bear Mountain Park in New York State with her ship. The sole survivor but comatose, Molly was found by the United States Air Force and hospitalized for over a year. During her convalescence, Molly's alien molecular structure and metabolic functions adapted to Earth's environment. She awoke, unable to speak any human language at first but learned quickly. Escaping from her hospital bed, Molly was chased by the military into downtown Coopersville, then a depressed former steel town. While being chased and filmed by the local media, Molly saved the life of a young child who was about to be hit by an army truck. Smashing the truck to bits, Molly was caught on film and the image of "The Princess of Finesse" (a satirical jab at her penchant for causing destruction wherever she goes) went viral.

A year later, flanked by the members of the newly formed D.A.R.T., and partnered with a young air force pilot named Lauren Holder, Molly made her official public debut.

POWERS & WEAPONS

Molly appears to look like a normal, healthy ten year old human female. This however is not the case at all. Due to her alien physiology, Molly is actually over thirty human years old. Her mental and emotional facilities seem to be arrested at the level of a child, while her ability to retain information is remarkably advanced. Molly possesses an abundance of military and tactical knowledge learned over the course of her career. She has a facility for languages as well as an understanding of advanced scientific theory.

Molly possesses superhuman abilities that make her one of the most formidable heroes on the planet. Chief among her powers are superhuman strength, which has been difficult to measure, as it has increased over the years. She has been known to lift weights equaling that of Sherman tank. She can leap long distances, covering several city blocks in a single leap. She possesses incredible speed and reflexes that, while not on par with her physical strength, allows her to run as fast as 50 miles per hour. She's practically invulnerable, able to shrug off small arms fire easily, and explosions. She doesn't need to sleep or breathe, nor does she have normal human body functions such as sweating, allowing her an incredibly high level of endurance. Her powers seem to stem from a single ability; being what D.A.R.T. lead scientist Phillip Leung calls, "Variable Molecular Control."

Molly possesses complete control over her molecular structure, instantaneously transforming giving her body the density of diamond like carbon. Her skin and bones become capable of surviving pressures as great as 70 gigapascals or 101,526,416 pounds per square inch. Despite this level of strength for some reason, she seems to have only one weakness. Highly charged electrical impulses like lightning have been known to temporarily render her unconscious. Whether this is due to her unique physiology or another factor is unknown.

Molly Danger created by and ™ Jamal Igle

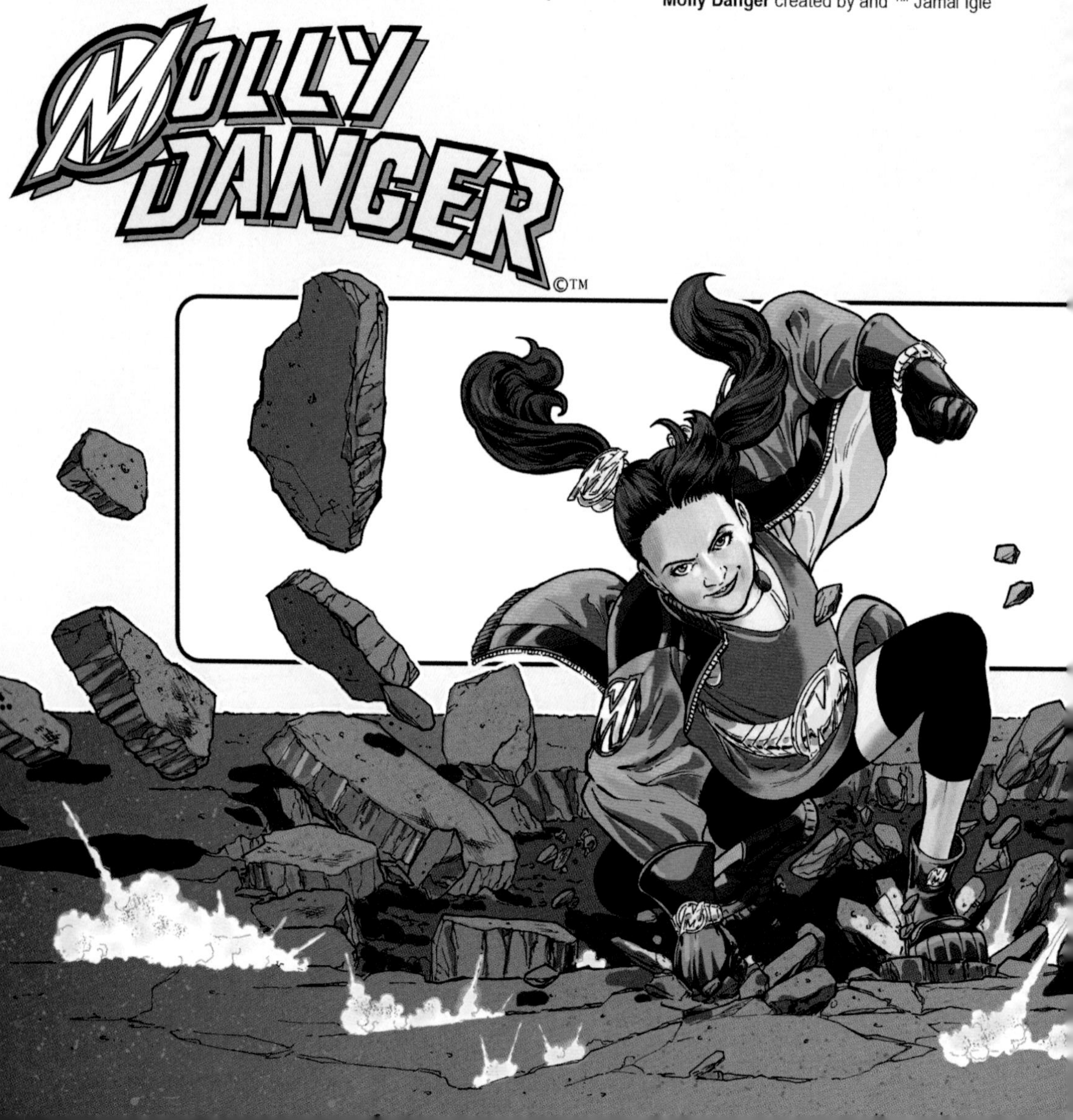
MOLLY DANGER
©TM

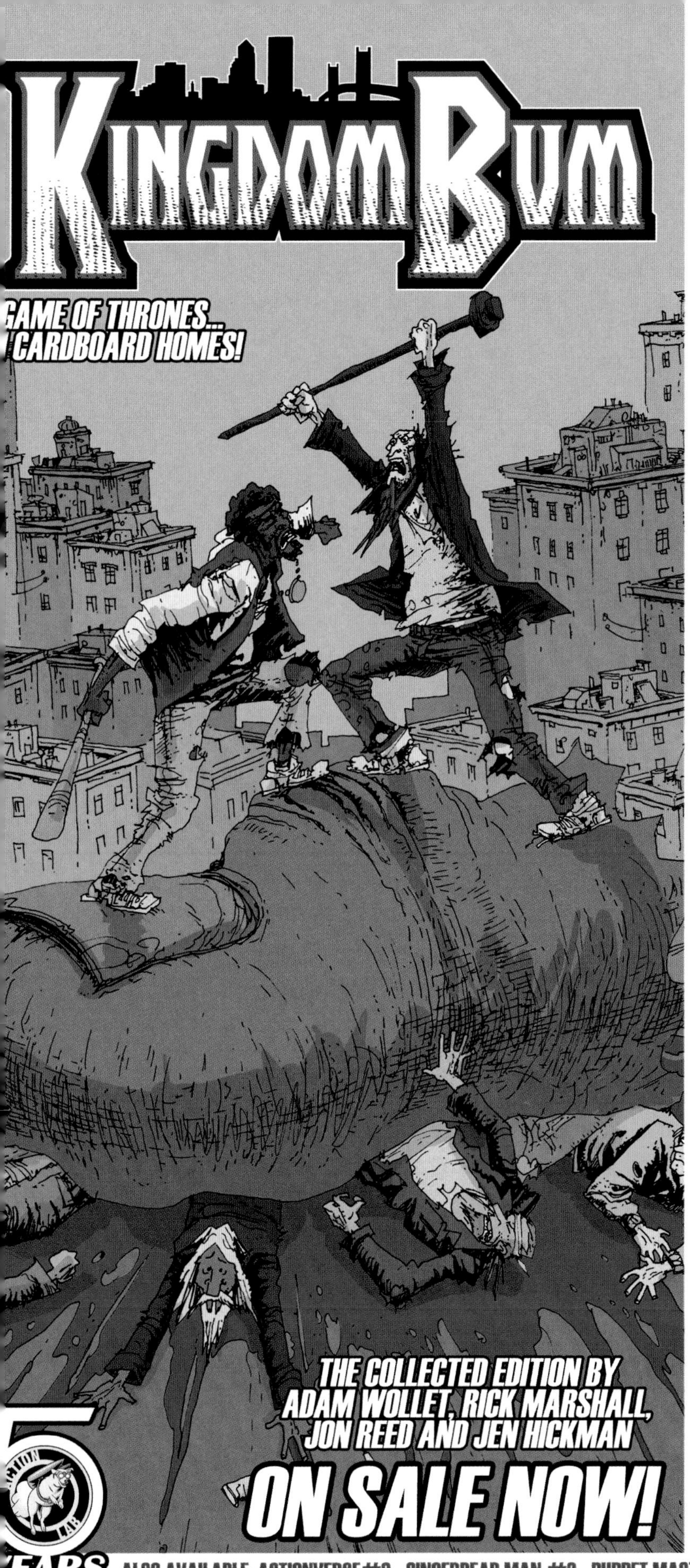
KINGDOM BUM
GAME OF THRONES...
CARDBOARD HOMES!
THE COLLECTED EDITION BY
ADAM WOLLET, RICK MARSHALL,
JON REED AND JEN HICKMAN
ON SALE NOW!

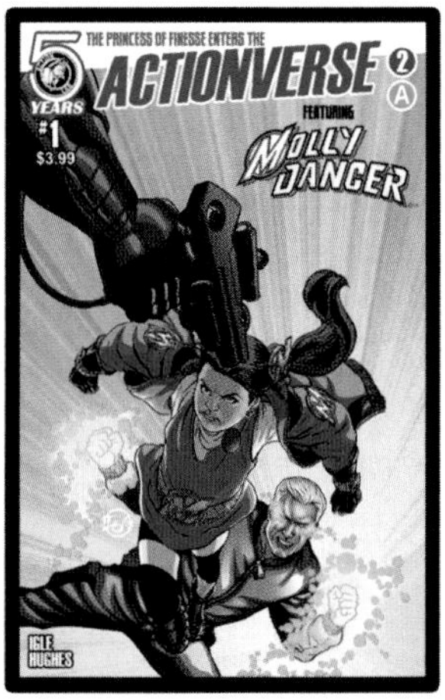
THE PRINCESS OF FINESSE ENTERS THE
ACTIONVERSE 2
FEATURING
MOLLY DANGER
5 YEARS
#1
$3.99
IGLE
HUGHES

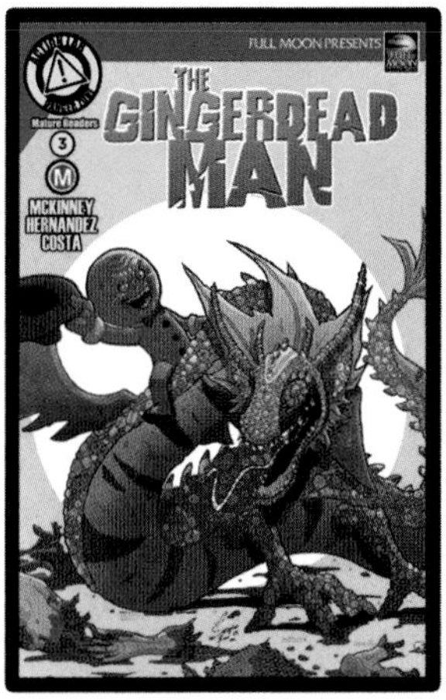
FULL MOON PRESENTS
THE GINGERDEAD MAN
Mature Readers
3
MCKINNEY
HERNANDEZ
COSTA

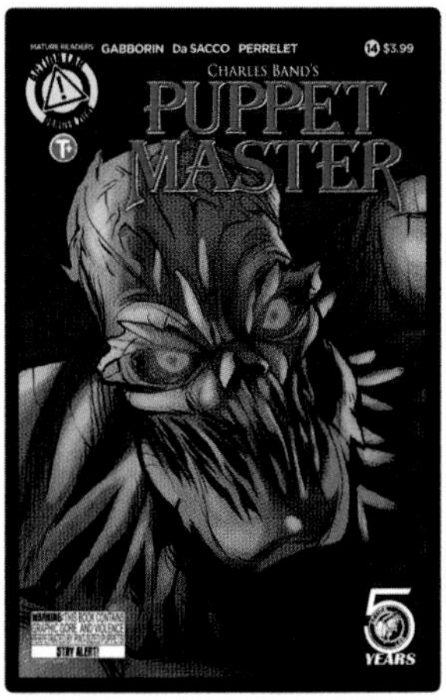
MATURE READERS GABBORIN Da SACCO PERRELET
14 $3.99
CHARLES BAND'S
PUPPET MASTER
5 YEARS

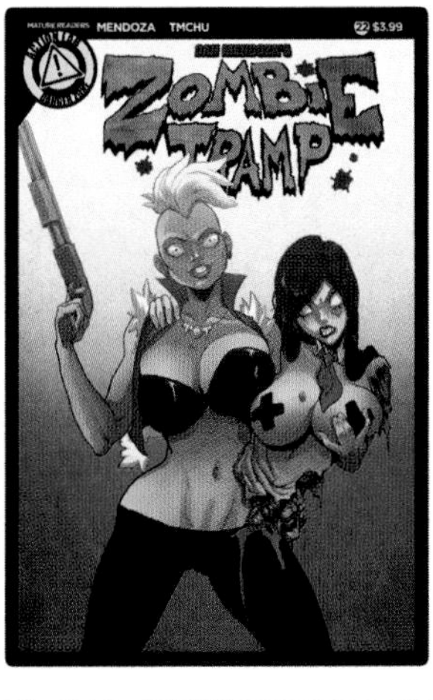
MATURE READERS MENDOZA TMCHU
22 $3.99
ZOMBIE TRAMP

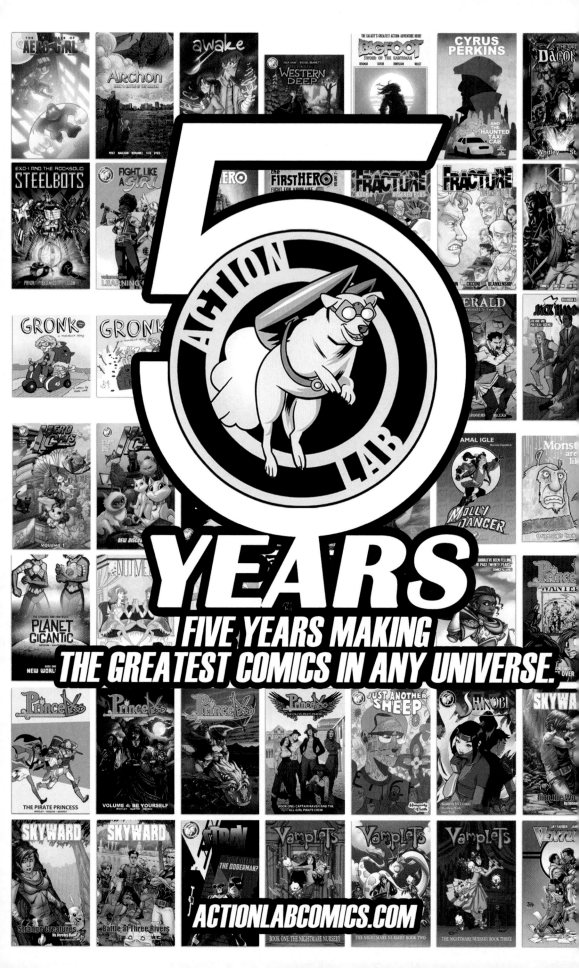

5 YEARS

FIVE YEARS MAKING THE GREATEST COMICS IN ANY UNIVERSE.

ACTIONLABCOMICS.COM

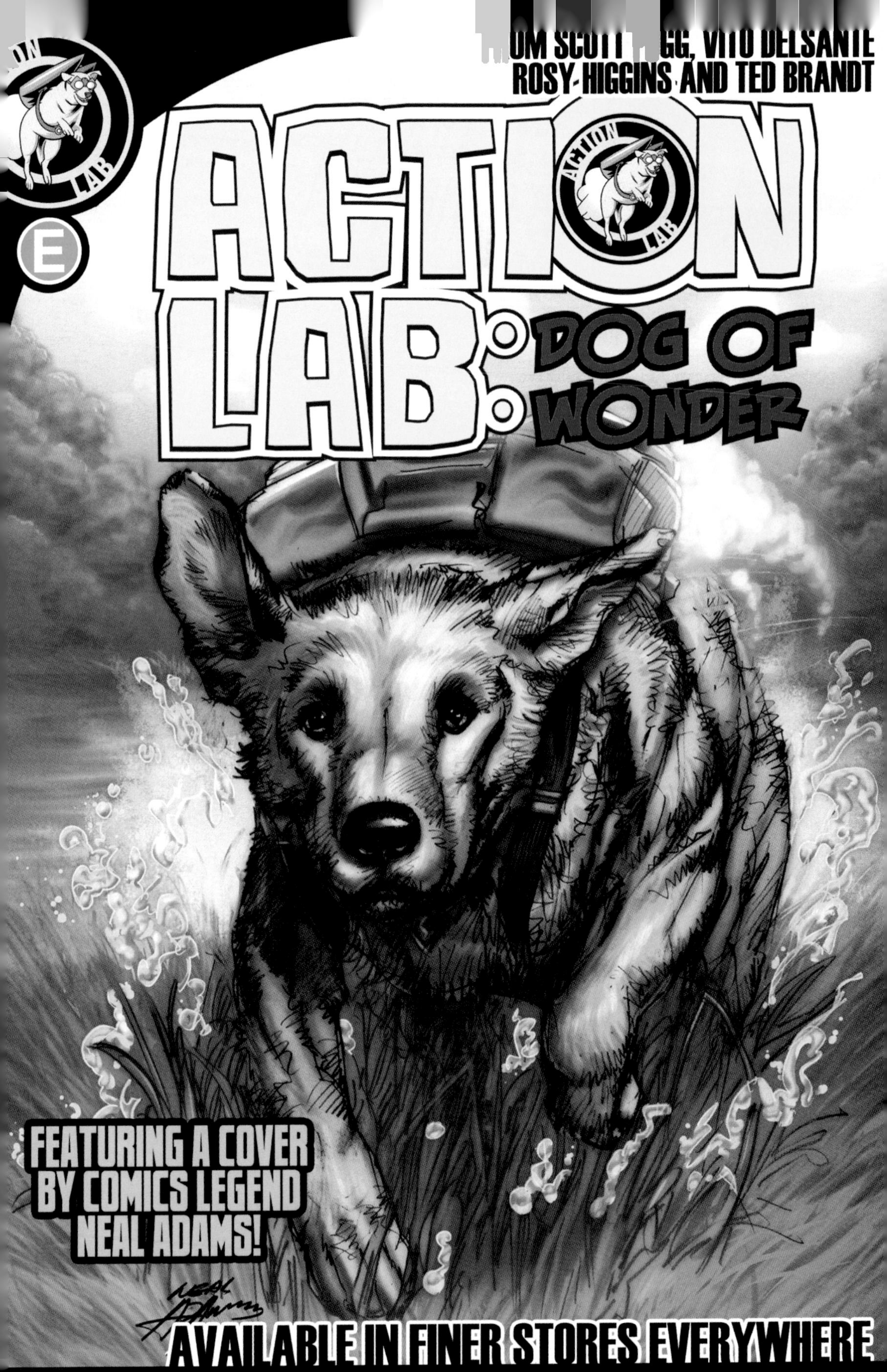

VITO DELSANTE
ROSY HIGGINS AND TED BRANDT
ACTION LAB: DOG OF WONDER
FEATURING A COVER BY COMICS LEGEND NEAL ADAMS!
AVAILABLE IN FINER STORES EVERYWHERE

For five years, readers have looked at the Action Lab Entertainment logo and wondered, "Who IS that dog with the jet pack?" Wonder no more! The story you never thought would be told is now an ongoing monthly title as ACTION LAB: DOG OF WONDER comes to

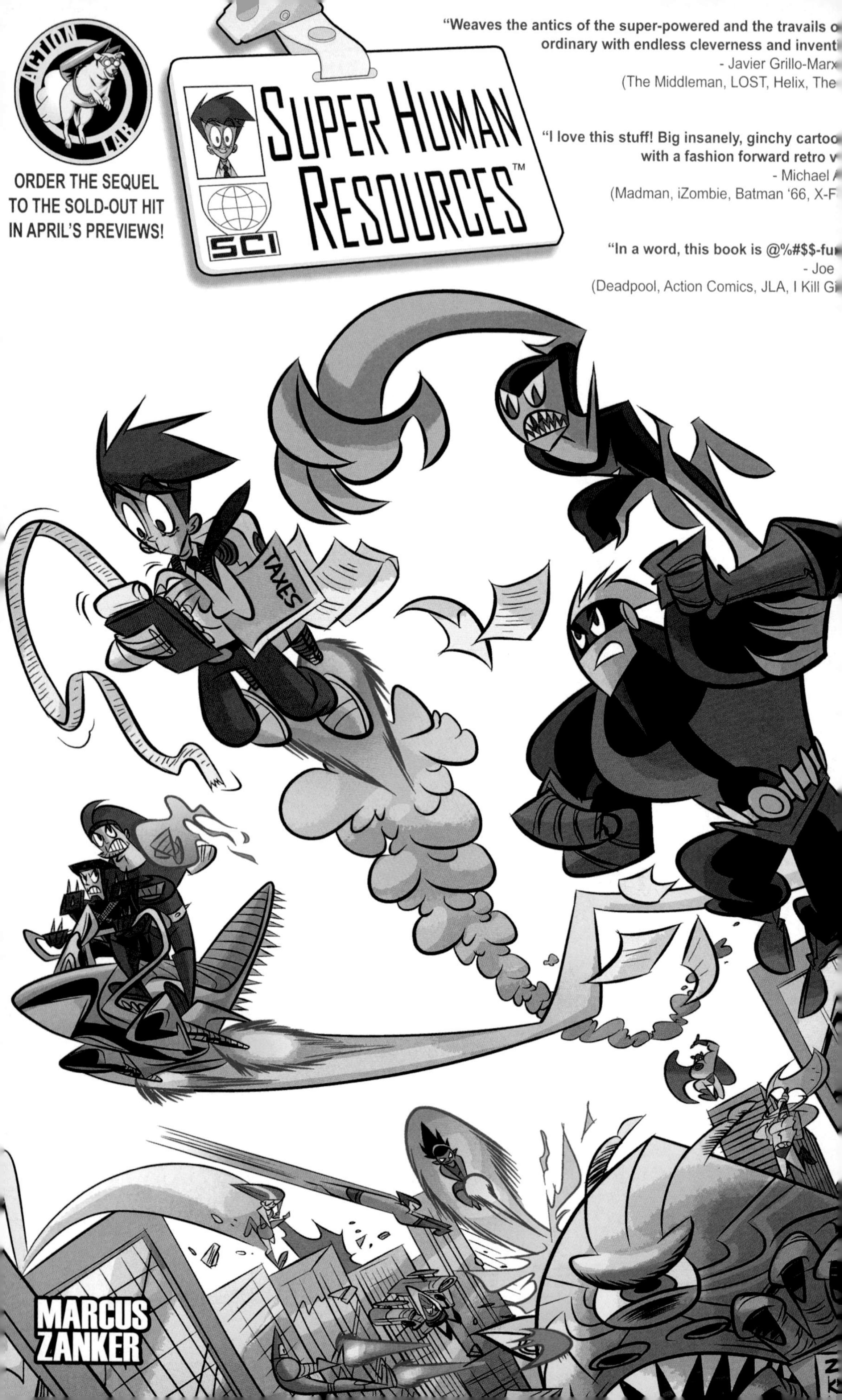
ACTION LAB
ORDER THE SEQUEL
TO THE SOLD-OUT HIT
IN APRIL'S PREVIEWS!
SUPER HUMAN RESOURCES™
SCI
"Weaves the antics of the super-powered and the travails o
ordinary with endless cleverness and invent
- Javier Grillo-Marx
(The Middleman, LOST, Helix, The
"I love this stuff! Big insanely, ginchy carto
with a fashion forward retro v
- Michael
(Madman, iZombie, Batman '66, X-F
"In a word, this book is @%#$$-fu
- Joe
(Deadpool, Action Comics, JLA, I Kill G
TAXES
MARCUS
ZANKER

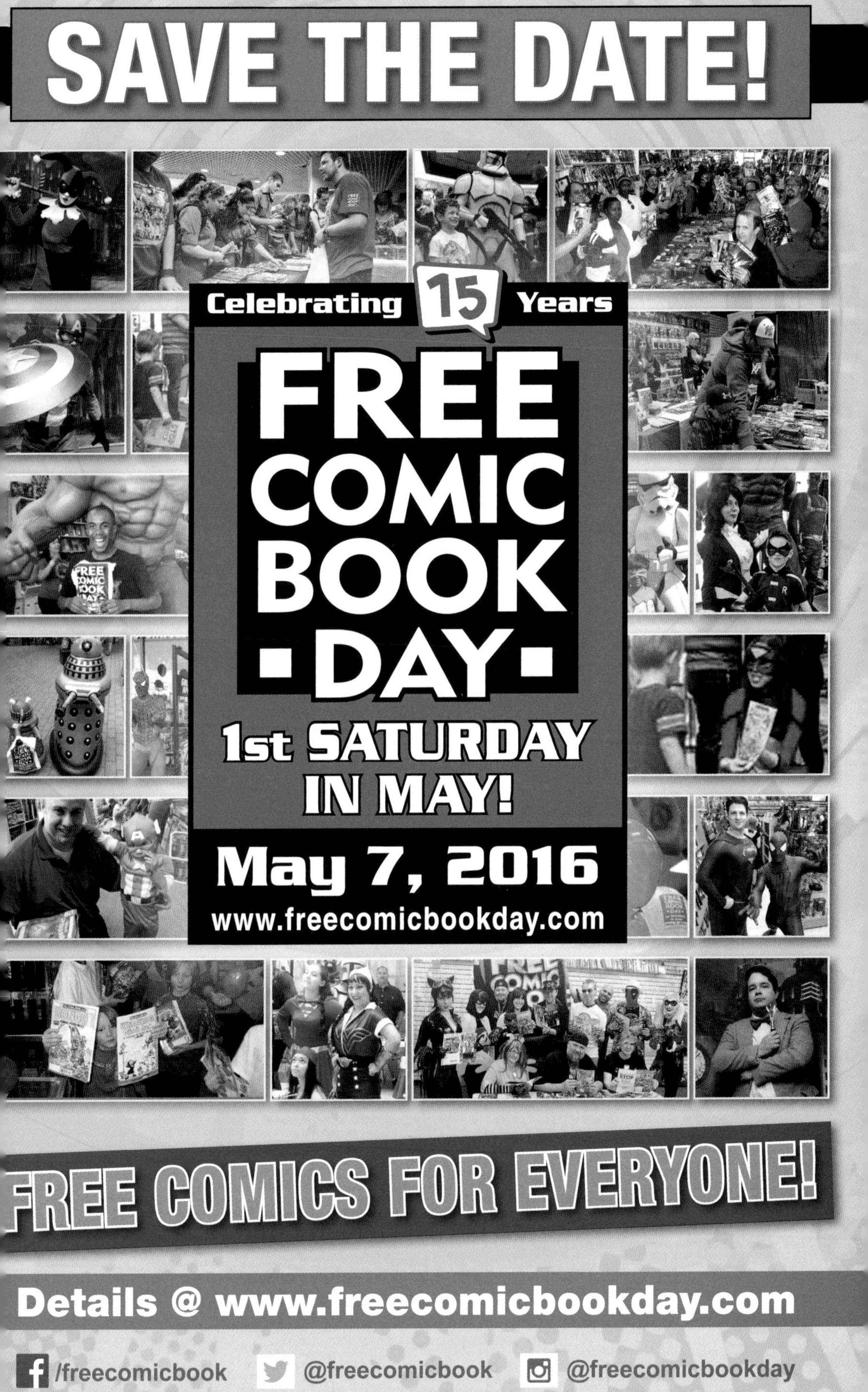
SAVE THE DATE!
Celebrating 15 Years
FREE COMIC BOOK DAY
1st SATURDAY IN MAY!
May 7, 2016
www.freecomicbookday.com
FREE COMICS FOR EVERYONE!
Details @ www.freecomicbookday.com
/freecomicbook
@freecomicbook
@freecomicbookday

READ MORE NOW

ACTIONLABCOMICS.COM

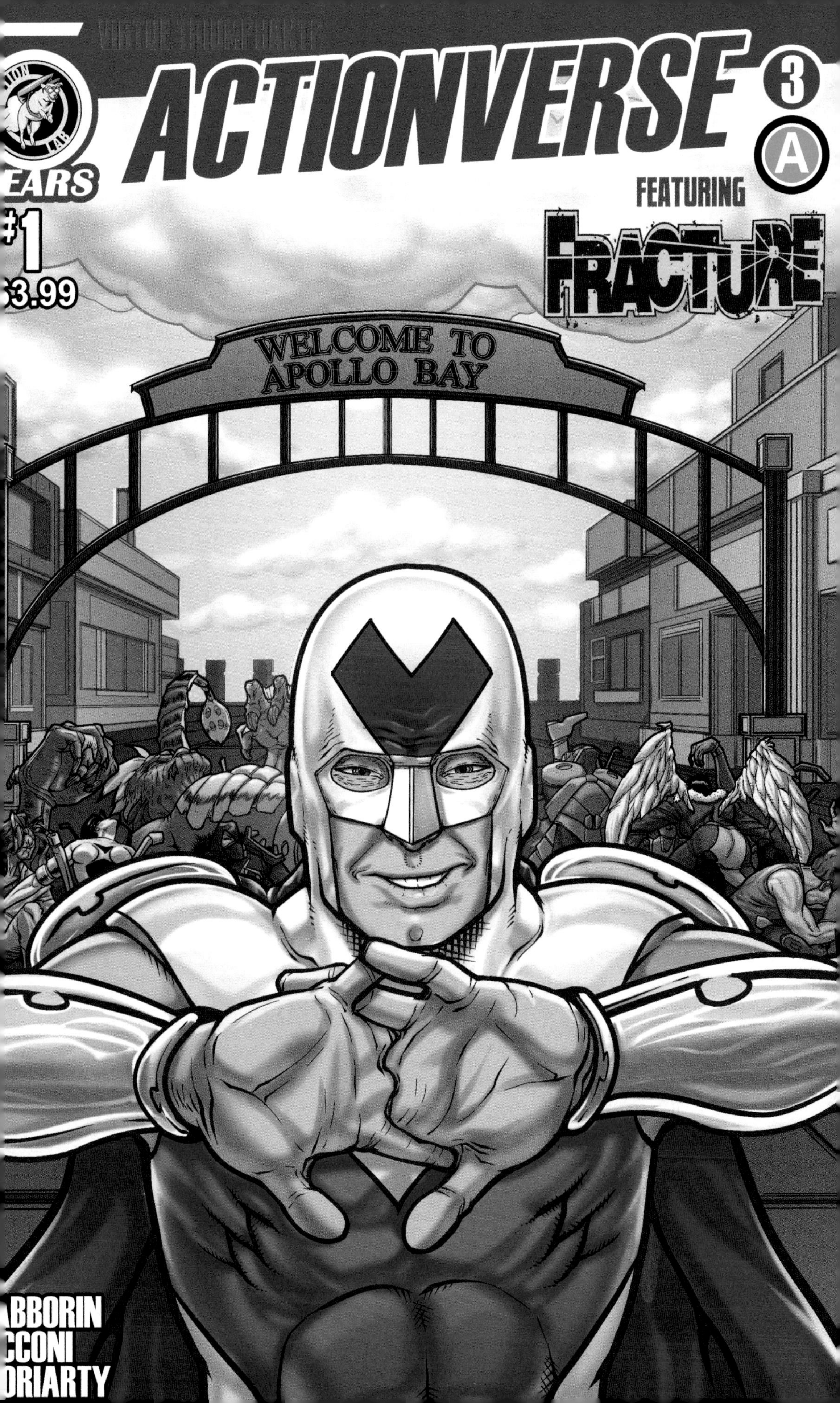

ACTIONVERSE
3
A
EARS
#1
$3.99
FEATURING
FRACTURE
WELCOME TO
APOLLO BAY
ABBORIN
CCONI
ORIARTY

ACTIONVERSE

FEATURING

Written by Shawn Gabborin

Drawn by Chad Cicconi

Colors by Meredith Moriarty

Letters by Full Court Press

Cover by Chad Cicconi

Variant Connecting Cover by Ron Frenz, Marc Deering
Ross Campbell and David Bednarski

Edited by Vito Delsante

FRACTURE and all related characters created by Gabborin and Cicconi

PREVIOUSLY

The former Malice, Kyle Scordato, has survived his first encounter with Molly Danger, but barely.
As he licks his wounds, and a new player arrives on our world, we learn Kyle's origin
and how he escaped from the Teritan world.

BRYAN SEATON - PUBLISHER
DAVE DWONCH - PRESIDENT
SHAWN GABBORIN - EDITOR IN CHIEF
JASON MARTIN - PUBLISHER, DANGER ZONE
JAMAL IGLE - VICE-PRESIDENT OF MARKETING
JIM DIETZ - SOCIAL MEDIA DIRECTOR
NICOLE D'ANDRIA - EDITOR
CHAD CICCONI - ...WAIT, HE DREW THIS ONE?!
COLLEEN BOYD - SUBMISSIONS EDITOR

ACTIONLABCOMICS.COM

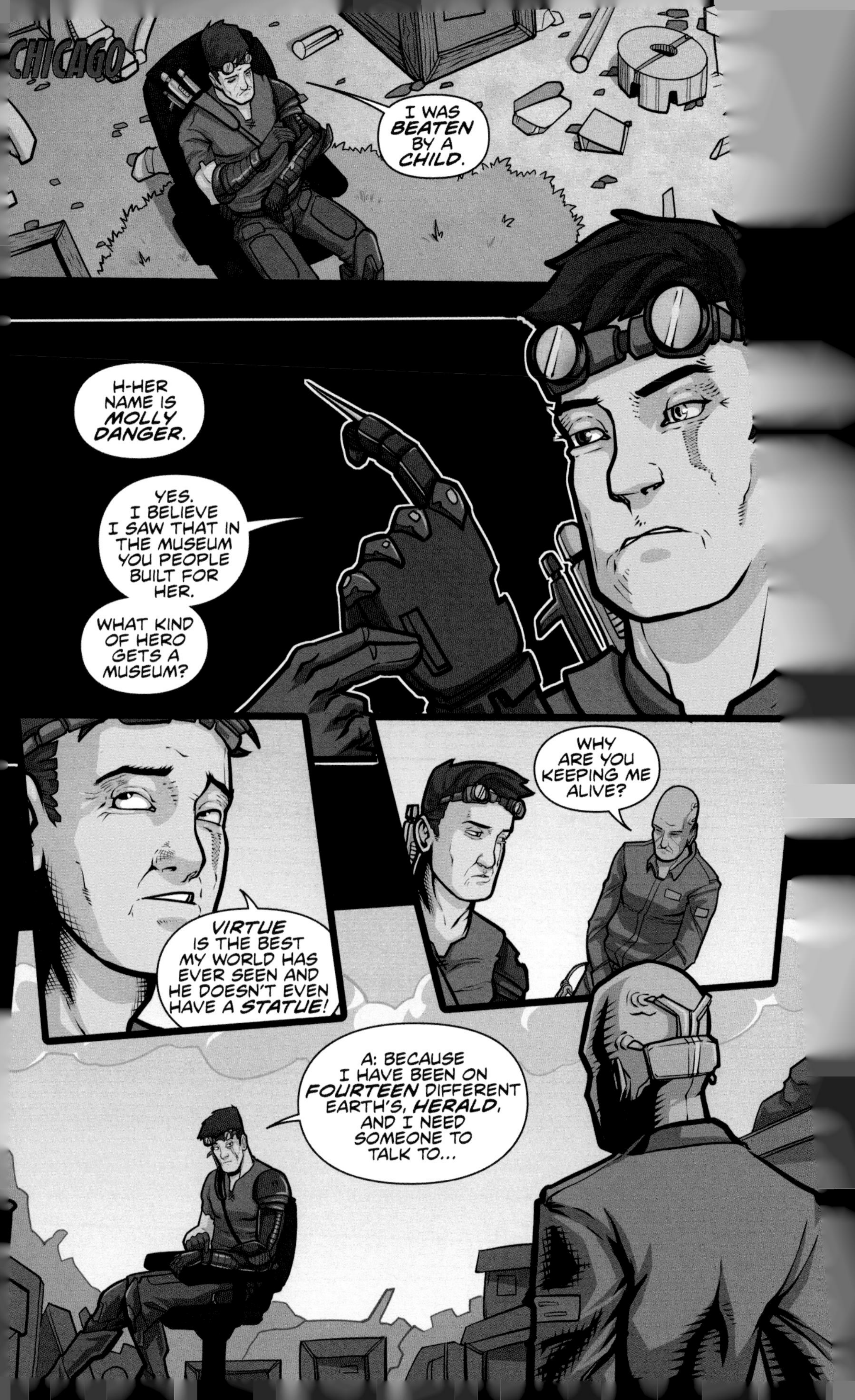
CHICAGO
I WAS BEATEN BY A CHILD.
H-HER NAME IS MOLLY DANGER.
YES. I BELIEVE I SAW THAT IN THE MUSEUM YOU PEOPLE BUILT FOR HER.
WHAT KIND OF HERO GETS A MUSEUM?
VIRTUE IS THE BEST MY WORLD HAS EVER SEEN AND HE DOESN'T EVEN HAVE A STATUE!
WHY ARE YOU KEEPING ME ALIVE?
A: BECAUSE I HAVE BEEN ON FOURTEEN DIFFERENT EARTH'S, HERALD, AND I NEED SOMEONE TO TALK TO...

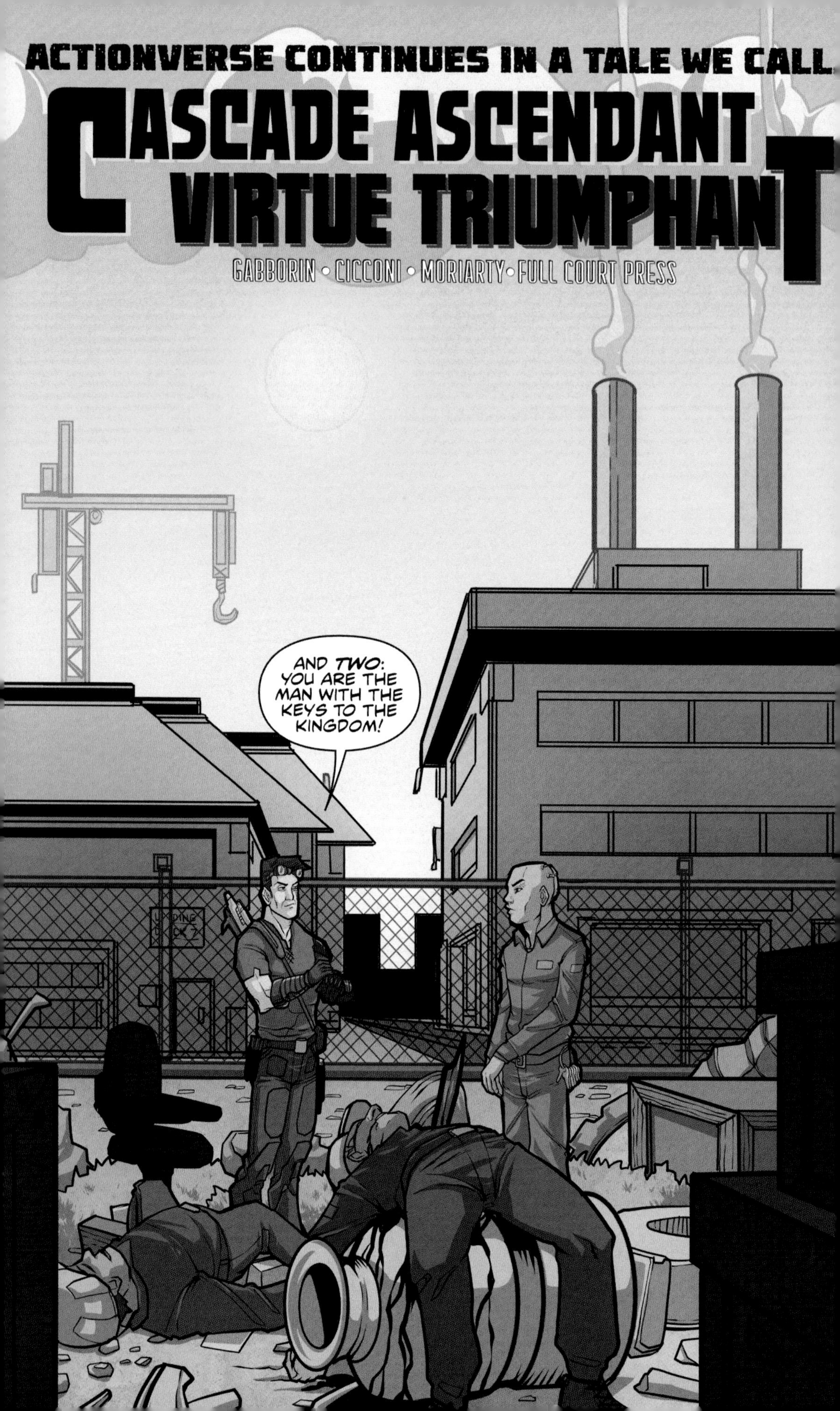
ACTIONVERSE CONTINUES IN A TALE WE CALL
CASCADE ASCENDANT VIRTUE TRIUMPHANT
GABBORIN • CICCONI • MORIARTY • FULL COURT PRESS
AND TWO: YOU ARE THE MAN WITH THE KEYS TO THE KINGDOM!

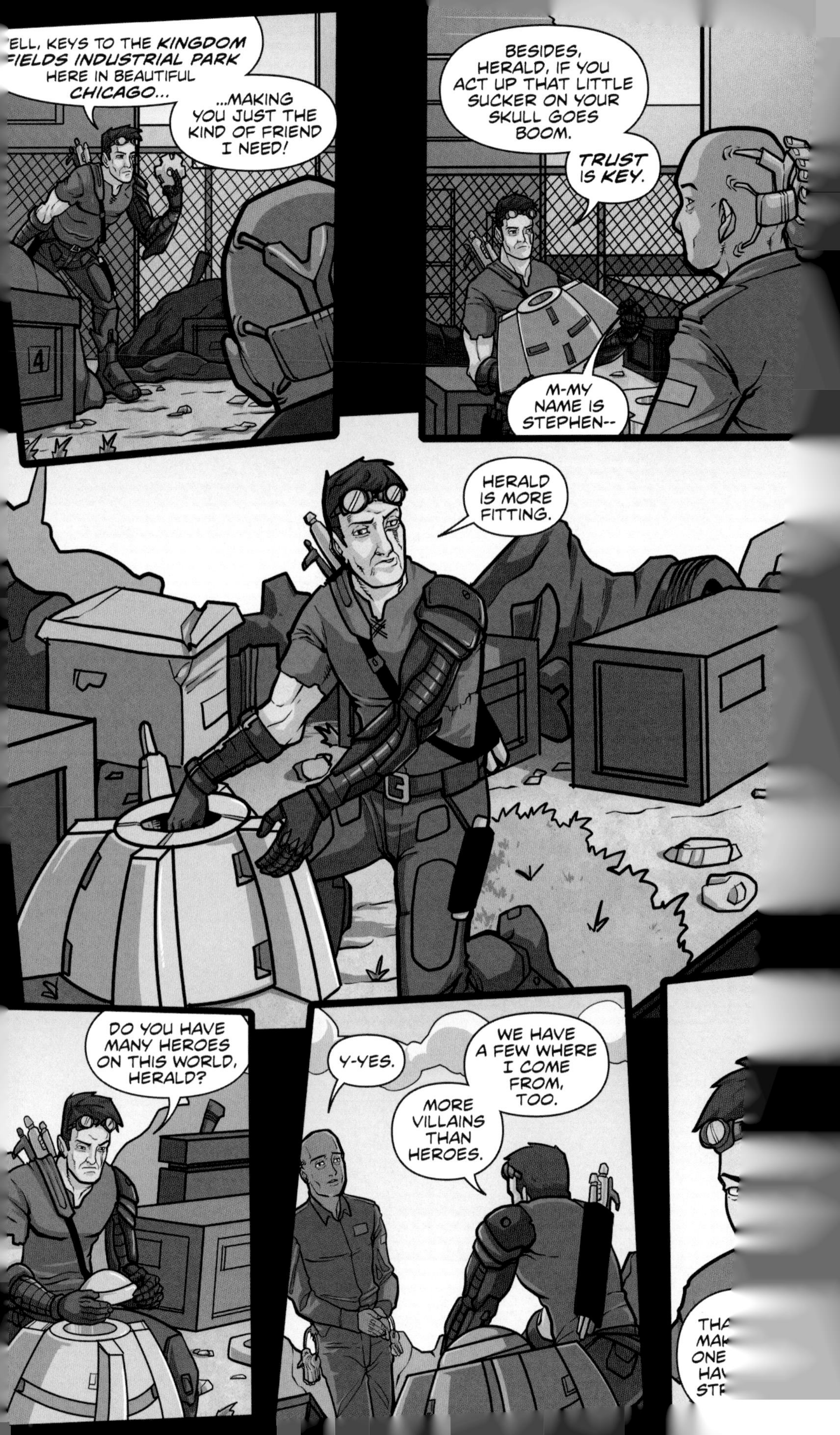
ELL, KEYS TO THE KINGDOM FIELDS INDUSTRIAL PARK HERE IN BEAUTIFUL CHICAGO...
...MAKING YOU JUST THE KIND OF FRIEND I NEED!
BESIDES, HERALD, IF YOU ACT UP THAT LITTLE SUCKER ON YOUR SKULL GOES BOOM.
TRUST IS KEY.
M-MY NAME IS STEPHEN--
HERALD IS MORE FITTING.
DO YOU HAVE MANY HEROES ON THIS WORLD, HERALD?
Y-YES.
WE HAVE A FEW WHERE I COME FROM, TOO.
MORE VILLAINS THAN HEROES.

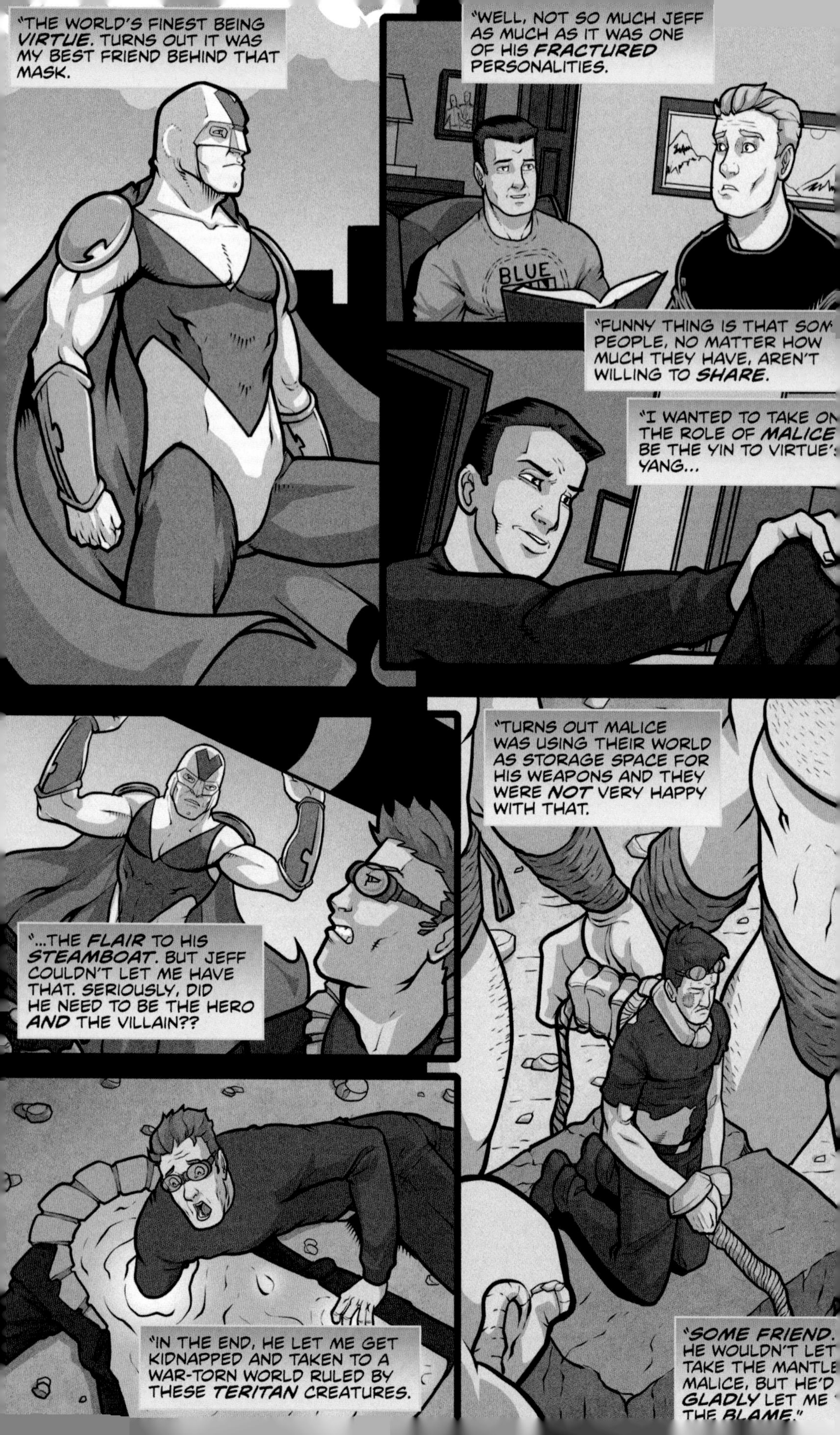
"THE WORLD'S FINEST BEING VIRTUE. TURNS OUT IT WAS MY BEST FRIEND BEHIND THAT MASK.
"WELL, NOT SO MUCH JEFF AS MUCH AS IT WAS ONE OF HIS FRACTURED PERSONALITIES.
BLUE
"FUNNY THING IS THAT SOM PEOPLE, NO MATTER HOW MUCH THEY HAVE, AREN'T WILLING TO SHARE.
"I WANTED TO TAKE ON THE ROLE OF MALICE BE THE YIN TO VIRTUE'S YANG...
"...THE FLAIR TO HIS STEAMBOAT. BUT JEFF COULDN'T LET ME HAVE THAT. SERIOUSLY, DID HE NEED TO BE THE HERO AND THE VILLAIN??
"IN THE END, HE LET ME GET KIDNAPPED AND TAKEN TO A WAR-TORN WORLD RULED BY THESE TERITAN CREATURES.
"TURNS OUT MALICE WAS USING THEIR WORLD AS STORAGE SPACE FOR HIS WEAPONS AND THEY WERE NOT VERY HAPPY WITH THAT.
"SOME FRIEND. HE WOULDN'T LET TAKE THE MANTLE MALICE, BUT HE'D GLADLY LET ME THE BLAME."

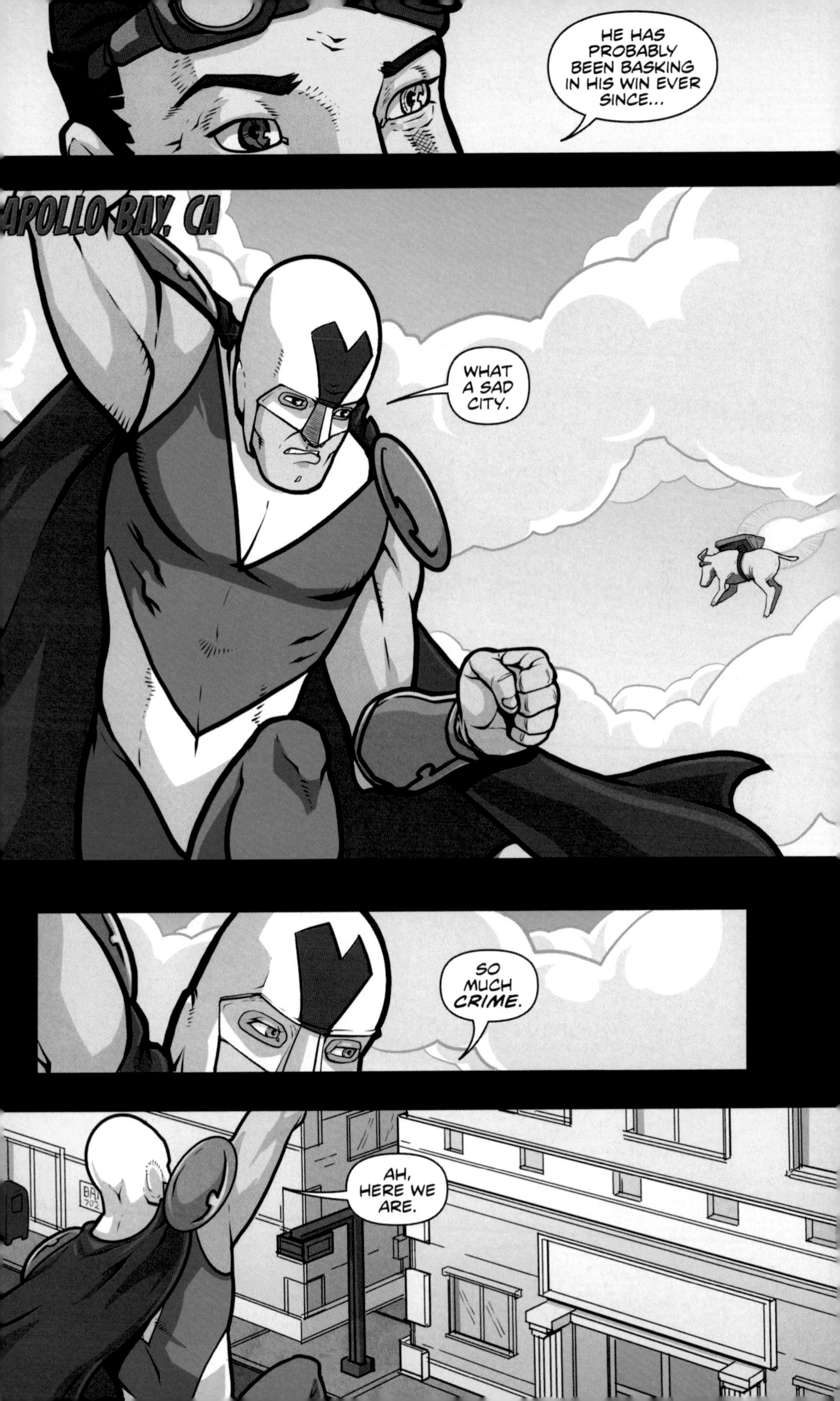
HE HAS PROBABLY BEEN BASKING IN HIS WIN EVER SINCE...
APOLLO BAY, CA
WHAT A SAD CITY.
SO MUCH CRIME.
AH, HERE WE ARE.

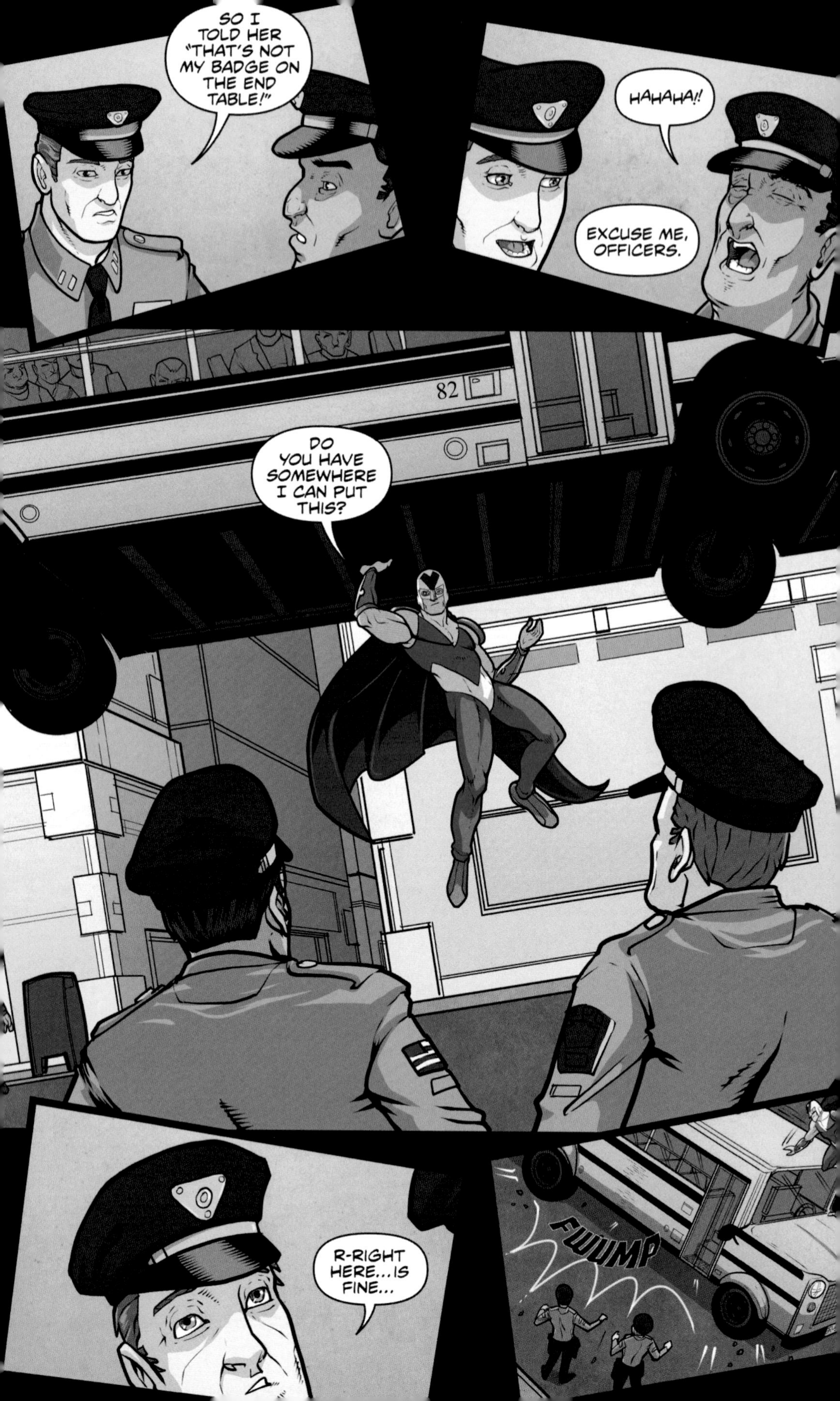
SO I TOLD HER "THAT'S NOT MY BADGE ON THE END TABLE!"
HAHAHA!!
EXCUSE ME, OFFICERS.
82
DO YOU HAVE SOMEWHERE I CAN PUT THIS?
R-RIGHT HERE...IS FINE...
FWUUMP

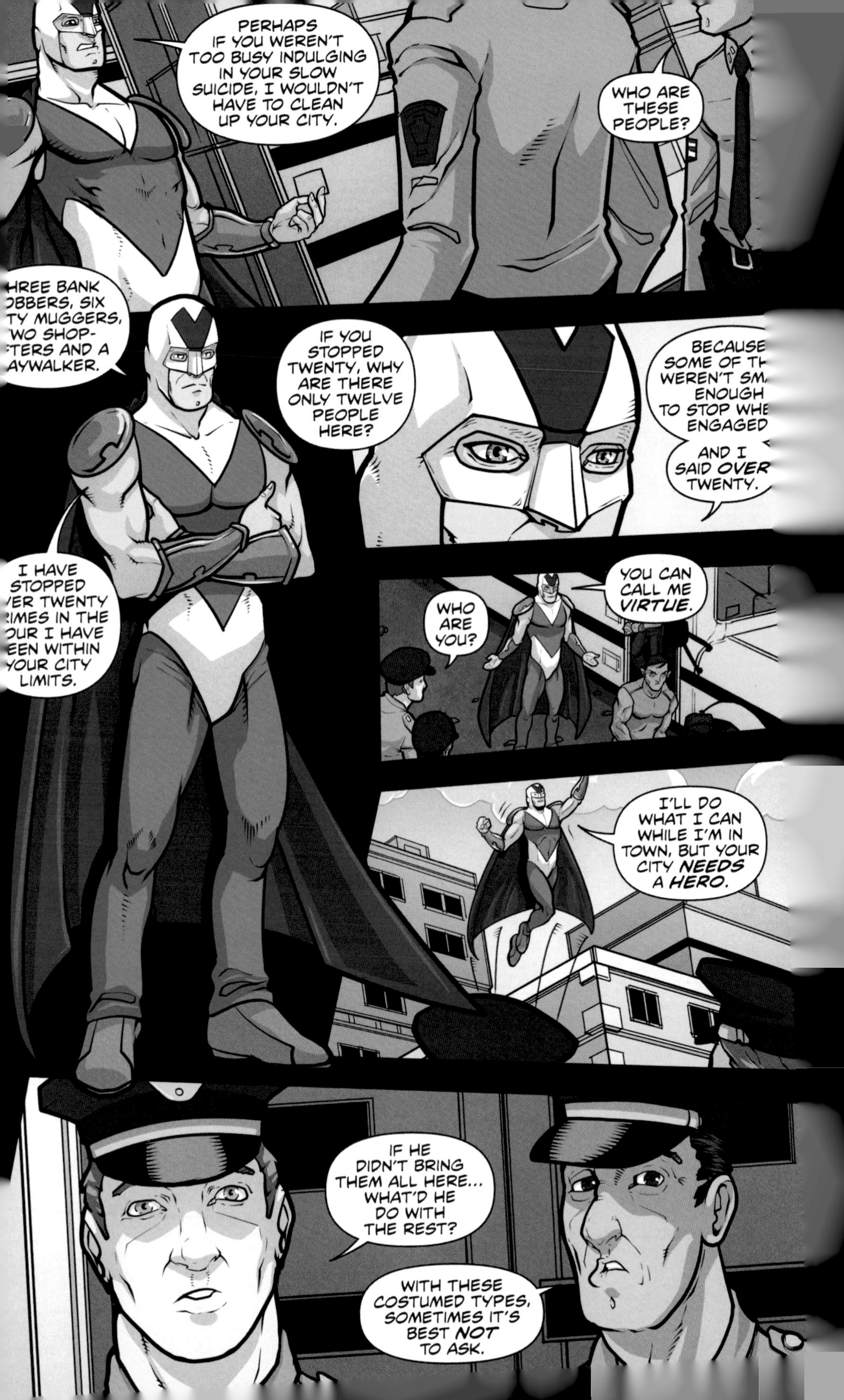

PERHAPS IF YOU WEREN'T TOO BUSY INDULGING IN YOUR SLOW SUICIDE, I WOULDN'T HAVE TO CLEAN UP YOUR CITY.
WHO ARE THESE PEOPLE?
HREE BANK OBBERS, SIX TY MUGGERS, WO SHOP- TERS AND A AYWALKER.
I HAVE STOPPED VER TWENTY RIMES IN THE OUR I HAVE EEN WITHIN YOUR CITY LIMITS.
IF YOU STOPPED TWENTY, WHY ARE THERE ONLY TWELVE PEOPLE HERE?
BECAUSE SOME OF TH WEREN'T SMA ENOUGH TO STOP WHE ENGAGED
AND I SAID *OVER* TWENTY.
WHO ARE YOU?
YOU CAN CALL ME ***VIRTUE***.
I'LL DO WHAT I CAN WHILE I'M IN TOWN, BUT YOUR CITY ***NEEDS*** A ***HERO***.
IF HE DIDN'T BRING THEM ALL HERE... WHAT'D HE DO WITH THE REST?
WITH THESE COSTUMED TYPES, SOMETIMES IT'S BEST ***NOT*** TO ASK.

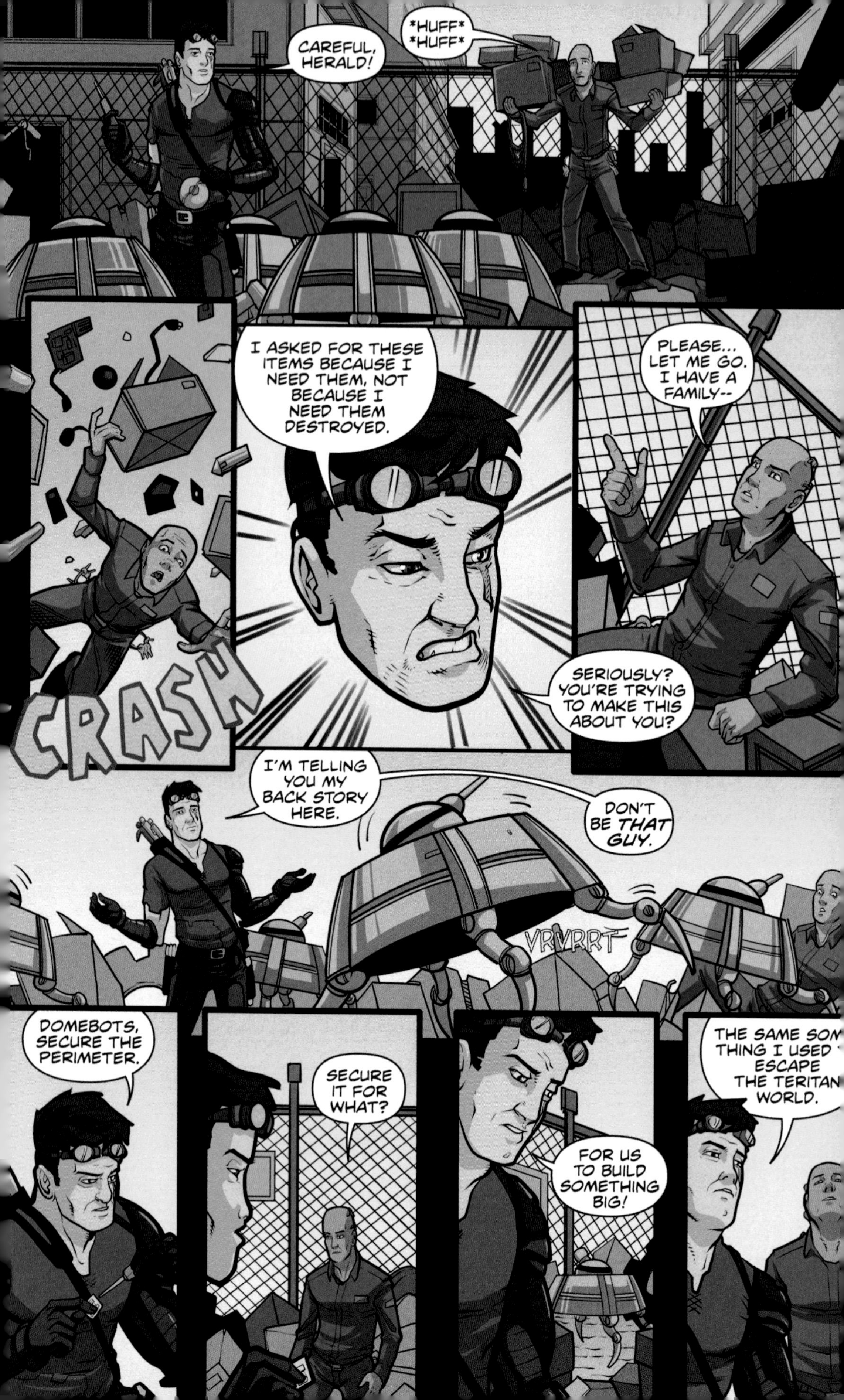
CAREFUL, HERALD!
HUFF *HUFF*
CRASH
I ASKED FOR THESE ITEMS BECAUSE I NEED THEM, NOT BECAUSE I NEED THEM DESTROYED.
PLEASE... LET ME GO. I HAVE A FAMILY--
SERIOUSLY? YOU'RE TRYING TO MAKE THIS ABOUT YOU?
I'M TELLING YOU MY BACK STORY HERE.
DON'T BE THAT GUY.
VRRVRRT
DOMEBOTS, SECURE THE PERIMETER.
SECURE IT FOR WHAT?
FOR US TO BUILD SOMETHING BIG!
THE SAME SOM THING I USED ESCAPE THE TERITAN WORLD.

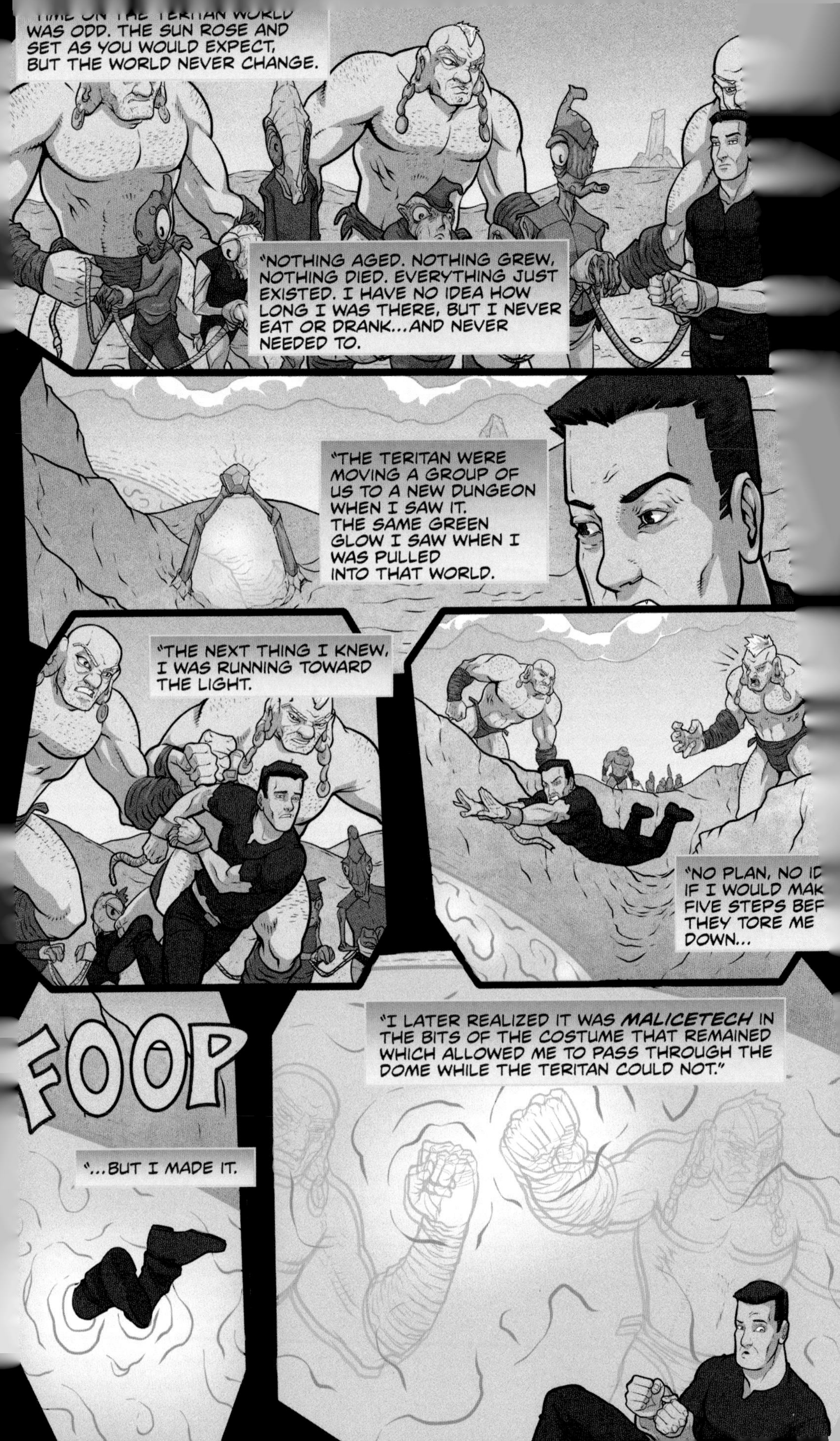
"TIME ON THE TERITAN WORLD WAS ODD. THE SUN ROSE AND SET AS YOU WOULD EXPECT, BUT THE WORLD NEVER CHANGE.
"NOTHING AGED. NOTHING GREW, NOTHING DIED. EVERYTHING JUST EXISTED. I HAVE NO IDEA HOW LONG I WAS THERE, BUT I NEVER EAT OR DRANK...AND NEVER NEEDED TO.
"THE TERITAN WERE MOVING A GROUP OF US TO A NEW DUNGEON WHEN I SAW IT. THE SAME GREEN GLOW I SAW WHEN I WAS PULLED INTO THAT WORLD.
"THE NEXT THING I KNEW, I WAS RUNNING TOWARD THE LIGHT.
"NO PLAN, NO ID IF I WOULD MAK FIVE STEPS BEF THEY TORE ME DOWN...
FOOP
"...BUT I MADE IT.
"I LATER REALIZED IT WAS *MALICETECH* IN THE BITS OF THE COSTUME THAT REMAINED WHICH ALLOWED ME TO PASS THROUGH THE DOME WHILE THE TERITAN COULD NOT."

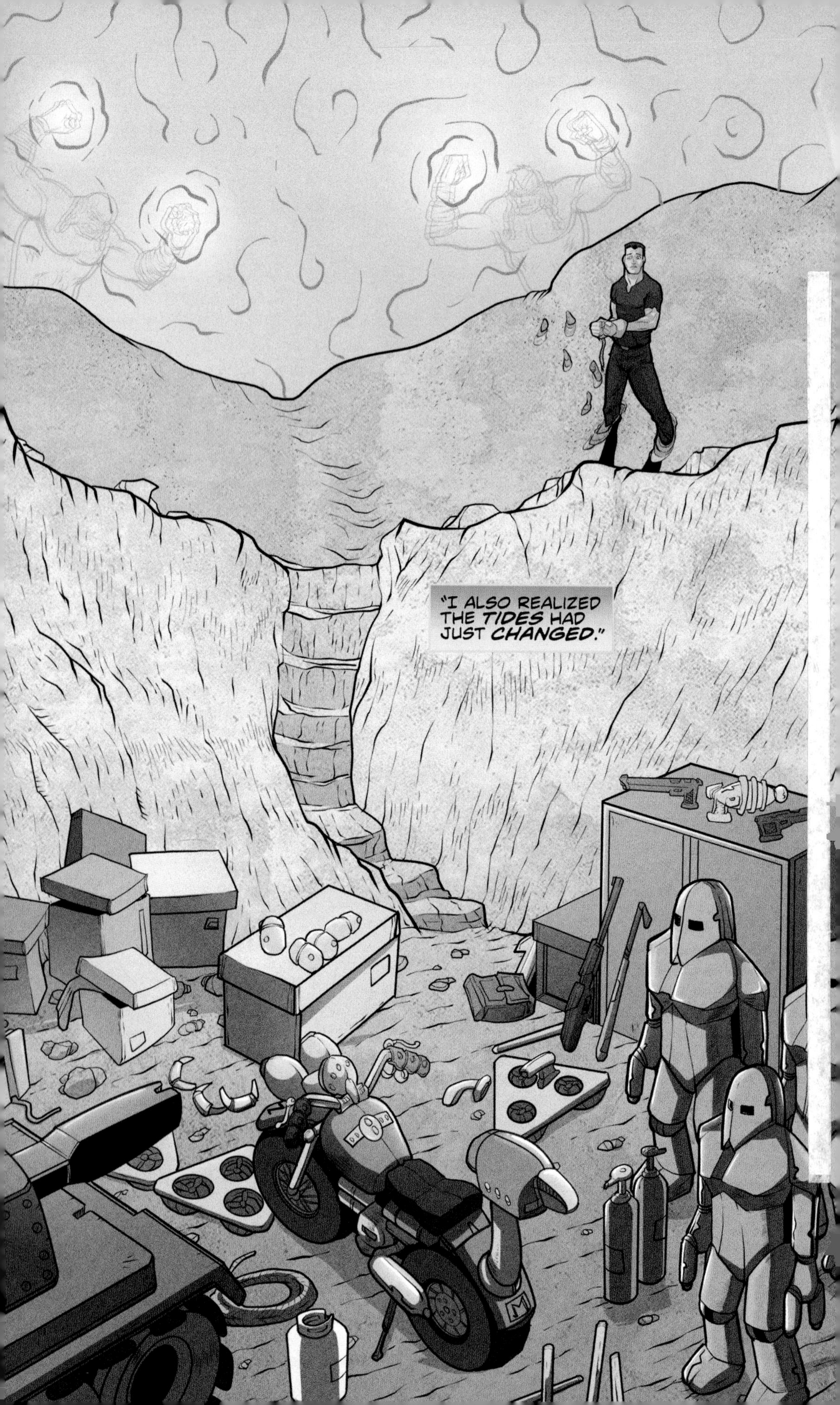
"I ALSO REALIZED THE TIDES HAD JUST CHANGED."

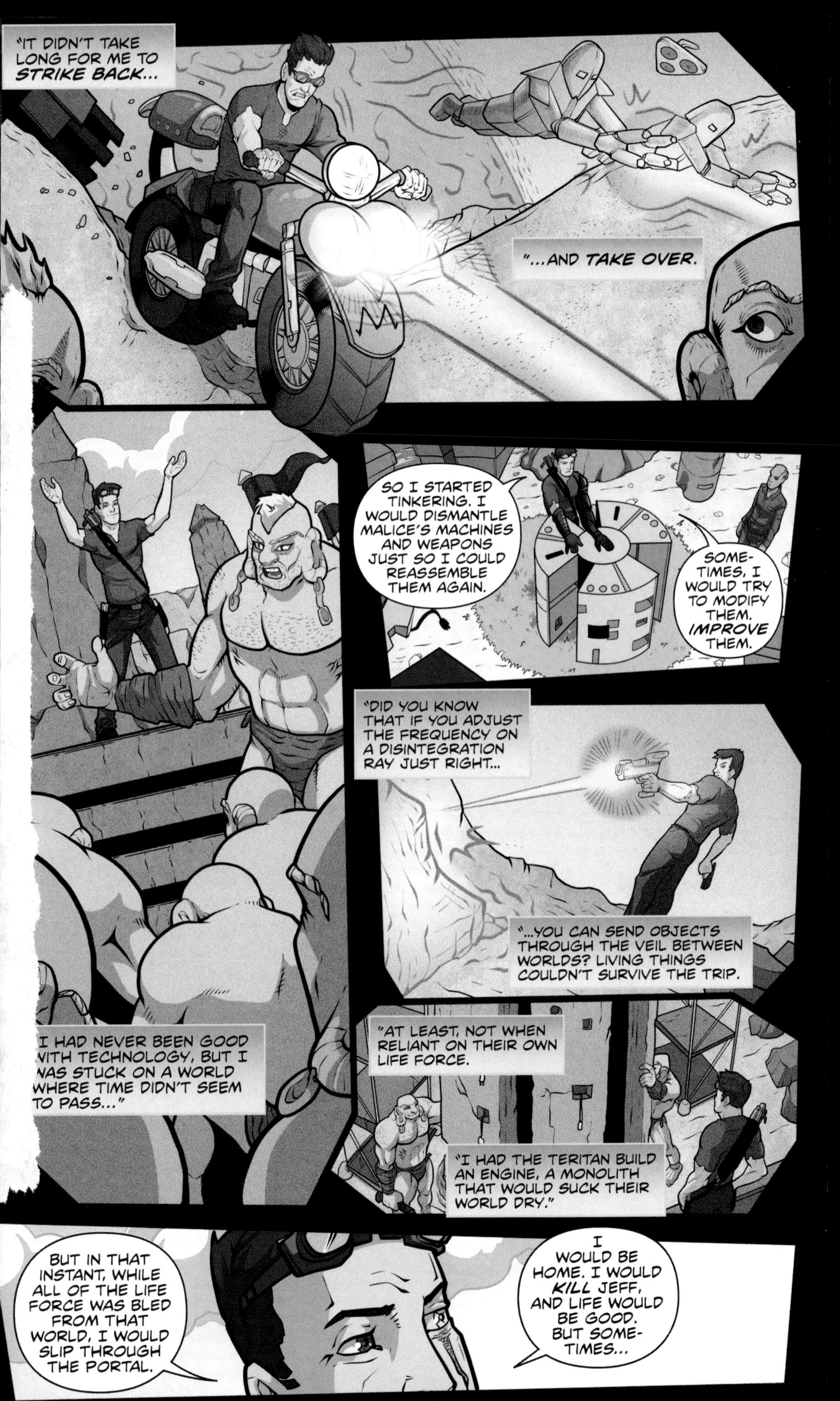
"IT DIDN'T TAKE LONG FOR ME TO STRIKE BACK...
"...AND TAKE OVER.
"I HAD NEVER BEEN GOOD WITH TECHNOLOGY, BUT I WAS STUCK ON A WORLD WHERE TIME DIDN'T SEEM TO PASS..."
SO I STARTED TINKERING. I WOULD DISMANTLE MALICE'S MACHINES AND WEAPONS JUST SO I COULD REASSEMBLE THEM AGAIN.
SOME-TIMES, I WOULD TRY TO MODIFY THEM. IMPROVE THEM.
"DID YOU KNOW THAT IF YOU ADJUST THE FREQUENCY ON A DISINTEGRATION RAY JUST RIGHT...
"...YOU CAN SEND OBJECTS THROUGH THE VEIL BETWEEN WORLDS? LIVING THINGS COULDN'T SURVIVE THE TRIP.
"AT LEAST, NOT WHEN RELIANT ON THEIR OWN LIFE FORCE.
"I HAD THE TERITAN BUILD AN ENGINE, A MONOLITH THAT WOULD SUCK THEIR WORLD DRY."
BUT IN THAT INSTANT, WHILE ALL OF THE LIFE FORCE WAS BLED FROM THAT WORLD, I WOULD SLIP THROUGH THE PORTAL.
I WOULD BE HOME. I WOULD KILL JEFF, AND LIFE WOULD BE GOOD. BUT SOME-TIMES...

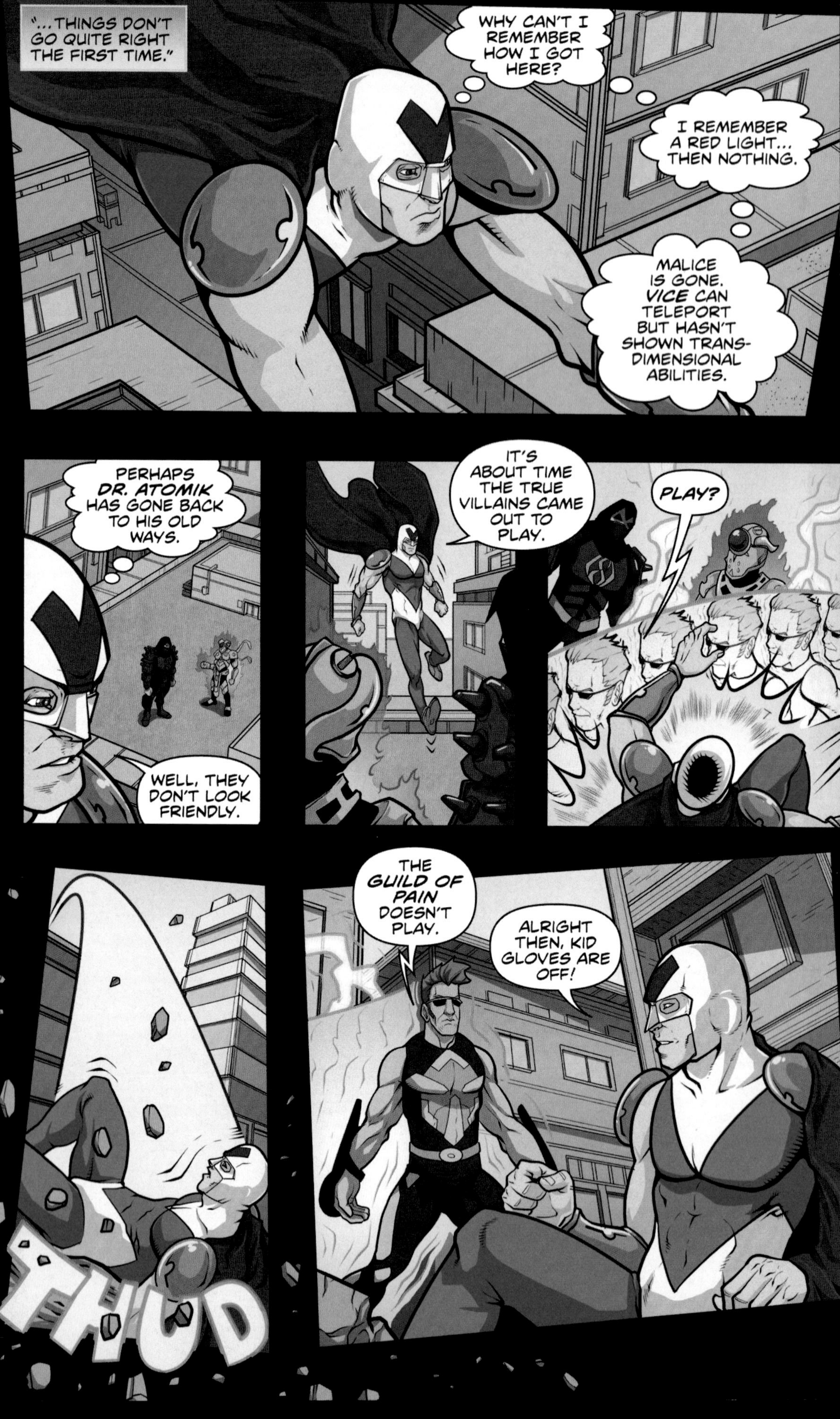
"...THINGS DON'T GO QUITE RIGHT THE FIRST TIME."
WHY CAN'T I REMEMBER HOW I GOT HERE?
I REMEMBER A RED LIGHT... THEN NOTHING.
MALICE IS GONE. VICE CAN TELEPORT BUT HASN'T SHOWN TRANS-DIMENSIONAL ABILITIES.
PERHAPS DR. ATOMIK HAS GONE BACK TO HIS OLD WAYS.
WELL, THEY DON'T LOOK FRIENDLY.
IT'S ABOUT TIME THE TRUE VILLAINS CAME OUT TO PLAY.
PLAY?
THUD
THE GUILD OF PAIN DOESN'T PLAY.
ALRIGHT THEN, KID GLOVES ARE OFF!

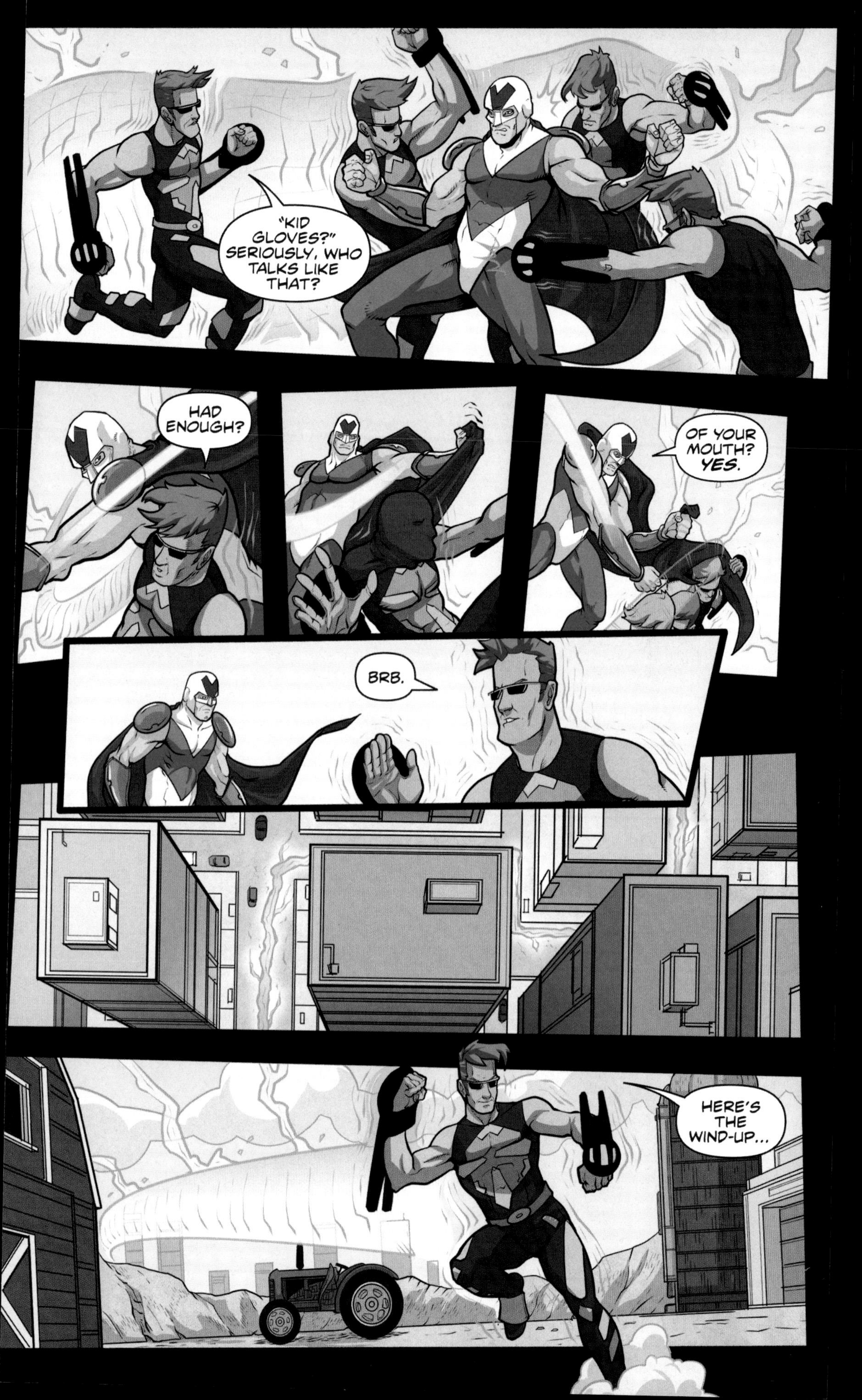
"KID GLOVES?" SERIOUSLY, WHO TALKS LIKE THAT?
HAD ENOUGH?
OF YOUR MOUTH? *YES.*
BRB.
HERE'S THE WIND-UP...

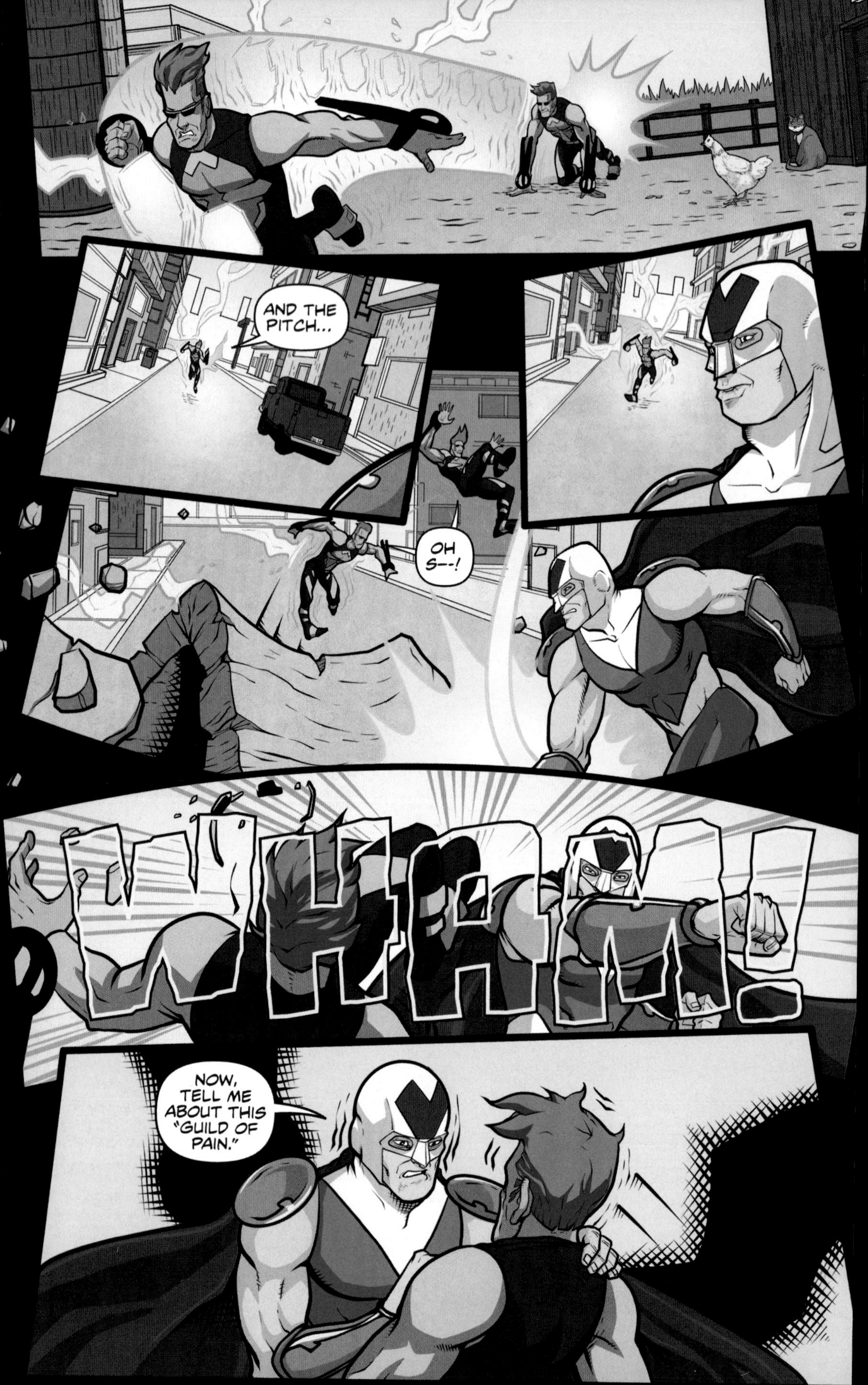
AND THE PITCH...
OH S--!
WHAM!
NOW, TELL ME ABOUT THIS "GUILD OF PAIN."

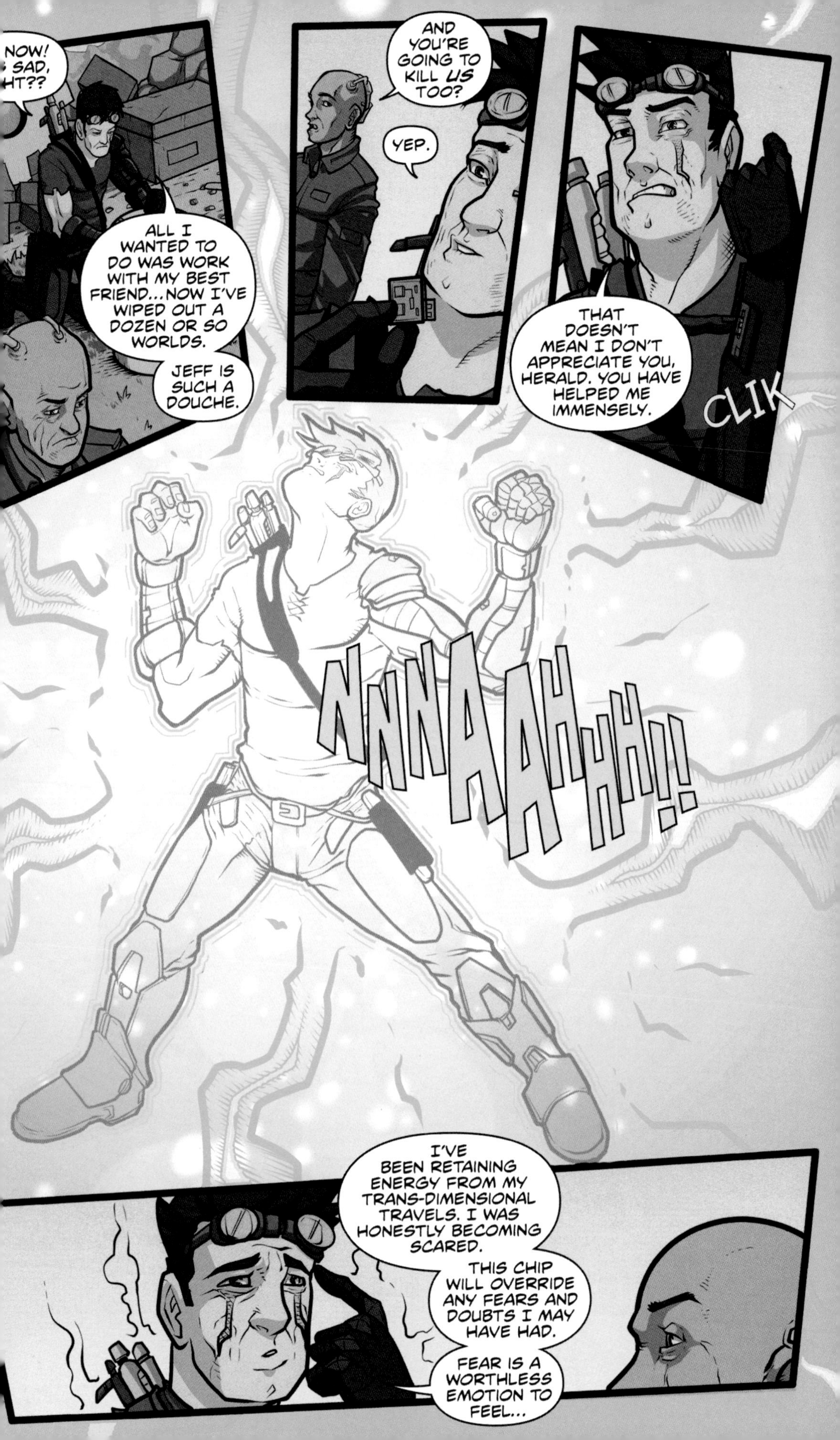

NOW! ...S SAD, ...HT??
ALL I WANTED TO DO WAS WORK WITH MY BEST FRIEND...NOW I'VE WIPED OUT A DOZEN OR SO WORLDS.
JEFF IS SUCH A DOUCHE.
AND YOU'RE GOING TO KILL US TOO?
YEP.
THAT DOESN'T MEAN I DON'T APPRECIATE YOU, HERALD. YOU HAVE HELPED ME IMMENSELY.
CLIK
NNNAAHHHH!!!
I'VE BEEN RETAINING ENERGY FROM MY TRANS-DIMENSIONAL TRAVELS. I WAS HONESTLY BECOMING SCARED.
THIS CHIP WILL OVERRIDE ANY FEARS AND DOUBTS I MAY HAVE HAD.
FEAR IS A WORTHLESS EMOTION TO FEEL...

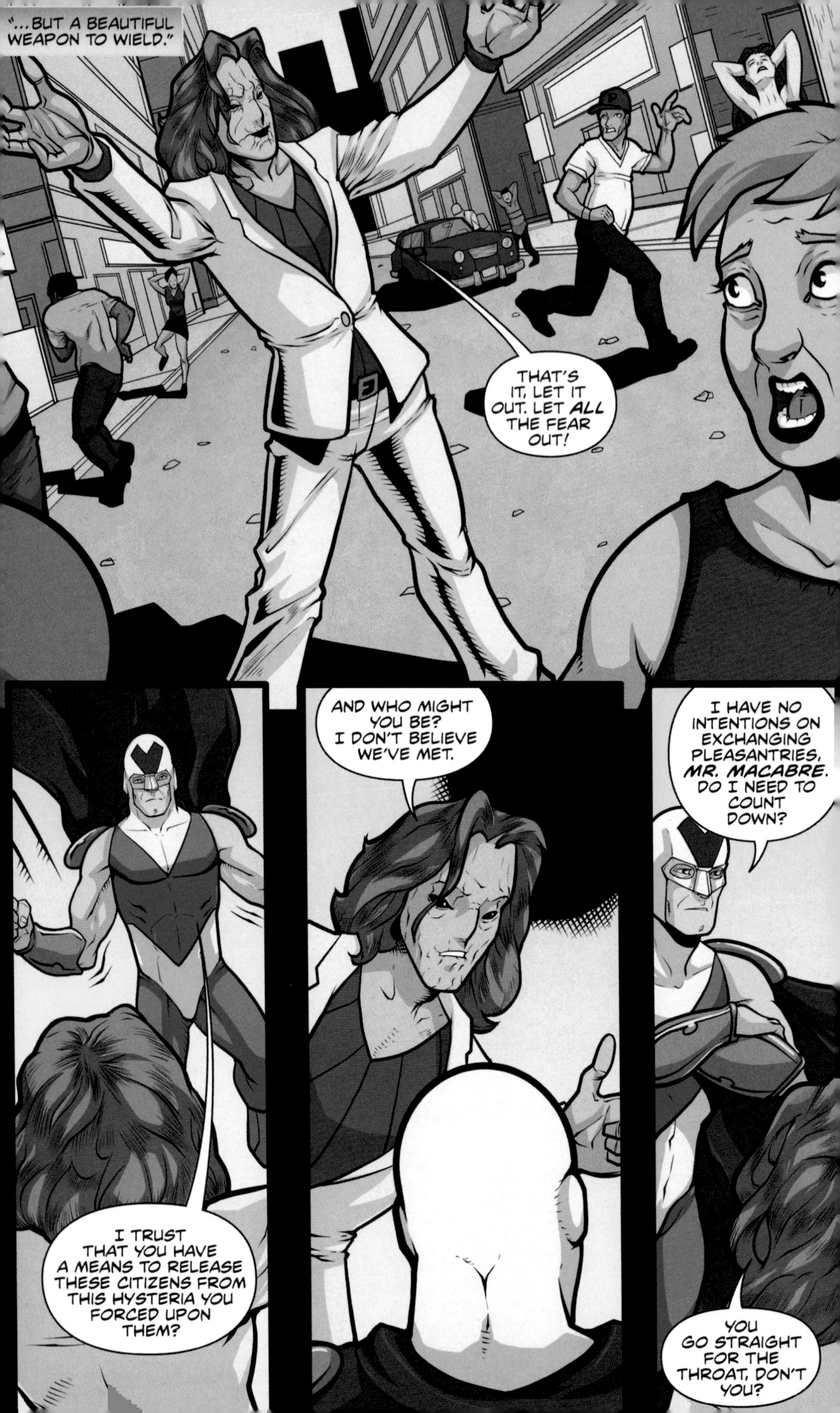
"...BUT A BEAUTIFUL WEAPON TO WIELD."
THAT'S IT, LET IT OUT. LET ALL THE FEAR OUT!
I TRUST THAT YOU HAVE A MEANS TO RELEASE THESE CITIZENS FROM THIS HYSTERIA YOU FORCED UPON THEM?
AND WHO MIGHT YOU BE? I DON'T BELIEVE WE'VE MET.
I HAVE NO INTENTIONS ON EXCHANGING PLEASANTRIES, MR. MACABRE. DO I NEED TO COUNT DOWN?
YOU GO STRAIGHT FOR THE THROAT, DON'T YOU?

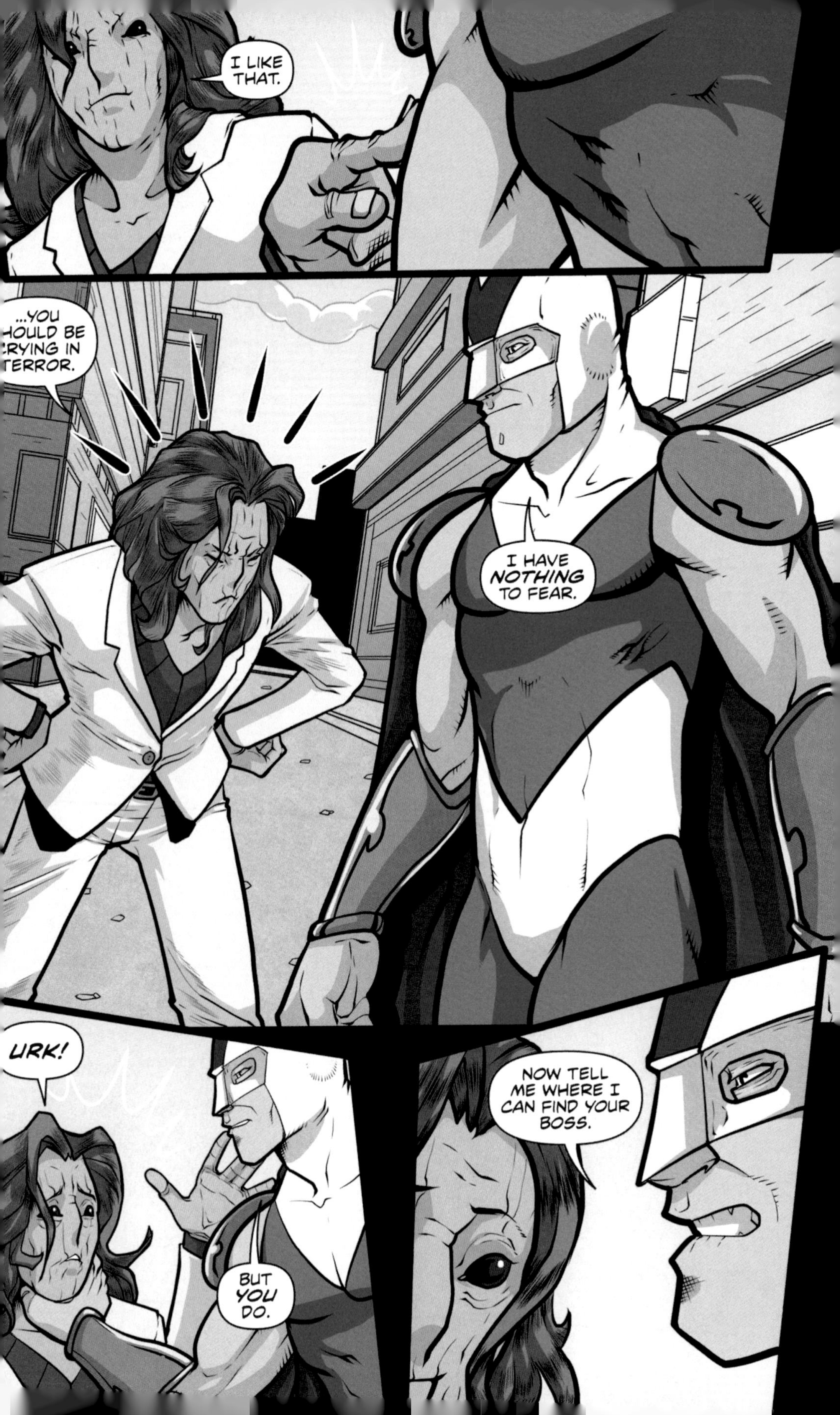
I LIKE THAT.
...YOU HOULD BE RYING IN TERROR.
I HAVE NOTHING TO FEAR.
URK!
BUT YOU DO.
NOW TELL ME WHERE I CAN FIND YOUR BOSS.

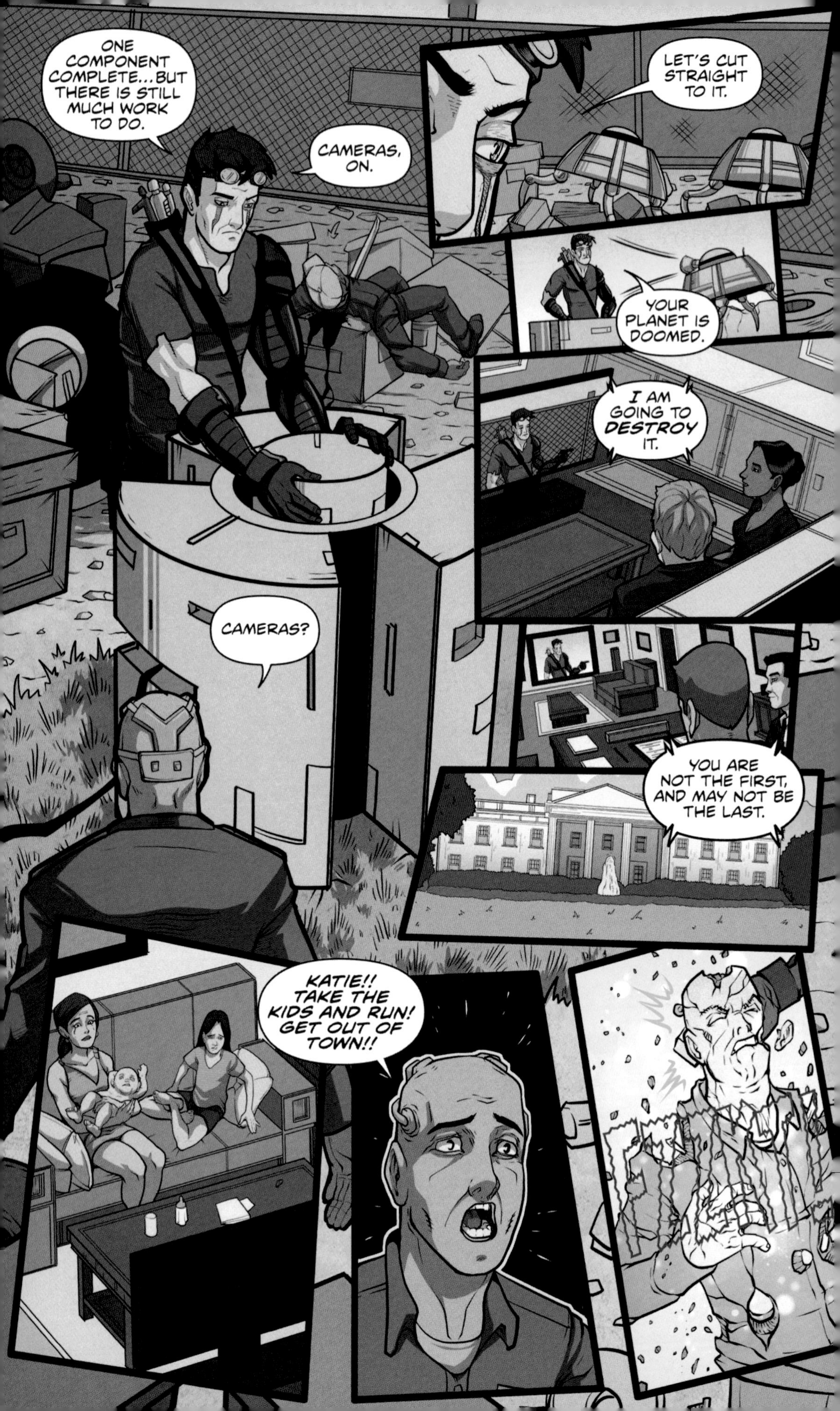
ONE COMPONENT COMPLETE... BUT THERE IS STILL MUCH WORK TO DO.
CAMERAS, ON.
LET'S CUT STRAIGHT TO IT.
YOUR PLANET IS DOOMED.
I AM GOING TO DESTROY IT.
CAMERAS?
YOU ARE NOT THE FIRST, AND MAY NOT BE THE LAST.
KATIE!! TAKE THE KIDS AND RUN! GET OUT OF TOWN!!

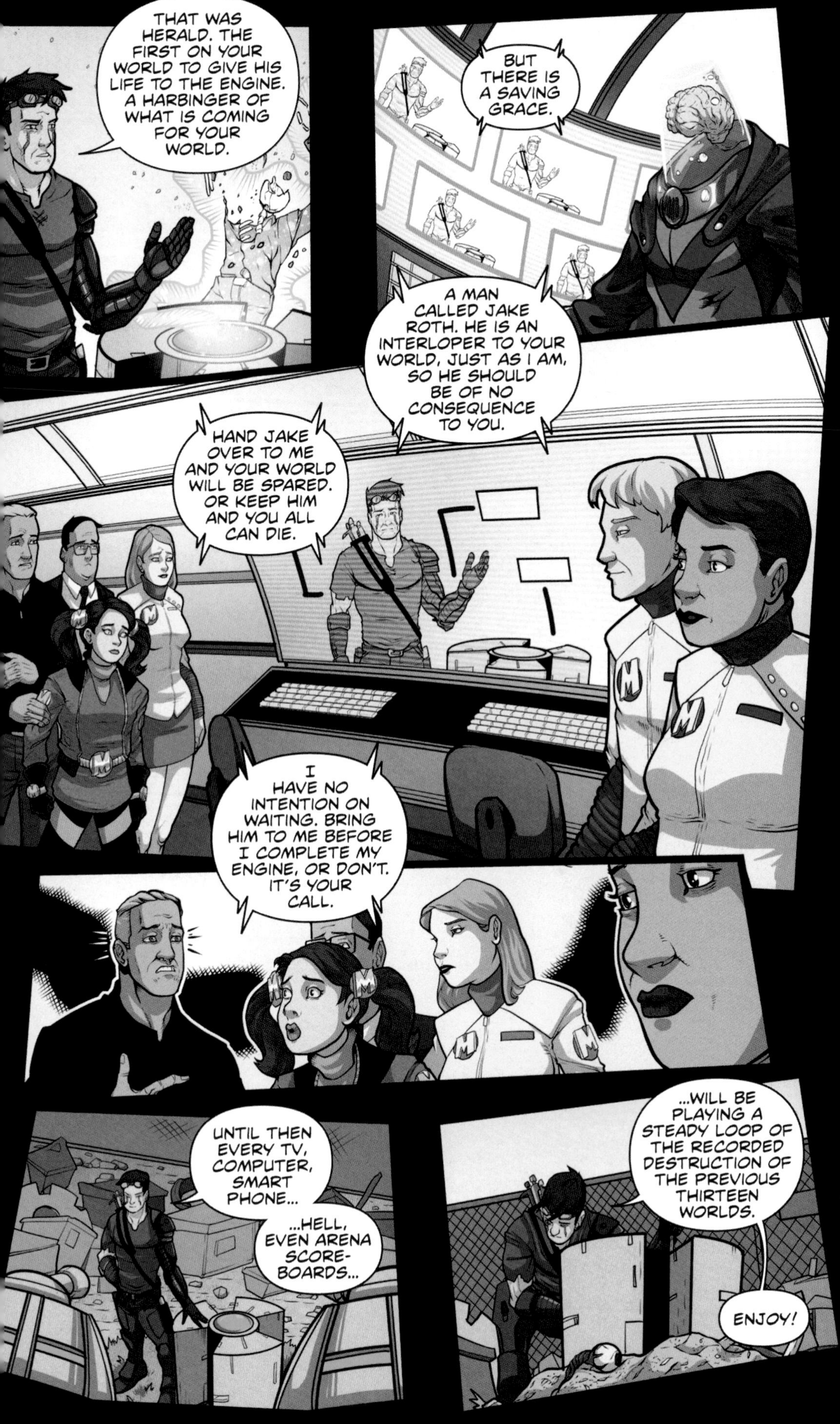
THAT WAS HERALD. THE FIRST ON YOUR WORLD TO GIVE HIS LIFE TO THE ENGINE. A HARBINGER OF WHAT IS COMING FOR YOUR WORLD.
BUT THERE IS A SAVING GRACE.
A MAN CALLED JAKE ROTH. HE IS AN INTERLOPER TO YOUR WORLD, JUST AS I AM, SO HE SHOULD BE OF NO CONSEQUENCE TO YOU.
HAND JAKE OVER TO ME AND YOUR WORLD WILL BE SPARED. OR KEEP HIM AND YOU ALL CAN DIE.
I HAVE NO INTENTION ON WAITING. BRING HIM TO ME BEFORE I COMPLETE MY ENGINE, OR DON'T. IT'S YOUR CALL.
UNTIL THEN EVERY TV, COMPUTER, SMART PHONE...
...HELL, EVEN ARENA SCORE-BOARDS...
...WILL BE PLAYING A STEADY LOOP OF THE RECORDED DESTRUCTION OF THE PREVIOUS THIRTEEN WORLDS.
ENJOY!

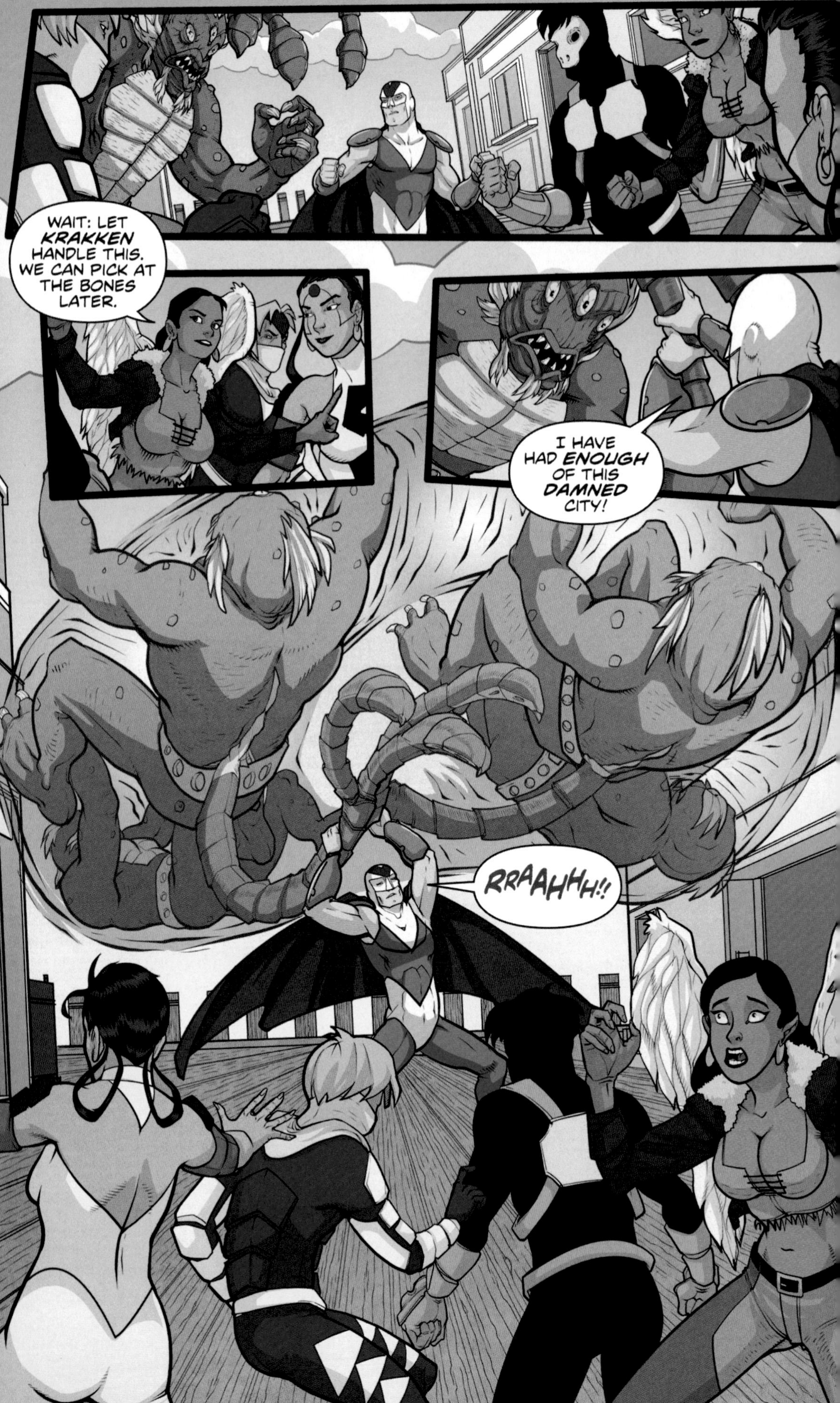
WAIT: LET KRAKKEN HANDLE THIS. WE CAN PICK AT THE BONES LATER.
I HAVE HAD ENOUGH OF THIS DAMNED CITY!
RRAAHHH!!

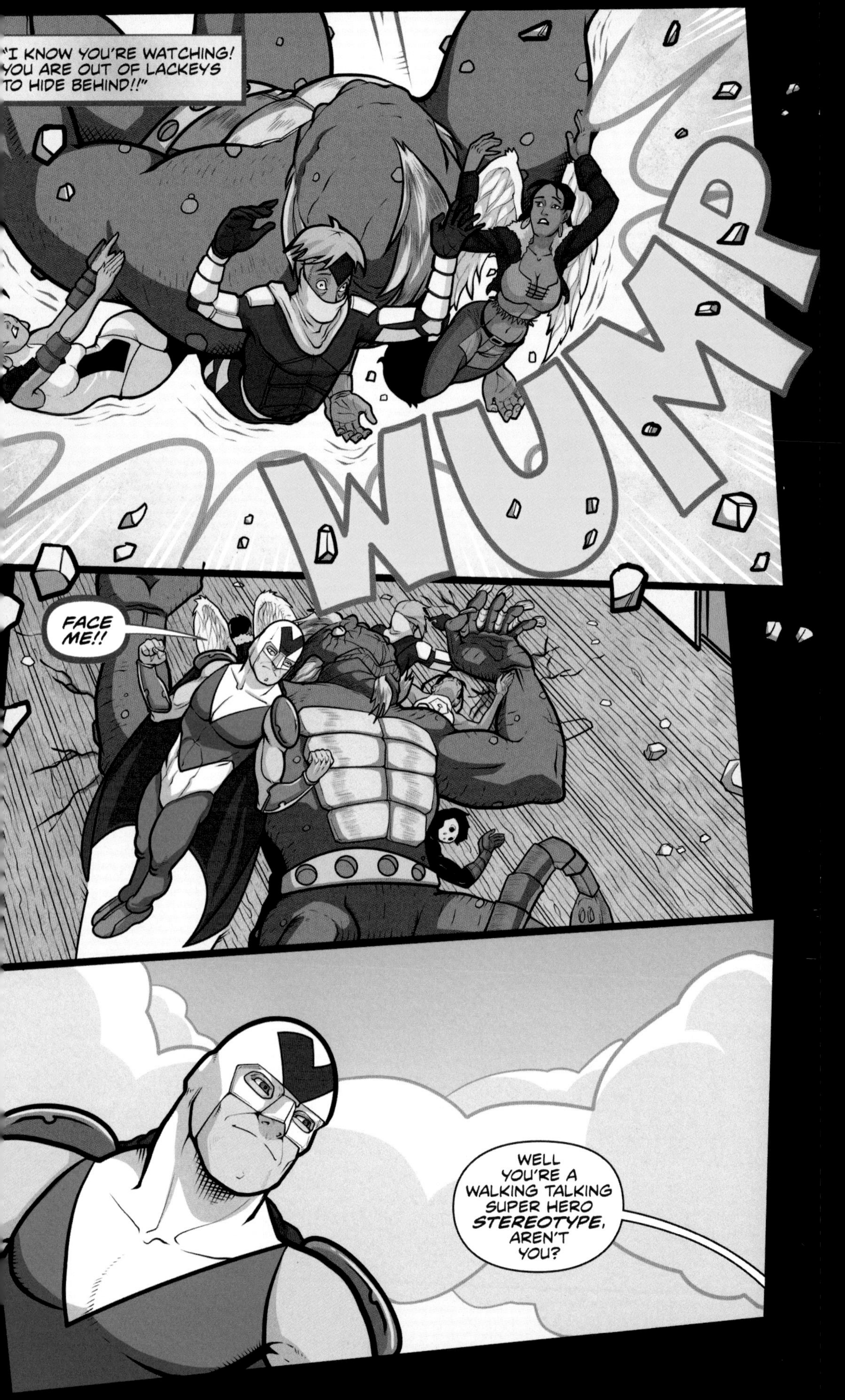
"I KNOW YOU'RE WATCHING! YOU ARE OUT OF LACKEYS TO HIDE BEHIND!!"
WUMP
FACE ME!!
WELL YOU'RE A WALKING TALKING SUPER HERO *STEREOTYPE*, AREN'T YOU?

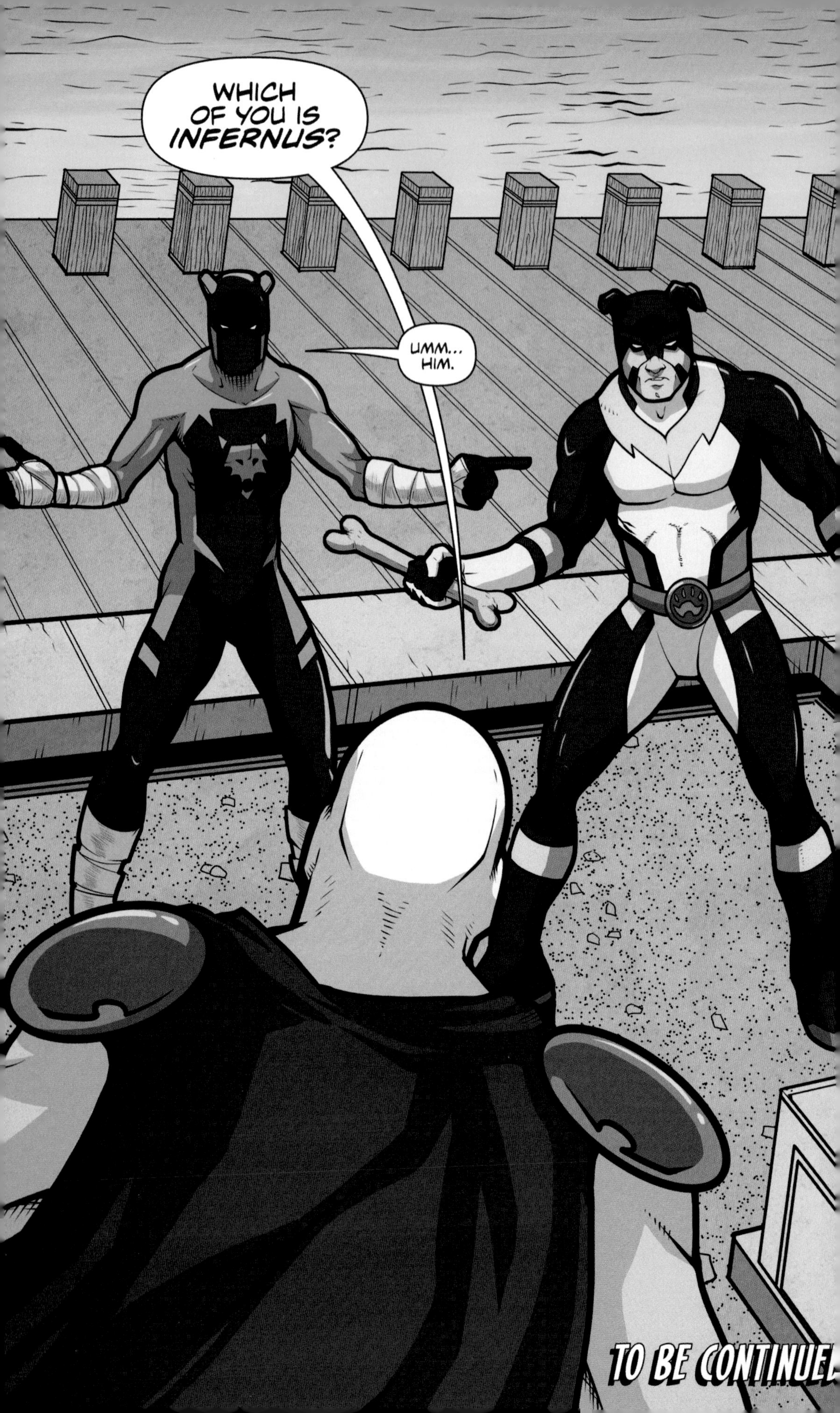
WHICH OF YOU IS INFERNUS?
UMM... HIM.
TO BE CONTINUED

...they asked me to write about how I felt drawing this ...sue. That was a loaded question.

...explain, I ran a full gamut of emotions while ...awing this issue. Let me try to share a few of them.

...st, I felt excitement. I was thrilled to be asked to be ...part of a once-in-a-lifetime, never before seen project ...this type. As far as we know, with apologies to Dave ...an's WAR OF THE INDEPENDENTS, this project is ...sentially the first time a publisher of creator owned ...rk took this large a group of creator-owned projects ...d mashed them together to interact in a persistent, ...ared narrative universe. Sure, Marvel, DC, Valiant ...d others have created shared narrative universes in ...ich multiple characters and multiple "properties" ...teract, but we haven't seen another example of this ...any creator-owned properties working together under ...independent publishing banner to form a persistent ...ared narrative space. There were legal issues to ...nfront, timing issues to confront, as well as script, ...sign, and narrative issues. We felt like we were ...ing something new, something different, and ...mething terribly difficult, and that's exciting.

...cond, I felt humbled. The level of talent involved in ...s massive project was staggering and intimidating. ...ce you've already read the issue, I can share that in ...final pages I got to draw a lot of characters created ...folks I really, really like and respect, and whom I ...ow are way more talented than I am. Getting to ...w the F1rst Hero, Stray, Midnight Tiger, and Molly ...nger in a context other than fan art was both ...azing and nerve wracking at the same time. Molly ...nger is only in 2 panels of this book, and Stray and ...are only in one, but trying to step up my game so ...se panels don't look like garbage compared to how ...u've seen those characters before was a daunting ...d exciting challenge.

Third, I felt exhausted. While drawing this book, I was also attempting to get to the finish line on the art for my other upcoming project, BLUE HOUR (coming in July, 2016 from Action Lab), while at the same time plotting and doing character designs for my planned project beyond that, THE NULL FAERIES. I'm not used to juggling that many projects at once, while still maintaining my life/work balance between family, comic work, and my full-time career as an attorney. There were a few late nights working on FRACTURE. But I wouldn't trade the experience for anything.

Fourth, I felt nostalgic and proud. FRACTURE was the first book from Action Lab that was accepted by Diamond for distribution in the direct market. In a very real sense, FRACTURE was instrumental in Action Lab's "birth" as a company, and the development into what it is today. That being said, in all honesty, the sales for FRACTURE didn't set the world on fire. After the publication of Volume II (Vice and Virtue) in 2014, there was great uncertainty as to whether we'd do another volume or indeed, whether we'd ever revisit these characters. That was partially based on sales, but also in large part due to the fact that I honestly wanted to do something other than super heroes for a while. But getting to do this single issue in the ActionVerse line brought back all the old memories of what I loved about these characters, what I loved about drawing a super hero book, and what I loved about working with Shawn. It was fun on a whole lot of levels.

Fifth and finally, I felt grateful. The opportunity to collaborate with the other creators who are a part of this project was amazing. Meshing art, plots, design, and timing with 20+ others in putting this together was wrenching, frustrating, and exhilarating. Being pushed to "up my game" so my book doesn't drag this series down, or look terrible in comparison to the others, was a fire under me that I've seldom experienced before. Candidly, I don't know if I'd sign up to do it again, but I'm tremendously glad I did. I can't wait to see where the ActionVerse ends up, and to see where the story takes us, takes Action Lab, and these characters. Please stick with us, and enjoy the show.

- Chad Cicconi
Pittsburgh, PA
March 23, 2016

VIRTUE

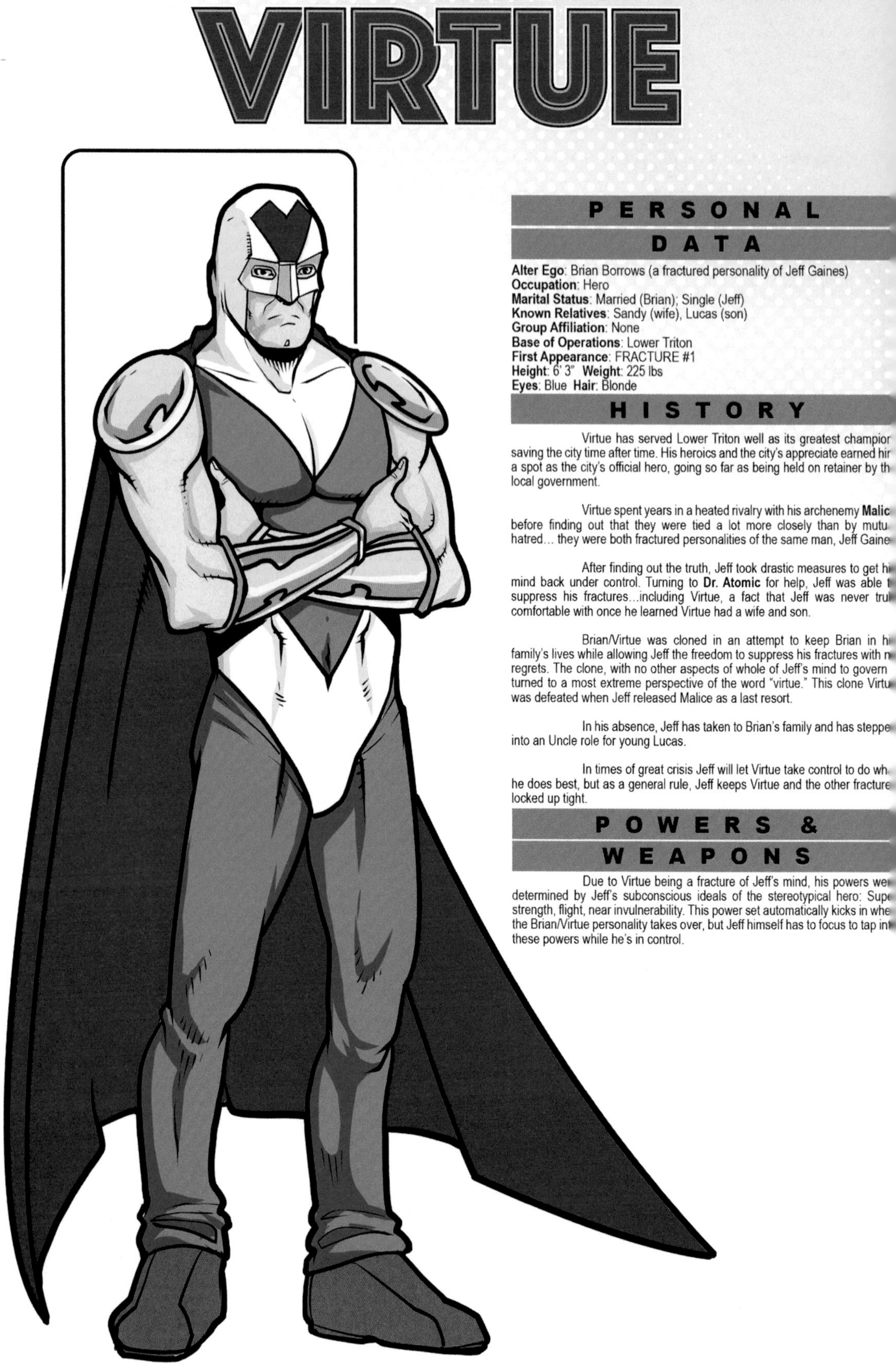

PERSONAL DATA

Alter Ego: Brian Borrows (a fractured personality of Jeff Gaines)
Occupation: Hero
Marital Status: Married (Brian); Single (Jeff)
Known Relatives: Sandy (wife), Lucas (son)
Group Affiliation: None
Base of Operations: Lower Triton
First Appearance: FRACTURE #1
Height: 6' 3" **Weight**: 225 lbs
Eyes: Blue **Hair**: Blonde

HISTORY

Virtue has served Lower Triton well as its greatest champior saving the city time after time. His heroics and the city's appreciate earned hir a spot as the city's official hero, going so far as being held on retainer by th local government.

Virtue spent years in a heated rivalry with his archenemy **Malic** before finding out that they were tied a lot more closely than by mutu hatred… they were both fractured personalities of the same man, Jeff Gaine

After finding out the truth, Jeff took drastic measures to get hi mind back under control. Turning to **Dr. Atomic** for help, Jeff was able t suppress his fractures…including Virtue, a fact that Jeff was never tru comfortable with once he learned Virtue had a wife and son.

Brian/Virtue was cloned in an attempt to keep Brian in hi family's lives while allowing Jeff the freedom to suppress his fractures with n regrets. The clone, with no other aspects of whole of Jeff's mind to govern turned to a most extreme perspective of the word "virtue." This clone Virtu was defeated when Jeff released Malice as a last resort.

In his absence, Jeff has taken to Brian's family and has steppe into an Uncle role for young Lucas.

In times of great crisis Jeff will let Virtue take control to do wh he does best, but as a general rule, Jeff keeps Virtue and the other fracture locked up tight.

POWERS & WEAPONS

Due to Virtue being a fracture of Jeff's mind, his powers we determined by Jeff's subconscious ideals of the stereotypical hero: Sup strength, flight, near invulnerability. This power set automatically kicks in whe the Brian/Virtue personality takes over, but Jeff himself has to focus to tap in these powers while he's in control.

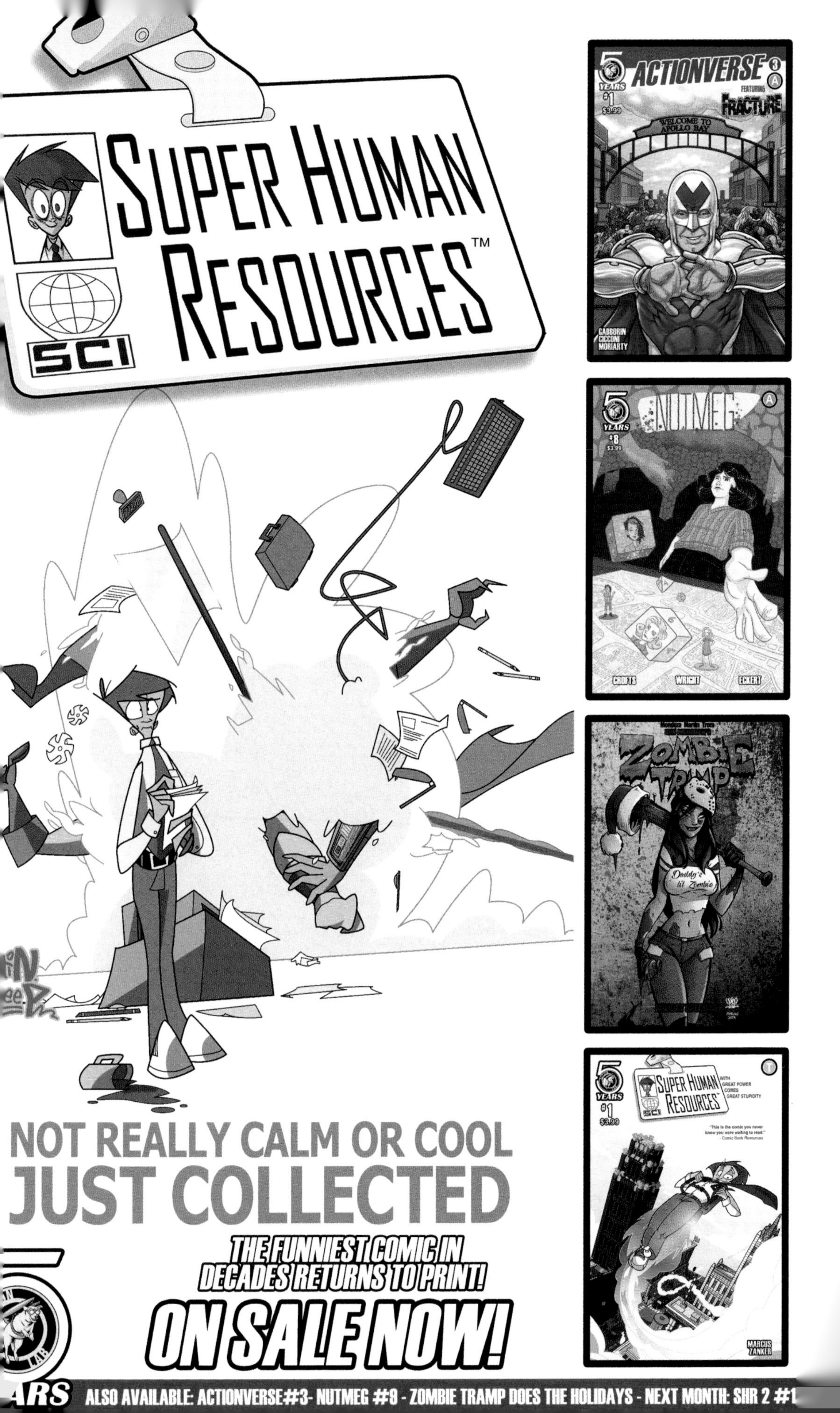
SUPER HUMAN RESOURCES™
SCI
ACTIONVERSE 3 A
FEATURING
FRACTURE
5 YEARS
#1
$3.99
WELCOME TO APOLLO BAY
GABBORIN
CICCONI
MORIARTY
NUTMEG A
#8
$3.99
CROFTS
WRIGHT
ECKERT
ZOMBIE TRAMP
Daddy's lil Zombie
SUPER HUMAN RESOURCES™
WITH GREAT POWER COMES GREAT STUPIDITY
SCI
T
#1
$3.99
"This is the comic you never knew you were waiting to read."
- Comic Book Resources
MARCUS
ZANKER
NOT REALLY CALM OR COOL
JUST COLLECTED
THE FUNNIEST COMIC IN DECADES RETURNS TO PRINT!
ON SALE NOW!
ARS
ALSO AVAILABLE: ACTIONVERSE#3- NUTMEG #9 - ZOMBIE TRAMP DOES THE HOLIDAYS - NEXT MONTH: SHR 2 #1

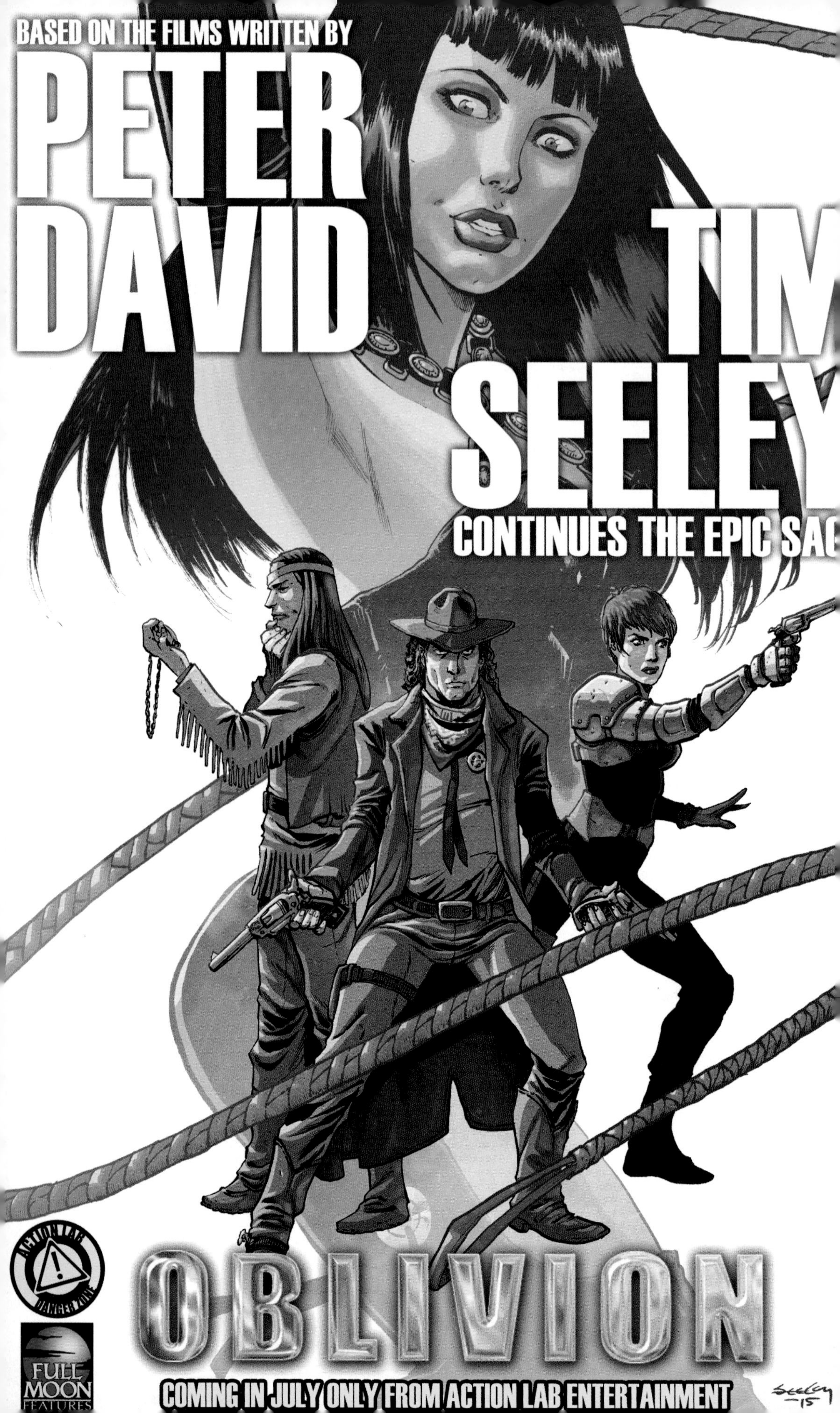
BASED ON THE FILMS WRITTEN BY
PETER DAVID
TIM SEELEY
CONTINUES THE EPIC SAG
ACTION LAB DANGER ZONE
OBLIVION
FULL MOON FEATURES
COMING IN JULY ONLY FROM ACTION LAB ENTERTAINMENT

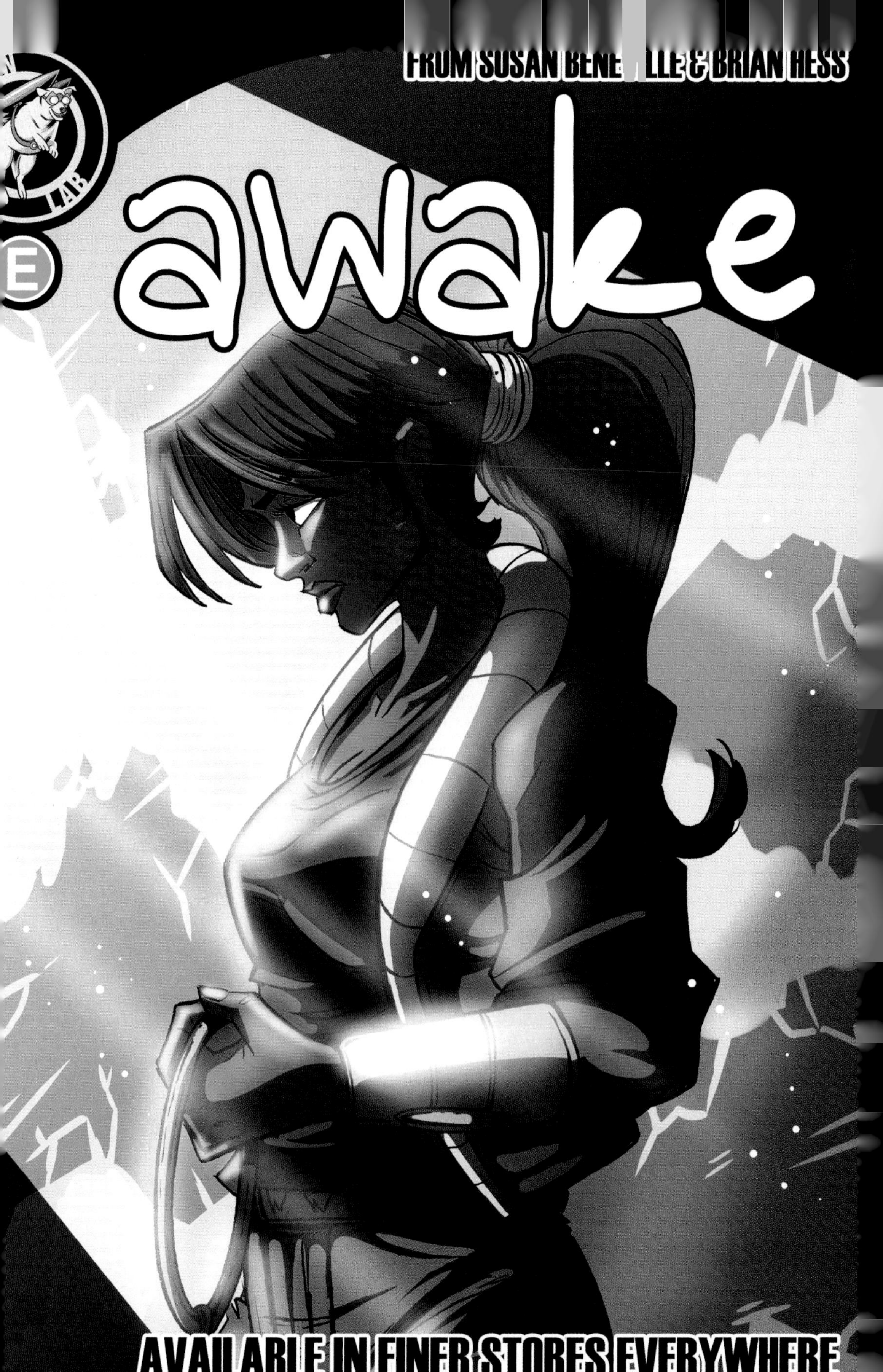

FROM SUSAN BENE LLE & BRIAN HESS
awake
AVAILABLE IN FINER STORES EVERYWHERE

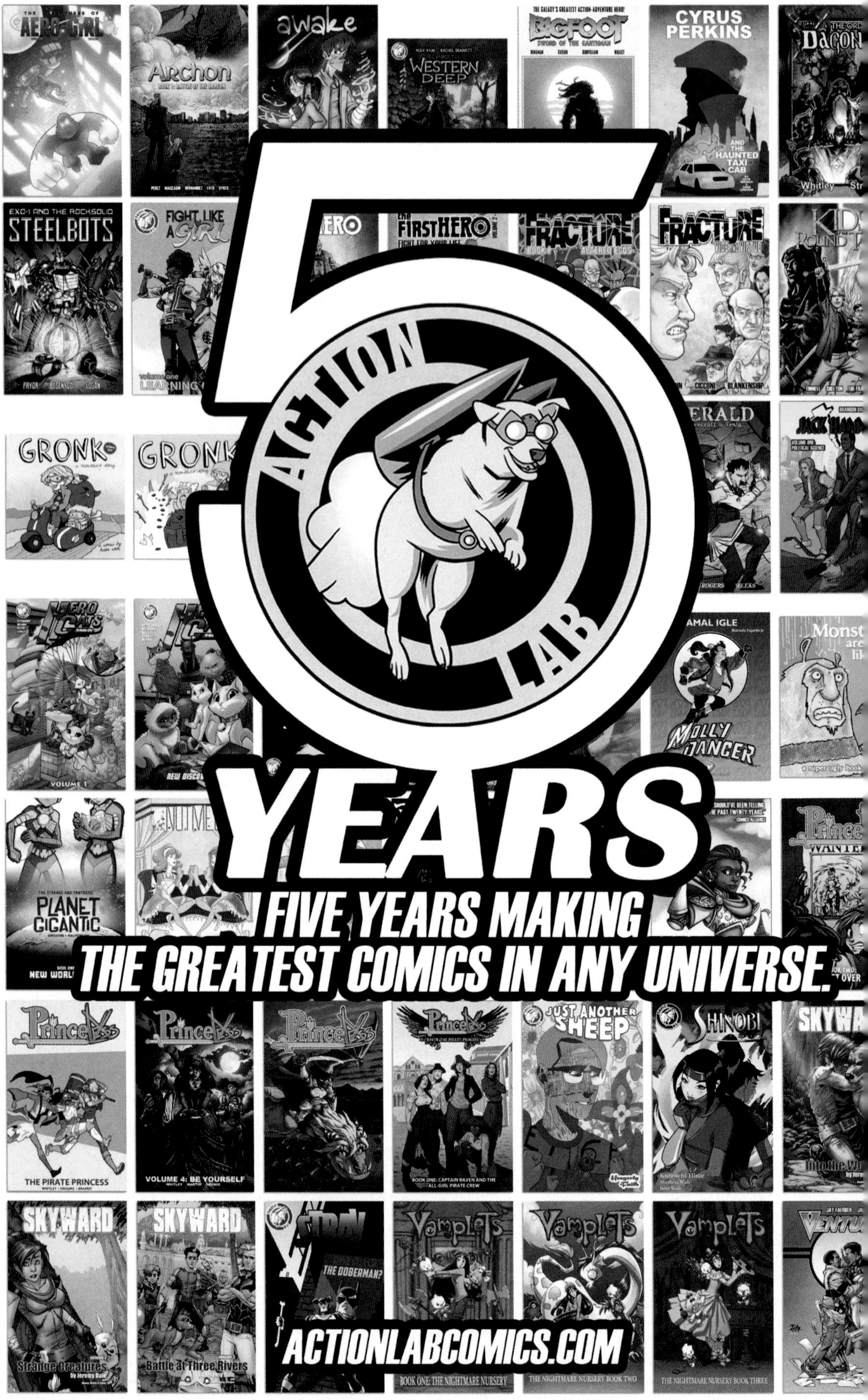
ACTION LAB
5
YEARS
FIVE YEARS MAKING
THE GREATEST COMICS IN ANY UNIVERSE.
ACTIONLABCOMICS.COM

SAVE THE DATE!

Celebrating **15** Years

FREE COMIC BOOK ·DAY·

1st SATURDAY IN MAY!

May 7, 2016

www.freecomicbookday.com

FREE COMICS FOR EVERYONE!

Details @ www.freecomicbookday.com

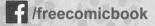

f /freecomicbook @freecomicbook @freecomicbookday

ACTION LAB

READ MORE NOW

Actionverse - Action Lab
www.actionlabcomics.com
00311
7 02382 69113 4

ACTIONLABCOMICS.COM

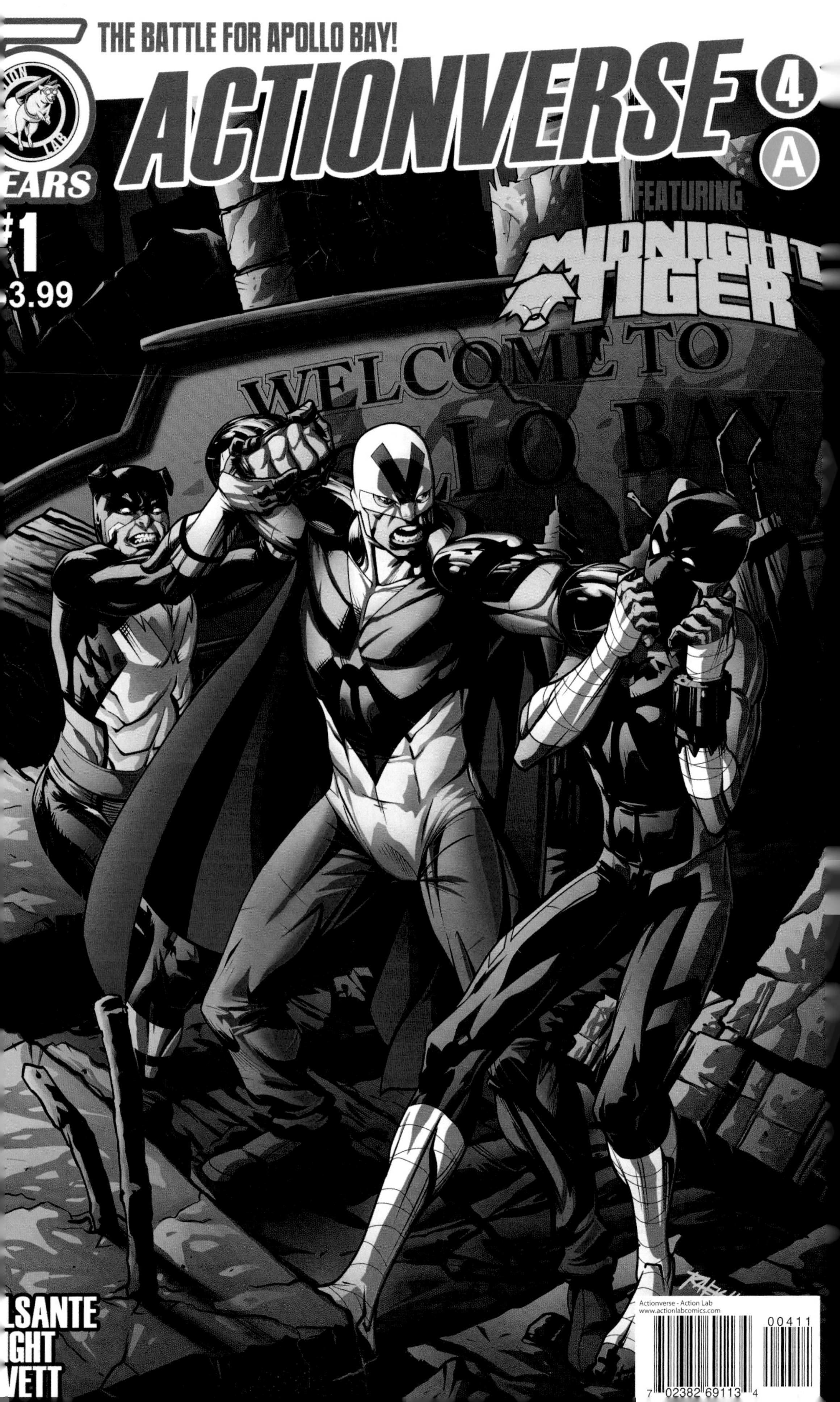

THE BATTLE FOR APOLLO BAY!
ACTIONVERSE
4
A
EARS
#1
3.99
FEATURING
MIDNIGHT TIGER
WELCOME TO
LO BAY
LSANTE
GHT
VETT
Actionverse - Action Lab
www.actionlabcomics.com
00411
7 02382 69113 4

ACTIONVERSE

FEATURING

Written by Ray-Anthony Height and Vito Delsante

Drawn by Ray-Anthony Height

Colors by Nate Lovett

Letters by Full Court Press

Cover by Height and Lovett

Variant Connecting Cover by Ron Frenz, Marc Deering
Ross Campbell and David Bednarski

Edited by Vito Delsante

MIDNIGHT TIGER and all related characters created by Ray-Anthony Height

PREVIOUSLY

Apollo Bay has been cleaned up by Virtue. All that stands in his way are Midnight Tiger, the defender of the Bay, and Stray, his new friend. They don't stand a chance. Meanwhile, Medula is ready to make his move from the shadows.

BRYAN SEATON - PUBLISHER
DAVE DWONCH - PRESIDENT
SHAWN GABBORIN - EDITOR IN CHIEF
JASON MARTIN - PUBLISHER, DANGER ZONE
JAMAL IGLE - VICE-PRESIDENT OF MARKETING
JIM DIETZ - SOCIAL MEDIA DIRECTOR
NICOLE D'ANDRIA - EDITOR
CHAD CICCONI - ...HELPLESS AS A KITTEN
COLLEEN BOYD - SUBMISSIONS EDITOR

ACTIONLABCOMICS.COM

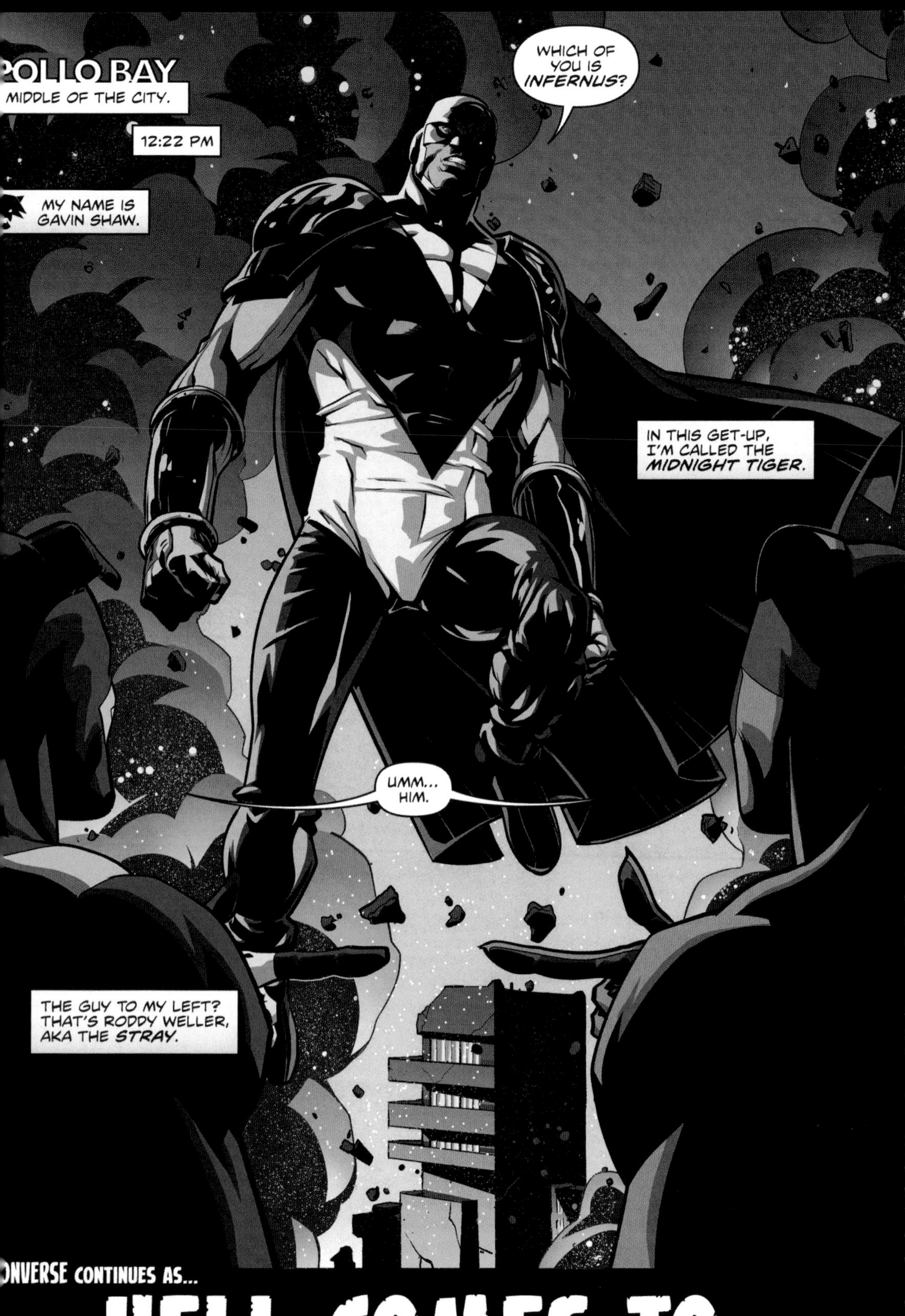
POLLO BAY
MIDDLE OF THE CITY.
12:22 PM
WHICH OF YOU IS INFERNUS?
MY NAME IS GAVIN SHAW.
IN THIS GET-UP, I'M CALLED THE MIDNIGHT TIGER.
UMM... HIM.
THE GUY TO MY LEFT? THAT'S RODDY WELLER, AKA THE STRAY.

ONVERSE CONTINUES AS...

HELL COMES TO APOLLO BAY!

DELSANTE ✶ HEIGHT ✶ LOVETT ✶ FULL COURT PRESS

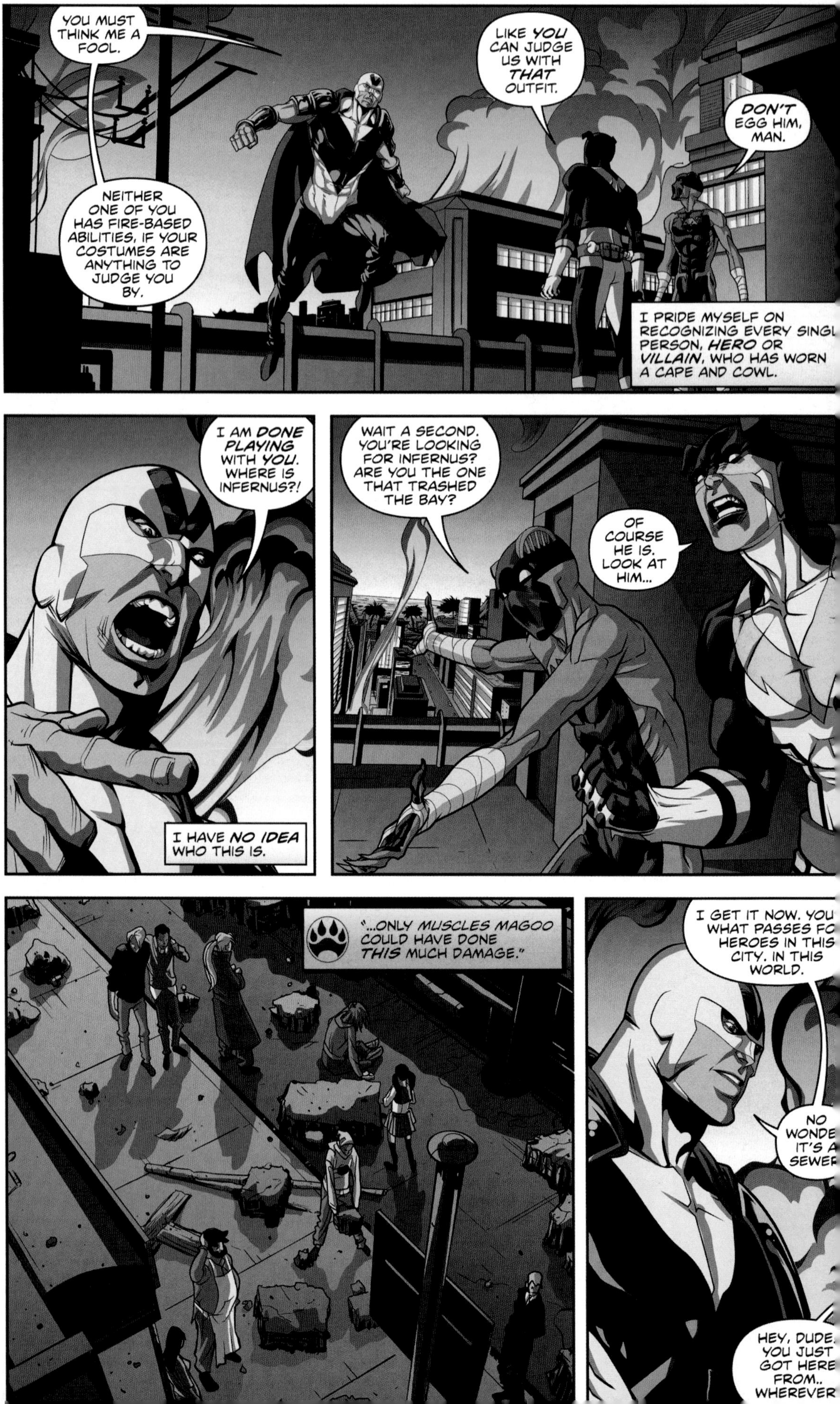

YOU MUST THINK ME A FOOL.
NEITHER ONE OF YOU HAS FIRE-BASED ABILITIES, IF YOUR COSTUMES ARE ANYTHING TO JUDGE YOU BY.
LIKE YOU CAN JUDGE US WITH THAT OUTFIT.
DON'T EGG HIM, MAN.
I PRIDE MYSELF ON RECOGNIZING EVERY SINGL PERSON, HERO OR VILLAIN, WHO HAS WORN A CAPE AND COWL.
I AM DONE PLAYING WITH YOU. WHERE IS INFERNUS?!
I HAVE NO IDEA WHO THIS IS.
WAIT A SECOND. YOU'RE LOOKING FOR INFERNUS? ARE YOU THE ONE THAT TRASHED THE BAY?
OF COURSE HE IS. LOOK AT HIM...
"...ONLY MUSCLES MAGOO COULD HAVE DONE THIS MUCH DAMAGE."
I GET IT NOW. YOU WHAT PASSES FO HEROES IN THIS CITY. IN THIS WORLD.
NO WONDE IT'S A SEWER
HEY, DUDE. YOU JUST GOT HERE FROM.. WHEREVER

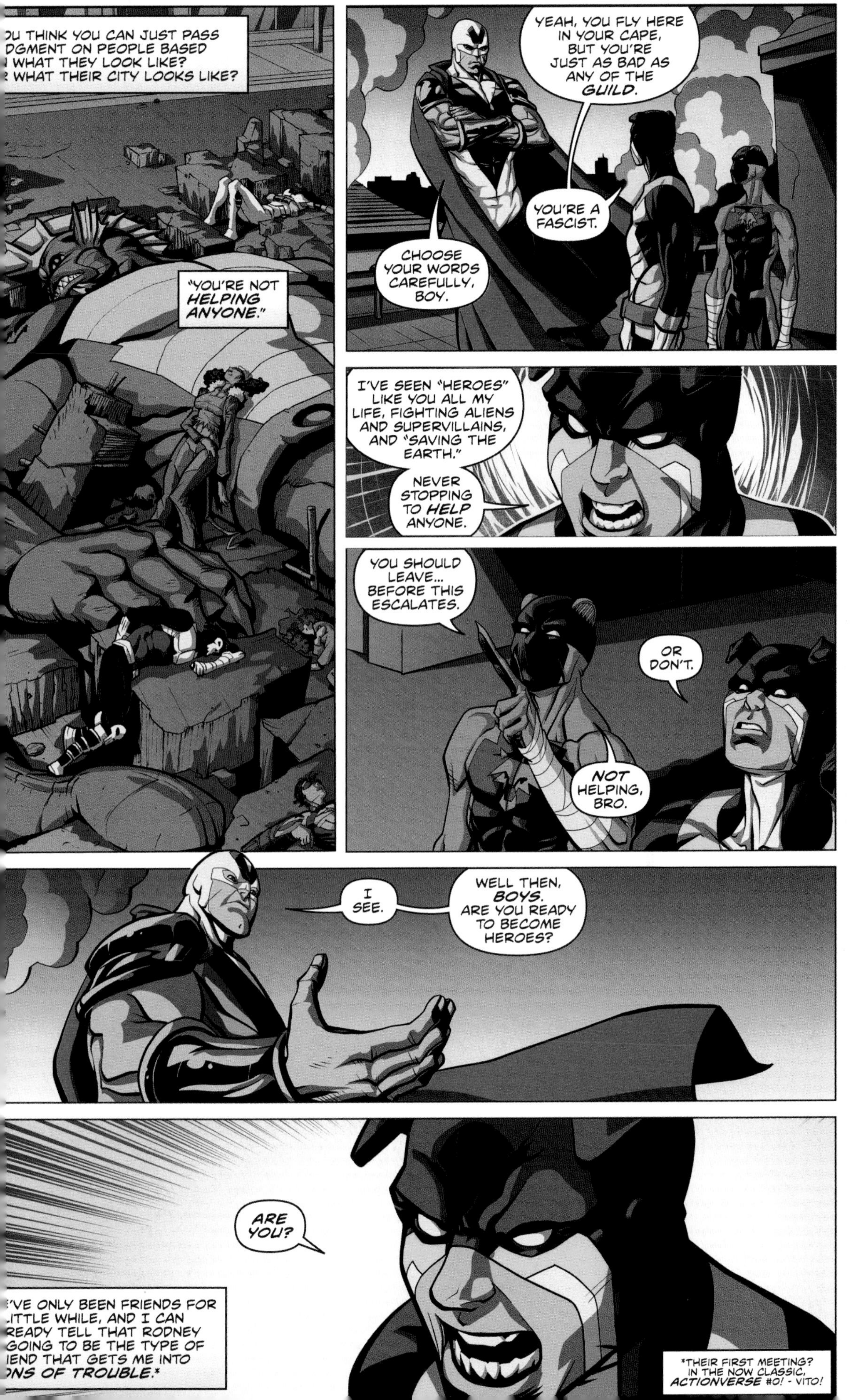

OU THINK YOU CAN JUST PASS DGMENT ON PEOPLE BASED WHAT THEY LOOK LIKE? R WHAT THEIR CITY LOOKS LIKE?
"YOU'RE NOT HELPING ANYONE."
YEAH, YOU FLY HERE IN YOUR CAPE, BUT YOU'RE JUST AS BAD AS ANY OF THE GUILD.
YOU'RE A FASCIST.
CHOOSE YOUR WORDS CAREFULLY, BOY.
I'VE SEEN "HEROES" LIKE YOU ALL MY LIFE, FIGHTING ALIENS AND SUPERVILLAINS, AND "SAVING THE EARTH."
NEVER STOPPING TO HELP ANYONE.
YOU SHOULD LEAVE... BEFORE THIS ESCALATES.
OR DON'T.
NOT HELPING, BRO.
I SEE.
WELL THEN, BOYS. ARE YOU READY TO BECOME HEROES?
ARE YOU?
'VE ONLY BEEN FRIENDS FOR LITTLE WHILE, AND I CAN READY TELL THAT RODNEY GOING TO BE THE TYPE OF IEND THAT GETS ME INTO ONS OF TROUBLE.*
*THEIR FIRST MEETING? IN THE NOW CLASSIC, ACTIONVERSE #0! - VITO!

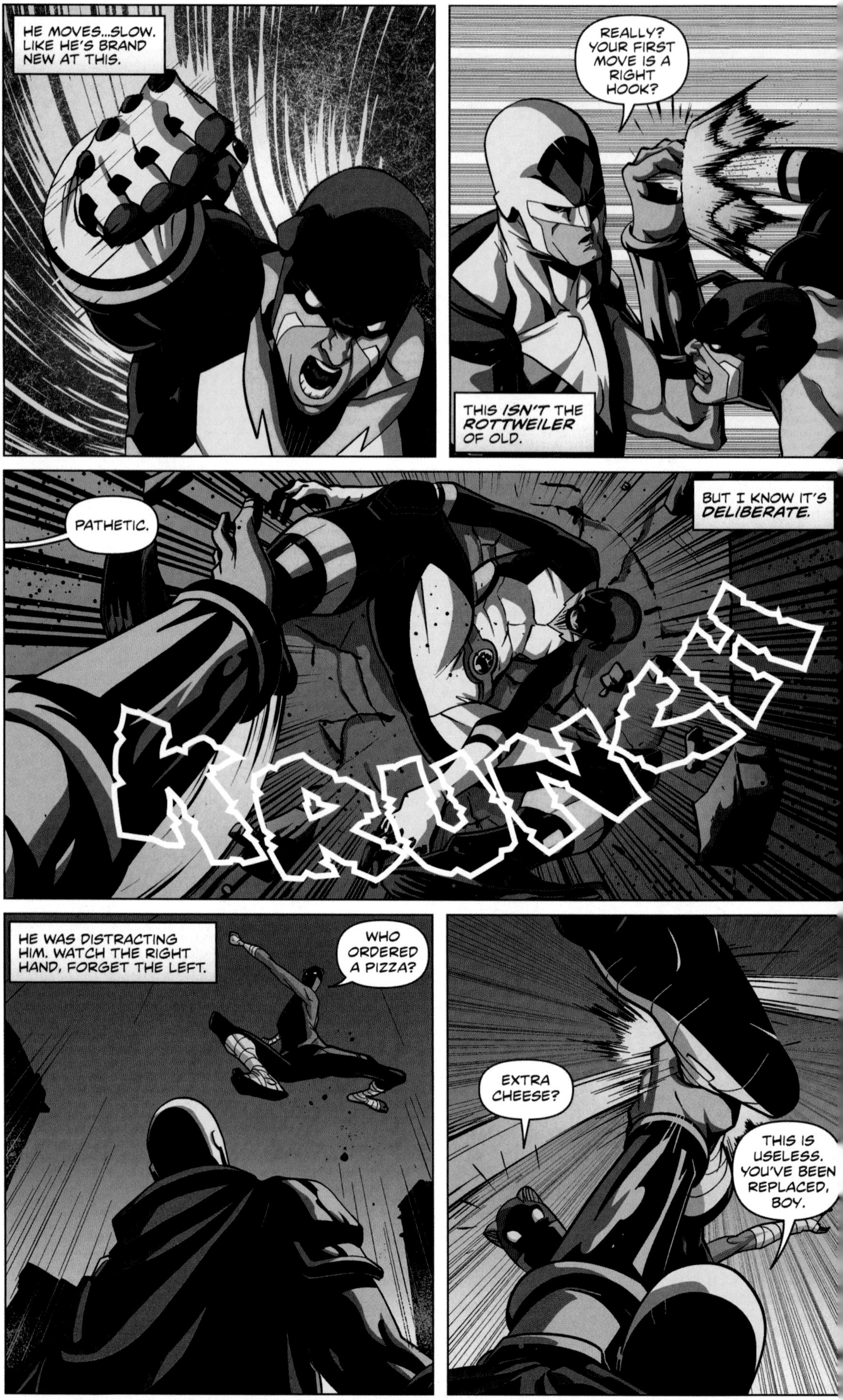
HE MOVES...SLOW. LIKE HE'S BRAND NEW AT THIS.
REALLY? YOUR FIRST MOVE IS A RIGHT HOOK?
THIS ISN'T THE ROTTWEILER OF OLD.
PATHETIC.
BUT I KNOW IT'S DELIBERATE.
KRUNK!!
HE WAS DISTRACTING HIM. WATCH THE RIGHT HAND, FORGET THE LEFT.
WHO ORDERED A PIZZA?
EXTRA CHEESE?
THIS IS USELESS. YOU'VE BEEN REPLACED, BOY.

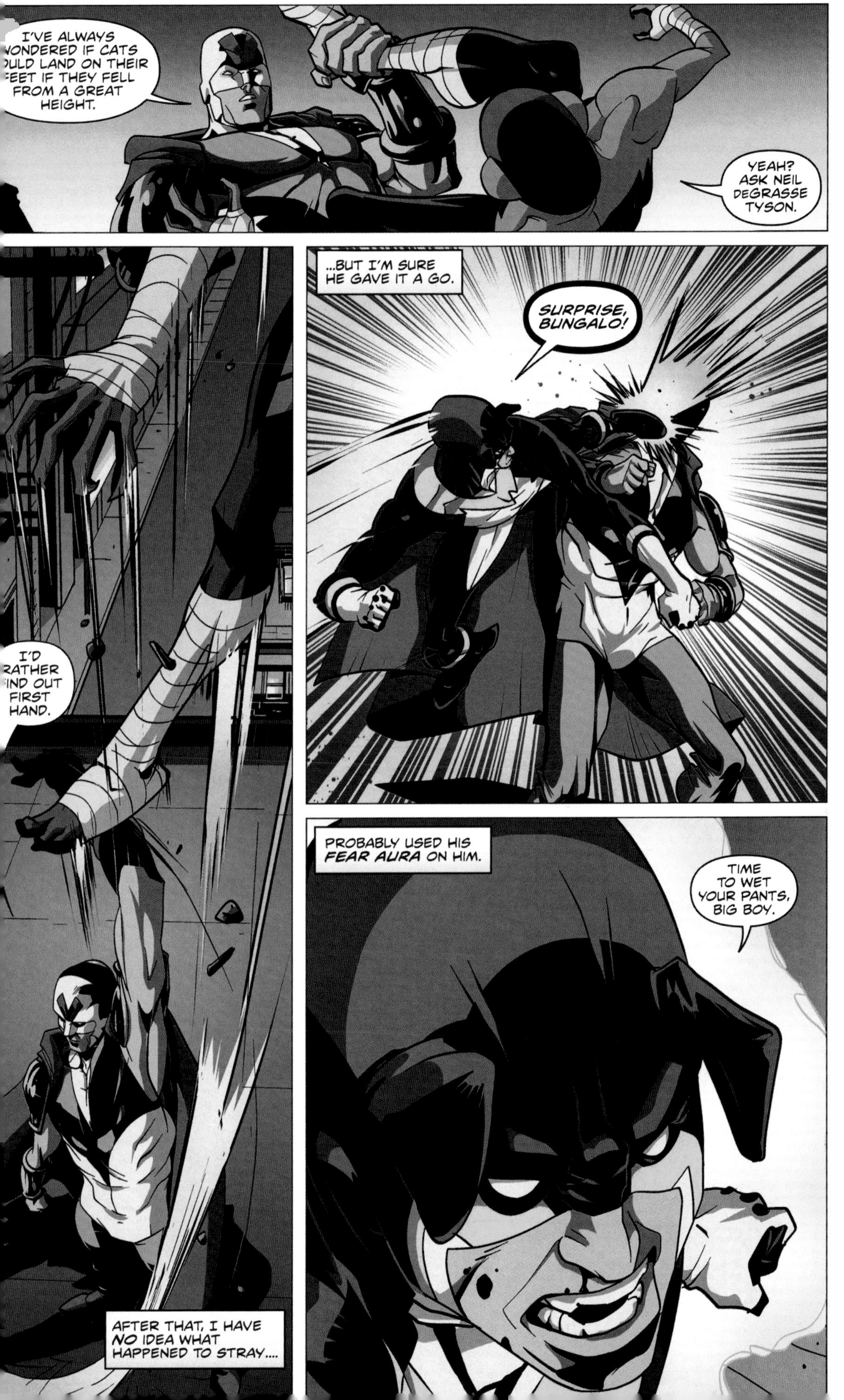
I'VE ALWAYS WONDERED IF CATS WOULD LAND ON THEIR FEET IF THEY FELL FROM A GREAT HEIGHT.
YEAH? ASK NEIL DEGRASSE TYSON.
I'D RATHER FIND OUT FIRST HAND.
AFTER THAT, I HAVE NO IDEA WHAT HAPPENED TO STRAY....
...BUT I'M SURE HE GAVE IT A GO.
SURPRISE, BUNGALO!
PROBABLY USED HIS FEAR AURA ON HIM.
TIME TO WET YOUR PANTS, BIG BOY.

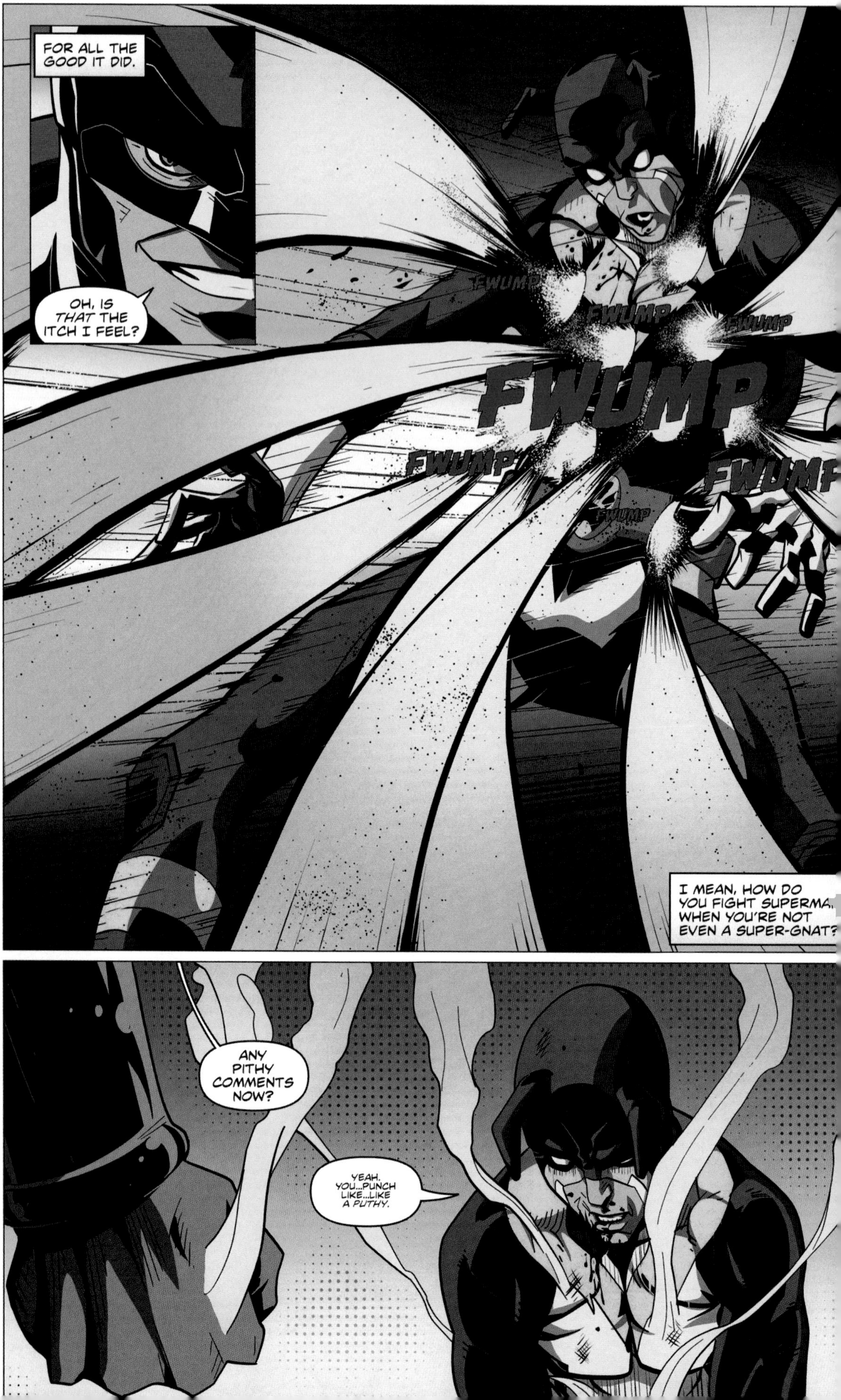
FOR ALL THE GOOD IT DID.
OH, IS *THAT* THE ITCH I FEEL?
FWUMP
FWUMP
FWUMP
FWUMP
FWUMP
FWUMF
FWUMP
I MEAN, HOW DO YOU FIGHT SUPERMA WHEN YOU'RE NOT EVEN A SUPER-GNAT?
ANY PITHY COMMENTS NOW?
YEAH. YOU...PUNCH LIKE...LIKE A *PUTHY*.

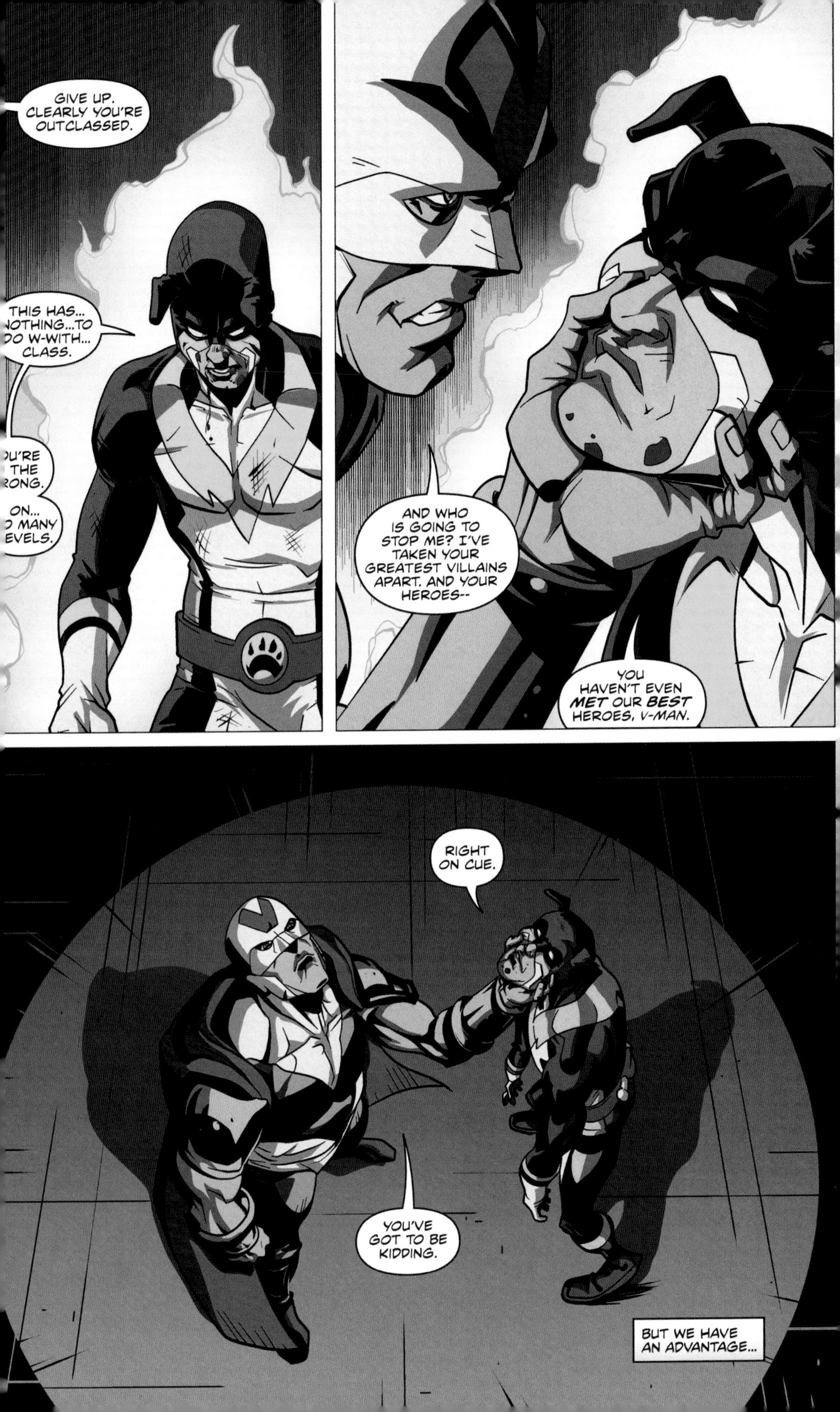
GIVE UP. CLEARLY YOU'RE OUTCLASSED.
THIS HAS... NOTHING...TO DO W-WITH... CLASS.
U'RE THE RONG.
ON... O MANY EVELS.
AND WHO IS GOING TO STOP ME? I'VE TAKEN YOUR GREATEST VILLAINS APART. AND YOUR HEROES--
YOU HAVEN'T EVEN MET OUR BEST HEROES, V-MAN.
RIGHT ON CUE.
YOU'VE GOT TO BE KIDDING.
BUT WE HAVE AN ADVANTAGE...

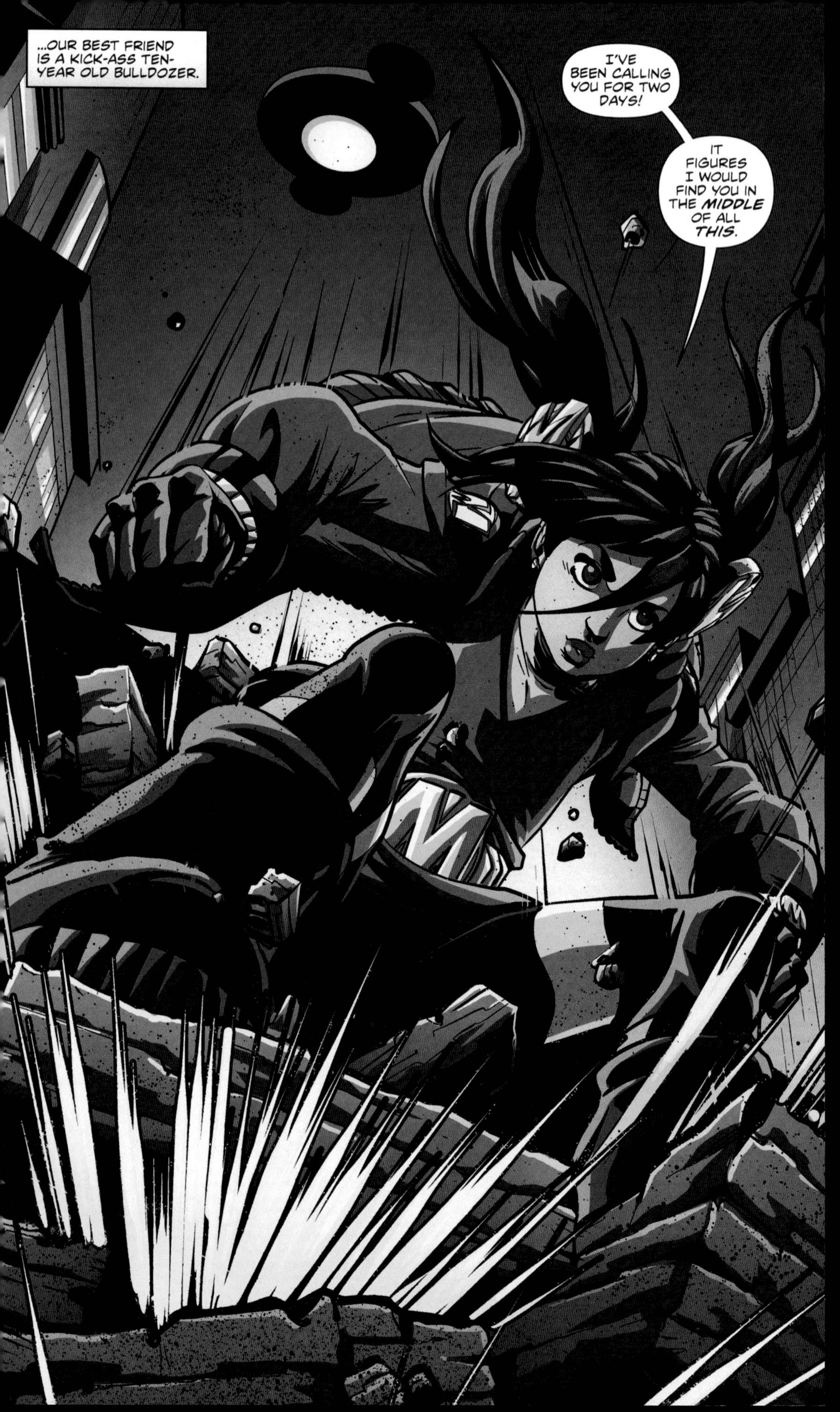
...OUR BEST FRIEND IS A KICK-ASS TEN-YEAR OLD BULLDOZER.
I'VE BEEN CALLING YOU FOR TWO DAYS!
IT FIGURES I WOULD FIND YOU IN THE *MIDDLE* OF ALL *THIS*.

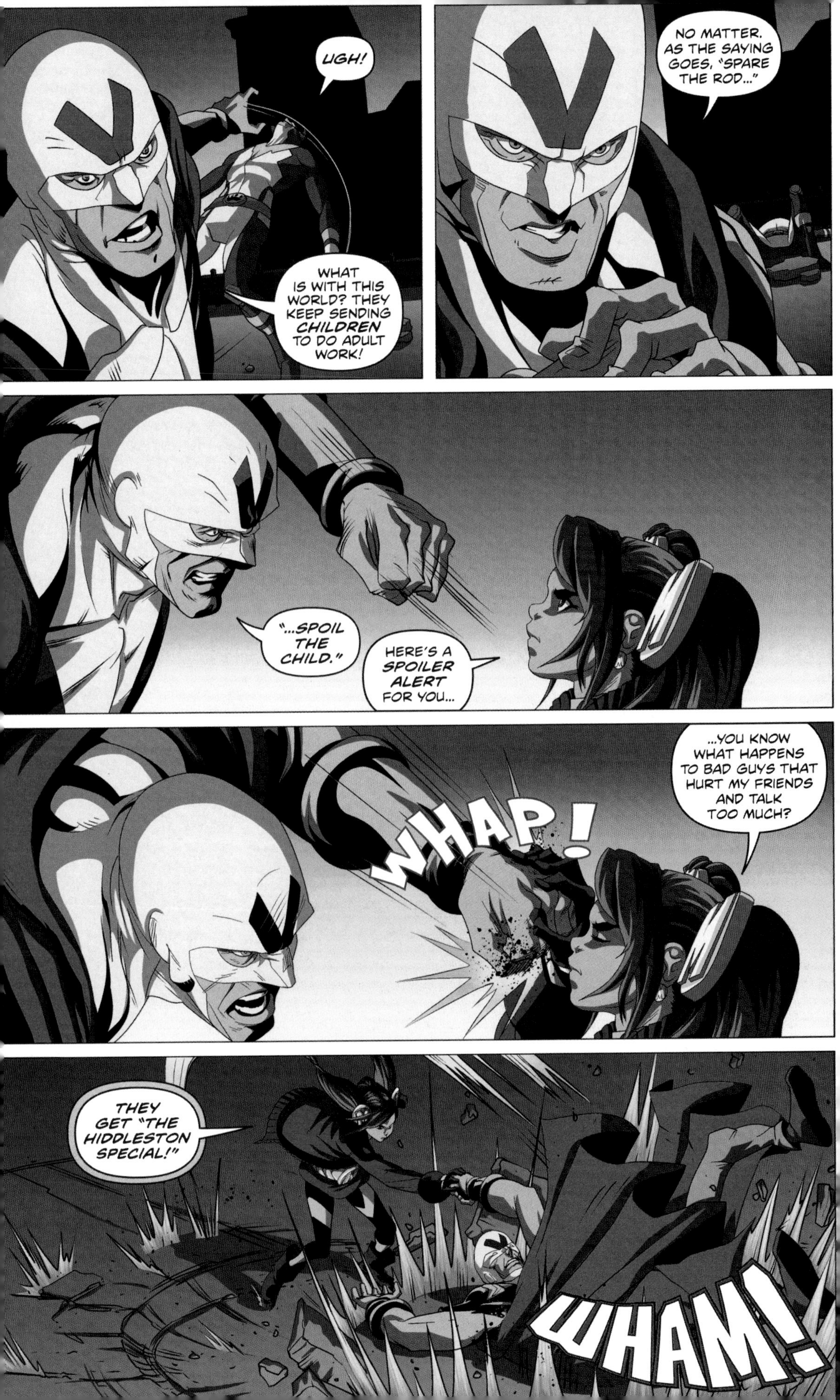
UGH!
WHAT IS WITH THIS WORLD? THEY KEEP SENDING CHILDREN TO DO ADULT WORK!
NO MATTER. AS THE SAYING GOES, "SPARE THE ROD..."
"...SPOIL THE CHILD."
HERE'S A SPOILER ALERT FOR YOU...
...YOU KNOW WHAT HAPPENS TO BAD GUYS THAT HURT MY FRIENDS AND TALK TOO MUCH?
WHAP!
THEY GET "THE HIDDLESTON SPECIAL!"
WHAM!

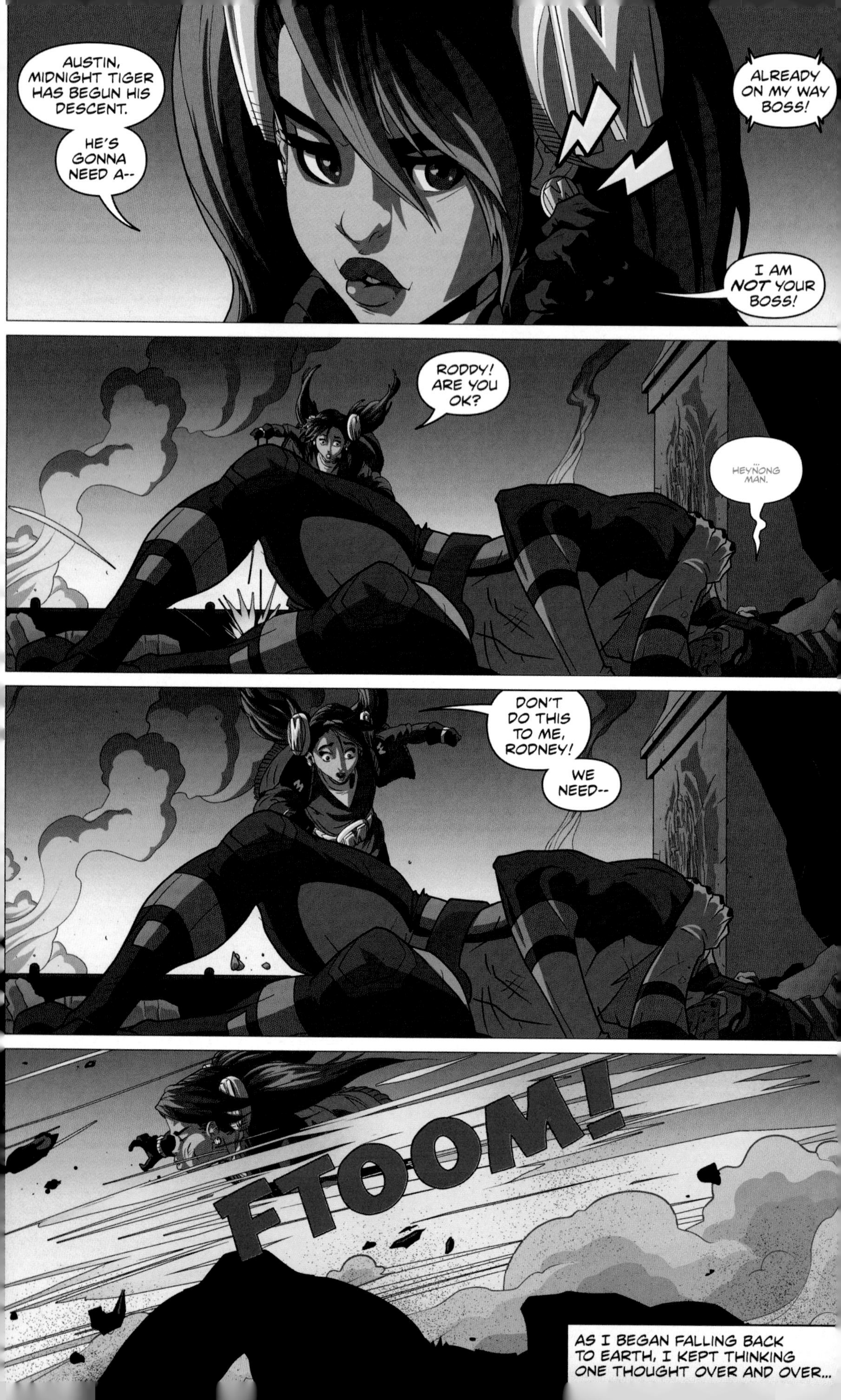
AUSTIN, MIDNIGHT TIGER HAS BEGUN HIS DESCENT.
HE'S GONNA NEED A--
ALREADY ON MY WAY BOSS!
I AM NOT YOUR BOSS!
RODDY! ARE YOU OK?
... HEY NONG MAN.
DON'T DO THIS TO ME, RODNEY!
WE NEED--
FTOOM!
AS I BEGAN FALLING BACK TO EARTH, I KEPT THINKING ONE THOUGHT OVER AND OVER...

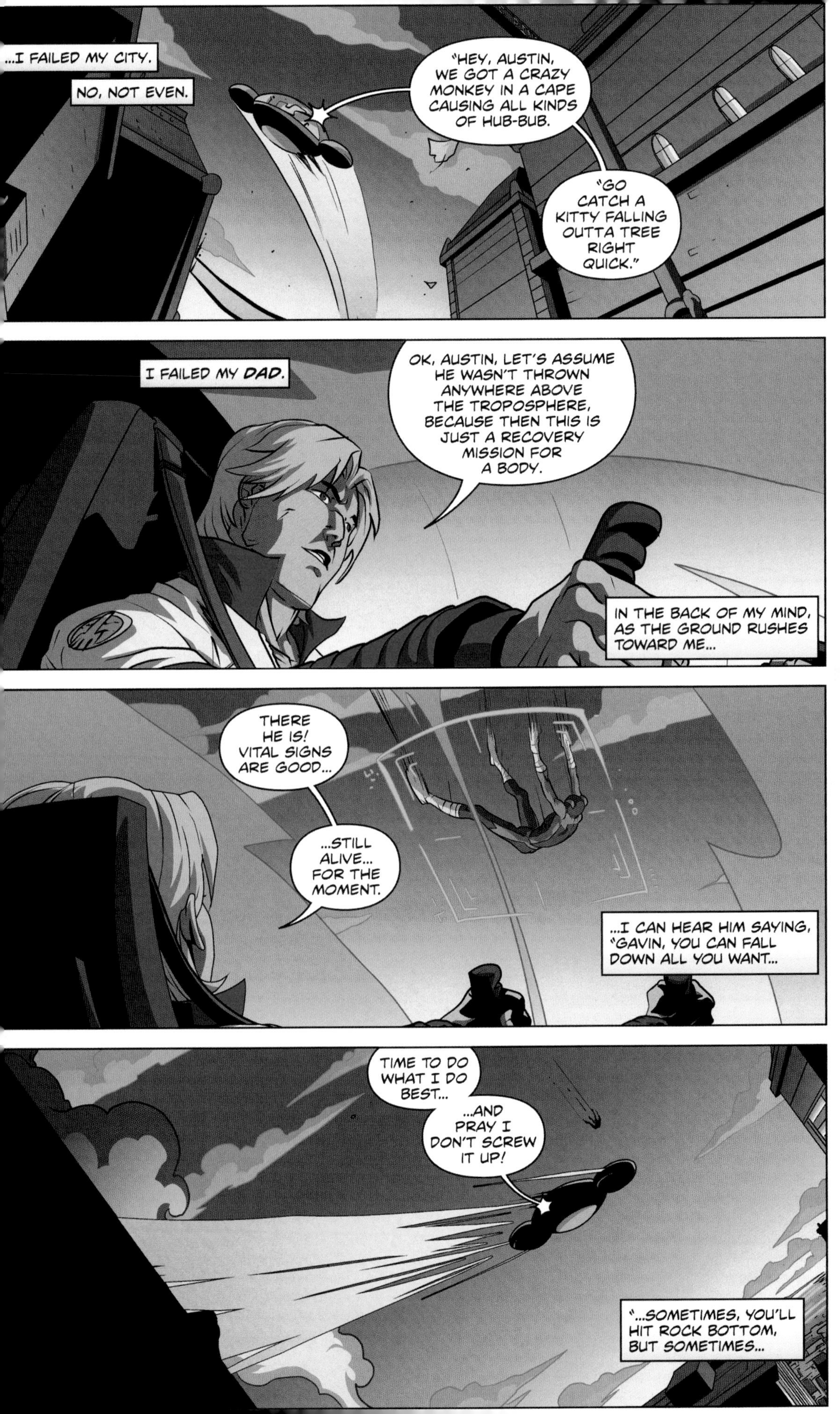
...I FAILED MY CITY.
NO, NOT EVEN.
"HEY, AUSTIN, WE GOT A CRAZY MONKEY IN A CAPE CAUSING ALL KINDS OF HUB-BUB.
"GO CATCH A KITTY FALLING OUTTA TREE RIGHT QUICK."
I FAILED MY *DAD*.
OK, AUSTIN, LET'S ASSUME HE WASN'T THROWN ANYWHERE ABOVE THE TROPOSPHERE, BECAUSE THEN THIS IS JUST A RECOVERY MISSION FOR A BODY.
IN THE BACK OF MY MIND, AS THE GROUND RUSHES TOWARD ME...
THERE HE IS! VITAL SIGNS ARE GOOD...
...STILL ALIVE... FOR THE MOMENT.
...I CAN HEAR HIM SAYING, "GAVIN, YOU CAN FALL DOWN ALL YOU WANT...
TIME TO DO WHAT I DO BEST...
...AND PRAY I DON'T SCREW IT UP!
"...SOMETIMES, YOU'LL HIT ROCK BOTTOM, BUT SOMETIMES...

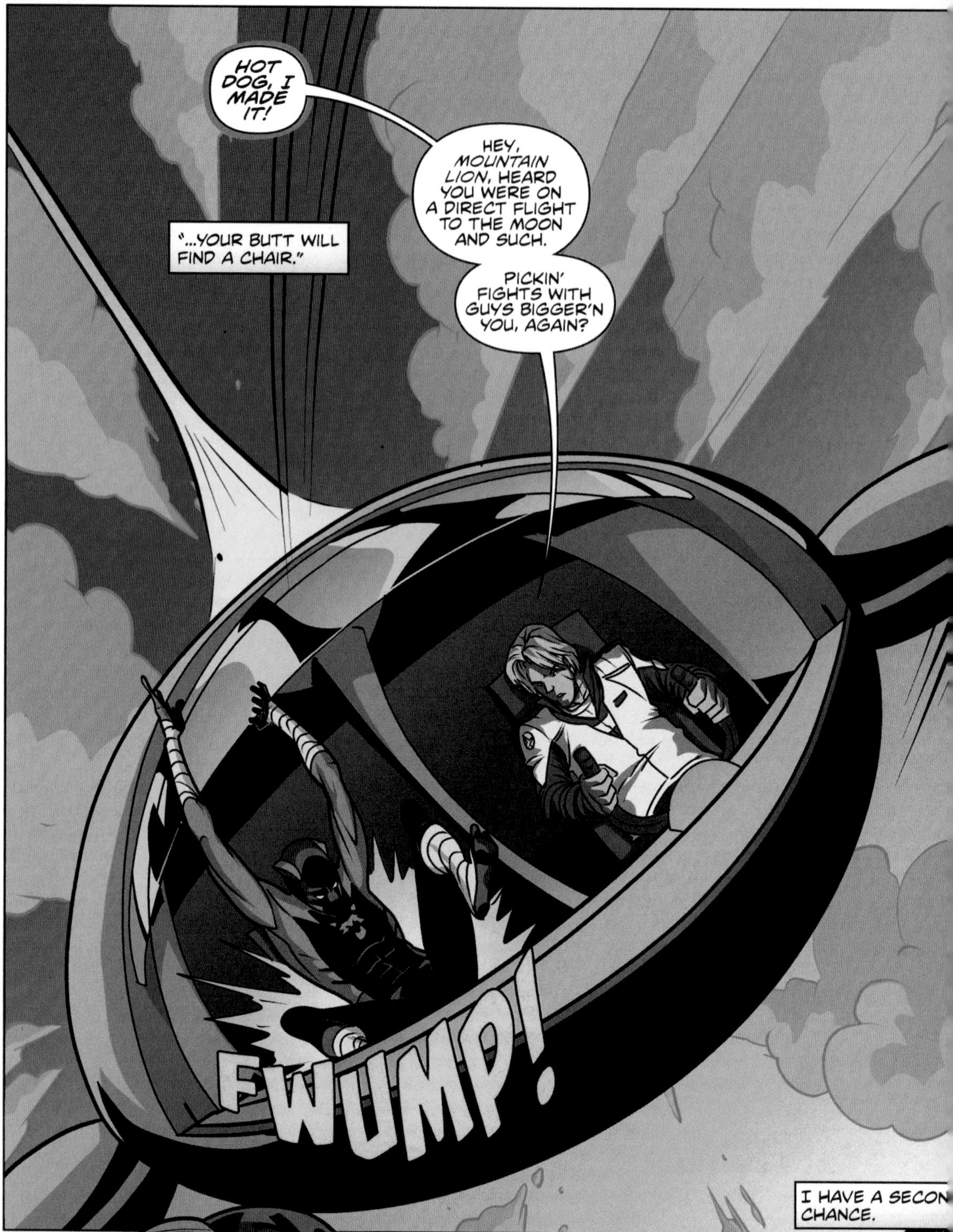
HOT DOG, I MADE IT!
"...YOUR BUTT WILL FIND A CHAIR."
HEY, MOUNTAIN LION, HEARD YOU WERE ON A DIRECT FLIGHT TO THE MOON AND SUCH.
PICKIN' FIGHTS WITH GUYS BIGGER'N YOU, AGAIN?
FWUMP!
I HAVE A SECON
CHANCE.

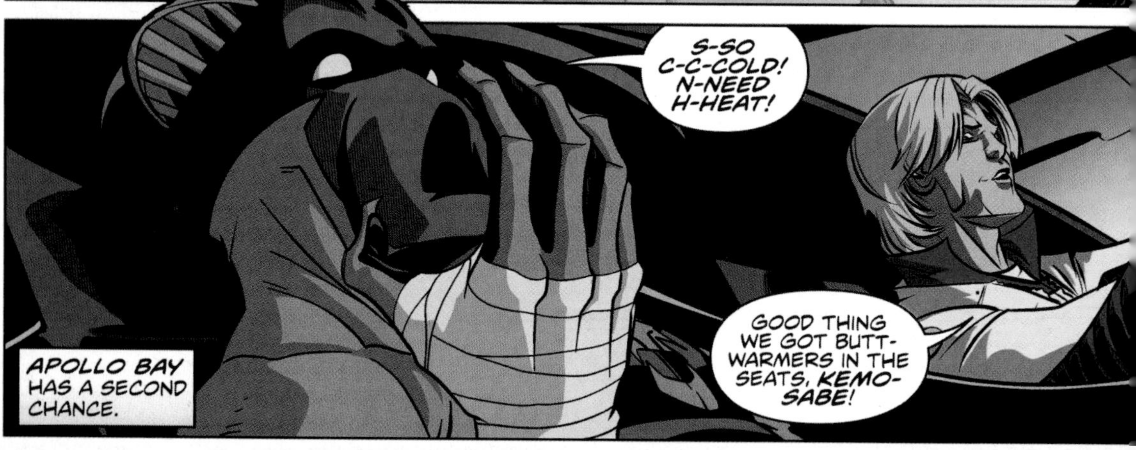
S-SO C-C-COLD! N-NEED H-HEAT!
GOOD THING WE GOT BUTT-WARMERS IN THE SEATS, KEMO-SABE!
APOLLO BAY HAS A SECOND CHANCE.

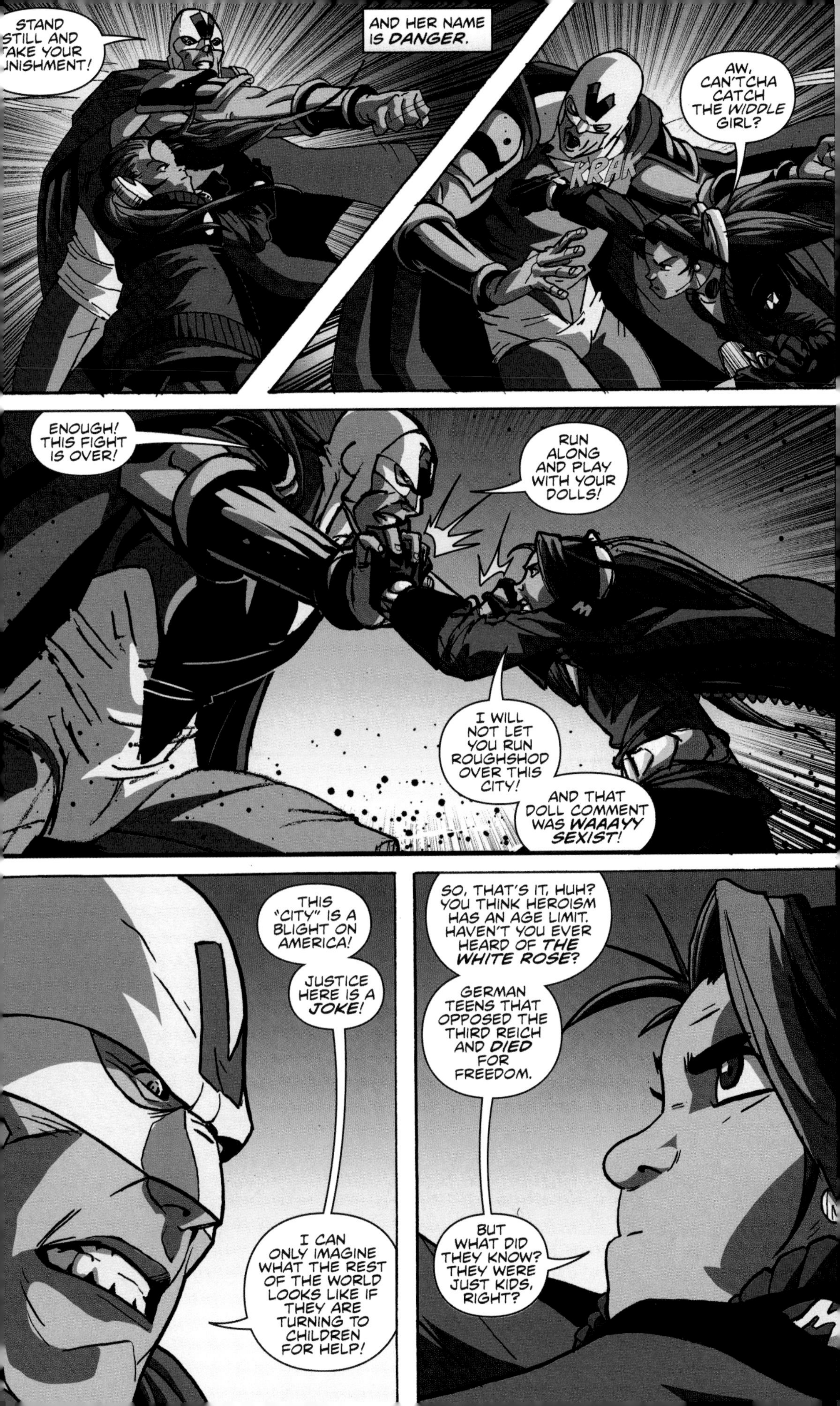
STAND STILL AND TAKE YOUR PUNISHMENT!
AND HER NAME IS DANGER.
AW, CAN'TCHA CATCH THE WIDDLE GIRL?
KRAK
ENOUGH! THIS FIGHT IS OVER!
RUN ALONG AND PLAY WITH YOUR DOLLS!
I WILL NOT LET YOU RUN ROUGHSHOD OVER THIS CITY!
AND THAT DOLL COMMENT WAS WAAAYY SEXIST!
THIS "CITY" IS A BLIGHT ON AMERICA!
JUSTICE HERE IS A JOKE!
I CAN ONLY IMAGINE WHAT THE REST OF THE WORLD LOOKS LIKE IF THEY ARE TURNING TO CHILDREN FOR HELP!
SO, THAT'S IT, HUH? YOU THINK HEROISM HAS AN AGE LIMIT. HAVEN'T YOU EVER HEARD OF THE WHITE ROSE?
GERMAN TEENS THAT OPPOSED THE THIRD REICH AND DIED FOR FREEDOM.
BUT WHAT DID THEY KNOW? THEY WERE JUST KIDS, RIGHT?

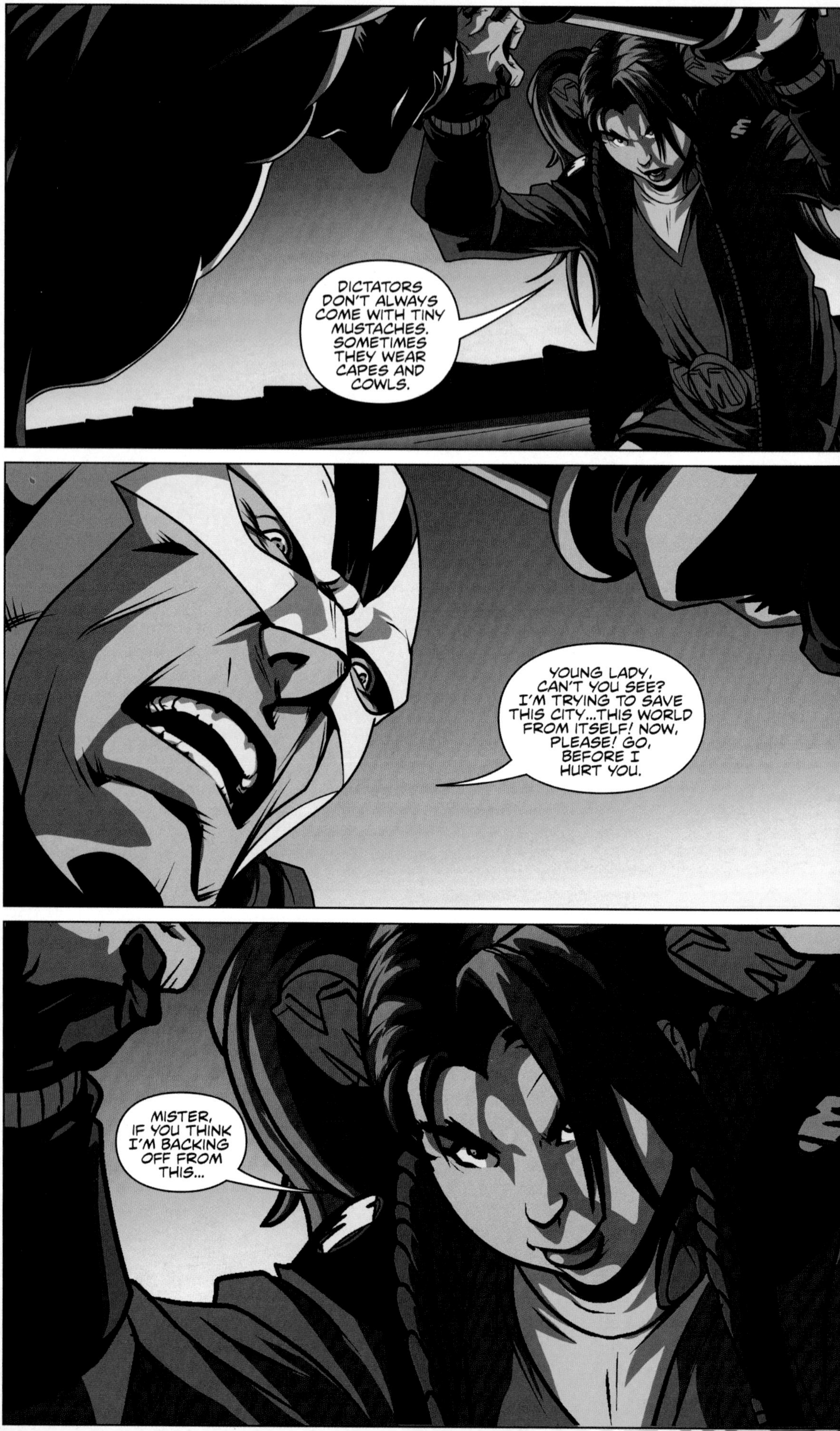
DICTATORS DON'T ALWAYS COME WITH TINY MUSTACHES. SOMETIMES THEY WEAR CAPES AND COWLS.
YOUNG LADY, CAN'T YOU SEE? I'M TRYING TO SAVE THIS CITY...THIS WORLD FROM ITSELF! NOW, PLEASE! GO, BEFORE I HURT YOU.
MISTER, IF YOU THINK I'M BACKING OFF FROM THIS...

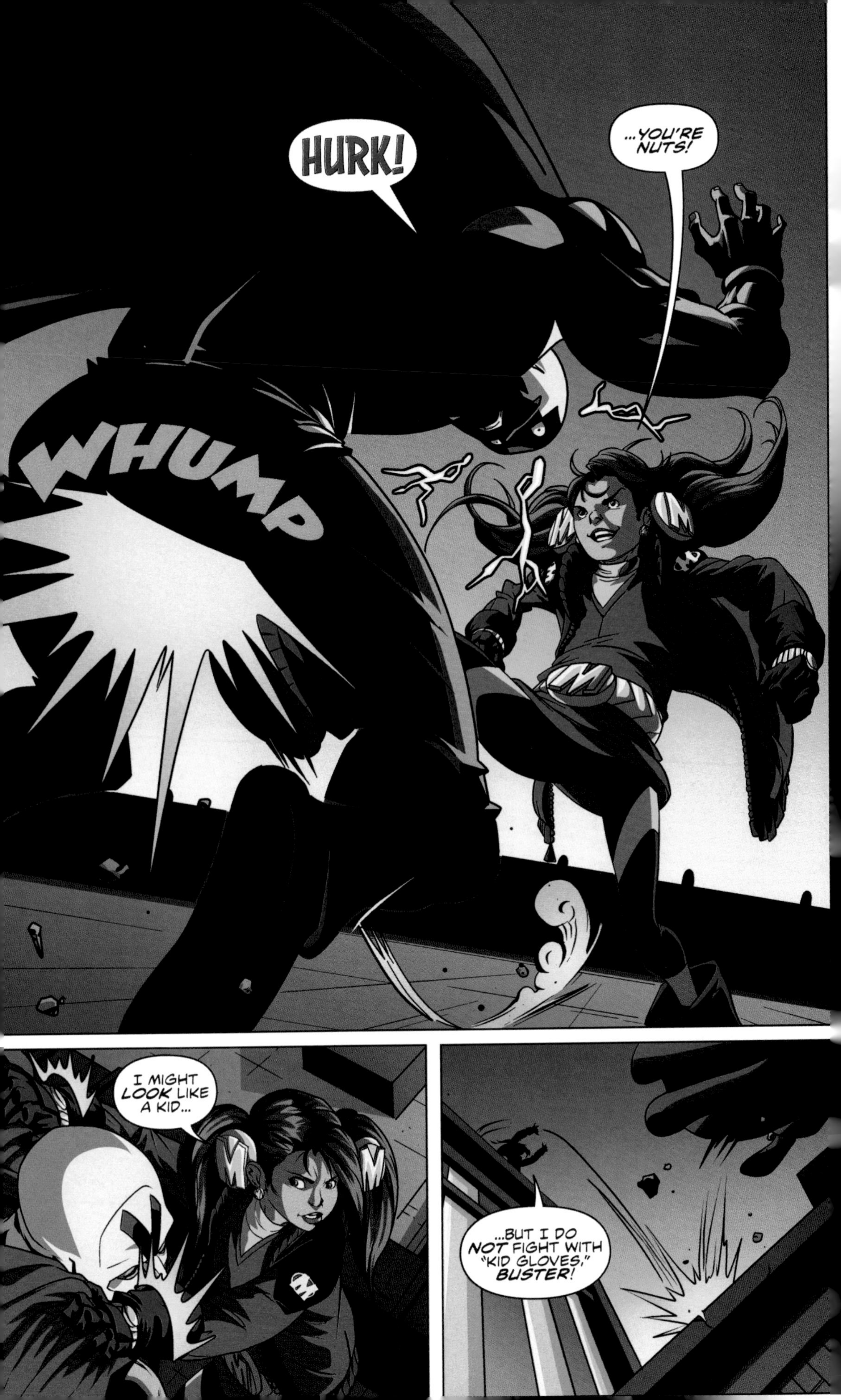
HURK!
...YOU'RE NUTS!
WHUMP
I MIGHT LOOK LIKE A KID...
...BUT I DO NOT FIGHT WITH "KID GLOVES," BUSTER!

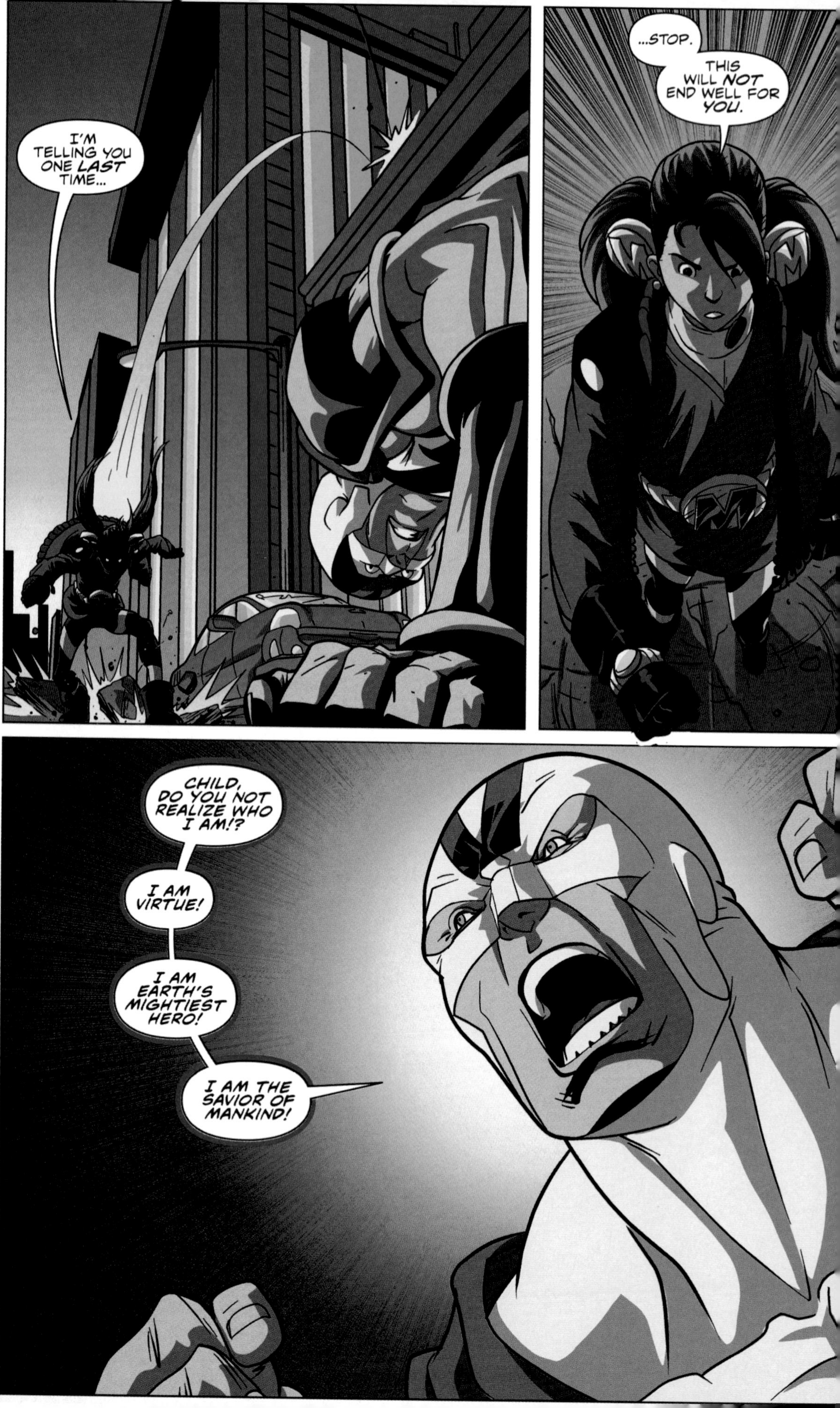
I'M TELLING YOU ONE LAST TIME...
...STOP.
THIS WILL NOT END WELL FOR YOU.
CHILD, DO YOU NOT REALIZE WHO I AM!?
I AM VIRTUE!
I AM EARTH'S MIGHTIEST HERO!
I AM THE SAVIOR OF MANKIND!

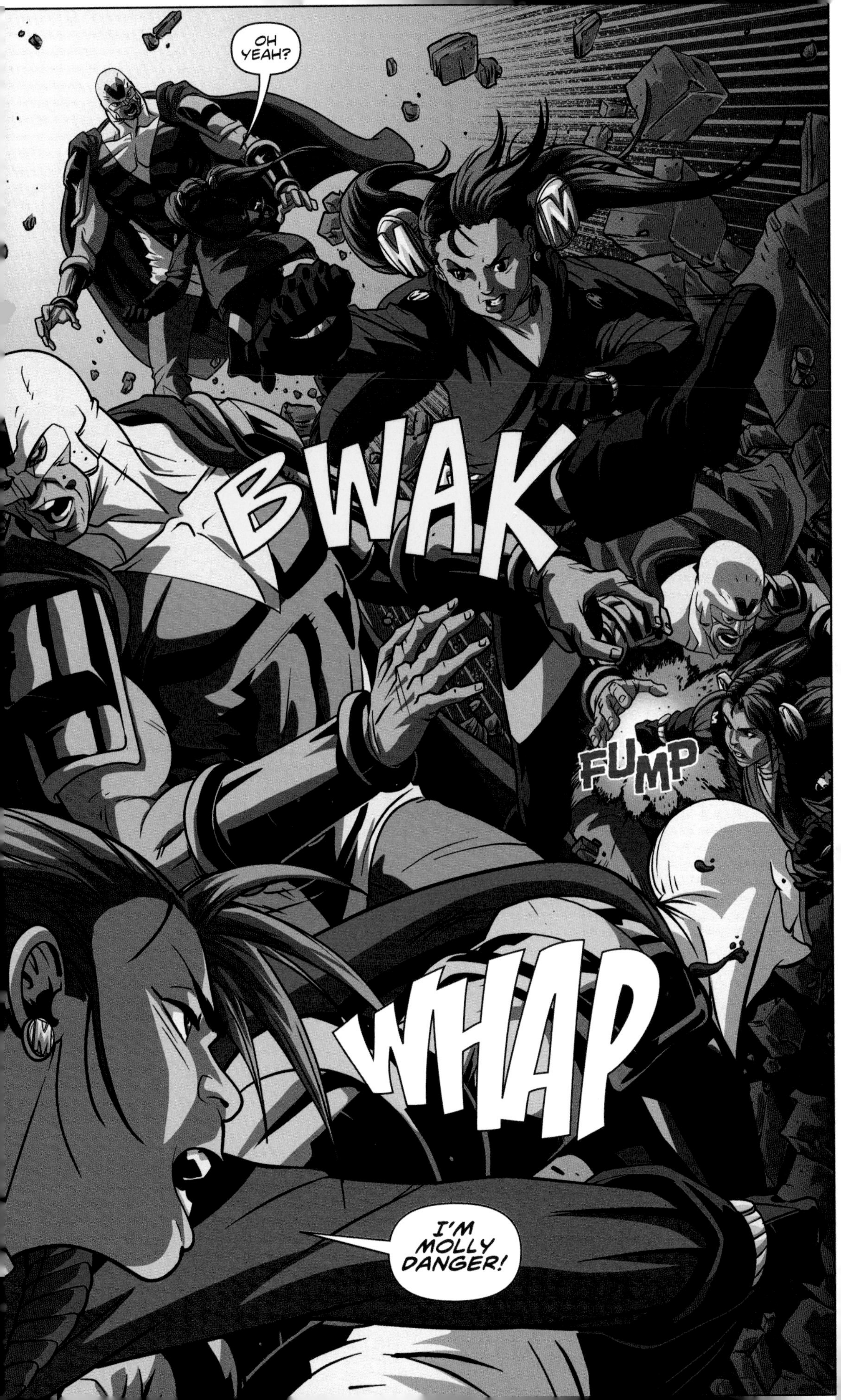

OH YEAH?
BWAK
FUMP
WHAP
I'M MOLLY DANGER!

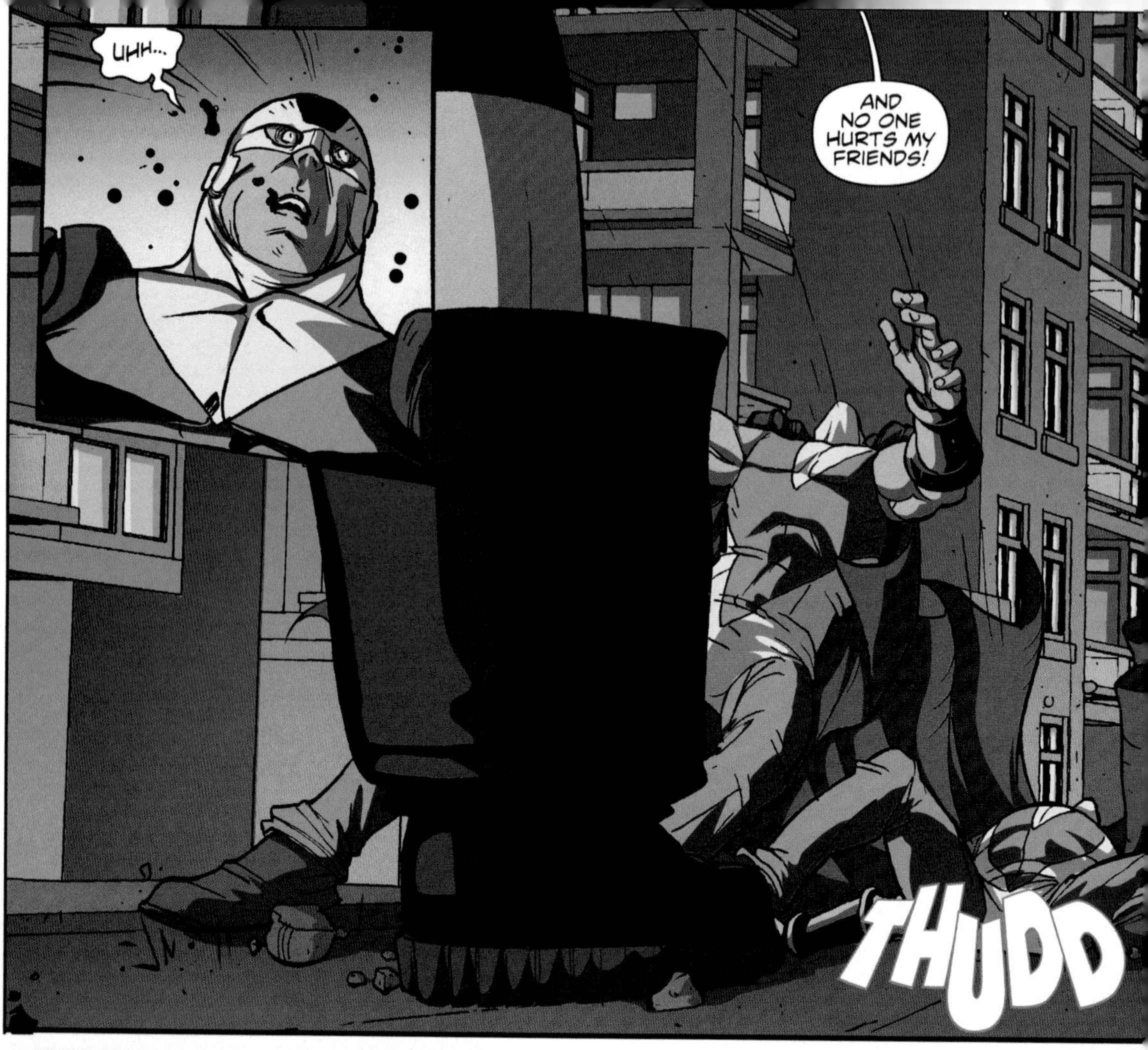
UHH...
AND NO ONE HURTS MY FRIENDS!
THUDD

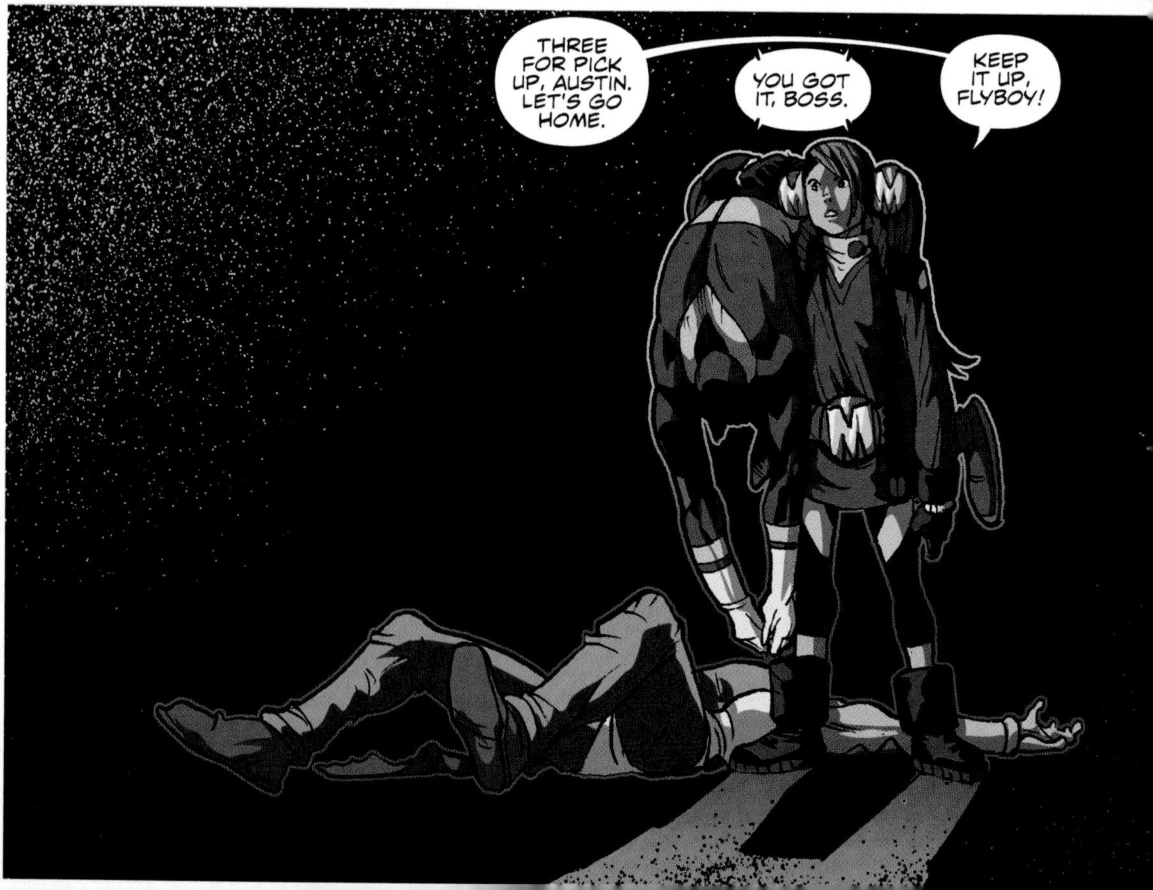
THREE FOR PICK UP, AUSTIN. LET'S GO HOME.
YOU GOT IT, BOSS.
KEEP IT UP, FLYBOY!

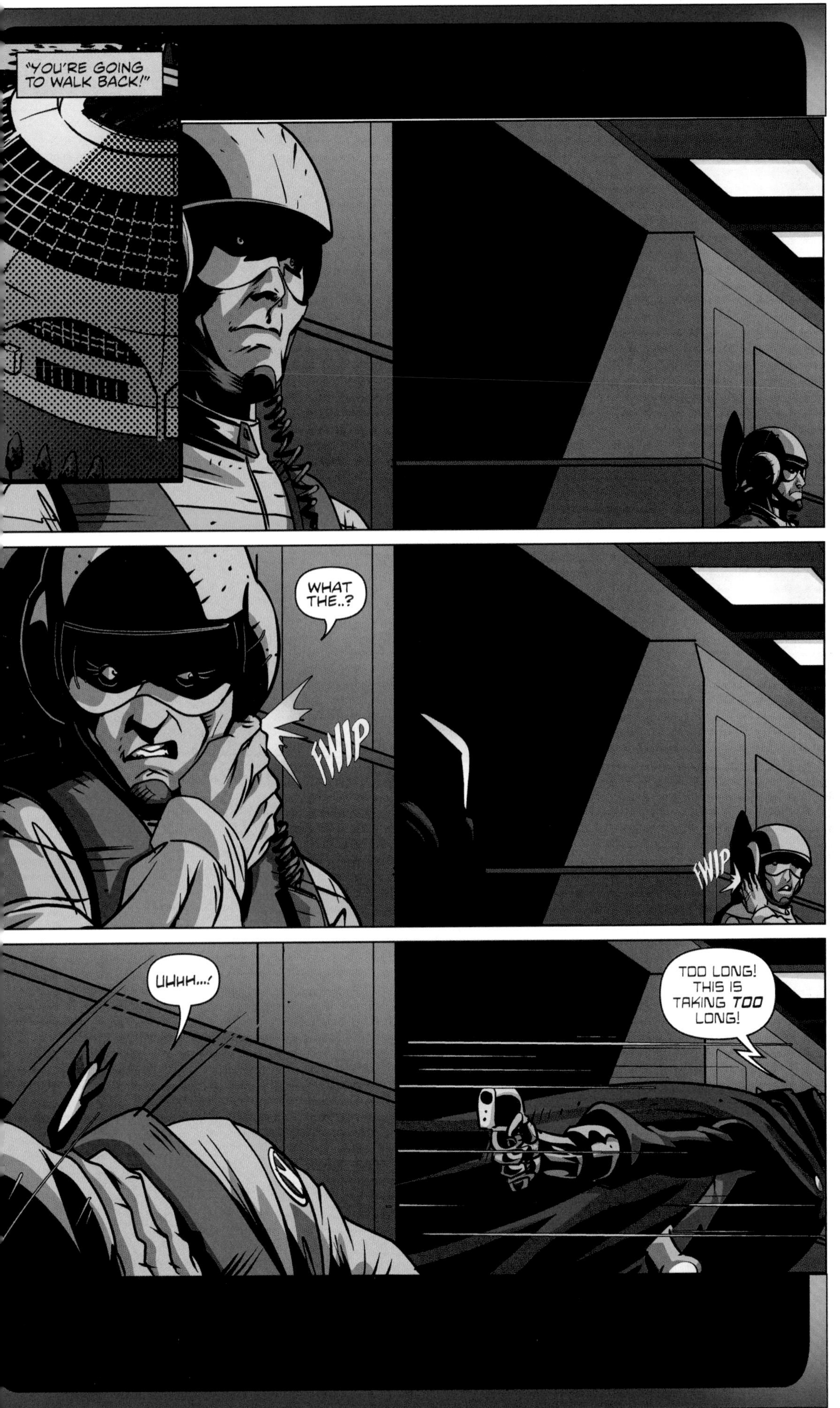
"YOU'RE GOING TO WALK BACK!"
WHAT THE..?
FWIP
FWIP
UHHH...!
TOO LONG! THIS IS TAKING *TOO* LONG!

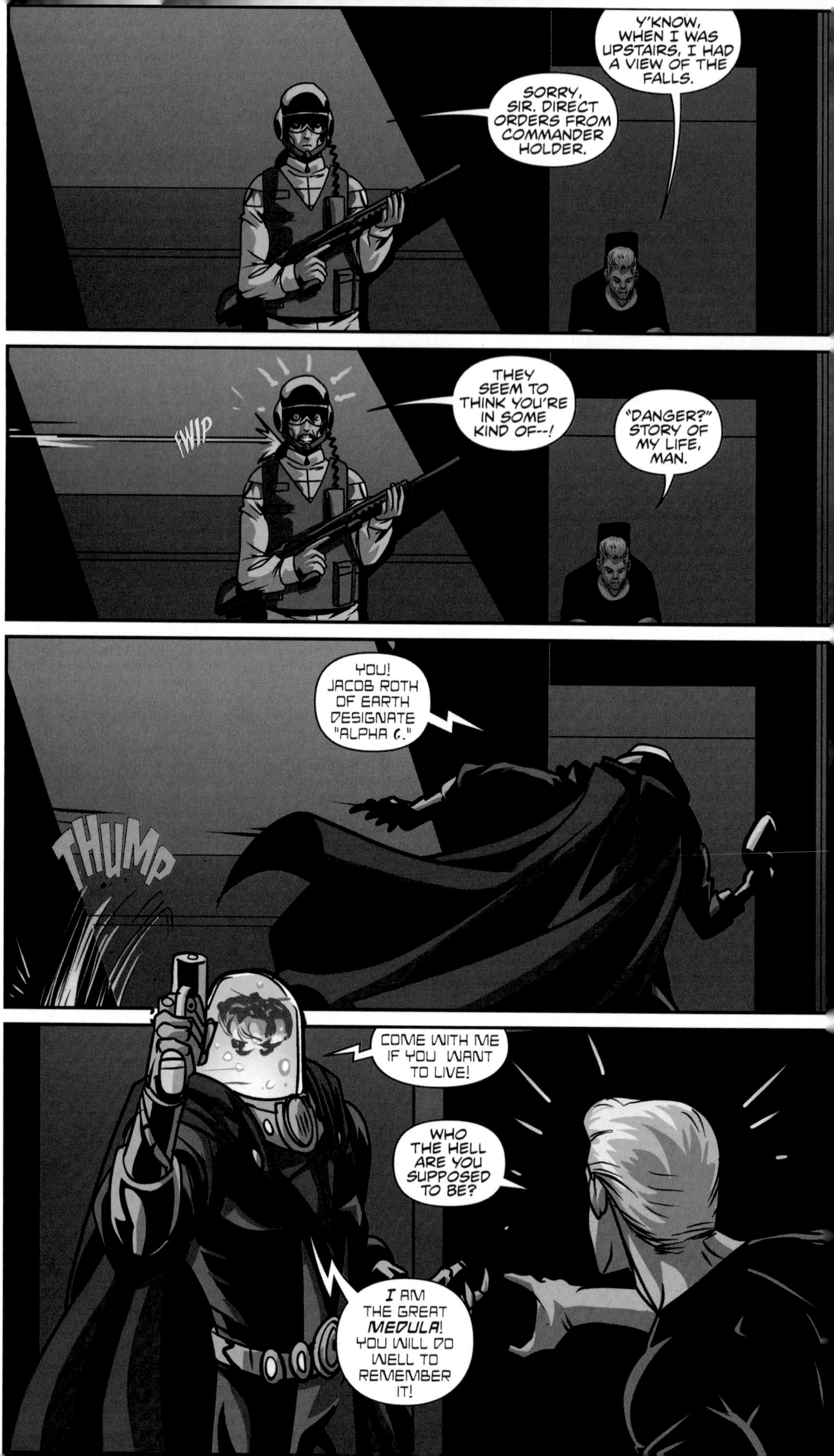
Y'KNOW, WHEN I WAS UPSTAIRS, I HAD A VIEW OF THE FALLS.
SORRY, SIR. DIRECT ORDERS FROM COMMANDER HOLDER.
"DANGER?" STORY OF MY LIFE, MAN.
THEY SEEM TO THINK YOU'RE IN SOME KIND OF--!
FWIP
YOU! JACOB ROTH OF EARTH DESIGNATE "ALPHA 6."
THUMP
COME WITH ME IF YOU WANT TO LIVE!
WHO THE HELL ARE YOU SUPPOSED TO BE?
I AM THE GREAT MEDULA! YOU WILL DO WELL TO REMEMBER IT!

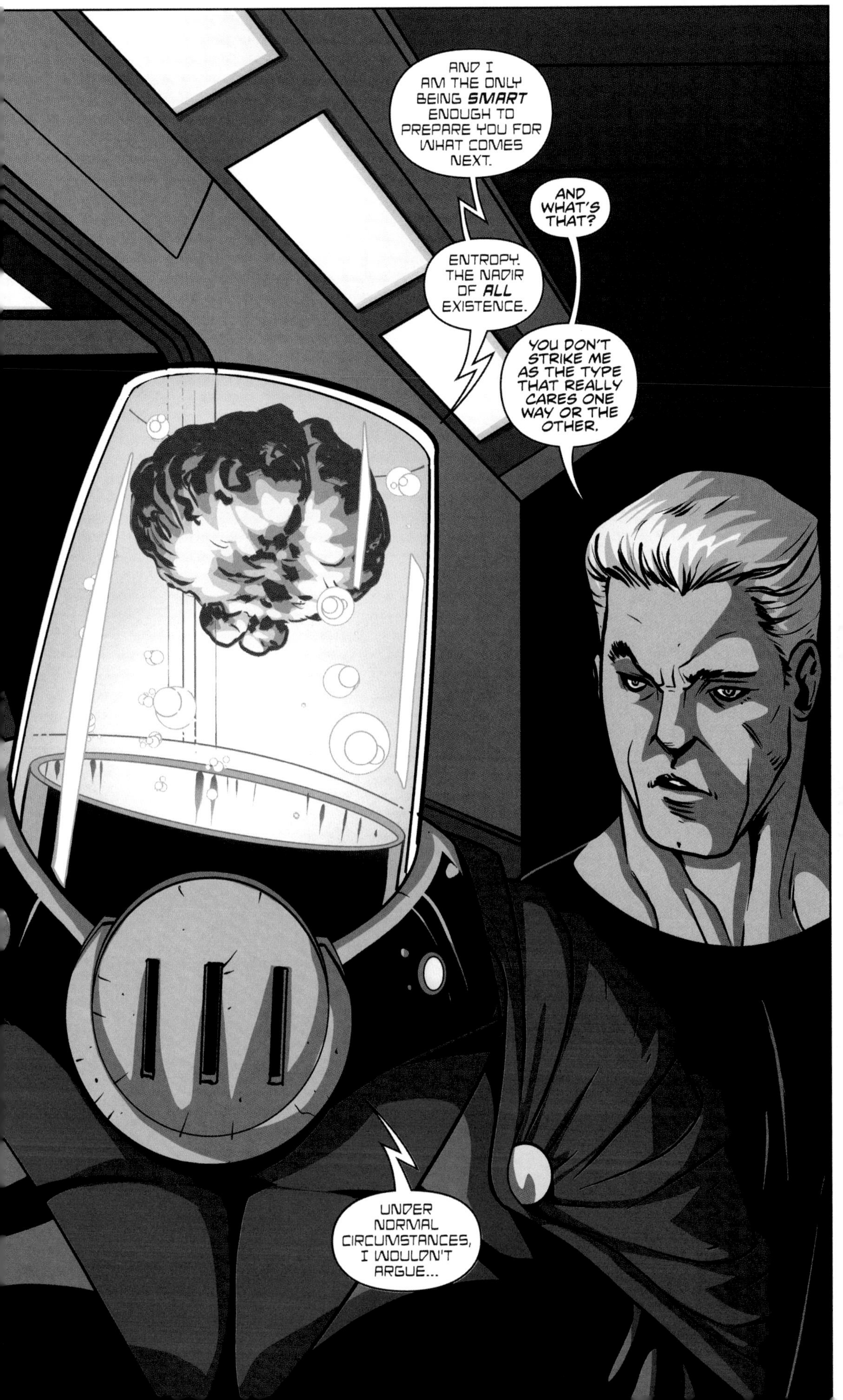
AND I AM THE ONLY BEING SMART ENOUGH TO PREPARE YOU FOR WHAT COMES NEXT.
AND WHAT'S THAT?
ENTROPY. THE NADIR OF ALL EXISTENCE.
YOU DON'T STRIKE ME AS THE TYPE THAT REALLY CARES ONE WAY OR THE OTHER.
UNDER NORMAL CIRCUMSTANCES, I WOULDN'T ARGUE...

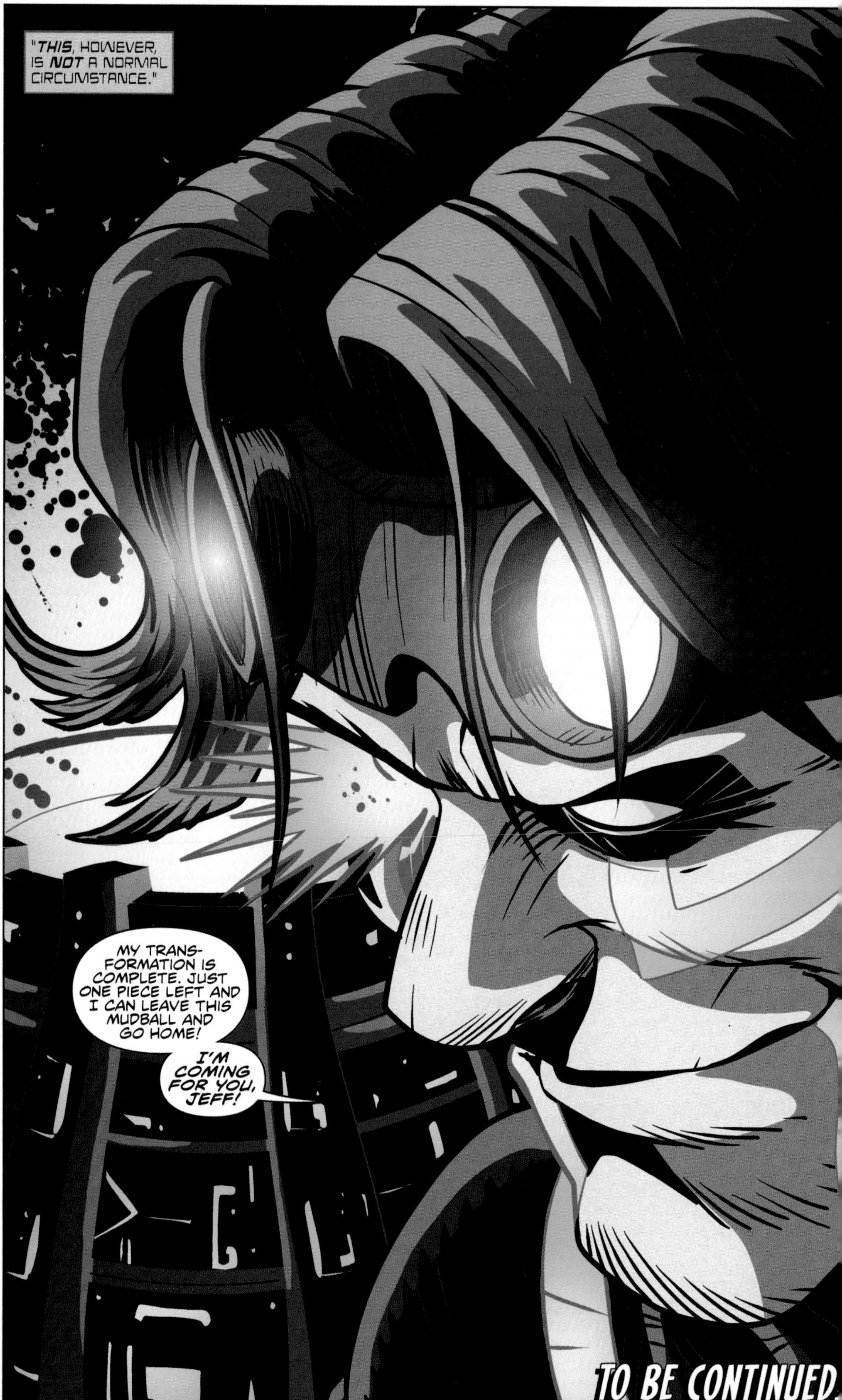
"THIS, HOWEVER, IS NOT A NORMAL CIRCUMSTANCE."
MY TRANSFORMATION IS COMPLETE. JUST ONE PIECE LEFT AND I CAN LEAVE THIS MUDBALL AND GO HOME!
I'M COMING FOR YOU, JEFF!
TO BE CONTINUED.

MIDNIGHT TIGER

PERSONAL DATA

Alter Ego: Gavin Matthew Shaw
Occupation: High School Student, Adventurer
Marital Status: Single
Known Relatives: Robert Frank Shaw (father), Rebecca Anne Shaw (mother), April King (sister)
Group Affiliation: The Icons (recruit/reserve member)
Base of Operations: Apollo Bay, California
First Appearance: MIDNIGHT TIGER #1
Height: 5' 9" **Weight**: 160 lbs
Eyes: Brown **Hair**: Black

HISTORY

Gavin Shaw is a young high school senior living in Apollo Bay, one of the toughest cities in California. Gavin's greatest desire was to find a way to do what the police had never been capable of doing...Release the stranglehold the gangs and drug dealers have had on his hometown.

On his way home from visiting his best friend, Dex, Gavin stumbles across the hero known as Lionsblood (a member of the superhero team called The Icons) who had been badly injured in an alley. Quickly running to the hero's aid, Gavin unknowingly placed himself in the line of fire between Lionsblood and the beast known as the Hyena who, moments before, he had gravely injured. After contacting the police and acting as a shield to protect the fallen hero, Gavin suffered a mortal wound delivered by the villain before he fled the scene.

Gavin awoke in a hospital bed almost completely healed after being in a coma for three days. Surprised that he was even still alive, the teenager would soon realize that Lionsblood, in an effort to save the boy's life, had to inject him with the same serum that gave the hero his powers. Unfortunately, his would-be mentor died shortly after saving the teenager's life which left Gavin having to figure things out on his own.

Wanting to put his new found abilities to good use and finally having the means to do something about the crime that ravages Apollo Bay, Gavin, inspired by heroes like the Doberman and Manticore, became the crime-fighter known as Midnight Tiger. Soon, he began to catch the attention of major criminals which he knew he had no hope of handling on his own. This prompted him to seek training from the ICONS Project, whom he initially turned down for membership after discovering they wanted to move him away from Apollo Bay. The Icons are a government sanctioned superhero team spearheaded by former superhero turned cop, Lt. Grant Goodrich. They're composed of young, moderately experienced heroes who stepped in during cases where the local authorities or even S.H.E.R.I.F.F. (Super Human Enforcement, Retrieval, and Investigation: Federal Facility) aren't capable of handling super-powered incidents. Though lacking the sufficient experience, Gavin is determined to protect the city of Apollo Bay from any and all threats and one day become one of the greatest heroes ever known.

POWERS & WEAPONS

Midnight Tiger possesses a number of superhuman attributes that are a result of a combination of a genetically altered version of ailuranthropy (a cousin to the virus that causes lycanthropy) and the anomalies found in Gavin's own DNA. Prof. Thaddeus Hadaway (Lionsblood), who had been infected by a direct strain of ailuranthropy himself, performed many genetic manipulations on the virus in order to cure it, but was ultimately unsuccessful. However, he did develop a strain that gave him more control of his bestial form that enabled him to retain his intelligence and personality no matter how animal-like his physiology transformed. Presumably, after testing Gavin's blood to gauge it's compatibility based on his specific DNA, a modified version of this strain was developed as a serum and administered to teenage Shaw during his coma.

Unlike Lionsblood who carried the original base virus for ailuranthropy despite his genetic tampering, Gavin does not undergo an outward physical transformation into a were-cat. So, aside from retractable claws on both hands and feet and canines that can grow at will (all capable of tearing through about 2" of steel coupled with his strength), his enhanced abilities have become innate and on the genetic level and he retains a human appearance.

Gavin's superhuman physical attributes of catlike strength (2 tons), speed, intelligence, agility, durability, flexibility, reflexes/reactions, coordination, balance, endurance and a kind of pheromone scent he gives off (which he calls his musk) reflect his namesake.

Though Gavin is still vulnerable to disease and illness, his enhanced physiology makes him capable of healing injuries superhumanly faster and more extensively than ordinary humans, including injuries as severe as broken bones or gunshot wounds within a matter of minutes.

He possesses superhumanly acute senses. His sense of touch is enhanced to the extent that he is able to feel the slightest variations on any surface. His vision and hearing are enhanced in a similar manner, enabling him to both see and hear sights and sounds that ordinary humans can't and to see and hear at much greater distances and in the dark. He also possesses a superhumanly acute sense of smell that he uses to track a target by scent.

Gavin originally utilized a freestyle version of Capoiera, but relied heavily on his enhanced abilities to compensate for his current lack of skill. However, he has begun training at Icons headquarters in several forms of martial arts disciplines best suited to his abilities by Wraith, the Icons combat instructor.

Midnight Tiger created by and ™ Ray-Anthony Height

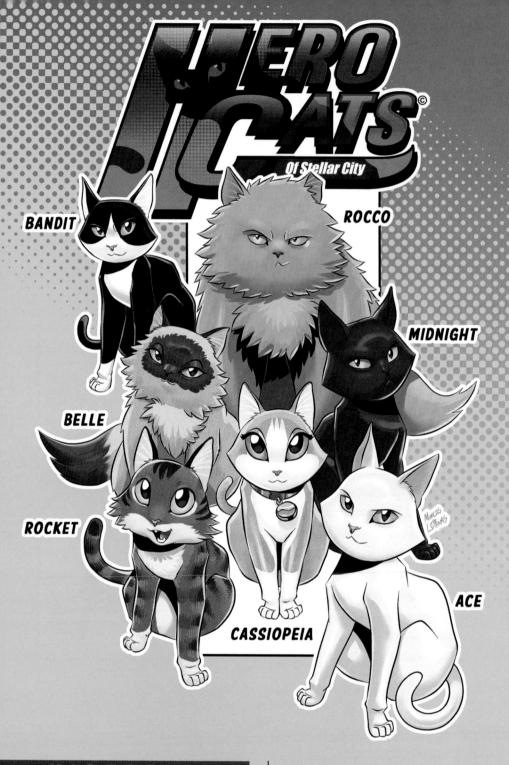

HERO CATS
Of Stellar City

BANDIT

ROCCO

MIDNIGHT

BELLE

ROCKET

CASSIOPEIA

ACE

HISTORY

There's more to the cats of Stellar City than people might imagine.
No costumes?
No capes?
No problem!
Hero Cats always find a way to save the day.

Ace, their fearless leader, has assembled quite an amazing team. Each cat is highly trained and has unique skills.

Midnight can leap from building to building and has a never ending grudge against criminals.
Belle can read people's minds and, despite her questionable past, she is wise beyond her years.

Rocket is the fastest cat in the world and loves computers. He also claims to be from outer space.
Rocco never loses a fight and loves movies.
Bandit is an undercover agent and specializes in acquiring rare items.
Cassiopeia is the most powerful of them all. She can read! This comes in very handy when the team is out on missions.

Cassiopeia also lives with the local super powered trouble magnets, **Galaxy Man** & **Cosmic Girl**.

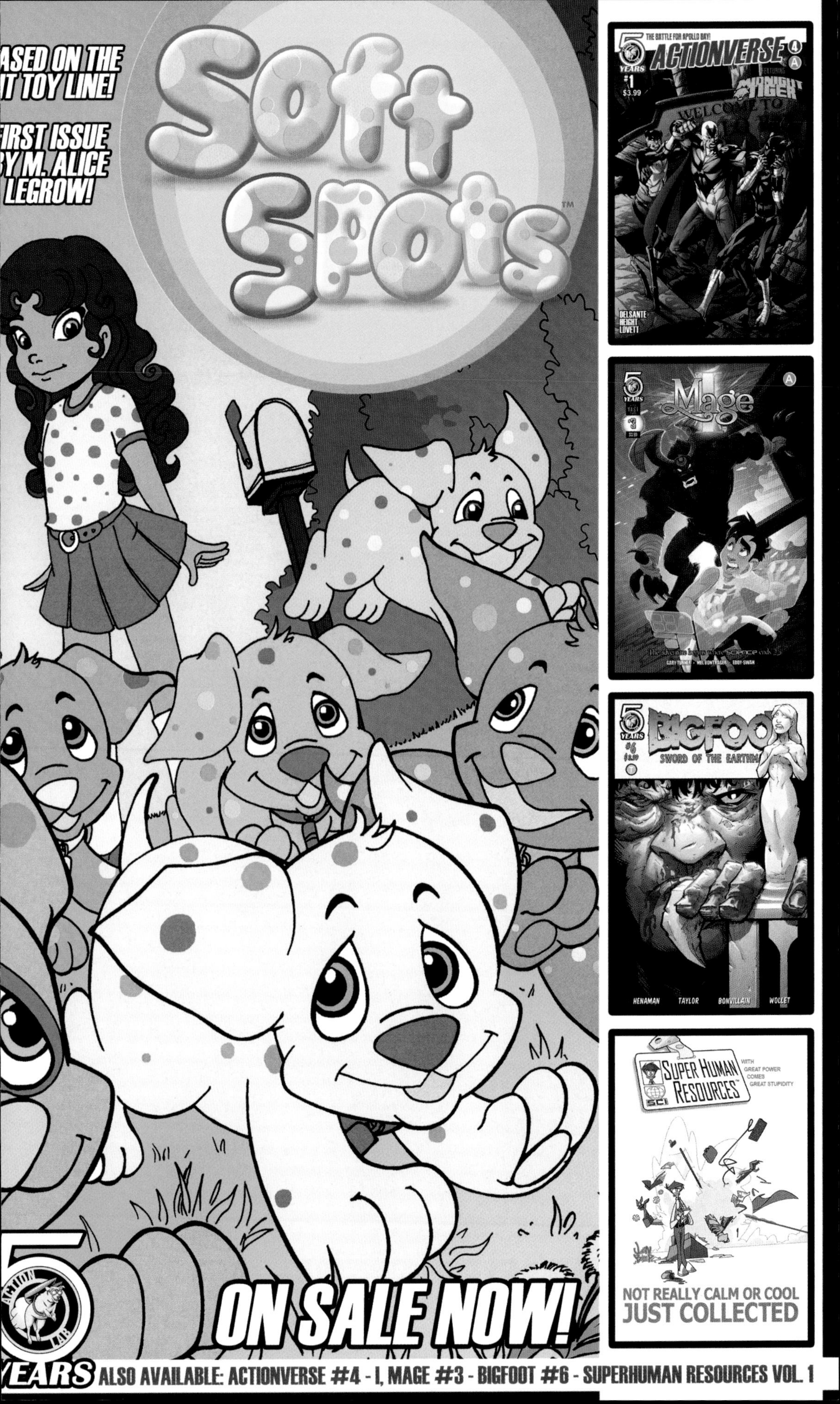
ASED ON THE
IT TOY LINE!
FIRST ISSUE
BY M. ALICE
LEGROW!
Soft Spots™
THE BATTLE FOR APOLLO BAY!
ACTIONVERSE
#1
$3.99
DELSANTE
HEIGHT
LOVETT
Mage
#3
The adventure begins where science ends
BIGFOO
SWORD OF THE EARTHM
#6
HENAMAN TAYLOR BONVILLAIN WOLLET
SUPER HUMAN RESOURCES™
WITH GREAT POWER COMES GREAT STUPIDITY
NOT REALLY CALM OR COOL
JUST COLLECTED
ON SALE NOW!
5 YEARS
ALSO AVAILABLE: ACTIONVERSE #4 - I, MAGE #3 - BIGFOOT #6 - SUPERHUMAN RESOURCES VOL. 1

FROM SCOTT FOGG, VITO DELSAN
ROSY HIGGINS AND TED BRAN

ACTION LAB: DOG OF WONDER

FEATURING A COVER BY COMICS LEGEND NEAL ADAMS!

AVAILABLE IN FINER STORES EVERYWHER

For five years, readers have looked at the Action Lab Entertainment logo and wondered "Who IS that dog with the jet pack?" Wonder no more! The story you never thought would be told is now an ongoing monthly title as ACTION LAB, DOG OF WONDER, comes to comic book shelves everywhere!

COMIC COLLECTOR LIVE

COMIC MARKETPLACE

YOUR FAVORITE

BUY.
SELL.
ORGANIZE

TRY IT FREE!

WWW.COMICCOLLECTORLIVE.CO

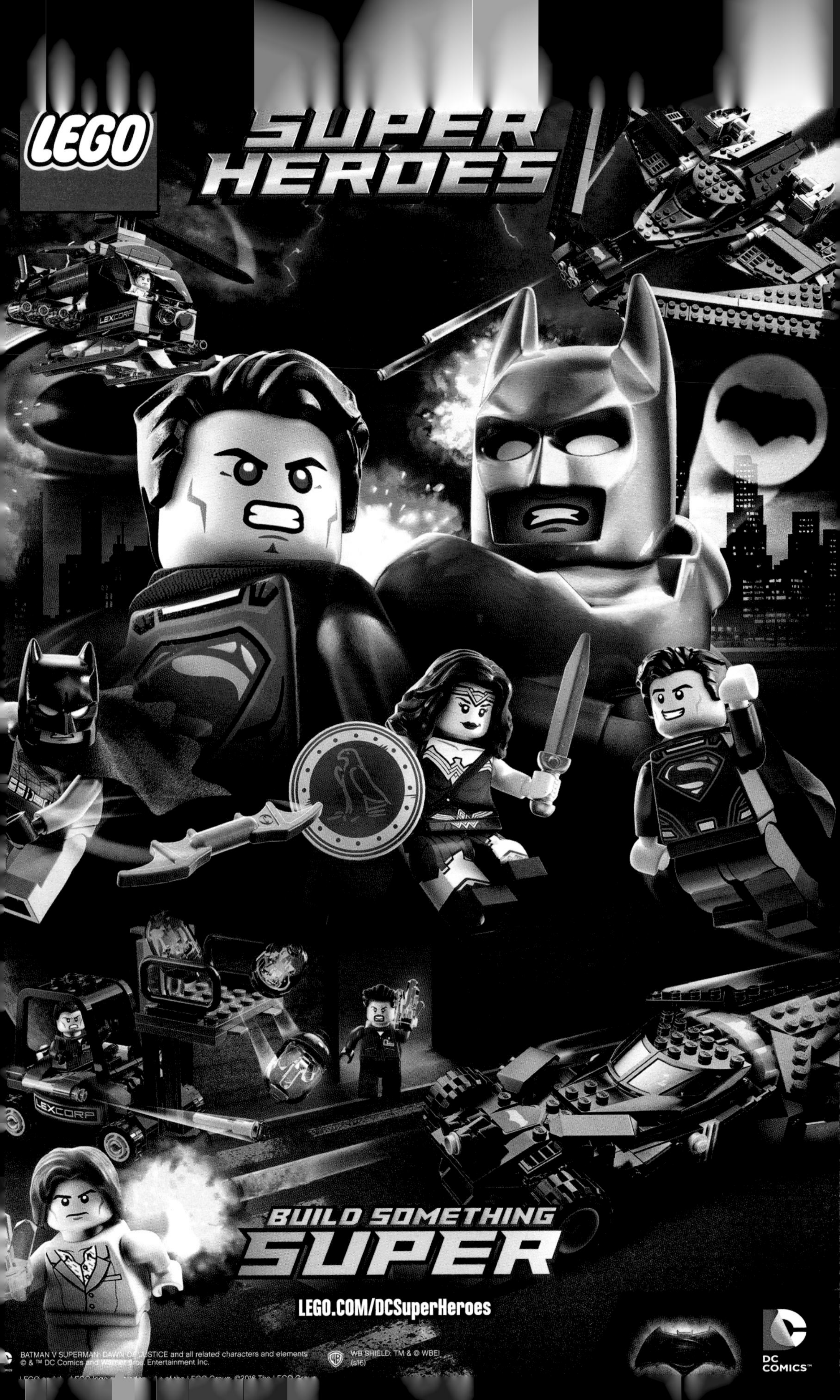

LEGO
SUPER HEROES
LEXCORP
BUILD SOMETHING
SUPER
LEGO.COM/DCSuperHeroes
BATMAN V SUPERMAN: DAWN OF JUSTICE and all related characters and elements © & ™ DC Comics and Warner Bros. Entertainment Inc.
WB SHIELD: TM & © WBEI (s16)
DC COMICS

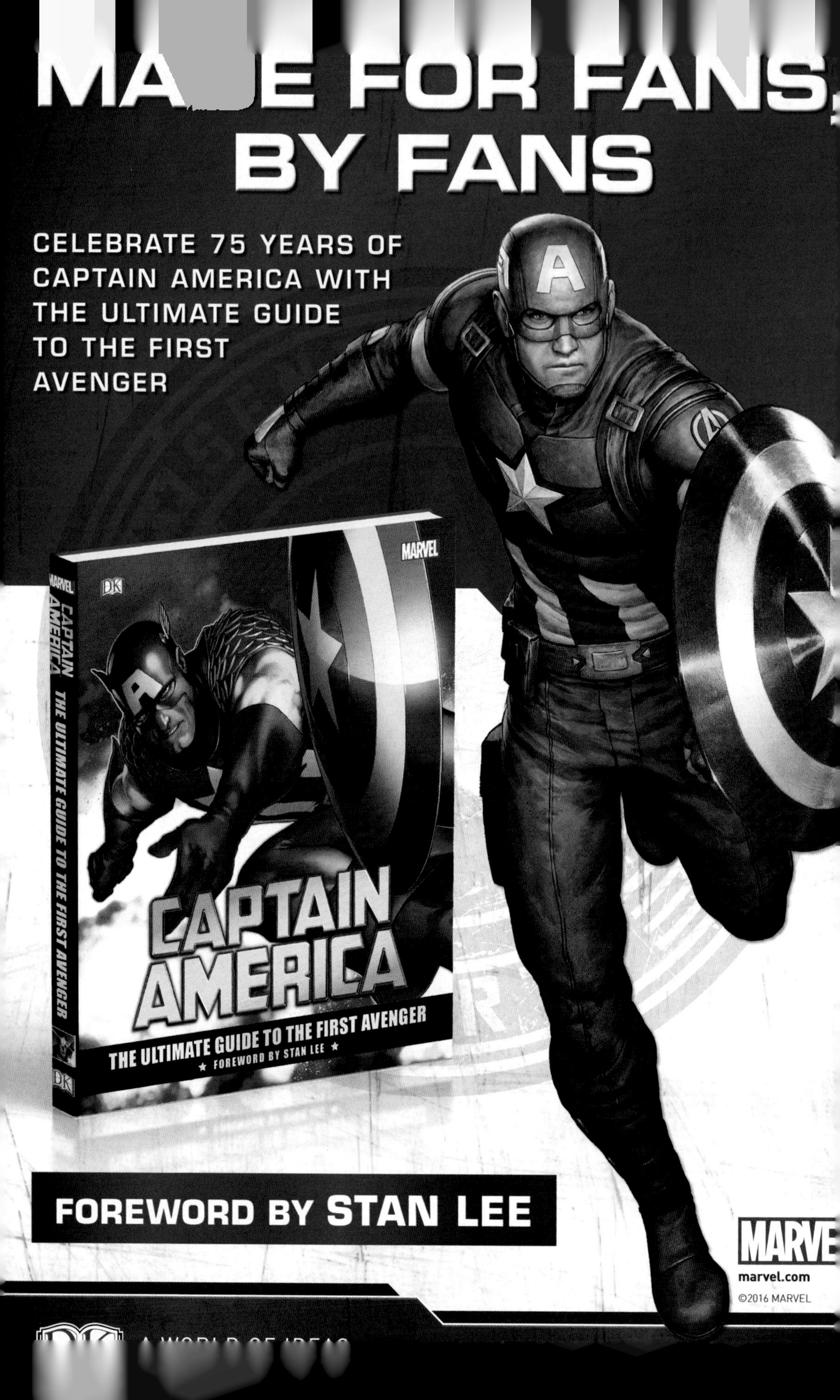
MA E FOR FANS,
BY FANS
CELEBRATE 75 YEARS OF CAPTAIN AMERICA WITH THE ULTIMATE GUIDE TO THE FIRST AVENGER
MARVEL
DK
CAPTAIN AMERICA
THE ULTIMATE GUIDE TO THE FIRST AVENGER
★ FOREWORD BY STAN LEE ★
FOREWORD BY STAN LEE
MARVEL
marvel.com
©2016 MARVEL

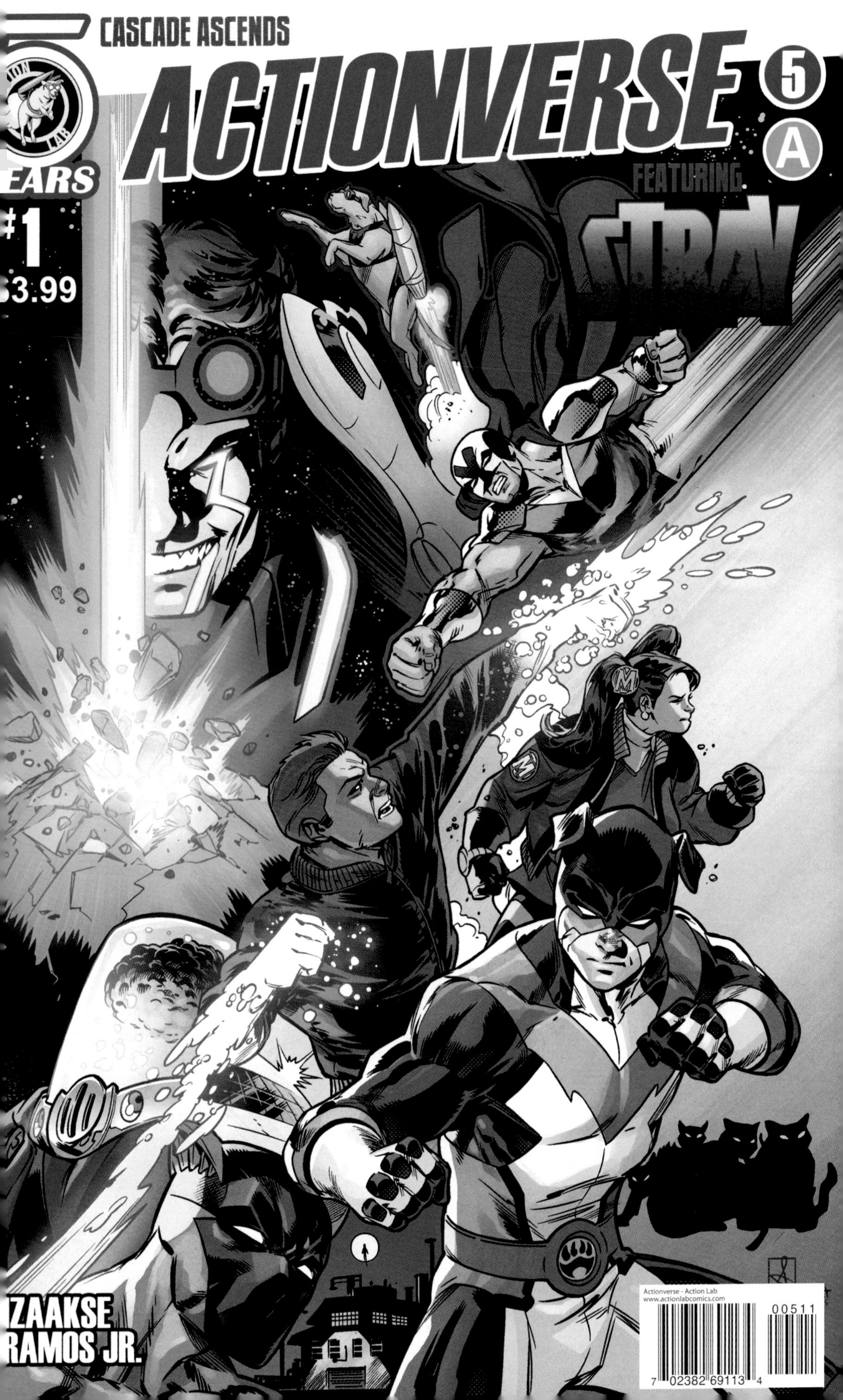
CASCADE ASCENDS
ACTIONVERSE
5
A
FEATURING
STRAY
EARS
#1
3.99
ZAAKSE
RAMOS JR.
Actionverse - Action Lab
www.actionlabcomics.com

ACTIONVERSE

FEATURING

Written and Drawn by Sean Izaakse

Colors by Wilson Ramos, Jr.

Letters by Full Court Press

Cover by Sean Izaakse and Mat Lopes

Variant Connecting Cover by Ron Frenz, Sean Izaakse
Ross Campbell and David Bednarski

Edited by Vito Delsante

STRAY and all related characters created by Delsante and Izaakse

PREVIOUSLY

Kyle Scordatto has fully transformed from Malice into Cascade. The heroes of our Earth have hours
before his portal engine powers up and leaves the world in ashes. If, and only if, they can cooperate.

BRYAN SEATON - PUBLISHER
DAVE DWONCH - PRESIDENT
SHAWN GABBORIN - EDITOR IN CHIEF
JASON MARTIN - PUBLISHER, DANGER ZONE
JAMAL IGLE - VICE-PRESIDENT OF MARKETING
JIM DIETZ - SOCIAL MEDIA DIRECTOR
NICOLE D'ANDRIA - EDITOR
CHAD CICCONI - THE GEARHEAD WITH MOTORBREATH
COLLEEN BOYD - SUBMISSIONS EDITOR

ACTIONLABCOMICS.COM

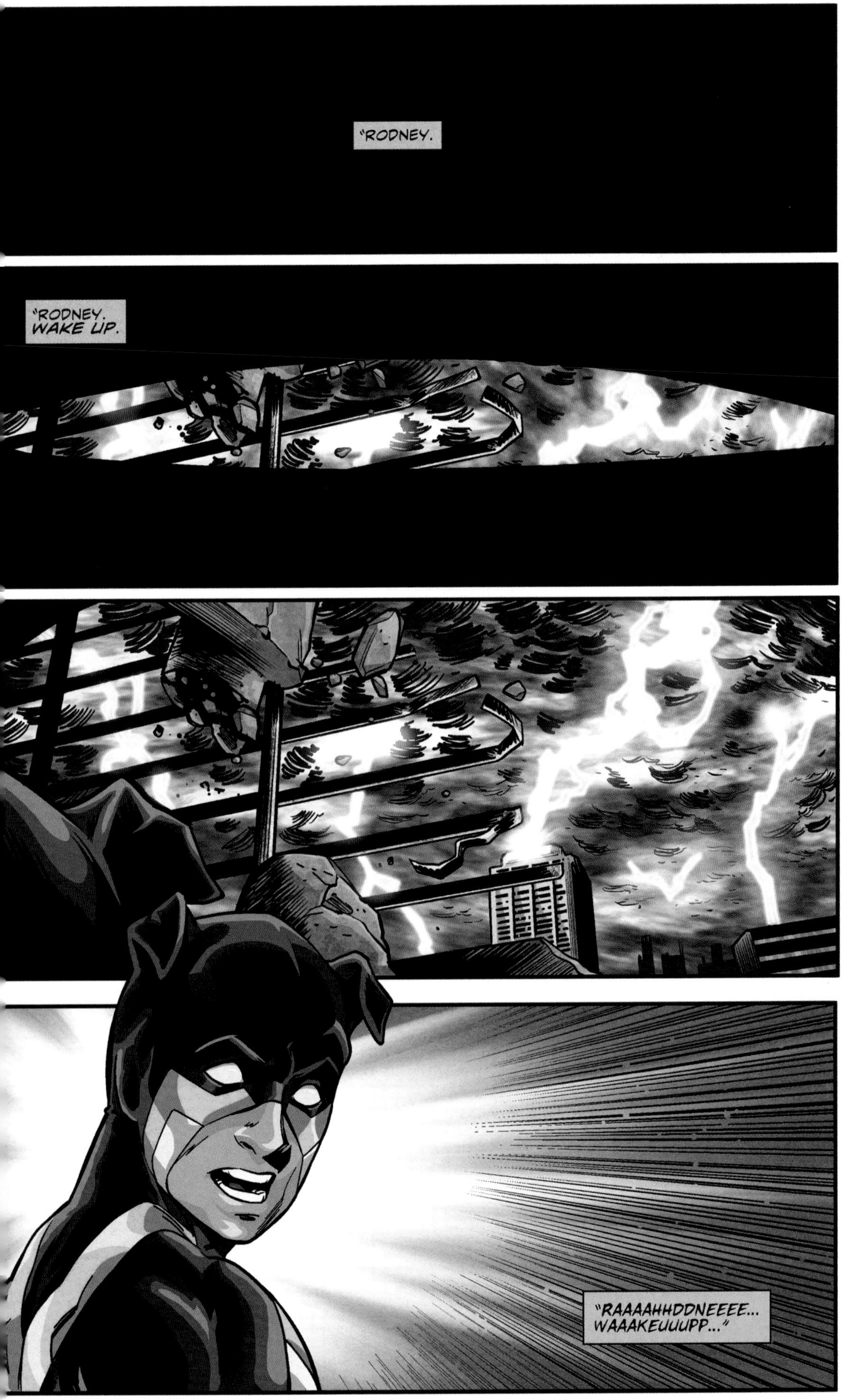
"RODNEY.
"RODNEY. WAKE UP.
"RAAAAHHDDNEEEE... WAAAKEUUUPP..."

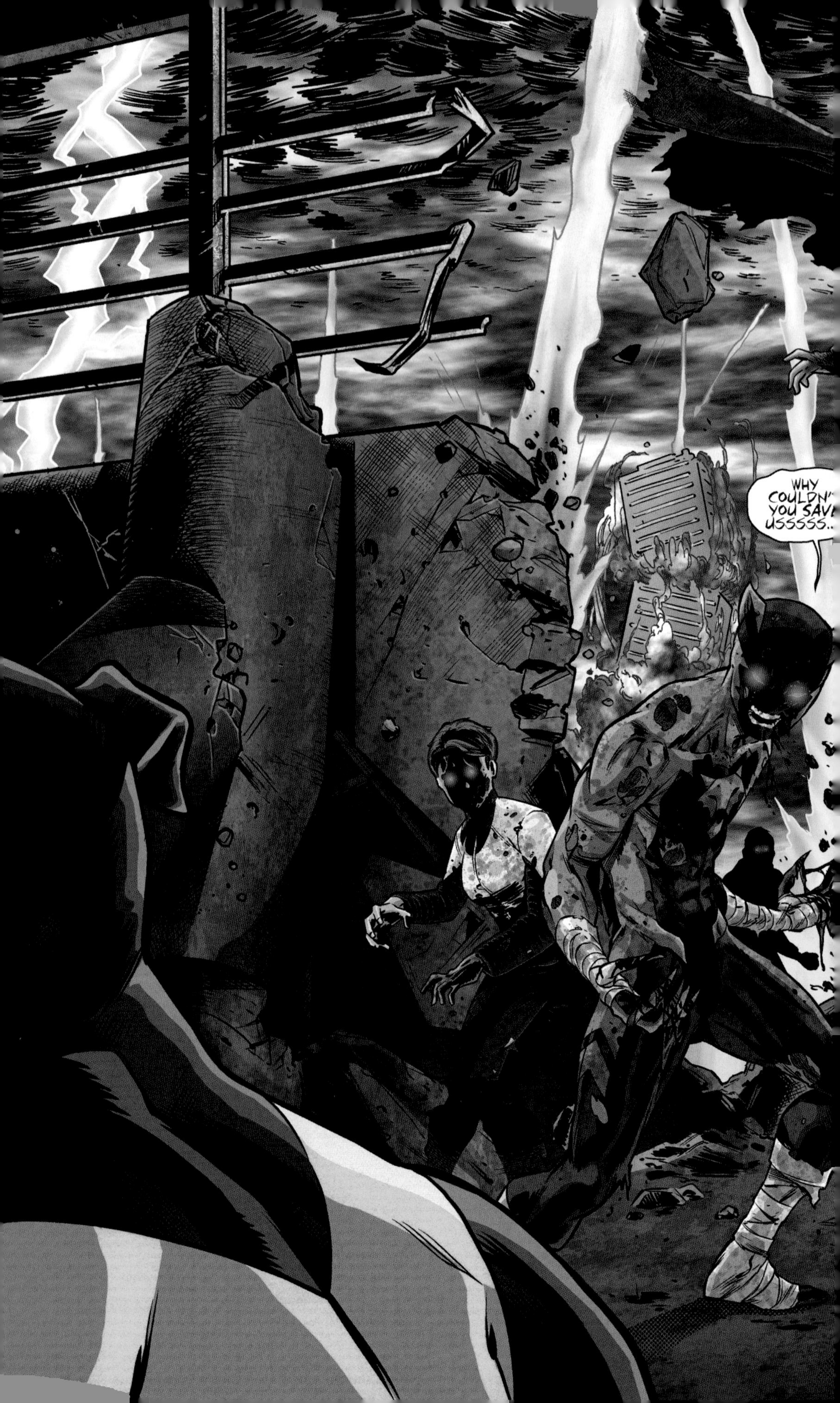
WHY COULDN'T YOU SAVE USSSSS...

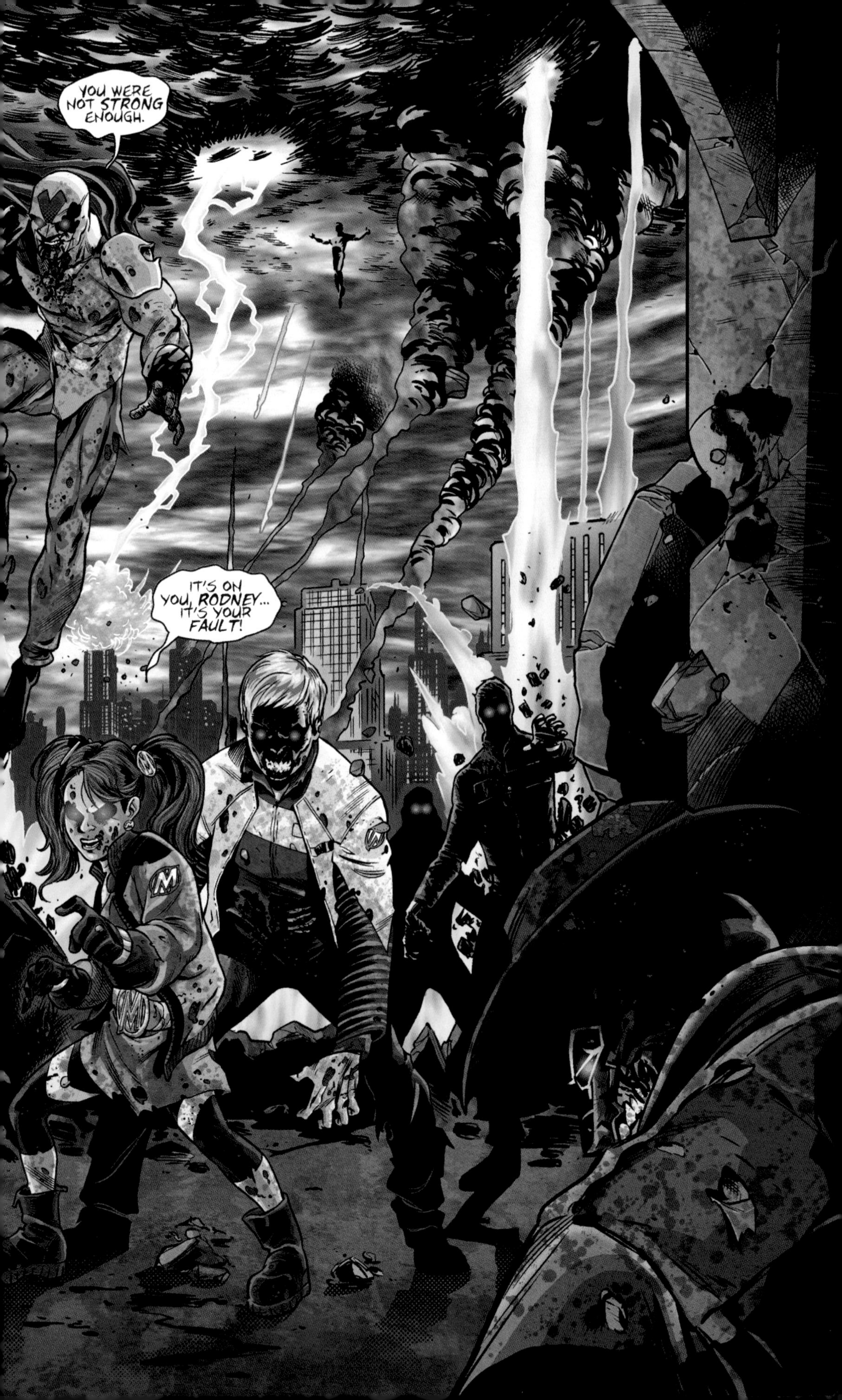
YOU WERE NOT STRONG ENOUGH.
IT'S ON YOU, RODNEY... IT'S YOUR FAULT!

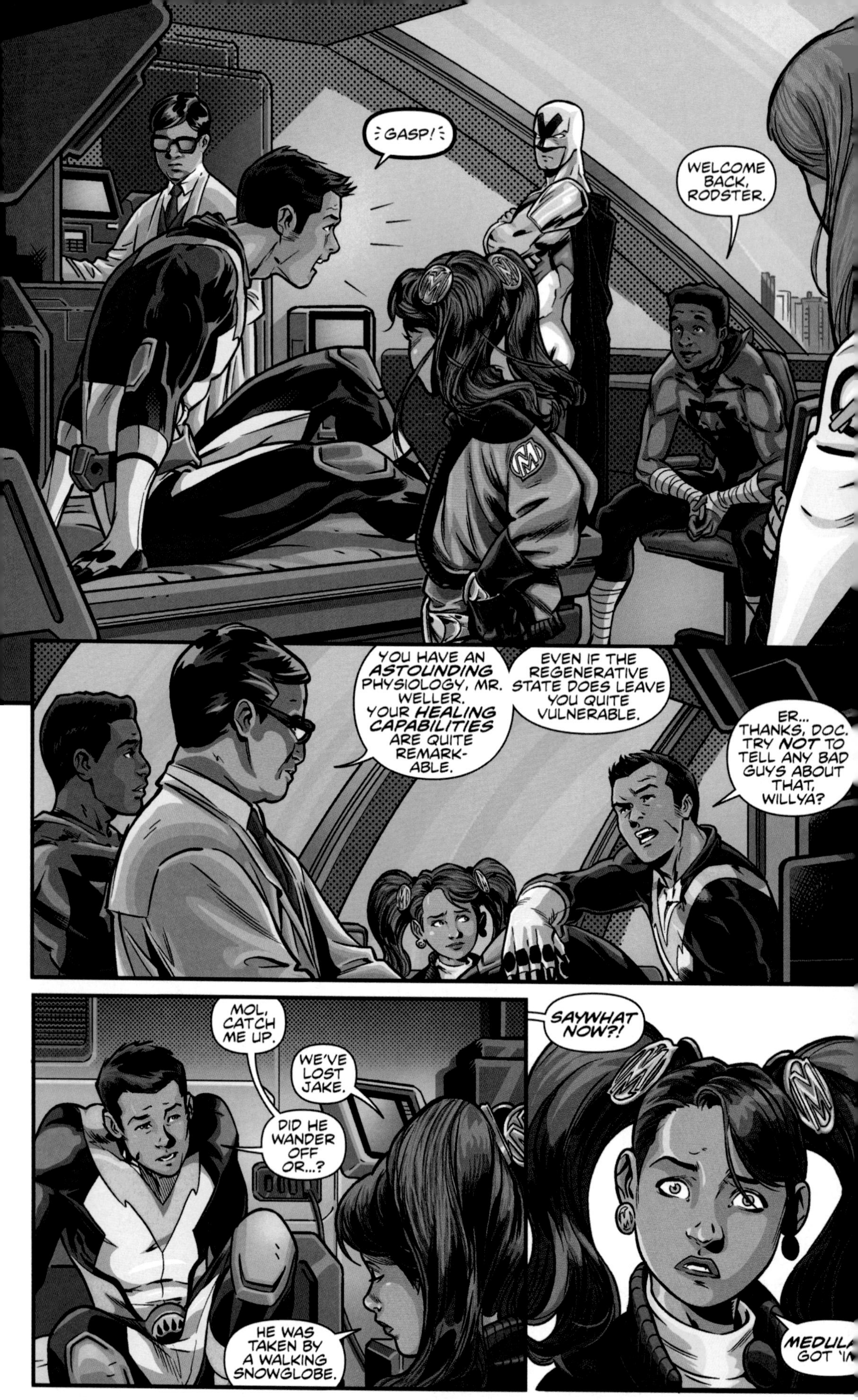
GASP!
WELCOME BACK, RODSTER.
YOU HAVE AN ASTOUNDING PHYSIOLOGY, MR. WELLER. YOUR HEALING CAPABILITIES ARE QUITE REMARK- ABLE.
EVEN IF THE REGENERATIVE STATE DOES LEAVE YOU QUITE VULNERABLE.
ER... THANKS, DOC. TRY NOT TO TELL ANY BAD GUYS ABOUT THAT, WILLYA?
MOL, CATCH ME UP.
WE'VE LOST JAKE.
DID HE WANDER OFF OR...?
HE WAS TAKEN BY A WALKING SNOWGLOBE.
SAYWHAT NOW?!

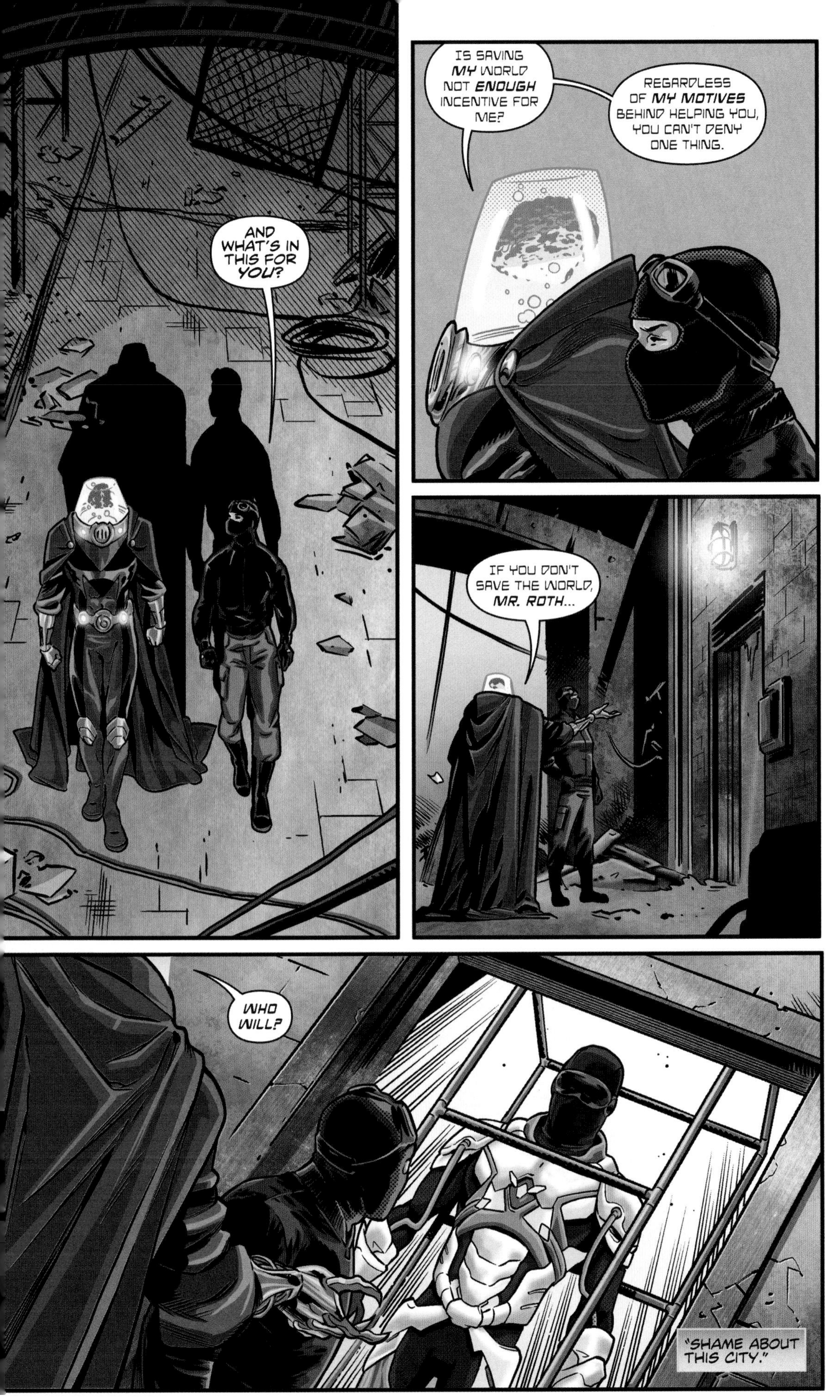
AND WHAT'S IN THIS FOR YOU?
IS SAVING MY WORLD NOT ENOUGH INCENTIVE FOR ME?
REGARDLESS OF MY MOTIVES BEHIND HELPING YOU, YOU CAN'T DENY ONE THING.
IF YOU DON'T SAVE THE WORLD, MR. ROTH...
WHO WILL?
"SHAME ABOUT THIS CITY."

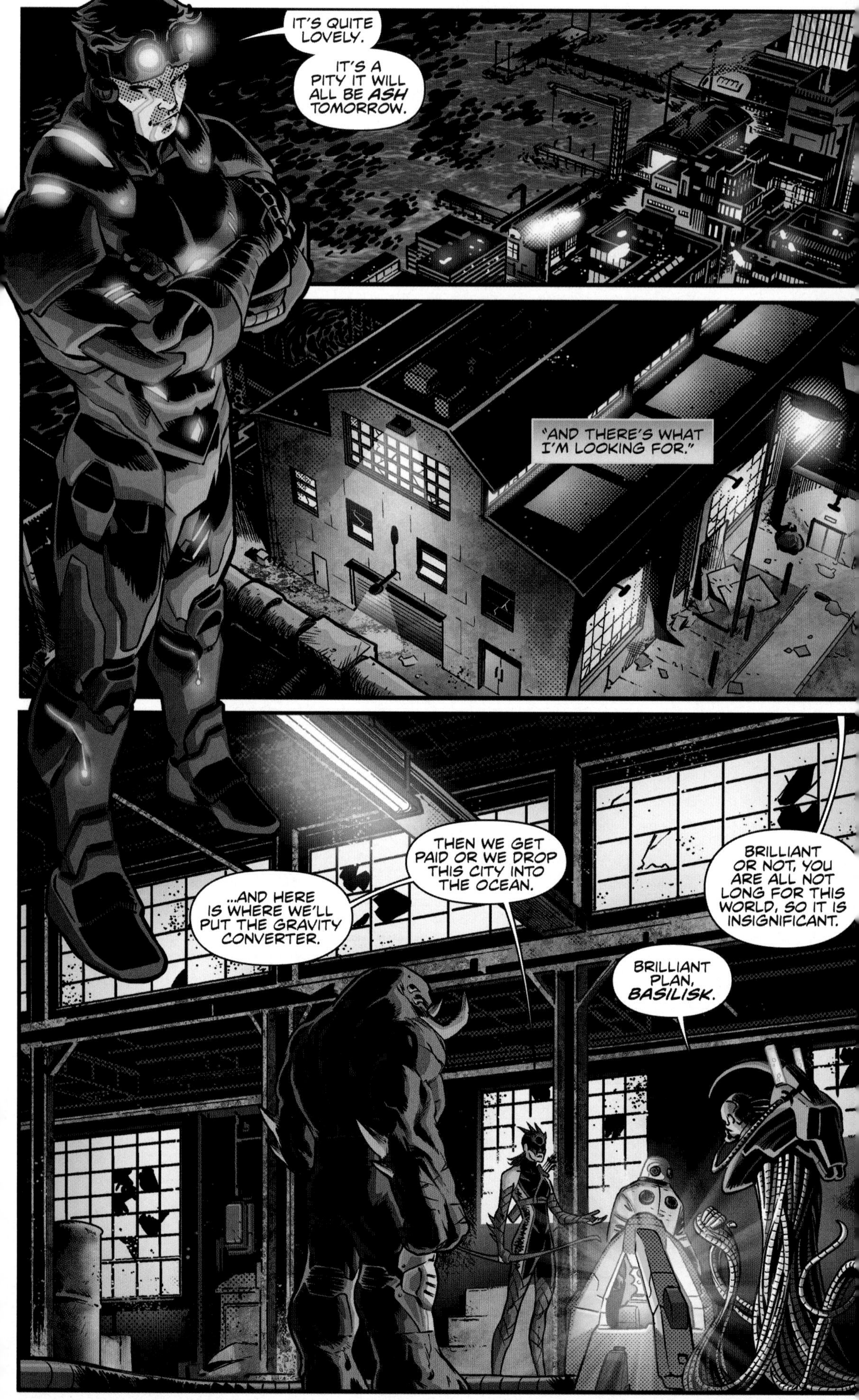

IT'S QUITE LOVELY.
IT'S A PITY IT WILL ALL BE ASH TOMORROW.
"AND THERE'S WHAT I'M LOOKING FOR."
...AND HERE IS WHERE WE'LL PUT THE GRAVITY CONVERTER.
THEN WE GET PAID OR WE DROP THIS CITY INTO THE OCEAN.
BRILLIANT PLAN, BASILISK.
BRILLIANT OR NOT, YOU ARE ALL NOT LONG FOR THIS WORLD, SO IT IS INSIGNIFICANT.

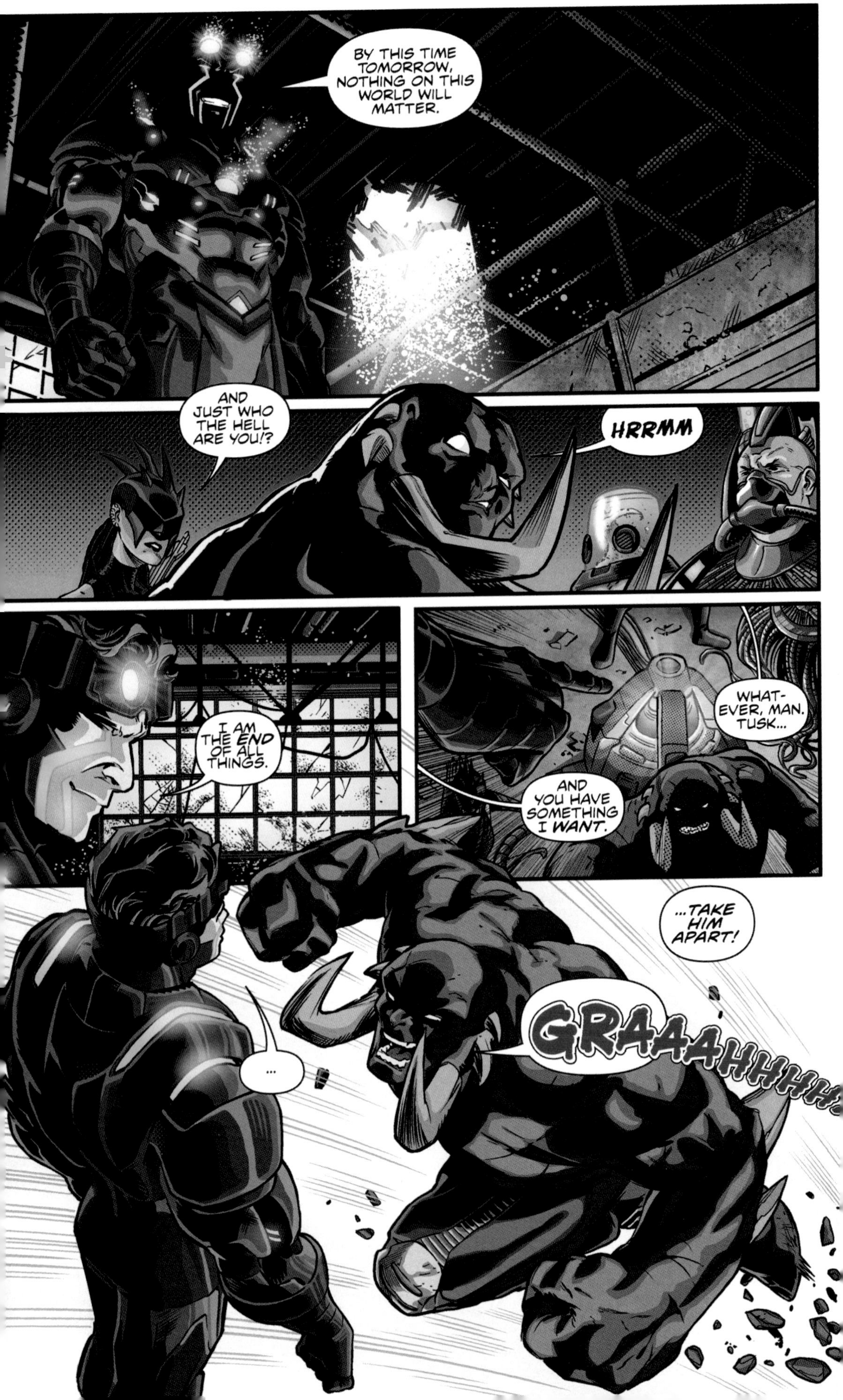

BY THIS TIME TOMORROW, NOTHING ON THIS WORLD WILL MATTER.
AND JUST WHO THE HELL ARE YOU!?
HRRMM
I AM THE END OF ALL THINGS.
AND YOU HAVE SOMETHING I WANT.
WHAT-EVER, MAN. TUSK...
...TAKE HIM APART!
...
GRAAAHHHH

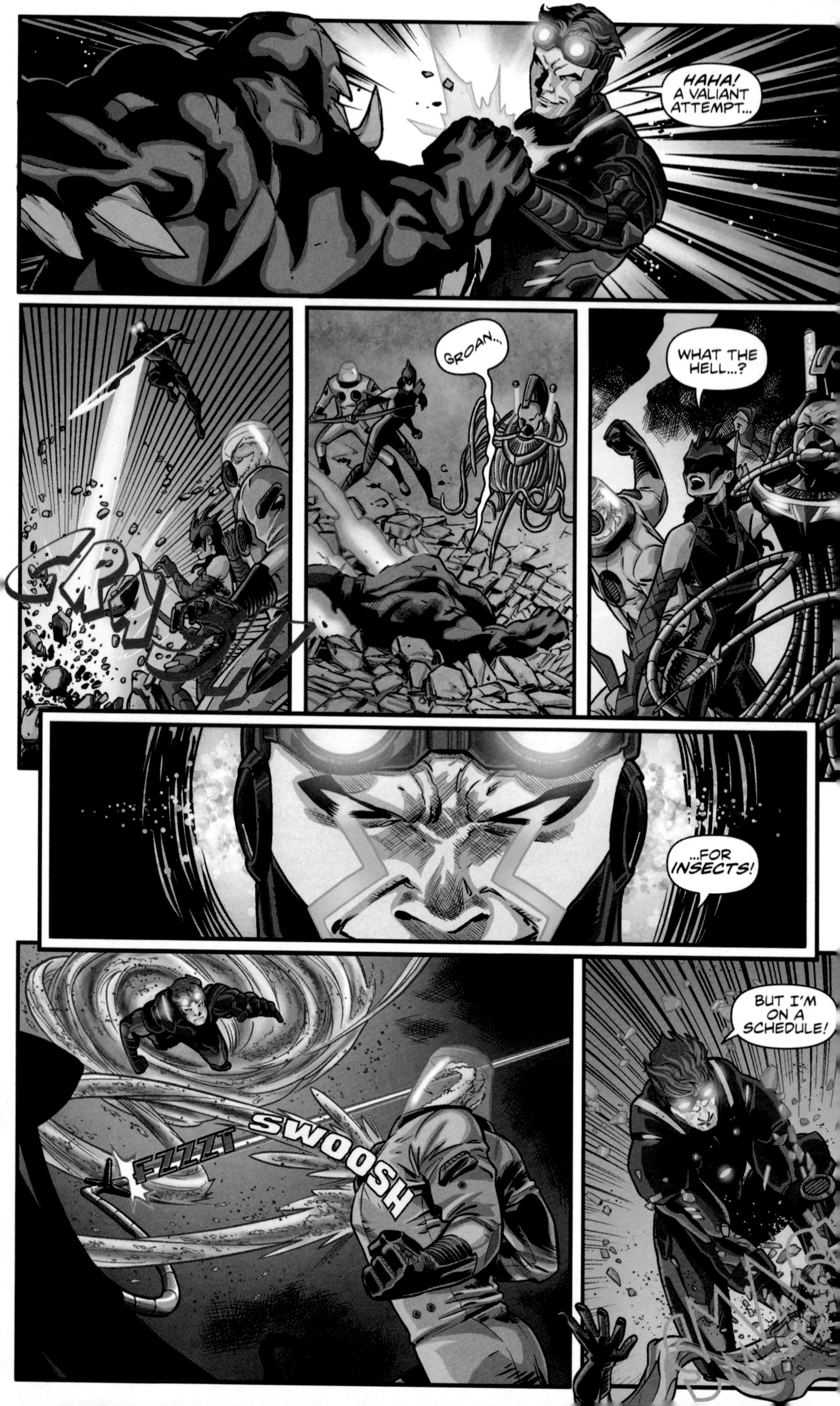
HAHA! A VALIANT ATTEMPT...
GROAN...
WHAT THE HELL...?
...FOR INSECTS!
SWOOSH
FZZZT
BUT I'M ON A SCHEDULE!

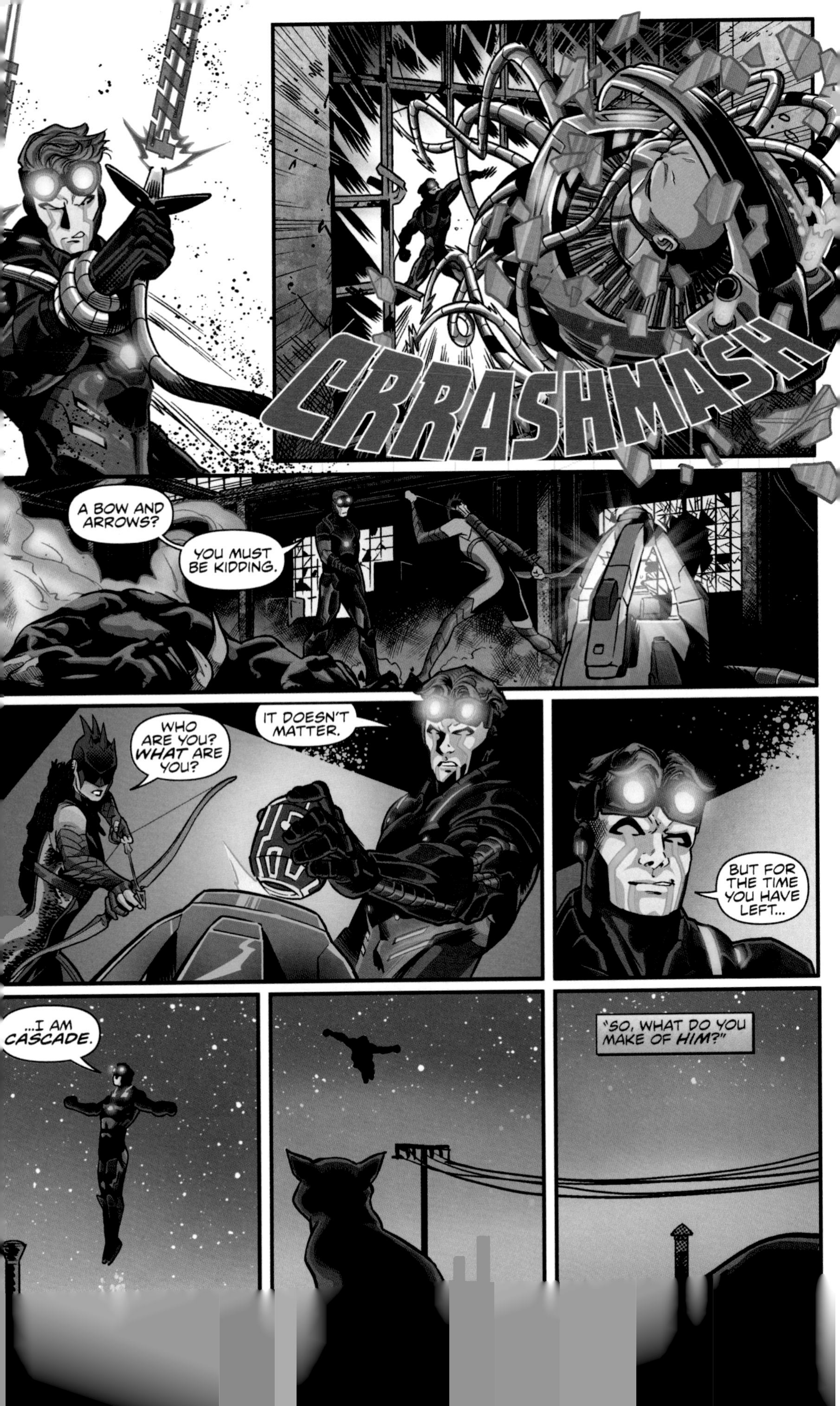
CRRASHMASH
A BOW AND ARROWS?
YOU MUST BE KIDDING.
WHO ARE YOU? WHAT ARE YOU?
IT DOESN'T MATTER.
BUT FOR THE TIME YOU HAVE LEFT...
...I AM CASCADE.
"SO, WHAT DO YOU MAKE OF HIM?"

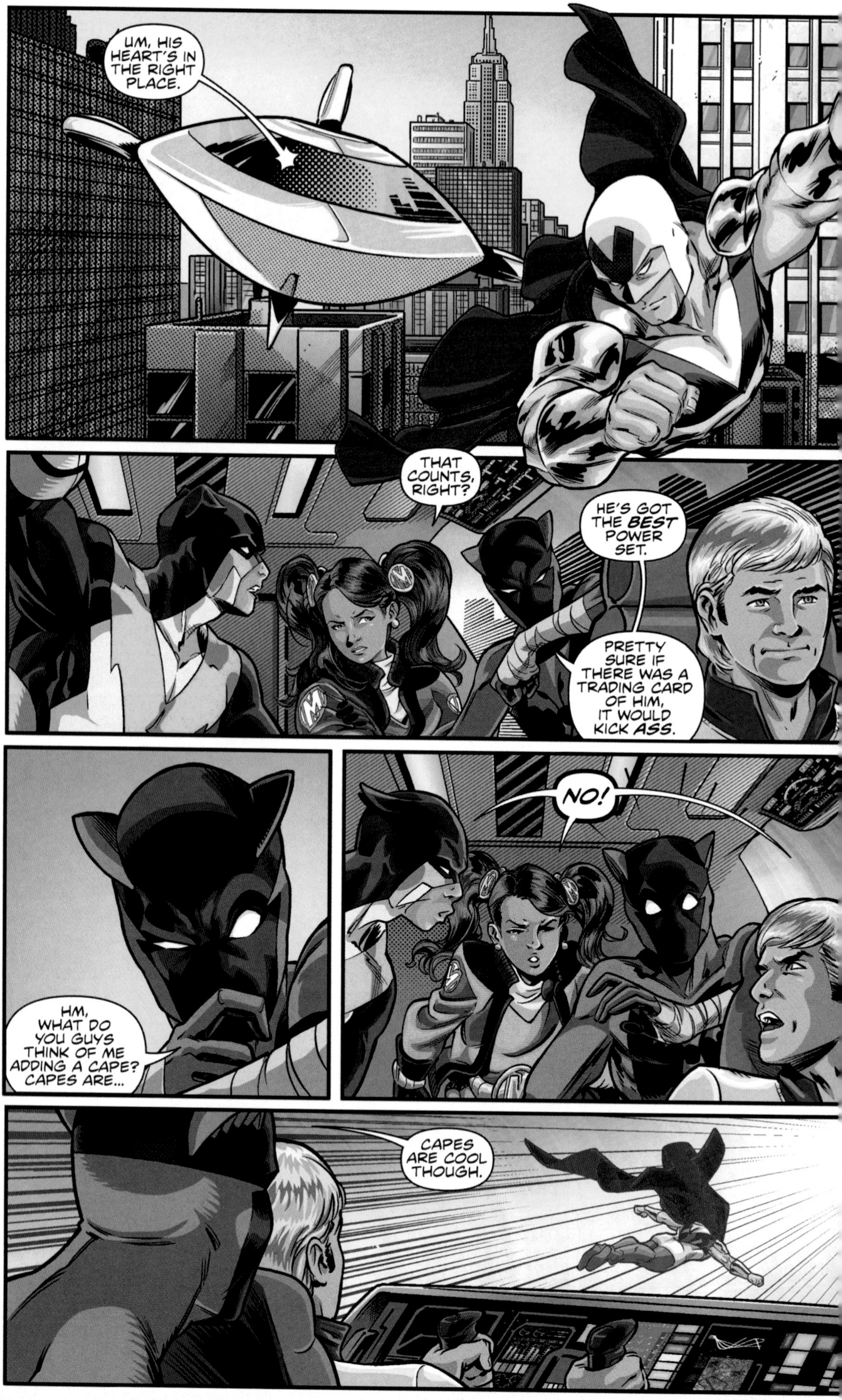
UM, HIS HEART'S IN THE RIGHT PLACE.
THAT COUNTS, RIGHT?
HE'S GOT THE BEST POWER SET.
PRETTY SURE IF THERE WAS A TRADING CARD OF HIM, IT WOULD KICK ASS.
HM, WHAT DO YOU GUYS THINK OF ME ADDING A CAPE? CAPES ARE...
NO!
CAPES ARE COOL THOUGH.

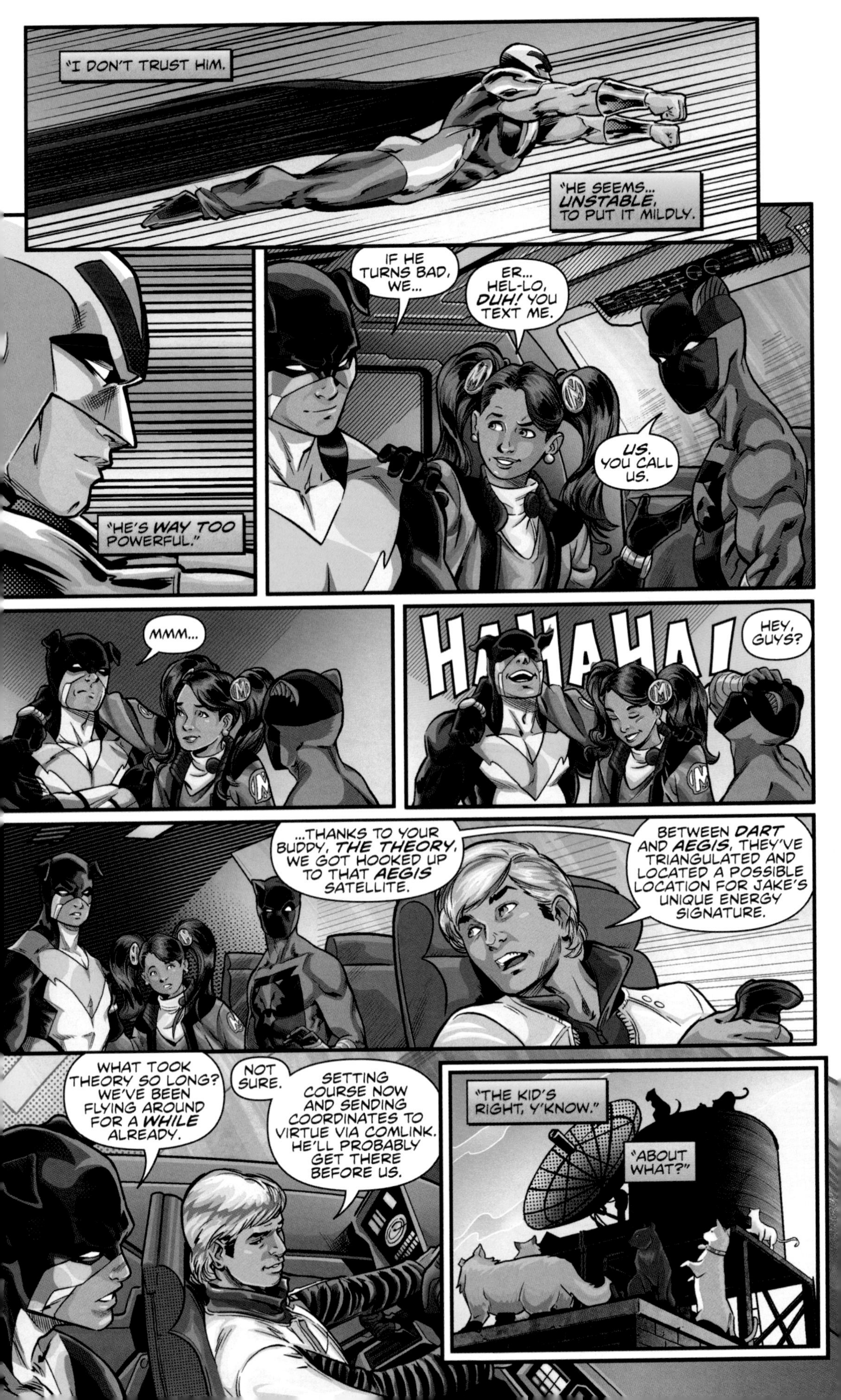
"I DON'T TRUST HIM.
"HE SEEMS... UNSTABLE, TO PUT IT MILDLY.
"HE'S WAY TOO POWERFUL."
IF HE TURNS BAD, WE...
ER... HEL-LO, DUH! YOU TEXT ME.
US. YOU CALL US.
MMM...
HAHAHA!
HEY, GUYS?
...THANKS TO YOUR BUDDY, THE THEORY, WE GOT HOOKED UP TO THAT AEGIS SATELLITE.
BETWEEN DART AND AEGIS, THEY'VE TRIANGULATED AND LOCATED A POSSIBLE LOCATION FOR JAKE'S UNIQUE ENERGY SIGNATURE.
WHAT TOOK THEORY SO LONG? WE'VE BEEN FLYING AROUND FOR A WHILE ALREADY.
NOT SURE.
SETTING COURSE NOW AND SENDING COORDINATES TO VIRTUE VIA COMLINK. HE'LL PROBABLY GET THERE BEFORE US.
"THE KID'S RIGHT, Y'KNOW."
"ABOUT WHAT?"

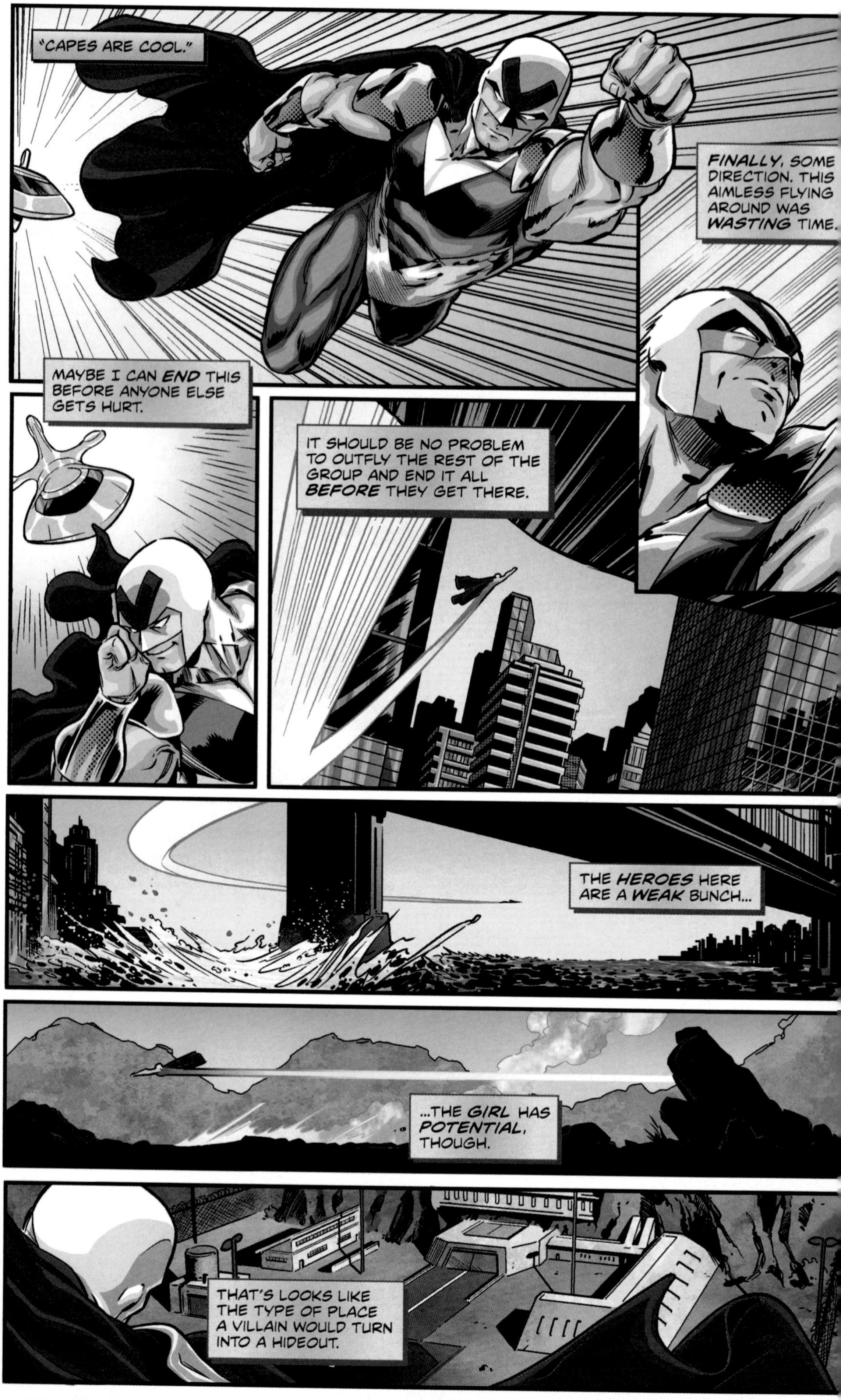
"CAPES ARE COOL."
FINALLY, SOME DIRECTION. THIS AIMLESS FLYING AROUND WAS WASTING TIME.
MAYBE I CAN END THIS BEFORE ANYONE ELSE GETS HURT.
IT SHOULD BE NO PROBLEM TO OUTFLY THE REST OF THE GROUP AND END IT ALL BEFORE THEY GET THERE.
THE HEROES HERE ARE A WEAK BUNCH...
...THE GIRL HAS POTENTIAL, THOUGH.
THAT'S LOOKS LIKE THE TYPE OF PLACE A VILLAIN WOULD TURN INTO A HIDEOUT.

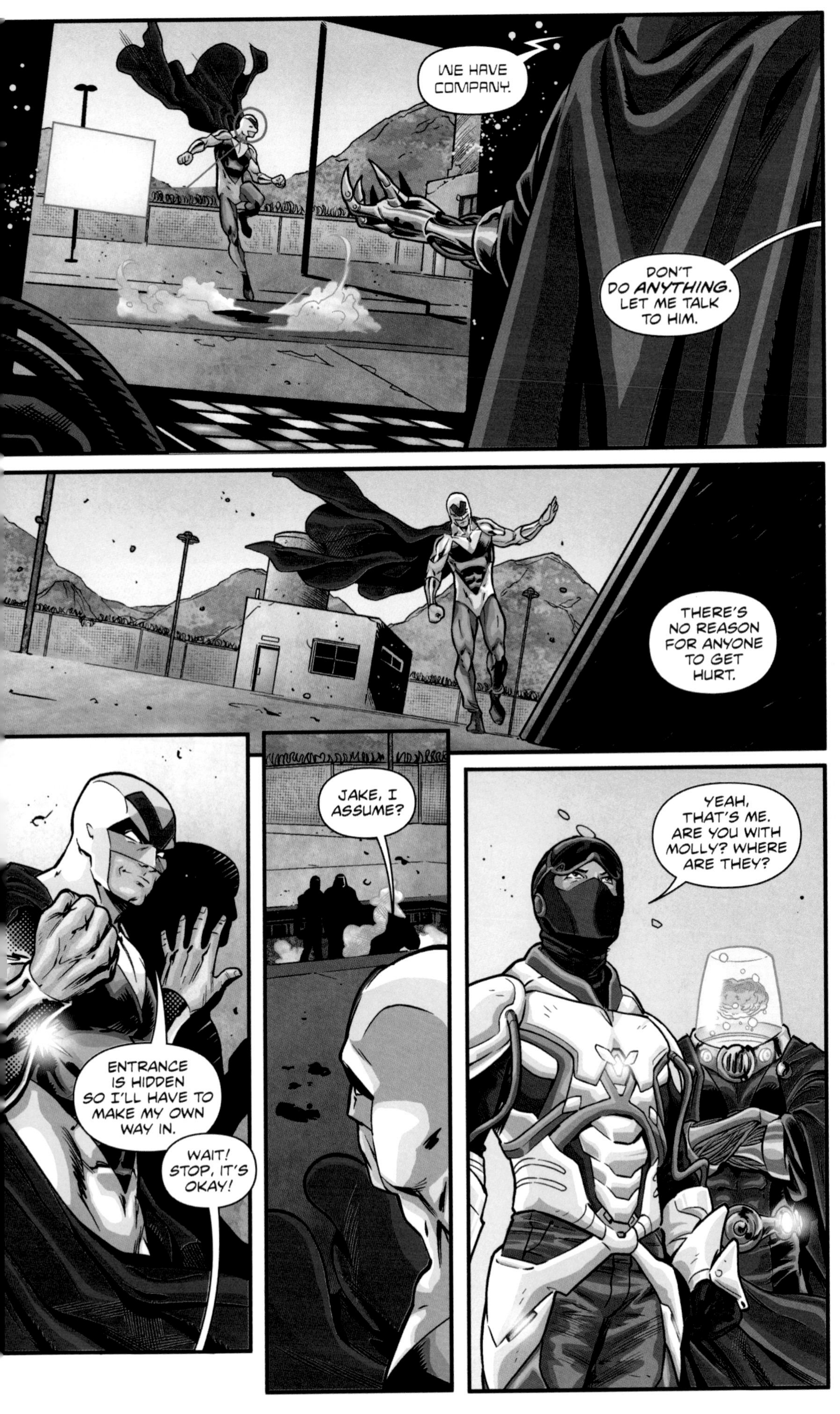
WE HAVE COMPANY.
DON'T DO ANYTHING. LET ME TALK TO HIM.
THERE'S NO REASON FOR ANYONE TO GET HURT.
ENTRANCE IS HIDDEN SO I'LL HAVE TO MAKE MY OWN WAY IN.
WAIT! STOP, IT'S OKAY!
JAKE, I ASSUME?
YEAH, THAT'S ME. ARE YOU WITH MOLLY? WHERE ARE THEY?

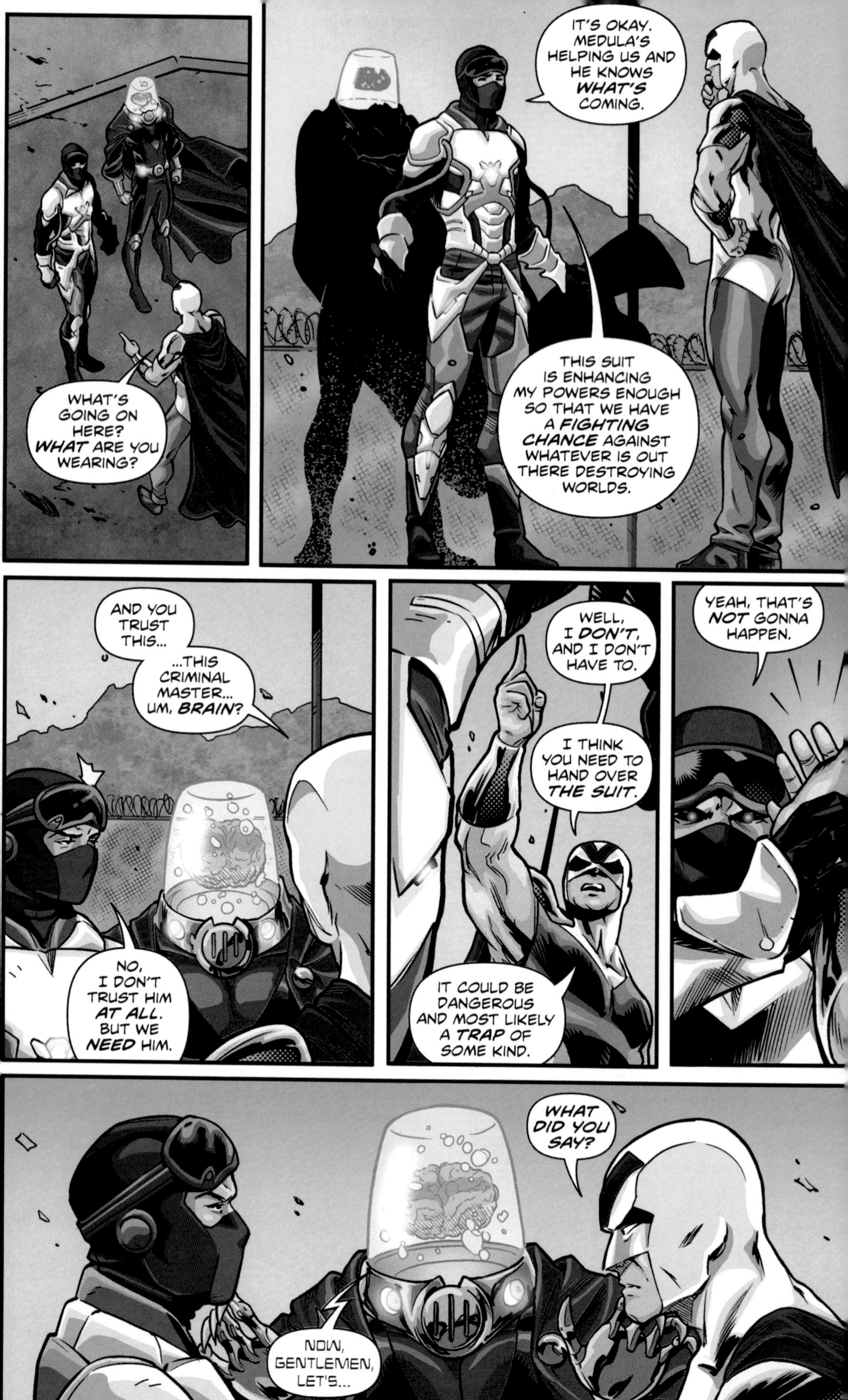
WHAT'S GOING ON HERE? WHAT ARE YOU WEARING?
IT'S OKAY. MEDULA'S HELPING US AND HE KNOWS WHAT'S COMING.
THIS SUIT IS ENHANCING MY POWERS ENOUGH SO THAT WE HAVE A FIGHTING CHANCE AGAINST WHATEVER IS OUT THERE DESTROYING WORLDS.
AND YOU TRUST THIS...
...THIS CRIMINAL MASTER... UM, BRAIN?
NO, I DON'T TRUST HIM AT ALL. BUT WE NEED HIM.
WELL, I DON'T, AND I DON'T HAVE TO.
I THINK YOU NEED TO HAND OVER THE SUIT.
IT COULD BE DANGEROUS AND MOST LIKELY A TRAP OF SOME KIND.
YEAH, THAT'S NOT GONNA HAPPEN.
WHAT DID YOU SAY?
NOW, GENTLEMEN, LET'S...

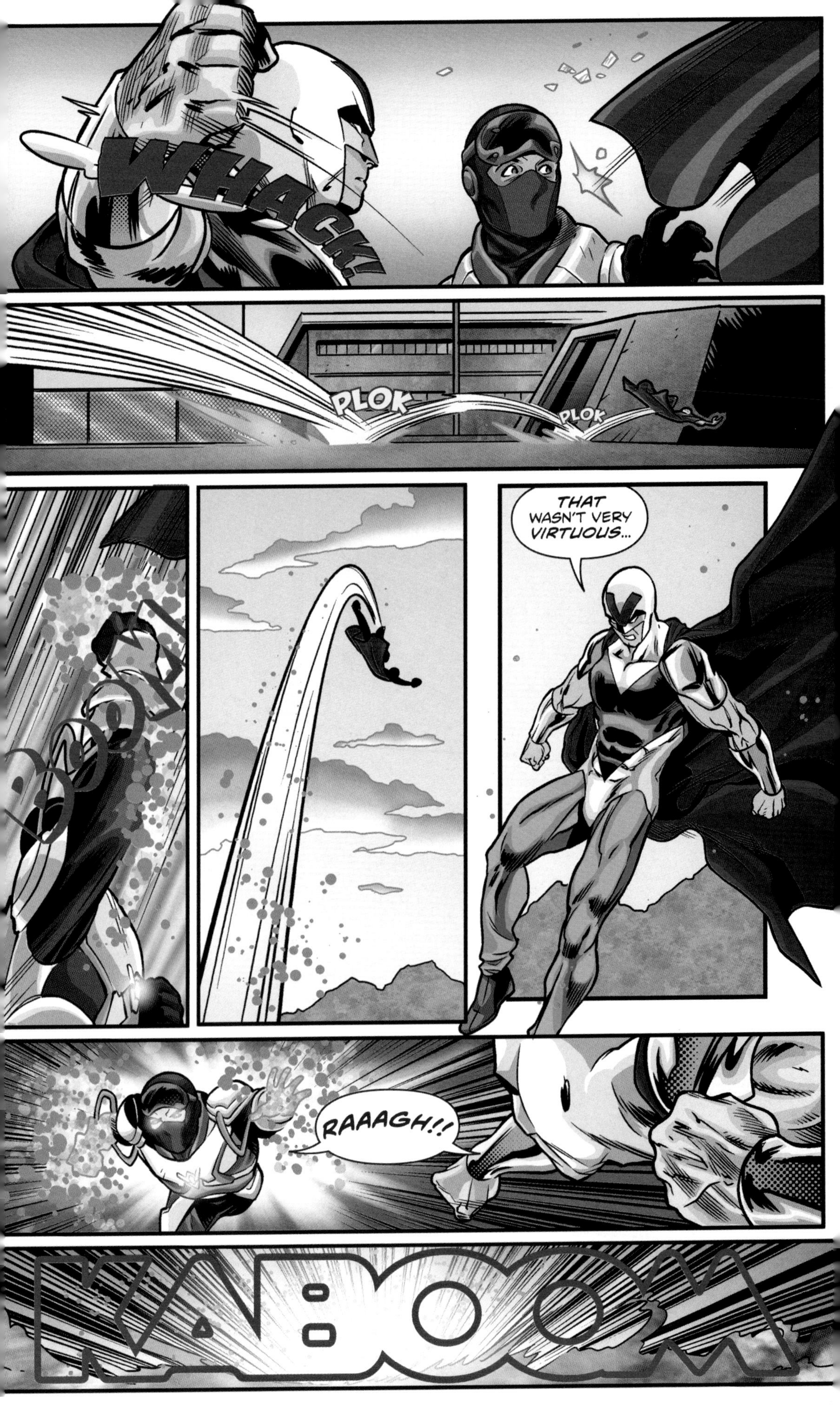
WHACK!
PLOK
PLOK
THAT WASN'T VERY VIRTUOUS...
RAAAGH!!
KABOOM

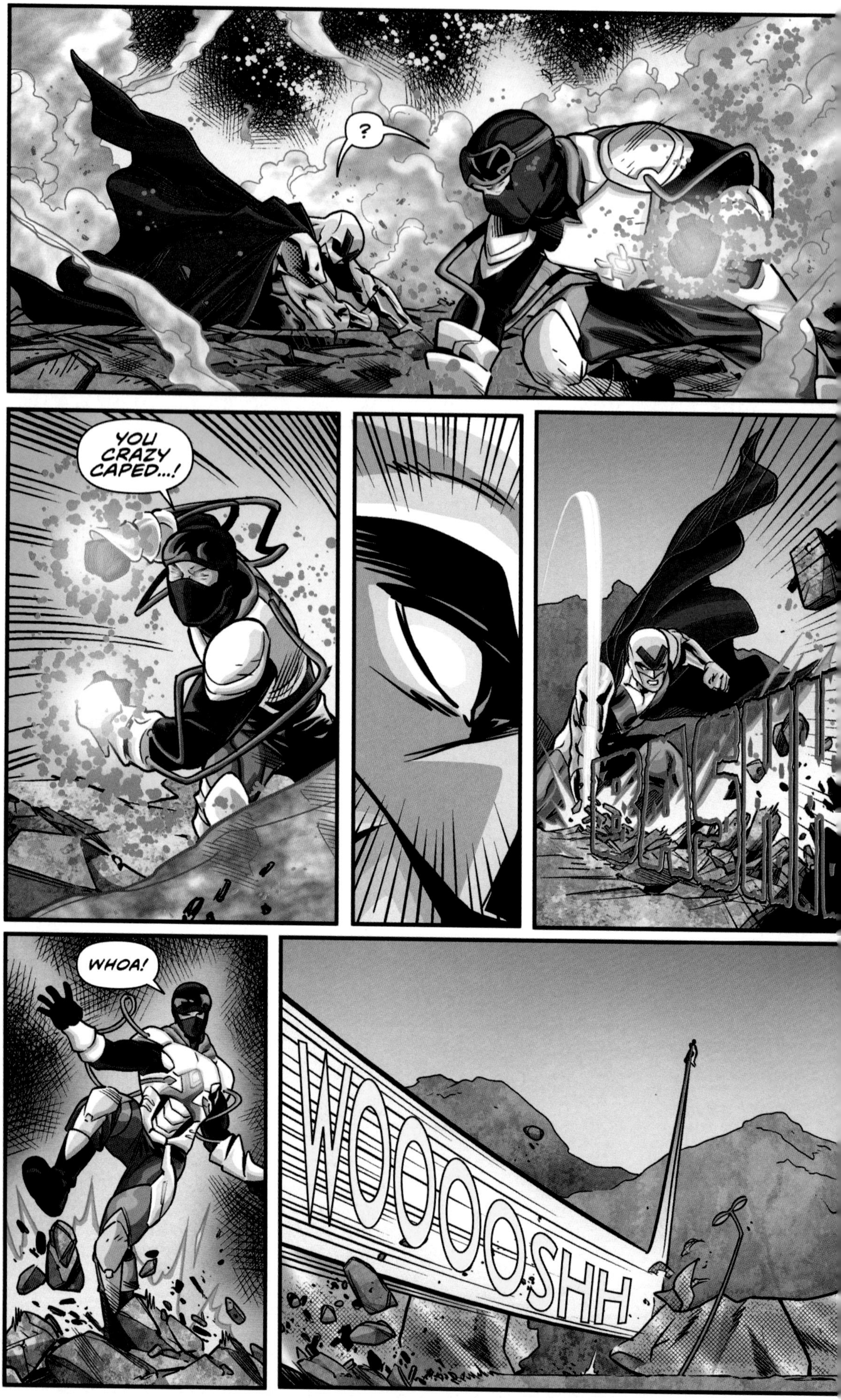
?
YOU CRAZY CAPED...!
WHOA!
WOOOOSHH

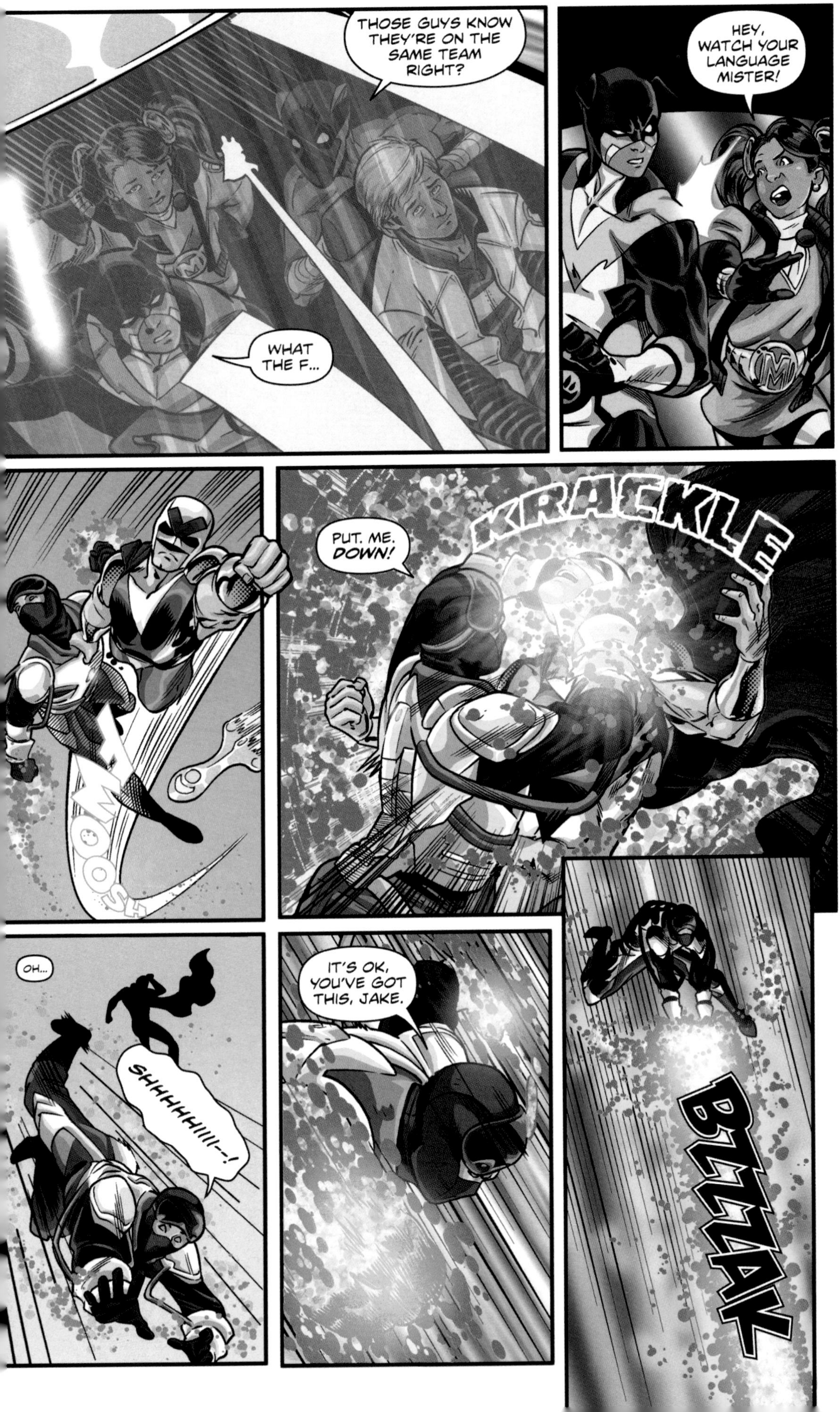
THOSE GUYS KNOW THEY'RE ON THE SAME TEAM RIGHT?
WHAT THE F...
HEY, WATCH YOUR LANGUAGE MISTER!
WHOOSH
PUT. ME. DOWN!
KRACKLE
OH...
SHHHHHIIIII---!
IT'S OK, YOU'VE GOT THIS, JAKE.
BZZAK

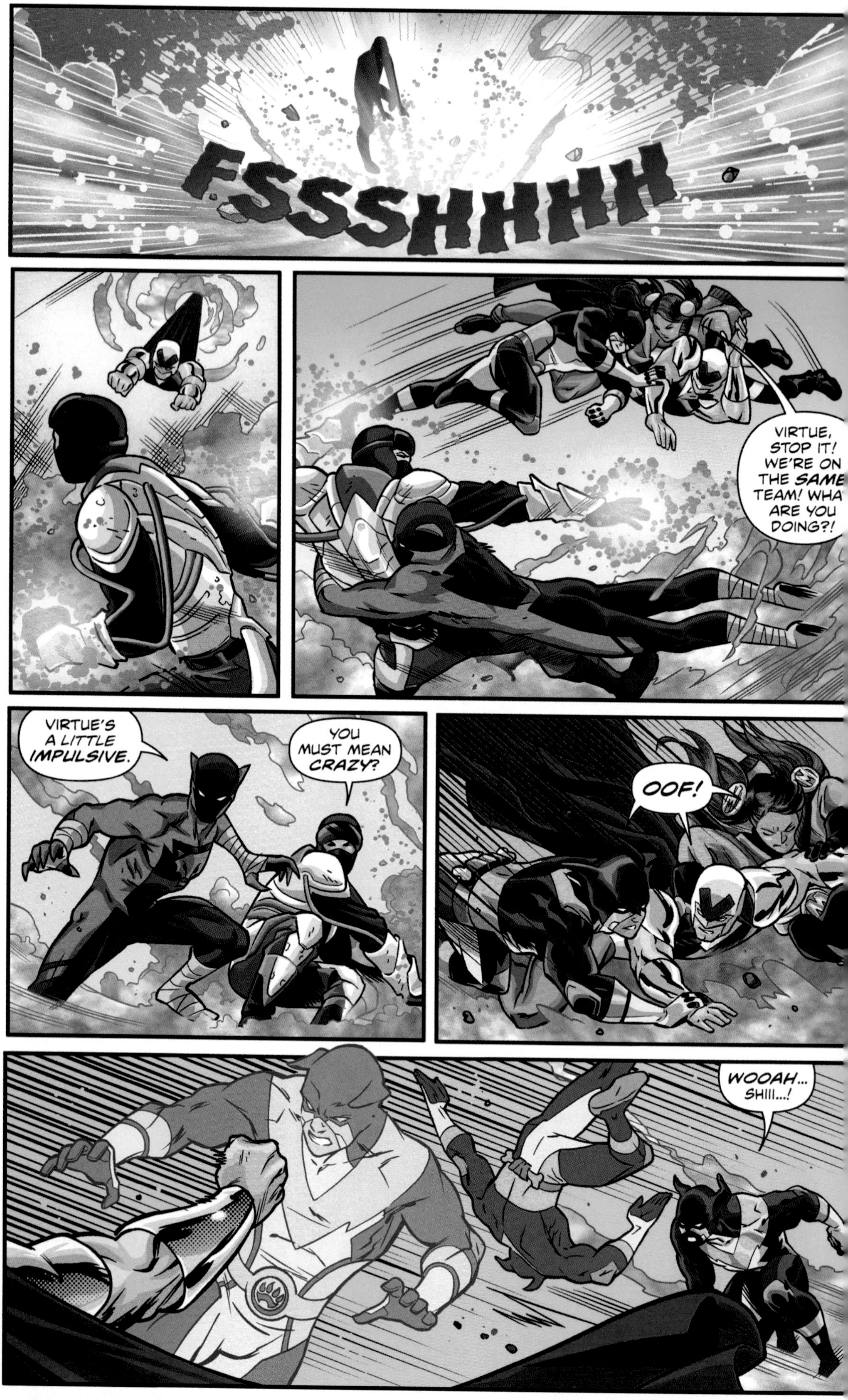
FSSHHHH
VIRTUE, STOP IT! WE'RE ON THE SAME TEAM! WHA ARE YOU DOING?!
VIRTUE'S A LITTLE IMPULSIVE.
YOU MUST MEAN CRAZY?
OOF!
WOOAH... SHIII...!

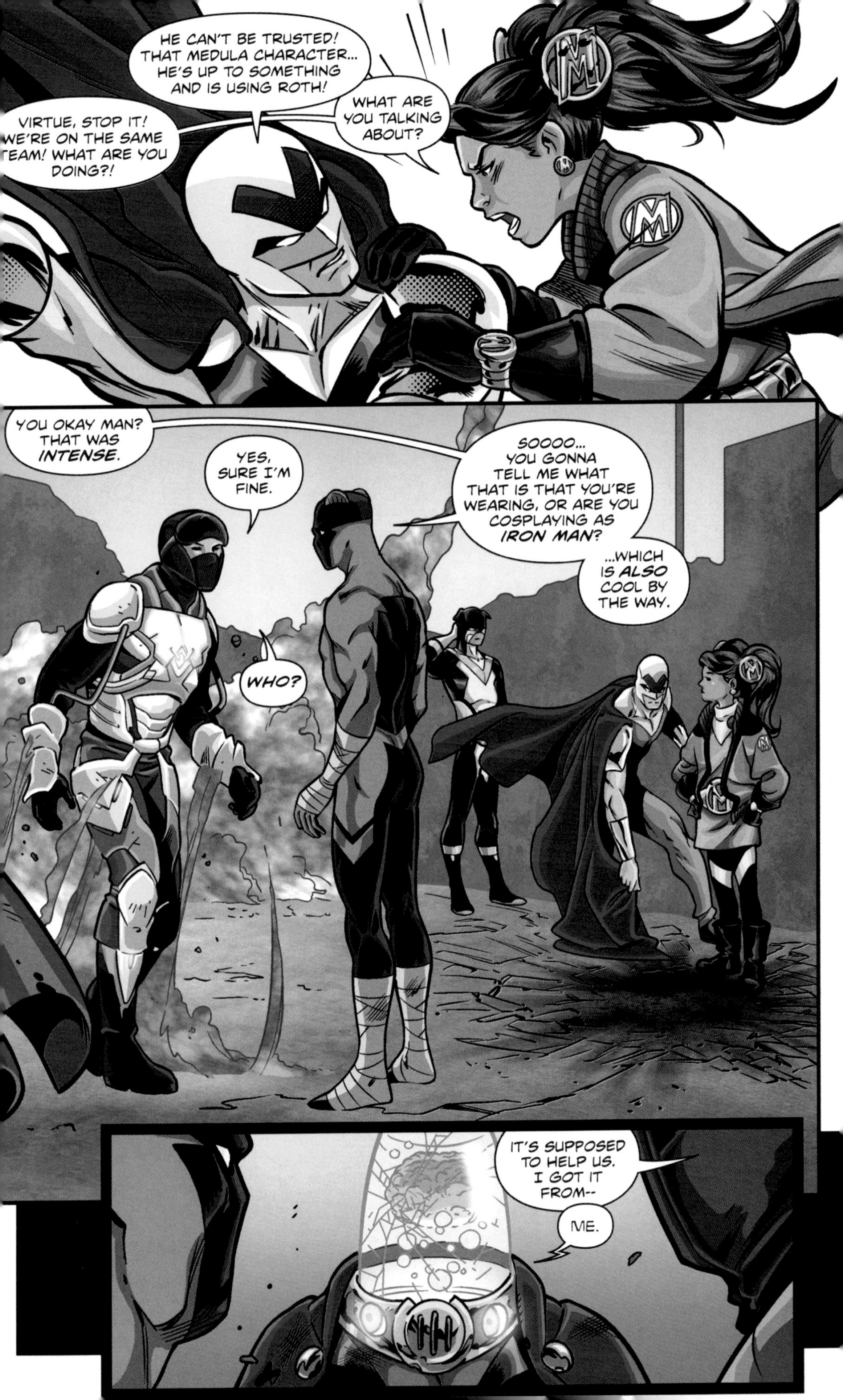

HE CAN'T BE TRUSTED! THAT MEDULA CHARACTER... HE'S UP TO SOMETHING AND IS USING ROTH!
VIRTUE, STOP IT! WE'RE ON THE SAME TEAM! WHAT ARE YOU DOING?!
WHAT ARE YOU TALKING ABOUT?
YOU OKAY MAN? THAT WAS INTENSE.
YES, SURE I'M FINE.
SOOOO... YOU GONNA TELL ME WHAT THAT IS THAT YOU'RE WEARING, OR ARE YOU COSPLAYING AS IRON MAN?
...WHICH IS ALSO COOL BY THE WAY.
WHO?
IT'S SUPPOSED TO HELP US. I GOT IT FROM--
ME.

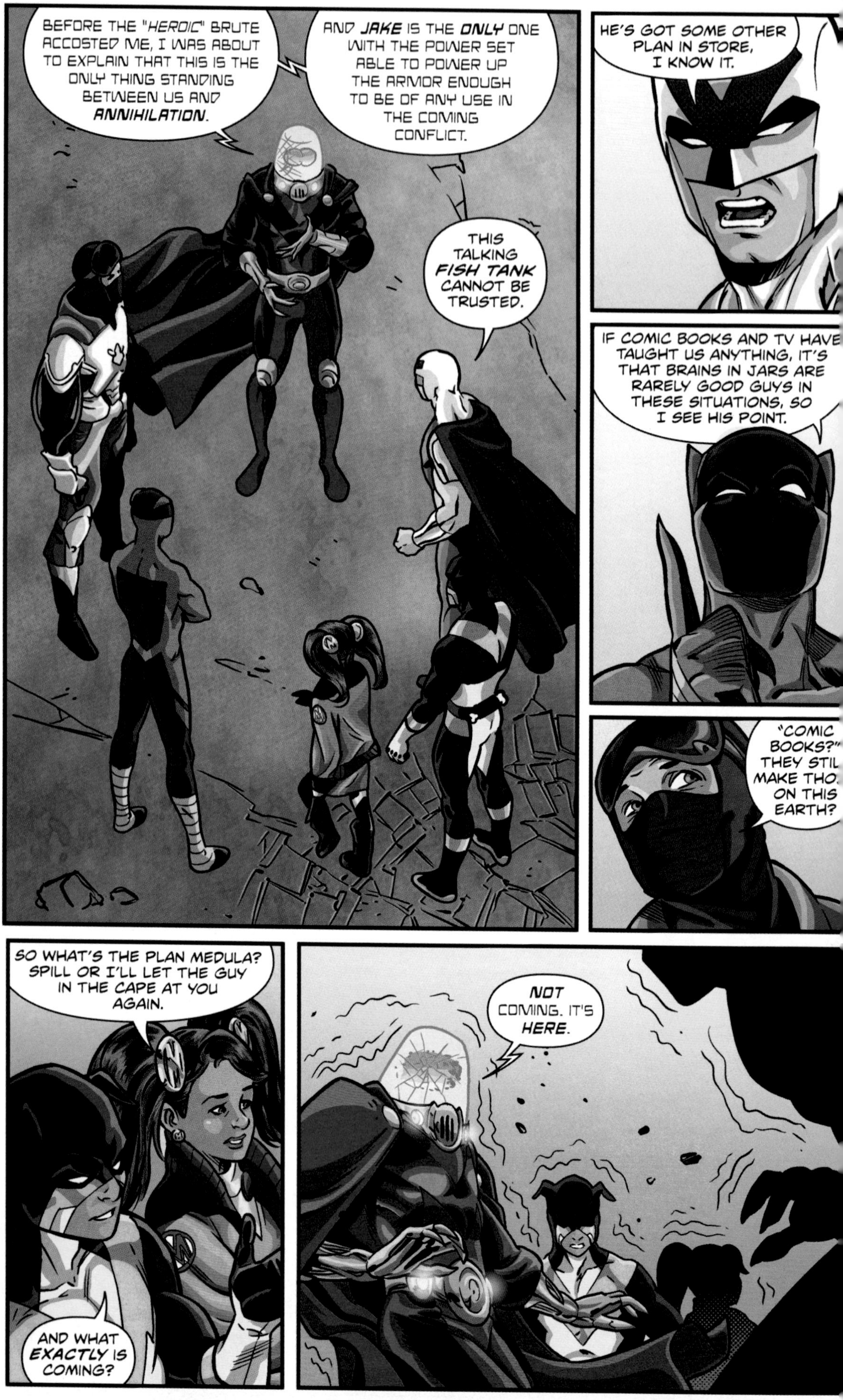
BEFORE THE "HEROIC" BRUTE ACCOSTED ME, I WAS ABOUT TO EXPLAIN THAT THIS IS THE ONLY THING STANDING BETWEEN US AND ANNIHILATION.
AND JAKE IS THE ONLY ONE WITH THE POWER SET ABLE TO POWER UP THE ARMOR ENOUGH TO BE OF ANY USE IN THE COMING CONFLICT.
THIS TALKING FISH TANK CANNOT BE TRUSTED.
HE'S GOT SOME OTHER PLAN IN STORE, I KNOW IT.
IF COMIC BOOKS AND TV HAVE TAUGHT US ANYTHING, IT'S THAT BRAINS IN JARS ARE RARELY GOOD GUYS IN THESE SITUATIONS, SO I SEE HIS POINT.
"COMIC BOOKS?" THEY STIL MAKE THO ON THIS EARTH?
SO WHAT'S THE PLAN MEDULA? SPILL OR I'LL LET THE GUY IN THE CAPE AT YOU AGAIN.
AND WHAT EXACTLY IS COMING?
NOT COMING. IT'S HERE.

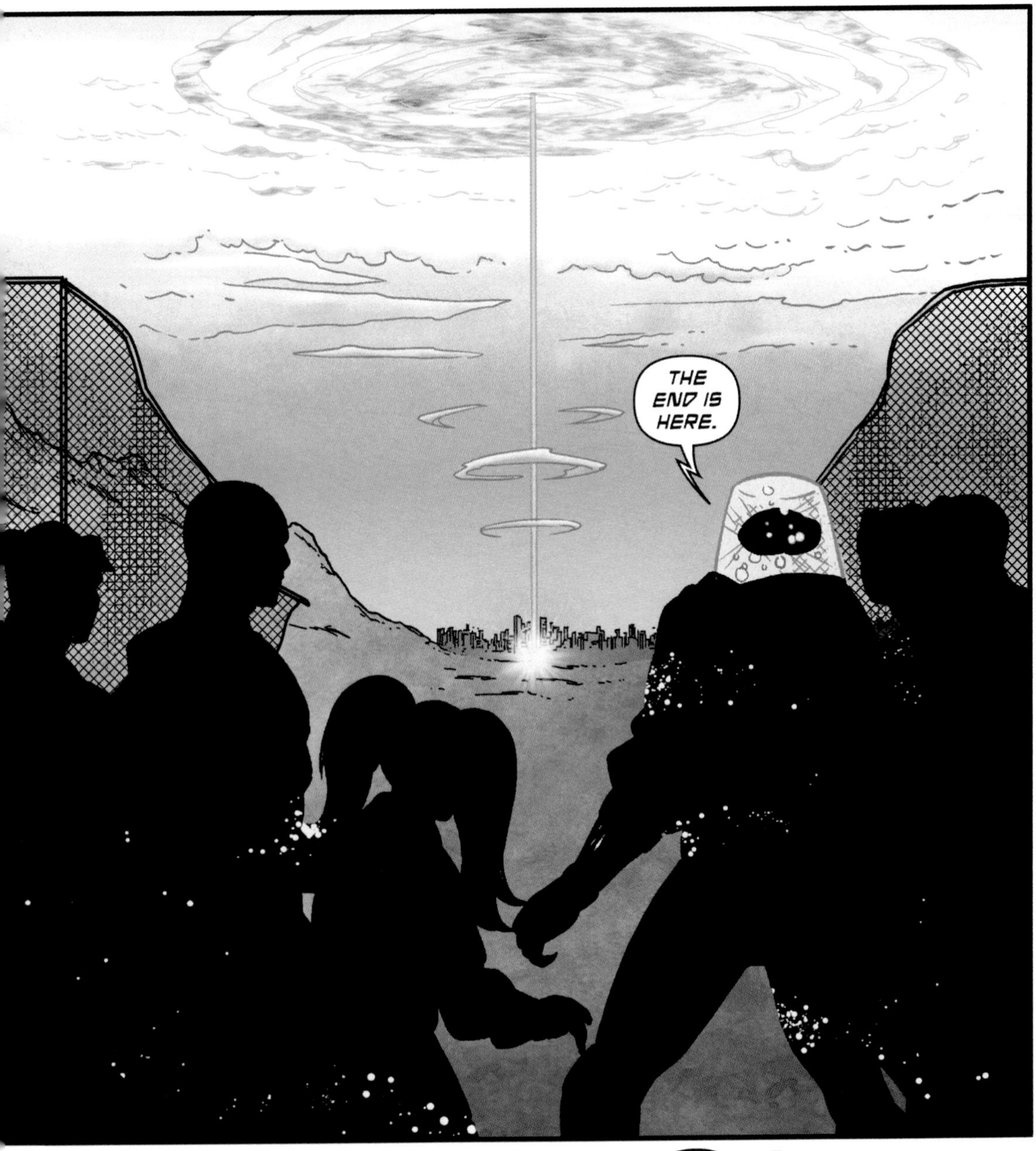
THE END IS HERE.

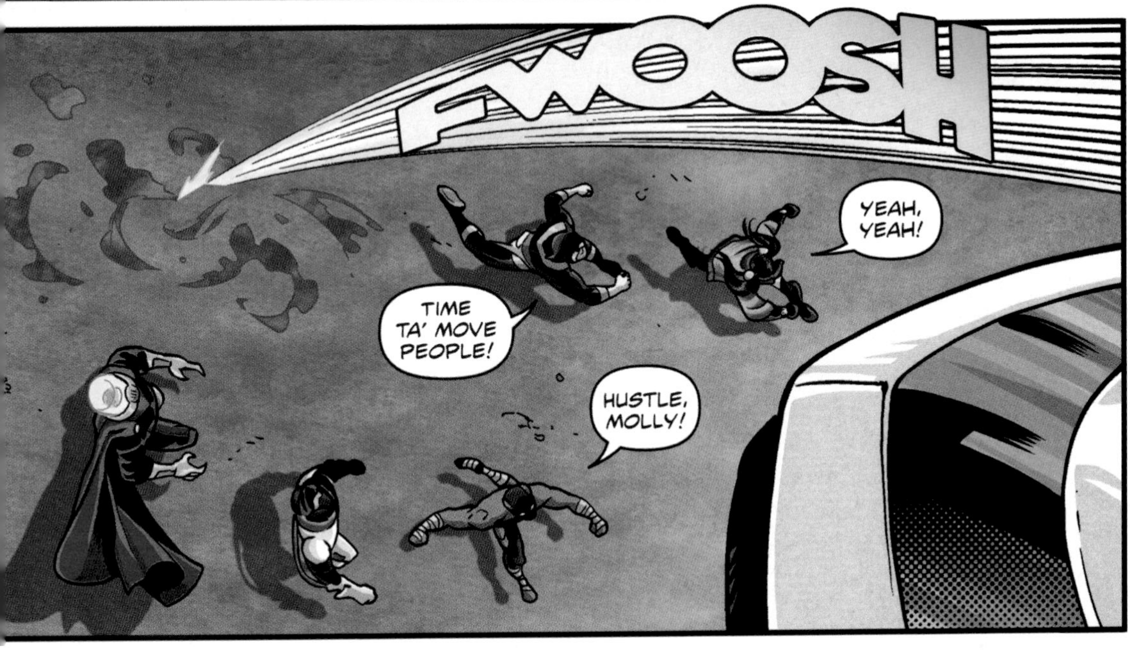
FWOOSH
YEAH, YEAH!
TIME TA' MOVE PEOPLE!
HUSTLE, MOLLY!

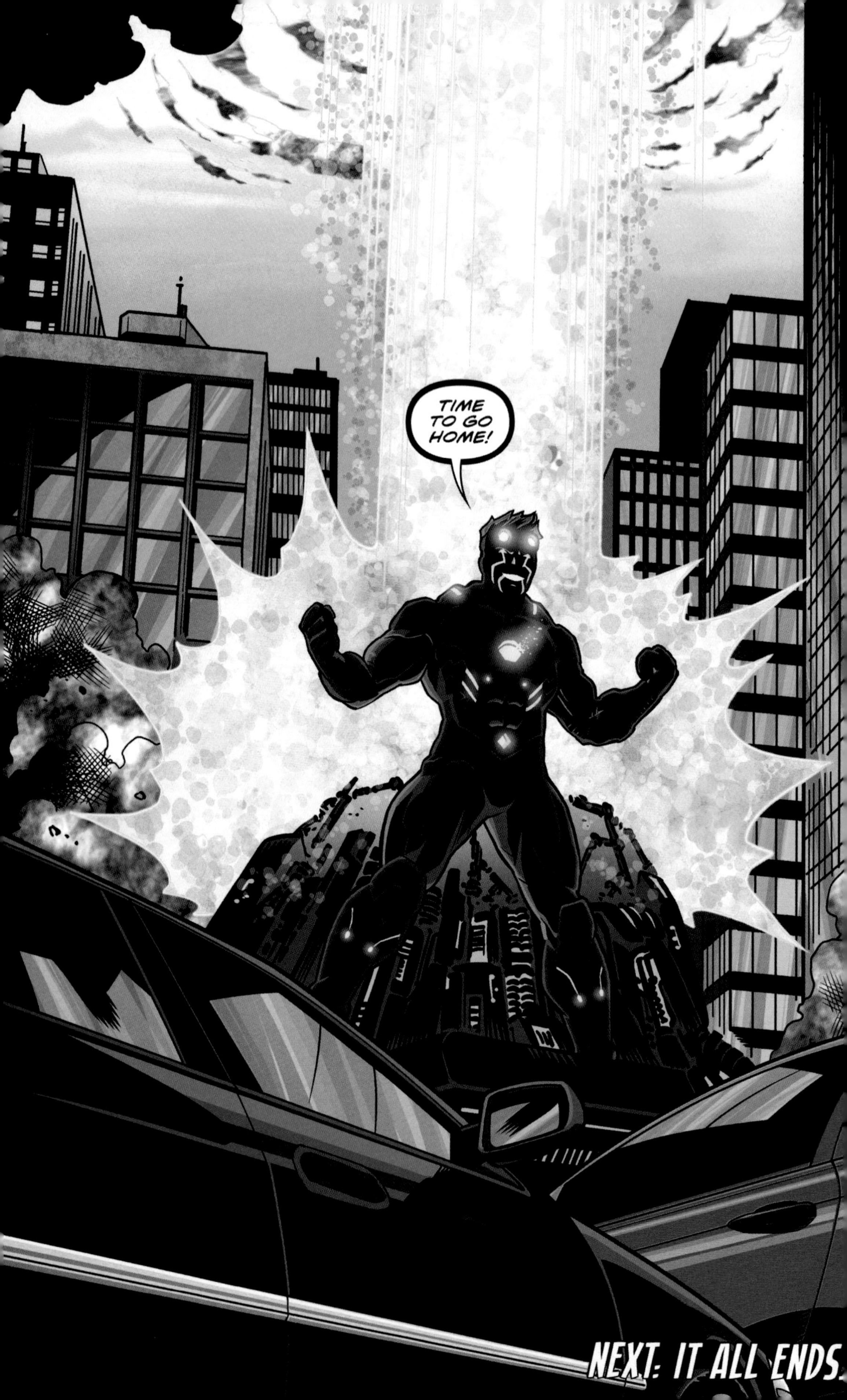
TIME TO GO HOME!
NEXT: IT ALL ENDS.

Here comes the part of the letter when I tell you why you should pick up STRAY when it comes back as a bi-monthly ongoing.

(Wait, grab the first trade and THEN get ready for the new ongoing.)

...st off, you've stuck around for five issues and you're reading a ...ter column. That shows commitment, and for that, we thank you!

...'s letter has been written three times now, and almost had a ...mpletely different tone.

...en we sat down to plot out ACTIONVERSE, the other creators and ...ad a very simple goal in mind; To expose our books to a new ...dience. A bigger one, we hoped, that would embrace all of the ...es. We were asked by the higher ups at ALE if we, the individual ...ators, were interested in doing a crossover. Understand ...mething; all of us, the creators on the books, are all comic book ...ders. Some of us read one book a month; some have pull lists ...th multiple titles. We knew what we were getting into doing an ...vent book." But, think about this...did you know about FIRST ...RO before this mini series? What about FRACTURE? Did you miss ...t on the MOLLY DANGER or MIDNIGHT TIGER Kickstarter ...mpaigns? This isn't an event book, by the standard definition. ...is is a crossover, sure, but in a way, it's more pure than your ...ndard event. Let me explain.

...an be argued that ACTIONVERSE, as a concept, started ten years ...o, before there was an Action Lab. Back then, there was another ...blisher that sought to make a shared universe. And that ...blisher from ten years ago had two creators in common with ...ion Lab today; Ray-Anthony Height and Vito Delsante. Mutual ...miration turned into, "I hope we get to work together someday," ...ich then turned into, "No matter what, our characters share a ...iverse." I won't take credit for what you're holding in your ...nds, and I don't think Ray would either...

...ut, boy, if that's not a heckuva coincidence.

...we stuck to just the two of us, you might not have gotten ...nething this big in scope. And that's why, when Jamal Igle ...nted to be a part of the same universe, we were ecstatic. Because ...thfully, we're not just friends, but fans of each other's work. I've ...own Jamal about as long as I've known Ray, and the desire was ...re to work with him as well. When Jamal got the gig on ...htwing at DC, I bugged him every week to see if I could just ...ch a done-in-one in the run. I love Nightwing, but this...THIS...is ...much better.

...ks might be shocked that Sean Izaakse not only drew this issue, ...t wrote it, too. I'm not. When you work with someone as close as ...have for the past three years, you know exactly what kind of ...ent a person has. Sean is incredibly talented. Seriously. It's ...nning and annoying, really. Hurts a little inside to think that he ...esn't need me to do a good comic, but then I get to read the book ...e everyone else and stand in awe. Sean is a true artist, and I was ...re than happy to step away from this issue. Like all true auteurs, ...just needed a chance.

As creators, the best thing that could happen with our creations is to see them grow on their own. Once an artist draws the first sketch from your description, that character is given life, and as a result, they start to breathe. They start to act like...well, like they do. Or, in some cases, like they always have...you just didn't know it. In short, they start to live. And Rodney, our hero, is just starting to live again. He's reinvented himself, and in someways, unbeknownst to him, he's reinvented the idea of the legacy hero.

(If you don't know, a "legacy hero" is someone that inherits the identity of a mentor. Usually a sidekick, but it's sometimes another hero or, in some cases, someone completely new and different.)

STRAY, the comic, is about a former sidekick who comes back to the world of masks and tights and questions who he is in this world. He knows who he used to be, but just like a wise man once said, you can never go home again. He grew up. He lived. And now, he's returned to a world that moved on without him. He's not an anachronism, per se, but just like every coming-of-age story, he's trying to figure out who he wants to be. He's like every one of us, looking for answers and a way to make it all make sense.

What's coming for STRAY, the comic, and Stray, the character? First, we're going to take a look at his past. I am hesitant to say that this was a storyline that the fans demanded...but no kidding, a ton of readers asked to see more of Rodney's years as the Rottweiler, so Sean and I are going to tell that story. We're going to be joined by a newcomer on art, Phil Cho. I call him a newcomer, but I've been a fan of his for a while. This is just his first mainstream independent (how's that for an oxymoron?) work.

Beyond that, we're going to be filling in a lot of blanks. Sean and I have been congratulated and slapped on the back a lot since Issue One because we have, in just four issues, redefined the phrase, "world building." How else to describe a world where you know none of the characters, but feel as if you've known them all along? So, that being said, we're going to continue doing what we've been doing. Building the StrayVerse, alongside the Actionverse. We're going to bring in new artists, like Phil, and maybe some well known ones, too. We're going to break our comic, so to speak, and rebuild it in new and exciting ways without having to reboot it every 12 months.

We have a lot of stories to tell.

We have many miles to go.

It'd be cliche to say we're just getting started, but...

- Vito Delsante
Pittsburgh, PA
April 2016

STRAY

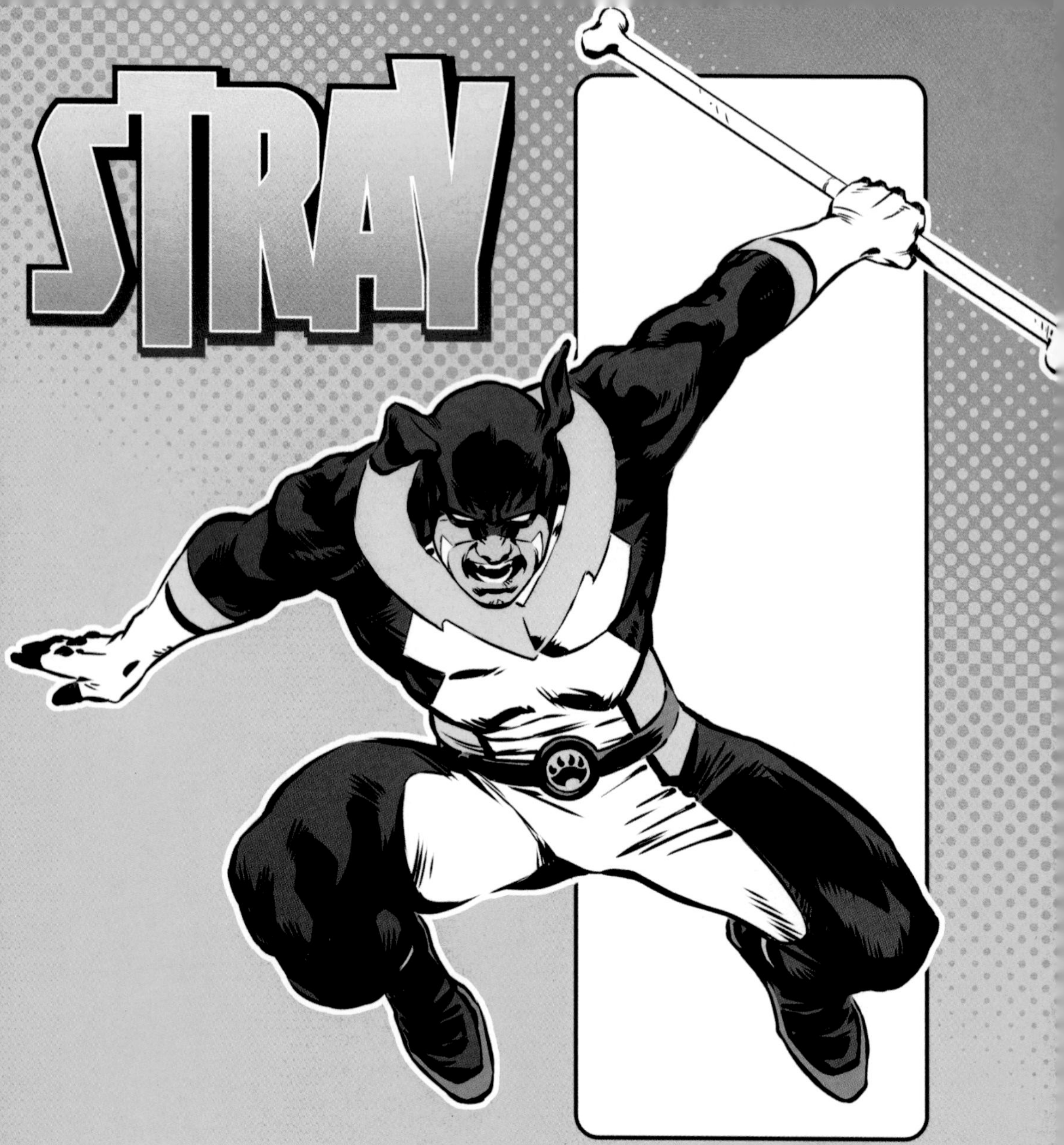

PERSONAL DATA

Alter Ego: Rodney (Roddy) Weller
Occupation: Adventurer
Marital Status: Single
Known Relatives: Daniel Weller (father, deceased), Emily (Emmy) Roth-Weller (mother, deceased), John Weller / Hans von Welle (grandfather, deceased)
Group Affiliation: Pax Mundi (former agent), The TeenAgents (former leader)
Base of Operations: New York City
First Appearance: STRAY #1
Height: 6' 0" **Weight**: 225 lbs
Eyes: Brown **Hair**: Black

HISTORY

Life was normal for Rodney Weller...except for the fact that his father was the hero known as the Doberman (NOTE: his grandfather was the first Doberman). When Rodney was around eight years old, his mother, Emily Roth-Weller, was killed in a car accident. The accident was made more tragic when it was discovered that Emmy was pregnant at the time. This drove his father, Daniel, into a frenzied state, which affected his ability to fight crime. Forced into a sabbatical, Daniel chose to train Rodney in martial arts and basic criminology. Two years later, the Doberman returned...with a sidekick; the Rottweiler (or, simply, Rotty).

Rotty would go on to inspire the first wave of heroes of the modern age, all teenagers. The teens teamed up with Rotty to save Astrea from Dire Wolf and elected him the leader of the TeenAgents, a new team of heroes. During a routine patrol, the Doberman and Rottweiler, (at the time 15 years old), busted a thief who was robbing a convenience store. The thief claimed that he was stealing to feed his family. Rotty had pity, and tried to convince his father to let the man go, but the Doberman disagreed. The disagreement caused a huge rift between father and son, culminating in Rodney quitting. The Doberman would take on another partner, a new Rotty (later known as Argos) soon after.

Rodney, now homeless, turned to drugs. While he would never (in actuality, could never) truly get addicted to them, he favored one, gSmack, more than others. A glamorous drug that only the very rich can afford, Rodney lives in luxury with some of NY's hippest junkies, but aware of how far he's fallen. It wasn't until he found out the Doberman was murdered that he would detox and return to crime fighting under the new name, Stray.

POWERS & WEAPONS

Stray has inherited a hyper-metabolism from his father, the Doberman, but, as mutations are known to do, Rodney's power is even more developed than that of his father's. While the Doberman was able to heal from most serious injuries and wounds, Rodney possesses an equilibrium factor that enables him to recover from any injury. What this means is that when Rodney is injured severely, his body shuts down at it's most "even" state and he falls into a semi-comatose state. To the observer, it looks as if he has passed out and is unconscious, but within, his body is repairing the damage.

He also has empathic manipulation powers, however, this is at a very low level and it seems to tax him when he uses it. Simply put, the angrier he gets, the more fear he can project. Theoretically, he can project an opposite effect as well, but he's unaware of how this works. The effectiveness this ability has on the target, or targets, depends on the strength of the targets control over their own emotions and the strength of their personalities.

Stray uses a shortened bo staff (called a "bone staff" due to it's appearance). The staff separates at the center to become two additional weapons; nunchaku or escrima sticks.

Stray created by and ™ Vito Delsante and Sean Izaakse

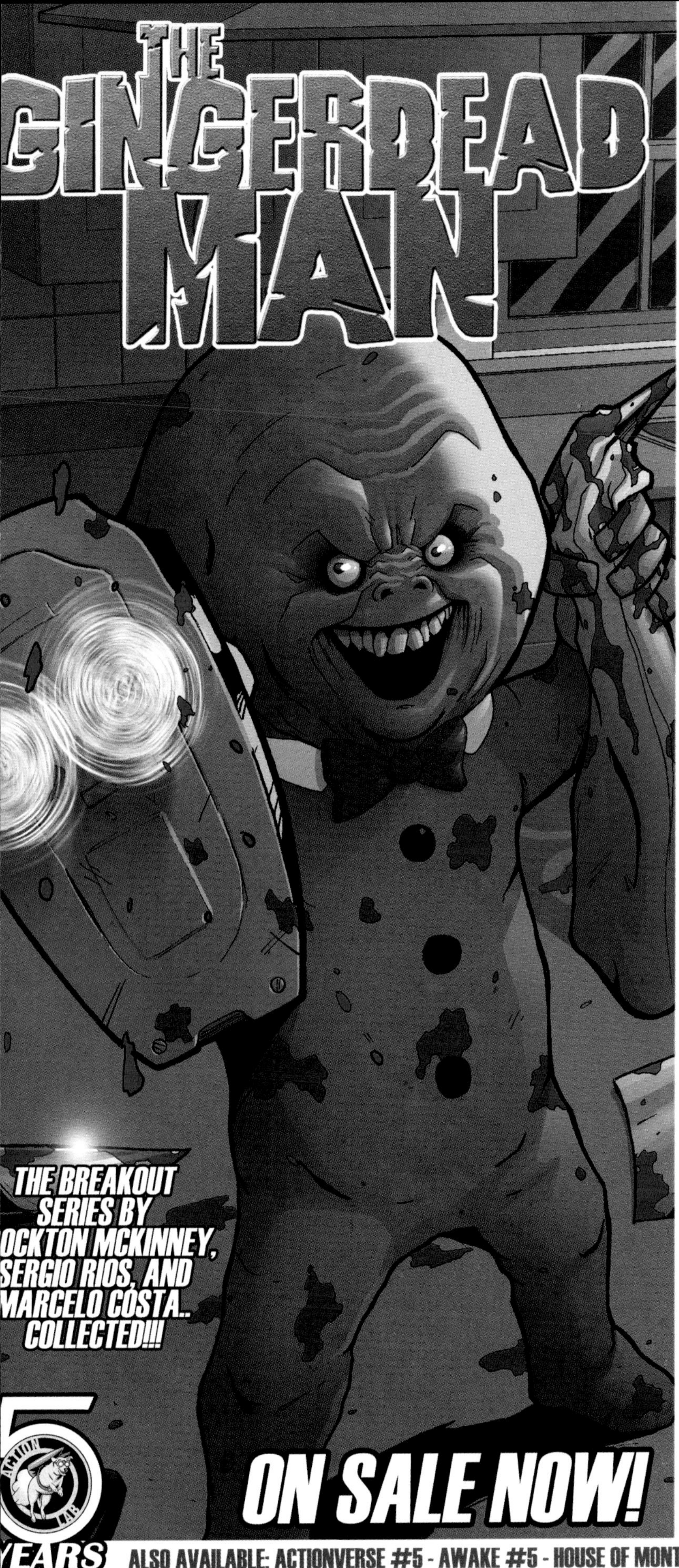
THE GINGERDEAD MAN
THE BREAKOUT SERIES BY
OCKTON MCKINNEY,
SERGIO RIOS, AND
MARCELO COSTA..
COLLECTED!!!
5
ACTION LAB
ON SALE NOW!

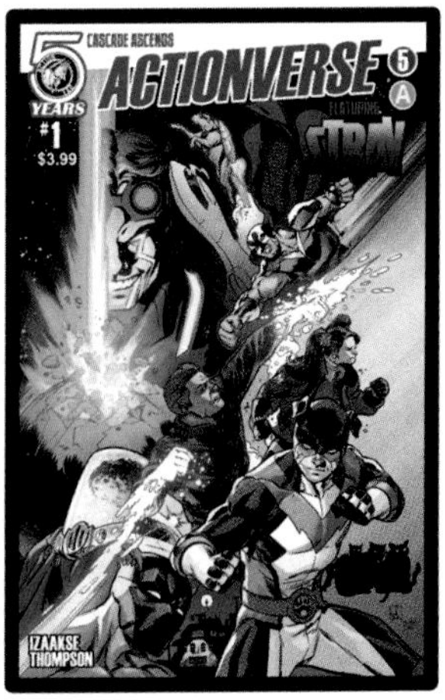
5 YEARS
CASCADE ASCENDS
ACTIONVERSE
#1
$3.99
IZAAKSE
THOMPSON

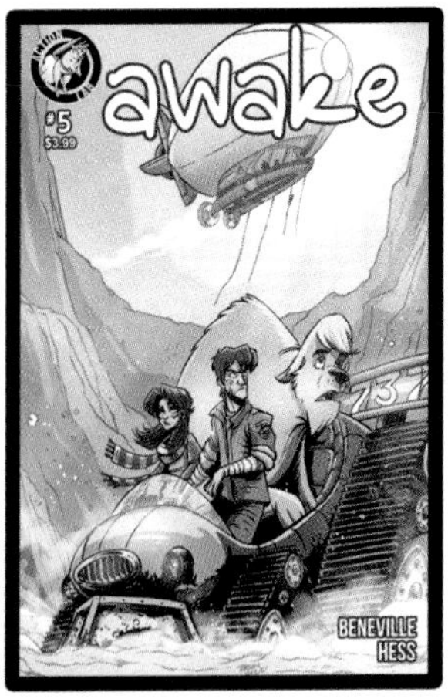
awake
#5
$3.99
BENEVILLE
HESS

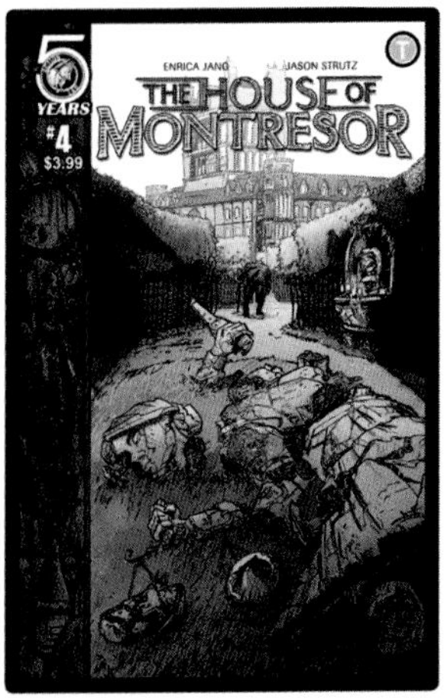
5 YEARS
ENRICA JANG
JASON STRUTZ
THE HOUSE OF MONTRESOR
#4
$3.99

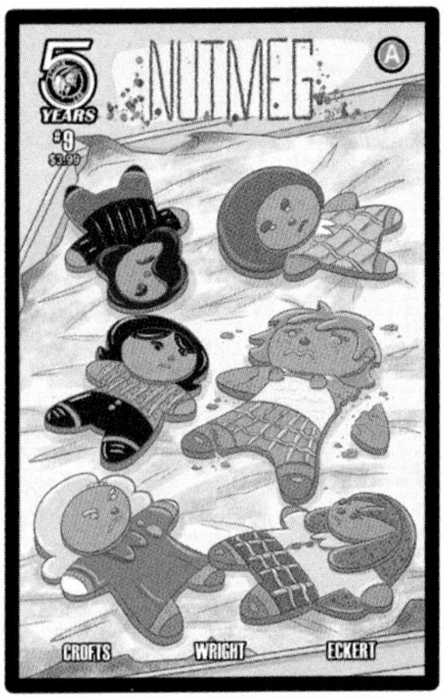
5 YEARS
NUTMEG
#9
$3.99
CROFTS
WRIGHT
ECKERT

YEARS ALSO AVAILABLE: ACTIONVERSE #5 - AWAKE #5 - HOUSE OF MONTRESOR #4 - NUTMEG #9

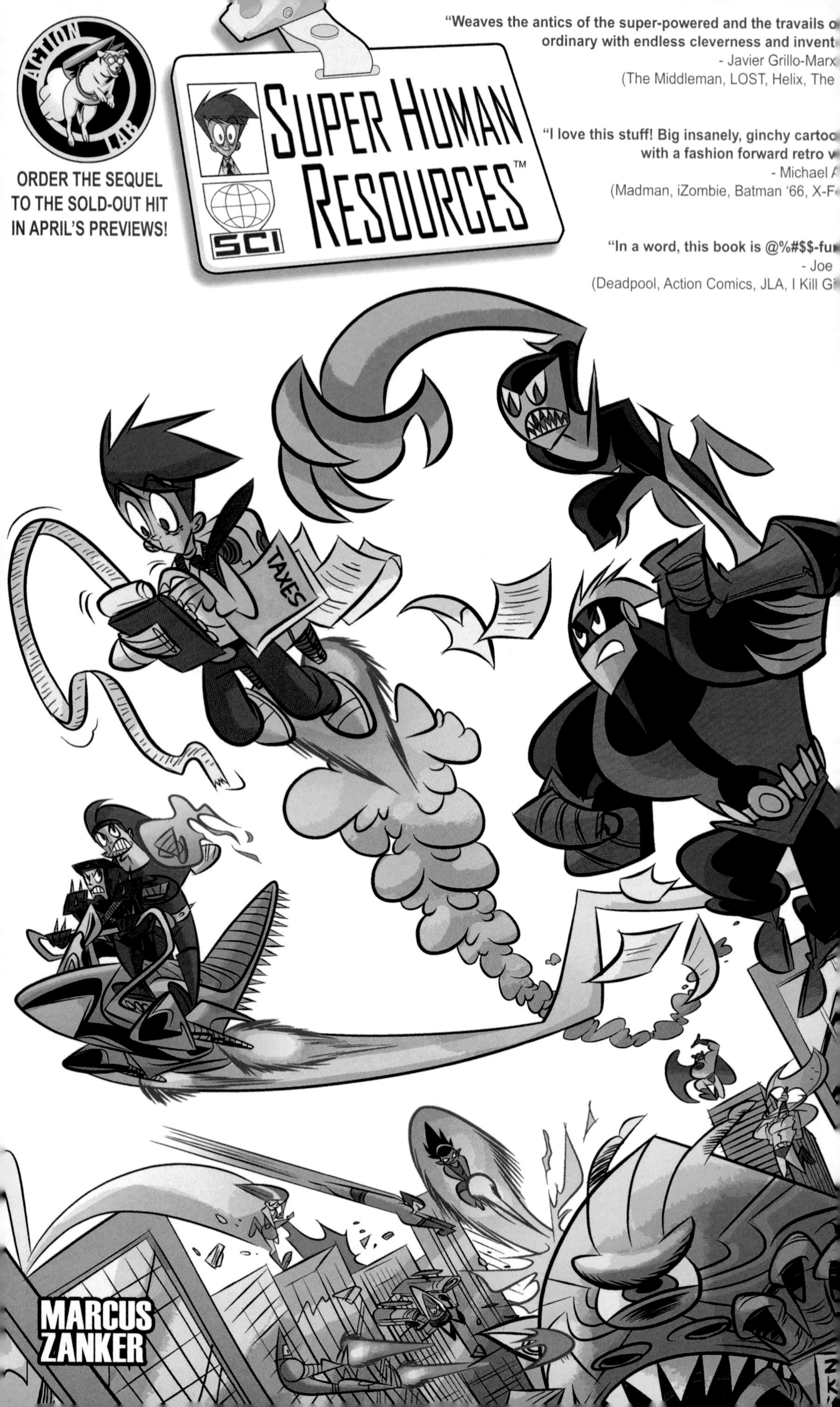
ACTION LAB
ORDER THE SEQUEL
TO THE SOLD-OUT HIT
IN APRIL'S PREVIEWS!
SUPER HUMAN RESOURCES™
SCI
"Weaves the antics of the super-powered and the travails o
ordinary with endless cleverness and invent
- Javier Grillo-Marx
(The Middleman, LOST, Helix, The
"I love this stuff! Big insanely, ginchy cartoo
with a fashion forward retro v
- Michael A
(Madman, iZombie, Batman '66, X-F
"In a word, this book is @%#$$-fu
- Joe
(Deadpool, Action Comics, JLA, I Kill Gi
TAXES
MARCUS
ZANKER

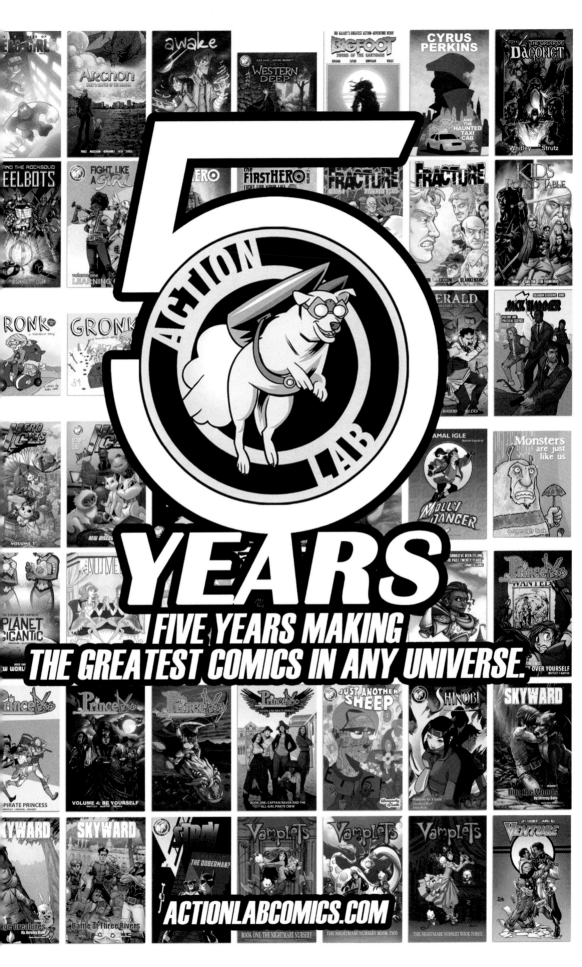

YEARS

FIVE YEARS MAKING
THE GREATEST COMICS IN ANY UNIVERSE.

ACTIONLABCOMICS.COM

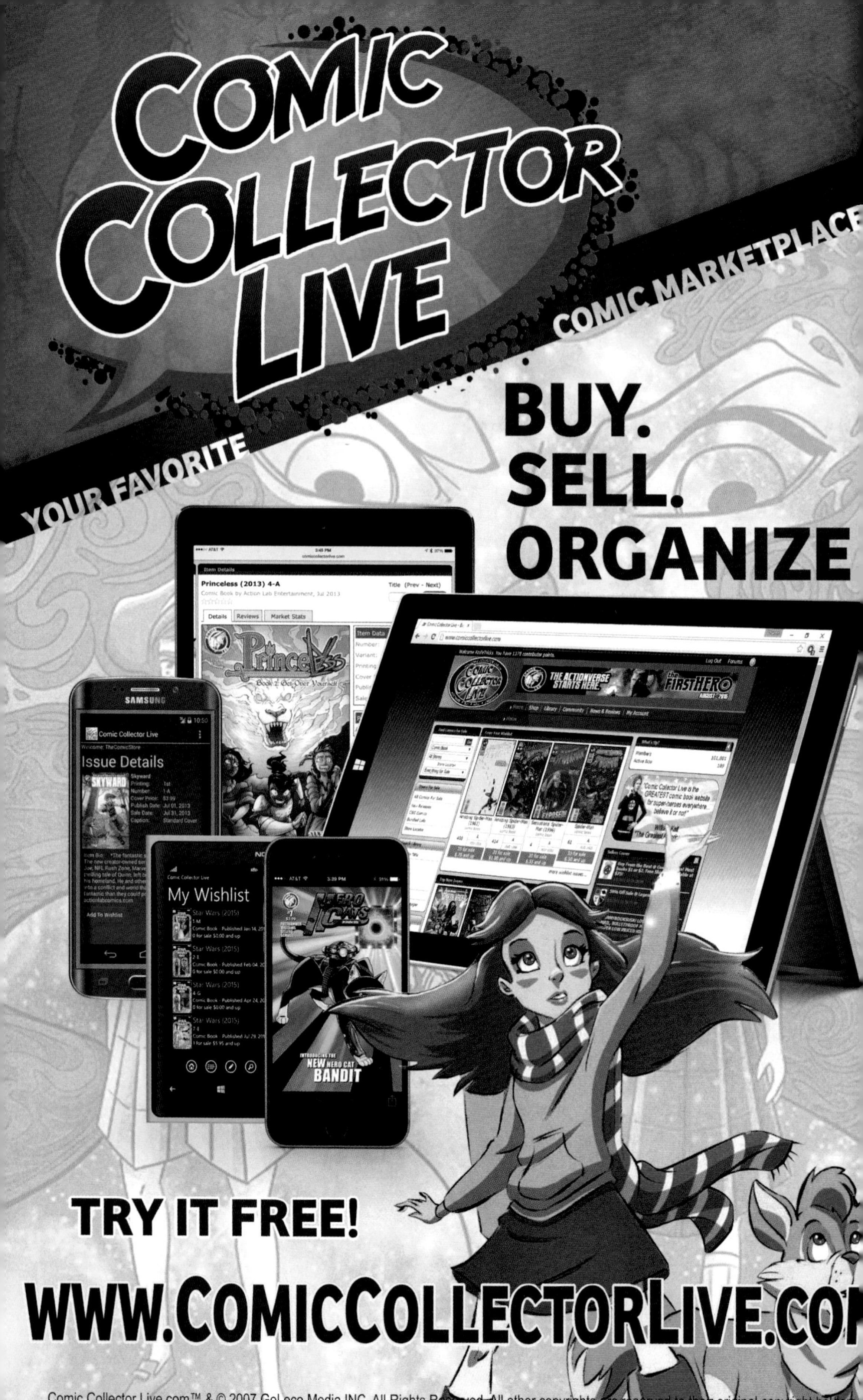
COMIC COLLECTOR LIVE
YOUR FAVORITE COMIC MARKETPLACE
BUY.
SELL.
ORGANIZE
TRY IT FREE!
WWW.COMICCOLLECTORLIVE.COM

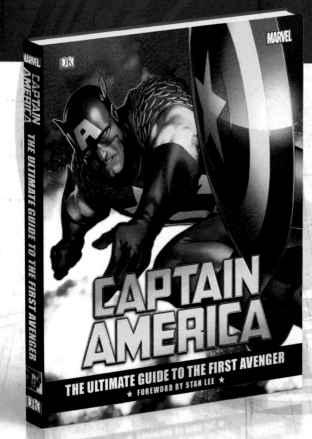

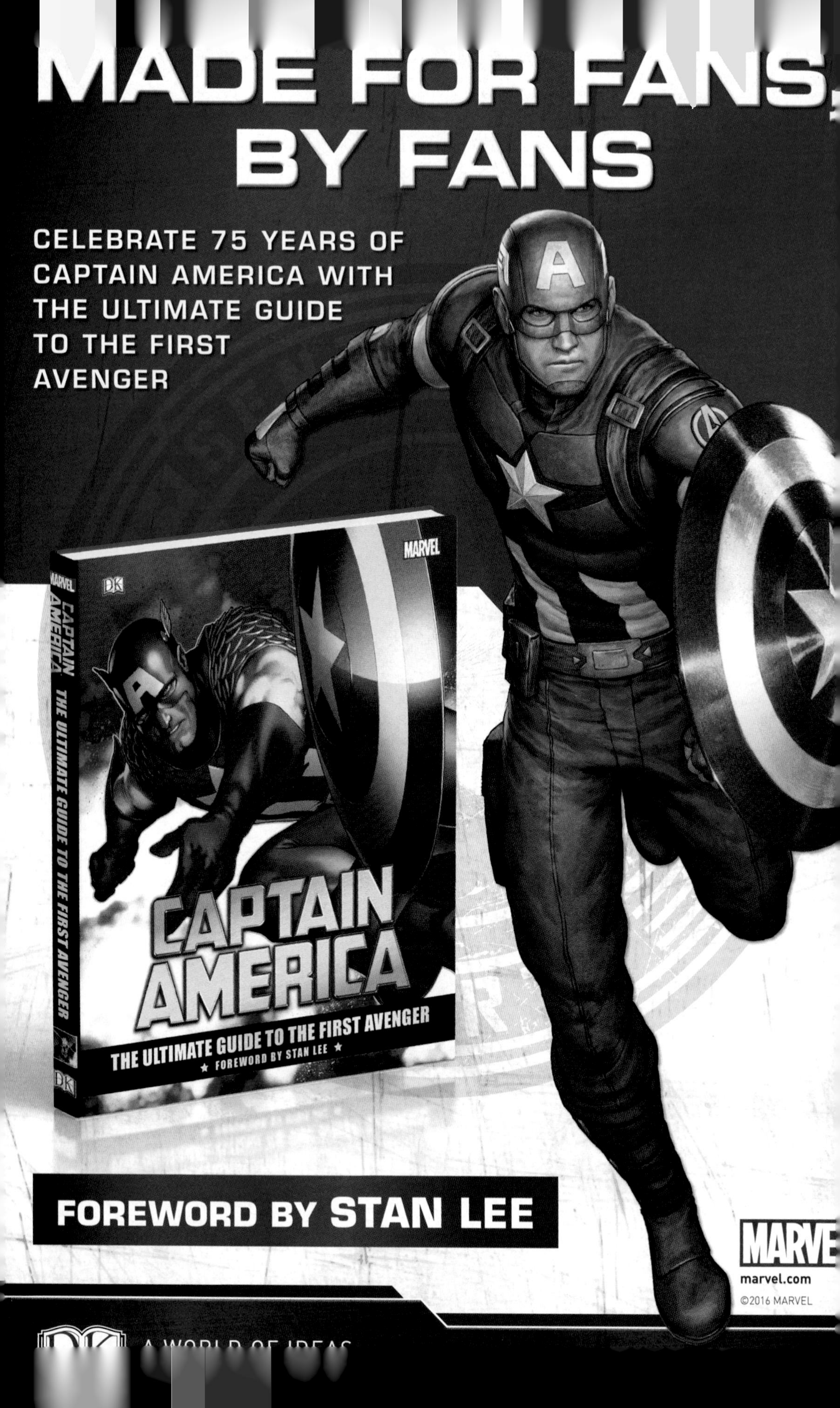

MADE FOR FANS, BY FANS

CELEBRATE 75 YEARS OF
CAPTAIN AMERICA WITH
THE ULTIMATE GUIDE
TO THE FIRST
AVENGER

FOREWORD BY STAN LEE

A WORLD OF IDEAS

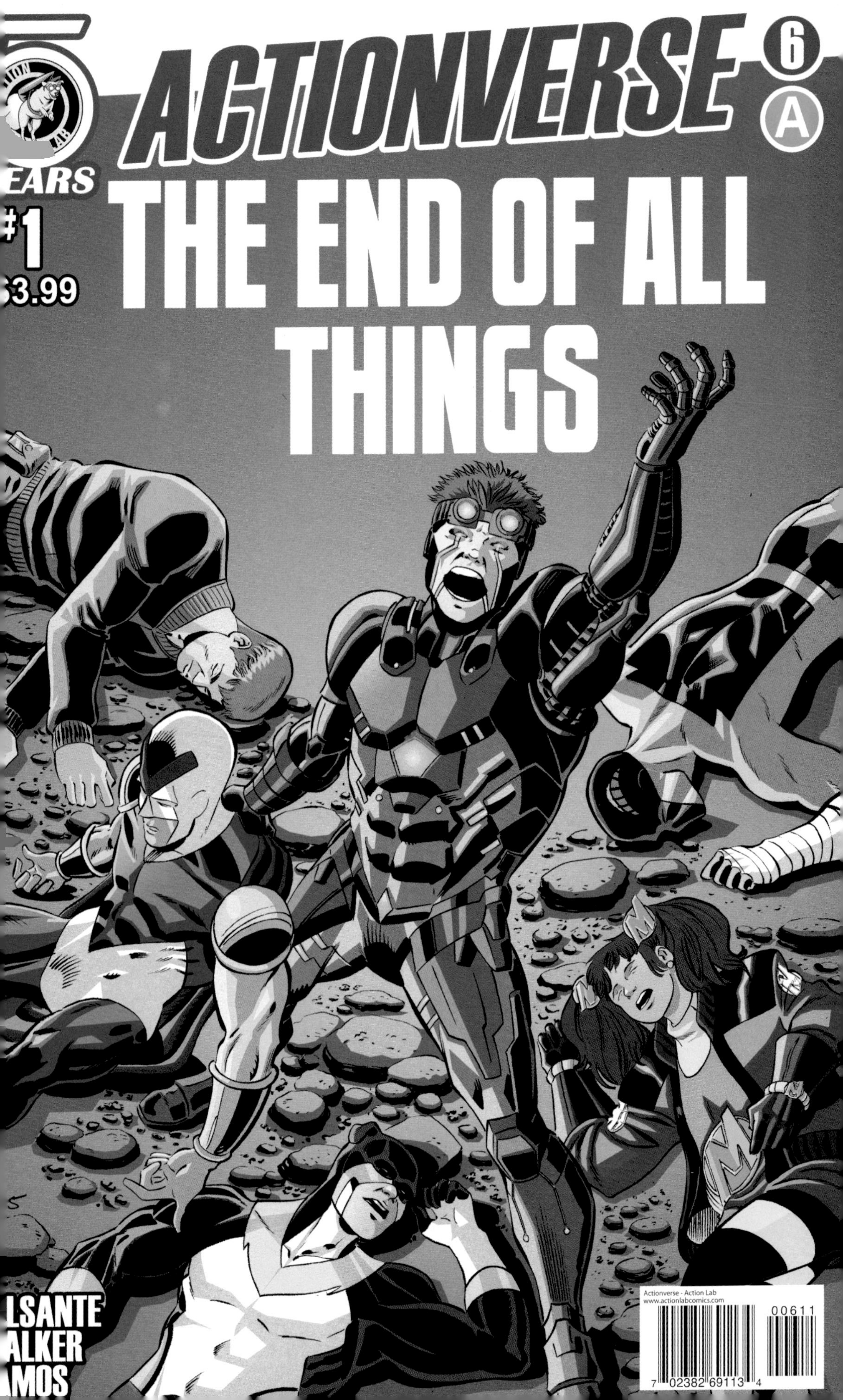

ACTIONVERSE
6
A
5 YEARS
EARS
#1
$3.99
THE END OF ALL THINGS
LSANTE
ALKER
MOS
Actionverse - Action Lab
www.actionlabcomics.com

ACTIONVERSE

Written by
Vito Delsante

Art by
Steve Walker

Colors by Wilson Ramos, Jr.

Letters by Full Court Press

Cover by Steve Walker

Variant Connecting Cover by Ron Frenz, Marc Deering
Ross Campbell and David Bednarski

Edited by
Vito Delsante

PREVIOUSLY

Time's up! Cascade has unleased the power of the portal engine and the world
begins to shake. Molly Danger and her friends are the only ones left to stop him.
All. Hope. Is. LOST.

BRYAN SEATON - PUBLISHER
DAVE DWONCH - PRESIDENT
SHAWN GABBORIN - EDITOR IN CHIEF
JASON MARTIN - PUBLISHER, DANGER ZONE
JAMAL IGLE - VICE-PRESIDENT OF MARKETING
JIM DIETZ - SOCIAL MEDIA DIRECTOR
NICOLE D'ANDRIA - EDITOR
CHAD CICCONI - ENGINE OF DESTRUCTION
COLLEEN BOYD - SUBMISSIONS EDITOR

ACTIONLABCOMICS.COM

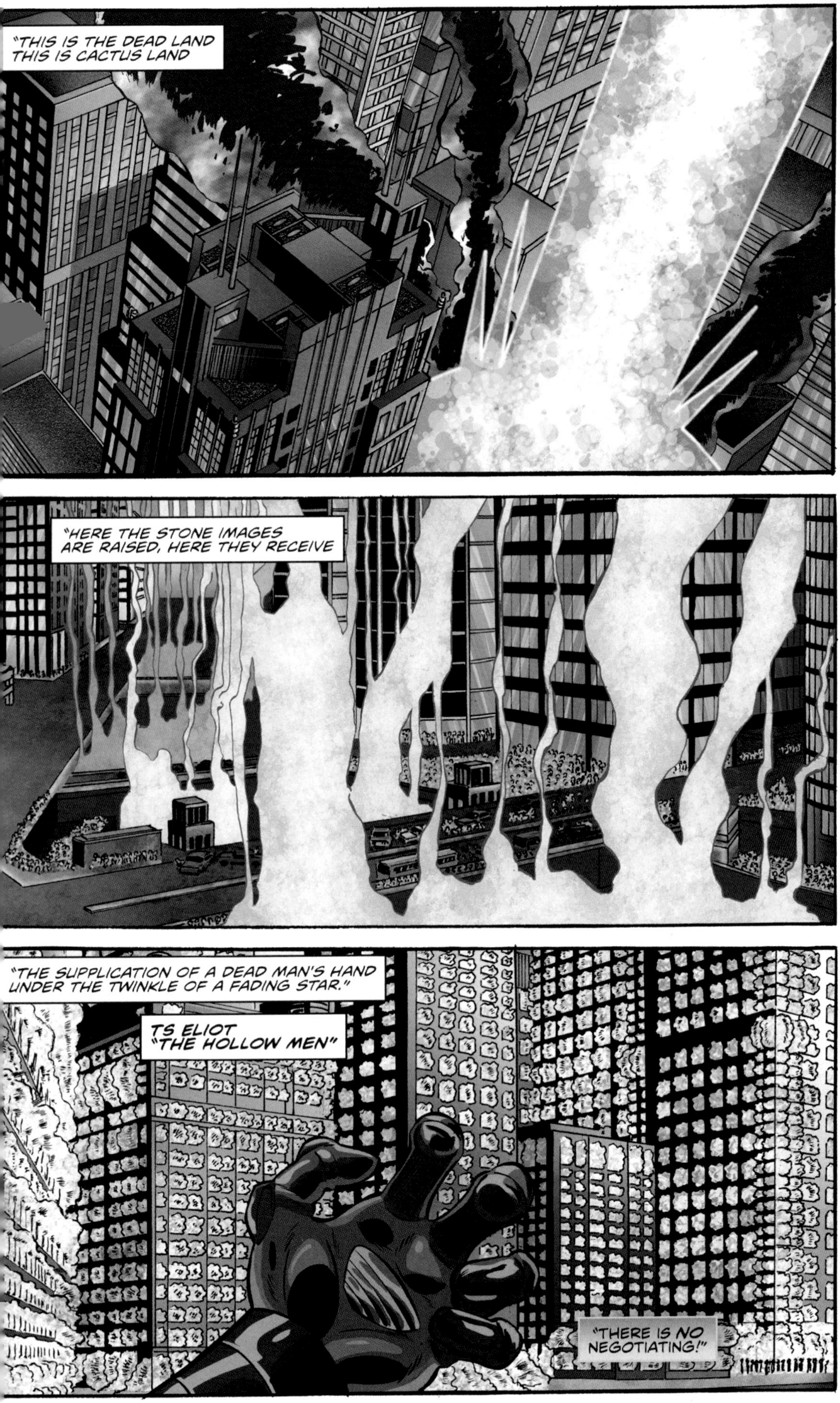
"THIS IS THE DEAD LAND
THIS IS CACTUS LAND
"HERE THE STONE IMAGES
ARE RAISED, HERE THEY RECEIVE
"THE SUPPLICATION OF A DEAD MAN'S HAND
UNDER THE TWINKLE OF A FADING STAR."
TS ELIOT
"THE HOLLOW MEN"
"THERE IS NO
NEGOTIATING!"

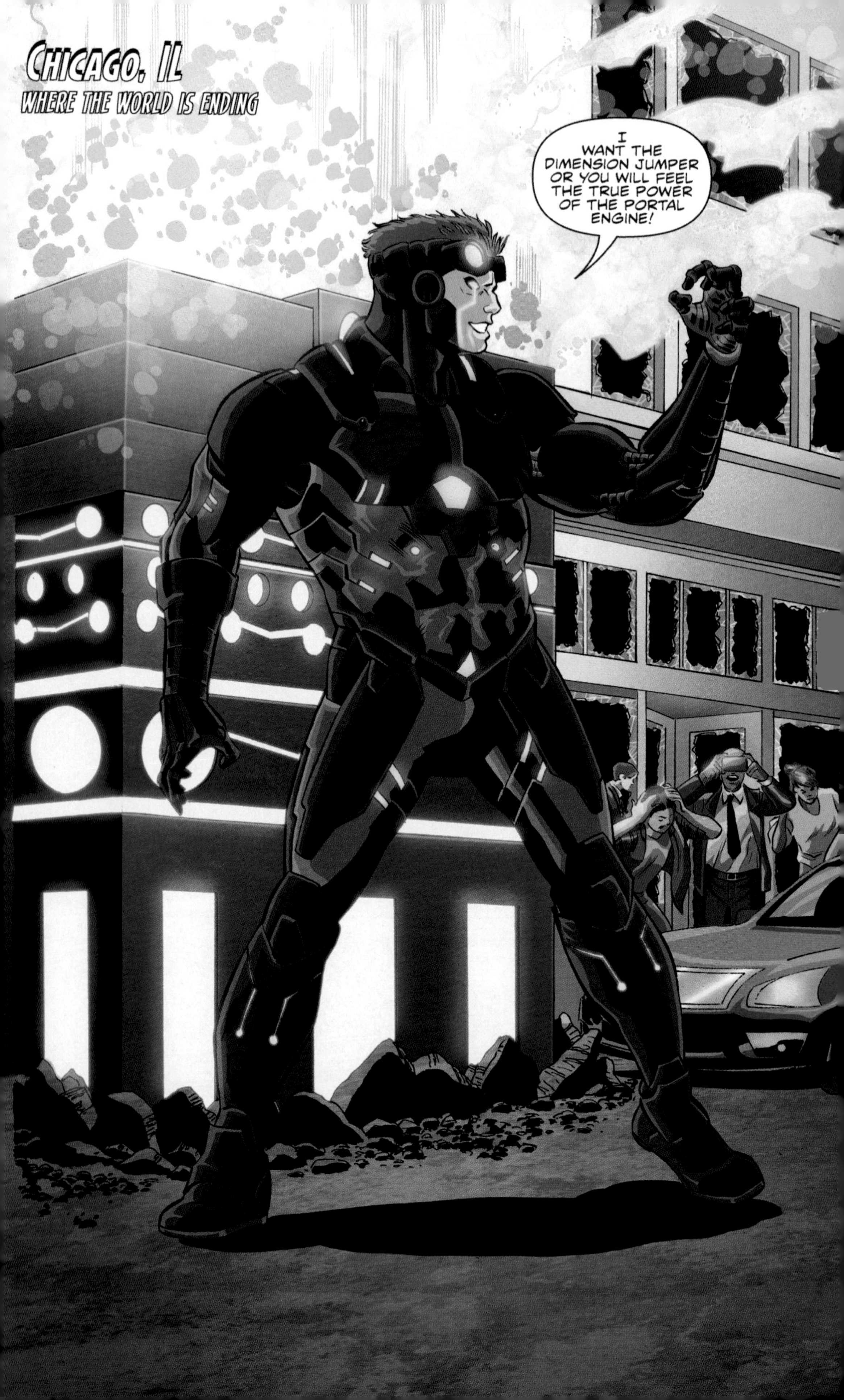
Chicago, IL
Where the World Is Ending
I want the dimension jumper or you will feel the true power of the portal engine!

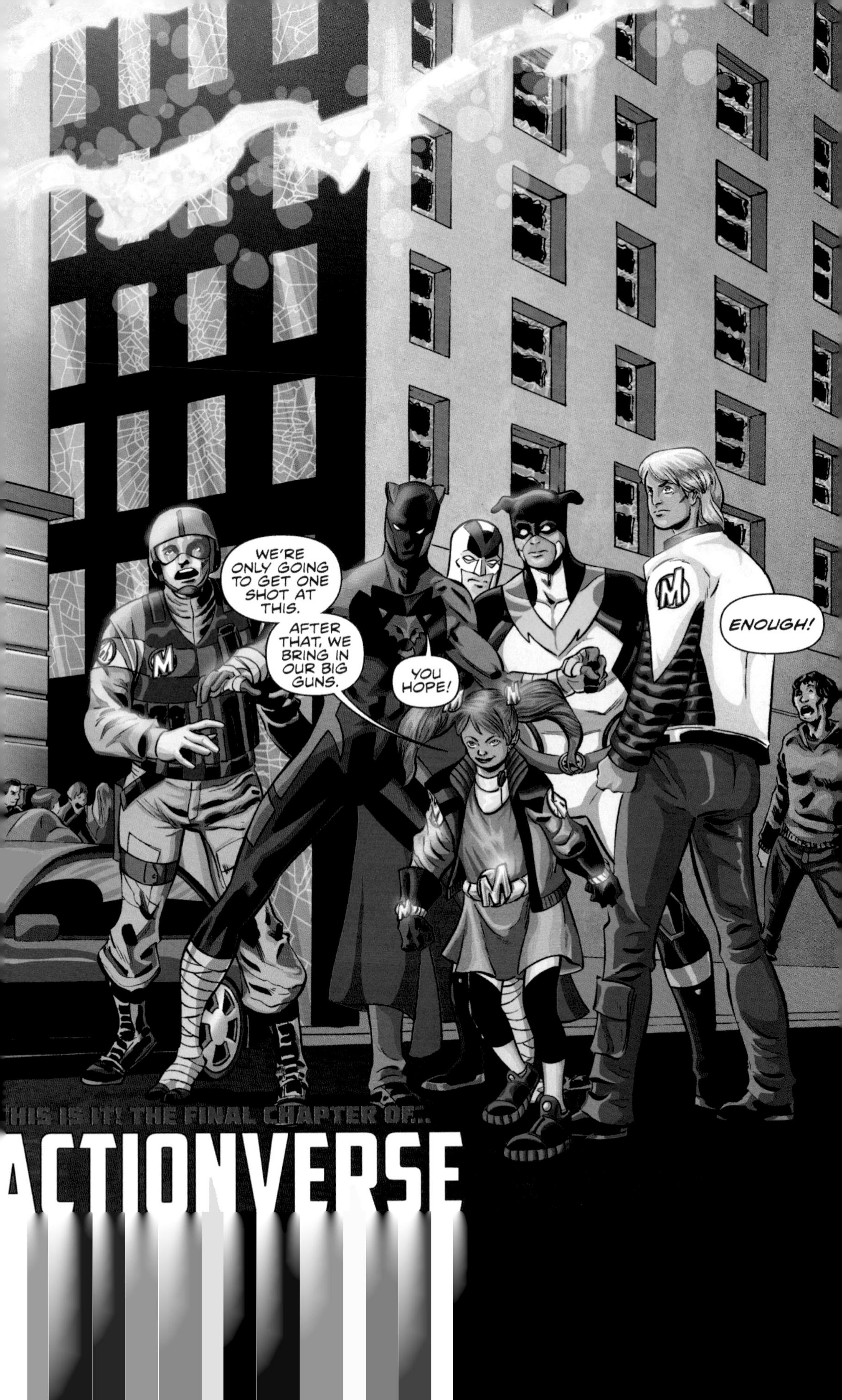
WE'RE ONLY GOING TO GET ONE SHOT AT THIS.
AFTER THAT, WE BRING IN OUR BIG GUNS.
YOU HOPE!
ENOUGH!
THIS IS IT! THE FINAL CHAPTER OF...
ACTIONVERSE

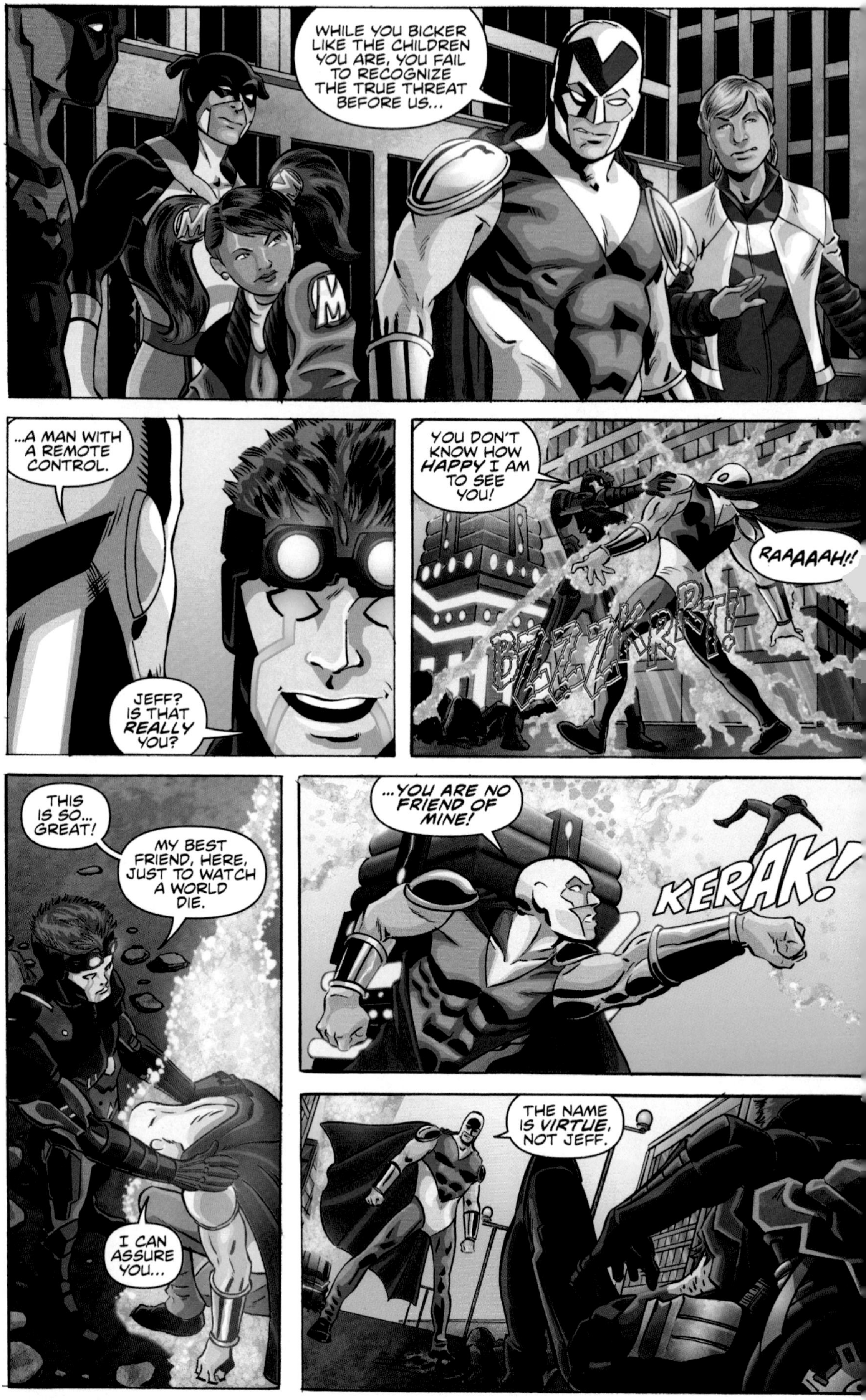
WHILE YOU BICKER LIKE THE CHILDREN YOU ARE, YOU FAIL TO RECOGNIZE THE TRUE THREAT BEFORE US...
...A MAN WITH A REMOTE CONTROL.
JEFF? IS THAT REALLY YOU?
YOU DON'T KNOW HOW HAPPY I AM TO SEE YOU!
RAAAAAH!!
BZZZKRRT!
THIS IS SO... GREAT!
MY BEST FRIEND, HERE, JUST TO WATCH A WORLD DIE.
I CAN ASSURE YOU...
...YOU ARE NO FRIEND OF MINE!
KERAK!
THE NAME IS VIRTUE, NOT JEFF.

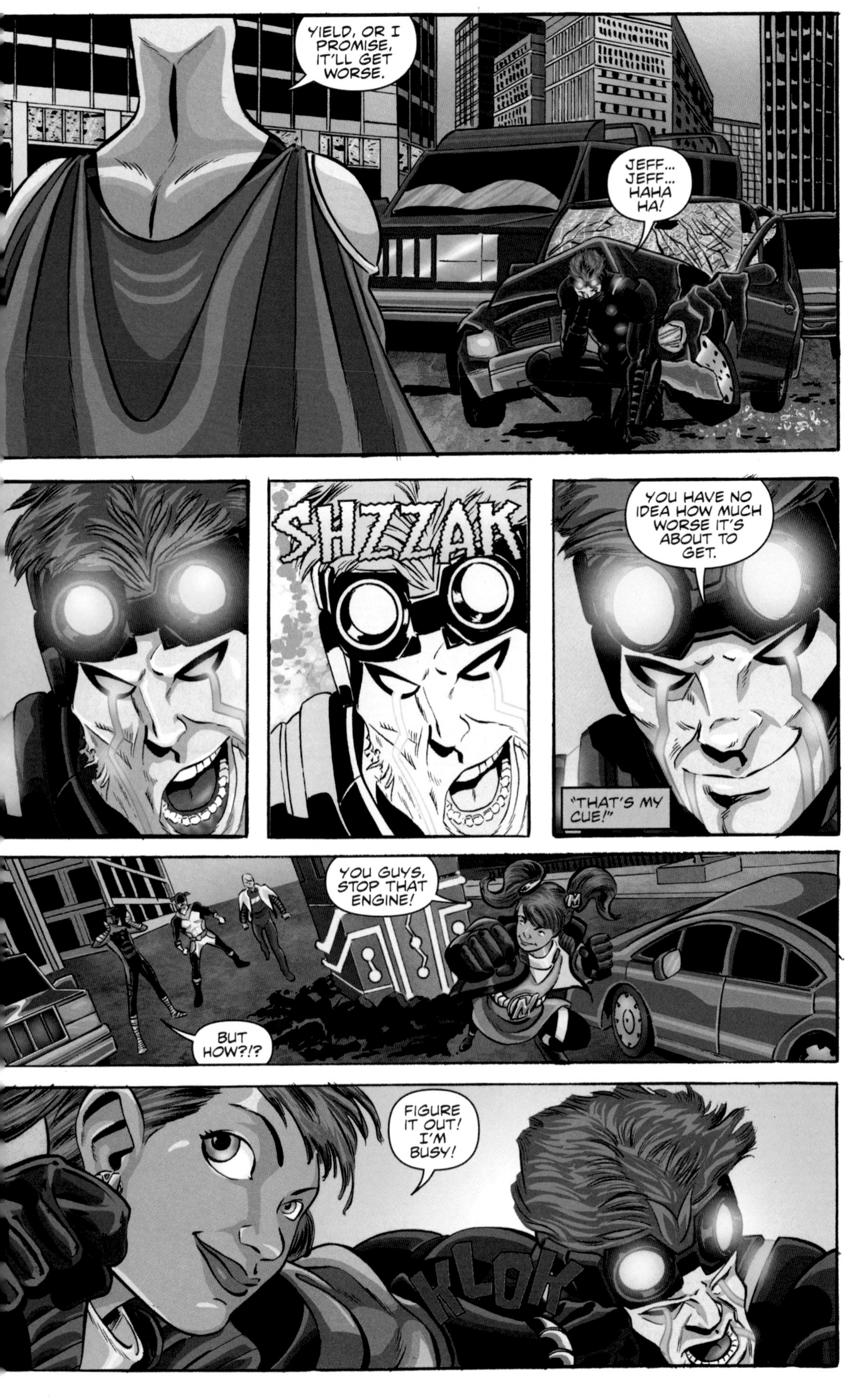
YIELD, OR I PROMISE, IT'LL GET WORSE.
JEFF... JEFF... HAHA HA!
SHZZAK
YOU HAVE NO IDEA HOW MUCH WORSE IT'S ABOUT TO GET.
"THAT'S MY CUE!"
YOU GUYS, STOP THAT ENGINE!
BUT HOW?!?
FIGURE IT OUT! I'M BUSY!
KLOK

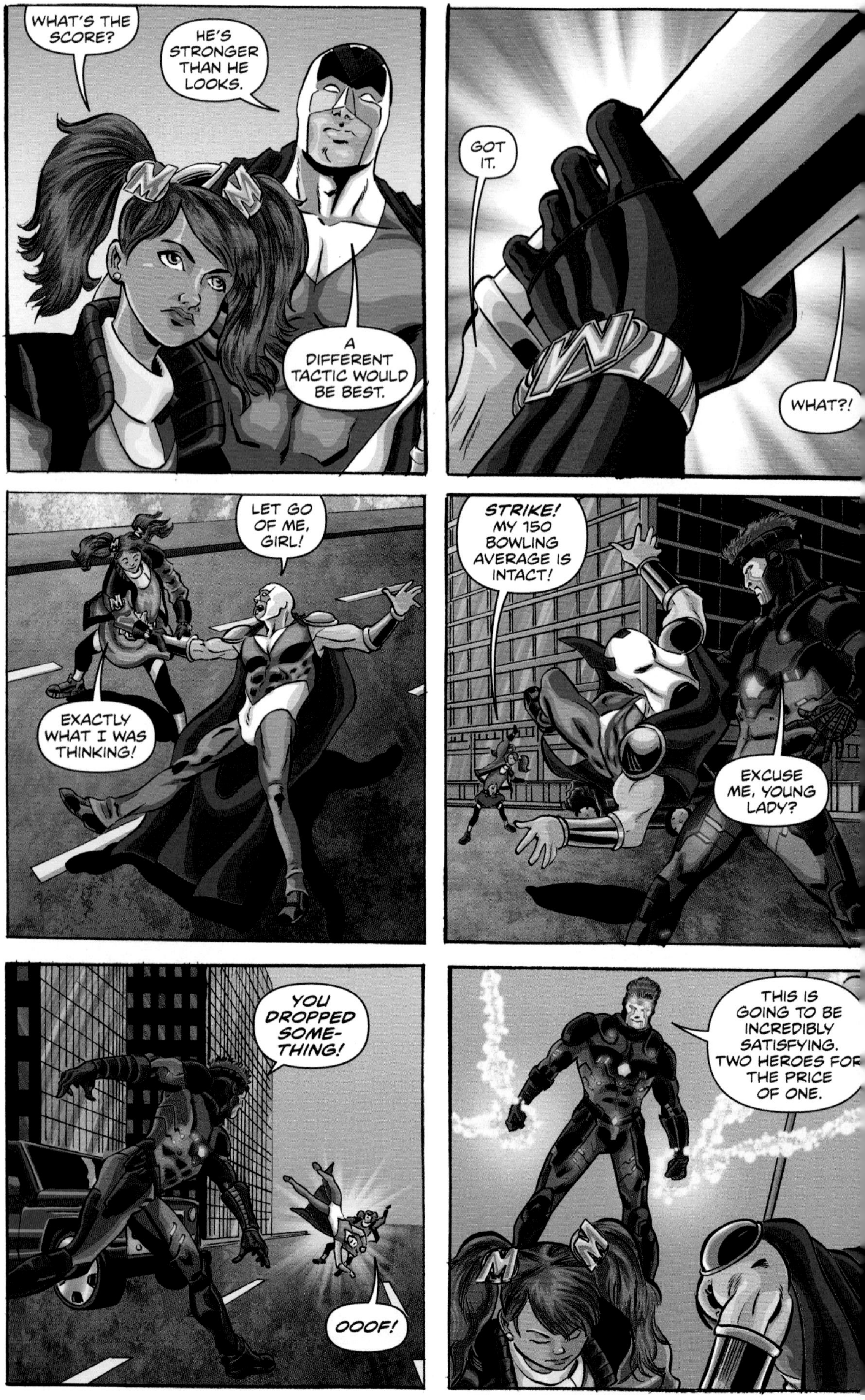
WHAT'S THE SCORE?
HE'S STRONGER THAN HE LOOKS.
A DIFFERENT TACTIC WOULD BE BEST.
GOT IT.
WHAT?!
LET GO OF ME, GIRL!
EXACTLY WHAT I WAS THINKING!
STRIKE! MY 150 BOWLING AVERAGE IS INTACT!
EXCUSE ME, YOUNG LADY?
YOU DROPPED SOME-THING!
OOOF!
THIS IS GOING TO BE INCREDIBLY SATISFYING. TWO HEROES FOR THE PRICE OF ONE.

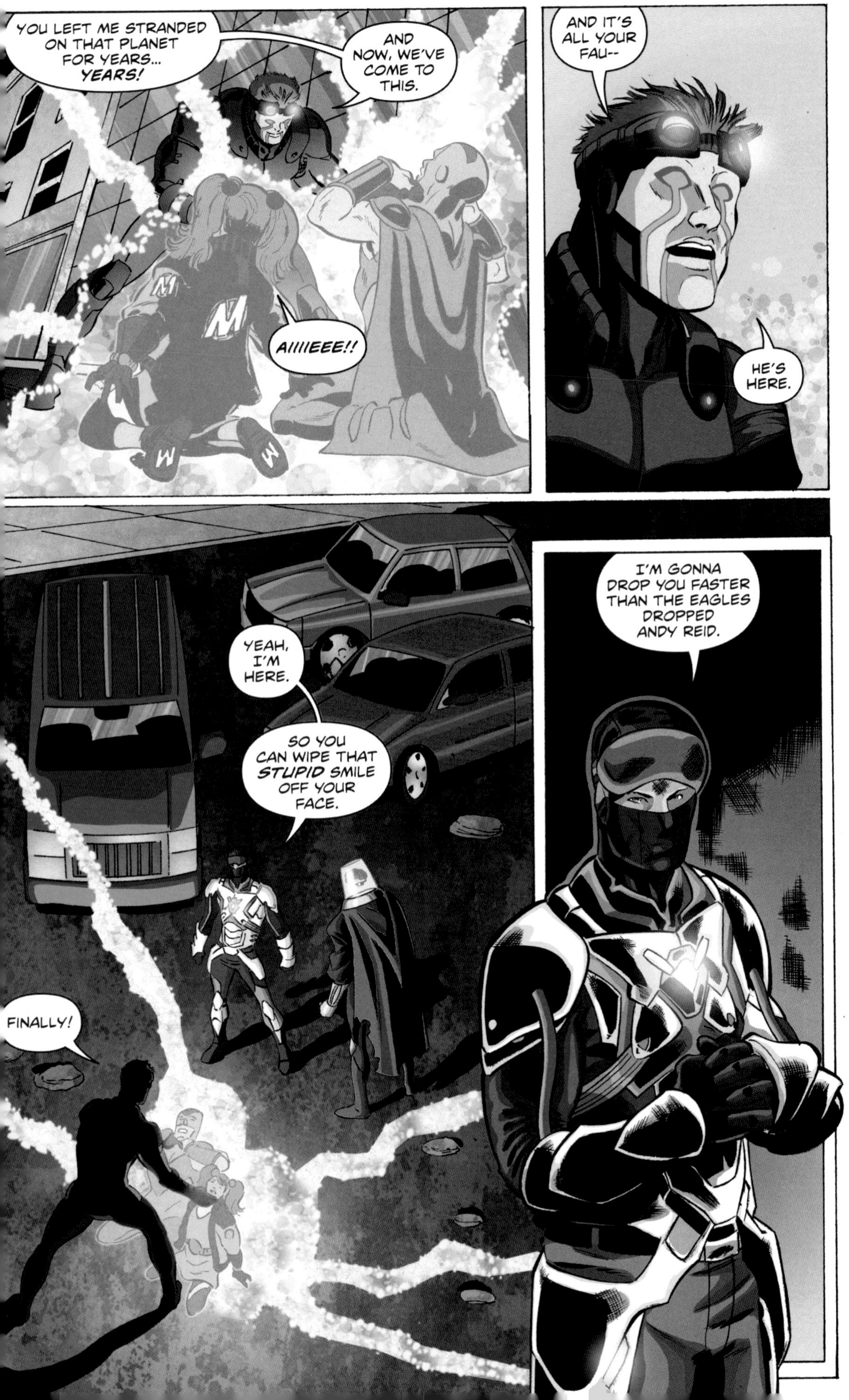
YOU LEFT ME STRANDED ON THAT PLANET FOR YEARS... YEARS!
AND NOW, WE'VE COME TO THIS.
AIIIIEEE!!
AND IT'S ALL YOUR FAU--
HE'S HERE.
YEAH, I'M HERE.
SO YOU CAN WIPE THAT STUPID SMILE OFF YOUR FACE.
I'M GONNA DROP YOU FASTER THAN THE EAGLES DROPPED ANDY REID.
FINALLY!

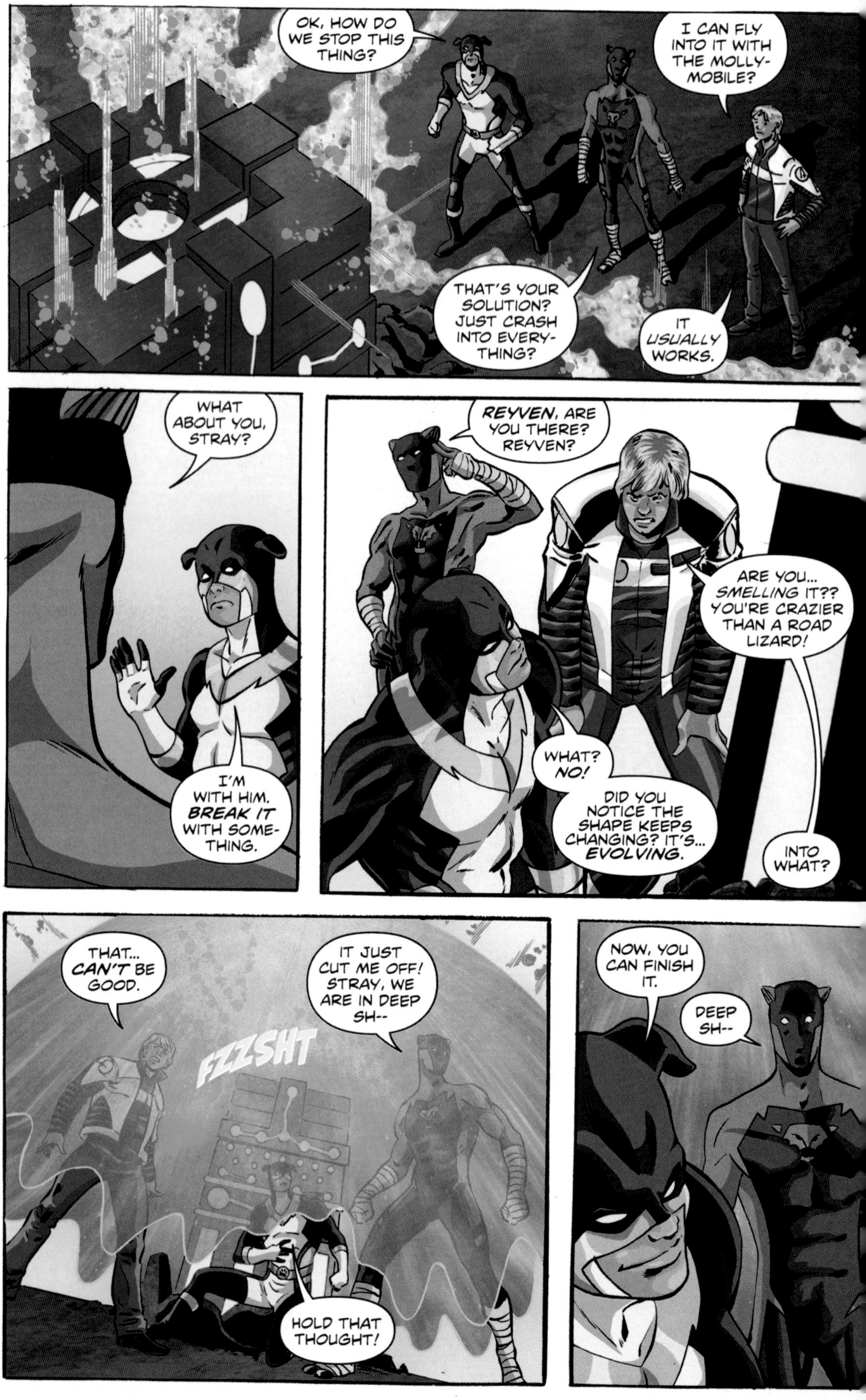
OK, HOW DO WE STOP THIS THING?
I CAN FLY INTO IT WITH THE MOLLY-MOBILE?
THAT'S YOUR SOLUTION? JUST CRASH INTO EVERY-THING?
IT USUALLY WORKS.
WHAT ABOUT YOU, STRAY?
I'M WITH HIM. BREAK IT WITH SOME-THING.
REYVEN, ARE YOU THERE? REYVEN?
ARE YOU... SMELLING IT?? YOU'RE CRAZIER THAN A ROAD LIZARD!
WHAT? NO!
DID YOU NOTICE THE SHAPE KEEPS CHANGING? IT'S... EVOLVING.
INTO WHAT?
THAT... CAN'T BE GOOD.
IT JUST CUT ME OFF! STRAY, WE ARE IN DEEP SH--
FZZSHT
HOLD THAT THOUGHT!
NOW, YOU CAN FINISH IT.
DEEP SH--

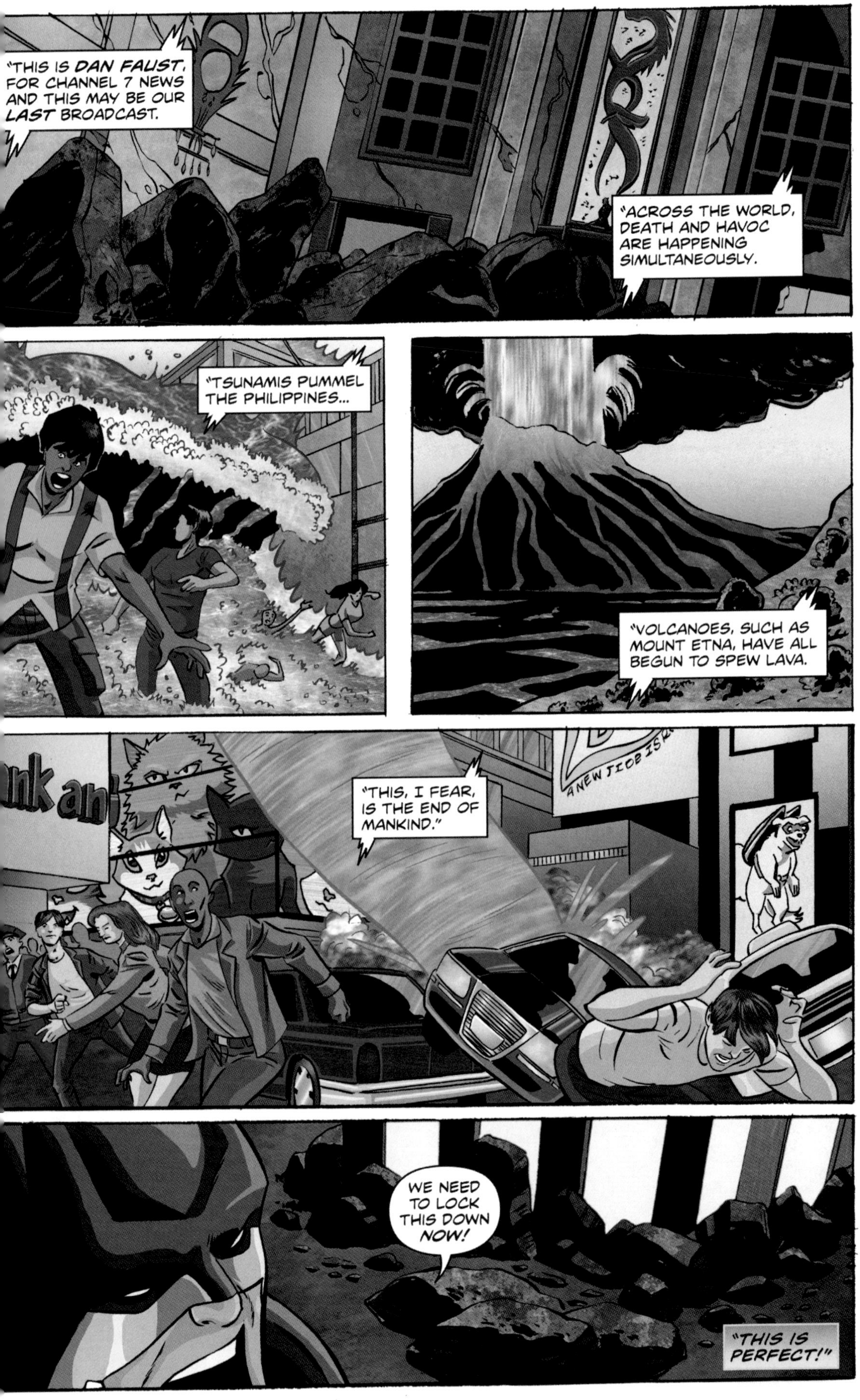

"THIS IS *DAN FAUST*, FOR CHANNEL 7 NEWS AND THIS MAY BE OUR *LAST* BROADCAST.
"ACROSS THE WORLD, DEATH AND HAVOC ARE HAPPENING SIMULTANEOUSLY.
"TSUNAMIS PUMMEL THE PHILIPPINES...
"VOLCANOES, SUCH AS MOUNT ETNA, HAVE ALL BEGUN TO SPEW LAVA.
"THIS, I FEAR, IS THE END OF MANKIND."
WE NEED TO LOCK THIS DOWN *NOW!*
"*THIS IS PERFECT!*"

I COULDN'T HAVE WRITTEN A BETTER ENDING.

I CAN LEAVE MY GREATEST RIVAL STRANDED ON A DEAD WORLD.

JUST LIKE HE DID TO ME.

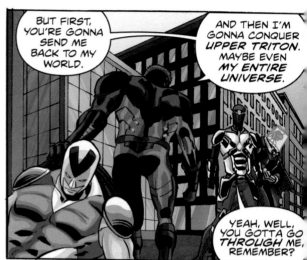

BUT FIRST, YOU'RE GONNA SEND ME BACK TO MY WORLD.

AND THEN I'M GONNA CONQUER UPPER TRITON. MAYBE EVEN MY ENTIRE UNIVERSE.

YEAH, WELL, YOU GOTTA GO THROUGH ME, REMEMBER?

HEH. FUNNY CHOICE OF WORDS.

YOU DON'T EVEN KNOW HOW POWERFUL YOU ARE, DO YOU?

MAN, YOU'RE INSANE IF YOU THINK I'M GOING TO HELP YOU.

THAT'S IT. KEEP HIM DISTRACTED WHILE I CALIBRATE.

HELP ME? YOU HAVE NO CHOICE.

NOTHING YOU DO CAN, OR WILL, HELP THIS WORLD.

YAAARRGH!

"HEH, YOU CAN'T EVEN HELP VIRTUE!"

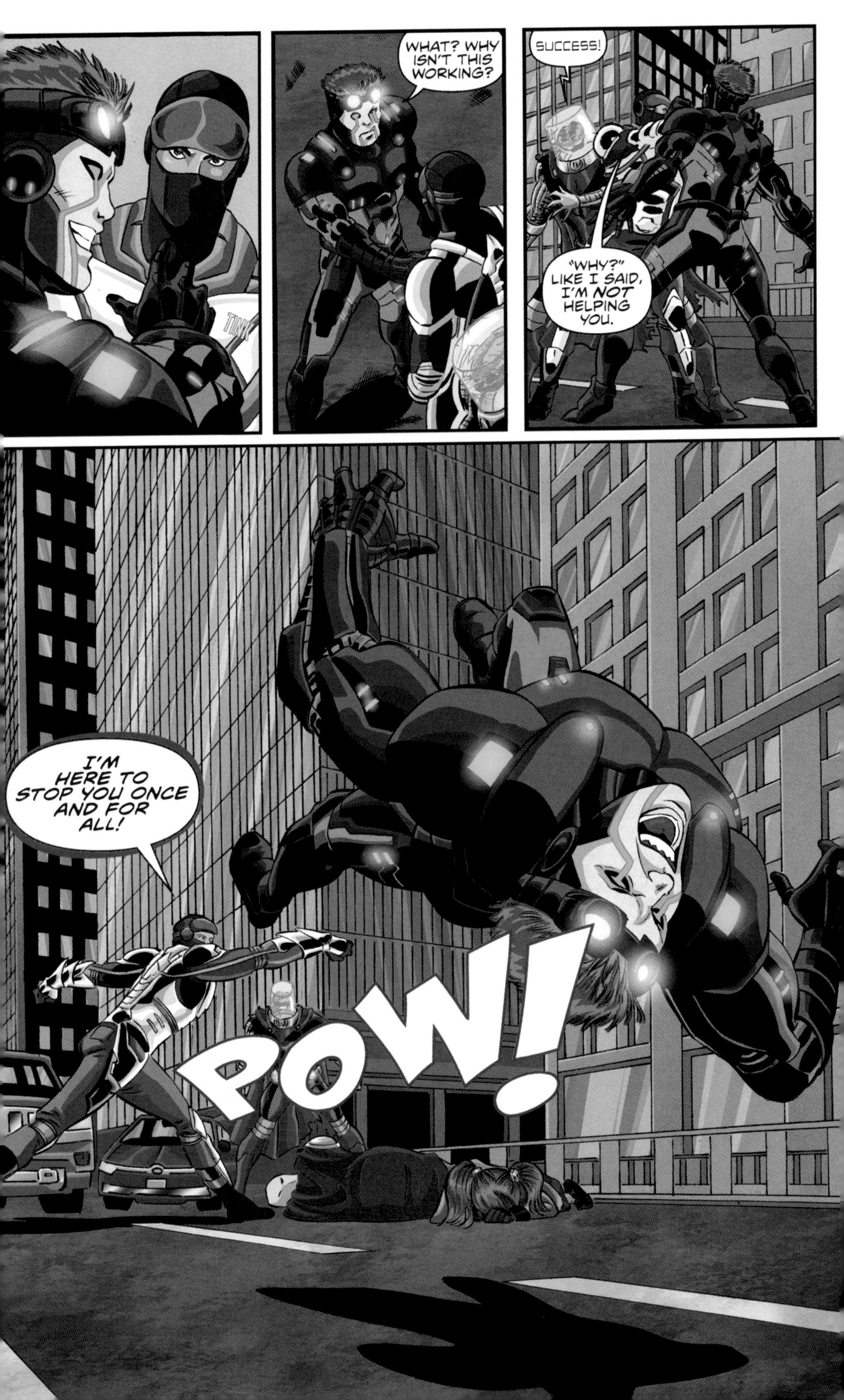
TINK
WHAT? WHY ISN'T THIS WORKING?
SUCCESS!
"WHY?" LIKE I SAID, I'M *NOT* HELPING YOU.
I'M HERE TO STOP YOU ONCE AND FOR ALL!
POW!

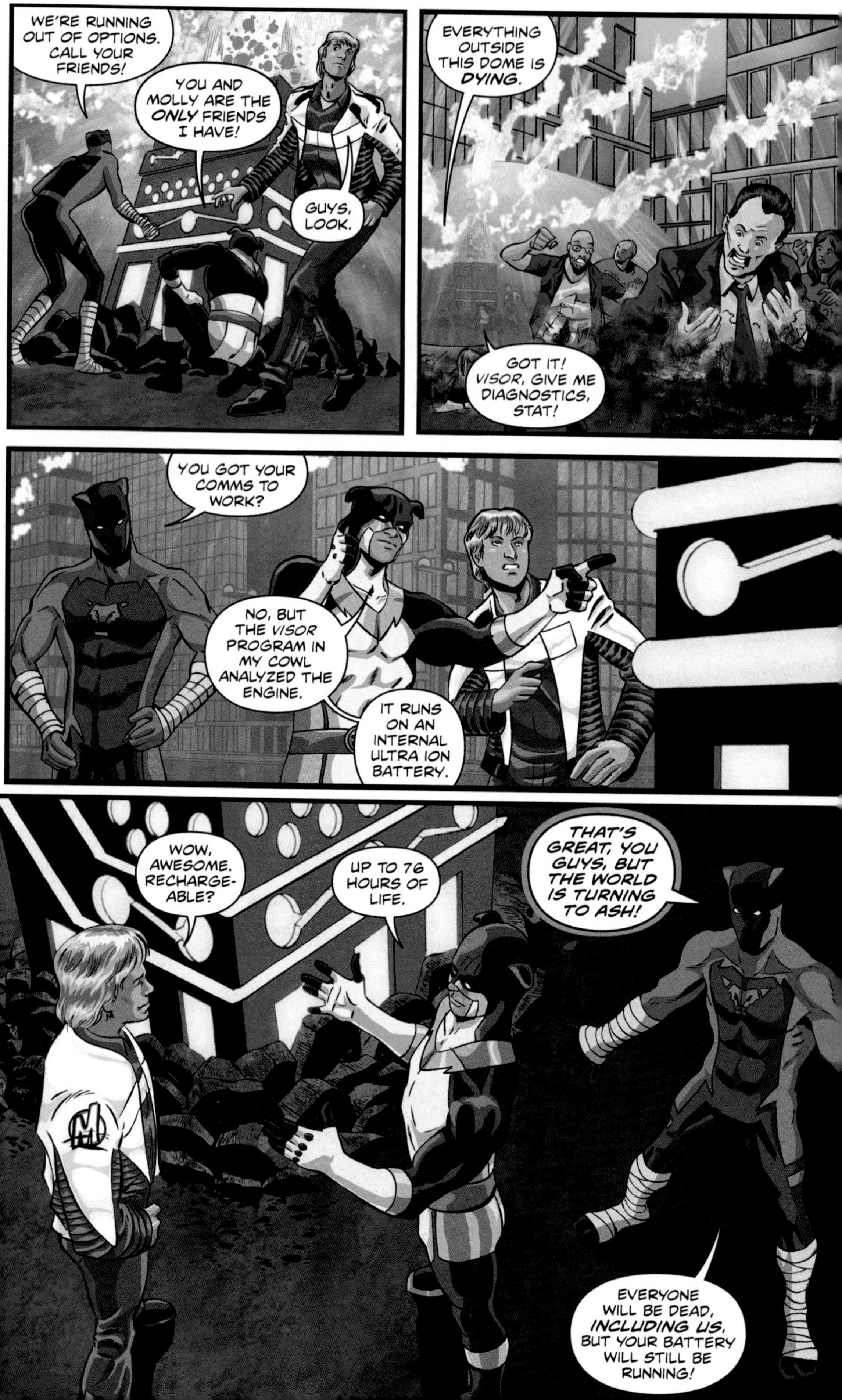
WE'RE RUNNING OUT OF OPTIONS. CALL YOUR FRIENDS!
YOU AND MOLLY ARE THE ONLY FRIENDS I HAVE!
GUYS, LOOK.
EVERYTHING OUTSIDE THIS DOME IS DYING.
GOT IT! VISOR, GIVE ME DIAGNOSTICS, STAT!
YOU GOT YOUR COMMS TO WORK?
NO, BUT THE VISOR PROGRAM IN MY COWL ANALYZED THE ENGINE.
IT RUNS ON AN INTERNAL ULTRA ION BATTERY.
WOW, AWESOME. RECHARGE-ABLE?
UP TO 76 HOURS OF LIFE.
THAT'S GREAT, YOU GUYS, BUT THE WORLD IS TURNING TO ASH!
EVERYONE WILL BE DEAD, INCLUDING US, BUT YOUR BATTERY WILL STILL BE RUNNING!

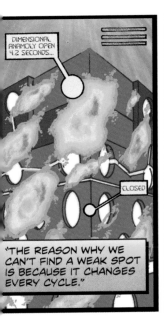

DIMENSIONAL ANAMOLY OPEN 4.2 SECONDS...

CLOSED

"THE REASON WHY WE CAN'T FIND A WEAK SPOT IS BECAUSE IT CHANGES EVERY CYCLE."

THIS ISN'T AN ENGINE AS MUCH AS IT'S A SIPHON.

AS IT SIPHONS THE INERT ENERGY, THE POWER GRID ACTUALLY SHIFTS.

SO...?

SO, IF WE TIME THIS RIGHT, WE'LL NOT ONLY SHUT IT DOWN...

"...WE MAY BE ABLE TO REVERSE THE DAMAGE BY RESTORING THE ENERGY!"

NOW, JACOB! FLIP THE SWITCH!

CLICK

URRRRR

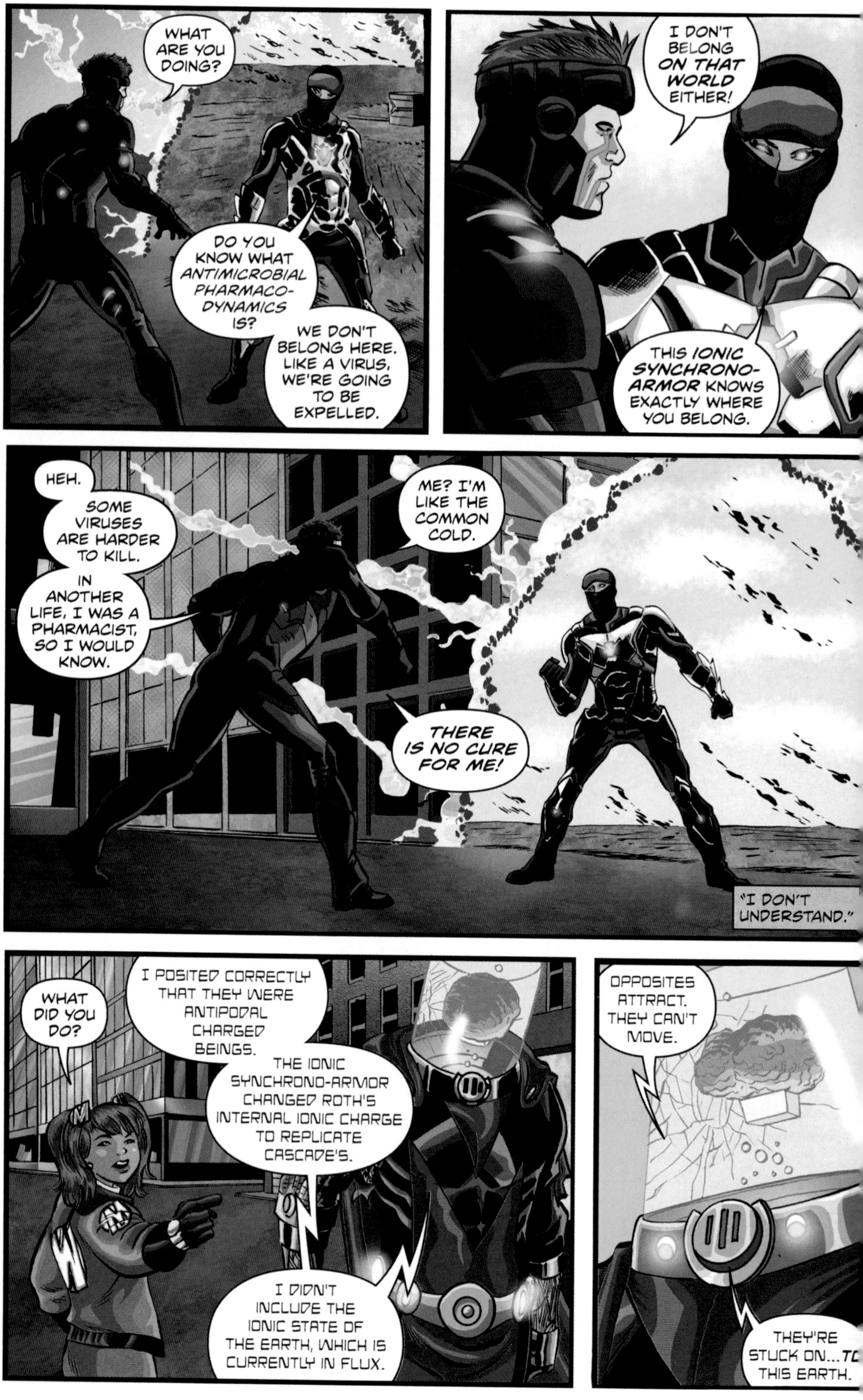
WHAT ARE YOU DOING?
DO YOU KNOW WHAT ANTIMICROBIAL PHARMACO-DYNAMICS IS?
WE DON'T BELONG HERE. LIKE A VIRUS, WE'RE GOING TO BE EXPELLED.
I DON'T BELONG ON THAT WORLD EITHER!
THIS IONIC SYNCHRONO-ARMOR KNOWS EXACTLY WHERE YOU BELONG.
HEH.
SOME VIRUSES ARE HARDER TO KILL.
IN ANOTHER LIFE, I WAS A PHARMACIST, SO I WOULD KNOW.
ME? I'M LIKE THE COMMON COLD.
THERE IS NO CURE FOR ME!
"I DON'T UNDERSTAND."
WHAT DID YOU DO?
I POSITED CORRECTLY THAT THEY WERE ANTIPODAL CHARGED BEINGS.
THE IONIC SYNCHRONO-ARMOR CHANGED ROTH'S INTERNAL IONIC CHARGE TO REPLICATE CASCADE'S.
I DIDN'T INCLUDE THE IONIC STATE OF THE EARTH, WHICH IS CURRENTLY IN FLUX.
OPPOSITES ATTRACT. THEY CAN'T MOVE.
THEY'RE STUCK ON... THIS EARTH.

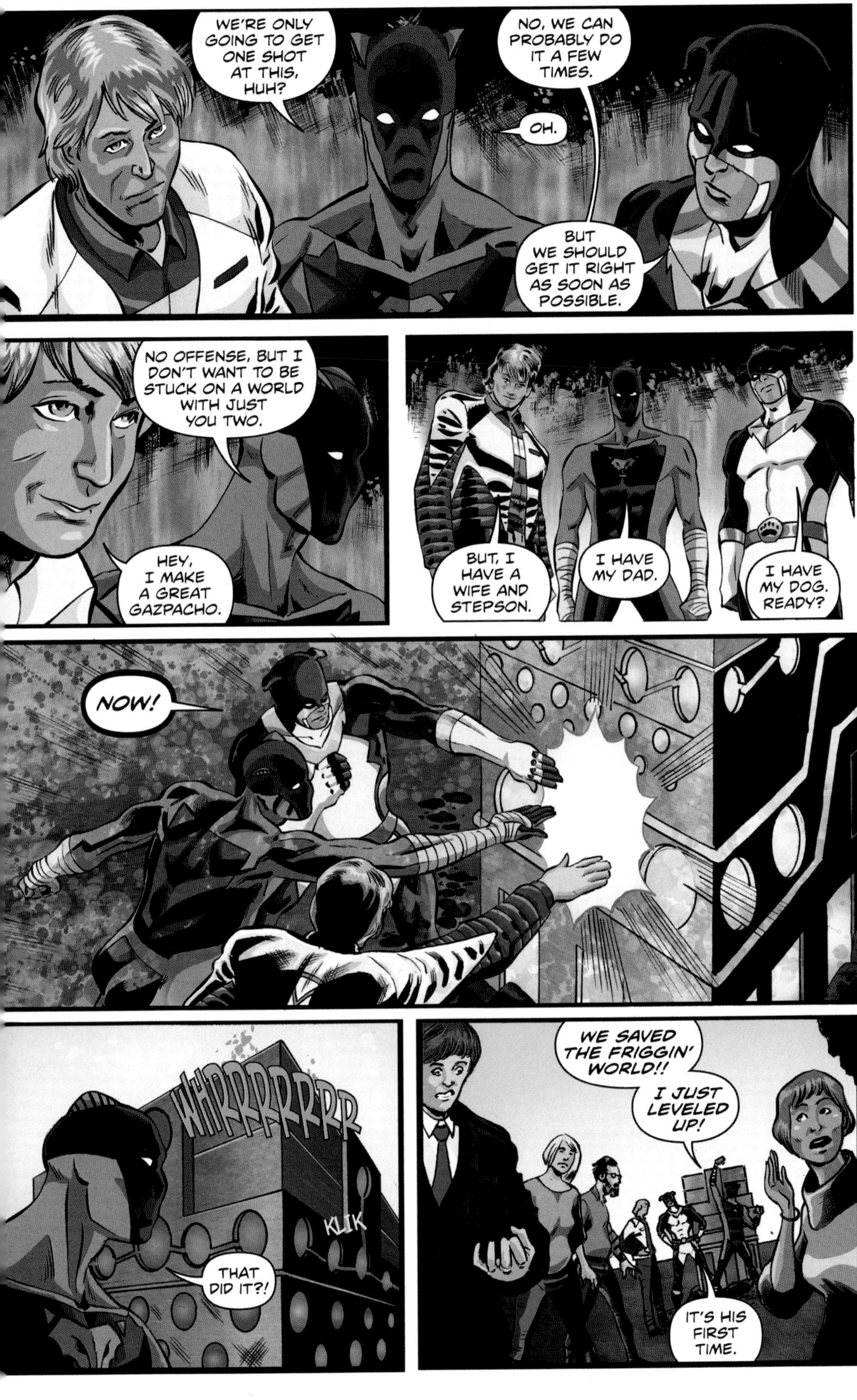
WE'RE ONLY GOING TO GET ONE SHOT AT THIS, HUH?
NO, WE CAN PROBABLY DO IT A FEW TIMES.
OH.
BUT WE SHOULD GET IT RIGHT AS SOON AS POSSIBLE.
NO OFFENSE, BUT I DON'T WANT TO BE STUCK ON A WORLD WITH JUST YOU TWO.
HEY, I MAKE A GREAT GAZPACHO.
BUT, I HAVE A WIFE AND STEPSON.
I HAVE MY DAD.
I HAVE MY DOG. READY?
NOW!
WHRRRRRRR
KLIK
THAT DID IT?!
WE SAVED THE FRIGGIN' WORLD!!
I JUST LEVELED UP!
IT'S HIS FIRST TIME.

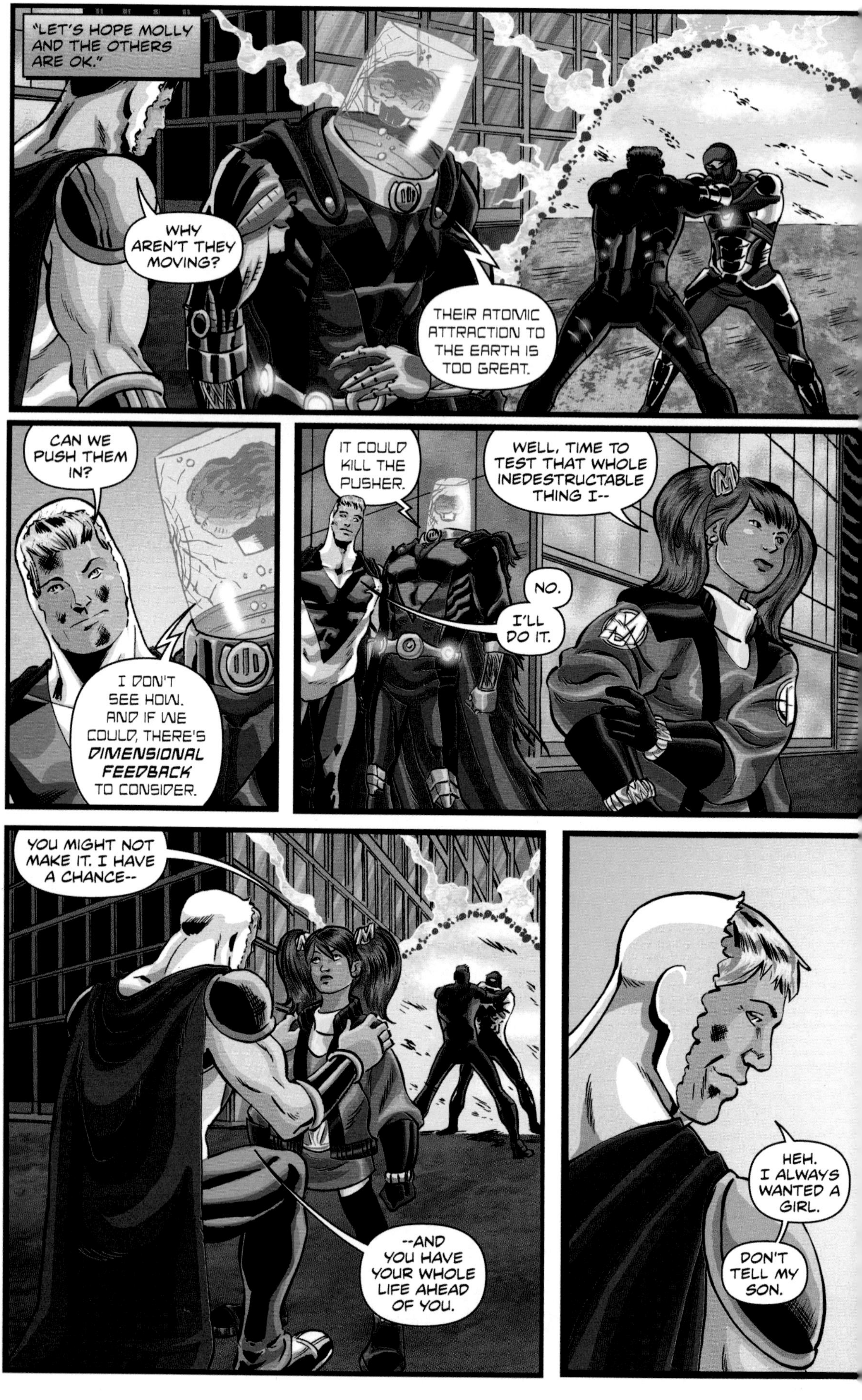
"LET'S HOPE MOLLY AND THE OTHERS ARE OK."
WHY AREN'T THEY MOVING?
THEIR ATOMIC ATTRACTION TO THE EARTH IS TOO GREAT.
CAN WE PUSH THEM IN?
I DON'T SEE HOW. AND IF WE COULD, THERE'S DIMENSIONAL FEEDBACK TO CONSIDER.
IT COULD KILL THE PUSHER.
WELL, TIME TO TEST THAT WHOLE INEDESTRUCTABLE THING I--
NO.
I'LL DO IT.
YOU MIGHT NOT MAKE IT. I HAVE A CHANCE--
--AND YOU HAVE YOUR WHOLE LIFE AHEAD OF YOU.
HEH. I ALWAYS WANTED A GIRL.
DON'T TELL MY SON.

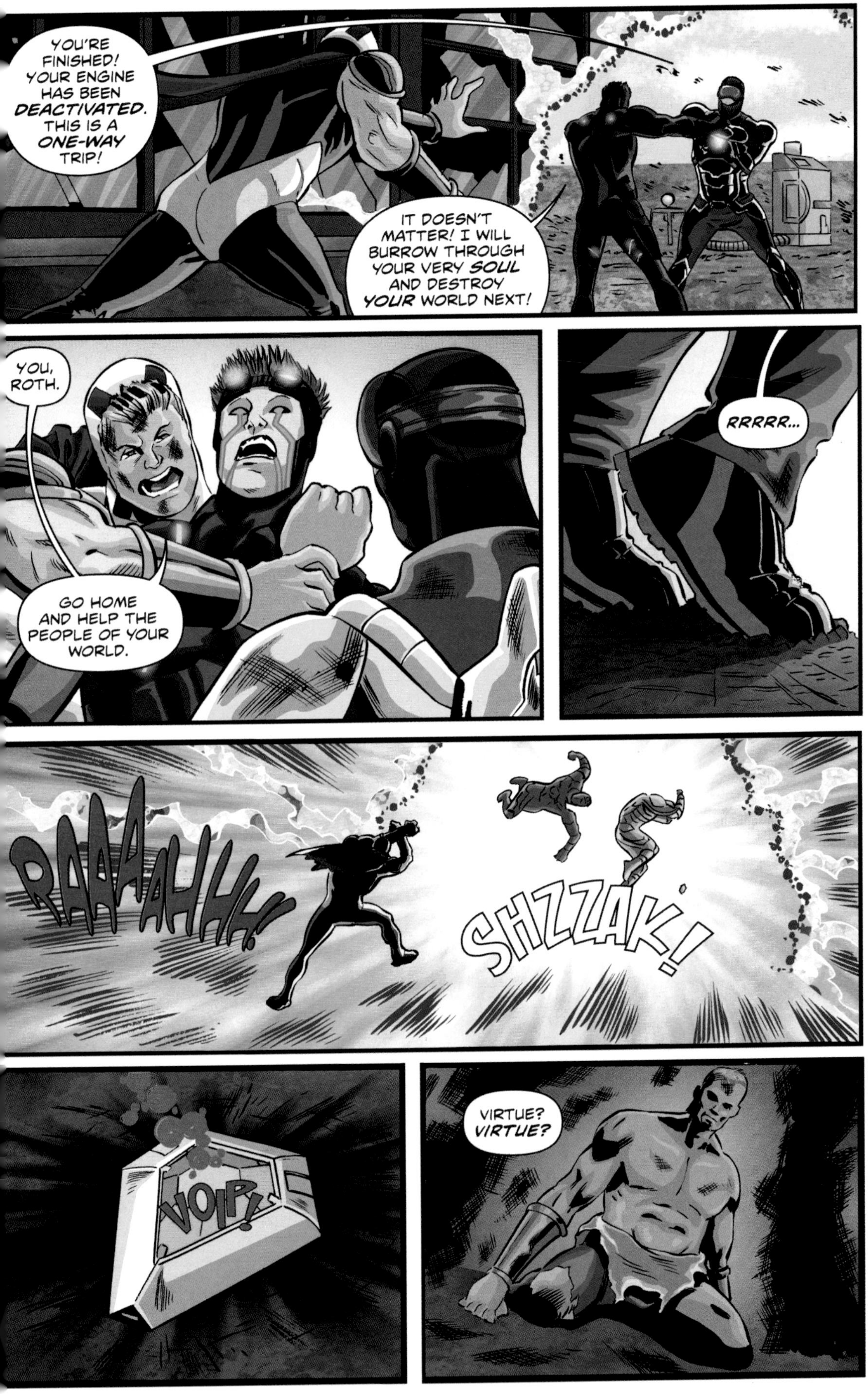

YOU'RE FINISHED! YOUR ENGINE HAS BEEN **DEACTIVATED**. THIS IS A **ONE-WAY** TRIP!
IT DOESN'T MATTER! I WILL BURROW THROUGH YOUR VERY **SOUL** AND DESTROY **YOUR** WORLD NEXT!
YOU, ROTH.
GO HOME AND HELP THE PEOPLE OF YOUR WORLD.
RRRRR...
RAAAAHHH!
SHZZZAK!
VOIP!
VIRTUE? **VIRTUE?**

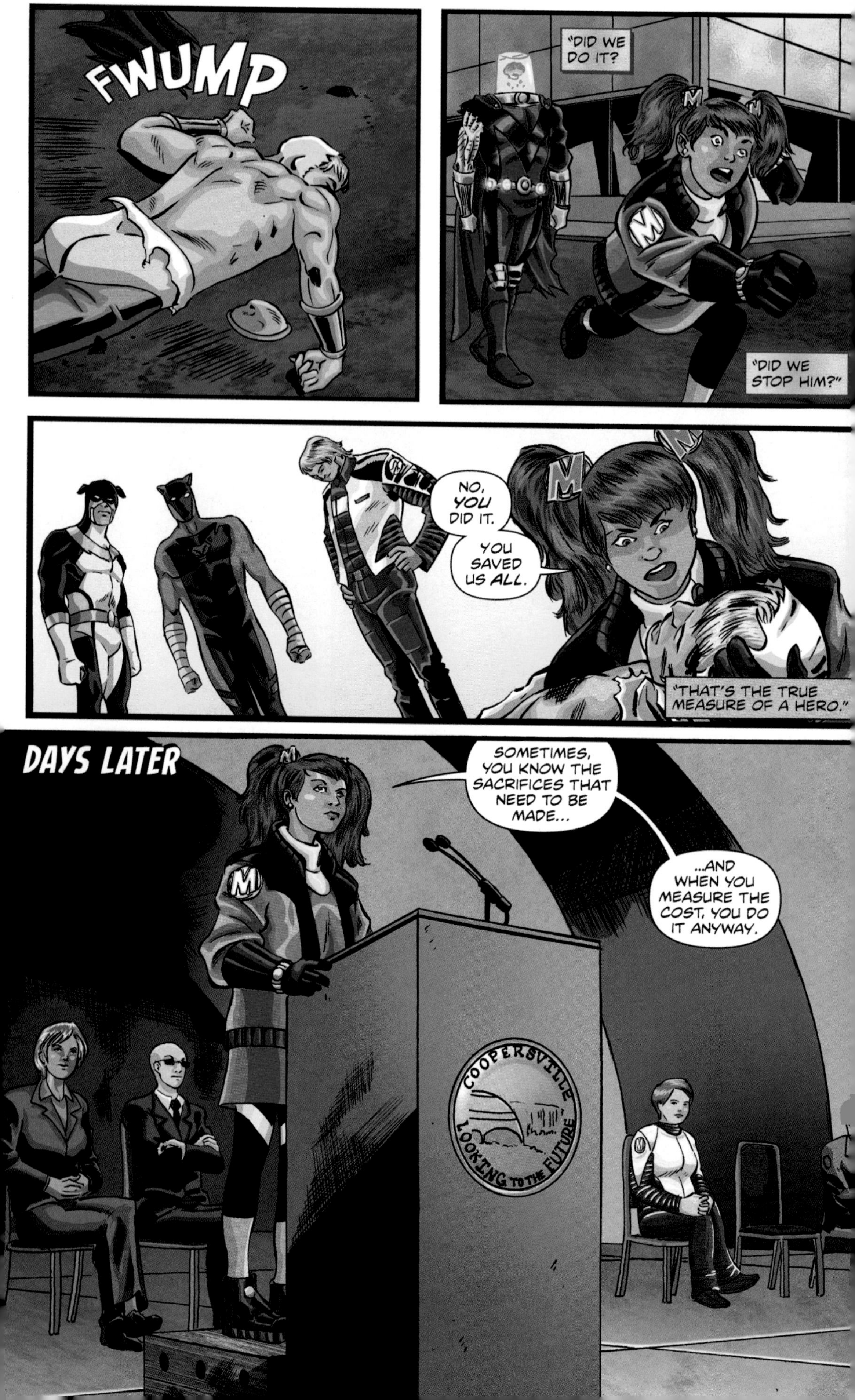
FWUMP
"DID WE DO IT?
"DID WE STOP HIM?"
NO, YOU DID IT.
YOU SAVED US ALL.
"THAT'S THE TRUE MEASURE OF A HERO."
DAYS LATER
SOMETIMES, YOU KNOW THE SACRIFICES THAT NEED TO BE MADE...
...AND WHEN YOU MEASURE THE COST, YOU DO IT ANYWAY.
COOPERSVILLE
LOOKING TO THE FUTURE

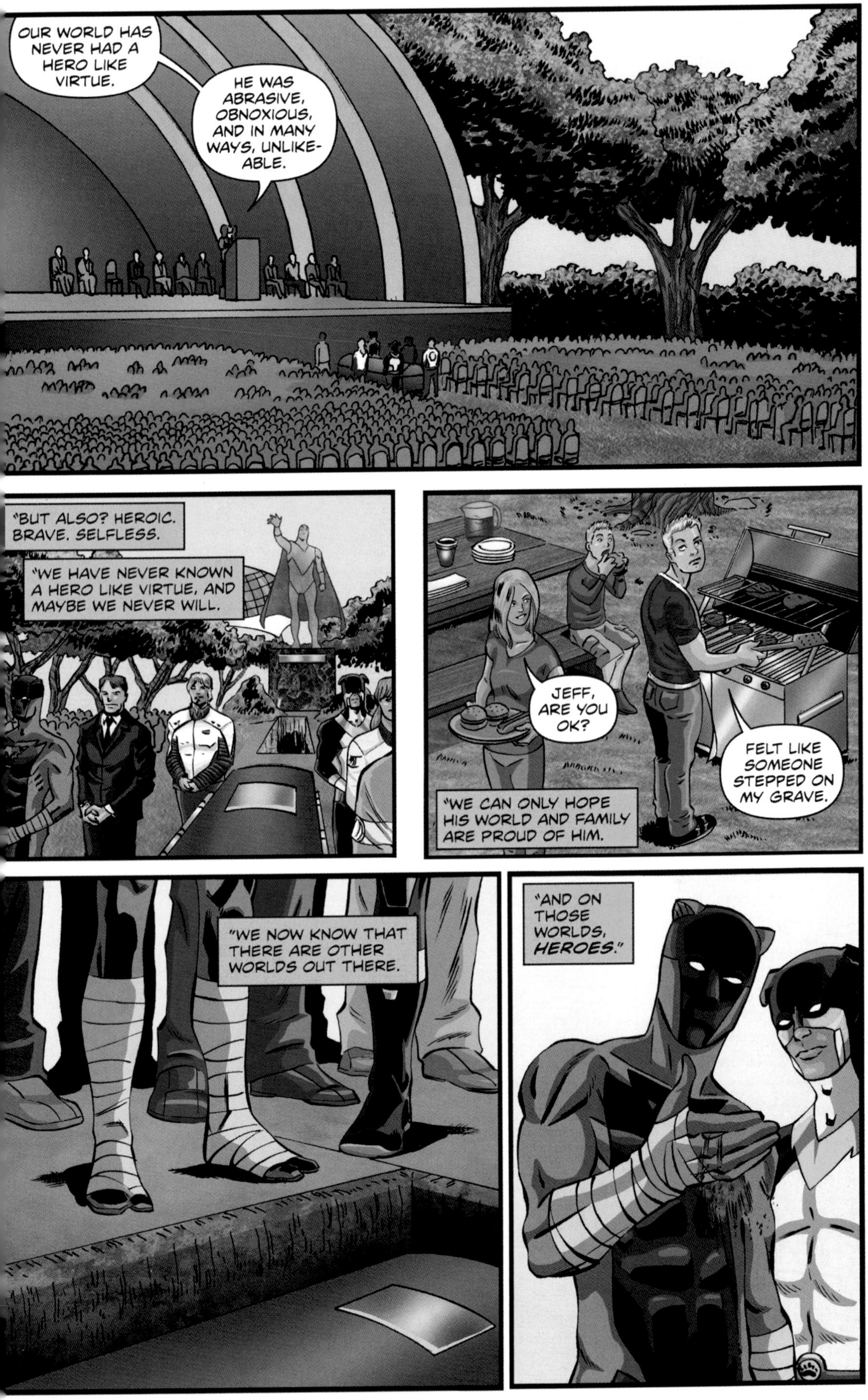
OUR WORLD HAS NEVER HAD A HERO LIKE VIRTUE.
HE WAS ABRASIVE, OBNOXIOUS, AND IN MANY WAYS, UNLIKE-ABLE.
"BUT ALSO? HEROIC. BRAVE. SELFLESS.
"WE HAVE NEVER KNOWN A HERO LIKE VIRTUE, AND MAYBE WE NEVER WILL.
JEFF, ARE YOU OK?
FELT LIKE SOMEONE STEPPED ON MY GRAVE.
"WE CAN ONLY HOPE HIS WORLD AND FAMILY ARE PROUD OF HIM.
"WE NOW KNOW THAT THERE ARE OTHER WORLDS OUT THERE.
"AND ON THOSE WORLDS, *HEROES*."

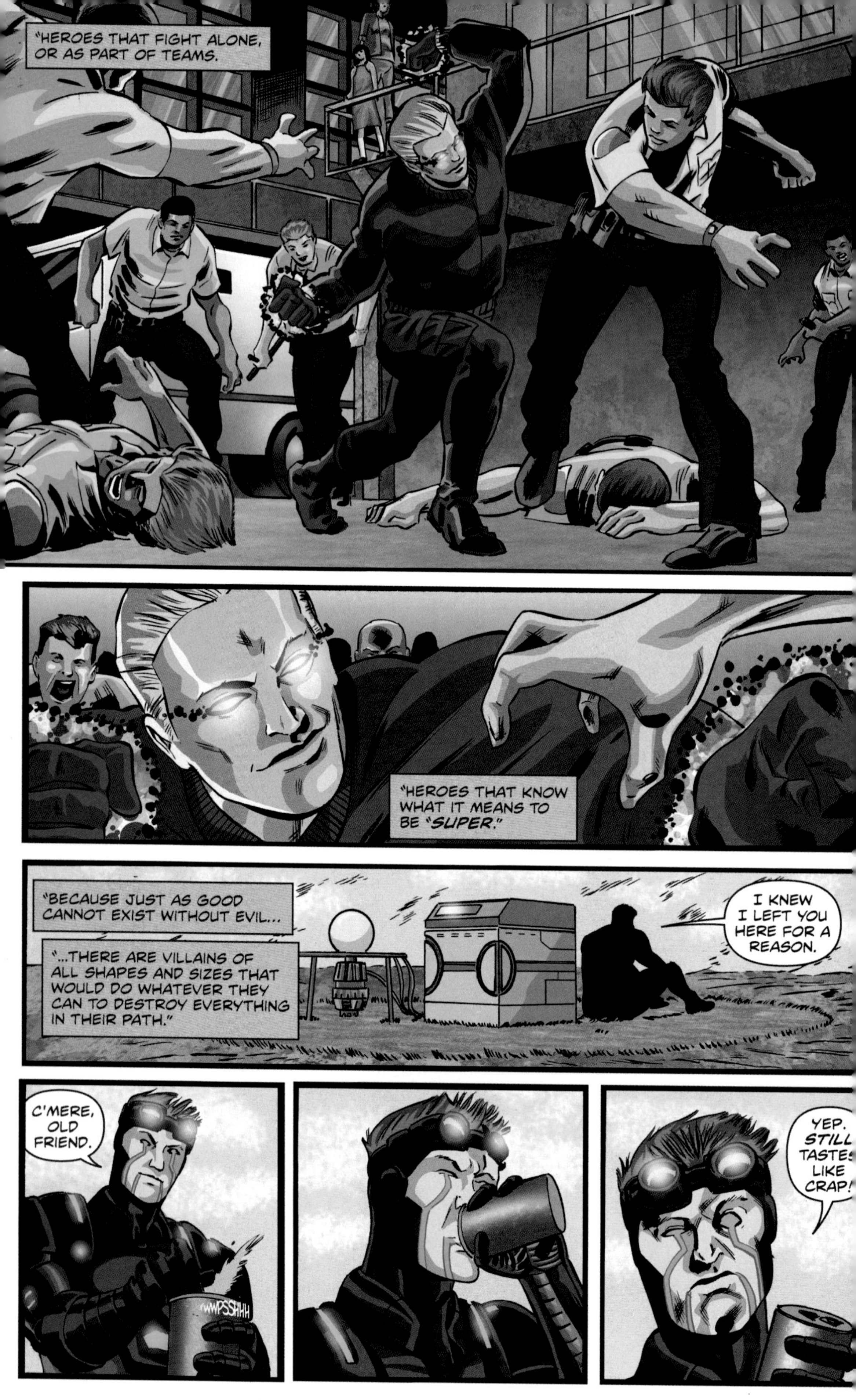
"HEROES THAT FIGHT ALONE, OR AS PART OF TEAMS.
"HEROES THAT KNOW WHAT IT MEANS TO BE "SUPER."
"BECAUSE JUST AS GOOD CANNOT EXIST WITHOUT EVIL...
"...THERE ARE VILLAINS OF ALL SHAPES AND SIZES THAT WOULD DO WHATEVER THEY CAN TO DESTROY EVERYTHING IN THEIR PATH."
I KNEW I LEFT YOU HERE FOR A REASON.
C'MERE, OLD FRIEND.
FWWPSSHHH
YEP. STILL TASTES LIKE CRAP!

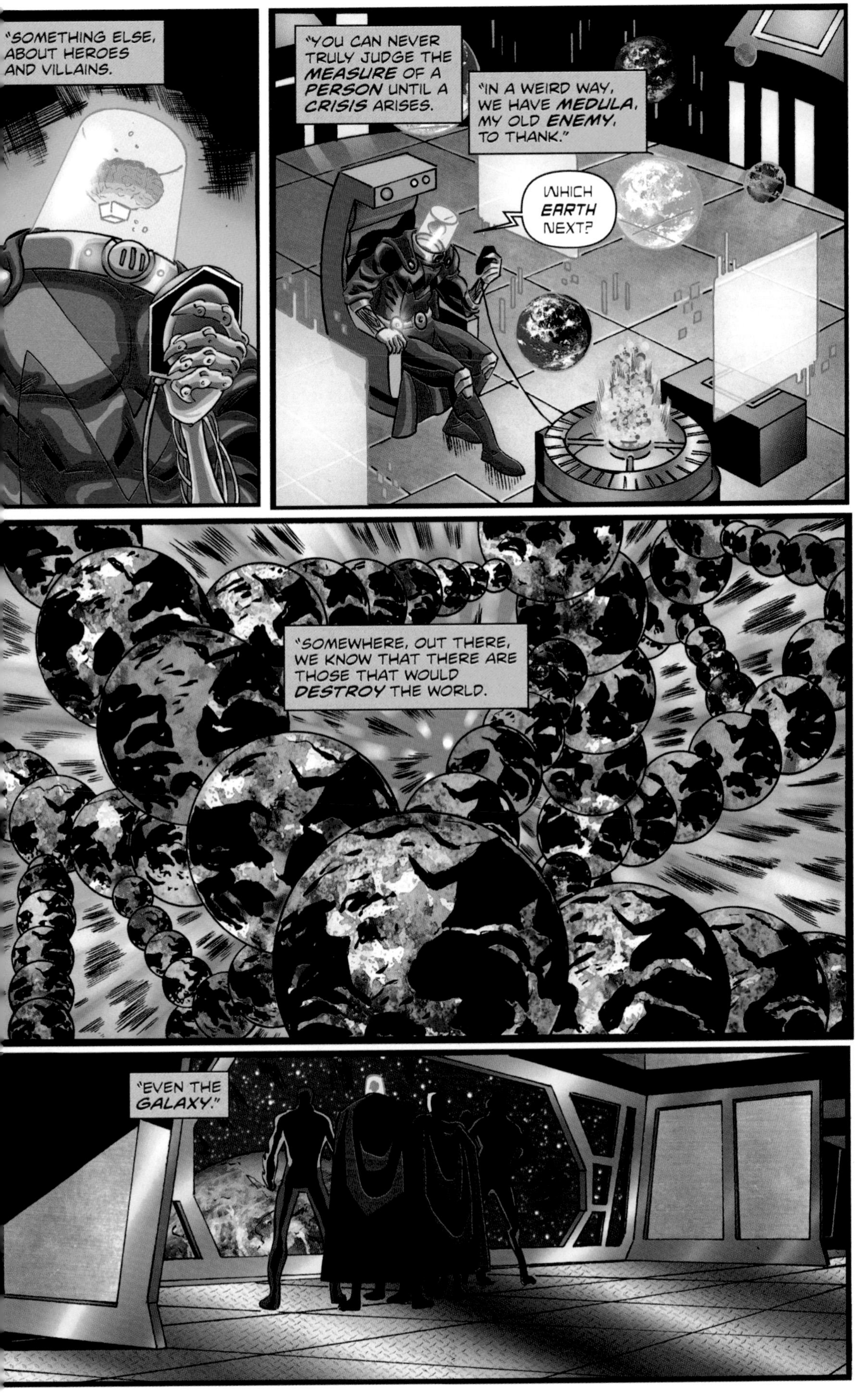
"SOMETHING ELSE, ABOUT HEROES AND VILLAINS.
"YOU CAN NEVER TRULY JUDGE THE MEASURE OF A PERSON UNTIL A CRISIS ARISES.
"IN A WEIRD WAY, WE HAVE MEDULA, MY OLD ENEMY, TO THANK."
WHICH EARTH NEXT?
"SOMEWHERE, OUT THERE, WE KNOW THAT THERE ARE THOSE THAT WOULD DESTROY THE WORLD.
"EVEN THE GALAXY."

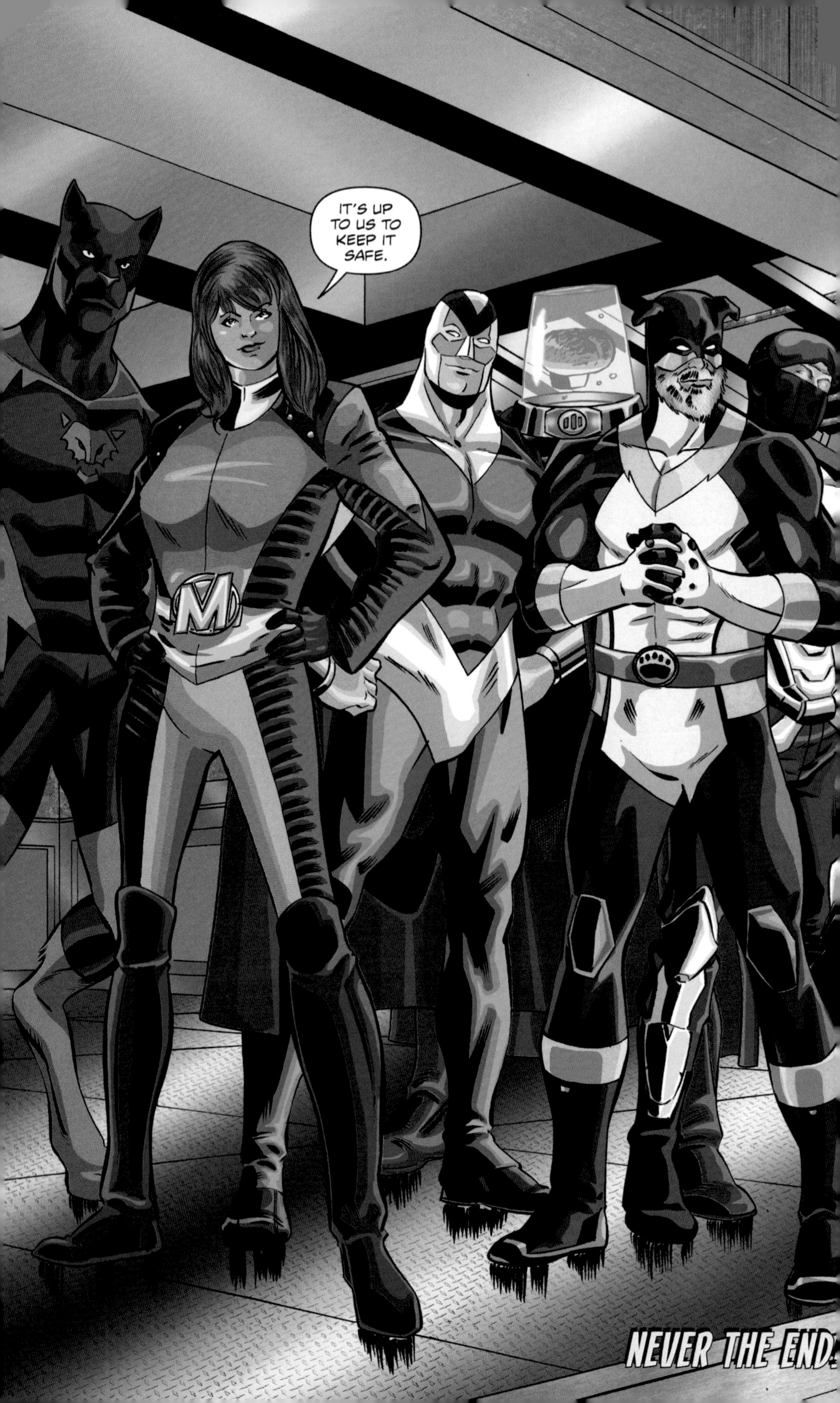
IT'S UP TO US TO KEEP IT SAFE.
NEVER THE END.

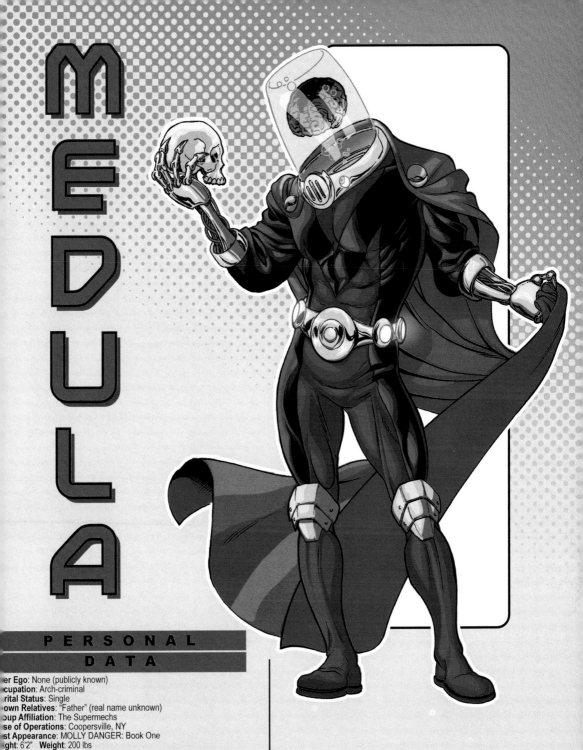

MEDULA

PERSONAL DATA

ter Ego: None (publicly known)
cupation: Arch-criminal
rital Status: Single
own Relatives: "Father" (real name unknown)
oup Affiliation: The Supermechs
se of Operations: Coopersville, NY
st Appearance: MOLLY DANGER: Book One
ight: 6'2" **Weight:** 200 lbs
es: None **Hair:** None

HISTORY

Medula showed up in Coopersville, New York, a year or so after appearance of Molly Danger. A clearly psychotic individual, Medula ships technology to the point that he had his brain and vital organs vested and placed into the cyborg body he inhabits. He believes that nanity will never advance unless they completely abandon their flesh and od bodies. He attempted to poison the water supply of the town dam when ly stopped him. Vowing revenge, Medula returned shortly thereafter in a ly weaponized APC (armored personnel carrier) and nearly destroyed all owntown Coopersville, until Molly stopped him again.

Each capture and escape has made Medula more and more ermined to destroy Molly, and each encounter escalates. Medula, a master nologist is able to build complex robotics from junk parts. He's built msday machines from scrap and giant robots from used car and truck ts. He continues to try to spread his gospel but deep down, Medula is a ard. Preferring to hide behind his machines rather than a straight frontation, he rarely expands his ministry beyond the boarders of Coopers-

POWERS & WEAPONS

Medula has no superpowers, however his cybernetic body possess enhanced strength and speed. He's capable of seeing in 360 degrees at once in radar like fashion. His one true advantage is his enhanced intellect. A super-genius, Medula is capable of creating complex machinery from the simplest of tools and parts. He has designed weapons and components so intricate and complex that they can barely be reverse engineered.

Medula created by and ™ Jamal Igle

CASCADE

PERSONAL DATA

Alter Ego: Kyle Scordato
Occupation: Pharmacist, criminal, would-be supervillain
Marital Status: Single
Known Relatives: Unknown
Group Affiliation: None
Base of Operations: Lower Triton; the Metaverse
First Appearance: FRACTURE #1 (as Kyle), ACTIONVERSE #1 (as Cascade)
Height: 5'8" (as Kyle) 6'6" (as Cascade) **Weight**: 160 lbs (as Kyle) 670 lbs (as Cascade)
Eyes: Brown (as Kyle) Iridescent green (as Cascade)
Hair: Black (as Kyle) Auburn (as Cascade)

HISTORY

Kyle Scordato lived a life of relative anonymity. Working as a pharmacist in Lower Triton, Kyle's best friend, Jeff, changed his life when he revealed that he had not one, not two, but three different personalities: That of **Malice**, a supervillain inventor, **Virtue**, his heroic arch-nemesis and Brian, a husband and father. Kyle gave Jeff some medication (illegally) that, for a short time, helped Jeff control the "*fractures*," but Kyle wanted more. Seizing the opportunity to make a name for himself, he stole the Malice costume and technology, and drew Virtue out of hiding by kidnapping his/Brian's family. Their conflict raged across Lower Triton, but in the end, Kyle was dragged off into a pocket dimension via the coat he wears. There, he became a prisoner of the **Teritans**, the race of aliens who lived in the dimension where Malice stored his weapons. Kyle's story ended here...or so it was believed.

Because Malice stored his weapons in the Teritan dimension, Kyle was able to overthrow and conquer the Teritans once he found the weapons cache. Over the next few years, he began to build a machine that could siphon the energy of every living being on a planet and open a portal to a parallel and corresponding Earth. The end result of this "portal engine" would leave behind a dead world of ash and stone, where nothing could live or grow. As Kyle would find himself on a new Earth that was not his own, he kept building the machine, slowly (and unknown to him) internalizing much of the dimensional energy that separated the different worlds. However, he's unable to harness that energy, and slowly, on every world, builds a new containment suit. As a result, Kyle is not only losing parts of himself, but parts of his humanity. To him, however, it's worth the sacrifice in efforts to get back home and have his revenge on the man who started him on this path: Virtue.

POWERS & WEAPONS

Kyle himself has no powers to speak of, but as a result of falling through to the Teritan dimension, he has endless inventions of mass destruction at his fingertips. Over time, Kyle has learned to tinker with some of these weapons and not only improve their function, but find other uses for the technology.

As Cascade, Kyle is able to travel through the dimensional barriers that separate the different worlds in the Metaverse, but at a cost. Since he is just a man with no extra-normal abilities, the energy that exists between dimensions is actually killing him without his knowledge. He keeps on absorbing it, without a way to release it (unlike Jake Roth, aka **the F1rst Hero**, who doesn't absorb it, but is able to channel it and release it as a blast). As a result, Kyle has had to slowly build a containment suit to keep himself alive.

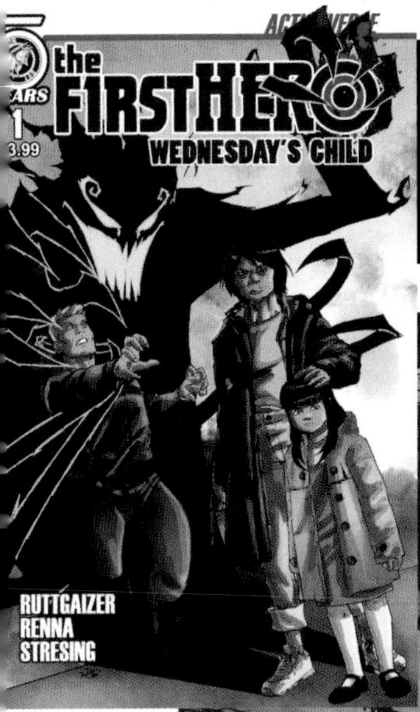

the FIRST HERO
1
3.99
WEDNESDAY'S CHILD
RUTTGAIZER
RENNA
STRESING

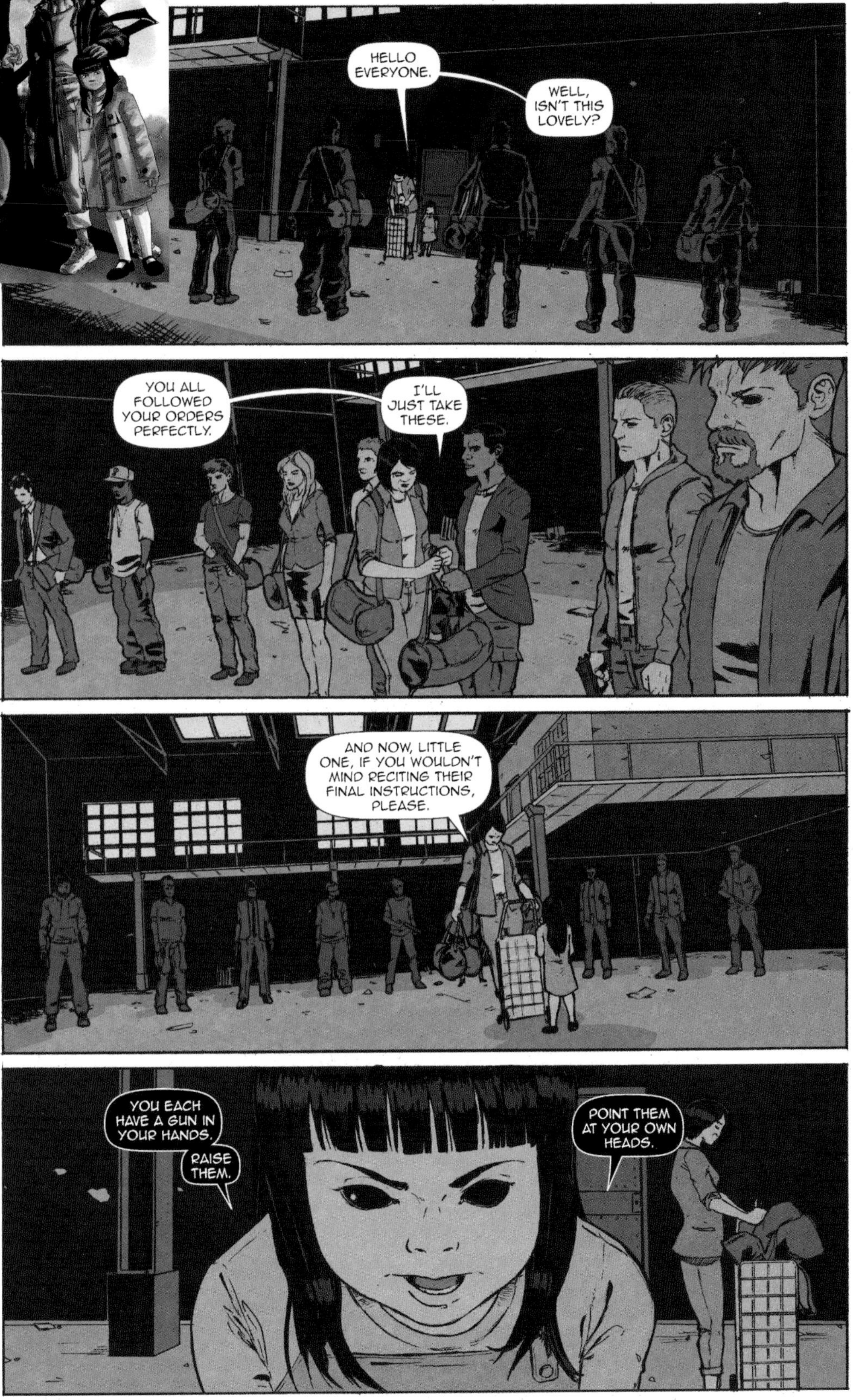

HELLO EVERYONE.
WELL, ISN'T THIS LOVELY?
YOU ALL FOLLOWED YOUR ORDERS PERFECTLY.
I'LL JUST TAKE THESE.
AND NOW, LITTLE ONE, IF YOU WOULDN'T MIND RECITING THEIR FINAL INSTRUCTIONS, PLEASE.
YOU EACH HAVE A GUN IN YOUR HANDS.
RAISE THEM.
POINT THEM AT YOUR OWN HEADS.

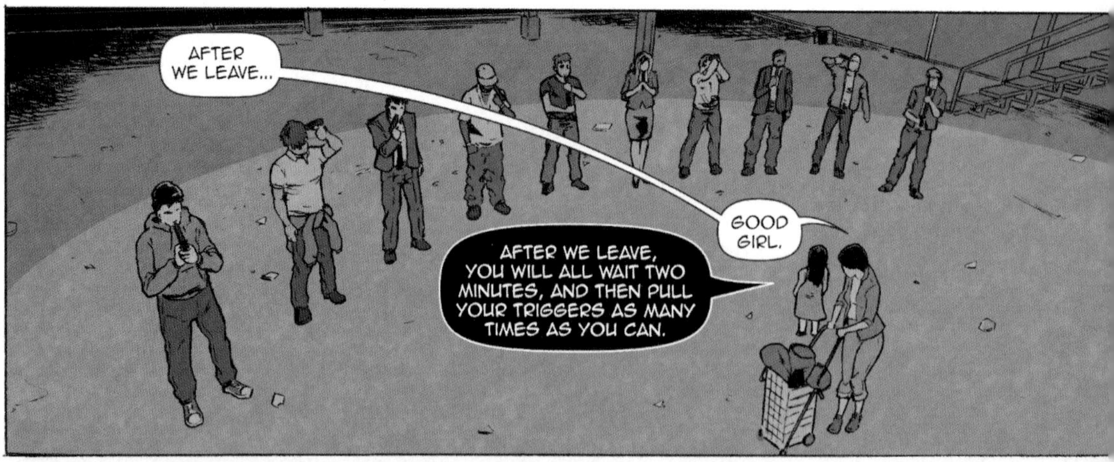
AFTER WE LEAVE...
GOOD GIRL.
AFTER WE LEAVE, YOU WILL ALL WAIT TWO MINUTES, AND THEN PULL YOUR TRIGGERS AS MANY TIMES AS YOU CAN.
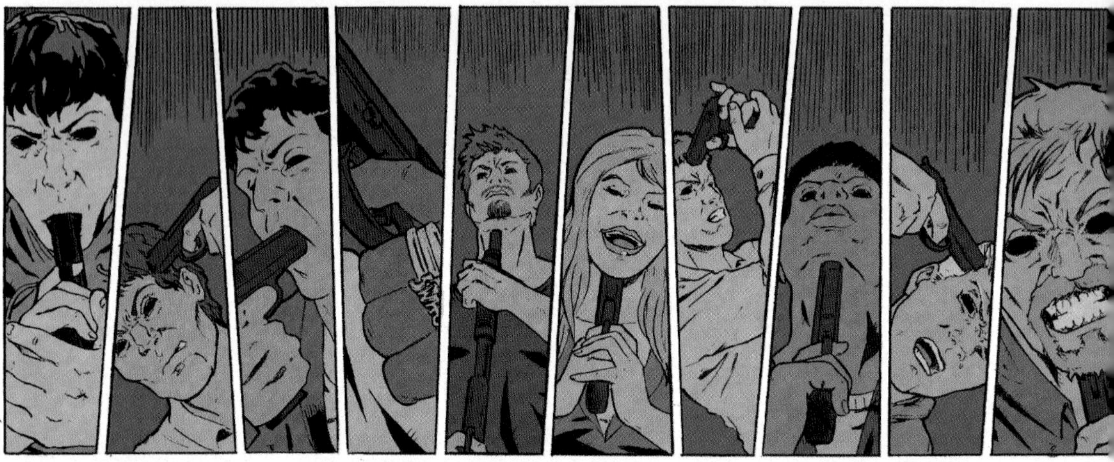
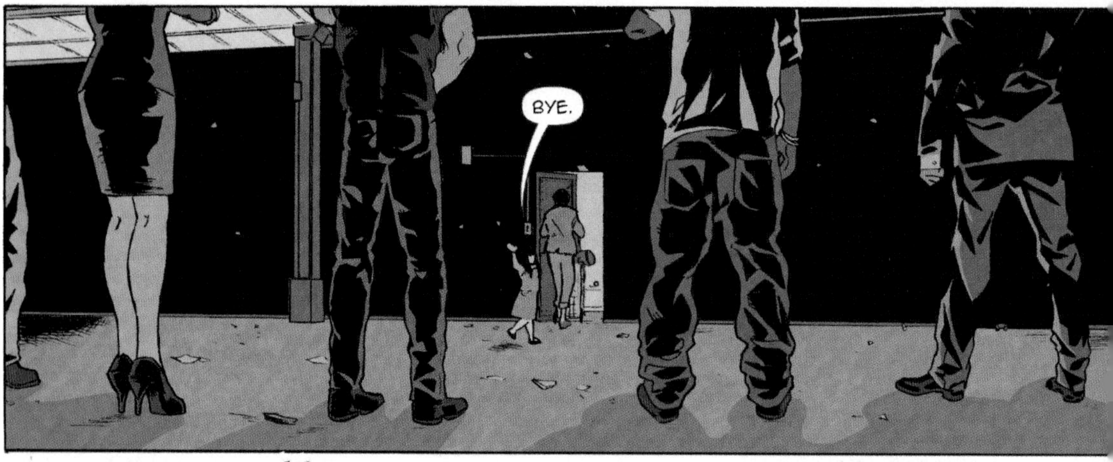
BYE.
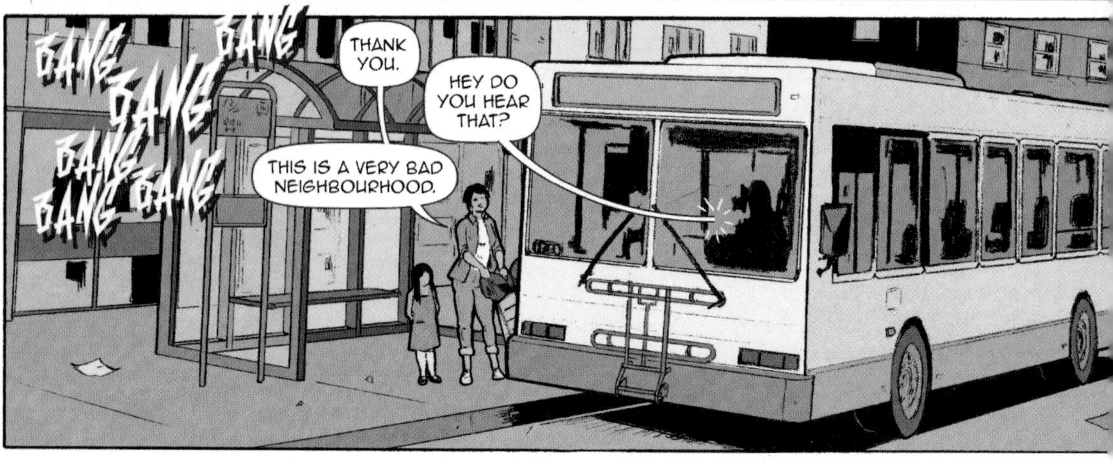
BANG BANG BANG BANG BANG BANG
THANK YOU.
THIS IS A VERY BAD NEIGHBOURHOOD.
HEY DO YOU HEAR THAT?

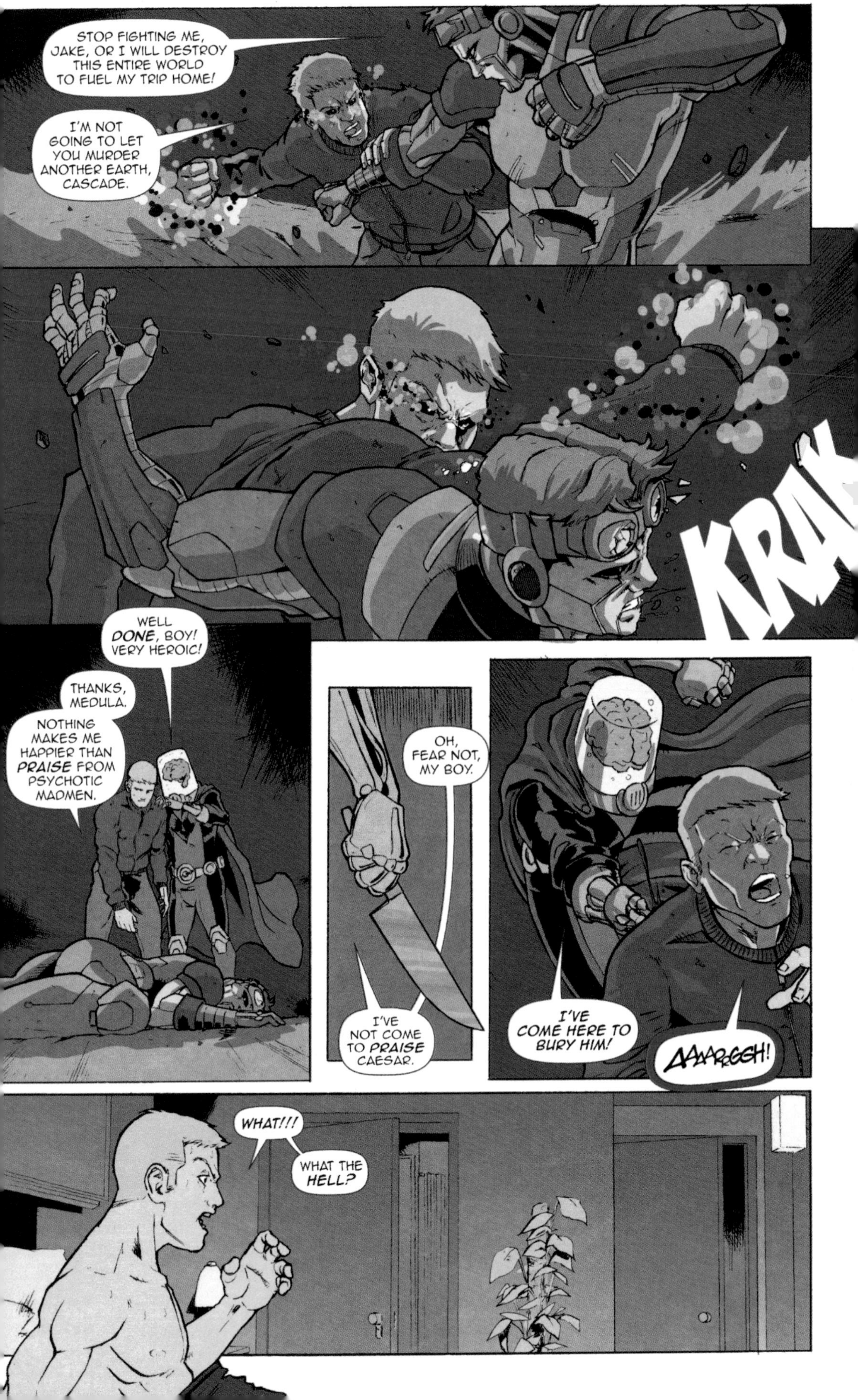
STOP FIGHTING ME, JAKE, OR I WILL DESTROY THIS ENTIRE WORLD TO FUEL MY TRIP HOME!
I'M NOT GOING TO LET YOU MURDER ANOTHER EARTH, CASCADE.
KRAK
WELL DONE, BOY! VERY HEROIC!
THANKS, MEDULA.
NOTHING MAKES ME HAPPIER THAN PRAISE FROM PSYCHOTIC MADMEN.
OH, FEAR NOT, MY BOY.
I'VE NOT COME TO PRAISE CAESAR.
I'VE COME HERE TO BURY HIM!
AAAARRGGH!
WHAT!!!
WHAT THE HELL?

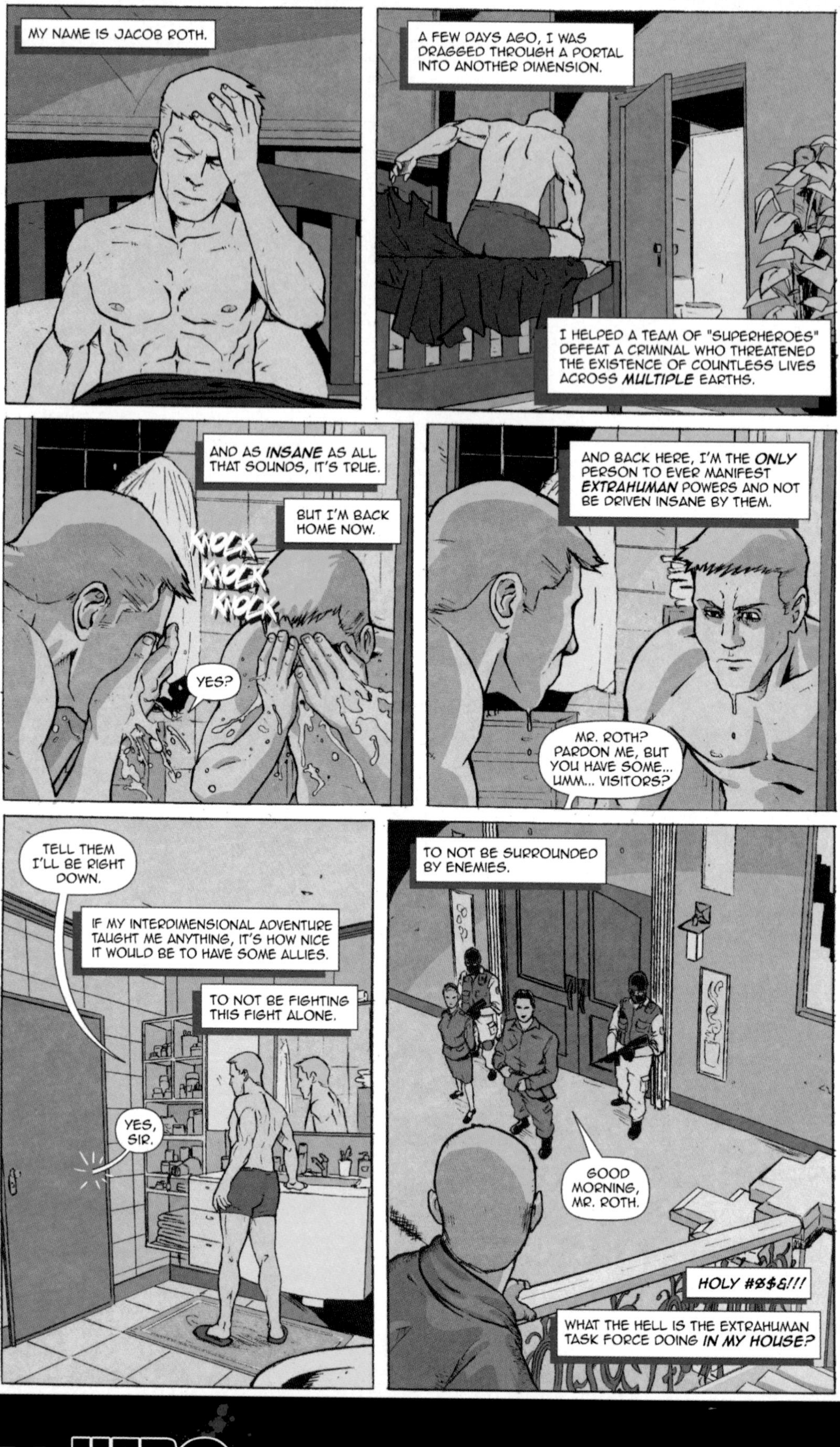

MY NAME IS JACOB ROTH.
A FEW DAYS AGO, I WAS DRAGGED THROUGH A PORTAL INTO ANOTHER DIMENSION.
I HELPED A TEAM OF "SUPERHEROES" DEFEAT A CRIMINAL WHO THREATENED THE EXISTENCE OF COUNTLESS LIVES ACROSS *MULTIPLE* EARTHS.
AND AS *INSANE* AS ALL THAT SOUNDS, IT'S TRUE.
BUT I'M BACK HOME NOW.
KNOCK KNOCK KNOCK
YES?
AND BACK HERE, I'M THE *ONLY* PERSON TO EVER MANIFEST *EXTRAHUMAN* POWERS AND NOT BE DRIVEN INSANE BY THEM.
MR. ROTH? PARDON ME, BUT YOU HAVE SOME... UMM... VISITORS?
TELL THEM I'LL BE RIGHT DOWN.
IF MY INTERDIMENSIONAL ADVENTURE TAUGHT ME ANYTHING, IT'S HOW NICE IT WOULD BE TO HAVE SOME ALLIES.
TO NOT BE FIGHTING THIS FIGHT ALONE.
YES, SIR.
TO NOT BE SURROUNDED BY ENEMIES.
GOOD MORNING, MR. ROTH.
HOLY #%$&!!!
WHAT THE HELL IS THE EXTRAHUMAN TASK FORCE DOING *IN MY HOUSE?*

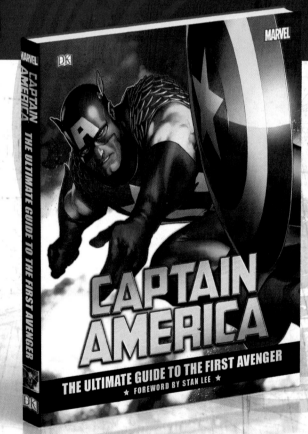

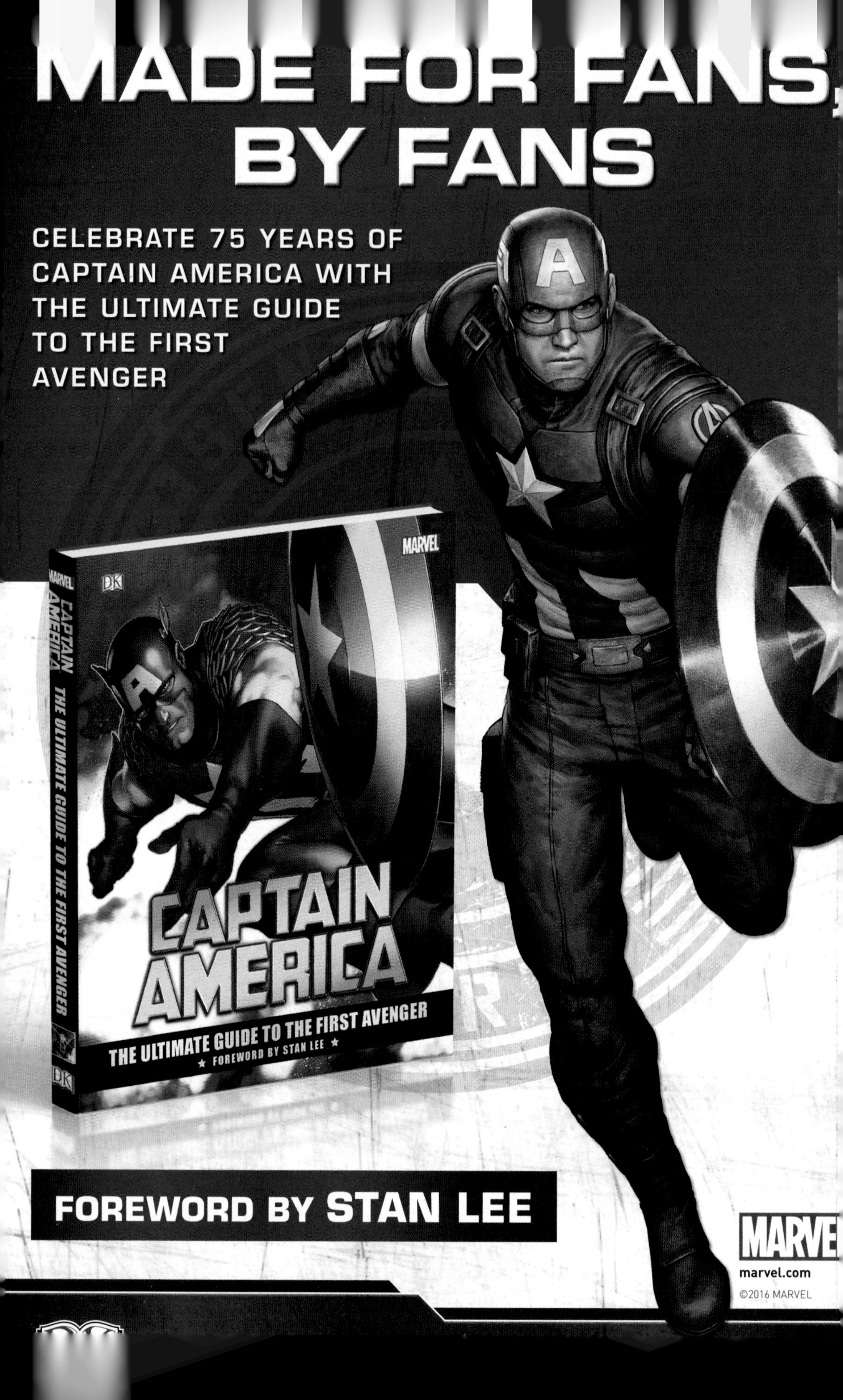